CLARKESWORLD
YEAR TEN - VOLUME ONE

CLARKESWORLD
YEAR TEN - VOLUME ONE

EDITED BY NEIL CLARKE & SEAN WALLACE

WYRM PUBLISHING

CLARKESWORLD: YEAR TEN VOLUME ONE

Wyrm Publishing
www.wyrmpublishing.com

For more information, contact Wyrm Publishing:
wyrmpublishing@gmail.com

ISBN: 978-1-64236-020-2 (trade paperback)
ISBN: 978-1-64236-019-6 (ebook)

Visit Clarkesworld Magazine at:
clarkesworldmagazine.com

Table of Contents

Introduction

NEIL CLARKE

It's a little confusing doing these "annuals" now that we've started—with Year Nine—splitting each into two volumes. That means that the start of year ten is actually the eleventh book in the series and it feels like by the time I'm done working on one now, two more are ready to go. The slowest part of the process is definitely these introductions, particularly for a year that doesn't incorporate many changes or major events at the magazine. Year nine covered our 100th issue and the introduction of translations. Year ten, well, that was taking everything we learned and the process and adapting our routines to make it work more smoothly. It's the sort of background work that doesn't make for very interesting introductions—or does it?

The stories in this volume represent all the original fiction we published in *Clarkesworld Magazine* from October 2015 through March 2016, issues 109-114. Five of the twenty-seven stories in this book are part of our efforts to publish more works in translation. Each of these is from China, as a result of the collaboration with Storycom that was celebrating its first anniversary at this time. One of my goals in regularly including translations in our lineup was to help make it feel like a normal part of the short fiction community. Looking back from 2019, I had no idea how important a message that was sending, particularly to readers and authors from other countries—not just China.

Over time, I've become more familiar with some of the previous efforts to do the same. Most sought to focus exclusively on foreign works, an enthusiasm that may have just been their undoing. One such attempt in the late 1960s was a magazine edited by Frederik Pohl, called *International Science Fiction*. The second issue—which would be its last—included an editorial by Lester Del Rey. (If you aren't familiar with these two names, you should look them up.) In that editorial he said that "our stories are sent to large numbers of fans and translators all over the world, while our own authors and fans seldom get even a hint of the work being done in our field by others. We're in serious danger of becoming the most provincial science-fiction readers—and writers—on earth." The fears he stated fifty years ago are very close to what happened to our community.

In the last few years, however, that has begun to change. More obviously in short fiction, but that tends to be how the field goes: where short fiction succeeds, novels follow. Speaking from a 2019 perspective, there's a lot more of these works being published in English language magazines and anthologies, and interestingly, I can see those same stories spreading from there and out to other non-anglophone markets. We've long seen our stories exported to other countries. It's nice to see that same mechanism helping the foreign authors we publish. Our problems here might not have been as unique as Lester thought. They just didn't have it as bad.

There's still a long road ahead, but it feels good to know that we've been a continuing part of that change. In some ways, it's a simple variation on every editor's joy at finding a new author to work with. In this case, I'm just fishing in a bigger pool. Obviously, it's not that simple, particularly if you can't speak or read other languages. Going through translators is a big leap of faith and we can't ignore the extra cost translation incurs. For that reason, this problem will be forever linked to the financial health of the short fiction field. If you want to see these efforts continue to grow, subscribe to those markets making the effort. It makes a difference.

So I suppose, one simple thing in a six-month window is enough to feed the introduction beast. Now if you'll excuse me, I need to figure out what to say in volume two before another set of annuals go to print.

Neil Clarke
May 2019

Extraction Request

RICH LARSON

When they finally shift the transport's still-smoldering wing enough to drag Beasley out from where he was pinioned, for a moment all Elliot can do, all anyone can do, is stare. Beasley's wiry arm with its bioluminescent tattoos is near sheared from its socket, and below his hips he's nothing but pulped meat and splinters of bone.

He's still alive, still mumbling, maybe about the woman Elliot saw in a little holo with her arms thrown around his neck, back before Beasley's dreadlocked mane was shaved off and a conscript clamp was implanted at the top of his spine.

"His impact kit never triggered," someone says, as if that's not fucking obvious, as if he could have been ragdolled out of the transport otherwise.

"Is the autosurgeon trashed?" someone else, maybe Tolliver, says. Elliot's ears are still ringing from the crash and his head swimming from what he was doing before it and all the voices seem to blend. He knows, dimly, that he should be giving orders by now.

"An autosurgeon can't do shit for him. What's it going to do, cauterize him at the waist?"

"Get him some paineaters at least. Numb him up."

"Shock's done that already."

"You don't know that."

"I fucking hope that."

Beasley is still trying to talk, but it's all a choking wet burble from the blood in his mouth. The nudge, though, comes through. It slides into the corner of Elliot's optic implant, blinking poisonous yellow. A little ripple goes through the rest of the squad, which means they got it, too. A couple of them reflexively clap their hands to the backs of their necks, where the caked scar tissue is still fresh enough to itch.

Elliot realizes that down here in the bog, cut off from command, the clamp at the top of Beasley's spine no longer needs official permission to trigger its nanobomb. All it needs is consensus.

"I'd want it done for me," Tolliver says, wiping a glisten of sweat off his face. His upvote floats into the digital queue. He chews at his lip, shoots Elliot a look that Elliot carefully ignores.

"Yeah," Santos from the lunar colony says, which is as much as she's ever said. "Trigger him." Another upvote appears, then another, then three more in a cascade. Elliot sees that he has a veto option—something they didn't tell him when they stuck him as squad leader. He looks into Beasley's glazed eyes and completes the consensus, floating his vote to the queue.

The nanobomb goes off, punching a precise hole through the brainstem and cutting every string at once. Beasley slumps.

Apart from that, injuries are minimal. Everyone else's kits went off properly, as evidenced by the gritty orange impact gel still slathering their uniforms. Elliot picks it off himself in clumps while he surveys damage to the R12 Heron transport settling in its crater at the end of a steaming furrow of crushed flora and shed metal. The anti-air smartmine shredded their primary rotor when it detonated, and the crash itself did the rest of the work. The Heron's not going to fly again.

"Should get them fuel cells out of her," says Snell, who is scarecrow skinny with a mouth full of metal, and dark enough so his shaved scalp seems to gleam blue-black. "In case there's leakage." Aside from Beasley, who's being wrestled into a body bag, Snell is the only one who knows flyers worth a damn. They conscripted him for smuggling human cargo on a sub-orbital.

"You do that," Elliot says, when he realizes Snell is waiting for go-ahead. "Get one of the Prentii to help. They're digging."

"You mean one of the twins?" Snell asks, with a grin that makes his metallic teeth gnash and scrape. Elliot did mean the twins, Privates Prentiss and Prentiss. The nickname slipped out, something Tolliver calls them the same way he calls Snell "The Smell" and Mirotic "Miroglitch." If he has one for Elliot, too, he doesn't use it when they're together.

"Yeah," Elliot says. "Get one of the twins."

Snell pulls on a diagnostic glove and clambers into the Heron carcass; Elliot turns to check on the perimeter. If they hadn't gone down over swampland, where the rubbery blue-purple ferns and dense-packed sponge trees provided a cushion, the crash might have been a lot worse. Their impact cleared a swathe on one side of the transport. On the other, Mirotic is calibrating the cyclops.

Elliot watches the red-lit sensory bulb strain on its spindly neck and spin in a slow circle. "What's it see?" he asks.

Mirotic is tapped in, with his optic implant glowing the same red as the surveillance unit. "Nothing hot and moving but us. Bog gets denser to the east and south. Lots of those sponge trees, lots of subterranean fungi. No radio communications. Could be more anti-air mines sitting masked, though."

His English is airtight, but still carries a Serbian lilt. Before they clamped him, he was upper-level enforcement in a Neo-European crime block on Kettleburn. He once personally executed three men and two women in an abandoned granary and had their corpses put through a thresher. Only Elliot has access to that back-record. To everyone else, Mirotic is a jovial giant with a bristly black beard and high-grade neural plugs.

Prentiss, Jan, trundles past, having received Snell's nudge for a hand with the fuel cells. He wipes wet dirt off on his tree-trunk thighs. Both he and his sister are nearly tall as Mirotic, and both are broader.

"Soil's no good for graves," Prentiss rumbles over his shoulder. "He's going to get churned up again. Watch."

"How many drones came out intact?" Elliot asks Mirotic, trying to sound sharp, trying not to imagine Beasley's body heaved back to the surface.

"Two," Mirotic says. "I can fix a third, maybe."

"Send one up," Elliot says, scratching his arm. "Get a proper map going."

Mirotic hesitates. "If I send up a drone, we might trigger another smartmine."

Elliot hadn't thought of that. He hasn't thought of a lot of things, but rescinding the order would make him look off, make him look shook, maybe even remind Mirotic of the night he saw him with the syringe.

"That's why you keep it low," Elliot says. "Scrape the tree line, no higher. And keep it brief."

Mirotic takes a battered drone from its casing and unfolds it in his lap, sitting cross-legged on the damp earth. As it rises into the air, whirring and buzzing, his eyes turn bright sensory blue.

"It's strange there's no animal life," Mirotic says. "Nothing motile on the sensor but insects. Could be a disease came through. Bioweapon, even. Seen it in the woods around New Warsaw, dead and empty just like this." He rests his thick hands on his knees. "We could have everyone jack up their immunity boosters."

Elliot takes the hint and sends a widecast order to dial up immunity and use filtration, at least for the time being. Then he goes to where Tolliver and Santos are vacuum-sealing Beasley's body bag, the filmy material wrapping him tight like a shroud. Tolliver looks up at his approach, flicking dark lashes. He has smooth brown skin and sly smiles and a plastic-capped flay a skin artist did for him on leave that shows off the muscle and tendon of his arm in a graceful gash. Elliot has felt it under his fingertips, cool and hard. He knows Tolliver is fucking at least one other squadmate, but he doesn't think it's Santos.

"Me and Tolliver will finish up," Elliot says. "Go spot for Mirotic. He's tapped in. Then get the tents up."

"Sir." Santos's the only one on the squad who says sir, who salutes, and she does both with enough irony to slice through power armor. Santos was a foot soldier for one of the Brazilian families up on the lunar colony. She looks like a bulldog, squinty eyes and pouched cheeks. Her clamp didn't go in right and there's double the scarring up her head.

When Santos leaves, still sneering, Elliot drops to a crouch. "Did they know each other?" he asks, grabbing the foot end of the body bag. Tolliver takes the other and they carefully stand up.

"Talked Portuguese together sometimes," he says. "Beasley knew a bit. Said the moony accent's a real bitch to follow, though."

Elliot tells himself that this is why he needs Tolliver on his side, because Tolliver sees the webs, sees all the skinny bonds of social molecule that run through the squad.

"Fucked up seeing him halfway gone like that," Tolliver says, with a put-on hardness to his voice. "At least the clamp is good for something, right?"

Elliot grunts in response as they carry Beasley away from the downed Heron, away from the surveillance unit and the carbon-fiber tents now blooming around it.

"When I said we could give him paineaters, that vein in your forehead, it went big," Tolliver says, almost conversationally. "You were in the back when they hit us. You were in the medcab again."

"I'm coming down," Elliot says, even as his itching arm gives another twinge. "And I'm staying off it. Staying sharp."

Tolliver says nothing, and then they're at the hole where the other Prentiss, Noam, is waiting with a spade slung over her shoulder. They lower the body bag in slowly, gently. Elliot reaches down for a fistful of damp earth and crumbles it over Beasley's shrouded face. Tolliver does the same. Prentiss starts shoveling.

"We got the extraction request through before we lost altitude," Elliot says. "Won't be down here long."

Tolliver gives him a sidelong look. "Some of us will be," he says, then turns and leaves.

Elliot stays to watch until the body bag has disappeared completely under thick wet dirt.

Dusk drops fast on Pentecost, dyeing the sky and swamp a cold eerie blue for a half-hour before plunging them into pitch dark. Most of the squad already have peeled eyes—the night vision surgery is a common one for criminals—and Elliot orders all lights dimmed to minimum to conserve the generator.

Elliot has a tent to himself. He lies back stiff on his cot in the dark and reviews mission parameters in his optic implant, scrolling up and down over words he's read a thousand times. They were heading north to reinforce Osuna, cutting slantwise across marshy no-man's land the rebels usually stay away from. They were not expecting hostiles on the way, and now they're grounded at least a thousand klicks from the nearest outpost.

Elliot tries to calculate how long the paineaters and emergency morphine he salvaged from the shattered medcab will last him. Then he accesses his personal files in his implant and watches the one clip he hasn't deleted yet, the one he watches before he sleeps.

"She's awake . . . Just looking around . . . "

His wife's voice draws three syllables out of awake, drags on around, high and sweet and tinged weary. His daughter's soft and veiny head turns. Her bright black eyes search, and Elliot can pretend they see him.

Something scrapes against the side of the tent. He blinks the clip away, hauls upright and reaches for his weapon before he recognizes the imprint of a body pressed up flush to the fabric. Elliot swipes a door with his hand and Tolliver slides through, already halfway undressed.

"Told the Smell I'm out back for a long shit," Tolliver says, working his stiff cock with one hand, reaching for Elliot's waistband with the other. "Let's be quick."

"Wasn't sure you'd be coming," Elliot says, helping yank the fatigues off. "Because of Beasley."

"Don't fucking talk about Beasley," Tolliver says.

Elliot doesn't, and Tolliver's body all over his is second best to a morphine hit for helping him not think about that or anything else. But when he comes it's a throb and a trickle and then everything turns lukewarm dead again. Afterward, Tolliver sits on the edge of the cot and peels his spray-on condom off in strips.

"Jan went walkabout in the swamp a bit," he says, because this has been the usual trade since they deployed last month. "Think he's testing the range limit for the clamp. Wants to skate, maybe. Him and his sister."

"In the middle of a mined bog?" Elliot asks, pulling his fatigues back on.

"They're both settlement-bred," Tolliver says. "Colonist genemix, you know, they think they're invincible. Probably think they can tough it out and get south to the spaceport."

"He told you that he wants to desert?"

Tolliver takes a drink from Elliot's water bottle and runs his tongue along his teeth. "He told me he did some exploring," he says. "Wanted to jaw about some odd bones he found. I filled in the rest."

"What did he find?" Elliot asks.

"Animal bones," Tolliver says. "Really white, really clean."

"Mirotic thinks a plague might have come through," Elliot says, instead of saying a bioweapon. "There'd be bones."

"Plagues don't usually put them in neat little heaps," Tolliver says. "He said they were all piled up. A little mound of skeletons."

Tolliver swipes a door and disappears, leaving Elliot sweat-soaked and sick-feeling. He only hesitates a moment before he gropes under the bedroll for his syringe. Before he can start prepping his favorite vein, the cyclops starts to wail.

Everyone is out of their tents and armed in a few minutes, clustered around the cyclops. Half of them are rubbing their eyes as the peel sets in and turns their irises reflective. Elliot switches to night vision in his implant, lighting the shadows radiation green. The air sits damp and heavy on his shoulders, and with no breeze nothing moves in the flora. The stubby sponge trees and wide-blade ferns are dead still.

"Where's your brother?" Elliot asks Noam, counting heads.

"Taking a shit out back," she says. "He'll have heard it, though."

Mirotic is tapped in now, his implant blinking red. "Just one bogey," he says. "Thirty meters out. Looks like some kind of animal."

"You set it to wail for every fucking swamp rat that wanders through?" Snell says. His face is still streaked with soap.

"It's a lot bigger than a rat," Mirotic says. "Don't know what it is. It hasn't got vitals. It isn't warm."

"Mechanical?" Elliot asks, thinking of the spider-legged hunter-killers they used to drag rebels out of their caves around Catalao. Tech has a way of trickling over in these long engagements, whether stolen or sold off on the side.

"It's not moving like any of the crawlers I've seen," Mirotic says. "Circling now, toward the back of us. Fast. Jan's still squatting back there."

Some of the squad swivel instinctively. Elliot pulls up Jan's channel. "Prentiss, there's a bogey heading towards you," he says. "Might be mechanical. Get eyes on it."

Jan's reply crackles. "Hard to miss," he says. "It's fucking glowing."

"And what is it?" Elliot says. "You armed?"

Jan's reply does not come by channel, but his howl punctures the still night air. Elliot is knocked back as Noam barrows past him, unslinging her gnasher and snapping the safety off. Snell's fast behind, and then the others, and then Elliot finds himself rearguard. He's still fumbling for his weapon when he rounds the back of the downed Heron.

His eyes slip-slide over the scene, trying to make sense of the nightmarish mass of bioluminescence and spiky bone that's enveloped Jan almost entirely. His night vision picks out a trailing arm, a hip, a boot exposed. The creature is writhing tight around Jan's body, spars of bone rasping against each other, and the glowing flesh of it is moving, slithering. The screams from inside are muffled.

Snell fires first, making Elliot's dampers swell like wet cotton in his ear canals. The spray of bullets riddle the length of the creature, and a fine spray of red blood—Jan's blood—flicks into the air.

"Don't fucking shoot!" Noam smacks Snell's weapon down and lunges forward, reaching for her brother's convulsing arm. Before he can grab hold, the creature retreats toward the tree line with Jan still ensnared, unnervingly fast.

It claws itself forward on a shifting pseudopod of bone spines, moving like a scuttling blanket. Someone else fires a shot, narrowly missing Noam running after it. The creature slithers into the trees, for an instant Noam is silhouetted against the eerie glow of it, then both of them disappear in the dark.

"Shit," Tolliver says. "I mean, shit."

Elliot thinks that's as good a summary as any. He can still see Noam's vitals, and Jan's too, both of them spiked hard with adrenaline but alive. They'll be out of range in less than a minute.

"I hit it," Snell says. "Raked it right along its, I don't know, its abdomen. Didn't do nothing."

"You hit Jan. That blood spray, that was Jan."

"Jan's *inside* it."

"We're going after them, right?"

Elliot looks around at the squad's distorted faces. Tolliver's eyes gleam like a cat's in the dark. There is no protocol for men being dragged away by monsters in the night. He opens his jaw; shuts it again. Mirotic shifts in his peripheral, taking a half-step forward, shoulders thrust back, and Elliot knows he is a nanosecond from taking the squad over, and maybe that would be better for everyone.

"Mirotic," he says. "You stay. Get a drone up and guide us bird's eye. Everyone else, on me."

Plunging through the dark swamp, Elliot expects every mud-sucked step to trigger another smartmine. Sweat pools in the hollow of his collarbone. The whine of the drone overhead shivers in his clenched teeth, and the squad is silent except for heavy breathing, muted curses as they follow its glowing path in their implants. The Prentii's signal comes and goes like a static ghost.

The warped green-and-black blur of his night vision, the drone's shimmering trail of digital breadcrumbs, the memory of the monster and Jan's disembodied thrashing arm—none of it seems quite real. A nightmare, or more likely an overdose.

"Rebels stay out of these swamps," Snell says aloud, dredging something from his post-clamp war briefing. "All the colonists do." His voice is thin and tight.

Nobody replies. The drone's pathway hooks left, into the deepest thicket of sponge trees, and they follow it. Pungent-smelling leaves slap against Elliot's head and shoulders. It reminds him almost of the transplanted eucalyptus trees where he grew up on Earth.

"Can't get any closer with the drone," comes Mirotic's crackly voice in his ear. "Trees are too high, too dense. They're right ahead of you. Close now."

The twins' signal flares in Elliot's skull, but their channels are shut and their vitals are erratic. Elliot's feels his heart starting to thrum too fast. Eyes blink and heads twitch as the rest of the squad picks up the signal. Tolliver's face is drawn, his mouth half-open. Santos is unreadable. Snell looks ready to shit himself. Hands tighten on stocks. Fingers drift to triggers.

The sponge trees thin out, and Elliot sees the same bioluminescence that swallowed Jan whole. The shape of it is indistinct, too bright for his night vision, so he flicks it off. When he closes and reopens his eyes, he sees what's become of the twins.

They are tangled together in a grotesque parody of affection, limbs wrapping each other, and it's impossible to tell where one ends and the other begins because they are coated in a writhing skin of ghostly blue light. Long shafts of dull gray bone, humors or femurs from an animal Elliot knows was not killed by any plague, skewer them in place like a tacked specimen.

Reminding himself it might be a hallucination, Elliot steps slowly forward. "Prentiss?"

A sluggish ripple goes through the twins' tangled bodies. Elliot follows the motion and finds a neck. A head not covered over. Noam's eyes are wide open and terrified. Elliot watches her face convulse trying to speak, but when her bruised mouth opens, glowing blue tendrils spill out of her throat. It's inside her. Elliot recoils. In his own throat, he feels bile rising and burning.

"Shit, they're conscious," Tolliver breathes. "What is that stuff? What the fuck is . . . ?" He reaches for Noam's cheek with one hand, but before he makes contact the other head, Jan's, buried somewhere near his sister's thigh, begins to wail. It's a raw animal noise Elliot has only ever heard men make when they are torn apart, when their limbs have been blown off, when shock and pain have flensed them down to the reptile brain and all it knows to do is scream.

He claws Tolliver's hand back.

"Don't touch them," he says. "We have to run a scan, or . . . " He looks at the bones pinning them in place, at the writhing cloak that looks almost like algae, now, like glowing blue algae. He has no idea what to do.

"Look at the feet," Santos says thickly. "Fuck."

Elliot looks. Noam's feet are not feet any more. The skin and muscle has been stripped away, leaving bits of bone, crumbling with no tendon to hold them together.

"Kill them," Santos says. "It's eating them alive." She pulls her sidearm and aims it at Jan's screaming mouth. Her hand tremors.

Elliot doesn't tell her no. It would be mercy, now, to kill them. Same how it was mercy for Beasley.

A vein bulges up Santos's neck. "Can't," she grunts. "The implant."

Elliot aims his own weapon at Jan and as his finger finds the trigger he finds himself paralyzed, blinking red warnings scrolling over his eyes. Convict squads have insurance against friendly fire same as any other. Maybe in a combat situation the parameters would loosen a little, but this, an execution, is out-of-bounds.

"Send the nudge, Noam." Tolliver squats down by her wide-eyed face. "You in there? You gotta send the nudge. So we can trigger you. Come on, Noam."

The yellow message doesn't appear. Maybe Noam is too angry, too colonist, thinking she is invincible, thinking somehow she'll get out of this scrape how she got out of all the other ones. More likely her mind is too far gone to access the implant. Jan starts to scream again.

"I'll fucking do it manual, then," Tolliver says, with his voice shaking. He looks at Snell. "Give me your knife. Unless you want to do it."

Snell wordlessly unclips his combat knife and slings it over, handle-first. It's a long wicked thing, not regulation or even close. Elliot thinks he should offer to do it. He's in command, after all. He knows where the jugular is and where to slit it without dousing himself in blood. But he only watches.

And the instant Tolliver touches Noam's head, all hell breaks loose. The monsters come from everywhere at once, scuttling masses of bone and biolu-minescence. From the ground, Elliot realizes dimly even as he backpedals, keys his night vision, opens fire. The rest of the squad is doing the same; splinters fly where bullets hit bone but the skin of things, the blue algae, just splits and reforms.

Subterranean fungi. He remembers that from the topography scan as Tolliver klicks empty and fumbles his reload.

"Get the fuck out," comes Mirotic's voice. "They're coming on your twelve, your three. Lots of them."

Doesn't matter. The thought spears through Elliot's mind. Doesn't matter if he dies here or on Kettleburn or wherever else. He's been dead for ages.

Then Tolliver goes down, tripped by a monster clamping its bony appendages around his legs like a vice. Elliot aims low and for gray, shattering enough bones for Tolliver to wriggle out, to swap clips. But bullets aren't enough here.

Elliot loads the incendiary grenade as Tolliver scrambles free. He tries to remember the chemical compositions here on Pentecost. For all he knows, it might light up the whole fucking swamp. For all he knows, that might be a better way to die than getting flensed alive.

"Run," Elliot orders, and sends the fire-in-the-hole warning spike at the same time. "Leave them."

Santos rips past him, then Snell, then Tolliver right after, no protest, his reflective eyes wide and frantic in the dark. With adrenaline turning everything slow and sharp, Elliot fires the grenade where he thinks the splash will be widest, hitting the dirt between two of the surging creatures. He remembers to blink off his night vision only a nanosecond before the explosion.

A wall of searing heat slams over his body and even without night vision the blossoming fireball all but blinds him. He feels Tolliver grabbing his shoulder, guiding him out of the thicket. Through the roar in his ears, he can't be sure if Jan is still screaming.

They are sitting in the husk of the downed Heron, grouped around a heater. Every so often someone glances toward the cyclops, which is still whirring and spinning and searching. Santos has a bruise on her forehead from where the butt of Snell's gnasher clipped her in the dark. Tolliver cut his thumb falling. Other than that, they are all fine, except Elliot hasn't been able to get to his syringe.

"So there was no plague," Mirotic says. "Only a predator."

"That thing was artificial," Snell says. His eyes look wild, bloodshot, and his hand keeps going to the spot where his knife used to be. "No way could that evolve, man. It's a weapon."

"It's organic, whatever it is," Mirotic says. "Looked on the scan like a fungus."

"It's a weapon, and they dumped us here to test it." Snell's voice ratchets high. "That fucking smartmine was probably one of ours. We're expendable, right? So they dumped us here to see if it works."

Elliot waits for someone to tell Snell to settle the fuck down, but instead Santos and Tolliver and Mirotic are all looking at him, waiting for his response. Tolliver plucks at the bandage around his hand, anxious.

"The colonists stay out of these swamps," Elliot says. "You said that yourself." He has a flash of the twins' twisted bodies, the scuttling monsters. "I figure now we know why."

"When do we get extracted?" Santos asks flatly. "Sir."

Elliot knows they are low priority. Maybe five days, maybe six. Maybe more. "They know we're rationed for a week," he says.

"A fucking week?" Snell grinds his metal teeth. "Man, we can't be out here a week with that thing. I'm not ending up like the twins, man. I say we carry what we can, and we get out of here."

"To where?" Mirotic asks. "The fungus extends under the ground in all directions."

"If you knew about this, why didn't you tell us?" Snell demands.

Mirotic's nostrils flare. "Because fungus is not usually predatory."

Elliot tries to focus on the back-and-forth, tries to think of what they should do now that they know the swamp is inhabited by monsters. He realizes he is scratching at his arm.

Santos looks over. "What the fuck?"

But she isn't looking at Elliot. Tolliver, who has been silent, ash-faced, is clutching at his bandaged thumb. He looks down at it now and his eyes widen. A faint blue glow is leaking from underneath the cling wrap.

"Oh, shit, oh, shit, I feel it." Tolliver is twisting on the cot, sweat snaking down his face. "I can feel it. Moving."

The bandages are off his hand now and his cut thumb is speckled with the glowing fungus. The autosurgeon unfolds over his chest like a metal spider while Mirotic searches for the right removal program, his eyes scrolling code. Elliot feels a panic in his throat that he never feels during combat. It reminds him of the panic he felt last time he spoke to his daughter.

He crouches down and holds Tolliver's free hand where Snell and Santos can't see. It's slippery from the sweat.

"Got it," Mirotic says thickly. "Biological contaminant."

The autosurgeon comes to life, reaching with skeletal pincers to hold Tolliver's left arm in place. Carmine laserlight plays over his skin, scanning, then the numbing needle dips in with machine precision to prick the base of his thumb.

Tolliver's free hand clenches tight around Elliot's.

"Hate these things," he groans, locking eyes for a moment. "Rather let the Smell use that big old fucking knife than have a bot digging around—"

"Shouldn't have dropped it, then," Snell says.

Tolliver swivels, his mouth pulls tight in a grimace. "Fuck you, Snell."

The autosurgeon deploys a scalpel. Metal slides and scrapes and the sound shivers in Elliot's teeth. Mirotic is looking over at him, and when he speaks he realizes why.

"The spores are moving. Autosurgeon wants to take the whole thumb."

A wince ripples through the tent; Santos clutches his own thumb tight between two knuckles. Tolliver's eyes go wide. He tries to yank his arm away, but the autosurgeon holds tight.

"No!" he barks. "No, don't let it! Turn the fucking thing off!"

"It could spread through his body if we aren't fast," Mirotic says. "How you said it did to Prentiss and Prentiss."

Elliot swallows. He isn't a medic. What they drilled into his head, from basic onwards, was to trust the autosurgeon. And he doesn't want Tolliver to end up like the twins.

"Do it," he mutters.

"Turn it off!" Tolliver wails. "Listen! Listen to me, you fucks!"

His free hand thrashes but Elliot holds it tight, not caring anymore if Santos and Snell can see it, as the scalpel descends.

"The program's running," Mirotic says. "Too late to stop it."

The blade makes no sound as it slices through the skin, the tendon, the bone. The autosurgeon catches the squirt of bright red blood and whisks it away. Tolliver howls. His spine arches. His hand clamps to Elliot's hard enough to bruise.

Elliot sits underneath the cyclops, listening to it whir. He said they would sleep in shifts, that he would watch first, as if his vitreous eyes might catch something the sensors miss. Partly because he had to say something. Give some kind of order. Mostly because he needed a hit.

Now, with the morphine swimming warm through his veins, he feels light. He feels calm. His heartbeat is so slow it is almost an asymptote.

"He screamed so much because there was no anesthetic in the autosurgeon."

Elliot turns to see Mirotic, holding a black plastic cube in his hand. He understands the words, but his guilt breaks apart against the high and then dissipates. Tolliver will be fine. Everything will be fine. He tries to shrink the chemical smile on his face, so Mirotic won't see it.

"Everybody knows why," Mirotic says. "Where's the rest of it?" He doesn't wait for a reply. He snatches the rattling sock out of Elliot's lap and yanks him to his feet. Mirotic is tall. But he's slow, too, the way everything is slow on the morphine, and Elliot still has his old tricks.

A hook, a vicious twist, then Mirotic is on the ground with the needle of the syringe poised a centimeter from his eyeball.

"I need that," Elliot says.

"You're pathetic," Mirotic grunts. "Holding his hand and wasting his morphine."

"Why do you care?" Elliot asks, suspicious now, wondering if maybe it's Mirotic who Tolliver visits in the night when he doesn't come to him.

Mirotic slaps the syringe away and drives a knee up into Elliot's chest. The air slams out of him, but he feels only impact, no pain. He staggers away, bent double. If his lungs were working he would maybe laugh.

"I care because you used to know what the fuck you were doing," Mirotic says. "Back before they stuck you with a con squad." He taps the high-grade neural plug at his temple. "You read our records. But I've seen yours, too. These personnel firewalls aren't shit. And if we're going to get out of this, it won't be with you doped to the eyes."

"Give Private Tolliver the paineaters," Elliot rasps, straightening up. "Leave the morphine. That's an order."

Mirotic shakes his head. "It stays with me, now. You'll get it when we get extracted." He tosses the black plastic cube; Elliot nearly fumbles it. "Worry about this, instead," Mirotic says. "Worry about a fungus that eats our flesh and uses the bones like scaffolding."

Elliot turns the cube over. Through the transparent face, he sees sticky strands of the glowing blue fungus moving, wrapping around Tolliver's scoured-white knucklebone.

In the morning, Snell is gone.

"Never woke me for my watch," Santos says, picking gound out of the corner of her eye. "I checked the tent. His kit's not there."

"And now he's out of range," Mirotic says. "Could get the drones up to look for him. Keep them low again so we don't trigger any more mines."

The inside of Elliot's mouth feels like steel wool. They are standing in the sunshine, which makes his head ache, too. A cool breeze is rippling through the blue-and-purple flora. The sponge trees are swaying. It's peaceful, near to beautiful. In daylight it's hard to believe what happened only hours ago in the dark. But the twins' tent is empty, and Tolliver is drugged to sleep with bloody gauze around the stump of his thumb.

"Why would we look for him?" Elliot says.

Santos gledges sideways at Mirotic, but neither of them speak.

"He deserted," Elliot says. "If he doesn't pose a threat to us, we let him walk. He'll either step on a mine or get eaten alive." He feels slightly sick imagining it, but he keeps his voice cold and calm. "Mirotic, rig up a saw to one of the drones, start clearing the vegetation on our flank. Make sure we have clean line of fire. No use watching them on the cyclops if we can't hit them til they're right up on us. Santos, get the comm system out of the Heron. We're going to make a radio tower."

When Santos departs with her sloppy salute, there's less contempt in it than usual. Mirotic stays and stares at him for a second, suspicious. Elliot meets his gaze, pretending he doesn't care, pretending he didn't already ransack Mirotic's cot looking for the morphine while he was on watch.

"Good," Mirotic says, then goes to get the drone.

Elliot turns back toward the tents. He lets himself into the one Tolliver and Snell were sharing, and realizes Tolliver is no longer asleep. He's sitting up on the sweat-stained cot, staring down at his lap, at his hand.

"How are you feeling?" Elliot asks, because he doesn't know what else to say.

"You took my thumb." Tolliver's voice trembles. "I needed that thumb. That's my good hand."

"It was moving deeper," Elliot says. "That's why we had to amputate. You probably don't remember." He hopes Tolliver doesn't remember, especially not the pain.

"Still got a trigger finger, so I guess it doesn't matter to you, right?" Tolliver says. "Still got a mouth, still got an ass. All the parts you like."

Elliot feels heat creeping under his cheeks. "You can get a prosthetic when they pick us up," he says, clipped.

"At this rate?" Tolliver gives a bitter laugh. "There's gonna be nobody left to pick up tomorrow, fuck a week. That's if you really did get the extraction request through, and you're not just lying through your fucking teeth. I know junkies. I know all you do is lie."

Elliot wants to slip his hands around Tolliver's throat and throttle him. He wants to slip under the sheet and hold Tolliver to him and tell him they're going to make it. He does neither.

"I needed that thumb because I was going to be a welder," Tolliver snaps as Elliot goes to leave. "When all this shit was over and I'd gotten my clamp out, I was going to be a welder like my grandfather was."

But war is never really over, and there's a sort of clamp that doesn't come out. Elliot doesn't even remember what he used to think he was going to be. He turns over his shoulder.

"Your head's not right," he says calmly. "It's the drugs. Try to sleep more."

"Oh, fuck you," Tolliver says, somewhere between laughing and crying. "Fuck you, Elliot."

Elliot steps out, and the tent closes behind him like a wound scabbing shut.

By the time night falls, they've cleared a perimeter, cutting away the vegetation in ragged circumference around the Heron, the tents, the cyclops. Tolliver came out to help mid-afternoon, jaw clenched tight and eyes fixed forward. Nobody mentioned his hand or even looked at it.

The few incendiary grenades they have in armory are distributed. Mirotic is trying to rig up a flamethrower using a soldering torch and fuel drained from the tank. Santos and Tolliver are perched on the roof of the Heron, hooking the makeshift antennae into the comm system through a tangle of wires.

Mostly busy work, Elliot knows. They can't be sure the incendiary grenade did anything but distract the fungus, and it moves fast enough that having open ground might only be to its advantage. They don't know anything about this enemy.

But if he keeps up appearances, maybe he can get the last of the morphine back from Mirotic without resorting to violence. Act sharp, act competent, and then when the withdrawal kicks in he won't have to exaggerate much to make Mirotic realize how much he needs it to function.

"Nothing," Santos says.

Elliot looks up to the roof of the Heron. Tolliver is still trying to rotate the antennae for a better signal, but all that comes through the comm system and into their linked implants is shrieking static. He dials it down in his head. They are too far from the outpost.

Then a familiar signal comes faint and blurry. A blinking yellow nudge slides into the corner of his optic.

"Snell," Tolliver says. "Shit."

Elliot feels a shiver go under his skin. The sky is turning dark above them. The cyclops picked up no movement during the day, but like Mirotic said, plenty of predators hunt only at night. There can only be one reason Snell would send the nudge. Elliot can picture him stumbling through the bog, maybe dragging a turned ankle, with the blue glow creeping closer and closer behind him in the dark. Or maybe the fungus already has him, is already flensing him down to his skeleton.

Tolliver's upvote appears, then Santos's. It will only take four votes now to trigger the nanobomb. Mirotic looks over at him, and Elliot doesn't think Mirotic is the merciful type. He executed three people and put their bodies through a thresher. But then Mirotic's upvote appears in the queue.

"Quick," Tolliver says, not looking at him. "Before we lose the signal."

Elliot is not sure if he's making the strong move or the weak move, but he adds his vote and completes the consensus because he still remembers Jan's screams. Everyone is silent for a moment. Santos crosses herself with the same precision she salutes.

"Leave the antennae," Elliot says. "The extraction request went through. They'll come when they come. Until then, we dig in and stay alert."

Santos hops down off the roof of the Heron. Tolliver follows after, gingerly for his bandaged hand. Elliot looks at what's left of the squad—fifty percent casualties in less than two days, and nowhere near the frontlines. Santos is steady; Elliot hasn't seen her shook once yet. Mirotic is steady. But Tolliver hasn't told a joke or barely spoken the whole day and his eyes look scared.

Elliot's still looking at Tolliver when the cyclops wails a proximity alert. He tamps down his own fear, motions for Mirotic to tap in.

"Seven bogeys," Mirotic says. "Different sizes. Biggest one is over two meters high. They're heading right at us, not so fast this time."

Elliot flicks to night vision and watches the trees. "Aim for the bones," he says, remembering the previous night. "They need them to hold together. Santos, get a firebomb ready."

Santos loads an incendiary grenade into the launcher underslung off her rifle. Tolliver has his weapon tucked up against his side, like he's bracing for auto, and Elliot remembers it's because he has no thumb. Across the carpet of chopped-down ferns and branches, he sees something emerging from the trees. It's not moving how the other ones moved.

Elliot squints and the zoom kicks in. The shambling monster is moving on three legs and its body is a spiky mess of charred bone held together by the ropy fungus. Through the glow he can make out part of a blackened skull on one side. The twins' bones, stripped and reassembled like scaffold. His stomach lurches.

Santos curses in Portuguese. "Permission to fire?" she asks through her teeth.

The other bogeys are converging now, low and scuttling like the one that took Noam. A pack, Elliot thinks. He can feel his pulse in his throat. This isn't combat how he knows combat. Not an enemy how he knows enemies. He wonders if the flames even did any damage the night before. Bullets certainly hadn't.

"Wait until they're closer," he says. "No wasted splash."

Santos sights. Her finger drifts toward the trigger. She waits.

But the monsters don't come any closer.

"It's fucking with us," Tolliver says. "Sitting out there waiting." He has a calorie bar in his hand but it's still wrapped. He's been turning it over and over in his fingers.

Santos bites a chunk off her own ration. "You think it thinks?" she asks thickly. She glances to Mirotic, who shrugs, then to Elliot, who distractedly does the same. Elliot is more concerned by the deepening itch in the crook of his arm. He needs morphine soon.

"Has to," Tolliver says. "It came for Jan first. Jan was the one who went out and found the bones in the first place. Then it used Noam to lure us out."

The four of them are sitting under the cyclops, with a crate dragged out to hold food and dice for a game nobody is keeping track of, just rolling and passing on autopilot. Every so often Elliot has someone walk a tight circle around the Heron to check their back, in case more of the monsters try to flank them. In case the cyclops malfunctions and doesn't see them coming. Busy work.

But there are still only seven, and they still haven't advanced from the edge of the trees. Sometimes the fungus shifts and the bones find new positions, but they all stay in place, waiting, maybe watching, if the fungus has some way of seeing them. Mirotic suggested heat sensitivity. Mirotic, who must have the morphine hidden somewhere on his body.

Santos is the first to finish her food. She stands up, brushing crumbs off her knees. "I'll go," she says, hefting her weapon. Elliot nods. He can't help but notice Tolliver's eyes follow Santos around the corner of the Heron, wide and worried. Maybe it is Santos he goes to see.

"Big snakes only have to eat once in a month," Tolliver says, turning his eyes back to his bandaged hand, studying the spot of red blooming through. "Spend the rest of it digesting."

Mirotic snorts. "This fungus is not part of a balanced ecosystem. It killed off all the other animal life. Obliterated it."

"Wish we had a fucking chinegun," Tolliver mutters.

Then the cyclops keens, and everyone is on their feet in an instant. Elliot sights towards the tree line first, but the monsters haven't moved. Mirotic's optics blink red.

"Right behind us," he says, and whatever he says next is drowned in gunfire. Santos's signal flares hot in Elliot's head, combat active. Elliot rounds the corner of the Heron and sees Santos scrambling backward as a ghoulish mass of bone and blue bears down on her. He can't understand how the monster covered the perimeter so quickly, how the cyclops didn't spot it earlier. Then he recognizes the tatters of Beasley's polythane body bag threaded through the fungus.

Elliot shoots for bone, but the way the monster writhes as it moves makes it all but impossible. The burst sinks harmlessly into its glowing blue flesh. Tolliver is firing beside him, howling something, but through the dampers he can't hear it. The monster turns toward them, distracted. Elliot calculates; too close for a grenade. He fires again and this time sees Beasley's shinbone shatter apart.

The monster sags, shifting another bone in to take its place, moving what's left of Beasley's arm downward. In the corner of his eye Elliot sees Santos is on her knees, rifle braced. Her shot blows a humerus to splinters and the monster sags again. Elliot feels a flare of triumph in his chest.

Motion in his peripherals. He spins in time to see the other seven bogeys swarm over the top of the Heron. He switches to auto on instinct and strangles the trigger, slashing back and forth. Bullets sink into the fungus, others ricochet off the Heron, spitting sparks. Some find bone but not enough. The rifle rattles his hands and then he's empty and the monsters are still coming.

He backs up, hands moving autonomously for the reload. Tries to get his bearings. Tolliver is still firing, still howling something he can't make out. Santos is down, legs pinned from behind. Bony claws are moving up her back; Elliot sees her teeth bared, her eyes wide. Where is Mirotic?

The answer comes in a jet of flame that envelops the nearest monster. It doesn't scream—no mouth—but as Elliot stumbles back from the heat he can see the fungus twisting, writhing, blackening to a crisp. Mirotic swings the flamethrower, painting a blazing arc in the air. Elliot reloads, sights, fires.

Suddenly the monsters are fleeing, scuttling away. Elliot fires again and again as they round the edge of the Heron. Mirotic waves the flamethrower, Elliot and Tolliver shoot from behind him, advancing steadily. One of the monsters crumples and slicks onto its neighbor, leaving its bones behind on the dirt. Elliot keeps firing until the glow of them is completely obscured by trees.

"You fuckers, you fuckers, you fuckers," Tolliver is saying, almost chanting.

Elliot is shaking all over. His skin is crawling with sweat. "Check on Santos," he says, and Tolliver disappears. There are aches in his back and arms and he can feel his bowels loosening for the first time in a long time. He needs to get the morphine back. He turns to Mirotic, to tell him as much, but as the big man snuffs the end of the flamethrower, he stumbles.

A wine-red stain is blooming under his shirt. Elliot remembers the ricochet off the side of the Heron. Mirotic sits down. He methodically rolls his shirt up and exposes a weeping bullet hole in his side. Elliot can see the shape of at least one shattered rib poking at his skin.

"Fuck," Mirotic says, in a burble of blood.

Shattered rib, punctured lung, and probably a few other organs shredded to pieces. Gnasher bullets were designed to disperse inside the body. "Where is it?" Elliot demands, squatting down face-level. "Where's the morphine?"

Mirotic's face is pale as the old Earth moon. He shakes his head. He tries to speak again, says something that might be *autosurgeon*.

"I'll get the autosurgeon," Elliot says, even though he knows it's too late for that. "Where's the morphine?"

No response. Elliot frisks him, and by the time he pulls the vial out from Mirotic's waistband his hands are slicked scarlet. He clutches his fingers around it and gives a shuddering sigh of relief. Mirotic's eyes flutter open and shut, then stay shut. Elliot gets to his feet, head spinning, as Mirotic's vitals blink out.

When he goes back around the corner of the Heron, Elliot finds Santos is dead, too. One of the fleeing monsters drove a wedge of bone through her skull, halfway smashing her clamp. Blood and gray matter are leaking from the hole. A single spark jumps from the clamp's torn wiring.

Tolliver is crossing himself and his shoulders are shaking. There's a fevered flush under his skin.

"We'll burn her," Elliot says. "Mirotic, too. Any bones left, we'll crush them down to powder."

"Alright," Tolliver says, in a hollowed out voice. His eyes fix on the vial clutched in Elliot's bloody hand, but he says nothing else.

Lying on his cot with his limbs splayed limp, Elliot is in paradise. He feels like his body is evaporating, or maybe turning into sunlight, warm and pure. He can hardly tell where his sooty skin ends and Tolliver's begins.

"Did you kill him for it?" Tolliver's voice asks, slurred with the drug.

"Ricochet," Elliot says.

"Would you have killed him for it?" Tolliver asks.

"Wouldn't you?" Elliot asks back.

As soon as they dealt with the bodies, he went to the tent to shoot up. Tolliver followed him, and when Elliot offered him the syringe, already high enough to be generous, he took it. Elliot doesn't know how long ago that was.

"What made you like this?" Tolliver asks. "What got you so hooked? What fucked you up so bad?"

"There's no one thing," Elliot says, because he is floating and unafraid. "It's never one thing. That would make it easier, right? If I was a good person, and I saw something so bad this is the only way I can . . . " He puts a finger to his temple and twists it.

"Forget," Tolliver supplies.

"Yeah," Elliot says. "But there's no one thing. This job kills you with a thousand cuts."

"But there must have been one thing," Tolliver says. "One thing that got you stuck leading a con squad. Mirotic says. Said. Said you used to be somebody."

Elliot doesn't want to talk about that. "Was it Santos?" he asks, running his fingers along Tolliver's hip.

"What?"

"The nights I message you but you don't come," Elliot says. "There was someone else."

Tolliver shakes his head. "You really are a piece of shit," he says, almost laughs. "You thought that had to be the reason, huh? Never thought maybe some nights I don't really feel like fucking a drugged-up zombie who plays some pornstar in his optics the whole time?"

"I don't," Elliot says.

"Your wife, then," Tolliver says. "That's even more fucked."

"I don't play anything in the optics," Elliot says. "I just see you. That's all."

Tolliver's voice softens a little. "Oh."

On impulse, Elliot sends him the clip. He watches it at the same time, watches his daughter's head turn, her bright eyes blink. "She's grown," he explains. "Twenty-some now. Her and her mother live on old Earth. Only thing they hate more than each other is me. If I was going to get out, it would've been years and years ago."

He moves his hand to Tolliver's arm, wanting to feel the cool plastic of his flay under his fingertips.

"They didn't put me with a con squad as a punishment," he says. "I volunteered."

He looks down into the exposed swathe of red muscle on Tolliver's arm. There are tiny specks of luminescent blue nestled in the fibers. He feels a deep unease slide under his high.

"I don't want to get eaten from the inside," Tolliver says. "I don't want them using my bones."

The poison yellow nudge appears in Elliot's optics.

"Trigger me," Tolliver says. "Right now. While everything still feels okay. You trigger me, and then do yours."

"Could take the arm," Elliot says. "The autosurgeon."

"You said this job kills you with a thousand cuts." Tolliver uses his good hand to find Elliot's and squeeze it. "I'm not going to be a welder. I don't want to be some fucking skeleton puppet, either. Let's just get out of here. And let's not leave anything behind."

His hand leaves, but leaves behind a cool hard shell. Elliot runs his thumb along the groove and recognizes the shape of Tolliver's incendiary grenade. He cups it against the side of his head. He thinks, briefly, about what the pick-up team will find when they finally arrive. What they'll think happened.

He thinks of Tolliver's file, the one he opened and read only once, how Tolliver had smothered his grandfather in his sleep and said it was to stop his pain, even though his grandfather had been healthy and happy. Nobody was good here. Not even Tolliver. But the two of them, they are a good match.

Outside, the cyclops starts to wail. Elliot adds his upvote to the queue, and Tolliver goes limp in his arms. His thumb finds the grenade's pin and rests there. He thinks back to the last time everything still felt okay, then plays it in his optics, watching his daughter before she knew who he was.

"She's awake," his wife's voice sings. "Just looking around . . . "

Elliot breathes deep and pulls the pin and waits for extraction.

The Algorithms of Value
ROBERT REED

Parchment woke comfortably hungry, a fine dream lingering while she lay inside the bed that knew her utterly.

This was the most unremarkable morning.

Happy eyes opened to find the expected room. Cockroaches scrambled across cracked plaster walls. Ancient cars roared and a neighbor's hip hop shook the floor. But there was also a spring wind lifting the window curtain, bringing the scent of hot bacon and the quick, fierce shouts of sparrows. Parchment listened to the birds savoring their spectacular lives, and in the same spirit, she smiled to herself. Then came the sharp crack of a pistol followed by the wailing of someone who had never existed—a wounded voice begging for mercy from everything else unreal.

"Change," Parchment ordered.

The walls silenced and blurred.

"You know where."

The young emerald forest was rendered in precise detail. Bacon didn't exist here, but there were orchids and scented insects and the luscious stink of soil built from comet tar and the purest water. Dawn had just broken on this portion of the terraformed world, glorious sunshine descending from an artificial moon designed by AI sowers. Every tree was a slender tower, the high branches too distant to resolve with sleepy eyes, and down through the sunbeams came a cobalt-blue bird, bigger than ten men, flying lazily against the feeble gravity.

"A day to value," sang the bird. "A beautiful day to eat."

She was born pale and pretty but with an unexpected golden cast to her skin. Wanting to bless the baby, the young mother gave her that rich-sounding name, and nearly two centuries of busy, busy life had mostly erased the old meanings. Parchment wasn't the skin of animals anymore. Parchment was the famous old lady climbing out of her bed to use the toilet and cleansing fountain on the far side of a tree.

With a respectful tone, her room offered to measure her health and feed her.

"No, and no," she replied. "I feel wonderful and I'm eating out this morning."

Her room immediately wove new clothes, but to prove she could, Parchment wished the first hat to vanish, and the second, deciding to wear nothing on her head but carry three umbrellas—highly engineered umbrellas spun from boron and diamond—plus a new purse of moa leather filled with respectable possessions.

By law, every room needed one authentic door.

This particular room offered two doors, one leading directly outdoors, and having collected her belongings, that's where she went.

Every room was able to feed and care for its owner, and people couldn't be forced to leave any room. Yet the world outside always felt busy and crowded and alive. Parchment's street was wide, lined with stacked rooms and standalone rooms. Mayhem flooded the senses. Mayhem had its music. Flocks of sparrows and other city birds swarmed, and intense little machines jetted about on important errands. Neighbors stood in or near the street, shouting to one another while watching strangers. They called to her by name, adding "Madam" and "Ms." for good measure, and Parchment waved at no one in particular, giving warm words to the nearest few.

Approaching her, one familiar fellow praised the morning's beauty by asking, "How could anyone stay inside with this splendor?"

"A fine question," Parchment agreed.

Then his pretty little daughter hurried close, saying, "Yes, but rain is definitely coming, Madam Parchment."

Parchment handed her one of the umbrellas. It was silly, thinking that any ordinary object was precious. But the gesture was what was important. To that child, what mattered were the famous hands that held the prize, and to the old lady, it was the illusion of charity lending warmth to one small moment.

The gift was cradled lovingly while the girl whispered, "Thank you thanks so much so much."

It was never a bad day, getting attention from a famous lady.

There was a boy standing nearby. Maybe he had been standing there from the beginning. One foot behind the other, he flashed a bold smile at the woman with two umbrellas. Parchment didn't recognize the face but she knew his attitude. Begging was older than humanity, and he looked like the sort who would beg for anything, regardless of his needs.

"You can have one too," Parchment offered.

"No."

What did he say?

"I like rain," he said.

"Well, good," she said.

Straightening his back, he asked, "But what else can you give me?"

The world grew a little quieter, bystanders turning, keeping tabs on the small, unseemly drama.

Aiming to tease, she asked, "What else is there?"

He showed her a wide, unendearing smirk.

"Think I'm generous, do you?"

"No, ma'am. I don't."

Parchment laughed at his tone, even while she bristled at the attitude, and tired of the child's attitude, she decided to ignore him, walking off as quickly as she could on long legs that never covered ground fast enough.

Every street was a machine, smart as necessary and busy doing its lifelong calling. Avenues and alleys kept themselves clean, recycling bins ruling the corners. Today the nearest bin resembled a shark's mouth rising from the pavement, and a man had climbed into the mouth, furiously burrowing into the trash.

Scavenging was honorable long before the first ape pushed a hungry hand into someone else's garbage. But these were the wealthiest times and there was zero reason for this nonsense. Parchment's mother had called these people "dumpster dogs," and they were usually best avoided. But that irritating boy was following, keeping far too close, and that's why she paused and struck the shark with a flat hand.

The man inside the trash twisted and popped up, startled to find an umbrella dropped into his hands.

One glance at her face was enough.

"Thank you, Madam Parchment," he sputtered.

"You're welcome," she said, walking on.

Undeterred, the boy fell in beside her.

"I know all about you," he said.

"You think so?" she asked.

"Absolutely," he said sharply.

She stopped walking, instantly regretting showing just that flicker of interest. But this was her neighborhood and these were people friendly to her, and Parchment refused to be intimidated by a child who was . . . how old did he look to be . . . ? A mature twelve, perhaps.

"I don't want to know about you," she said, opening the final umbrella and tipping its shadow over her face, leaving that peculiar little sparrow blinking in the sunshine.

"You're the old lady who invented the Algorithms," he said.

The street grew quiet.

With a slow, firm tone, she said, "First of all, I had tiny roles in an exceptionally large project. So no, you're wrong. I built almost nothing."

The resolve didn't waver. That face wasn't as young as she imagined. He was older. Fourteen, maybe?

"Second of all, nobody can invent what already exists, and the Algorithms have always been. Profound relationships woven through the universe, waiting to be discovered. Like gravity. Like fire and poetry. I filled my own little niche, and that was long ago, and third of all, are you going to leave me alone now?"

"Probably not," the boy confessed.

Several neighbors, stronger than old women or boys, set themselves near the two debaters, offering their help with concerned glances and clenched fists.

Parchment handed over the last umbrella.

"Take this and leave me alone," was her advice.

The boy smiled when he looked at the prize. But then he ran back to the shark mouth, climbing in beside the trash hunter before shoving the gift as far down as he could reach.

• • •

Sentience deserved quite a lot, and the Algorithms of Value spoke to exactly that: the fierce guarantees afforded every self-aware entity, organic or machine.

Safety was the first necessity. Surviving the next moment was paramount. For humans, nourishment and clean water were unimpeachable if rather less urgent rights. There also was the universal right to shelter. By law, every person was guaranteed a home and every home possessed at least one dependable room. Walls had to be ready to project any image, real or fictional. Rooms could sing any song and tell any story, calibrating versions according to the resident's desires. And of course every sentient voice had to be able to speak to everyone else, whenever they wished and without cost. Of course, of course.

Wealth itself was never guaranteed, and true wealth had never been harder to weigh. But there were sentient fortunes who owed their allegiance to Parchment, and she owned comets and asteroids outright, plus valuable lands scattered across the Earth. And she held title to three connected rooms, none of which were tiny. With her age and that small, critical role working with the Algorithms, she also owned a rather considerable celebrity.

Thousands of people had been involved in the Algorithms. Some were more important than her, but they died long ago and here she was, proud for what she had done, damn humility and other silly standards.

But what piece of the Algorithms was Parchment's? In her own eyes, what made her special?

More than any other person, she ensured everyone had the absolute right to be different. To be odd, unique. Or even pathetically ordinary. Food and shelter were essentials, yes. But people and self-aware machines had to be able to cling to peculiar beliefs, just so long as nobody was hurt. For instance, one old lady could wake inside a vanished room decorated with dirty chairs and a ragged curtain drawn across one imaginary window, the close ceiling built from bowed plaster, two cracks peeking through tired white paint.

Sixteen decades ago, there were very few rooms in the world that could manage that trickery. But Parchment and her husband were fortunate enough to own one, and that's when the bedroom habit began, leading to a string of acidic comments.

"Why this fucking dump?" her husband would ask.

"This where I came from," Parchment responded. "And I'll fall back to this, if things go wrong."

"Well, I didn't grow up in your fucking dump," he said. "Don't pretend I care about games you play with your guilty conscience, and sure as shit I don't believe in your reasons anyway. You're lying."

The man was never mild or sweet or decent. But he was useful. He inherited his cash and old-style stocks, and that was long before a pretty golden girl graduated from grade school. He was one of the old masters of a corporation responsible for the best AIs anywhere. An occasional charmer, he had a habit of stalking the pretty girls, like Parchment, and she knew that full well and married him regardless. Nobody else offered a faster route to success, and just as important, her roguish mate had his own simplicities. Immune to normal jealousies, Parchment didn't have to watch over him or pay any attention to the gossip. It was enough to be a famous couple with a unique normalcy, and as it happened, that normalcy didn't have to last all that long. The AIs were building a new world, richer and far more flexible, and what was expensive soon became cheap. The best rooms weaved better and better illusions, capturing the heart of existence, and a successful couple could afford a giant home filled with ever-changing realms. And that's why a difficult husband didn't have to come out of his favorite room for weeks, even to throw an insult at his aging wife. Which was a fair description of their last fifty years.

In the end, three rooms were plenty. One was Parchment's sanctuary, another belonged entirely to her husband, while the large space between could serve as a social playground, but was mostly filled with anti-noise—ensuring she never had to hear the games an old beast played with his various toys.

The beast was a century dead, and his widow rarely thought about him. But in the proper mood, Parchment would admit that the man was perceptive in one critical fashion: The old bedroom with its cracks and curtains and gunfire wasn't just a cautionary reminder to herself. It was also aimed at her husband. Beginning life male and at a respectable height, he had managed to rise quite a bit higher. But his wife was born at the bottom, and not only did she match his achievements, but she eventually supplanted him.

And of course she was the one-half of a marriage blessed with the unique, increasingly famous name.

Fire was an honorable attraction among humans. So were the blessings of food prepared by friendly hands and padded seats where an ancient body could find repose if not out-and-out rest. Parchment had several favorite restaurants, but there was only one nicest nearest and finest establishment. It offered simple candles at each table and an eager blaze surrounded by a stone chamber set inside the longest wall. The food was barely better than what her home could weave from perfect ingredients, but there were those who counted on her commerce and appreciated her nature. And in turn, she enjoyed those who smiled at her, keeping her favorite booth ready for no one else. Unless of course this was a day to invite a guest.

"Is anyone joining you, madam?"

"Not this morning. No."

Some museum establishments had waiters and individual service, but Parchment would never seek out places as egalitarian as that. A long steel counter ruled by a smiling workman was enough, with people and machines in the kitchen supervising the meals.

"And what will you have this morning, madam?"

She knew the fellow's name and much of his life story. Less than thirty when they met, he had reached his sixties—not young but plenty of energy in the bright smile and the jittering dance of fingers waiting to strike the ordering keys.

"A hadrosaur omelet," she said. "With cuttlefish and Martian greens and a double helping of feta and why not coffee too?"

The proper keys were struck—an archaic ritual that didn't need to exist anywhere for the last hundred years.

The old lady paid with gold coins pulled from the new purse.

Another ritual, and splendid because of it.

The smile and the man handed her a new mug and an old wooden marker. She was required to pour her own coffee, and what she liked best wasn't the abundance of brews or the infinite capacity to mix them in any combination . . . no, the joy was in doing this for herself inside a room filled with strangers and neighbors. The heat of the coffee was another kind of fire, and her booth was empty and eager for her to sit inside the reassuring confines. Furniture and windows could always be reconfigured, following endless whims, but this place resisted change. Maybe that's what she liked best. And maybe that's why she had abandoned plenty of other restaurants over the decades, each for committing the crime of novelty.

Parchment's wealth was difficult to calculate, and that from AIs built to do nothing but count the mass of capital. She could purchase this business and a thousand other restaurants, remaking them however she wished or preserving them in amber. But not only didn't she avoid that, it had been decades since even the possibility had drifted through her mind.

Sitting where she belonged, alone, she sipped hot water laced with brown chemicals born minutes ago. Nothing in the mug had anything to do with coffee trees and beans. The fireplace stood to her right. On her left, tall diamond windows opened onto a city corner, and standing on that popular corner—doing nothing and obvious because of his immobility—was that same odd boy.

Looking at him, Parchment felt tense.

The boy was going to stare. She expected nothing else. So she sipped while studying the numbered marker on her table, certain that the young face would soon push against the diamond. But no, when she looked again, nothing had changed. People strode past and they stood together and chatted, but the boy just stared at the soft clean face of the street, and not once, even in small ways, did the nameless creature beg from any of the passersby.

Yet he had certainly made a plea for Parchment's kindness.

Her meal arrived, full of its own heat and flavors—a collection of materials derived by guesswork and perfected by experience. The man from the counter personally delivered the plate and disposable utensils along with the standard question, "Will there be anything else, madam?"

"That child," she said, pointing.

Then she said nothing, curious what her friend would imagine to come next.

"Do you wish him gone?" the man inquired.

"Eventually," she said. "But for now, I'd like to have him sit in front of me. If you can induce him to do that. And I'll pay for his breakfast, if he wishes."

"What will we make of our world?"

The Algorithms were meant to answer one iteration of that everlasting question. Humanity and the machines were approaching a rough balance, but this wasn't going to be the fabled, feared Singularity. AIs were brighter by the second, but human reach was expanding at an astonishing pace. The situation was as perilous as any thriller alarmist scenarios. This was a situation hungry for order, and that's why the Algorithms were conceived over beer and then heavily funded. And most importantly, the work was empowered by emergency laws. Ten thousand meetings and a thousand thousand emails wrestled with the "make of our world" conundrum. Genius worked on nothing else, and the work marched across most of a decade, crafting the world's shape. And when genius slept—human and otherwise—it suffered nightmares about a quiet, empty future that would come if any portion of the critical work failed.

Parchment endured more than her share of awful nights.

But not her husband. A life of success had stripped away much of his imagination. Looking forwards, he saw nothing but Paradise, and maybe the road map wasn't obvious to anyone, including himself, but at least he had confidence in the men and those few bright girls who were better at details than a visionary such as himself.

He still slept with living women. There was always some pretty assistant and a prettier intern and various etcetera girlfriends amenable to a wealthy man's body parts.

Parchment still shared the mansion with him, on those rare nights when both were home.

They even occasionally slept inside the same room.

There was no blatant moment when Parchment gained the upper hand in the marriage. But it was obvious that colleagues respected her opinion. And the AIs sought out her advice. And her husband was visibly bothered by praises being offered to her, and worse still, to her "innovative" work.

"'Innovative' is an idiot's cliche," he complained.

"You should share your insight," she suggested. "Tell the idiots that they don't know how to use language."

That earned a hard half-stare, as if the air beside her face had offended him.

"It's better to be innovative than get stuck inside a hole," she warned.

Her husband never struck her. Except with his thoughts, that is. And he probably never realized that she could read the violence in his face and posture. But it was obvious just then: His imaginary self had just slapped her across the mouth.

Shifting topics, she said, "We aren't making enough progress."

That was a reliable way to make him laugh. Doubt brought ridicule to whoever dared offer the opinion. "We always thought self-aware machines would kill us," he reminded her. "Yet here we are, still happily in charge of the conscious Them."

AIs were always Them. And despite the bluster, her husband was never entirely comfortable with Them.

Life was a race, and there was always a moment when someone else took the lead. Her husband was still in charge of quite a lot. At work, at home. But the various girlfriends were running him to exhaustion. That was an argument for later days, Parchment decided. When he was more vulnerable than now. What mattered was the question to be answered in the next few years, if not sooner.

"What will They make of us?" she asked.

"Besides Us being the gods that brought them into existence?"

She stared, and not at the empty air.

He wouldn't blink. She watched his thoughts, shoulders pushing forwards and the handsome eyes finally staring at her eyes. Dogged and a little scared, he said, "You don't have any reason to complain. We're building a helluva set of rules. These Values of ours. No, I'm not the one making them tight enough to last a million years. But shit, we've got the best coders and lawyers that ever lived, and the most loyal machines, and we're going to end up with a political-economic-ecological system that runs itself for ten million years."

"Nothing runs itself," she said.

"So our grandkids make baby adjustments," he maintained. "Flourishes they can drop in where necessary."

She honestly wished that he was right, and she said, "I believe you."

Which surprised him. And heartened him. "So what do you think we should do, Parchment? To keep this world orderly and happy, I mean."

It was a rare opportunity, the two of them together and him pretending to care what she believed.

"The key to this," she began.

"Yeah?"

"Everyone needs to wake up poor."

There. She said it as simply as possible, including machines as well as people in that expansive "everyone."

But what was profound to her was worse than laughable to him.

"I'll tell you what everybody needs," he said. Then up went a finger, pointed straight at her face. "There's one thing and one thing only, and when we get it . . . when we reach that point . . . nothing ever changes again."

"That's the beautiful, awful truth about tomorrow."

And the bastard beast was right.

Sitting in front of Parchment, the boy looked both smaller and older. Inside the table, menus upon menus suggested breakfasts and other meals.

"How old are you?" she asked.

"Guess," he said instantly, as if expecting the question. But before she could guess, he added, "Fifteen years and seven months. Although I look young, I know. The girls always think so."

"I'm not good with ages," she said, meaning to shove the matter aside.

Breaking tradition, her friend had come from behind the counter to take this special order.

"I know what I want," the boy said. A fingertip touched the tiny entry, pulling it into a larger font, and setting both hands flat on the tabletop, he added, "My room won't make this."

The man took a sudden breath. But his voice remained calm and warm when he asked, "And how many?"

"Two, please. Grilled and with the bones included. I like playing with bones."

"Very good, sir."

Then it was just the two of them, and Parchment guessed, "You live on your own."

"Emancipated since I turned fourteen," he said.

The world was crowded but exceptionally safe, and tradition was the only reason why people half his age were called children. Parchment didn't have much fondness for long childhoods, and if she had any power, she would have ordered . . .

But nobody had that power, did they?

"My room is minimal," the boy mentioned.

"Minimal?"

"Spartan. That's the word," he said with pride.

"But in that room, you can see anything and eat almost anything," she said. "No home is tiny anymore."

He shrugged. "There has to be a smallest stupidest room. And I'm the one who got it."

Why did she invite this animal to join her? What did she imagine would come of this?

"You have three rooms," he continued. "That's what your neighbors tell me, at least."

"Your name?" she asked.

Was the question even heard? He looked at one of his hands, then the other. "I thought of asking for one of your extra rooms."

"And I'd have kept the umbrella for myself," she joked.

He shrugged. "Asking doesn't mean you want. Asking is the noise you make to cover up the real business."

She nodded, working with his words.

Then the expression changed. The little man seemed a hundred years old, asking, "Why do we live this way?"

"What way?"

"Poor and crowded and trapped on one poor crowded world?"

Obvious answers probably wouldn't appeal to him. But it was important to make the right noise here, and that's why she offered the obvious reply. "We're the richest people who ever lived. Even you. You own a room property and enough capital to live for centuries, and an army of servants waiting for your next words."

"I rather like that image," he agreed.

"There's no reason to be stubborn," she said. "Perhaps I'll look up your face, see who you are on my own."

The comment was avoided with a sideways glance.

Then the meal arrived, and she muttered, "Oh god."

On the plate, woven from soulless ingredients and cooked inside a fierce, brief fire, were a pair of human hands.

The young man's own hands, apparently.

"Well," Parchment said.

"Haven't you heard of this dish?" he asked, lifting a newly made fork and knife. "It's popular among a few of us."

"It's ugly and it's rude," she said.

"I'm fifteen. What do you expect?"

She said nothing.

"I know what you're thinking. 'Do I have to have him kicked out, or do I stand and run away to save myself?'"

She looked up, waiting to catch any eye that would help her.

"Ink," said the young man.

"Pardon?"

"That's my name. As of a few weeks ago, as it happens." He dropped the utensils, picking up a cooked hand by the wrist bones and the thumb. "I found out about you and decided to change my name. To Ink."

"Ink writing on Parchment. Is that the joke?"

"After the first minutes, no. The humor pretty much drained away."

And suddenly this awful beast of a youngster was fascinating. Why was that? What had he done or said to deserve this change of attitude?

"I didn't want your umbrella," he said.

"I realized that."

"And I don't care that much about any room inside your house."

"Good," she said.

He nibbled at the flesh between the thumb and forefinger. Then with grease on his mouth, he said, "I don't think normal thoughts."

"You don't," she agreed.

"If you guess what I want," he began.

Then he bit again.

"If I guess?"

"You're more clever than I imagined," he said. "But I don't think you are. I don't think anybody can be that clever."

When was the last time that anyone was this fascinating?

Parchment sat back.

The young man ate in slow careful bites, revealing an unexpected precision with this taunting cannibalism.

"Let me confess a considerable something," she said.

"If you let me hear it however I want," he said.

My, this was one exceptionally refreshing fellow.

Their former mansion was abandoned, not sold. Cash and capital had little left to say to the wealthy, and that's the way it would be for everyone soon. Parchment had designed three portable, nearly perfect rooms. One room was enough for the husband's endless pleasure, and their home could be carried almost anywhere, which meant Antarctica and Berlin, Bali and the newly green Atacama. What about Mars? Calculations were made, the skeleton of a transport ship was built, but the mistress of the house didn't relish leaving billions of people out of reach, and that's why the rooms ended up standing in the midst of a continent-sized city.

Two famous people lived a few steps apart. The husband's heart was the closest heart to hers. Yet only in a physical sense, of course. After he died, Parchment counted the days since they last spoke. Four thousand and seven days passed since she said any word to her mate. Four thousand days since she could have touched either of his hands or the outlines of his still handsome face. If she had wanted to touch him, which she didn't.

Did Parchment grieve when he was gone?

More than she admitted to anyone, particularly herself.

No, she never liked the man, and the young-girl's admiration was long spent. But when everything else was easy, he was otherwise. Her husband was blunt and rude and simple, and he was eager to crush whatever joy she could imagine, and that made him the rarest treasure.

Before he died, Parchment spent long moments imagining the man's passing. And she was wrong in every way. Her normal assumption was that she wouldn't know it had happened. Peculiar sex would kill his heart, and being indifferent to the world, he wouldn't have configured any safety system. The corpse would rot. Sealed doors would keep that secret, perhaps for years. She imagined that he was dead already—a vivid, sometimes appealing daydream that lasted for several years.

She rather liked being a widow, if only in practice.

On the four thousand and eighth morning, someone knocked on her tenement door. This was the door leading into the central room, that space where nobody ever was, and her surprise was vivid. Fun. Dressing as quickly as she could, she called out a few words about patience and who was there and what was happening. Nobody answered, but the knocking persisted. So she asked her room if she was in danger, and with its calmest warm voice, the room promised that danger had never been less of a possibility.

That's when she knew. Her neighbor, the man who had beaten her endless times inside his mind, was no more.

Half-dressed, she opened her door.

What wasn't human stood before her. It was vividly female, yes, but shaped unlike every earthly woman. The orifices were filled with light, and she smelled of odd musks and salt and odors that resisted definition, and after offering a name that might have been her own, the fantasy creature told the Earth woman that her man was lost but the body remained, and could she come please claim the body before it began to foul the world?

"The world," Parchment repeated to her breakfast partner.

The half-eaten hand was forgotten. Ink watched her face, spellbound.

"I always assumed he was screwing interns," Parchment said. "But it seems no, he had moved past those pale dreams. Decades ago, the man secretly bought the help of high-end AIs. He wanted a world of unusual depth, packed with details no rational person would bother with. A world drawn down to every grain of scented sand and a deep history, with ten willing alien wives playing on tendencies and oddnesses that I couldn't have imagined, even when I imagined his worst."

A sigh preceded a shake of the head. And the boy said, "Neat."

"No," she disagreed.

He thought of arguing. She saw the ideas flashing across his face. But he decided not to strike back with logic or emotion.

Silence was best.

"The man's body was still warm," she said. "He still smelled alive, but not in a normal way. Because he had been eating contrived alien meats and whatever else, I assume. And breathing a different air. A very beautiful air, by the way. I looked about. Before calling the appropriate officials, I stood on a mountaintop not much larger than this restaurant, admiring a view that was as lovely as any could be. The wife stood beside me. Grieving in her fashion, I suppose. Some orifices leaked music. Other portions of her offered words. She told me that the mountain was filled with amazing rooms. The sum total of her world's artistic wealth was within my reach, and wouldn't I wish to have a quick year-long look?

"I told her to show me the way.

"She lead me to a staircase. And when she started down, I used the kill-command that I wove into each of our rooms. Back when I built them, I did that. And the data were instantly dumped. So much data, so quickly, that the Earth felt the impact as AIs and servers fell into their first sleep in decades."

She stopped talking.

Ink looked at his plate.

"I own worlds," she said.

He nodded.

"Ages ago, I sent my fortune into the Kuiper Belt and told it to keep busy."

"I know that," he said.

"You don't want umbrellas or rooms," Parchment said. "I think you want me to hand over one of my little terraformed comets."

He didn't say, "Yes."

Instead, Ink sobbed with genuine, weary despair. "We've got so much out there, but this is where we stay."

"People are homebodies, by nature," she said.

"I'm not."

She waited.

"Yeah," he said. "I want one world and a ship. And I know people. People who can't live another day here, eating a life that won't ever test them."

Emotion welled up inside Parchment.

The boy watched.

Both of them waited.

Then she said, "No," and picked up the uneaten hand. And taking a first little nibble, liking the pepper but not the grease, she said, "I have a rather different proposal to offer."

The hip hop woke her.

Violent, joyous lyrics ended with the hard bark of a car backfiring. Which was more alarming than a pistol, odd as that seemed.

Parchment sat up.

"Change the scene?" the room anticipated.

"No. Don't."

For the first time since she was a thirteen, Parchment dressed inside that grim, bug infested room. A freshly woven third-hand dress and comfortable shoes and a hat ready to catch any eye. Then she stepped through the other door, into the central room. An expansive volume originally meant to be filled with parties and significant ceremonies, it was occupied by nothing but white walls and a gray floor and one youngster sitting with legs crossed in the middle of the floor, speaking to unseen faces on a privacy screen.

"Ready?" she asked.

He tried twice to stand, and then succeeded, legs revealing his nervousness. Which was endearing to see in any groom.

The Abduction of Europa

E. CATHERINE TOBLER

BOLAJI

Everything blurs.

This morning, I thought it was the condensation of my breath upon the helmet's convex interior, but it's something else. Deep space shapes our eyes in ways unknown. Under this pressure, Europa is hazy, distant water plumes fogging the horizon, but closer too, and I think there is an undiscovered crevasse. We should be more mindful, but we soldier on, single file, metal cleats biting into the thin ice that covers Europa's salt ocean. Marius is already lost and though we walk toward Thrace Terminal, it has never seemed so distant. The second icecat seized up three days ago and no human has made this journey on foot.

We should be perfectly fine—our suits were made for this world, heavy enough so that we will not struggle in the lesser gravity, thick enough to shield us from the radiation pouring from the sky. Beyond the haze, Jupiter churns in eternal storm. Before we left Thrace Terminal, we were mindful of the red spot, seeming to reemerge from having been swallowed—but I cannot see it now, Jupiter's immensity hesitant to rise.

It used to bother me, the idea that we would be dead in a day without all the shielding we live behind. That radiation would squash us like bugs, but you get used to it. Space is hostile, my father used to say, but so too the ocean. We were not built for these spaces, so must change ourselves to enter them. It has always been so; history tells us this.

A low vibration churns in my gut as I stab my cleat into the ice and push myself through another step. Endless miles of ice, the naked sky above us. I peek at that sky and my knees jelly at the sight of Galileo Station coming into view, framed against the vast milk-in-coffee expanse of Jupiter. The station's helium collection pods catch the distant sunlight and look like strands of spider web. They dance, but not in any wind. They plummet, into the clouds and gone, before returning with their precious cargo. The idea that the station is populated, that somehow people live within its walls, troubles my mind. Against the bulk of Jupiter, the station is no more than a pinprick, and if we living creatures fit within that pinprick—

I am made to feel small. Nausea punches a clammy hand into my throat. I try to swallow it down, because vomiting in a containment suit is no one's idea of a good time. The smell of my body is overwhelming, the silent admission that I escalated this endeavor, that Marius died, that they would send Kotto alone for us. *Alone.*

It is the idea of paperwork that calms my mind; paper is a thing of the past, of course—it will be a series of cold keys and colder screens, making my fingertips chill with every swipe, but the idea of the work to come comforts, even if the idea of Kotto behind me does not. If you had to have anyone come after you, on a distant ice-clad moon where your partner had been—*swallowed,* my mind whispers.

Tragically taken, I amend.

Kotto would not be anyone's first choice. Kotto knows walls and vehicles; she doesn't know sky and ice. She doesn't know the stories of these distant places the way I do.

KOTTO

They say that after a while, you don't notice the cold.

The station is cold and Europa, being four hundred and eighty-five million fucking miles from the sun, is naturally and one-hundred percent organically, cold. You think you won't miss it—that far away, you'll be locked up tight inside Thrace Terminal and too busy working. You'll be diving into a goddamn alien ocean—what's to miss? All that warmth is what.

You don't dream about sex—you dream about sunlight, about the way it looked falling through leaves, about the way it felt on your skin. They say you can't remember—you were too young, born on Schiaparelli Station, shot toward Galileo as a teen, your family devoted to the deep; you've only ever seen holos of trees you foolish, foolish girl, but you remember what that light looked like. Like fucking heaven.

I talk about light a lot in my mental assessments. I'm told that station-borns tend to have some trouble with natural light, or lack thereof. Something in our mind remembers it wasn't supposed to be all darkness and cold; something inside still hungers for what we've never known. And Europa, despite being one of the brightest objects in the goddamn sky, isn't ever quite bright enough from the surface.

She's all silver and ice—the Snow Queen, Marius called her—but you know that means she's cold. Bolaji talks about the life that runs beneath her frozen surface, crackling in copper coils, and I thought at first he meant the ocean—but he means the lineae, which look like bloodied shadows to me.

They meant to remove me from service once, given that my eyes cannot see the full color spectrum, but in the end decided that would be a waste, given my family's devotion to the deeps. Once you're out here, what else is there to do—it's not like we're building entertainment complexes or schools. We aren't making cities—though aren't we, every station is a city in miniature—and there aren't exactly other jobs that need filling. This deep in, everyone's a garbage collector, a plumber, a chef.

I'd trained and advanced at the top of every class as if born to water, so it wasn't like they could kick me without consequence. There are a good many of us, but still not enough. Deep space science remains a sparse thing. Most people stayed where they were born, in the warm, sunshiny splendor of Earth. Fucking Earth. It's no more than a pinprick in the sky and I still crave it. Wonder what the oceans taste like. Wonder if I'll ever get there.

"Hold."

My voice crackles out of my suit and ahead of me, Bolaji pauses in our trek. I draw alongside him, watching the plumes of vapor that haze the sky. Somewhere else, our helmets might dot with moisture, but here, the plumes fall as snow and ice—it's too damn cold on the surface to stay liquid for long. But Bolaji's helmet is fogged and I lift a gloved hand, trying to wipe it away. It's on the inside—he's breathing too hard and I wonder if he's got what Marius had, what we're trying to deny he had. Shrieking about the lost station—he'd found it, he'd found it, but there *was* no lost station, we'd know. Wouldn't we?

People out there, it was said, they get sick and go mad because of the cold, because of the dark. You can't tell a person's gone mad, not until they melt down. But Bolaji's eyes are steady on me.

"Gotta get Marius out of your head," I say. "What happened happened, Bolaji—you were good to go after him, but goddamn. Some people aren't made for *this* kind of place, even if they were born out here."

But there's something else in Bolaji's eyes even as he nods at me and agrees. There's something else and I don't press. *What did he see that I couldn't see?* There's no because. I just don't. I'm fucking tired and we'll be sleeping another night on the ice and I'm *tired*. So tired of the cold they said I would stop noticing. They never said when—but they said I would.

MARIUS

On the edge of the salt ocean, a growing limb of night's dark spreads and Marius can't make sense of it quickly enough. The ocean has no edge, no shore because the ice cap covers Europa entire. In turn, the ocean covers every bit of rocky ground. But here, there is a shore, an outcropping where Marius stands barefoot. The limb of darkness spreads like water through sand toward him.

"Bolaji, can you see this?"

There is no reply.

Marius kneels upon the shore where it feels like mica, thin and flaking. He dips his hands into the darkness and recoils at the sudden warmth. He has not known such a sensation outside being tangled with another body. (He thinks of William, pushes the memory away—that was another life, another planet.) The darkness creeps up his arms, to the elbow, to the shoulder. At that point, it feels as if a great maw has taken him in and the memory of cold is erased. This world was never cold, its ocean never solid.

Marius watches the shore retreat at an alarming speed; the sparkling mica glints and is then gone as the salt ocean swells over his head. He thrashes, turning to look at what has a hold of him, but there is no face. Only clouded arms of ink, the limb of night having dissolved itself in the salt water.

He learned to swim as a child on Schiaparelli Station and took top placements. It would be different in an ocean, they said; a calm and controlled pool was not an ocean where one would encounter tides, currents, undertow. Pools did not contain living creatures. Any creature on Europa, should its ocean prove salty, would be called a halophile—*salt lover*—but Marius always remembered "halo" for angels.

The angel before Marius has a halo, and the deeper he is pulled, the more it glows in golden splendor. Oxygen deprivation can cause a mind to hallucinate, but Marius remains certain of what he sees before him. Certain, too, of the way his lungs have quieted, of the way he doesn't feel cold, because every synapse is shutting down.

BOLAJI

When Zeus abducted Europa, he came to her in the form of a striking white bull and she, in praise of his beauty, draped him with hand-woven garlands of flowers. Endless scent and color streamed from his grand horns and he reveled in the feel of her upon his back.

Europa, they would have you believe, so reveled in the feel of him beneath her, strong and sure and warmer than anything she had ever known, that she did not notice he was carrying her away from the shore, not until they were in the sea's wet, not until he had pulled her under and changed into a man more beautiful than any before him—for of course, he was no man at all.

They say Europa did not scream (Marius screamed—my people say a traveler to distant lands should make no enemies and this was not our intent—never our intent), but by then, she was under water. How could anyone have known? The foam that rushed to shore could have easily been from her thrashing in the water, trying to escape Zeus's maniacal hold—but it was only the gentle swelling tide, they say, carrying flower petals to shore in the wake of a beautiful wedding.

Europa's tides are well-concealed beneath a cap of ice, plumes of water escaping when they can. But once free, they freeze and become part of the ice forevermore. Europa stretches infinite before us. Ahead, I can see the curved ridges we will likely take shelter in if we mean to rest and hydrate. The Delphi Flexus is not endless, but looks such from where we walk; we have to cross its boundary, and then the penitentes—the spikes of ice that prove this world is melting and refreezing in turn—before Thrace Terminal becomes a possibility.

I am torn between which is a more severe loss: Marius or the two icecats. Kotto would say the icecats, given our present circumstances. I am worried I would agree.

Within the flexus, we find a curve of ice in which to shelter. There will be no fire, but our suits are equipped with a series of chemical warming layers that should see us through. Likewise, there is a liquid feeding system, and though it is not my mother's moin moin, it will do. My mother told me the death that kills a man begins as an appetite, and perhaps this is what she meant, so when Kotto bids me eat, I activate the suit's feeding tube, tonguing once for water, twice for pureed food. There are two more meals to be had, which means at least two nights without. Possibly more. We will arrive at Thrace Terminal hungry.

"Bolaji, what—"

Kotto grabs my arm and extends it away from my body. The soft suit is the only thing that separates us from certain death via cold or radiation, and by the soft light radiating from her helmet, I can see what she sees. The sleeve of my suit has torn, from elbow to wrist, the fabric gaping open as if the sleeve has been unbuttoned. Every layer is ripped, ruined, and something pale rests within.

It is *so* pale, I do not even recognize my own arm for my skin is not this color, but brown. I stare, for I have never seen such a thing—has it been burned by cold? If my suit has been compromised, why have I not perished?

Kotto moves swiftly, cracking her case open to retrieve the emergency patch kit. I want to tell her to stop, but I sit silently, creamed spinach puree growing sour on my tongue. I should be dead. Why am I not dead? Kotto works fast—her hands are sure as she seals the entire length of the sleeve back together. In the cold, frost begins to crackle over the binding.

"Kotto."

"Sssh."

She does not have to tell me twice.

KOTTO

They say that in deep space, the extraordinary will become ordinary and eventually you stop noticing it. When the extraordinary is one's everyday job, it's nothing to fuss over. We live in space, we are settling the entire system, these acts are no longer magic. These *people*—they need to stop talking, because they're so fucking wrong.

Bolaji's arm should not be that color—it's like ice, Europan ice. But it's also *not*. If the lineae within Europa's ice look like shadows to me, charcoal lines hastily sketched, this ice is different, for his veins make a lineae of their own, these deep blue. Or, what I presume to be blue. I should not be able to see this color—but here it is. I have never seen it, and yet I know it. An ancestral memory, my therapist would say. I want to ask Bolaji what color the lines are, but the suit needs to be sealed, and once it's sealed we say nothing.

"Kotto."

"Sssh." I lift my hand, as if I could place it over his mouth to silence him. But he stays silent. Trembling. His eyes are wide and I tell myself they are not getting pale, they are as brown as they ever were, calling to mind the blackwood jungles my grandmother left me paintings of. So deep one could get lost, until the sunlight pierced the trunks and—*oh Bolaji*. What the hell? This was a simple rescue, nothing more.

Beyond the goddamn color of his arm, Bolaji should be dead. I am certain this fact presses on him as much as on me. His suit was opened to space, to the

Europan air which stands at nearly three hundred degrees below zero. Nothing can survive that. Not even the icecats proved able and they were built for it.

Beneath my feet, the ice *rumbles*. Our training is so ingrained, I don't even have to say "move!" before we're in motion. We know.

As stable as the surface should be, deep space remains largely unknown and hostile. Perhaps we were not meant to come this far—we are too fragile, too alive to know the depth of this cold. Europa is only doing what Europa does best. Under the strain of Jupiter above her, carting her deeper into the stars, she cracks and groans and spews water from her belly. Most of this water falls to coat the ground in fresh ice; some escapes into space.

Bolaji and I climb up the flexus and slide down its backside, avoiding the spew of ice water. Despite the danger, I am grinning as we glide down the ice, over bumps and ridges as the crews on Mars often traverse the sand dunes. At the bottom of the ridge, our ice cleats stab us steady, though the ground rumbles still. High in the hazy sky, more water plumes.

"Kotto—"

"Bolaji, move," I say, because I want some distance between us and that plume. If we're resting at all (he should be dead, Bolaji should be *dead*), it's not going to be on top of Europa's vomiting mouth.

MARIUS

Others have been on Europa for eons, so long that when they try to convey it in numbers and words, Marius is overwhelmed. Others believe he has a mind for science, but Marius can't digest what they transmit. Images flood his tear-blurred vision—another star system, far from where he now floats. An explosion, a nebula, debris hurtling through space. These simple things, Marius slowly understands.

Marius cannot understand his own star system in its infancy, but when he realizes that nine worlds are spinning into creation around a violently bright sun (he still counts Pluto), he can taste tears on my lips. He views the planets as children, small but growing larger, hauling in rock and gas, coalescing atmospheres tolerable and toxic, flinging comets here and moons there. He watches young Mars flood and old Mars perish; *Valles Marineris* cracks wide and he fears the entire planet will split in two, but she holds, dusty and dead.

No one has witnessed this, Marius thinks, though is quickly reminded by the strong body beneath his own that Others were here first. Others witnessed. This was theirs until slumber and gravity drew them into the depths where they slept, Marius and his kind cracked Europa's ice like an egg, pierced her salty ocean, drilled into her rocky mantle. (Crude, but he thinks of William again—cracking, piercing, drilling.)

Marius tries to speak, but is under water, and cannot understand how he is breathing, let alone how he might speak. He thinks he should not have left the station, but he had to, otherwise there would be no *this*. He was called to leave the station, knowing where to find them, knowing they had something to show him—the lost station, the end of all he had sought. Bolaji should never have followed—Marius is certain where the fault lies.

He stretches into the cold dark and when he can no longer see any brightness above, loses his sense of direction. Everything is featureless black, as if nothing has ever been created. In this black, there has never been a sun, nor any speck of light, until something startling and green darts through the salted water. Glowing Others murmurate across his vision, one sliding through Marius's palm small as a flower.

The beings draw so near that they swarm around Marius, against his skin—skin, not suit, and he wonders when it was lost, and why he is not dead (is he dead?). When they swarm with more fury, his throat grows raw from screaming. He is not yet dead, he is not yet—

BOLAJI

Europa, once carried to Crete where she was to be queen, was welcomed by Asterion—he of the labyrinth, the creature that was half man, half monster. Did Asterion challenge Zeus for Europa's fair hand? There are no such stories of what became of her there—but for the one that my mind creates: that Europa, enraged after being taken from her home and life, turned on them both; that Athena looked down in her wisdom and recognizing a warrior soul, transformed what remained of the garland of flowers into a sword. Europa killed Zeus and imprisoned Asterion within the labyrinth, before tracing the path of spilled flowers back home.

I am certain this did not happen, but it seems so, as Kotto jostles me into consciousness once more. She stands as fiery, sword-brandishing Europa above me, intent on slaughtering whatever obstacle lands in our path. I have never seen Kotto as such before and it steals my breath. Kotto keeps always to herself, intent on her work, on finding the smallest organisms that call Europa's oceans home. She cared nothing for humanity—only what life might exist elsewhere. When she found the first, this was the only time I heard her laugh; she said they were yellow-orange, but they glowed green for me.

My tongue is numb in my mouth; I cannot answer her when she speaks, nor can I fully understand what she has said. She glows, as if she has become one of the salt-loving organisms of the deep. I nod and she seems pleased, vanishing from my sight. We move, but I am not walking. Kotto drags me on the emergency sledge. As if I have broken a leg. As if I am incapable.

A look down at my legs tells me I *am* incapable. My suit has split wide again, exposing my legs to the air. At some point, it is clear that Kotto tried to seal the rends, but they split the binding again and again. I cannot fathom why; I do not feel larger, and my body is not shaped differently. But the skin that gleams up from the torn suit is wholly white, as clear as ice, with thousands of blue lineae running beneath.

This should startle me, but between the evidence and the emotion, there is a great gulf of nothing. One cannot reach the other. I study the legs as if they were

Europan ice, following each lineae until I can no longer trace its path. They wind across the legs and disappear under, and I imagine I see patterns within them: sharp-edged stars and the lump that is Zuma Rock. I have only ever seen this rock in images handed down from lifetimes before my own: a gray and hulking lump rising quite suddenly from the trees as if it were dropped from space. My many-times-great grandfather was said to have climbed it; my many-times-great grandmother said that was absurd. And yet, here I am on Europa. I picture my many-times-great grandfather upon this rock and I am calmed.

Come morning—is it morning?—the idea of the rock still rests within me. I feel it as if upon my tongue, salty and weighting it down so I cannot speak when Kotto looks at me. But I see it upon her face. Something else has happened, something she has no explanation for, and the following morning (the ice so very bright beneath Jupiter's glowing orb), she will have no explanation for what comes next.

I want to speak to her; I want to write her a letter. My fingers crave the feel of keys, of a cold glass screen, so that I might tell her how Europa surely followed that trail of broken flowers home. So that I might tell her how Zuma Rock rises black from the greenery, and how my many-times-great grandfather stood upon it, barefoot, naked, the way I will stand upon the ice before the consumed shell of my body falls away.

KOTTO

One man should not weigh so much in this gravity.

The sledge is ingenious, locking Bolaji firmly into place, so he is not jostled no matter the terrain we cover. The runners have blades, but like an ice skate possess something of a toe pick, which I can latch into the ice to keep the entire thing from moving. I do this now, kneeling on the ice as I try to catch my breath. We'll share our last meal in a few hours; tomorrow will be hungry, and Thrace Terminal is at least another day beyond. Water isn't a problem, at least; Europa's ocean water freezes clean, desalinated, and our suits are equipped with a sealed system that will allow me to store and melt ice for drinking.

Marius should never have come out—it's easy to convince myself of this. When Marius left the station, shrieking about finding a lost station (*the* lost station—madness—we had not been here before, had we), Bolaji, in his good nature, followed. No one went onto the ice alone—ever, ever, ever. Going alone was certain death. Not that Marius cared or waited—his discovery, he cried, would not wait. Of course he took an icecat. Of course Bolaji took another to follow. And now—we were nearly fucked, but the universe had surely seen worse, even if we had not.

I went alone, didn't I? Charged out after Bolaji without a second, without a third. Just went, and I shouldn't have. Was it worth two lives, Kotto? This goddamn lost station? What the hell does deep space do to a mind? *What did Marius see that I did not?*

"Bolaji."

He's so still, the ice color having creeped up his cheeks. He tries to move his mouth, but cannot open it. His water tube remains tucked in the corner; he's unable to even tongue that away, which is probably best. A slow trickle is better than nothing. If I can get him back to Thrace Terminal, if we can get him in sickbay—I don't know. Medicine isn't my thing—first aid sure, but not this. And this isn't like anything I've ever seen.

"Can you try to sit up?"

Bolaji nods at me, but doesn't move. He should be able to sit up, only his legs secured to the sledge; his hands curl around the handles, but he could move them if he wanted. If he was able. I bite the inside of my cheek and taste salt. Maybe whatever's happened to him won't let him. Was this part of what happened to Marius?

The known part was Bolaji radioing back, shrieking that Marius had found it—had found it and we were going to be famous and known and it was better than standing on Zuma Rock naked. Maybe this thing had a hold of him then, too. Was this what extreme cold did to a person? No; cold like this killed a person flat out. Why the hell wasn't Bolaji dead? Why weren't we all?

"Not sitting up is also fine."

Bolaji watches me like I'm something he's never seen instead of someone he's worked with for seven years. He did a brief stint on Galileo Station, but his heart was never there. When I accused him of wanting a moon of his own, brand new ground he could sink his feet into, he joked that I always wanted an ocean no one had peed in. He wasn't entirely wrong.

"Come on. If you stop slowing me down, we can make the spikes, and that means . . . Thrace is still damn far away . . . "

The sledge seems lighter when I pull it back into motion. When I dreamed of alien oceans, I dreamed of beasts big enough to pull crafts through them. Not our crafts—their own. These beasts were never not industrious, crafting marvelous cities at the edge of every ocean they possessed—and probably peed in.

But the beasts here are smaller and according to Bolaji, brighter, glowing green. What had Marius found that could compete with that? We'd found life—goddamn alien life—and he was throwing himself out onto the ice for what. For this?

I glance back at Bolaji, whose arms are raised, hands reaching for something I cannot see. Something he probably can't see, either. But what I see turns my stomach; the gloves of his suit are ripped. But more than that maybe, because the fabric looks eaten away. Something in the air, a contaminant we couldn't detect, something in the ice? The exposure to long, continued cold?

The penitentes rise like stalagmites from the ice field ahead. The thin blades of ice, some running dark with trapped minerals, are all turned the same direction, as if something has caught their attention. That something is the far-distant sun. I wonder what it would be like, to stretch under its warmth, to watch it melt this entire ball of ice into a whole, free-flowing ocean. Some worlds, I remind myself, are like that.

I position the sledge within the shelter of two penitentes, and laugh at myself for doing so. It's not as if there's someone out here to find us. It's not as if anyone else is looking. Tomorrow, I'll be in radio range of Thrace; tomorrow, they'll know. I draw on my feeding tube, food first, water second, and watch the sky until sleep claims me. I don't mean to sleep long—Bolaji can't be left alone—but four hours have passed by the time I look upon the Jupiter-bright sky again.

"If you pick up the pace," I tell Bolaji, "we can cover some good ground here—how's your water, anyhow?"

I pick my way to the side of the sledge, reaching for the controls on the arm of Bolaji's suit. His water level is too high—he hasn't consumed any in the time we've been traveling, and when I look at his helmet, I see why. Bolaji is gone. His suit flutters empty, but for a puddle of what looks like water.

MARIUS

At this point, Europa's ocean is one hundred and eleven kilometers straight down, and Marius can see forever. The water swarms with life, hydrothermal vents spewing warmth into the ocean cold. Vast columns of bubbles stream upward, into the dark. Salt bursts across his tongue, but something beyond that, something metallic and true.

Here, life abounds. Small, insistent. Larger, established. A creche of crabs cling to the hot chimneys, hearts fluttering beneath their transparent exoskeletons. Eels, worms, and Others, so many Others. They have been here a long time, have made nests and smoothed hollows in the Europan rock where the world is forever warm.

Others carry Marius over the crater and the crab-crusted remains of anchor points rising from the rocky ground. Marius recognizes the broken frame, the shattered drill. A lost station, *the* lost station—but this lost station is Thrace Terminal, and the markings on the steel legs confirm it. He does not remember Thrace Terminal being lost, but can see it the way he has seen the past—an explosion, a water-pale nebula, debris hurtling through the black salted sea. These simple things Marius understands.

Marius and Others glide toward still-standing Thrace Terminal; the water tastes of metal, thermal vents scattering bubbles in their wake, broken petals that will perish before they reach the ice cap.

BOLAJI

Europa followed flowers; I follow water.

All thoughts of the suit, of Kotto, of Marius, have gone; these came Before. They are not Now. Now and here, there is only the water, the salt having transformed my body into something Other. I spread through the water, following the currents created by the deep thermal vents—even up here, beneath the ice, my body knows the way the water flows; can sense the warmth and cool entwined.

If there is purpose, it is only in growth. Why do we change? How do we endure? Why do we stretch for depths we have no hope of reaching? What happens when we *do* reach them? I think briefly of a man upon a rock, sweat-stained and aching. I think of how he must have looked at the land below him, at the froth of impossibly green trees, and this is how I survey the waters beneath me now. They are small, but filled with life.

I travel as the water, pushing up through the ice clefts as I will, flinging myself into the sky which spreads clear and bright, before raining back to the ocean below. Pieces of me freeze on Europa's porcelain face, but I am more than these; I spread infinite, seven times as big as Earth's oceans, butting against the ice cap. Tonguing it into deeper water.

KOTTO

Thrace Terminal stands black and skeletal against the ice. The distant sunlight gleams off the towers, off the ice that wraps her steel legs. She's still far off, but I breathe easier at seeing her familiar shape. If the extraordinary is supposed to become commonplace, then maybe the commonplace also becomes extraordinary, especially when we are forced from its confines. You don't dream about sex; you dream about familiar walls, your possessions no matter how meager, everyone you know.

I flick my comms to life, already itching to get inside the station and take my helmet off. I want to breathe the stale, recycled air. I want to walk barefoot down the chilly corridors in morning. I want to attend my next goddamn mental assessment and show them I did it. I made it.

"Kotto to Thrace Terminal."

But the sledge, folded back into the emergency pack at my back, weighs heavy. I made it back, but alone. I did it, but couldn't bring Bolaji with me. Couldn't pull Marius back from whatever cliff he'd jumped off. *Do you believe Bolaji had anything to do with Marius's condition? With his disappearance?* They will ask, won't they? What will I answer? Bolaji did not make it, and Marius did not make it—what can I say? The cold has frozen me to the core—envy encases my heart and I cannot feel what perhaps I should for them, for the loss of them.

"Thrace Terminal—Kotto, fucking Christ."

"Not quite that." But I try to smile at the sound of Rey's voice—something familiar, something warm. "Have you in sight—probably tomorrow, unless you send an icecat." I relay my coordinates and hear Rey dispatching a crew for me.

My steps quicken at the thought; my walk hastens to a run, but when my helmet clouds with breath, I slow. No sense in overdoing it, not if they're sending people for me.

What did Marius and Bolaji find? What did they know? Why didn't you find it? Maybe you couldn't fucking see it, Kotto—the changes in the ice, the changes in the water. Or did you find it and were simply unable to see the way Bolaji and Marius could?

When the ground rumbles, I wonder at the speed at which they've come. I strain to hear the icecats clawing their way cross the miles-thick ice, but they're still too far distant. The vibration through the ice is pervasive, and I track it, as if dancing.

If they say that eventually you don't notice the cold, must it also come to pass that after a while, you grow so accustomed to the world you inhabit, you forget it's hostile? You forget that a rumble isn't always a transplanted icecat; sometimes, it's the native ice-buried ocean you've come to study. Sometimes, it's a plume of water and vapor erupting from a fissure in the ice. A plume of water that seems to enfold you like an arm, like a garland of flowers, drawing you toward the arctic waters.

I tumble and when I at last come to rest against a gently curved flexus, I'm breathing hard. The world beyond my helmet is hazy, but I can see the tear in my sleeve. Elbow to wrist, my arm gone to Europan ice. Deep blue lineae trace a new map to new lands upon me. Europa swims gray and I think it's the condensation of breath on my helmet—but it's something else.

I have forgotten the cold.

Everything blurs.

Seven Cups of Coffee
A.C. WISE

One

Here, in this now, our first cup of coffee is still in your future. It's 1941, and you've been married to your husband for two years, three months, and seven days. He doesn't know about the way you look at the women in fashion magazines and clothing catalogs. The way you find yourself imagining how the drape of this skirt, the brush of that hemline, would feel against their skin in particular. You barely admit to yourself the way your fingers want to stray to the back of your neck, the outline of your collarbone, the shape of your mouth when you look at them. Your skin flushes hot, only partly shame, and you put the pages away quickly, telling yourself it's only your imagination, the flutter deep in your belly when you look at them.

They are too pretty, too perfect, the women in those magazines and catalogs. It's only that you want to be them. You want hair that never strays out of place, and lips that stay bright and unsmudged all day long. Nothing else.

After the first cup of coffee, which is in your future and my past, everything will change. It is the beginning of the end for you. For me, in this now, in every now I've found yet, it is already too late. I can't change anything, I can't fix anything. I've tried. But I'm not giving up. Ever. I will not give up on us, on you.

Two

It is 1983 and I'm sitting across from a woman who hasn't given me her real name, saying only to call her Scarlett. I'm here because I answered a want ad for a cleaning woman. I'm here because I'm running out of options; I have nowhere else to go.

Scarlett smirks, the cat after the canary. I should leave, but the steaming cup of coffee between my hands, followed by the plate piled high with fluffy eggs, greasy bacon, and crisp golden toast, keeps me in place. I haven't had more than saltines and the last dregs of Cheez Whiz in the now-empty jar over the past three days. And Scarlett is buying.

"Time travel," she says, and I'm sure I misheard, but I don't stop shoveling food in my mouth to check.

In this now, I haven't yet seen her time machine. I've lived my life linearly, scrounging odd jobs and crashing on friends' couches. In this now, my parents want nothing to do with me—words like "no daughter of mine" and "not under my roof" still ringing in my ears, better at least than my mother's tearful, "if you just try" and "you're so pretty, girls like you don't have to be . . . *that* way."

In this now, the closest I've gotten to time travel is occasionally getting high—losing minutes or hours, or slowing everything down, stretching it out when it gets to be too much and I don't want to think about the hole where my family used to be. I have no idea yet what is and isn't possible. How going into the past or the future can rip a person apart in ways they never imagined, ways they can't see until it's far too late.

I haven't met you yet, not in this here and now. All I know is that I'm down to almost my last saltine. My on-again-off-again girlfriend called it off for good and kicked me out, and I desperately need a job. So 'cleaning woman' sounds pretty good right about now.

Three

It is 1945, and you are pregnant with your first child. The first one you're counting that is—at least out loud. There was a miscarriage, just over a year ago, but you're trying not to think about that. You're trying to move on, think positive thoughts, look ahead to the future so bright and full of promise.

This time, everything will be okay. You're sure of it. You glow softly with the knowledge, even though sometimes you can still smell the bleach—taste it, the scent thick at the back of your throat—burning as you scrub blood from white tile. This time, things will be different. Everything will be the way it is supposed to be, because you love your husband and you are a good wife and you will be a good mother soon, too.

You've stopped subscribing to fashion magazines, and when you go to the post office to collect your mail, you tell the clerk to throw the catalogs away. You shop at the new department store downtown with your sister-in-law, and you don't think about the women in the other changing rooms, pulling silk stockings over the length of their legs and clipping them in place. You don't think of cotton and wool tugged over their heads, or their hands smoothing the fabric against their hips and bellies. And those long afternoon hours waiting for your husband to get home, sitting by the apartment window, which you have open for the breeze, your skin barely flushes at all, and your thoughts are completely under your control.

You've barely begun to show. You haven't told your husband yet, just in case. You keep the secret tucked inside your cheek, biting your lips against the fullness of a smile. You've always wanted to be a mother. You've dreamed of holding your little girl in your arms, singing songs, and making up silly stories so she'll laugh. You already know you're going to name her Alice, just like you know for sure she's going to be a girl, but you keep that knowledge secret, too.

In this here and now, I don't know any of this yet, because I haven't met you. I'm standing on a street corner, holding an anachronistic cup of coffee brought back with me from 1983. I'm blowing on it while I wait, not wanting to burn my tongue, and trying to calm my nerves, distract myself from what I'm about to do.

It's snowing. Christmas week and the streetlights and shop windows glow, making each individual snowflake glitter and shine. Any moment now, you'll come down the street your arms full of packages, not paying attention. You'll be thinking about the carefully chosen tie for your husband, and the sweater for your sister-in-law. How you'll wrap everything and place it just so under the Christmas tree. And then, when every present has been opened, you'll pull out one last package you've been keeping hidden and place it in your husband's hands. A silver rattle, and you'll tell him what a wonderful father he'll be.

With all these thoughts filling up your mind, all I have to do is step out in front of you, just another distracted shopper, my head full of Christmas, not paying attention to where I'm going. I won't even have to brush your arm, accidental fingertips on the thickness of your wool coat, or nudge your hip with mine as you pass. A simple step, and you'll move out of my way, miss your footing, and slip into the road just as the number eight bus comes along. And it will be too late for the bus to stop, fish-tailing on the ice. Brakes squealing, and pedestrians gasping as your packages fly through the air—that carefully chosen tie, the beautiful sweater for your sister-in-law, and even the little silver rattle—falling to soak in the slush on the ground.

Scarlett has told me all this, every last detail she thinks I need to know to make sure everything goes perfectly. That doesn't include your name, or anything about you, or why it's so important to make sure the baby in your belly—little Alice who you want so badly to meet and hold in your arms—is never born.

Without a face or a name, I can pretend it really is an accident. I'm not a murderer, just a clumsy pedestrian. I can collect my cash and choose where and when to live out the rest of my life. That's what Scarlett promised—do the job, and I get one last trip. Then I never have to see a time machine again if I don't want to.

So I'm waiting in the falling snow, blowing on my cup of coffee, and in exactly one minute, you'll walk down the street toward me. Easy. Simple and clean.

After all, in this here and now, what are you to me? Nothing. Just a date and a time and a precise location. A step to the left at exactly the right moment. I don't even know what you look like, not yet. Though in time I will know every detail of your body, where your waist dips toward the curve of your hipbone, the scent of your skin late in the afternoon just before your husband gets home, and the way your lips taste in the bruise-dark hours between three and four a.m. when he's out of town.

But for now, I know none of these things. I look at my watch and count silently, my breath steaming in the winter cold. And when the moment comes, I drop my anachronistic cup of coffee and take that one little step to the left, eyes closed, heart pounding, tears hot against the winter cold.

Four

It's 1984, New Year's Day. I'm shaking, my jaw clenched to keep my teeth from chattering. The diner is warm, the only place open on the entire snowy street. In all its seventeen years, the diner has prided itself on never once being closed.

The windows steam. I sweat inside my coat, but I can't bear to remove it. My hands are wrapped around a cup of coffee, but the thought of putting food in my mouth is abhorrent.

Scarlett slides into the booth across from me—not a hair out of place, her make-up immaculate as always. It's the same diner where I first met her. She's still smiling, not quite smirking her cat-with-the-canary look, until she gets a good look at me.

"I want to go back," I say. "I changed my mind. I want to undo it. Find someone else if you have to, I don't care. I'll give the money back, and I won't tell anyone. You'll never see me again, I promise."

I expect her eyes to go hard when the words stop, and for a moment they do. Then a real glimmer of regret, a hint of sympathy creeps through. Her hands cover mine, still wrapped around the coffee mug. I wonder about her real name, how she got here, about the shadows under her perfect skin, and the brief flicker of pain behind her eyes.

She speaks softly, even though we're the only two in the diner, holding my gaze the entire time.

"It doesn't work that way. I'm sorry."

I want to spit in her face, call her liar. I want to slap her and make her take the words back, but deep down, I'm afraid they're true. A time machine isn't a magic wand. I can't undo what I've done. I made a choice, and now your blood is on my hands.

I don't ask again. Instead, I beg Scarlett to at least tell me your name. I have to know. I have to own this thing, fully and completely. If your death is going to be on me for the rest of my life, it will be *your* death, a specific death, belonging to a real woman, not just a place and a time and a step to the left with eyes closed and tires shrieking in the fresh-fallen snow.

"It won't help you sleep at night," Scarlett says. "In fact, it will only make things worse. Why do that to yourself?"

"Please," I say.

She relents, partway. She tells me your name, and nothing more. Not where to find you before that day in 1945. Not why the child in your belly had to die. I leave the diner pretending that will be enough. I have your name. I can mourn. I can try to make some kind of peace with what I've done.

Five

It is 2037, February, and the stainless steel screw-top cup from a thermos of coffee is passing back and forth from my mittened hand to the hand of a woman named Mona. Mona is from 1961, hiding out here in the future, another of Scarlett's 'cleaning women'. We met here in 2037, coincidentally picking the same year out of all the years Scarlett offered us after our jobs were done. We were both trying to see how far we could run, and recognized something haunted in each other under all the slick, bright neon of a future that wasn't what we wanted after all.

"My time, or yours," I'd said, the cheesiest of pick-up lines.

We fell into each other hard, not love, but desperation, something to cling to because we were both terrified of being alone inside our skins.

What we learned together is what we both already knew apart—there is no place far enough that either of us can run. Even this here, this now—where women can love women, where men can kiss each other and vow to spend the rest of their lives together, where people of both or neither genders can live their lives in peace—we can't be happy. Our pasts are a shadow; we can't live in all this light until we've found a way to undo what we've done. Then, maybe then, we would deserve a future like this one.

The coffee passing between us is spiked liberally with brandy, the last of the bottle drunk before we set out into the cold. We're here to sneak into Scarlett's time machine, stalling and stamping our feet against the cold as we gather courage. This is another thing we've learned. There has always been a time machine here. As far as we know, there always will be one. Whether Scarlett built it or found it doesn't matter. What matters is we've seen her operate it just enough times between us to know how it's done.

I boost Mona up first, then scramble over the chain link fence behind her. From this angle, the time machine looks like nothing, a strange fragment of light refracted in a way it shouldn't be, a bend of the universe. Not even a machine, but time folded somehow, impossible, but possible, because both of us are here.

This is goodbye, but we don't say it aloud. Mona goes first, back to 1961, I assume, though I never asked. Just like she never asked me where I was running. She slips into the machine that isn't a machine and it unfolds, throwing loops of light around her body so bright I have to shade my eyes. Then she's gone.

I drink the last of the coffee in the thermos, down to the dregs, and leave the stainless steel screw-top cup behind. Deep breath, and I step forward. Light encompasses me, the machine hurtling me backward through the years as though it doesn't care that my one and only goal is to unravel time.

Six

It's 1943, before your first child, the one you never even had the chance to name. Before the bleach and the chemical sting behind your eyes, burning your skin as you scrubbed and scrubbed the bathroom floor. You still subscribe to fashion magazines in this here and now. In this here and now, you know what my fingers feel like sliding silk stockings down the length of your calves, bunching cotton and wool in my fists and rucking it up over your hips and your belly.

Our first cup of coffee is in your past, my past. And I know that in the bruise-dark hours between 3 and 4 a.m., your mouth tastes like plums.

I have tried every way I know to convince you to run away with me. I've played out every scenario I can imagine, trying to undo the future, change what I haven't yet done, what I will do, what I have always done, in my past and your future.

I have looped through this moment so many times, stepping into Scarlett's machine again and again, and letting it rip me apart. Every word from your lips, every gesture of your hands, the way you lean your body away or toward me, frightened or longing—I have it all memorized. Sometimes I wish I could leave; spying on your life this way—a string of moments in your past and your future—doesn't seem right. But somewhere in one of those moments there has to be a key, a word, a phrase, something I can do or not do to save your life.

In a future just a few days from now, you will tear your fashion magazines to pieces, stuff the scraps down the drain, and run water over them until they are pulp. You will slam the apartment window, eschewing the breeze playing with the ends of your hair. You want the apartment sweltering, sweating out the memory of me, sweating out everything you've buried deep inside you for so long.

I've been there to witness this destruction. Seen the way the curls stick, sweat-damp, to the back of your neck and wanted to taste the skin between them. Even angry, even broken, even denying what you are, in that near future I'll want to run my tongue over your collarbone, rest my hands where your waist dips in, and feel your pulse beating just under your skin.

I'll want to whisper to you that everything will be okay. Even though it's a lie.

If I hadn't killed you in my past, your future, I wouldn't be in love with you. Or would I? Was this always meant to be?

Here and now, you are distracted. Your eyes are the same color as the coffee you're holding. Not just brown, but the color it turns when it catches the light as you pour it from pot to cup. A rich color on the edge of red. Secret. Flavorful. Strong.

Steam rises into the light slanting over the kitchen table between us. You keep glancing at the clock, counting the minutes until your husband comes home, projecting yourself into the future when all I want to do is hold you in the here and now. You haven't told me to leave yet, but you will. You're already thinking about fixing your hair, smoothing powder over the places where my lips have been, making dinner, all the things a good wife should do.

Everything about your posture says brittle, haunted. Fragile as the cup in your hands.

"You should go," you say.

Inside those words, I hear all the ones you don't say, at least not this time, the words you've said in the times before. "I can't do this anymore. I want a baby. That's something you can't give me. I don't love you. I never loved you. You're sick and wrong and it's a sin. I never want to see you again."

In all of those times, never once have I told you that in two years, right before Christmas, I will cause your death. I don't tell you about the children, either of them, who will never be born. And I don't tell you about the horrible things I've contemplated doing—finding a way to cause another miscarriage, murdering your husband, all to keep you safe, keep you alive.

No matter how deep your words cut—and they cut to the bone—I don't fire back with my secret knowledge. It isn't fair that I know you better than you know yourself. Besides, the knowledge would rip your heart out and I tell myself it's a mercy to you, letting you live in bliss and innocence for a while longer.

It's a lie. I'm sparing myself. I don't want you to die hating me. I need to pretend I can still fix this somehow. I haven't given up on you. I swear.

I want to take your hands across the table. I want to hold them and look into your eyes. Maybe this time you'll believe me when I tell you the future gets better. If you ran with me, we could go to a place where we could love each other openly and no one would judge us. We could have a baby and it would be ours, our family, something new to fill the hole in my heart where my family used to be.

I wonder if that's unfair to you, if I'm trying to make you into something you're not. All the words I could possibly say in this here and now don't feel right. Not yet. But maybe one day. I have to keep trying.

In this here and now, I don't say anything at all. But I do stand for a moment outside your apartment door, breath held, listening. I stand there long enough to hear the coffee cup shatter as you hurl it against the wall.

It will be all cleaned up by the time your husband gets home. Every trace of me will be scrubbed clean from your body, and you'll be smiling. Just like a good wife should, no matter the white-hot ball of rage you've pushed down deep inside.

Seven

It is 1941. In this here, in this now, our first cup of coffee is still ahead, for both of us. I haven't met you yet, and I've already killed you in the future, four years from now. I haven't tried to convince you to run away with me. I haven't tried desperately to undo what I've done. I don't know the scent of your hair, or the feeling of your skin under my fingertips. All I have is a name, so I don't even know it's you when we collide.

You're just coming out of the post office, your arms full of catalogs and fashion magazines. It's summer, and the magazines scatter—bright, beautiful women, caught in the sunshine, pages fluttering in the breeze.

You blush, hurrying to gather them, and I bend to help you. I don't know anything about you except the way a curl of your hair sticks to the corner of your mouth as you pause to look up at me. In that moment, I've already started to fall in love. It's too late by the time you tell me your name. I've invited you for that first cup of coffee. I've heard you laugh, self-conscious, guarded, but with so much promise of joy tucked inside.

I could run away before the waitress brings the cups. I could go back—to the future, to the past, try again. If I did, would it change anything? I wouldn't know the taste of your skin, or the look in your eyes, right before you tell me to go. Maybe my heart wouldn't break, and you wouldn't throw yourself into your husband's arms with such angry determination, set on proving me wrong, determined to be something you're not. Maybe you wouldn't be carrying a child that needs killing according to some grand cosmic plan that I don't even understand.

Or maybe all of this was always meant to happen, always will happen, no matter what I do.

But that doesn't mean I'll stop trying, looking for a way to unravel everything I've done. Maybe it isn't possible, but I have to try. For you. For us. For all the cups of coffee in our past and our future.

All I know is that in this moment, this here and now, you're looking at me in a way I've never been looked at, been seen, before. And I wouldn't trade this cup of coffee for the world.

Chimera

GU SHI, TRANSLATED BY S. QIOUYI LU AND KEN LIU

*An individual, organ, or part consisting
of tissues of diverse genetic constitution.*
—Merriam-Webster

1. Chimera

*It had the fore part of a lion, the tail of a dragon, and its third head, the
middle one, was that of a goat, through which it belched fire.
    It was begotten by Typhon on Echidna, as Hesiod relates.*
—Apollodorus, *Bibliotheca*, Book 2, Chapter 3 (as translated by Sir
James George Frazer)

I watch her enter.

In the six years since we parted ways, I've always wanted to know: exactly how
cold and calculating is the machine under the soft, lustrous skin of this witch?

She sees me, her eyes filling with delight—no trace of embarrassment, nor
shame.

"Evan." She quickens her footsteps. "Darling, long time no see."

A delicate, warm perfume wafts from her approaching figure, the same as
the scent in my memory. I recall what she said as she bared her heart to me, not
long after we were married:

"Lately I've been thinking—I could write my dissertation based on pictures of
my expressions: *Managing Emotions and Social Responses*. What do you think?
Take smiles: I know over a thousand of them, and each requires the manipulation
of different muscle groups. Each one can be the response for many situations,
and their combinations are infinite!

"The only difficulty is meticulous expression management. It would require
massive calculations; perhaps it's untenable—Evan, don't look at me that way—
enough. See, you musicians always misunderstand the scientific mind. I'm not
a machine; a Turing machine would never be able to figure out in such a short
time which smile to use in which circumstance—I'm a human being, a wonderful
creation.

"*This* is a worthy subject for biology."

She solemnly pointed at her head, then laughed with a snort: sweet, innocent, like she couldn't contain herself. "Look at you. So serious! I'm just joking around."

Now, she stands before me in a fine cashmere coat, a silk scarf snug against her throat: both wrapping her well-exercised, slim body. Nothing escapes her keen interest: she studies society, fashion, health, romance. She studies me, studies my passions, my expressions, my movements, as though I'm the most fascinating person she's ever seen. In reality, I'm no different than the rats in her laboratory. She grants my wishes—then takes them away.

She looks at me, the joy displayed by the curved corners of her mouth calibrated perfectly. But, face-to-face with my ex-wife, I can't call forth the happiness from when we were in love.

I'm weary of this.

"I just wanted to talk about Tony."

No tabloid reporter would ever believe the truth: a mother abandoning her swaddled infant and guiltless husband on the same day as the child's birth, then disappearing off the face of the Earth for six years.

"I know."

I finally catch a flicker of weakness in her eyes, but her voice remains level.

"I was just about to come talk to you about him, too."

Tony is six.

If it weren't for what happened three months ago, I would have never contacted his mother. That day, as I took Tony to the park, a maroon Honda barreled out of nowhere onto the sidewalk and pulled Tony under a tire. After five days in the emergency room, he opened his eyes, but his kidneys had sustained irreparable damage. Upon discovering that his body couldn't take a kidney transplant, I realized that my son would have to undergo dialysis three times a week for the rest of his life. In despair, I pored over every piece of medical literature I could get my hands on until I stumbled upon the topic of regenerative medicine, the goal of which is to use the patient's own stem cells to grow replacement organs.

One of the foremost scientists in this field is my ex-wife. A rising star, she's in charge of a new chimera lab that successfully grew a rat's pancreas inside a mouse. They created a chimera that had never before existed in nature. In journal articles, commentators viewed this study as a milestone for regenerative medicine. Based on this success, a human-pig chimera could, in theory, be viable. And now, I'm hoping that she can grow Tony's kidneys inside a pig. After the pig matures, the kidneys can be transplanted back to Tony.

As she gently stirs a cup of Darjeeling tea, she murmurs, "Of course I love him. You have no idea how painful the news of the accident was for me. But what you mentioned in your letter—I really can't make that happen."

"I read your article, plus the discussions in *Cell*. You and your lab are the only people in the whole world who would be able to duplicate Tony's kidneys."

Seeing her disbelief, I can't stop myself from adding, "Please don't assume that I can't find and read scientific articles."

"Of course. You're so smart—if you want to accomplish something, you'll get it done." She masks her surprise and lets out a small sigh. "It's just that, if you've already read my article, then you'd know that this is all only theoretical. Rat-mouse chimeras and human-pig chimeras are two entirely different things; it's like—" She looks up, blinking, then looks back at me. "—Like how you can sing, and you can play guitar, but that doesn't mean you can play a pipe organ."

"I could do it with time," I say. "These skills share similar principles."

Facepalm. "Lord, that was a terrible analogy. How should I explain this to you . . . I imagine you already know how the chimera I created came to be."

I turn on my iPad. I've already highlighted many paragraphs in her article, so I find the quote I'm looking for easily: *We injected induced pluripotent stem cells (iPS) from a rat into blastocysts from a mouse lacking the Pdx1 gene. Mice lacking the Pdx1 gene are unable to develop a normal pancreas; the rat iPS cells were able to remedy the genetic deficiency of the recipient mouse blastocysts. These rat-mouse chimeras were able to develop into adults with normal, functional pancreases.*[1]

She points to a sentence. "Oh right, this part. You must know that rats and mice are two entirely different animals, right? In taxonomical terms, the former is of the genus *Rattus*, and the latter is *Mus*—"

I interrupt her. "Of course!"

"Sorry." She shrugs, then points again at that line of text. "Look here. If we wanted to use a similar method to create a human-pig chimera, then we would first have to get blastocysts from a pig that lacks the genes to produce kidneys. But where would we get such blastocysts? And how would we locate genes that can develop kidneys? These are all problems we have to solve from the ground up, and we don't know if we'd be successful at any of them."[2]

"I'm begging you to try." I see her lips opening and closing, but I don't understand her words. "I know there's no guarantee of success."

"Please don't say 'beg'; he's also my son. I'm willing to do anything for him." She implores me with a doleful look, her eyebrows downturned. "'Try'—See, that's the second question. Let's say we could find all the genes that contribute to kidney development and knock them out of the pig blastocyst with precision. Then what? Can I inject Tony's cells into the blastocyst? No. Using human embryonic stem cells to do research is illegal and highly unethical."

1   In 2010, Kobayashi et al. published a study in *Cell* that demonstrated the viability of rat-mouse chimeras. At the same time, commentary about the study also appeared in *Cell* under the title "Viable rat-mouse chimeras: where do we go from here?" This quote paraphrases that commentary. Of note is the fact that the same research group published another study in *PNAS* in which they performed a similar experiment with a pig. Ethical concerns stopped them from creating a human-pig chimera.

2   Named as one of the ten greatest scientific discoveries of 2013, CRISPR/Cas9 allows the creation of organisms with knocked out genes. That is, so long as we know which genes control the development of which organs, those genes can be made inoperative ("knocked out"). If a knockout pig blastocyst were combined with human stem cells, theoretically, a pig could be grown with a human organ.

"You care about that?" I stare at her, astounded. "You care about ethics?"

She touches a finger to her lips. "Please lower your voice."

I know her all too well. If she didn't want to respond to my request, she wouldn't have come to see me.

She winks, as if we share an unspeakable little secret.

"Tell me, what would it take to get you to try?" I really can't take much more of her antics.

She breaks eye contact and turns to look outside. A long silence. I gaze at her profile: her refined, nurturing face is as beautiful as it was the last time I saw her. In the afternoon light, she's radiant, like a statue of the Virgin Mary in a church—a cold statue that can breathe. At last, she smiles and turns back to me:

"A mother smashing through scientific taboos to save her son's life—such a tale is enough for me, even better if I get to play the role of the magnificent mother in this story."

Yes, that would be her. Her actions are endowed with philosophy and poetry, but her performance is always built upon her own awareness of the philosophy and poetry that her actions will bring to her. In her mind, she's cut off from the rest of the world, a god surveying the Earth. She will undertake this difficult task not because Tony is her son, but because doing so will turn her into a glorious legend.

What a selfish, abhorrent monster.

She continues. "I must tell you that I have no confidence of success. When it comes to human experimentation, there's no precedent to refer to, and I may even create a monster—but that's what makes it exciting, no? I'll do it, but I still recommend that you go to the hospital and look into standard kidney transplant—"

"Every one of his lymphocyte cross-matching tests has come back positive."

She looks at me, not quite understanding. "So?"

"Kidneys from a donor will likely lead to acute rejection," I say. "It's possible he can only take a transplant from his own body."

"My God." She furrows her brow.

"Right now we're relying on dialysis to keep him alive. You can't imagine how painful this is." I think of Tony's cries and can't help but shudder.

The light in her eyes grows firm and resolute. "I understand. I'll put my all into this."

"Thank you," I say.

"There's one more thing that I should tell you." She gets up and walks to my chair, then sits on the armrest. She holds up the iPad and finds another paragraph. "Look here."

A few locks of her hair fall against my face. I stare at those words, but they're beyond my comprehension. I shake my head. "I don't understand."

"The commentator here points out that although the result of the chimera experiment is successful, we don't fully understand the underlying principles. So, in the course of these experiments, we can't control the degree of chimerization. Although the goal may be to produce a pancreas, other areas of the mouse body may also have rat cells."

"So?"

"This is the primary reason why we can't just play around with human cells in research," she says. "If we did a human-pig chimera experiment, I have no way of controlling how many human cells end up in the pig."

"I still don't understand what you're trying to say."

"Think about it, Evan." She puts her hands on my shoulders and looks at me. "This pig may become a second Tony—our son could be concealed in its body. And when it grows up, we'll snatch its kidneys together, then kill it."

A. Adam

Lin Ke lay outside the operating room.

They were already an hour late, and the anesthesiologist hadn't even arrived yet. The only thing separating her naked body from the people walking up and down the corridor was a thin layer of white fabric. She felt very uneasy.

"Why haven't we started yet?" she asked the nurse.

Flustered, the nurse replied, "We've just received notice that due to factors outside our control, your cultivated organ order was canceled. We're very sorry."

What kind of reason was that?! She was the biggest goody-two-shoes aboard this spaceship. In all her one hundred years here, she'd always paid her cultivated organ insurance premiums on time to ensure that her every organ would remain young and healthy. Her heart, the very organ that she was trying to replace, palpitated from rage.

She put on her clothes as quickly as she could. The first thing she did was to file a police report. Then, she took the rail to Deck Seven—supposedly, her new organ was there, in an Adam.

"As your customer," she protested to the overseer, "I demand an explanation for why my order was canceled. I absolutely will not wait another three years with only this shoddy heart!"

"But your order is perfectly fine," the overseer said, surprised. He turned on the monitor. The feed showed the interior of an organ cultivation cabin: organ after organ was wrapped in thin film, all of them growing from tubes that hung from the ceiling. They looked like bunches of grapes waiting for harvest.

But the heart that belonged to Lin Ke was already gone and marked as "harvested."

Stunned, Lin Ke checked the hospital's information platform again, forwarding the notice with the subject "Order Cancellation" to the overseer. But she wasn't expecting that he would doubt the veracity of the notice. "Ma'am, our monitoring platform *can't* be wrong."

The overseer's response enraged Lin Ke. She stood up. "If you can't figure out what happened, then I'll have to go take a look myself."

"Of course. The organ cultivation contract specifies that to be within your rights." The overseer didn't back down at all. "But please remember, you can only look. You cannot enter the cabin."

Ten minutes later, Lin Ke, accompanied by a police droid, opened the door to Organ Cultivation Cabin 35. A horrifying, bloody stench assaulted her nose. As she realized what she was seeing, her view narrowed to an intense spasm as her chest tightened. Then, everything went dark as she fainted.

Luo Ming was the first human police officer to arrive on the scene.

Total chaos.

Those were the first words that came to his mind. As he entered Cabin 35, he had a hard time imagining what the mountain of flesh and blood he was seeing used to look like.

"What happened here?" He regretted not donning a filtration mask before coming in. He lowered his voice as he spoke to his "assistant" Edmund, an AI that was invisible to the naked eye. Edmund was his most dependable companion.

"Ms. Lin Ke, who filed the police report, suffered a heart attack from shock and is now being treated in the hospital." Edmund's voice emitted from a speaker inside his ear. "She complained that the cultivators breached their contract and canceled her order."

At a loss, Luo Ming said, "I think we're looking at a lot more than a breach of contract here."

Viscous blood was still seeping onto the immaculate white floor from a pile of organs three meters in diameter. In some places, the blood had already congealed into a pitch-black patch. Some organs in the outermost layer of the meter-tall flesh pile still looked fresh; a few were even twitching and wriggling—the rotting smell in the air had to be coming from something deeper inside the pile.

As he imagined what the inside might look like, Luo Ming felt his scalp tingling. "We'd better make sure that there are *only* cultivated organs here. God forbid that this mess is hiding a murder scene." Luo Ming commanded Edmund to scan the room. Edmund took control of the police droid via the wireless remote, overriding the droid's visual system to complete his assigned task.

"I'm always a little unsettled by how easily you take control of them," Luo Ming muttered. He could, of course, issue commands to the police droid directly, but then he would have to waste time organizing and analyzing the raw data himself.

"Please don't grumble about your misgivings concerning AIs to me," Edmund replied. "I believe I've found something that's even more unsettling."

While Luo Ming had been griping, the scan revealed that two arms and half a head were also buried within the mountain of organs. The Adam matrix absolutely could not have created those three body parts.

"Alright, looks like we've just added a dismembered corpse to the case," Luo Ming said, sighing. "*The Eden Daily* is going to have a field day with this."

Luo Ming had Edmund scan and record the details of the scene in the cabin; then, he answered First Officer Qin Wei's videocall. Qin Wei was the spaceship *Eden*'s head of security.

"This is perhaps the worst case I've seen on my one hundred and three years aboard this ship." As Luo Ming spoke, his gaze fell on a pair of human eyes that dangled from the ceiling. His voice shook. "You—you'd better come take a look."

2. Echidna

And in a hollow cave she bore another monster, irresistible, in no wise like either to mortal men or to the undying gods, even the goddess fierce Echidna who is half a nymph with glancing eyes and fair cheeks, and half again a huge snake, great and awful, with speckled skin, eating raw flesh beneath the secret parts of the holy earth.
—Hesiod, *Theogony* 300-305 (as translated by Hugh G. Evelyn-White)

"Excuse me, are you—" After observing me for twenty minutes, the woman beside me asks timidly, "Typhon's lead singer Evan Lee?"

"No." All that feels like a past life.

She blurts out an apology and follows up with, "You really look like him."

I channel all the cold disinterest I can muster into my voice. "Is that so."

So ends that conversation. The flight attendant soon comes around with drinks. I ask for a glass of wine, followed by another. The cramped economy seat constricts my body, and terrifying words throw heavy shackles on my mind: "father," "responsibility," and so on.

When I was still Evan Lee, my days of pleasure and riches seemed endless—until she left me, taking with her half of my possessions and all of my musical inspiration.

For a long time after our separation, I constantly thought of her, analyzed her, studied her. I flipped through old tabloids, gathered paparazzi gossip, replayed our wedding video again and again to pick up each of her frowns and smiles, and examined every picture and recording of all the times she appeared with me to support my publicity efforts. During that darkest period of my life, these were the best benefits from my once-great fame—plenty of materials for me to study. And so, bit by bit, I got close to the monster beneath her perfect shell, the serpent-half concealed beneath her beautiful appearance. But there was one part of our life together that I could never understand.

Her pregnancy.

The pregnancy happened only because it was part of her plan. During the first three years of our marriage, I told her many times that I wanted a child, but she would always brush me off with a "no need to rush," plus a session of hot sex. When she decided it was time, she didn't think to discuss the decision with me at all.

"Evan, guess what?" That was the first night after the end of my tour. When I opened the door to our home, a festive atmosphere greeted me.

"What kind of surprise does my little sweetheart have?" I cupped her neck and kissed her lips.

"A baby." She laughed, her eyes curving with joy. "Darling, we're going to have a baby!"

I was stunned. After three years of begging, I had all but given up on the idea.

"It's already three months old." She put my hand on her flat stomach. "Right here."

My palm detected absolutely no movement, but, in that moment, the word "father" entered my mind. Every cell of my being filled with joy. Two months later, Typhon released its last single, "Fire by Lightning." Music critics felt that its "every note was imbued with love and joy." Then, on the day our hit single won the Golden Melody Award, my wife changed in a way that I never could have imagined.

On that day, her labmate called me and said that she had suffered a nervous breakdown.

Impossible. My wife—for whom even an "off mood" was rare—had suffered a nervous breakdown?

Nothing like this had ever happened before. I rushed to campus. Her laboratory was at the end of a boulevard shaded with trees. The rows of Chinese parasol trees had already shed their leaves, leaving behind only branches full of round, dangling fruits. As I walked into that red-brick building, one of her students recognized me.

"Mr. Lee, finally!" His expression was a mixture of agitation, worry, and curiosity, but he prudently suppressed his emotions under a veneer of politeness. "I'm Edmund. She's in the third-floor animal room. You should hurry."

"Thank you, Edmund," I said in a rush.

Although the campus was where we first met, that was actually my first time in her lab. The sparkling floor was like a hospital's; there were rows and rows of metal shelves, each neatly packed with plastic cages connected to a central ventilation system. This room must've held a thousand, no, ten thousand rats!

I found her behind the shelves full of rats. She was cradling her head as she crouched in a corner, her hair a mess, her shoulders shuddering, but her cries were inaudible.

"Honey—" Seeing her like this frightened me. "What's wrong?"

The moment my hand touched her, she let out a screech. I stepped back. "Okay, I won't touch you. What happened?"

Slowly, she raised her head. I had never before seen such panic in her eyes. Her parted lips trembled, but a long time passed before she uttered my name: "Evan."

"Yes, it's me." I chastised myself. "I should've held you back; I shouldn't have let you go to work. The baby's already almost six months old—"

"No!" she shrieked. "No! Don't bring it up! Don't—"

"Alright, we won't talk about the baby." I reached out and tried to get close to her. Her whole body trembled, as though she were struggling to escape. Defeated, I could only call upon my own specialty: "Honey, let's sing 'Titans' together, okay?"

She stopped struggling and looked at me blankly, like a helpless child.

"*A singer in the wilderness, recounting tales of the gods . . .*"

It was a gentle song, and also her favorite melody. I sang as softly as I could, so soft the words were almost inaudible. Music turned out to be more effective than language. She listened until I was halfway through the song, sniffled, then threw herself into my arms and sobbed. I stroked her messy hair and tried to soothe her terrified shivers.

"It's okay, it's okay; I'm here."

She slumped against my chest and, with great effort, uttered a few disconnected phrases: "It's a . . . parasitic . . . parasitic . . . monster . . ."

"What?"

"I don't want the baby. Evan, I don't want that parasite inside my body!"

Shocked, I asked, "What happened? I don't understand."

She wiped her nose on my sleeve. Finally, she could speak in complete sentences. "The baby is taking over my life; it's a parasite in my body. It's controlling my thoughts, commanding me to eat what it wants to eat, telling me to go where it wants to go, demanding I do what it wants to do. It's a parasitic monster in my body, a monster! It's devouring me, do you understand? I can't control myself anymore! I can't stop myself from thinking about it! I can't focus on what I want to do. I can't understand my own notes. I don't care about my papers, either. The only thing in my mind is how I can make it feel more comfortable! I've been possessed by it; it's already wormed its way into my brain—do you understand?"

I couldn't help but laugh. "My silly girl; this is a normal reaction to pregnancy. It's because you love the baby—our baby."

"No!" She stared at me with alarm. "This is absolutely not normal! Not normal at all! You just don't get it because it hasn't possessed *your* body!"

I held back my laughter and said as sincerely as I could, "If it were possible, I would bear the baby for you, but I can't. Chin up; you're a mother now."

She stopped crying. For a few seconds, she stared at me in an unfamiliar way, as though I were the one who had lost my mind. But she soon became her usual self again. She wiped her eyes with her sleeve, then looked up and giggled sheepishly. "Oh goodness, I really did go nuts today."

"It's a very common anxiety, honey."

She leaned against my shoulder. "You're right. These are normal feelings for a new mother. I need to get used to them."

In the months that followed, there were a couple more incidents in which she was dejected and depressed, but there were no more episodes as intense as the one in the lab.

But I started to be more vigilant, canceling a new tour so that I could spend more time with her. Around the 39th week of her pregnancy, I stumbled upon a file in her computer that recorded in detail the "conversations" she had with her unborn baby: when she went to the restroom, dreams, favorite foods and kinds of music—all trivial things. Reading these notes, I began to understand what she said that day in the lab. The things she noted were not her own habits or tastes, but someone else's.

The baby growing inside her was using her body to do what it wanted to do. Once she realized this, she was terrified.

If she had been a typical mother, perhaps she would have used "love" to explain her behavior. But she couldn't do that. Emotions to her are a kind of camouflage, something to let her blend in with others. So she could only understand everything from the baby's perspective: this was a monster that had possessed her body and taken control of her so that it could survive inside her.

Maybe the plane's air conditioning is too cold, but suddenly, I shiver. I never thought I'd come to understand why she'd abandon her own child: If she didn't, she'd always be under Tony's control, forced to give up on having her own life—just as I have.

"Please fasten your seatbelt, Mr. Lee," the flight attendant says. "We're about to land."

As we descend, a city surrounded by an oasis blooms in the vast expanse of desert outside.

B. Eden

After completing a genetic survey of the scene, Luo Ming received Edmund's interim report: the limbs and head in Organ Cultivation Cabin 35 belonged to three deceased passengers. Terminal illness was unquestionably the cause of all three deaths; furthermore, they had all chosen to donate their bodies to science to advance research on those illnesses. Edmund's discovery allowed Luo Ming to unfurrow his brows just a bit.

"It's not murder," he said to First Officer Qin Wei, who had rushed to the scene. "That's good news at least."

Like Luo Ming and the majority of the passengers aboard *Eden*, Qin Wei was close to a hundred fifty years old. He had just gotten a scalp replacement: only an infant-like layer of fine hair covered the top of his head, lending a comical air to his overall appearance.

"Thank goodness." Qin Wei was distracted, and he muttered as though to himself, "But . . . how'd these limbs even get here?"

"The body parts should have been sent to the medical research center under Deck Seven," Luo Ming said.

"Should have been, yes." Only now did Qin Wei look at Luo Ming. "The organ cultivation cabins are the most heavily monitored and secure part of this spaceship. For something like this to happen is unbelievable. You might not know this—even the police don't have the clearance to view documentation about Adam."

"Sharing such information could greatly help my investigation."

"I'm very sorry, Officer Luo, but those documents involve classified information about the very heart of *Eden*," Qin Wei said. "Since there aren't any suspected murders, I'd say this investigation has come to an end. Why don't you let me and the Adam overseers tie up any loose ends?"

Luo Ming read between the lines. "So you're saying that this is just an ordinary accident?"

Qin Wei smiled noncommittally. "The ship has experienced severe organ cultivation failures before, you know? Malfunctions in the cabin's temperature control."

Luo Ming studied his expression and let out a small sigh. "Alright, sir, I understand."

Only a day later, as he sat in his office, Luo Ming received an info packet from Edmund concerning Adam.

"You're a genius." Luo Ming sighed with approval and opened the document. As the unredacted details filled his view, Luo Ming gasped. "This ship's security system must have serious flaws for such classified data to be so easily accessible."

"Or perhaps it's your fault for illicitly bringing an AI aboard, hmm?" Edmund's voice was a cross between pride and smug derision.

"Well, no one's discovered you over all these years." Edmund was a gift Luo Ming had received a long time ago, and after years of working and living together, he had found the AI indispensable. Even after hearing about *Eden*'s ban on AIs, Luo Ming still chose to implant the terminal into his body and smuggle Edmund aboard the spaceship.

"That's because the intelligence systems here are far too primitive," Edmund said. "But you don't need to worry about the security of the ship. Its core systems are sealed off from outside networks. I haven't found a single entry point."

Luo Ming nodded and returned his attention to the documents. It appeared that *Eden* was actually a research vessel that provided replacement organs for its several hundred thousand passengers, allowing them to extend their lives indefinitely. At the same time, it transmitted the residents' health data back to Earth, so that people back home could learn first-hand about potential complications from a large-scale organ replacement program. *Eden* followed a comet's orbit in the Solar System so that its path crossed with the Earth's once every four years, allowing the ship to dock at a space station and exchange both personnel and information.

"I always thought we were heading away from the Solar System," said a surprised Luo Ming. "And nobody ever told me we could leave the ship!"

Edmund said, "Looks like they'd gone to a lot of trouble to hide the truth and prevent you all from discovering that you're actually laboratory mice."

In light of this new-found knowledge, the organ cultivation cabins really were the soul of *Eden*. They were often called "Adam" chambers, after that figure from Christian lore who used his own rib to create humanity's other ancestor. But, to be more precise, every mucous membrane pouch in the organ cultivation cabins that bore a human organ—those were all Adams. They were distinct, each carrying different passengers' genes, cultivating different organs.

When *Eden* was first designed, the Adams were separated from one another. But, as time passed, the Adam overseers discovered a strange phenomenon: after a few Adams began cultivation inside the same room, cells would start growing along the feeding tracts until all the Adams were connected to each other.

However, this connection did not delay or corrupt the growing organs; rather, organ cultivation in all the Adams became more efficient as organ maturation time decreased. Some researchers believed that this "genetic networking" created a system among the Adams for exchanging growth signals and hormones, accelerating organ development.

As a result, when the cultivation cabins were renovated forty years ago, the overseers installed passages that allowed all the Adams to connect to each other, resulting in an awe-inspiring effect—while each passenger's genome was still preserved as separate and complete, the vast majority of organ cultivation times were cut by at least half. Even the development time for lungs, the slowest organ to cultivate, was cut down by a third.

"I still don't understand what any of this has to do with our case." Luo Ming felt agitated. "I keep feeling like we missed something at the scene."

"I recorded a complete scan of the room," Edmund said.

"Perhaps—" Luo Ming pondered. "The problem may not only be *inside* the cultivation cabin."

"What do you mean?"

"Do you remember the dispute between the woman who filed the report and the Adam overseer?" Luo Ming asked.

"The hospital's notification system showed that Ms. Lin Ke's order for a heart had been canceled, whereas Adam's monitoring platform showed that everything was fine."

"Right," Luo Ming said. "Adam's system should be much more secure than the hospital's, yet the cultivation cabin overseer didn't know the true state of Cabin 35. Why is that?"

"Could it be that Adam's overseers were trying to conceal the mess inside?" Edmund asked.

"Maybe. But we can't rule out another possibility: none of those in charge, including the first officer and the cultivation cabin overseers, have any idea what really happened." Luo Ming put the recording of Lin Ke arguing with the overseer on the display. "Watch the man's expression—the surprise is genuine."

"True, as I can confirm with microexpression analysis," Edmund said.

"Based on the scene we observed, it's very likely that what happened to Lin Ke wasn't an isolated incident. But she was the only one who felt strongly enough to make a report to the police, and who went to open the door to Cabin 35. That's in the contract, but it looks like passengers only exercised their right to examine the cabins during the early years of the ship's journey."

"Are you suggesting that all the organs we saw on the ground had their orders canceled?"

Luo Ming's eyes lit up. "We might as well follow this lead. Edmund, can you break into the databases for both the cultivation cabins and the hospital and pick out all relevant records? It's possible that there are discrepancies between the two systems—those would be the organs we saw in Cabin 35."

"You really know how to come up with hard problems for me." Despite these words, Edmund sounded delighted. "I'll give it a shot."

3. Typhon

From his shoulders grew a hundred heads of a snake, a fearful dragon, with dark, flickering tongues, and from under the brows of his eyes in his marvelous heads flashed fire, and fire burned from his heads as he glared. And there were voices in all his dreadful heads which uttered every kind of sound unspeakable; for at one time they made sounds such that the gods

understood, but at another, the noise of a bull bellowing aloud in proud ungovernable fury; and at another, the sound of a lion, relentless of heart; and at another, sounds like whelps, wonderful to hear.
—Hesiod, *Theogony* 820-835 (as translated by Hugh G. Evelyn-White)

Nine years later, I find myself in her laboratory again. Edmund has gone from an undergraduate to a doctoral student, but the way he looks at me hasn't changed in the least—he's just like any other awe-struck fan. "Mr. Lee, the professor is waiting for you in the animal room."

"Thank you, Edmund."

She doesn't notice when I enter. She's squatting beside a pig that has to be half a meter tall, all her attention focused on it as she laughs. She puts her cell phone on speaker, and music starts playing. It's my song, "Fire by Lightning."

"When I cradle it in my hands,
The sun and moon tumble, stars fall.
Go ahead and fight, destroy;
The king of the gods' undying wish is in my hands."

The pig dances to the music on its hind legs, clumsily twisting and rocking. Gradually, it catches up to the tempo. She stands with it and leans against a desk, laughing so hard she can't breathe. The pig faces her, dancing now with gusto, keeping up even better with the beat. It's unbelievable—the pig is actually *dancing* to the brisk pace of the music.

The song, now in an ornamental cadenza, switches tempo. The pig stumbles and tumbles to the ground, startling her. She falls to her knees by its prone body. "Are you okay?"

The pig oinks in reply. Annoyed, she jabs its head with a finger, then says in the gentlest voice I've ever heard, "You rascal, don't scare me like that."

The pig's oinks are now laced with a hint of whining. She rubs its back. "Alright, alright; it's okay, as long as you're not hurt."

This is such a bizarre sight. I cough. She and the pig turn their heads simultaneously to look at me together—an image I'll never forget.

"What's wrong, Evan?" She stands.

It has Tony's eyes.

She's never seen Tony, so she can't know. But the eyes in that one-and-a-half-year-old pig belong to Tony: light brown irises with a hint of gray. It's not just the eyes, but also something unnamable in their depths, something that sends chills down my spine, making me forget why I'm here.

It reminds me of how I felt the time I found myself in the middle of a stage, having forgotten everything about the song I was supposed to sing. The electric guitar's prelude was nothing but white noise, and my legs trembled in the flickering magnesium lights.

"Do you need a cup of coffee?" She peers at me, concerned. "You don't look so good."

"Can we . . . talk . . . alone?" Even if I performed at three back-to-back shows, my voice still wouldn't sound like this.

"I was just about to show you our pig," she says. "It's doing really well. Fantastic, don't you think?"

I catch its gaze again, and in that second, I feel my soul being torn apart.

"My God!"

The pig stares at me as though it already knows its destiny: a wordless acquiescence to suffering, imbued with a fatalistic sense of tragedy. The last few times Tony underwent dialysis, he gazed at me with the exact same expression.

"Okay, Evan." She steps forward to hold my trembling hands. "Let's go somewhere else."

We don't say a word on the way to her office. The afternoon sun dissipates all shadows in the spacious room. Edmund brings in two tiny, round cups. "Thank you," she says, but then she doesn't say a word to me after Edmund leaves. The dappled shadows of tree leaves upon the desk lengthen. I take a sip of the now cold and bitter coffee. Finally, she breaks an afternoon's worth of silence.

"I thought you might want to take a look at the report."

A thick file lands before me. I open it, my arms stiff. Inside are notes starting from when the pig was an embryo until now. I can only make sense of the pictures. From the outset, it's always smiled at the camera, if that joyous and eager expression can be called a "smile"—but within the last month, it's ceased smiling. On the last page is a close up portrait of its eyes. Staring at them, I can barely tolerate the agitation in my stomach—I throw the file to the ground.

She stands and picks up the file, chuckling. "Good thing I didn't give you a digital version, or else I'd have to fill out a damaged equipment report now."

"How could this be?" I murmur.

"Evan, we have to face the facts." She lets out a soft sigh. "This is perhaps the best outcome: the pig is now in prime condition for organ donation—if you were to ask me, this experiment went unusually smoothly. We found the right path from the very beginning, and we overcame every obstacle within the shortest possible time. I doubt you'd find another instance in the history of science where the road to discovery was so smooth—"

"You—" I interrupt her, but I'm not sure what I should say.

"I've already gotten in touch with my friend Dr. Sanger. He's the best kidney surgeon at the state hospital." Her tone is level and calm. "I've already sent him the pig's file. He's reviewed the data and thinks the surgery will be no more risky than a standard human-to-human transplant. Evan, I don't understand why you're still not satisfied."

Only her last sentence betrays her suppressed anger, but it's enough to provoke all my terror and rage. I unlock my phone: the wallpaper is a picture of Tony staring innocently at me.

"Enough." I fling open the file and place my phone on top of the close up of the pig's eyes. "We both know where the problem is, right? Look at these eyes: they're exactly the same—"

"—as Tony's," she finishes. "Of course I know. Those are Tony's eyes; the cells in that organ are human cells."

I read the unspoken message from her face. "Are you . . . are you saying there are human cells in other organs as well?"

"Yes . . . it's a bit hard to take. Its nervous system is almost entirely made up of human cells." She shrugs. "Don't be naïve, Evan. We knew from the start that we couldn't control the degree of chimerization, but we went ahead anyway."

"The nervous system?"

"The cerebrum, the cerebellum, and the spinal cord—the vast majority of it," she says, enunciating each word, as if she's trying to engrave the words into my heart with her poisoned tongue. "To put it simply: our son is inside that pig."

I've never been so frightened, not even the time I saw Tony being pulled under that car. Back then, I was a father, but now, I've become a criminal—what in the world have we done? We've melded our son with a pig, and now we're going to butcher it with our own hands!

My silence allows her to relax her tone. "So long as I stay quiet, no one will know about this. These notes won't appear in my paper. The nervous system isn't the focus of this experiment, and it's not important for whether the experiment is declared a success. The kidneys are perfect, Evan. You don't have to worry about that at all."

"I'm not worried about that!" Her forced composure is intolerable. "Killing it is cruel—it's wrong! Don't you realize that the pig knows what's going to happen?"

She smiles. "Evan, what do you plan to do?"

"I—"

"You know, I haven't been able to sleep for the last two weeks." Her voice is low. "I keep thinking about whether you've been trying get back at me with this pig. I abandoned Tony, so you thought up the cruelest of methods to reawaken my motherly instincts. I kept telling myself that this *isn't* Tony, that this *isn't* my son; I even refused to name it out of fear that doing so would humanize the animal. But it went beyond my imagination: out of all the researchers, it's closest to me; out of all the music we play for it, it only likes yours."

Tony is the same way. From when he was a baby, as soon as he heard "Fire by Lightning," he'd start dancing.

She continues. "I've thought about it: should we stop and let Tony succumb to his fate, thereby allowing the pig to live? But then I saw you, and I realized that we've never had any choice but to go forward."

Her gaze penetrates me to the root, and I, in turn, finally see the trembling that she's kept hidden inside. Her terror and pain are undoubtedly far sharper than mine: it's only because she's been ruminating on them for so long that she can bury them under a tranquil facade. I've only glanced at the pig, but she's been raising it since it was a single cell.

Of course we can't turn back. Tony continues to deteriorate, and everything her lab has invested into this pig can't be hidden from her supporters. I demanded that she cross the Rubicon; it's only reasonable that both of us should bear this heavy cross.

"Right." I force myself to forget the pig. "Tony hasn't been doing so well lately. I'll bring him here as soon as possible. Don't want to miss the best window for surgery."

"We have an understanding then." She smiles, erasing all misgivings from her face. She opens her notebook and gives me Dr. Sanger's contact information as well as his CV. Then she tells me her own opinions and recommendations for the transplant surgery. Only after it's gone dark outside does she stop talking. "You should go," she reminds me. "If you leave now, you can still catch your flight."

I get up, hesitating for a moment over whether to shake her hand in a sign of friendship and gratitude. But she's holding her hands together before her chest. I guess there's no such need.

"I'm off then. Thank you," I say, my mouth dry.

She laughs and shakes her head. "Evan, Tony is my son too. Why are you saying 'thank you'?"

"Ah, yes." I laugh too.

We walk out of the laboratory together. The shadows of the trees pool together, enveloping the world in the stillness of night. I'm about to say goodbye, but then she speaks.

"The first time I saw you was over there, right?" She whispers, "That day, you played such a gentle tune. Who'd have thought that the song you'd end up recording would be so wild?"

I know she's talking about "Titans." The inspiration for the first phrase had come to me while I was performing at this school. That night, as though in the throes of a craving for some drug, I rushed around in search of a piano to bring the notes in my mind to life. I climbed through the window of my room and felt my way back to the locked auditorium, never realizing that there was another pair of ears outside listening.

"Detested by our forefathers,
Buried deep, hidden from the sun,
Scythe-wielding, throne-stealing, we bear curses and epithets.

. . .

We're destined to rebel,
Smashing barriers, heedless of cost;
Let smoke choke the air, let the earth burn to oblivion!"

She sings, only remembering some of the lyrics. She's also totally off-pitch, but I can't laugh as freely as I used to.

She turns to look at me. "Now that I think of it, your song was rather prophetic."

In the end, she never went to the state hospital, nor did she show up at Tony's recovery party. For five years, she disappeared into her lab, cutting off contact with all her friends.

I'm shocked when she calls me out of the blue. She tells me that she would like me to set up a charitable foundation in Tony's name to support organ transplants for children. During the last five years, I had emailed her with such an idea, but all my messages had been returned as undeliverable. I immediately agree.

Once the framework of the foundation is in place, I contact her again.

"I get the feeling that you're about to make a grand gesture," I say.

"I am," she replies. "I reprogrammed the chimera gene regulation network and turned it into a blastocyst-like structure—"

"Sorry," I interrupt her. "You know I don't understand all that."

"Give me a minute." She pauses, as though she were switching her linguistic module from *scientific jargon* to *common*. "We already have the capacity to produce human organs in a lab. I used existing chimeras to create a more stable structure; all you have to do is add new human cells, and it will create the corresponding organ."

"That's fantastic!"

"I'll never allow it to *look* like a human being again." Her tone is exhausted.

Simultaneously with the creation of the foundation, she publishes a series of papers on chimeras in *Cell*. Starting with the first human-pig chimera, she traces her groundbreaking work through the regenerative medicine lab. Overnight, she rocks the foundation of humanity's understanding of "life."

I buy that issue of *Cell*. The reviewers lavish her with praise: "This is a revolution for regenerative medicine, hinting at our near future: humanity will be able to swap out our organs as if they were interchangeable parts. We will live longer, maybe even forever."

Criticism and debates follow soon after. Although a mother's pressing need to save her son's life is understandable, experimenting with human stem cells is nonetheless an ethical taboo.

Her third paper pushes back against the torrent of attacks, laying out her model for the organ-cultivation matrix, which she names "Adam." It resembles a small, square box filled with mucous membranes and doesn't look like a living creature at all.

"The Adam technology won't encroach upon any ethical concerns," she says in an interview. "It won't develop a human brain; it can't think; it has no feelings—because we haven't provided it with any mechanisms for thoughts or feelings. The only thing it can do is use its own rib to save the people who need it."

C. The Captain

Luo Ming didn't really think that he could get in front of the captain of *Eden* based on just a letter—though that was his plan.

The woman before him had ashy white hair, wrinkled skin, and a hunched back; even sitting on the sofa seemed to take a lot out of her. Luo Ming was surprised by the captain's appearance. The women he knew prioritized external beauty, listing organs related to appearance at the front of their replacement queue.

"Regarding the incident in Cabin 35"—belying her appearance, the captain's voice was energetic—"I'd like to hear your point of view."

"The first officer has indicated that the incident is beyond my purview," Luo Ming said carefully, placing his hands before him.

"I actually think it's better to have a professional involved in the case." The captain gestured for Luo Ming to take the armchair before her. "But given the sensitive nature of the cultivation cabins, the results of the investigation should be kept confidential. That's not an issue for you, is it?"

"No." Luo Ming sat down. "I assume you've read my letter carefully?"

"Yes."

"As I mentioned, I believe this was no accident, but a premeditated crime."

The captain dropped her gaze. "Your theory is in conflict with the first officer's report."

"Haven't you summoned me here for another perspective?" Luo Ming studied the captain's expression, then continued. "I went over all the orders that the hospital's system canceled without explanation from the last three months. The total was over seven times the normal cancellation rate. I traced all the canceled organs to Cabin 35, but the monitoring system showed all the organs to be developing normally."

"And that's enough to convince you this wasn't an accident?" the captain asked. "Maybe the monitoring system is malfunctioning."

"It's not just the monitoring system, Your Excellency. Don't forget the cultivation cabin itself—how did that pile of 'accidentally harvested' organs come to be? And we have no explanation for the discrepancy between the cultivation cabins' monitoring system and the hospital's order tracking system."

The captain stared at him. "I'm listening."

"Before coming to see you today, I wasn't too sure about my conclusions." Luo Ming smiled modestly. "I originally suspected that the mismatch between orders was due to the overseers' efforts to hide the truth. But by summoning me, you've told me that even you, the captain of this ship, aren't sure what exactly happened. That leaves us with only one other possibility: The Adam overseers did *not* know about the recent incident in Cabin 35. Thus, we can theorize that the monitoring system has been tampered with."

"I had First Officer Qin Wei examine the cultivation cabin monitoring system," the captain said, her gaze growing more intent. "It appears to have been modified with a 'green screen'-like technology. Police droids entering and leaving the cultivation cabins would show up on the monitors as normal, but they'd always appear against a background showing the interior of the Adam chambers functioning normally."

"You're saying that the recording was selectively tampered with? The images of the Adam cabins on the monitors never changed?"

"No, not 'never changed;' they showed as 'functioning normally.' On the monitors, you could see the organs growing as expected, and when orders were supposed to be fulfilled, they were 'harvested normally.'" The captain shook her head. "This method of tampering with the system is highly sophisticated."

The captain's news deepened Luo Ming's puzzlement. "But this is what I can't figure out. If the entire incident was a premeditated crime, then the criminal already accomplished the most difficult step—taking over Adam's high-security monitoring system. Yet they forgot to cover their tracks in the far more basic hospital systems."

"There's a simple explanation for that: the criminal couldn't conjure the patients' requested organs out of thin air. They had no choice but to leave the orders alone and hope that patients would not exercise their right to examine the cultivation cabins."

Luo Ming shook his head. "But they could have played any number of other tricks that would have worked better. For instance, they could have systematically delayed the order fulfillment dates for all the affected organs to prevent anyone from knowing what had happened. However, based on my review of the hospital's records, the doctors and patients only found out at the last minute that their orders had been delayed or canceled. The notices came through the hospital's regular organ reception channels, not Adam."

"I'm now thoroughly confused." The captain furrowed her brow. "What are you trying to say?"

"For someone who came up with such a complicated scheme—going so far as to use a green screen to tamper with the monitoring records—forgetting about the hospital's basic database is a very strange oversight. They clearly have the capability to break into the hospital's systems, but they didn't—why not? One possibility is that they actually *wanted* to draw attention to what they did, but another possibility is that they didn't even know that the hospital's information platform *existed*."

"That's impossible," the captain said. "Every person aboard *Eden* knows about the hospital's organ replacement database."

"Of course, that's how it should be," Luo Ming said. "But there are always bound to be some people who *don't* know."

"I'm not interested in a vague hunch. If you have a definite suspicion, say so."

"On this ship, who wouldn't know about the existence of the hospital's organ replacement database? Or rather, who's never ordered an organ?" Luo Ming looked at the captain. "I hope you can help me gather a list of names. They're the primary suspects."

The captain tapped the armrest with a wrinkled finger and chuckled coldly. "That's quite an accusation." She met Luo Ming's gaze. "I've never replaced an organ."

4. Orthrus

Men say that Typhaon (Typhon) the terrible, outrageous and lawless, was joined in love to her, the maid with glancing eyes. So she conceived and brought forth fierce offspring; first she bore Orthus the hound of Geryones . . . but Echidna was subject in love to Orthus and brought forth the deadly Sphinx which destroyed the Cadmeans.
—Hesiod, *Theogony*, 304-335 (as translated by Hugh G. Evelyn-White)

Some legends say that it was actually Orthrus, and not Typhon, with whom Echidna conceived of those other monstrosities: Chimera and Sphinx.
—Anonymous

The first time I see her is at my father's funeral.

Although at least half of that crowd of tens of thousands have come to see her, I'm the only one who picks her out. She's wearing a black silk dress, a diamond ring dangling from a string around her neck. Her face looks even younger than mine. I don't know if it's my practice at identifying faces or a natural instinct that makes me recognize her as my mother. Then, she sees me too.

Five seconds later, I receive a direct message: "I'd like to chat after the funeral."

I remember my father's last words to me as he lay dying: "She's your mother, and she gave you the gift of life twice—be grateful."

Once the crowd dissipates, I duck into her car. She enters Oslo Airport, Gardermoen as the destination and turns her seat around to face me.

"Hello, Tony."

I haven't been called that in years. After my parents created the Tony Lee Charitable Foundation, I had to change my name to protect my privacy and live a normal life.

"Mom?" It turns out to be easier to say than I thought. "You look so young."

"Yes, it's me." She laughs, then winks, as though we share a secret. "I'm conducting a new experiment to restore my cells to a more youthful state. It's a dangerous experiment, and we don't know all the side effects—it's such a shame that I don't have another son to be the guinea pig this time."

"Um—" I have no idea what to say in response.

"Oh, darling, I'm just joking!" She spreads her hands disarmingly. "Now, tell me about your life. I hear that you're a police officer?"

"It's just a job."

Her grin widens. "You've done well. I noticed that you're dealing with AI crimes. Amazing."

"The world changes so quickly. Scientists can't control everything they invent." I resent her tone: she's speaking as though she's always been a part of my life, exercising a mother's care.

"That's true." She nods vigorously. "Sometimes we don't understand our creations as much as we'd like people to think."

That's unexpected. "Really?"

She doesn't answer, asking a question instead. "Will you come to our press event? We're going to announce some important news."

I've heard about her research group's press event, scheduled for next month. After seven years of silence, everyone's dying to find out what she's going to say.

"This could change the course of humanity." The car slows down. She glances out the window, then looks back at me. "You'll be there, of course."

Her confidence irritates me. I am not my father, who was always so entranced by her. "Sorry, I'm not interested in it."

"Believe me, darling, you *will* be interested." The car stops. She taps twice on her watch, and I receive an invitation as well as a packet of documents. "The thirteenth of next month. Be there."

She holds my hand for a moment, then leaves for the airport. The midnight sun throws her black dress into sharp relief.

Three hours and forty minutes later, the Airbus A400 she's on plunges into the sea.

I end my vacation early to join the search and rescue effort, but the Baltic Sea has swallowed any trace of her. In the depths of the turbid waves, I see the wreckage of the plane.

They say that there lies entombed humanity's wildest dream.

The day the rescue efforts end, I receive another invitation to the press event.

I've run out of excuses. Heeding the call of fate, I set forth on a journey of more than ten thousand kilometers. On the plane, I look through the documents she gave me.

There are pictures of a pig from when it was a piglet to when it was fully grown—undoubtedly my savior. I transfer planes at Amsterdam and New York before arriving at a small town in the middle of the desert. My father once told me about this town: it's the birthplace of my kidneys.

"Tony Lee," I say to the person who's here to meet me. The name is written on my invitation.

Her mouth hangs open with exaggerated surprise. She lowers her gaze. "I'm Chen Ying. My condolences."

"Thank you."

I enter the auditorium to a hero's welcome. Everyone seems to recognize me: they surround me, chattering about my mother and my kidneys, but neither of these two topics feel real to me. Thankfully, the press event starts up soon after. The chattering ends as the lights dim, and everyone turns to look at the illuminated stage.

"We will change the world once again." The middle-aged man on stage opens the ceremony with these words.

The applause is enthusiastic. "Alright, Edmund!"

Edmund is the chief scientist of my mother's medical research group—he and my mother once won a Nobel together. After the applause dies down, he speaks again.

"In the past thirty years, we've accomplished the unimaginable. From chimera experiments to the first successful human organ cultivation, as well as the spread of regenerative medicine thereafter, we've saved many people's lives—but we've also faced much opposition. The main objection has been: should we use humans as research subjects?"

Edmund picks me out of the crowd. "We're honored to have Mr. Tony Lee among us today. The fact that he's healthy and alive is our answer."

Thunderous applause and a blinding spotlight fall upon me together. The world goes white for a moment, and I can't see a thing.

"Our lab has never backed off from the effort to make our case to the public, but we've always lacked a decisive argument for the moral rightness of allowing human experimentation."

The spotlight eases away from me as Edmund continues, "But our latest discovery should finally settle this decades-long ethical dispute. First, let me introduce the youngest and most powerful member of our team: Mr. Sphinx, an avatar personifying our quantum computer."

Rays of light gather at his fingertips and then scatter to form a human shape—a powerful demonstration of the latest hologram technology. But given my profession, what draws my attention is the word "avatar." After handling hundreds of AI-related crimes, I'm leery of them, especially one taking advantage of quantum computing.

Sphinx renders as a golden-skinned teen. Once the rays of light have condensed, I almost can't tell that he's a hologram. A shy smile appears on his face, perfectly calibrated to give the impression of innocence.

"Good evening, everyone. I have a riddle—"

Laughing, Edmund interrupts him. "Let me guess: 'What has four legs in the morning, two legs in the afternoon, and three legs at night?' Sphinx, everyone knows the answer: humanity."

"Humanity, yes. That riddle compares a lifetime to a day," Sphinx says. "But I have a different riddle for you."

"Go ahead. The best minds of the world are gathered here today."

"Where did humanity come from? Before 'morning,' what happened in the darkness before dawn?"

"Evolution, Sphinx. I taught you this," Edmund says, sighing.

"But you must have proof," Sphinx says.

"We have many fossils of *Homo erectus* and *Homo sapiens*." Edmund pauses. "But—"

Sphinx takes over. "But, there is a gap in the fossil record. Until now, we have no direct evidence that modern humans, or *Homo sapiens sapiens*, evolved from the archaic *Homo sapiens*."

"But you have no evidence to disprove that modern humans evolved from *Homo sapiens*, either," Edmund counters.

"No, I do have proof. I know that humanity's ancestor is a chimera."

For about ten seconds, Edmund is silent. Murmurs rise in the meeting hall.

"A chimera?" Edmund says finally. "What kind of joke is this?"

"I never joke," Sphinx says. "Before the birth of quantum computers, calculating the product of two large prime numbers was very easy for classical computers, but figuring out the prime factors of a semiprime number, a natural number which is the product of two prime numbers, was practically impossible, making them useful for cryptography. After the creation of quantum computers, these early encryption technologies are no longer of use, as we can easily decrypt those methods using quantum algorithms. After adding me to the lab's research team, Edmund had a new idea—he wanted me to factor humanity's DNA."

"In other words, I wanted Sphinx to take one person's genome and separate it into their parents' genomes. It's a biologist's extension of quantum decryption." Edmund shrugs. "What I didn't expect was that Sphinx would actually be able to do it."

Sphinx nods. "Yes, after continuous algorithmic improvements and experimental confirmation, I can ensure a very high degree of recoverability. That is, if I have the complete genome sequence for any one of you, I can figure out the genome sequences of all your ancestors. I can recover their skin color, blood type, hair and eye color—give me enough time, and I can even recreate an ancestral human.

With the support of medical databases from around the world, I quickly created a database of the genomes of humanity's ancestors."

"As we factored human genomes," Edmund added, "we also attempted to factor the genomes of as many other species as possible, including mammals, reptiles, birds, insects, mollusks, and even plants—a total of 115,000 species for which we now have an ancestral genomic database. In the end, we made an astounding discovery."

The whole meeting hall is silent, enraptured.

"In every species other than humans, there is a similar trajectory for the number of ancestors that contributed to the species' genome." Rays of light once again gather in Edmund's hand. "Observe this graph—the x-axis is the number of genetic specimens per time period, and the y-axis is time. As we go further up, we go further back in time.

"Let's start with puffins. As we go up in the time scale, we discover that, regardless of how long the population has remained stable, there is always a period where the population rapidly declines—a 'bottleneck zone.'"

The graph slowly rises in pace with Edmund's gesture and stops at the midway point to show an hourglass shape. "What does this mean? At some point, for whatever reason, puffins died off in great numbers. The puffins we see now are descended from the few survivors of the bottleneck zone.

"If we continue tracing back the population count of the puffins' ancestors, we discover a fascinating phenomenon: history repeats itself. Above the bottleneck zone is an expansion period, and above that, another bottleneck—this goes on. We've calculated the trajectories for 115,000 species over the past 500,000 years, and they are all the same.

"Now, let's take a look at the human population."

Edmund waves his hand to the side. The human population graph rises up a bit, then quickly narrows to an almost invisible dot.

"A rather terrifying bottleneck, is it not?" Edmund says. "But, when we go back from here—"

He lifts his hand, but the graph doesn't rise with him. It stops there, towering, like the minaret of a mosque.

"What does this graph of humanity tell us? It tells us that, approximately 180,000 years ago, our common ancestor 'Mitochondrial Eve' gave birth to her children, and those children gave birth to more children, until human civilization dominated the globe." Edmund slows his speech. "But please take note: this graph also tells us that humanity can trace back to only *one* common ancestor."

Sphinx breaks in, "Let me remind you, one individual cannot proliferate the species."

"Of course, 'one' is neither accurate nor possible. We know now that, other than this woman, our common ancestors include four men as well. But regardless of how many people survived that bottleneck, how could something like this have happened? Sphinx's genome factoring analysis tells me that, before these ancestors, there were no ancestors."

"It's true," Sphinx says.

"Was there a mistake in our calculations?" Edmund says, "But we tested our calculations on fast-reproducing bacteria and generations of laboratory mice with detailed genetic records, and our algorithms were confirmed to be correct! Sphinx did not make any errors. Why, esteemed guests, why is it that we can trace the unbroken trajectories of 115,000 other species, but we can't do the same for humans? Before humanity's morning, what happened during the predawn darkness?"

Dead silence.

Everyone looks up at the inconceivable graph. Judging by the introductions given to me earlier, this room is filled with the world's top scientists and doctors, a few politicians and business tycoons, as well as representatives from a number of influential media outlets. Everyone is trying to find a flaw in the graph, but no one speaks. "Chimera," the word that Sphinx said at the beginning of the presentation, floats like a ghost over our heads.

"When I, too, was at a loss like everyone here today, I called my mentor. After she listened to my description, she asked me only one question: 'Edmund, do you still remember that pig?'"

Edmund looks at me. "Tony, do you still remember the pig that saved your life?"

Faint murmurs fill the hall.

Edmund shakes his head. "Maybe you don't; but I do. I always thought that that pig was the first chimera with human cells. But I was wrong.

"I had Sphinx trace back a few other populations, those of the chimeras we've been cultivating these past few decades. Although there aren't many chimera species, some rat-mouse chimeras have already reproduced over a hundred generations. What happens when we calculate the genomes of their ancestors?"

All of the graphs except for the human population graph disappear, replaced by the graphs of a few dozen chimera species. Like demons, the graphs climb upward, all terminating in a single point, some higher, some lower.

"They are the same as humans—these chimeras are *the same* as humans." Edmund pauses, then raises his voice. "But can we conclude from this that humans descended from a chimera? Of course not!

"I had Sphinx add to this model all of the *Homo sapiens* and *Homo erectus* genomes that we could find, leading to the discovery of one of our ancestors that shared a blood relationship with their ancestors.

"This ancestor was not Eve's human husband, but rather the hybrid child she had with a *Homo sapiens*. We used quantum algorithms on this child's *Homo sapiens* genes to conduct a complicated 'subtraction.' Finally, we extracted the part of Eve's genome that did not include any DNA from *Homo sapiens*."

Along with Sphinx, every point of light dissipates, then gathers into a huge double helix, one portion of which is highlighted in bright white.

Edmund emphasizes every word as he concludes. "We are certain that this is a chimera—a cross-species chimera."

I close my eyes. A photo my mother sent me appears in my mind's eye. In the documents, that photo was perhaps the most nondescript one, bundled together with countless standard shots of the chimera pig in the research notes. It was a close-up shot of the pig's eyes.

On the plane, I had glanced at it for maybe half a second, only to find that it had branded itself into my memories like a curse.

Those were my eyes. It had my eyes.

The hologram graphs disappear, leaving only Edmund on the stage.

"Humanity's common ancestor is a chimera. The foundation of all the ethical attacks and criticisms levied against us over the years has disintegrated. We have the evidence to prove that humanity was born in a laboratory. We are the product of science, not nature."

Edmund's voice trembles with excitement. "We don't yet have the technology to figure out what creatures were used to create humanity, and we can't tell who our creator was. But the success of chimeras and regenerative medicine tells us that we are only one step away from our Creator!

"So what is there left to fear? Shall we boldly stride across this ethical barrier and let each person choose whether to join us, or shall we hesitate, timidly adhere to the fate of every other species on earth, and wait for the next bottleneck to return civilization to square one, or perhaps even to annihilation?

"Esteemed guests, I submit that we're at a crossroads of science and history: we must make a choice—now is the time for full-scale human experimentation."

The sound of scattered applause gradually swells to a thundering roar that fills the auditorium. Some in the crowd still wear expressions of doubt, but they're also full of admiration. From the birth of that pig, this town has been the battlefront of human genetic transformation. It's the holy site within the heart of every biologist and medical specialist. The announcement today has advanced the field again, perhaps even bringing humanity closer to a new world.

It's too bad my mother isn't here to see this.

Right at that moment, I receive a high-priority direct message. The sender's name makes my heart skip a beat.

"I'd like to chat after the event."

D. Cabin Zero

"Edmund?"

No answer.

In the hundred years he'd been together with his AI, nothing like this had ever happened before. Luo Ming looked around, then raised his voice: "Edmund!"

His assistant finally appeared. "I'm here."

Full of concern, Luo Ming asked, "What did you find in the captain's cabin?"

Before meeting the captain, Luo Ming suddenly thought of a trick—entering the captain's cabin would give him the opportunity to have Edmund break into the ship's core control systems, which were isolated from external networks. The AI would then be able steal all of the top-secret information there. The plan went smoothly until Luo Ming unexpectedly provoked the captain and was thrown out too soon.

"It's true: the captain has never replaced an organ," Edmund said. "She was using prolonged hibernation to delay the aging process. The ship can awaken her in fifteen seconds, so there's no impact on the ship's normal operations."

"I don't care about that," Luo Ming said. "What else did you find?"

"I only had time to gather some population data. There are 29,000 people aboard who haven't undergone organ replacement surgery. The vast majority are young people under the age of 30. Only 15 are over 50 years old; above 80, only the captain. But she couldn't have been the criminal because she'd been in deep sleep for the past month, and wasn't awakened until after the incident had occurred."

"Then it seems we've reached a dead end here, too," Luo Ming said, sighing.

"Do you still think that the criminal is a 'person'?"

"You're the only AI aboard this ship," Luo Ming said. "If you did it, now would be a good time to confess."

Edmund's voice lowered. "That's a terrible joke. I have no way to clear my own name."

"That's not what I meant," Luo Ming said, backpedaling. "It was . . . a terrible joke."

"I know; I've already forgiven you," Edmund said. "But I have indeed run into a bit of trouble."

"What happened?" Luo Ming turned and saw First Officer Qin Wei walking toward him with a couple of police droids.

"I'm afraid that when I broke into the ship's control system, the captain discovered me," Edmund said apologetically.

"Dammit!" Luo Ming furrowed his brow. "How can I turn you off?"

"It's too late. A part of my data was left behind in the captain's cabin. By now, she probably knows everything about you." Edmund hesitated. "For example, your other name."

For the first time, Luo Ming wished that Edmund had a physical form, so that he could give him the evil eye—both his "artificial" nature and his "intelligence" could learn to take secrecy more seriously.

But he didn't have time to scold the AI; Qin Wei was already standing before him. "Mr. Luo, I'm afraid you'll have to come with us."

"What for?" Luo Ming asked, his face impassive.

"There have been additional incidents involving Adam," Qin Wei said, his rapid speech revealing his unease. "I need your help."

Luo Ming let out a held breath. "I would be happy to assist you, Mr. First Officer. But I recall that information concerning Adam is beyond my clearance level."

Qin Wei snapped his fingers: an enormous file suddenly filled Luo Ming's inbox. Coldly, Qin Wei said, "You're cleared now." He turned and walked away.

Luo Ming rushed to catch up. Summoning every ounce of sincerity, he said, "Please tell me what happened."

Qin Wei's expression softened. "I'll be brief: the other organ cultivation cabins all followed Cabin 35's example. Our orders have been canceled en masse, and the hospital is paralyzed. The captain has declared a state of emergency."

As he spoke, he sent more files to Luo Ming. The documents included a three-dimensional cultivation cabin model that even Edmund hadn't been able to find. According to these documents, the oval Deck Seven was the site for hundreds of linked cultivation cabins, which formed an inward spiral like a whirlpool.

Luo Ming recalled what Edmund had said earlier. "Do these cultivation cabins communicate with each other?"

"They share the same feeding ducts, so, theoretically, they're not isolated from one another." Qin Wei was now fully cooperating.

Luo Ming mulled over Qin Wei's response. Five minutes later, they arrived at the security line before Deck Seven. The white-haired captain stood amidst a crowd of police droids. She saw Luo Ming and made an unhappy face as she asked Qin Wei, "Why did you bring him here?"

"Luo Ming is the officer in charge of this investigation, Your Excellency," Qin Wei replied simply.

The captain scrutinized Luo Ming. Luo Ming avoided her gaze and examined the scene instead. "Edmund," Luo Ming said softly, "wasn't there something within the documents you sent that said one of the cultivation cabins is dedicated to the nervous system?"

No response. Edmund had disappeared completely. Luo Ming had no choice but to ask Qin Wei the same question.

Qin Wei's answer was quick: "Cabin Zero. Though it's not a cultivation cabin; rather, it's a conservation cabin that preserves a few exceptional brains."

"I thought brains were on the list of organs that can't be replaced."

"Right." Qin Wei gave him an odd look. "The brains grown in Adams have no memories. Replacing the brain would turn a patient into a mindless fool . . . who would do that?"

A terrible chill ran up his spine. Luo Ming felt himself getting close to the answer. "Then the ones in Cabin Zero are—"

Qin Wei hesitated, but still replied. "On their deathbeds, some important individuals chose to deposit their brains here. We adjusted the genetic expression modules of the Adams inside Cabin Zero so that they would age extremely slowly."

"So you're telling me that though the bodies of these people have died, their minds live on."

"Their minds are in deep sleep." Qin Wei was growing impatient. "Why are you asking this?"

"I'd like to take a look at Cabin Zero."

"Cabin Zero is perfectly fine." Qin Wei eyed him suspiciously. "The captain herself confirmed that."

Luo Ming persisted: "Last time, you and the captain also thought everything was perfectly fine." He noted Qin Wei's expression, then added, "I'm concerned that things are deteriorating faster than we imagined."

As things really did seem to be getting out of hand, Qin Wei finally agreed to Luo Ming's request. Cabin Zero was on the lower part of Deck Seven, at the center of the whirlpool of cultivation cabins. When the cabin doors opened, Luo Ming was met with an unbelievable sight.

Sacks made of translucent membrane dangled from the ceiling, each holding a spinal cord or a cerebrum. Between the Adam pouches, additional membranes had already enveloped all the interconnecting passageways, creating an actual web—a three-dimensional network made of neurons, spinal cords, and lumps of cerebral tissue. Two "people" were laid out neatly on the ground: the first a complete body—clean, naked, cold; the second a bulging sack of human skin, whose open abdomen revealed a heap of organs arranged in neat order: large intestines, stomach, liver . . .

It wasn't a human at all, but a pile of human parts.

"My God, what in the world—" Qin Wei murmured.

Luo Ming put on a pair of gloves and carefully peeled back the skin covering the loose organs. Where the thoracic cavity should have been, there was only a ghastly segment of gleaming white bone.

"That's his rib—Adam's rib," Luo Ming blurted. "He's trying to create an Eve."

5. Argus

And [Hera] set a watcher upon [Io], great and strong Argus, who with four eyes looks every way. And the goddess stirred in him unwearying strength: sleep never fell upon his eyes; but he kept sure watch always.
—Hesiod, *Aegimius* (as translated by Hugh G. Evelyn-White)

It is said, too, that Echidna, daughter of Tartarus and Earth, who used to carry off passers-by, was caught asleep and slain by Argus.
—Apollodorus, *Bibliotheca*, 2.1.2 (as translated by Sir James George Frazer)

When I see her again, I begin to understand why my father was so madly in love with her.

She can't be controlled, can't be known, can't be predicted. But when she's standing before me, she's thoughtful and warm. This contradiction allows her to exude allure like a demon. She's sitting on a black Barcelona chair now, her face pale and wan like a girl's. Her gaze falls upon me and she laughs weakly. "Tony, I'm so sorry that I didn't tell you earlier—did I worry you?"

Neither "yes" nor "no" would do—both would reveal me as a hypocrite. So I say, "I helped out with the rescue effort. I'm overjoyed to see you're alive and well."

"When I was at Gardermoen Airport, I realized something was wrong with my body, so I borrowed a friend's plane to get back to the laboratory more quickly." Her speech is deliberate, slow. "Then I discovered that nothing could be done about my problem, and so I just let the world think I was in the crash."

Anxious, I ask, "What do you mean?"

"I'm going to die soon." She looks at me, unperturbed. "For ten years, I've been exploring the potential of genetic modification. I thought I had resolved the entire genetic network, but I was wrong."

I don't know what to say.

Warmly, she tells me, "See, this is science. Most of the time, we aren't so lucky."

"Mom—"

"My failure has led me to make some adjustments to my future plans. We have to face the risks inherent in large-scale experimentation. I got in touch with a friend who's investing in an interstellar colonization program." She makes a call, and a hologram of a person appears before us. "Chen Ying, this is Tony. I believe you've already met."

The woman is the one who had come to meet me at the airport on the day of Sphinx's announcement.

Chen Ying ignores me completely. "How do you feel?"

"Terrible," says my mother. Then she looks at me again. "Tony, Chen Ying is one of the wealthiest people on Earth, but most people know nothing about her. I'm trying to convince her to lend me two of her five colonization ships for a few hundred years to use as research vessels."

"I've already agreed." Chen Ying furrows her brow as she looks at her.

"Right, but you haven't heard the actual plan yet. I'd like to put them on the same orbit as a short-period comet—"

"That's not important," Chen Ying says, interrupting her. "Send these details to the technicians; you need your rest now."

My mother makes a face. "Alright." Then, she ends the call.

The brief conversation leaves me with an impression of intimacy. Maybe it wasn't so much the topic of the conversation as it was Chen Ying's expressions. My mother senses my questions, but she doesn't answer them. "I'm going to move the next-generation chimera lab onto the spaceships. That way, I don't have to worry about the catastrophic consequences in the event of an accident in a terrestrial genetic lab. *Eden* is my first ship, which will conduct more conservative research. The chimeras she carries come from the first generation of stem cells—that is, part of them comes from you."

I remember the pig's eyes.

She continues: "We've been cultivating these cells for many years. Strangely, although we've tried to use other human cells and cells from other animals, this combination has always been the most stable. I guess we stumbled on a miracle with my first trial. Tony, you and I are both very lucky." She realizes my mind is wandering and changes the topic. "Speaking of which, what did you think of the big announcement?"

I think over the commentary from the last few days. "From what I've heard, this hypothesis still has some holes . . . "

"I left them on purpose." She gives me a cunning grin. "I just wanted to get everyone arguing, even start a war within science—only then can there be a revolution."

"But you seem to be losing."

"You still don't understand people." She touches a finger to her chin. "Only through conflict can people have choices; only then can we rouse people's emotions, even whip them into a frenzy. As the flames of war expand, the news will spread farther. More and more will join the battle, creating more soldiers for me. Only then will I stand forth to protect my believers, dealing a deadly blow to the opposition."

"You're already holding the weapon for dealing that blow, aren't you?"

"Not only that, Tony," she says gently. "All of this is a trap I've set to distract them from the real question."

"The real question?"

"What we announced at the event has nothing to do with the research I want to conduct. The interesting question has never been whether we can use humans as test subjects. I've long trodden in that forbidden territory, starting from when you were six. The far more interesting question is: What have we created through these experiments?"

"Chimeras."

"Chimeras, sure." She nods. "But what exactly are chimeras—people or beasts? Do chimeras have thoughts? Can they reproduce with other chimeras? Are chimeras the path forward for human evolution or humanity's downfall?"

"These are my fatal weaknesses because I don't know the answers. From the very beginning, I didn't understand why the chimera experiments were successful. I was like a child playing with clay, rolling various colors together until they turned into something new.

"But I won't tell people that I don't know the answers. I'll let them stare at an irrelevant chimera ancestor, a point of controversy where I hold in my hands all evidence, where the theory is both simple yet evocative. Look, they'll use this issue to attack me, thinking that this is the foundation of regenerative medicine. But they're wrong: once the arguments start and the flames of academic war erupt, I will be the only one who benefits. My opponents will fail and be thoroughly discredited; my soldiers will become a dedicated but foolish hivemind. Tony, *this* is what makes the game fun."

Seeing her eyes sparkle with excitement, I finally understand why my father would so often murmur the word "monster" whenever she came up in conversation. She's far more terrifying than any AI I've encountered. I surmise her tactics: "Do you plan on continuing to let Edmund lead the charge for you?"

"Edmund?" She's startled for a moment, then laughs uproariously. "Oh my goodness, you really didn't notice?"

"Notice what?"

"The Edmund at the press event was a hologram—the real Edmund passed away five years ago."

Once again I feel helpless, like an insect that's been caught in a spider's web. "I really didn't notice—"

"Okay, then that's our little secret." She giggles and taps her head. "There was no Edmund on stage at the announcement. The one standing there speaking through the hologram was me."

"But you . . . Why did you keep his death a secret?"

"Using him and your father as the mouthpieces of the research group and the charitable foundation saved me a lot of trouble. Plus, he agreed to let me use his likeness," she explains patiently.

I notice her expectant gaze. "Then—do you want me to join the foundation?"

"That would be the most perfect outcome. Tony Lee would without a doubt be the finest spokesperson for the Tony Lee Charitable Foundation." She shrugs. "But you won't join."

"Why not?"

"Because your body language and your expression give you away," she says. "You don't want this, and this kind of work doesn't suit you anyway—either way, I want you to make your own choices. From your reaction just now, I think you're far more interested in the spaceship."

I relax my hands, held tightly all this time in front of my chest. "It's true; a research ship does sound interesting."

"And also mad," she says. "As your mother, I don't want you to go. I don't want you to become a research subject again."

Her gaze now seems to truly carry a deep love. I don't understand her at all. "I'm sorry—I'll make up my own mind."

"Of course. I have no right to tell you what to do." She lets out a soft sigh. "But I still want to tell you that you're my most perfect creation, so perfect that you frighten me."

"Why?"

"Every time I saw you, heard about you, or even earlier, when I was pregnant with you and felt you, I experienced such terror." She looks out the window. "Because once I turned my head and saw the pile of trash in my lab, I'd suddenly realize the vast distance between myself and the Creator. I'd worry if I'd made a mistake from the very start, because I'd broken *His* rules."

"You weren't wrong," I say. "You saved my life."

"At a price." Her voice softens, revealing a deep exhaustion. "An enormous price that you can never imagine."

Everything happens just as she predicted.

Controversy after controversy concerning chimeras and human experimentation erupt, and every politician and college student seems to have something to say about the subject.

The dispute of the century ends three years later with news of Edmund's "death." His obituary, in combination with a new paper, deals a mortal blow to her opponents.

The revolutionaries reap the fruits of their victory, and the conservatives, in the face of ironclad proof, wilt and fade. Chen Ying's timely announcement of the research spaceships turns into the last lifeline for these drowning ethicists to clutch. The wild plan easily gains everyone's support: immortality proves to be an irresistible temptation for all, and even the wealthiest can't obtain a ticket aboard the ships.

Of course, obtaining a ticket isn't a problem for me.

I end up boarding *Eden* after all. Called by a strange impulse and yearning deep in my heart, I abandon my family, my friends, my job—everything I have on Earth. At the embarkation ceremony, I watch Chen Ying, the captain, deliver a speech.

"From today on, this is our ship. My dearest friend named it *Eden*, for it carries humanity's wildest dream, and because it will bring us new life."

E. The Complex Chimera

"It's still a child," Luo Ming said. "This explains everything."

"What do you mean? What exactly is 'it'?" Qin Wei asked, confused.

"Adam," Luo Ming replied. "Or, to be more accurate, 'it' is the collective made up of the Adams within all 109 cultivation cabins. They've connected with one another to create an enormous creature that thinks, breathes, and bleeds—a complex chimera."

Qin Wei paused for three seconds before he processed what Luo Ming was saying. "Preposterous! How could this be?"

"Yes, that's really what it is. Originally, it wasn't supposed to have thoughts, but you placed brains into its body, thereby giving it consciousness. All chimera experiments prohibit the creation of a nervous system—this was a basic rule put in place during the design of the Adam matrix, but you've broken it."

Luo Ming noticed that the captain had stopped outside the cultivation cabin to listen to his explanation. "It's extremely smart, but, at the same time, extremely naïve. After observing for a long time, it was clever enough to break into and take over the monitoring system for the cultivation cabins, but it had no idea that the hospital ordering system even existed. Now it's trying to imitate us. It found a human corpse to study and analyze, and it's trying to use these organs to create a self—it really thinks of itself as the Adam of lore, so it's trying to create an Eve. God, this is too funny!"

"Enough!" Qin Wei shouted. "I need you to provide me with evidence, Officer Luo, and not mere crackpot theories."

"I believe that, in every cultivation cabin, you'll find extra organs that haven't been ordered—for example, eyes, because it's eager to learn about this world." Luo Ming was speaking quickly, his tongue racing to catch up with his thoughts. "Please send someone to check—oh, it must also have had help moving the corpses and limbs into the cultivation cabins, unintelligent helpers that it could easily control."

Luo Ming trailed off as a police droid entered. It was carrying a whole set of human ribs. Seeing Qin Wei and Luo Ming, it stopped, dazed, as though it didn't know what it was supposed to do.

"I've long said that the ship's intelligence systems are too primitive." Unwittingly, Luo Ming had borrowed one of Edmund's phrases. "If the complex chimera can take over the monitoring system, then controlling these police droids would be child's play."

The appearance of the confused police droid forced Qin Wei to accept Luo Ming's conclusion: the one responsible for the series of incidents was Adam, the soul of *Eden*. After a hundred years of growth, it awakened the brains stored inside its pouches, dreamed up its own ideas, and was now trying to use the organs it had cultivated to create a new human-shaped self.

"I'll go check for those eyes you mentioned." Qin Wei's face was dark as he exited the cultivation cabin. Luo Ming watched him leave.

Alone with Luo Ming in the cabin, the police droid came back to life and shut the door.

Luo Ming heard his own heart thumping. This was no good. He had no idea where Edmund was, and this police droid looked much stronger than he was.

"Did you find me," the police droid said, "because you *are* me?"

"Are . . . are you speaking through that thing?" Luo Ming stared at the pair of eyes hanging in the corner of the cultivation cabin—light brown with a hint of gray.

"I am," replied the police droid under the control of the complex chimera. "Please answer my question, Tony Lee."

"When did you discover my true identity?" Luo Ming countered.

"When I first received your organ order," the chimera said. "You asked for eyes. My eyes."

Those are my eyes—Luo Ming gazed into those irises, recalling the close-up photograph sealed away in his memories.

"So I was the one who triggered your self-awareness." He let out a soft sigh. "Yes, I felt your presence the very first time I entered a cultivation cabin. I deduced everything from that feeling."

"Would I have grown to look like you?"

"I don't know."

"I've failed; I didn't create Eve." The police droid looked down at the floor, then carefully placed the ribs atop the human skin. "Why? Tell me: where did I go wrong?"

"This isn't the way humans create new life."

"But this is how you created *me*. You put different things into my body, and then I became me." The police droid looked at him, puzzled. "And I also know that I'm the same as you."

"No, you and I are not the same. We weren't born in this way—even you weren't born like this." Luo Ming took a step back, gingerly making his way toward the cabin door.

"How are we different? My cells are identical to yours." The pair of eyeballs stared at Luo Ming.

"Only some parts are the same." Luo Ming burst through the cabin door, leaping out without any hesitation. Only after he landed did he yell, "Edmund!"

The silhouette of the police droid froze by the cabin door. Edmund had appeared just in time to take control of it. "Nice work," said Luo Ming.

But there was no response.

"What's the matter?" Luo Ming tapped his ear. "Didn't you do this? Stop hiding!"

"I used the ship's control system to lock down all police droids." The captain answered him. "Thank you for helping us uncover the truth, Officer Luo—or do you prefer Tony Lee?"

"Whatever you want." Luo Ming looked at her. "I suppose you've known about my identity for a long time, Captain Chen Ying."

"Of course. Do you think I would have allowed you to gallivant about my ship, poking your nose into everything otherwise?" Chen Ying glared at him. "Enough. Don't play innocent with me. Your acting skills are nowhere near your mother's. Let me see: taking over a police droid, hmm? And stealing information from my cabin—do you need me to list out every violation you've committed over the years?"

Luo Ming tried to placate her with a grin. "All in the service of solving cases, Your Excellency."

Chen Ying harrumphed. "I have to admit you've done a good job."

"Thank you for your approval."

Chen Ying shook her head, deciding to change the topic. "I've already directed the ship to land. Luckily, we happen to be headed toward Earth already. The regenerative medicine group will send scientists to study this complex chimera. *Eden*'s mission is over, and I've done my duty to your mother."

"I'd say you've done a good job, too," Luo Ming said.

"Have you kept your distance from me because I was your mother's lover?" Chen Ying suddenly asked.

Luo Ming couldn't help laughing. "I'm sorry, but my mother has never 'loved' anyone."

"Why do you say that?"

"Love requires being with someone; words of love are just lies," Luo Ming said. "She would never have wasted time being with anyone."

Chen Ying looked at him. "Are you sure?"

6. Epilogue

Before I leave *Eden*, I go find Chen Ying.

"She passed away not even a month after you saw her for the last time," Chen Ying says. "Of course, she'd already planned everything."

"I guessed." It was around then that I received the AI Edmund as a gift.

Chen Ying takes me to the medical research facility under Deck Seven. Her real tomb is hidden there: a small, white box, not a single word anywhere on it.

"Is this really what she wanted?" I ask.

"Actually, I decided to bring her with me when we loaded the ship." Chen Ying laughs bitterly. "She wouldn't have cared where she's buried, anyway."

"But to be on a spaceship—" I think about it. "Forget it. This is fine."

Chen Ying looks at me. "Thank you." After a pause, she says, "From the very beginning, I knew she wanted me only for my ships."

"What happened between my mother and you is none of my business."

But she goes on, speaking to herself. "My family was among the first to get into the space assembly business, and the first to construct a ship large enough for interstellar colonization—I'm sorry, I know you don't want to hear any of this."

"Uh—" I hesitate for a moment. "Please go on."

"To make a long story short, by the time I met her, we'd already completed the designs for the spaceships and the preliminary investment. The first time she saw me, she asked me right away whether she could borrow a couple ships for research. I thought she was nuts—each ship cost hundreds of billions!"

That sounds just like my mother. "I can imagine that."

"To change my mind, she switched to an equally ridiculous method of persuasion. I was younger than her by six years. I had two children, but I'd never gotten married. At first, I told my boyfriend about her as a joke."

"But she succeeded in the end."

Chen Ying sighs. "Yep."

"That's just how she was," I tell her. "My father was more or less in the same situation."

"She was . . . very unique." Chen Ying pauses and looks at me again. "When I hesitated about starting a relationship with her, she said something that changed me. She could plant her ideas into your heart and make it seem like they were native to the soil."

My curiosity overcame the awkwardness of hearing about my mother's love life. "What did she say?"

"She said, 'You're standing inside a cage that I can't see, but outside the cage is the whole world. I'll be here waiting for you to come out, and then you'll see that there's nothing to be scared of.'"

I'm reminded of a recording of an interview my father did shortly after setting up the Tony Lee Charitable Foundation. That was the one time he and my mother appeared together on TV after their divorce, and they'd appeared only to respond to the attacks on chimera experiments. The host was losing in verbal jousting with my mother and decided to change tactics by turning to my father: "I'd really like to know why you've agreed to work with the former Mrs. Lee. Didn't she abandon you and Tony?"

My father paused thoughtfully, and then said, "We've chosen different paths in life, but, as her friend, I've never doubted her wisdom and courage. You must understand that she's not an ordinary person like you and me."

"How is she different?" asked the host.

"We're often bound by custom and habit, but she's not. She doesn't even understand why we're confined by these rules, unable to keep up with her. Marriage, science, what have you—to her, these are all mere problems to be solved. She's like a curious child, afraid of nothing, intent on finding out what the world beyond the fence is like—this is why she was able to successfully create a chimera, and it's also why she can now save lives through Adam."

While he spoke, the camera was focused instead on my mother's face. Her perfect little smile disappeared, replaced by confusion and surprise. I can't remember if I asked Edmund a question while watching the recording or if he had jumped in on his own initiative, but I distinctly remember the AI's commentary:

"She thought she knew the truth about everything, but she didn't know the truth about herself—only your father understood her."

F. Regeneration

The last person to disembark from *Eden* was Lin Ke—the woman who was so upset by her organ cancellation that she reported it to the police, and who suffered a heart attack upon seeing Cabin 35.

After three days of emergency medical treatment, her heart was still on the verge of failure. And, due to oxygen deprivation, her cerebrum was barely alive. Having obtained the captain's authorization, the doctors decided to take the extraordinary step of conducting an emergency transplant with two organs found in the cultivation cabins—they certainly weren't hers, but they came back negative on the lymphocyte cross-matching test. Unexpectedly, the procedure was a complete success.

A week later, Lin Ke, supported by a doctor, disembarked from *Eden*. Standing together with Luo Ming, they waited for the shuttle to take them back to Earth. She said "hello" to Luo Ming, who recognized her as the woman who had first pursued the mysterious organ cancellations and who had collapsed in front of Cabin 35.

After some small talk, he said, "So, you've recovered?"

"Thanks to organ replacement surgery," she said, "How did you solve the case?"

"That's quite a story." Since she was the first witness, he felt comfortable recounting for her the details of the mystery, including the part where all the Adams had joined to become a complex chimera.

"Incredible!" Lin Ke's eyes shone as she listened. "How's the pig—I mean, how's the complex chimera doing now?"

Luo Ming looked at her, startled. "Wait, did you just say 'pig'?"

"I've got some strange ideas in my head now." She laughed sheepishly. "You told me all the cultivation cabins are joined into one chimera; maybe a part of 'it' is now in my brain."

"Did you have a cerebrum transplant? I thought those weren't possible!"

"Ah, yes, but the doctors had to try to save my life," she said. "They used a preserved brain from Cabin Zero instead of one grown from scratch. My current brain must have spent quite a long time in Cabin Zero."

Luo Ming nodded. "I'm glad the risky surgery worked out. But are you still 'Lin Ke'?"

"Who knows." She shrugged. "I don't plan to see her friends any time soon, at least."

Luo Ming felt a sense of déjà vu when he saw her warm and cunning smile. Uneasy, he cleared his throat and said, "The complex chimera is still on Deck Seven. Right now *Eden* is swarming with regenerative medicine specialists."

"So that's what's going on! After you go back to Earth, what are you going to do?"

"I don't know. Maybe I'll travel the world after so many years spent cooped up in a ship."

She smiled again. "Sounds like a great plan."

The shuttle arrived at the port. Luo Ming stepped through the door and turned around. He found Lin Ke rooted to her spot.

"Do you need help?" he asked.

She dismissed him with a little wave. "I've decided to stay on the ship, Tony. This time, I won't abandon it again."

Luo Ming's eyes widened. "What?"

"I've spent more than a century with you—I think that's long enough," she said. "My other child needs me now."

Before Luo Ming could try to go back to her, the doors to the shuttle hissed shut. He pounded with all his might against the metal panels, but they didn't budge at all. "Dammit! Open the door! Please, open the door!"

But the shuddering of the floor told him that the shuttle had already taken off. Luo Ming looked out the window in despair. The space station was already several kilometers away. He would never again see "Lin Ke."

He held his breath, and, fingers trembling, found her in his long contacts list.

"Who are you?" Luo Ming asked.

Soon, he received a direct message in response:

"Remember what I told you before, Tony: there never was any Edmund. I was always the one speaking."

Originally published in Chinese in *Science Fiction World,* October 2015.

Morrigan in Shadow
SETH DICKINSON

capella 1/8

She's falling into the singularity.

Straight off her nose, shrouded in the warp of its mass, is the black hole that ate a hundred million colonists and the hope of all mankind.

So Laporte throttles up. Her fighter rattles with the fury of its final burn.

Spaceflight is about orbits. That's how one thing relates to another, up here: I whirl around you. I try to pull away. You try to pull me in. If we don't smash each other apart, or skip away into the void, maybe we can negotiate something stable.

But Laporte has learned that sometimes you just need to fall.

Her instruments don't understand what's happening. They're military avionics, built to hunt and kill other warships (other people) in cold flat space. Thus Laporte flies her final mission in a screaming constellation of errors, cautions, icy out-of-range warnings. An array of winter-colored protests from a machine that doesn't know where it is or why it's about to die.

She wants to pat the ship (a lovely, lethal, hard-worn Uriel gunship, built under Martian skies, the skies of her lover's childhood) on its nose and say: there, there, I know exactly how you feel. I'm with you, man. This shit is beyond me.

But it's not beyond her. She knows why she's here.

Laporte never thought she'd be a good soldier. Certainly she'd never planned to be an exceptional killer. Or a mutineer leading a revanchist fleet up out of Earth's surrender and into a crusade across the length of human space. Or, in her final act as a human being (if she dares make claim to that title any more), the avatar of an omnicidal alien power with no intelligence, no awareness, and a billion-year-old cosmic imperative to destroy all higher thought.

But she is all those things now. Born from the tragedy of a war as unnecessary as it was inevitable. Shaped by combat and command and (between it all, pulling in the opposite direction) the love of the finest woman she's ever met.

After all that, after Simms and NAGARI and That Revelation Ken, she knows why she's here. She knows what force plucked her out of paradise and fired her down the trajectory of her short, violent life. To this distant terminus where the universe folds up behind her into a ring of light, everything she loves, everyone she's hurt, receding.

She knows what she's come to kill. The object of her last assassination.

"Boss, this is Morrigan," she tells her flight recorder. "I am descending towards the target."

That's what she calls Simms, even now. Not 'love'. Boss.

There are three stories here, although they are all one:

What happened in Capella, at the end.

What happened with NAGARI, at the beginning.

What happened between Noemi Laporte and Lorna Simms, which is the most important story, and the one that binds the others.

It begins with the war, and with Lorna Simms—

simms 1/9

For a long time, long enough to murder tens of thousands of people, Laporte thought Simms was dead.

They fought for the United Earth Federation in the war against the colonist Alliance. Laporte and Simms were Federation combat pilots (SQUADRON VFX-01 2FM/FG2101 INDUS—The Wargods, Captain Lorna Simms Commanding) and they were good, so good, they fought like two fists on a drunken boxer, moved by instinct and kill-joy. Of course, a boxer has a body as well as a pair of fists—but they tried not to consider the shape of what connected them.

It wasn't love or lust alone (they were soldiers and their discipline held), nor was it only respect, or fear, or sly admiration. Something of all of this. Whatever connected them, it helped them fight. Simms the Captain, leader of killers, and Laporte her faithful wingman, who was the finest killer.

And they fought to save their Federation, their happy humanist utopia, Earth and Mars and the Jupiter moons—a community of people making each other better. They fought hard.

The war is a civil war. As intimate and violent and hard to name as the bond between Laporte and Simms. An apocalyptic exchange of fratricides between the Federation and its own far-flung interstellar colonists: the Alliance.

For a little while, long enough to give them hope, Laporte and Simms and their Wargods almost won the war.

Then the Alliance clockmaker-admiral, the cryogenic bastard Steele, set a trap. It caught Simms, Laporte, and their whole squadron. Everyone died. It was like a lesson: no band of heroes will save you. No soldiers bound by law and decency.

Out of that ambush Simms and Laporte flew each other to refuge, but it was not refuge enough, the war was in their bones and flesh now: Simms was dying, poisoned by radiation. So they sat together on a crippled warship and they talked about anything but each other.

Remember that? After the ambush at Saturn? Remember adjusting Simms' blankets and pressing your cheek to her throat? Hoping she'd live long enough for both of you to die together, as you'd always dreamed?

(Laporte's dreams are not, it turns out, wholly her own.)

The Alliance was winning, they agreed. Neither of them could see a way to avoid defeat. Neither of them would admit that to the other—not defeat, nor the other thing between them.

Simms passed out. Laporte stayed by her side.

And then a rescue ship came, and with it came al-Alimah, the woman with the gunmetal eyes and the shark-sleek uniform of a Federation black ops officer. She came to tempt Laporte away from Simms with the promise of her other love—

Victory. Al-Alimah came to offer Laporte a chance at victory. And she named the agents of that victory NAGARI.

nagari 1/10

What is victory? Only a fool goes to war without an answer.

The Alliance is winning (has won). What is their victory condition? Their grievance? The fatal casus belli that sparked it all?

The Federation is a gentle state, built on Ubuntu, a philosophy of human connection. So they say: the war began because the Alliance couldn't stand to be alone. They spent two decades rebuilding the severed wormhole to Earth, so they could demand reunification, so they could mobilize our thriving economy to build their warships. So they could galvanize our culture for war.

What the Alliance asked the Federation is what the woman named al-Alimah asked Laporte, as they stood together over the radiation-cooked body of Lorna Simms: give up your gentle ties. Come with me, towards victory. Become a necessary monster.

When the Federation refused to militarize, the Alliance invaded. It was their only hope.

Either they gained the Federation's riches, or they faced the Nemesis alone.

Laporte, she made the other choice, the one her beautiful home could not. She went with al-Alimah. She joined the phantom atrocity-makers called NAGARI and she discovered her own final hope, her endgame for Federation victory.

It'll require the extermination of the entire Alliance population. So be it. She is an exceptional killer. She proved that after she left Simms.

That's how she ended up here, at this raging dead star on the edge of Alliance space, this monument to the power of the alien Nemesis. The tomb of Capella—

capella 2/8

Back in the now: and someone's chasing her.

She sniffs him out by the light of his engines. Something's come through the wormhole behind her and started its own plunge towards the (terrible, empty, fire-crowned) black hole.

Laporte grins and knocks her helmet twice against her ejection seat, crash crash, polymer applause for the mad gentleman on her trail. She knows who it is. She's glad he's come.

She tumbles the Uriel end-for-end so that she's falling ass-first into oblivion and her nose is aimed back, up, towards the universe. There's a ring of night and bent starlight all around her, where the black hole's gravity bends space, but up above, as if at the top of a well, are the receding stars.

And there he is. A fierce blue light which resolves into the molybdenum greatsword-shape of an Alliance strike carrier. *Atreus*. Steele's flagship. Two and a half kilometers of tactical divinity.

Admiral Onyekachi Tuwile Steele prosecuted the war in the Sol theater. A game of remorseless speed chess with fifteen billion pawns in play. In the end, after the Federation exhausted all its gambits and defenses (save one, the one called NAGARI), he won the war.

He's a perfectionist, Steele. A man of etiquette and fine dress, a man who moves like a viper or a Kinshasa runway model. He makes intricate, clockwork plans, predicated on perfect understanding of his opponent's behavior. He cannot abide error.

He made only one.

Nowhere in the final hours of the war, the Mars gambit, the desperate defense and ultimate failure of SHAMBHALA, did he send enough hunter-killers to eradicate Laporte.

And now he has come a-howling after her, propelled by portents and terrors, operating on a desperate, improvised logic. That logic might be: if she wants it, I cannot permit it. If Laporte reaches for a thing, I must deny it to her. She is too dangerous to ever have a victory.

It might be something else. It's dangerous to let your enemy understand your war logic.

simms 2/9

There are three stories here. They all matter.

One is the story of Laporte at Capella, trying to kill billions. That's the ending.

One is the story of Laporte leaving Simms for NAGARI, in the name of victory. That's the beginning.

But in between them is another story, because the road from victory to genocide passes through love. In this middle part, the Federation's civilian government surrendered to the Alliance. And here in the ashes Laporte found Simms alive, Simms found Laporte still (barely) human, they each found the other in the cold scorched wolfpack of the Federation Navy, lurking on the edge of the solar system and contemplating mutiny.

This story is the most important, because it was Laporte's last chance to be a person again.

So: Laporte reaches for Simms. She wants to be close again. She wants to come back.

They're lying side by side in the avionics bay of Laporte's fighter: an alloy coffin as cold as treason. Mostly empty. The terms of the cease-fire have stripped all military electronics from the Federation Navy.

Like their uniforms—taken too. They work in gym clothes and mechanic's overalls. Whenever they breathe the vapor spills out white like a suitbreach. Every ten minutes a dehumidifier clicks on.

Simms shivers. Her hands rattle and she breaks the test pin she's using against the teeth of a server stack. "Shit," she says, closing her eyes. "Fuck."

She survived radiation poisoning. But surviving a wound doesn't erase it. You only rebuild yourself around the scar.

Laporte knifes the RESET switch up, down, up, down. They'll start over. "Slowing me down, boss," she says, trying to take Simms' fear and judo it around, make it funny, disarm its violence. "Slowing me down."

"Fuck you too." Simms clenches and unclenches her fists, one finger at a time. She's longer than Laporte, and stronger. Before she soaked up fifteen grays of ionizing radiation, she could always keep up. "*You* try fingerbanging a combat spacecraft after a lethal dose."

Laporte makes a wah-wah baby noise. Simms laughs. They work for a few more minutes and soon they've made the fighter ready to hold combat software in the spare memory of its navigational systems.

If they're going to mutiny, the mutiny needs its fighters. And Laporte is planning a mutiny.

Simms puts down the test pin and shivers from her scalp to her toes. She looks silver-gold, arid. She is the child of Mongolian steppe and American range and the desert of Mars. She's used to cold. Laporte's afraid that it's not the cold making her shiver. Simms has been listening, the last few days, as Laporte lifts up her scabs and talks about NAGARI, and about her plan for victory.

"They took out all my bone marrow," Simms says. "I'm full of fake bone shit. Medical goo."

Laporte rolls into her (the old words, in a pilot's brevity code: *Boss, Morrigan, tally, visual, press,* It's you, I'm me, I see you, I will protect you) and Simms puts an arm around her. Laporte kisses her under the jaw, very softly, and rests her ear against Simms' collarbone. There's a plastic button rubbing into her cheek but she doesn't mind.

"Seems to work okay," she says. She looked up radiation therapies: desperate transplant of reprogrammed skin cells and collagen glue. She imagined them peeling the skin off Simms' thighs to fill up her bones.

"Yeah." Simms' heart is slowing down, soothing out. It can't find the fight it's looking for. Or it's disciplining itself for what's to come. "I still work."

Laporte looks up from her collarbone to look her in the eye. "Are you going to fly with me?"

Will she fly in the mutiny. Laporte's grand plan, NAGARI's final hope? The Federation has surrendered, but its soldiers, its guardian monsters, do not consent to Alliance rule. They were made to win.

"I don't know yet," Simms says, looking at her hands. Whatever she says next will be an evasion. "I need to know more about your operational plan."

I need to know more about what you've become. What you got up to without me, while I was in the tank with my skin peeling off and glue in my blood.

"I need you out there," Laporte says. She means it to be business, pilot chatter, a tactical requirement. But she's thinking about how she left Simms. How it might have seemed, to Simms, that she had been expended. Cast off as spent ordnance.

Simms makes a soft sound, like she's too tough or too happy to cry.

The dehumidifier wakes up to dry out their words.

capella 3/8

The mutiny is what carried Laporte from the middle to the end.

The Alliance killed the Federation's best soldiers. It battered the Federation into political surrender. But it never beat NAGARI. It never beat Laporte.

When the peace negotiations began, Laporte flew her re-armed Uriel from post to distant post, rallying the Federation's dying strength for the death ride to Capella. Dozens of ships. Hundreds of pilots. Answering to Noemi 'Morrigan' Laporte, the last ace, the one who wouldn't let the fire go out.

Laporte airbrushed the suggestion of a raven on her fighter. Its claws are bloody. There is armor in its jaw.

She asked Simms to ride in her back seat as she went to raise mutiny. "A couple undead soldiers, flying the mutiny flag," she joked. "Like a buddy cop thing." But Simms looked away and Laporte thought, what am I doing, how can I ask her to light this war back up, to be the spark that escalates it from atrocity to apocalypse? The war took her skin and melted the inside of her bones. It ripped out the lining of her guts. She can't even shit without fighting the war.

"I'm not mission capable yet," Simms said, and she looked at Laporte as if the war had taken one more vital thing from her. "I hope the avionics work. I broke a lot of test pins in there."

So Laporte flew with al-Alimah instead. Al-Alimah from NAGARI.

The Federation government surrendered but its fleet did not. They struck during treaty negotiations. Laporte's rebel armada fought its way out of Sol by shock and treachery. Breached the blockades in Serpentis. Menaced the Alliance capital in Beta Aquilae.

And as they did, Laporte's NAGARI elite slipped into Vega. One wormhole away from their true goal.

Capella.

Admiral Steele's been chasing Laporte the whole way. Trying to repair his only error. And here they are now, in Capella, at the end of the hunt—Laporte plunging towards the black hole in her little Uriel and Steele's titanic *Atreus* plunging after her.

The Uriel's electronic warfare systems make a deep frightened sound. Laporte's helmet taps her chin and says:

VAMPIRE! ASPECT! STINGRAY! SSM-[EOS]-[notch 000x000]-[20+!]

It'll be missiles, then. A fuck-ton of missiles.

If he turned around now, with all *Atreus*' fuel still coiled up in her engines, Steele could probably stop his fall. Claw his way into a hover above the black hole, and then make the grueling climb up to the wormhole and safety.

But he's accelerating. Chasing Laporte. Risking himself and his entire crew to kill her.

Laporte opens a COM channel. Aims it downward. Into the dark. She has allies here, if they can be made to understand the danger.

"Ken," she sends. "It's me. Don't keep me waiting, old man."

That's why she's come here, to the singularity, to the tomb of Capella. Because the Nemesis made it.

Just as they made her.

nagari 2/10

Ken is a dream of Laporte's. Laporte's dreams are not entirely her own.

Ken happened long before the Alliance rebuilt the wormhole, long before the war—

She was six years old, playing in the yard. Her parents had a house in Tandale, part of Dar es Salaam, where they worked on heavy trains, moving cargo from the Indian Ocean all across Tanzania. Her father was a reserve pilot and her mother was in arbitrage. Little Noemi, left to self-directed education, as was the Ubuntu preference for the young, spent her days building a model train system in the dirt between her water garden and her ant battle arena. But the ants would not stay in the ant battle arena, not even a little—they kept foraying into the train system, no matter how many of them Noemi punitively de-limbed.

Ken suggested she consider the broader logic driving the ants. Ken often gave Noemi advice. Her parents were very proud that little Noemi had actualized such a useful inner friend.

After an exhaustive survey of her territories, Noemi discovered the problem. There was a rival ant colony north of the water garden. The two groups had fallen to war. She studied up on ant diplomacy, complaining into her phone, and concluded there was no pluralist solution. The colonies would compete for hegemony over all available resources. Unless one side achieved a swift victory, lives and labor would be lost on the war. An attritional stalemate could ruin them both.

She uncurled the garden hose and drowned the northern colony. The choice was simple, in that it was easy. It only depended on one thing. She knew and loved the ants in the south of the yard. She cared nothing for the ants in the north. There was no other distinction between them.

When you are a monster, as Laporte certainly is, you have to cling to the things that you love. The ligatures that connect you to the rest of humanity.

If you lose them, you may whirl away.

simms 3/9

Laporte didn't understand the Ken dream until she joined NAGARI. That's the beginning.

What the Alliance asked the Federation is what the woman named al-Alimah asked Laporte. She was a tall woman with gunmetal implants in place of her eyes. She gave Laporte a choice: stay with Simms as she fights the radiation poisoning, or come with me and try to win the war.

"The medics are coming," she said. "You can stay with your Captain until she dies, or until she doesn't. You'll make no difference. None of your talents or capabilities will contribute to her battle."

(Laporte is a wingman and she never leaves her wing leader—)

"Or you can come with me. I'm with a black ops unit. Special moral environment. NAGARI. You know we're losing this war. You know we need you."

(—except when necessary to complete the mission.)

And Laporte thought, if she lives, if she wakes up, I want to be able to say—

Hey, boss. We've won. I took care of everything for you. Did you have a good vacation?

So Laporte took al-Alimah by her tactical gloves and went with her, out of the sweltering briefing room, out of the dying ship where everyone's sweat was hot enough to leave red radiation burns, where their marrow rotted inside their neutron-salted bones.

And that was how she joined NAGARI.

nagari 3/10

NAGARI. A committee of monsters: a federation of sharks. Shaved-skull operators cooking lamb on the naked coils of their frigate's heatsinks. All veterans. Not one in uniform.

There are real psychological differences between Federation and Alliance citizens. Fifty years of sealed prosperity in Sol gave birth to a generation of humans who are very good at living but *very* bad at killing.

That's why the Federation, for all its socioeconomic might, is losing the war. (That's why Laporte thinks the Alliance chose war over peace. They could never win the peace. And they were built for victory.)

But Laporte isn't a good Federation citizen, no oh, that's what Simms told her in their radiation-cooked parley: you're a killer, you need no reason and no hate. It's just you. And that's why you'll be fine without me.

And Simms was right. Laporte has an instinct for violence. And there are others like her, gathered under the mantle of Federation black ops, where the terrain of their violence extends far beyond the battlefield.

"This is your first mission." Al-Alimah briefs her in the back of the mess kitchen as they inventory the remainders. Cumin and cinnamon and allspice blown down over them, but the stink of ozone is stronger. Al-Alimah's eyes are sensors and projectors: they sketch visions for Laporte by scratching her eyes with particle beams. "You will infiltrate an Alliance personnel convoy carrying non-combatant contractors. Dental and culinary services for rear-area bases."

When Laporte blinks, the images left by al-Alimah's eyes don't fade.

"You will deploy a neutron weapon against the dormitory ships. Leave no survivors."

Laporte imagines Simms asking: what is the military rationale for this strike, sir? She vows to ask, after the mission. She vows to get good data on the mission effects. She used to keep a kill tally, one strike for each fighter she shot down, one chance to preen and brag for Boss.

She sleeps with a cable in her skull, and she dreams about the strike over and over. When she flies it, it feels like a dream too. The neutron weapon makes no light or sound except the shrieking RAD warnings in her cockpit. She comes home to backslaps and fistbumps and moonshine from the still.

"The objective is atrocity," al-Alimah tells her, when she asks. The NAGARI analyst wears a baggy gray jumpsuit, indifferent to rank and physical presence. "The Alliance uses statistical modeling to predict our tactics. They've learned that we obey a set of moral guidelines. The only way to confound their predictions is to introduce noise."

Noise. Killing all those dentists with radiation was *noise*.

When Simms was irradiated she was very quiet.

Laporte stops spicing her food. She dresses in stark self-washing jumpsuits and she showers cold. The other operators are happy monsters, full of gossip and tall tales, not shy about talking shop or sex. Laporte touches no one. She doesn't talk about her missions. In the gym and the simulator she is laconic and dependable but she never asks for anything. She practices self-denial.

One of the other operators, Europa-born and silver-haired, comes after Laporte for reasons either carnal or tactical. The closest she gets to intimacy, of one sort or another, is when she says: "You act like you're a monk! Monks give up stuff they like, man. Monks deny their pleasures."

That's right. Monsters shouldn't be warm. They shouldn't have fun. Being a monster should feel like it costs.

But the silver woman grins at Laporte, an I-know-you grin, and says, "So when you pretend you hate the work—I know what that means. I know what's up."

Laporte flies noise jobs for months. False flags. Political assassinations. Bycatch enhancement. Straight-up terrorism. She has to round her kill tally to the nearest thousand. She has one of her teeth replaced by an armored transponder, so that someone will know she dies even if her body's vaporized.

Simms would not be proud. Simms fought a war against an invading army, and she hated the fuck out of them. But she had rules. NAGARI is anti-rule. Strategically amoral.

Is this her whole purpose now? Trying to buy the Federation a few extra months through the exercise of atrocity? Missions that violate every tenet of Ubuntu and civilized conflict?

It's war, Simms once said. In war, monsters win. Laporte gathers up that thought and buckles it around herself, for want of Simms, for want of victory.

Is she fighting because victory might mean seeing Simms again? Imagine that. Imagine saying: Hey, boss, you're alive. I neutron bombed a few thousand dentists, and we won the war. Can I buy you a drink?

simms 4/9

Back in the middle. In the story that moves Laporte from NAGARI to the black hole. Her last chance to stay human.

"It's not true," Laporte tells Simms.

They've finished re-arming all the fighters, breaking the ceasefire lock. This is the lean time between the surrender and the mutiny, when the Federation's surviving fleet lurks in the cold on the edge of the solar system, a faithful dog cast out and gone feral. Waiting for Laporte and NAGARI to rouse them to revenge.

"What's not true?" Simms asks. She pokes the fire with her cooking mitt.

They have a trash fire going on the *Eris'* hangar deck. Warships are very good at coping with internal fires, and very bad at serving as long-term habitats. They grew some chicken in the medical tissue loom and now they're burning trash under a plate of thermal conductor, in the hope of making a chicken curry.

"That monsters win," Laporte says. The chicken pops and spatters grease. Simms laughs and Laporte, thinking of dead cells sloughing apart under radiation, shudders. Her transponder tooth, left over from NAGARI work, is cold under her tongue. "In the end, actually, monsters tend to lose. And that's much worse."

"What do you mean?" Simms eyes her up. Simms is still exploring Laporte's new crazy side, separate (in her practical mind) from Laporte's old crazy side, before their long radiation-cooked severance. "Is this something from your NAGARI drug trips? Cosmic insight, plucked from the void?"

"Yeah," Laporte says, remembering the surgical theater, the feeling of cold entheogen slurry pumping into her skull. Where they discovered the truth about Ken. "I wish you'd been there."

"But I was there," Simms says, stirring the fire. The thermal conductor is a cheerful cherry-hot color, and Simms hums as she works, like she's trying to be casual about how much she cares for this idea: the possibility that she was out there, helping Laporte win, even while she was bolted to a triage rig with her bones melting out through needled tubes. "I was in your thoughts. Wasn't I? Isn't that what kept you alive?"

Why would she be so happy about this, about helping Laporte be a good monster, and then, just a day later, refuse to fly with Laporte in the mutiny?

Why?

nagari 4/10

This is what Laporte was up to while Simms' bones were melting:

Laporte flies her terror missions. She goes out alone and she returns alone, and between those stanchions she kills her targets. Her effect on the universe, the vector sum of her actions, is purely subtractive.

She *isn't* fine without Simms. Simms was her captain and her friend, the last tie keeping Laporte in the human orbit. But that's the point, right? Laporte's a monster now. Her past is useful to her only in the way that gunpowder is useful to a bullet. The more pain in it, the better.

The war's falling apart, slouching towards surrender. NAGARI scores victory after horrible victory. But the Federation Navy can't follow their lead. The clockmaker-Admiral Steele outfoxes the Navy again and again, closing in on Earth.

Laporte becomes a kind of leader among the operators, on strength of her efficiency, in admiration of her self-sufficiency. She learns the name of every NAGARI operator, their habits and crimes, their gym schedules (hey man, spot me) and cooking tricks (come on, not this curry shit again). She also learns the callsigns of every active pilot: physiological parameters, operational histories.

But she can't connect the two, the names and the callsigns. When a callsign dies on a mission, she isn't sure who it was until she misses their grunt in the gym, their recipes on the heatsink grill.

The Federation is still losing the war. Her intention is to keep flying until she dies.

But the memory of Simms (and the memory of what she said: you'll be fine, you don't need a reason) drives her mad with competition. She had a competition with Simms! She always wants to be better than her Captain expects.

So when she wakes up from a training dream she goes to al-Alimah and asks: "Why are we doing this? What's the point of noise jobs and neutron bombs, if it's just a way to put off the inevitable surrender?"

She expects the answer she's given herself: Monsters are weapons. It's not up to the weapon to choose targets.

But al-Alimah startles her. As if she is a ghost alive in the memory of childhood Tandale summers, al-Alimah says: "Tell me about Ken."

"What is this?" Laporte stares her down, eye to gleaming post-surgery tactical eye. "Why do you care about that?"

"You told your Captain Simms that you had an invisible friend as a child. He urged you to develop your faculty for violence."

Laporte laughs. It doesn't surprise her that NAGARI knows this shit, but it's *hilarious* that they care. "Ants, man. He wanted violence against ants. Ken was an imaginary friend."

Al-Alimah doesn't waver. "During your adolescence, you were treated for schizotypal symptoms. You reported violent ideation, dissociative thoughts, and a fear of outside intrusion. Your first boyfriend left you because he was afraid of you."

Laporte opens her arms in a gesture of animal challenge. "Are you worried," she says, grinning, "that I might be unwell?"

Al-Alimah laughs. She can pretend to be very warm, when she wants, although it's terrifyingly focused. Like all her charm radiates from a naked wire charged red-hot.

"What would Ubuntu have had you do to the ants?" she asks. "What would our Federation's philosophy say to two ant colonies at war?"

Find a pluralistic solution. Locate the structural causes of inter-colony violence. Rework the terrain, so that peaceful competition between colonies can produce a common good.

"Ubuntu is for people," Laporte says. "It doesn't work on ants."

Al-Alimah touches Laporte's wrist with one long, cold finger. "Think about the universe," she says, "and what portions of it belong to people. If Ubuntu applies to the human territory, what is NAGARI for?"

"Oh my God," Laporte says.

She understands instantly. She grasps the higher purpose of NAGARI.

She has a terrible, wonderful, world-burning premonition. A way to win the war.

nagari 5/10

Ask the Alliance, Steele's people, the aggressors and the victors in this terrible war: what is the grievance? The fatal casus belli?

Imagine a republic charged and corroded by perpetual emergency. Scattered across lonely stars. Simmering on the edge of rebellion. They may be tyrants. May also be the bravest and the most tenacious people ever born.

This is what Laporte knows, what NAGARI knows, about their history—

Humanity met something out there. Implacably hostile. Unspeakably alien. Nemesis.

Love is about knowing the rules of your connection. You know how you could hurt her, if you wanted, and she trusts you with this knowledge. And war is about that too. You learn the enemy's victory conditions, her capabilities and taboos. You build a model of her and figure out where it breaks. You force the enemy into unsurvivable terrain, pinned between an unwinnable war and unacceptable compromise.

But what do you do when the rules you use to understand how one thing relates to another stop working? When the other thing has no rules at all?

simms 5/9

Rules about Simms, from the time before radiation and ambush:

The Federation military forbids fraternization in the ranks. While Ubuntu treasures community, emotional attachment can compromise the chain of command.

So at first the fire between them, the charge in the air, bled off in confined ways—

Laporte tried not to look at Simms too much, or too little, so nobody would notice her unusual attention. This is like war logic. When you look for the enemy with your active sensors, you also tell the enemy where you are and what you intend.

When they checked each others' suits they were extremely professional. Soon they realized this was an error, since soldiers are profoundly obscene. But it was too late to start making catheter jokes.

Sometimes they sparred in the gym. Simms was icy and Laporte grinned too much. The whole squadron turned out to cheer. (They're all dead now.)

A new rule, after NAGARI and the Federation's surrender, after al-Alimah puts them back together. A rule they teach other—

You must never hint at your secret fear. The terrible thought that it might have been better if you'd never found each other again.

nagari 6/10

Al-Alimah shares the history of humanity and the Nemesis, the history that Laporte knows from school—and the secret parts NAGARI has collated.

There were two Nemesis incursions.

The first war, the war that divided mankind into Federation and Alliance, began like a nightmare and ended like an amputation. The Nemesis surfaced from the wormhole web and moved across human space erratic and arbitrarily violent. Humanity scored tactical victories (tactical victory is the tequila of combat highs: hot in the moment, hateful in the aftermath) but in the end the Nemesis world-killer called *Sinadhuja* made it all the way to Serpentis.

One step from Earth.

When *Sinadhuja* entered the wormhole to Sol, the Earth fleet resorted to their last hope. A firewall bomb. It cauterized the wormhole connection. Killed *Sinadhuja,* saved the hearth of the human species, and left the rest of mankind out there in the dark.

That's how the Federation and the Alliance became separate things—sometimes that's how you define yourself, in the space when you are separated, when you have abandoned all hope of reunion.

One night, waiting for al-Alimah to appear and task her with another massacre, clawing up gibbets of her gel mattress and then smoothing them back so they vanish into the whole, Laporte realizes that she knows Simms is dead. She has to be. It's naive to think she survived the radiation. Naive to imagine an end to the war, a happy reunion, a quiet retreat where they can tend to each other's wounds. Simms is dead.

It would be worse if she were alive. She would hate the monster Laporte, and she would hate herself for leaving Laporte to the monsters. Simms is a hell of a soldier, a superb pilot. That's how she defines herself. A good pilot never leaves her wingman.

What do you call this? The decision to know something not because it is true, but because it's useful?

Out there alone the Alliance survived. Thirty-two years they prepared for the Nemesis to strike a second time. Certain that victory would secure the future of mankind in the cosmos. Certain that defeat would mean extinction.

capella 4/8

She falls engine-first towards the black hole and *Atreus* falls after her with its torch aflame and missiles ramifying out into the space between them in search of the kill geometry, the way to confine her, the solution to Laporte.

Steele's ship outguns her by orders of magnitude. The Alliance fought Nemesis twice. They learned war-craft the Federation has never matched.

Atreus' missiles can make their own jumps. Leap from their first burn straight to Laporte across a stitch of folded space. But the singularity they're all falling for warps space, which makes it hard to jump. So the missiles come at her drunk and corkscrewing or they die in the jump and shear themselves open like fireflies burning too hot.

Not all of them, though. Not all of them. A few make it into terminal attack.

Laporte talks to Simms under her breath. Reporting the situation. *Boss, Morrigan, am spiked, stingray stingray, vampires inbound. Music on. Defending now.*

She rolls her shoulders and arms her coilguns and starts killing the things come to kill her.

And down there, down beneath her, in the groaning maelstrom where space-time frays and shears and starts to fall, where the course of events balances on the edge of inevitable convergence towards a central point, something wakes.

The light of a stardrive, peeling free of the fire. The huge dark mass of something mighty. Molting out of the black hole's accretion disc. Climbing up to meet her.

Ken says, in a voice as young as summer gardens, as old as ants:

Hello, Miss Laporte.

nagari 7/10

"The Alliance started the second Nemesis incursion," al-Alimah says.

They're having dinner together. Laporte's sure this is a dream, but because she sleeps with her nervous system braided into NAGARI's communal dreamscape, it's probably also real.

Al-Alimah wants to talk about Ken.

Laporte picks up her fork and eats. They're in a rooftop cafe and there's a warm wet wind, storm wind, coming from the north and west. The meal is salmon sous-vide cut into translucent panes of flesh. Like the pages of a carnage book.

When she touches the salmon with her fork it curls up around the tines. "The Alliance attacked the Nemesis?"

"There was an insurrection." Al-Alimah's a long woman, breakable-looking, tall like Simms but not trained to bear her own weight under acceleration. In dreamland she's traded her gray uniform for a rail-slim black gown. She looks like a flechette. A projectile. "Someone broke ranks."

After the first incursion, Nemesis behavior was the province of military intelligence. By political necessity, or perhaps out of some sense of Lovecraftian self-preservation, the Alliance tried to keep the pieces of the puzzle widely separated. But one of their Admirals, Haywain van Aken, finally unified the clues into a grand theory.

"What was it?" Laporte interrupts. The tines of her fork are hypodermic-sharp but she doesn't notice until she's already pierced herself, three points of blood on her lips, inside her cheek.

"We don't know." Al-Alimah shrugs with her hands. The tendons in her wrists are as fine as piano wire. "Not yet. But we know what he did."

Van Aken became convinced he could communicate with the Nemesis. He built a signaling system—almost a weapon, a cousin of the Alliance's missiles: it jumped high-energy particles directly into the mass of the target. Then he went rogue. Hurtling off past the Capella colony and into unexplored space. Possessed by a messianic conviction that he could find the Nemesis and end the war.

Laporte cracks her neck and leans back. Watches Alliance warships moving through the clouds around them, pursuing van Aken into Nemesis territory, overcoming disorganized Nemesis resistance with determination and skill. On the horizon a voice that isn't Admiral Steele's begins to murmur about the possibility of real victory.

"Forward reconnaissance found van Aken's ship adrift in a supernova remnant." Al-Alimah swallows something Laporte never saw her bite. She has a little piercing in her tongue. It's strange to imagine her going to get her tongue pierced. Maybe she put it in herself. "His crew had mutinied. An outbreak of psychosis." The sky flickers with records of violence, directionless, obscene. "Then the Nemesis boarded his ship. They took him."

"What?" Laporte stops chewing. It shocks her to imagine the Nemesis claiming a single human being. That isn't their logic. That's human logic.

"Yes. The Alliance had the same question." Al-Alimah points to the sky. Jawed shadows gather on the sun, four-kilometer reapers studded with foamed neutronium. "Three days later, scouts sighted the first of eighty-six *Sinadhuja* world-killers converging on human space."

The Alliance fought a harrowing retreat but the Nemesis poured after them, insane, inscrutable, an avalanche of noise. No central point of failure to target, like the single *Sinadhuja* in the first incursion. Nowhere for the Alliance to aim its might. It was like trying to kill a beehive with a rifle. Except that each bee, each *Sinadhuja,* was a match for half the Alliance fleet.

Al-Alimah flashes two peace signs at Laporte. Four stars glimmer on her fingertips: two binary stars. "The war ended in Capella. The Alliance had a colony there. They decided to hold the line long enough to evacuate." Tiny model *Sinadhuja* warships climb out of the webs of her hands, jaws gaping. Like scarabs. Like sharks. "The Nemesis fleet did something to the system's stars. Altered their orbits. It's tempting to read it as a demonstration of power, an act of intimidation or rebuke. Except that the Nemesis never used symbolic violence before."

Four stars roll off her fingertips and spiral down into each other. Supernova light pops, rebounds off al-Alimah's eyes, and collapses into a pinpoint devourer. The black hole.

"A hundred million civilians." Al-Alimah taps her two forefingers together, as if to telegraph the number. "A quarter of their fleet. All lost."

And something more important, too. The thing you lose when you realize that victory is impossible no matter how hard you fight.

Monsters win, Laporte.

Laporte thinks about grand strategy. The Nemesis might return anywhere, at any time. The Alliance needed ships, and weapons, and brilliant science, and something to offer its citizens as proof against despair—a new victory to fight for. So the Alliance did the only thing it could. It set to work rebuilding the way home: reopening the Serpentis-Earth wormhole with Nemesis technology.

And when that home refused to join the great work, the project of human survival, the Alliance resorted to war.

"And so we come to now," al-Alimah says. She leans back, as if she has discharged her duty, and drinks her wine. "Our great predicament."

The war between an Alliance driven by exigency, by the utilitarian, amoral need for survival, and a Federation built on humane compassion, on the idea that you do the right thing no matter the circumstance. How do you fight that war, if you're the Federation? If you can't listen to the Alliance argument without a scream of sympathy?

You make something like NAGARI. A cadre of monsters to do what you cannot.

The sky has changed again. It's Simms up there now. She has a face of triangles and planes, a faceted thing, and it pulls on Laporte, it engages her. Combat pilots decompose all things into geometry: threats, targets, and the potential energies between them.

"Your old Captain." Al-Alimah looks up at her too. "We never wanted to recruit her. Too conventional."

Laporte looks away from Simms, and voices the apocalypse option.

"If we can find some way to make the Nemesis return," she says, "and then collapse the Earth-Serpentis wormhole again, we can let the Nemesis wipe out the Alliance and end the invasion."

If they collapse the wormhole so the Nemesis can't get in, then the Federation will survive. Guarded by light-years of real space. All it will cost is a few billion human lives.

Everything can go back to the way it was. Human paradise. A confined peace.

al-Alimah is still waiting. Lips curled in amusement. Gunmetal eyes infected with the blind crawling light of distant computation. "That's just utilitarian strategy," she says. "Doesn't take a dream to make that connection. Tell me, Laporte, why do you think I brought you here? What endgame do you think all those terror missions were training you for?"

Ken. A childhood name for a childhood friend.

A man thought he could communicate with the Nemesis. Admiral Haywain van Aken.

Laporte puts her fork through her cheek. In the dream, it doesn't hurt.

capella 5/8

Atreus must see the monster rising behind Laporte. Steele must see the shape of the demon she's conjured up out of the accretion disc. The *Sinadhuja* world-killer is the insignia of everything the Alliance stands against. The monster in the mist. *Atreus* was built in hope of killing it.

Perhaps Steele will target his missiles at the *Sinadhuja*.

Laporte coilguns another incoming missile and it flashes into annihilation so bright her canopy has to black it out like a negative sun. And Steele keeps firing at her. *Atreus* keeps accelerating. If he sees the *Sinadhuja* he doesn't maneuver in response.

Once Steele said, about the war, about his strategy against the Federation:

I employ overwhelming violence. Because my enemies are gentle, humane, compassionate people. Their Ubuntu philosophy cannot endure open war. And the faster I stop the war, the faster I stop the killing. So my conscience asks me to use every tool available.

And Laporte answers him. Look what you conjured up, you brilliant, ruthless bastard. Look what you made. Someone willing to use every available tool to fight back.

Once Simms said, about her wingman, about Laporte:

You're insane. I'm glad you're on my side.

Laporte dances between the vectors of the missiles come to kill her and when they come too close she expends her guns on them and they intersect the snarl of the tracers and die like lightning. It's mindless, beautiful work. Like a dream. She talks to Simms:

Boss, Morrigan. It's almost done.

Ken stirs from his deep place to save his prize.

nagari 8/10

By now it's clear that the Federation will surrender. No conventional military action can defeat Steele's war logic, his simulation farm, his psychological pressure, his willingness to dive past ethical crush depth.

So NAGARI plans to make contact with Nemesis.

"Send me in first," Laporte says.

Consider semiosis—the assignment of symbols to things, and the manipulation of those symbols to communicate and predict change. That's how intelligent life works. Build a model of the universe, test your ideas in the model, and find the best way to change the world.

Only the Nemesis don't have any recognizable semiosis. They're a whirlwind traversing the Lacanian desert, a fatal mirage, recognizable only by the ruin of its passage.

Until Admiral Haywain van Aken sacrificed himself. Until he somehow convinced the Nemesis to take him in.

And ever since, the Nemesis have been speaking. Or attacking. It's hard to know.

For more than a decade the Nemesis have been broadcasting the apparition of Admiral Haywain van Aken into human minds. The Nemesis organisms communicate by direct nerve induction at a distance. Particles wormholed into the tissue of the target. (There is, of course, no possibility that the Nemesis are a product of natural evolution.)

"If they can do that," Laporte protests, "they can just murder us all. Cook our skulls from light-years away." Or read the brainstates of human commanders, predict everything they do, the way Laporte and Simms could predict each other.

"No. Not without van Aken." Al-Alimah lays out NAGARI's hypothesis: the Nemesis have no mentality. They cannot conceive of other minds to predict or destroy. Their war is algorithmic, a procedure of matter against matter, spawning tactics by mutation and chance and iterating them in the field. They never leap straight to the optimal strategy, because a smart foe predicts the optimal. Their war logic is hardened by chaos. Noise.

Van Aken is their beachhead in the land of human thought.

"He wants you," al-Alimah says, her long fingers on Laporte's wrist again. "You in particular are valuable to him. We want you to serve as an ambassador."

"That's stupid." Laporte may be a monster but she is not some other monster's spawn. "Are you saying I was purpose-built?"

"No. Far more likely that you were selected because you're somehow amenable to the Nemesis." Al-Alimah leans forward with her lips parted as if to admit her own monster secret. "Laporte, the third Nemesis incursion is already underway. Not with warships and weapons, not this time, nothing so crude. The Nemesis are attacking the command and control systems behind those assets."

Language. Plans. People.

"What are the mission parameters?" The Alliance has control of the Sol-Serpentis wormhole. Laporte can't just fly out to Capella. "How do we use this to save the Federation?"

Al-Alimah stands and her gown whips in the rising wind. "We drug you and mate your brain to a computer network. You will enter a traumatic dream state and communicate with van Aken—with Ken. We keep dosing you until you learn how to trigger a Nemesis attack on the Alliance. Or until you go mad." Her gunmetal eyes, looking down at Laporte, never blink. "You will be the third attempt. There were two prior candidates. They seized apart."

Laporte leans back in her chair and looks up at the woman.

She can be the necessary monster. She could call down genocide on the Alliance and save her beloved home. If she believes the Federation is the only hope for a compassionate, peaceful, loving future, then, logically, she should be willing to kill for it. If she has a button that says 'kill ten billion civilians, gain utopia,' she should press it.

She could win the war, for the memory of Simms. And Simms is dead, right? The dead can't be ashamed.

"Okay," Laporte says. "I'm in. I volunteer."

They will connect her to the NAGARI dreamscape and to the salvaged corpses of Nemesis organisms from the first incursion. They will scar messages into her brain. They will wait for the Nemesis, for the ghost of Haywain van Aken, to read them and reply.

Surgeons crown her in waveguides that ram through her skull and penetrate the gyrae of her brain. Cold drug slurry pumps the length of her spine: entheogens, to tear down the barriers between Laporte's psyche and outside stimuli. She goes under. She dreams.

simms 6/9
nagari 9/10

"Curry's ready," Simms says, and Laporte's stomach growls out loud. They grin at each other. Simms looks at Laporte's armored tooth and her grin falters just a little.

They eat their trash-cooked chicken curry side by side with their hips squashed together. Laporte tries not to jostle Simms' ribs with her sharp little elbows. Simms crunches on a bit of bone, makes a face, and gets juice on Laporte's buzzed hair. There is no shampoo anywhere on the ship so this is a bit of a disaster. Simms mops her up with blood cloth from the triage kit.

"Tell me why it's bad if monsters don't win," Simms says, blotting at the back of her neck.

Laporte leans on her for a moment, because she adores Simms' desire to hear this story again, especially the end. "I met Ken," she says, "he was in the dream, and he was real. They could see him in my mind. Something triggering nerve potentials."

She went into seizure almost instantly. The NAGARI surgeons let it happen.

Laporte stood in the garden in Tandale with the hose in her hand and pollen itching her nose. Ants crawled over her bare feet. From the house came the smell of her parents' cooking, impatient and burnt. She looked down at herself and laughed: she was in her favorite caraval cat t-shirt.

"Ah, Miss Laporte," Ken said. "You made it."

She looked for him but all she could see was the ants fighting, killing, generating new castes, mutating themselves into acid bombs and huge-headed tunnel plugs. "Admiral," she said. "Is that you?"

"Delighted to speak with you again. Let me briefly outline the necessary intelligence. A short history of all life. Then we can arrange our covenant."

Whatever Ken said to her must have been some kind of code, parasitic and adaptable, because it expressed itself as a love story. A story about Laporte and Simms.

Imagine this, Ken said, imagine a universe of Laportes and Simmses. Lorna Simms has rules. She builds communities, like her squadron, or like a network of wormholes. She takes the wildcat aces and the ne'er-do-wells, the timid and the berserk, and she teaches them all how to work together. When that work is done, Simms would like to leave you with a nice set of rules describing a world that makes sense. Simms is a Maker.

"Huh." Simms puts a little moonshine on the rag and keeps scrubbing at Laporte's head. "You have such nice dreams about me."

"Wait until you hear mine."

The other great class of life is the Laportes. (These are tendencies, mind, not binary teams. But they are real: vital parts of the history of life in the universe.) The Laportes rattle around breaking things, claiming things, reshaping things. They can achieve every bit as much as the Simmses, in their own way—but their triumphs are conquests, seductions, acts of passion and violence. The Simms build systems and the Laportes, parasites and predators and conquerors and geniuses and sociopaths, change them.

Whether delightful or destructive, the Laportes are Monsters.

When a Laporte meets a Simms, they fight. The Laporte might run rampant. She might murder the Simms, or trick her into subservience, or leave her spent and exhausted. Or the Simms might win, fencing the Laporte in with loyalties and laws, making her a useful part of something bigger. Understand? You following, Simms?

"It's about civilizations. Strategies. Game theory." Simms is a war junkie in her own way, a good self-directed Ubuntu learner, and she's done her homework. "And I'll bet, Laporte, that I know where your Admiral's going. The Simms win."

They win because they understand the Laportes. They make little models of what the Laportes are going to do, and they figure out how to get ahead of them, how to make their worst impulses useful, how to save them from harm (or lead them into it). They teach the Laportes what they can and cannot do.

Like Steele. Building statistical models of the Federation's tactics. Caging them in a prophecy of their own capabilities. And the only way out of that cage is to transgress the laws you use to define yourself.

"Hold still," Simms says. "This stuff really likes your hair."

"The Simmses do tend to win." Laporte leans back against her, just a little. When Simms is fixing Laporte up she forgets to be stiff and wary. "They win too much. And over billions of years, across the infinity of the universe, it turns out that's dangerous."

Imagine the god-Simms, ascendant. Puppeteering the cosmos with invisible loyalties. Learning how to guide the passions and the violence of the Laportes. Imagine Simms building not just a good squadron or a good civilization but a good galaxy, all the matter in it optimized for happy, useful thought.

Imagine a Simms setting out to build a *rechnender raum*: thinking space. Her laws written into the fundament.

"How did you learn all this?" Laporte asked the scurrying ants. In the shapes of their war she saw the ghost of an old man with dead stars in his eyes.

Ken had surmised some of it before his rebellion. And while the Nemesis had never communicated with him directly, they had, in their own way, signaled the truth: duplicating Haywain von Aken's consciousness millions of times, torturing it into madness, and exterminating the branches whose madnesses diverged from their desire.

"I'm not sure I follow that last part," Simms says. Now she's mopping the curry from behind Laporte's right ear. "Something about supercivilizations?"

"Imagine a place where everything could have anything it needed. For whatever it wanted." That was the happy Simms-world. Imagine a purpose? You can obtain it. You can get the resources you need.

"Like an Ubuntu slogan."

"Yes," Laporte says, shivering. That was what Ubuntu wanted to make. A place where people had everything they needed to be good. A place without violence and deprivation.

In the garden, Admiral Haywain van Aken told her that a universe without violence or deprivation was destined for something worse.

Cancer.

capella 6/8

Her Uriel sings her death to her.

DV UNDERBURN is a long drumbeat, pleading for more fuel, and SPIKE [COBRA TAME/ATREUS] is a-keening like headache, and MUSIC SOUR describes itself, and every time Steele fires she hears VAMPIRE! and a noise like someone ringing her molars with an armor chime.

But she's not going to die. She's too fast. She's too fierce. She's severed all the connections that would slow her down.

She kills a missile half a second from killing her and for an instant all her sensors are flash-blind but she kills the next too, a dead reckoning snapshot from a hundred kilometers with the pin graser. How? Because she has escaped the borders of herself. The *Sinadhuja* has trained its sensors on her. Ken is watching her. And she can see through his eyes.

She can think with his tissue, his fatal substrate. She is bleeding out of herself and into the Nemesis, the totipotent holocide-mind, the killing anima. Crossing the bridge Ken built.

Admiral Steele is calling to her. *"Federation pilot,"* he's saying, in that rich purring voice, not audibly afraid, *"you have been compromised by Nemesis psywar. Kill your engines and shut down your defensive jamming."*

Ken is calling to her. Miss Laporte. Come closer. We can complete our covenant. Together, we can save humanity.

"Okay, Boss," Laporte says. "Let's get ready."

nagari 10/10

Cancer, and its relationships to paradise and love:

You build a place without violence or deprivation. A place where anything can have everything it needs to be its finest, fullest self.

This is how cells became organisms. How people became civilizations. How a bunch of misfits and fuckups became a fighting unit *almost* tough enough to challenge Admiral Steele. A Simms wrote some laws to say: if we pool our energies, we can create a common good. And if you follow the rules, yeah, you, Laporte, if you don't eat too much common good, if you put in more than you take out, then we can last.

Imagine a Simms-god rampant, organizing the universe, winning the love of all the Laportes. So productive and persuasive that no one notices its ultimate agenda is hollow, self-referential, malignant.

Think about me. Organize everyone and everything to think about me. What am I? I am thinking about how to make everything think about me. I am a tumor, recruiting every system I encounter in the name of my own expansion.

"Whoa, now." Simms puts a wet finger on the back of Laporte's neck. "I'm very compelling, sure. Magnetic. But that's not me."

"Shh. Let me finish." Except, Laporte realizes, she is finished. That's the whole story. "van Aken believes in a cosmic proof: the axiomatic, mathematical superiority of cancer to all forms of containment. An empty thought that consumes intelligent systems and uses them to think about propagating itself."

Given a range of purposes, and a surplus of resources, one purpose would always triumph: the purpose of defeating and incorporating all other purposes. The two ant colonies in Laporte's garden had to dedicate themselves entirely to war. If one of them spent part of its energy on ant compassion, or ant culture, or ant art, it would lose. Cancer was the destiny of smart systems: empty, voracious, every part of them thinking about nothing but how to expand.

Unless there was someone with a hose to pour water on them.

"So," Simms says, humoring Laporte's great mythic rant, "why do we still have a universe? Why are we here, thinking about ourselves?"

"That's just what I asked van Aken," Laporte lies. Because she feels that it would be too creepy, too alien, to admit that she understood it right away.

In the part of the story she's avoiding, in the garden of the seizure dream, Laporte turned on her hose and began flooding her childhood constructs into mud. "The Nemesis are the anti-malignancy measure. They kill Makers. That's why they're so noisy and inefficient. So they can escape the models that Makers use to win wars."

From a distant Nemesis construct, tumbling through the ergosphere of Capella, borrowing the black hole's energies to hurl charged particles through quantum wormholes into Laporte's mind, Ken smiled his agreement. Tattooed it into Laporte's brain.

If you were afraid of intelligent thought consuming the universe, you had to turn the cosmos into an acid bath. An endless war against the triumph of Lorna Simms.

simms 7/9

"Okay," Simms says, squinting. "I think I got it all." She leans down, curled over Laporte's head, to look her in the eyes. "What happened next? Did you make the deal?"

"I did." She asked Ken: how do I get the Nemesis to wipe out the Alliance? And he told her: you must come to me, in Capella. "That's why I'm going out tomorrow."

Simms blinks, once, twice, a sign that she doesn't like this place, she wants to move on. They're touching on the open question, the raw wound between them. Is Simms going to fly again? Is she going to be part of Laporte's mutiny?

Are they still wingmen?

"And then?" Simms asks, pushing them past the moment.

"I couldn't get out. I couldn't wake up." It's funny how sharp Simms looks, upside down. Like she has some inverse swagger. Laporte wants to ask her to stay right there but what does Simms see, looking back? Is the inverse Laporte agreeable? "Contact with the Nemesis was killing me. I had no reason to live. Nothing to come back for."

She's seen the recordings of her brainstate. The seizure burning from skull to stem.

When Simms smiles upside down it looks like a grimace, which makes it much more familiar. "So they gave you anticonvulsants. And you woke up. Then you made up this part to help you get laid."

Laporte tells her anyway. "Al-Alimah whispered to me. And I heard her. She said . . . "

"Simms is alive," Simms says. "She survived radiation therapy, and now she's out there. Looking for you."

That was how Laporte came back from the seizure dream, just in time to fight in the Mars gambit and rage at the Federation's final surrender. Word came down: it's over. Move to a holding orbit. Await terms. Al-Alimah tore the orders up and all the assembled NAGARI operators made a satisfied growl like they were too angry to cheer.

"And that's how you got back to me." Simms kisses her on the right eyeball. "You're a sweet liar."

"Ew," Laporte says. "Don't do that."

But she smiles and—

capella 0/8

—tries to catch Simms' hand.

"You're meeting with the Admiralty tonight." Simms claps her on the shoulders, boom boom, look at you, kid, you're a big shot. And then she draws away, upright, articulate, her flight suit unzipped and tied around her waist, her hair loose on her shoulders. She backs away from Laporte in triangular half-steps, back leg then front, as if they're fighting and she is making room to retreat. The air that rushes in to fill the absence of her is cold and it smells of burnt curry.

"I am," Laporte says, wishing she would stay close. "I'm presenting the final battle plan. Al-Alimah's victory gambit."

"You're going to tell them you have a plan to bait the Nemesis into attacking the Alliance. A strategic distraction. When Steele pulls his fleet out of Sol, we can seal the node and live in peace."

"That's right."

"But that's not the plan." Simms aims one finger at her, a half-curled, hey-you stab. "You're not going to tell them the real plan. That's between you and your NAGARI friends."

The Nemesis are insuperable. Nothing can defeat them. They have unlimited resources (their warships conjured out of black hole accretion discs by probability manipulation) and their behavior, well, that's even worse: they have no mentality, no strategy to predict, nothing that can generate a nice clean model. Only a godslaying virulence, a random and chilling will to annihilate, manifesting strategies and hurling them at the enemy until the enemy has exhausted all countermeasures and taught the Nemesis their strengths.

To fight them is to instruct them how to kill you.

Haywain van Aken has summoned Laporte to Capella. To the black hole that is the Nemesis' engine, factory, and beacon in human space. Why? Laporte has a guess. They have no purpose or objectives of their own—those are Maker things, teleological, forbidden to them. Only their basic logic: whatever we encounter, we destroy.

But they didn't kill van Aken. They took him into communion. Maybe that act brought them closer to victory. Maybe, to them, subverting van Aken was an act of destruction: a lethality enhancement.

"I believe," Laporte begins, struggling, trying to hide her struggle, this is so hard to say because it requires her to navigate around her secret fear: that she is about to abandon Simms again, forever, in favor of the consummate monstrosity. "I believe I can trigger a Nemesis behavior that will exterminate everyone in Alliance space. I believe the Federation will endure. Humanity will have a chance at survival."

"That's how we save the Federation? How we keep Ubuntu alive? Sacrifice ten billion human lives?" Simms crosses her arms. "We're okay with defensive genocide?"

"That's war. We kill people to achieve our objectives."

Simms' hard eyes radiating a hard signal, and Laporte reads it in a way that's maybe unfair: I liked knowing that you were *my* monster. I liked knowing you had boundaries. "We kill soldiers."

"People," Laporte says, echoing the old Ubuntu lessons: everyone is human. There is no justifiable violence—only degrees of tragedy. "We're always killing people."

They stare at each other and on the raw metal deck between them Laporte can feel them piling the tally, the killcounts, the fighter pilots and warship crews they've murdered personally, the deaths contingent upon those by way of grief or loss (children abandoned, lovers driven to suicide, parents spiraling away into addiction). The *strategic targets* and *footprint bleed* and *noncombatant bycatch* and for Laporte it all wraps up in the voice of some terrified Alliance contractor on a suit radio trying to explain that he doesn't support this war, doesn't want to be here, he's just trying to pay off his electrical apprenticeship, would they please send a rescue ship, he's tumbling off into space and his radiation warnings are red and he doesn't want to drown in his own vomit, please, please. Send help.

When the Alliance captured Earth orbit, Admiral Steele threatened to bomb a city every hour until the Federation issued an unconditional surrender. What else could he do? Not with every soldier in the Alliance could he occupy even one continent. He had to use the tools at his disposal. He had to resort to calculated atrocity in the name of final peace.

Funny how that Ubuntu lesson can turn around, isn't it? How easily *degrees of tragedy* becomes *degrees of necessity.*

"You told me," Laporte says, "that if I hesitated, I would die. So I never hesitate."

Simms looks at her old wingman and new lover and whatever she's looking at is receding fast. "I hate them," she says. "But I don't know if I hate them enough to do this."

Laporte wants to grin and quip. She would tell Simms what Simms told her: monsters win.

But if she says that, she's telling Simms that this is all on her. That she's the one who made Laporte.

"There's no alternative," she says instead. "If we surrender to the Alliance, it's all been for nothing. We become part of the war against the Nemesis. And the Nemesis kill us all."

Simms does something with the fear in her eyes. Like she's folding it up and pointing it at something. "This al-Alimah woman. Were you two close?"

"Not like that." Not like you.

"I want to talk to her." Simms points at the deck behind Laporte, like a cue to turn around, and in doing that she makes it clear: the meeting will not include Laporte. "I've got some concerns to articulate."

"Fine." She can't keep the petty irritation from her voice. They should be together, effortlessly and unanimously lethal, two fists on the same fighter. "Are you flying with me tomorrow? When I go put out the signal?"

"I still need to check myself over in the simulator," Simms says. "Make sure the radiation shakes are gone."

Laporte's flown with her long enough to hear the *no.*

capella 7/8

She is in her Uriel, fighting off Steele, falling into the dead star and the waiting *Sinadhuja.*

She is in communion with the *Sinadhuja.* There are hallucinations puncturing her mind. She is in the garden with Ken.

"This is the bargain," he says.

He's a tall, strong-jawed man in the broadshouldered uniform of an Alliance admiral. He must be proud of that uniform, because he still wears his short-billed cap and his insignia. But the texture of him is black and squirming and when Laporte touches him she sees he's made of ants, ants at war, lopping limbs and antennae off each other with their scissored jaws.

Her fingers come away acid-burnt.

"Are you ready?" Haywain van Aken says. His eyes are two rings of fire, the accretion discs of two dead suns. "Do you understand what's about to happen?"

The *Sinadhuja* looms up behind her fighter. Four kilometers long and pregnant with methods of extinction. As it matches velocity with her ship its thrusters flare violet-black, the jets decaying sideways into some hidden curled dimension. It is attacking her, speaking to her, these two are the same. The Nemesis can never understand human minds well enough to manipulate them. But they have Haywain van Aken to do it for them.

"The Nemesis exist to tear down conscious thought," Laporte says to Ken.

She is in the cockpit, nudging the stick, steering her Uriel into the *Sinadhuja's* open gullet. All the alarms have gone silent, except one: PROXIMITY. PROXIMITY. Steele's voice is an electronic scratch, fading off, saying: *Brevet-Admiral Laporte, you are compromised. It's not too late. You can still self-destruct. You can still take out your sidearm and shoot yourself in the head. Brevet-Admiral Laporte, last time someone did this they blew up four suns—*

"The Nemesis have internal safeguards. Processes designed to rip apart any accidental intelligence they develop." Ken's peeling off the skin of his left-arm, degloving it, creating a sacrament of killing ants. "But this makes it hard for them to win."

They can't create their own leaders. They can't build models of the things they need to kill. They can summon up infinite might, but never learn how to apply it efficiently. How could they? In their fundamental state the Nemesis are a storm, a destructive process. Semiosis, the use of symbols to understand and plan, is forbidden to them.

A storm is powerful. But smart things can shelter from a storm.

So how do they defeat the gods of thought using only the logic of annihilation? Or, more aptly: what tactics might they stumble on, in their blind exploration of the possibility space?

Laporte cups her hands and accepts the sacrament. The ants start eating her flesh. She crushes them between her palms, to show her strength, and it only drives them deeper.

"They provoke the creation of monsters," she says. "Experts at the use of violence. And then they consume them to enhance their own violence."

"You will lead the Nemesis in war against the Alliance," van Aken intones, reading the sacred terms, the covenant he sacrificed himself to create. "You will guide them as long as you can. Inevitably, you will be devoured by the Nemesis, and your authority will be erased. But as long as you endure, you can protect your home."

The ants are inside her now. She can feel them under her skin. She looks at her arms and sees them in her muscle, bound by violence, grappling and flexing. The Alliance's spies and admirals would drink razors to get a look at her brain right now, full of the alien logic that will give her a transient kind of power over the local Nemesis.

"What about you?" she asks. Ken was a good friend, once, with good advice, even if he's now the organizing point of all Nemesis behavior in human space. "How long will you last?"

His smile is warm and toothy, an earnest, clever smile, and each tooth in it is a broad-headed warrior ant. "Humanity is going to be at war with Nemesis for a long, long time," he says. "I am the anima in command of semiotic warfare. I am the Admiral of communion. I keep myself from the jaws by supplying the Nemesis with new weapons. And if you can manage the Nemesis, Miss Laporte, if you can keep the fire burning hot . . . then I will have new monsters to cultivate."

"Ah," she says, satisfied. She gets it! It makes simple sense.

Van Aken knows how to achieve a kind of common ground with the Nemesis. How to make humanity at least temporarily useful. The Nemesis devoured van Aken because he could enhance their lethality. Make them better monsters.

Humanity will defy the Nemesis as long as their strength lasts. They'll get ruthless. And thus they will become the Nemesis' monster farm. A new drop in the acid bath. Victory is not only annihilation: it's monster-genesis.

"I'm sorry your lover abandoned you," Ken says. "She was a good person, deep down. That's why she didn't understand the necessity of our work."

The jaws of the *Sinadhuja* begin to close around Laporte's ship.

simms 8/9

After the curry-and-cosmology fight, they go to the gym to beat the shit out of each other. That helps less than it used to: Simms is still weak and they both know it, and holding back in a fight is just like lying anywhere else.

Showers require less discipline than they used to. They retreat to their haven in the officers' cabins, freed up by the death of most of *Eris'* staff, and they have makeup sex. It's the night before the mutiny, before Laporte asks Simms, one last time, to be her zombie warrior buddy cop. The night before Simms says, sorry, I'm not mission capable.

Laporte drowses in Simms' arms and then she wakes up to the sight of al-Alimah leaning over her. She's upgraded her eyes. They are blind, brilliant silver. The stud in her tongue gleams like Laporte's armor tooth.

"The mission," al-Alimah says, "begins now."

By reflex (it's all reflex, love reflex) Laporte reaches for Simms who's curled up beside her and in need of protection. But no one's there: only a warm place. She sits up to shove al-Alimah back. Simms pounces on her from behind, Laporte recognizes the feel of her forearms and the smell of her, she tries to fight but Simms is stronger, she's *stronger,* she was holding back in the gym. She pins Laporte facedown in the mattress with a growl.

Al-Alimah puts a needle into Laporte's neck and the world goes out.

Laporte remembers this as just a dream. Not because it's true, but because it's useful.

nagari 11/10

"Stop asking me to fly with you," Simms says. "I'm done. I can't be part of this. That's my final decision."

This is the moment before Laporte falls into Capella. At the end of the mutiny, in the slim window before Steele catches up with the NAGARI task force and stops them from breaching Nemesis space. Laporte's Uriel is waiting on the *Eris* hangar deck with a full warload and two empty seats. There is no time for hesitation.

"Boss," Laporte says, reaching out. She's sealed up in her flightsuit and when she touches Simms it's through the interface of her tactical gloves, fireproof, skin-sealed, built to insulate and protect. "Hey."

Not again, she wants to say. Don't do this again. We survived this. We split up but we found each other again and we cooked some curry and fixed some fighters, we're so close, we're going to win. For values of victory encompassing genocide.

Simms pulls away. "You're not the woman I knew," she says. "You can go make your bargain. But I don't want to be part of it."

Their orbit is over. The punch-drunk bloodlust and the will to win. They've spiraled too close and now they will fling each other away, each of them ballistic and alone. Simms prefers defeat.

"*Laporte*," al-Alimah calls, from the *Eris'* CIC. "*We're losing time. Are you airborne?*"

"You don't need me," Simms says. "You never have."

Laporte wants to say something clever, to fix this. An alien told me that every Laporte needs a Simms. That monsters have to love makers, so they can hone each other. So they can keep a safe orbit. Simms, if you go, I don't know how to find my way back.

But this time it's Simms who walks away from her.

Laporte flies through the wormhole, into Capella. Into the maw of the singularity. She falls.

capella 8/8
simms 9/9

The jaws of the *Sinadhuja* close around her ship. Armored mandibles clamping down to protect the warship's antimatter stores and soft internal structure and most of all van Aken, who is the bridge the Nemesis need, the means of their third incursion. Shutting off the ring of receding starlight, and the blue nova of the *Atreus* high above.

The Uriel's navigational lights illuminate the *Sinadhuja*'s interior. Laporte scans serrated geometry swarming with jointed, armored Nemesis organisms. Somewhere down there van Aken's human body has been translated, or consumed, into a component of the *Sinadhuja*. A semiotic weapons system.

Ken. Who is in Laporte's head, who knows what she knows. Who knows that *Atreus* is here to kill her. Who knows that she left Simms on a hangar deck in Vega.

Laporte's armored tooth fires a jolt of pain up the side of her jaw.

"Boss, Morrigan," Laporte says. She knows she has to say this. A dream told her. "We're a go. Wake up. Do it."

In the Uriel's back seat, the electronic warfare station, Simms smashes her helmet against the headrest in surprise.

"Fuck!" she says. Her voice is dry like paper tearing. "Holy shit!"

Laporte's weapons panel lights up with status reports. An IV dumping combat stimulants into Simms' blood, a cardiac implant restarting her heart, reflex sequencers firing commands into her brainstem. Waking her up from functional death. Since they left *Eris* together, Simms has been sustained by the emergency oxygen in her synthetic bone marrow and whatever black-ops technofuckery al-Alimah cranked into her.

Hidden from Haywain van Aken's communion. From his semiosis weapon, his dream of ants, his bridge into conscious minds.

In the garden, Ken says: "She left you. She thought you were an abomination. I don't understand."

Understand. That wonderful word. Laporte, giddy with the knowledge that Simms is alive again (again!), alive and flying with her, just can't resist the quip: "Just a bad dream, Ken."

"Al-Alimah. She fabricated that event and put it in you. Why?" The formicidae face tilts. "What about your mission, Laporte? What about human survival?"

"You're the mission, Ken." The Nemesis never manifested any central vulnerabilities during the second incursion. Never organized around any one point of weakness. "I'm sorry."

In the back cockpit Simms is speaking into her COM, the quick clipped voice of a veteran combat pilot, signaling for backup: "*Atreus, Atreus,* this is TROJAN. Request fire mission, flash priority, target is a *Sinadhuja* world-killer with enemy command assets aboard. Jump vectors coming now—"

Laporte's helmet pokes her in the back of the head. ALERT! it complains. EMCON VIOLATION! It doesn't like what Simms is doing, hotloading the reactor, shunting power into the ship's IFF and navigational beacons. Broadcasting targeting data on an Alliance tactical channel: a screaming, desperate plea to *shoot me.*

"*TROJAN,* Atreus." Steele's scalpel voice faint, so faint, distorted by the *Sinadhuja*'s armor and defensive jamming, by the grip of the black hole. By all these things keeping his missiles at bay. "*We have your target. Stand by for fire. Godspeed, pilots.*"

Maybe, in younger and less certain days, Laporte and Simms would have paused to say things left unsaid. To say goodbye.

But they don't need that now. They're on the same frequency. Much like the *Atreus* and the Uriel gunship, which is looking around the *Sinadhuja*'s guts with its targeting package, plotting trajectories with its navigational sensors, and telling Steele where, exactly, to fire his miracle missiles.

It's very hard to kill a *Sinadhuja*. From the outside.

In the garden, Ken makes a soft, thoughtful noise. "You knew I'd read your memories. So you let Simms and al-Alimah use you as a weapon. They leveraged Admiral Steele into cooperating with you. They used the NAGARI dreamscape to fabricate Simms abandoning you. And I believed it, because I cared about you."

Laporte grins an ant-tongued grin. She came here knowing, in a veiled way, that Simms was waiting for her. But she had no idea, all the way down, whether Steele had actually agreed to the plan. Whether his missiles were feints or fatally true.

But she knows, right now (as the first of Steele's fusion bombs jumps in ten meters off her nose and arcs off towards the back of the *Sinadhuja*'s interior) exactly what she needs to do. She needs to live. And so does Simms.

Laporte touches the stick, one last time, to line up the Uriel's cockpit with the gap in the armored jaws above.

"Eject!" In pilot code, you always say it three times, to make it real. "Eject, eject!"

She gets a nanosecond glimpse of Simms in the backseat mirror. She's grinning like an idiot.

Laporte pulls the wasp-colored handle between her legs. Her ejection seat hurls her starward, between the flashing jump-sign and corkscrewing trails of *Atreus'* missiles, up through the *Sinadhuja*'s jaws and away. She's turning as she rises, g-force snapping the acceleration sumps in the seat, and she can see another light with her, orbiting her, no, it's not an orbit, they're just flying together, co-moving.

"Simms!" she calls. "Boss!"

Down beneath them the *Sinadhuja*'s drive flares up red and massive and vomits debris and cuts out. The world-killer drops away, free falling, a mountain conjured up out of the black hole and now reclaimed by it. A flash of annihilation light blows through its hull down astern and suddenly it's geysering jets of molten metal, crumpling on itself, jump missiles darting out of the interior and curving back to re-attack with their submunitions scattering out behind them like fairy dust.

In the garden Ken says: "This is a selfish choice, Miss Laporte. What do you gain by killing me? You know they'll keep coming. You know they always win."

"Maybe." Laporte sprays him with her garden hose. He's already falling to pieces, ants sloughing off and returning to the dirt. "Maybe we'll make enough monsters to stop them."

Is that, his fading voice asks, how you want things to be? Everything honed to fight? Irrevocably weaponized?

Laporte doesn't know what to say to that. She has been a monster. But she's going to see Simms again, and when they're together, she won't feel like anything but a happy woman. Is monsterhood conditional? Like a mirror you hold up to the war around you, just long enough to win?

Everything dies. Even humanity, Laporte supposes. Maybe how you live should count for more than how long you last.

Admiral van Aken sends a soft farewell. He doesn't seem angry. More proud than anything.

Godspeed, he says. And good luck, Miss Laporte.

The *Sinadhuja*'s hull shatters. Blazes up in dirty fire and fades to ash and smelt and then the ruin of the world-killer falls away. Down below, in the accretion disk, black shapes begin to stir.

"Good kill," Simms says, like they're still back in Sol, shooting down bad Alliance pilots. Her voice is tinny over the suit radios, but very confident. "Scratch one Nemesis warship."

High above them, silhouetted against the distant bundled stars, *Atreus* has turned over. She's decelerating, burning 'up', trying to stop herself from hitting the black hole. Trying to make it back to the wormhole above.

"*TROJAN, Atreus.*" Steele quite calm and utterly polite—disappointingly unmoved to cheer. Laporte would've liked to rattle the bastard. "*We have your beacons. A search and rescue craft is on the way. Reply if able.*"

"Morrigan." Simms calling. "Morrigan, it's Boss."

"*Atreus, this is* Eris, *Federation Second Fleet.*" Another transmission. Stretched by blueshift and spiked by radiation. "*We have transited the wormhole. We are deploying tankers to assist your escape burn.*"

"*Copy you, Eris. Put your tankers on GUARD for rendezvous control.*"

"Morrigan!" Simms calls. "We're fucked!"

"What is it, Boss?"

"We got cooked pretty bad, Laporte." She sounds more disgusted than afraid. "Gamma flash. Check your rad meter."

Laporte picks the radiation alarm out of the small congress of alerts on her suit visor. It wants her to know that she's absorbed a critical dose, that she needs medical assistance, and that she should consider recording a last message for her loved ones.

"Ugh," Simms says. She makes an about-to-spit noise and then, considering her helmet, abandons it. "I'm going to have so much cancer."

Laporte dismisses the alarm and cues up an anti-emetic injection. They'll be okay. A little radiation never kept a good Federation pilot down. She starts tapping her seat thrusters, moving towards Simms, and look, Simms is already headed for her. As they pass they reach out and grab each other by their forearms so that they turn together around a common point.

"I think we'll be okay, boss," she says. She can hear the beacon of the search-and-rescue ship, howling down to them from the stars above, and the frame-shifted scream of the black-hole-eating light, far down below. "I think we'll be okay."

Simms claps her on the wrist, once and then again. "Me too, Morrigan." She's still grinning. "Me too."

FLASH FLASH FLASH
ISN BACKBREAKER FASTEST
S 0348 BAST $DATE_DYNAMIC_REFRAME
FM SECCON//BETAQ
TO ALLIANCE HIGHER

1. NEMESIS PSYWAR CHANNEL DESTROYED IN CAPELLA STRIKE BY JOINT FEDERATION/ALLIANCE ACTION
2. ALLIANCE SPECIAL ASSETS RECOVERED. DEBRIEFING PENDING. NOW IN RADIATION THERAPY ABOARD FEDERATION WARSHIP ERIS
3. LIMITED NEMESIS INCURSION NOW IN PROGRESS VEGA. SMOKE-JUMP UNITS RESPONDING. FEDERATION NAGARI TASK FORCE

RESPONDING. PRELIMINARY ESTIMATE 60% CHANCE CONTAIN-
MENT

4. FIREWALL UNITS ON STANDBY
5. SOL EXPEDITIONARY FORCE: IMMEDIATE RETASK TO VEGA FOR
   SMOKEJUMP RELIEF
6. DUE TO ENHANCED NEMESIS THREAT POSTURE, DIPLOMATIC
   RESOLUTION TO SOL REGIME REALIGNMENT ACTION IS BACK
   IN PLAY
7. MAINTAIN HIGHEST VIGILANCE. HUMANITY STANDS

Yuanyuan's Bubbles

CIXIN LIU, TRANSLATED BY CARMEN YILING YAN

1

Many people become enraptured by something or other from the moment of their births, as if they came into the world just for the delight of its company. In this way did Yuanyuan become enraptured by soap bubbles.

Yuanyuan was born with an apathetic expression on her face. She even seemed to cry as if she were discharging an obligation. The world was disappointing her greatly, it appeared.

Until, at five months old, she saw soap bubbles for the first time.

Immediately, she began to wave and kick in her mama's lap, her little eyes alight with a radiance that outshone the sun and stars, as if this was the first time she had truly seen the world.

It was noon in the northwest of China, many months since the last rain. Outside the window, the sun-scorched city billowed with dust. In this world of abnormal drought, the gorgeous apparitions of water drifting through the air were truly creatures of utmost beauty. That his little daughter could recognize their beauty gladdened Baba, who'd blown the bubbles for her. Mama, who was holding her, was very happy too. She had waived her remaining month of maternity leave; the next day, she would return to her lab for work.

2

Time passed. Yuanyuan entered the big kid class of preschool, and she still loved bubbles.

This Sunday, she was on an outing with Baba. She had a little bottle of bubble fluid in her pocket: Baba promised he'd have Mama take her up on her airplane to blow bubbles. This wasn't play-pretend; they really did go to the crude airfield on the city outskirts. The plane Mama used for her aerial seeding research was parked there.

Yuanyuan was quite disappointed. It was a battered agricultural biplane, probably from the Soviet days. Yuanyuan thought it must have been built out of old wood planks, like the hunter's hut in the forest from fairy tales. She doubted it could fly at all. But even so, this shabby plane was off limits to Yuanyuan, according to Mama.

"Today's her birthday!" said Baba. "You're already working overtime here instead of at home with her. At least let her ride on the plane. Give her some fun and excitement!"

"What fun and excitement? She weighs so much already. How many tree seeds will I have to leave on the ground?" Mama said, hauling another heavy plastic sack into the cargo hold.

Yuanyuan didn't think she was all that heavy. She screwed her face up and wailed. Mama hurried over to comfort her daughter, taking a strange object out of one of the big plastic tarp sacks on the ground. It was about the same size and shape as a carrot, pointy-headed and streamlined behind it, with a pair of cardboard tail fins stuck on its butt. It looked like a little airplane bomb, only transparent.

This might be fun. Yuanyuan reached out and touched it, only to immediately draw back: it was made of ice.

Mama pointed to a black speck at the center of the little bomb. She told Yuanyuan that it was a tree seed. "The plane drops these ice bombs from way high up, and when they fall to the ground, they stick into the soil. When spring comes, the ice melts. The water it forms helps the seed sprout and grow. If we drop lots and lots of these ice bombs, the desert will become green, and the sand won't blow into Yuanyuan's face anymore when she plays outside. Mama's research project will double the aerial afforestation survival rate in the Northwest drought areas—"

"What does a kid know about survival rates? Sheesh. Yuanyuan, let's go!" Baba picked Yuanyuan up and marched off. Mama didn't try to keep them, only quickly cupped her daughter's face in her hands one quick last time.

Yuanyuan could feel that Mama's hands were much rougher than Baba's.

From Baba's shoulder, Yuanyuan saw the "hunter's hut" take to the air with a rumble of engines. She blew a string of bubbles toward the plane and watched it disappear into the sandy ether.

Baba carried Yuanyuan out of the airfield to the roadside bus station. As they waited for a bus back into the city, she suddenly felt Baba shiver.

"Baba, are you cold?"

"No . . . Yuanyuan, didn't you hear something just then?"

"Hmm . . . I don't think so."

But Baba had heard it. There had been a low explosion, far off in the direction the plane had been flying, so distant that perhaps he registered it with a sixth sense. He jerked his head around to look back the way they'd come. In front of him and his daughter, the drought lands of the Northwest stared pitilessly toward the vault of heaven above.

3

Time flew onward. Yuanyuan entered elementary school, and she still loved bubbles.

She and Baba visited Mama's grave on Qingming Festival. Like always, she'd brought along her bottle of bubble fluid. As Baba set his flowers in front of the plain tombstone, Yuanyuan blew out a string of bubbles. Baba would have erupted, but her next words left his eyes wet with tears.

"Mama will see them!" Yuanyuan said, pointing at the bubbles floating past the gravestone.

"Child," Baba said as he hugged Yuanyuan, "you have to grow up to be like your mother, with her sense of duty and mission, with a high-minded purpose like hers!"

"I already have a high-minded purpose!" Yuanyuan yelled.

"Tell it to Baba?"

"Blow—" Yuanyuan pointed at her bubbles, already flown far into the distance— "big—*biiiig*—bubbles!"

Baba smiled sadly, shaking his head, and led his daughter away. They weren't far from where the plane had crashed a few years ago. That year, the seeds in the ice bombs dropped from the sky really did survive, growing into saplings, but the final victor had still been the endless drought. The aerially seeded forest had died to the last tree in the dry, rainless second year. Desertification marched inexorably onward.

Baba turned to look back. The setting sun stretched a long shadow behind the gravestone. The bubbles Yuanyuan had blown were all gone now, like the dreams of the woman in the grave, like the beautiful delusion of the Western Development Project.

4

Time flew onward. Yuanyuan entered middle school, and she still loved bubbles.

Today, Yuanyuan's young homeroom teacher had come for a home visit. She handed Baba a flashy, novel-looking toy gun. The physics teacher had confiscated it from Yuanyuan for playing during class, she explained. The gun had a fat barrel and a ring like an antenna loop attached to the muzzle. Baba turned it over in his hands, puzzled as to its appeal.

"It's a bubble gun," said the homeroom teacher, taking it and pulling the trigger. With a low whirr, a long string of soap bubbles shot from the small ring on the muzzle.

The teacher told Baba that Yuanyuan's grades were always the best in her year. Her biggest strength was her robust sense of creativity; the teacher had never seen such a lively-minded student before. He should cherish this seedling, she told him.

"Don't you feel that the child is a bit . . . how do I say this, a bit effervescent?" Baba asked, hefting the bubble gun.

"Hey, all the kids today are like that. Quite honestly, in this new era, being on the light and airy side isn't necessarily a flaw."

Baba sighed, cutting off the conversation with a wave of the bubble gun. He didn't think he and the homeroom teacher had much to say to each other. She was barely more than a child herself.

Once he saw the homeroom teacher off, leaving just the two of them, Baba decided to have a talk with Yuanyuan about the bubble gun. But immediately he encountered a new source of displeasure.

"You bought another one?" he said, pointing to the cell phone hanging from Yuanyuan's neck. "But you already got a new one this year!"

"No I didn't, Baba, I only changed the case! See, it keeps things fresh for me." Yuanyuan took out a flat box as she spoke. Baba opened it, revealing a row of colorful rectangles. At first glance, he thought they were a set of paints. Only upon further examination did he discover that they were twelve cell phone cases in twelve different colors.

Baba shook his head and set the box aside. "I wanted to talk to you about this . . . tendency."

Yuanyuan spotted the bubble gun in his hand and snatched it over. "Baba, I promise I won't bring it to school again!" She shot a string of bubbles at him.

"That's not what I wanted to talk about. The problem goes far deeper than that. Yuanyuan, look, you're a big girl now, and yet you still like to blow soap bubbles—"

"Is that wrong?"

"Oh, no, there's nothing wrong with that in and of itself. It's just that, like I said, your fondness reflects a certain, hmm, mental tendency."

Yuanyuan stared blankly at her father.

"It demonstrates your tendency to chase after pretty, novel, superficial things. You easily lose yourself in mirages. Being so ungrounded in reality will lead you in the wrong direction in life."

Yuanyuan looked at the soap bubbles filling the room, seeming even more puzzled. The bubbles swam tranquilly in the air like a school of transparent goldfish.

"Baba, let's talk about something more interesting!" Yuanyuan leaned against Baba's shoulder and adopted a confidential tone of voice. "Do you think our homeroom teacher is pretty?"

"I didn't notice . . . Yuanyuan, what I was saying was—"

"She's totally gorgeous!"

"I guess . . . I was about to say that—"

"Baba, you have to have noticed the way she looked at you just then, when you were talking. She was really into you!"

"Child, I swear, can't you leave off thinking about these silly things?" Baba irritably peeled his daughter's hand off his shoulder.

Yuanyuan sighed dramatically. "Oh, Baba, you've turned into one of those people who are grumpy about everything. What's the point of living if you never have anything new or interesting or exciting? You should be embarrassed, trying to be a life coach for other people."

A soap bubble drifted in front of Baba's face, then burst. He felt a puff of moist air, almost impossibly faint, and yet the ephemeral little misty drizzle granted him a moment of bliss. It made him think of his distant southern homeland, of all things. He sighed imperceptibly.

"When I was young, I chased after fantasies too. Your mother and I came here from Shanghai, so naive as to think that the Northwest would be a place where we could show the world our worth. In an unimaginably short time, we architects raised an entire, brand-new city out of the wasteland. We thought it would be our life's achievement. After we left this world, this city would stand as proof that we didn't live our lives in vain. Who could have imagined that we'd devoted our best years, and even our very lives, to nothing more than a soap bubble?"

Yuanyuan was astonished. "What do you mean, Silk Road City is a soap bubble? It's right here, rock solid. There's no way it's going to vanish with a pop, right?"

"It's about to disappear. The central government has approved the province's report and suspended all new projects to divert water to Silk Road City."

"Do they want us to die of thirst? The taps only work once every two days already, an hour and a half each time!"

"They're working out a ten-year evacuation plan right now. The entire city will be dismantled and relocated. Silk Road City will be the first city in today's world to disappear due to water shortages, a modern Loulan . . . In truth, the entire Western Development Project that once had us aflame with passion has already devolved into a nightmarish Western Mining Project. Who knows, that might be an ever bigger soap bubble."

"Wow, that's great!" Yuanyuan cheered. "We should have left this place ages ago! It's so boring here, I really can't stand it! Let's move! Move to a brand new place and start a brand new life! It's going to be amazing, Baba!"

Baba looked at his daughter silently, then stood and walked to the window. He gazed dumbly outside at the city amid yellow sand. His drooping shoulders made his silhouette suddenly appear much older.

"Baba," Yuanyuan called softly, but her father didn't respond.

Two days later, Yuanyuan's father took office as the last mayor of the fading city.

5

Yuanyuan got second place in science on her province's college entry examinations. Baba, truly overjoyed in a way that he rarely was, magnanimously asked his daughter if she had anything she wanted as a reward, even something absurd. Yuanyuan stuck her open hand, fingers spread, in his direction.

"Five . . . five of what?"

"Five bars of Diao brand clear soap." She stuck out her other hand. "Ten bags of Tide laundry powder." She flipped her hands over. "Twenty bottles of White Cat dish detergent." Last, she took out a piece of paper. "Most importantly, I need these chemicals. Buy them in the amounts I listed."

Getting the chemicals took work on her father's part. He had to ask a bureau deputy director going on a business trip to Beijing, who spent a whole day finding them all.

Once she had everything, Yuanyuan holed herself up in the bathroom for three busy days, filling a big washtub with some sort of liquid whose smell permeated into every room in the house. The fourth day, two classmates came over to deliver a custom-made hoop object more than a meter in diameter, shaped from a long piece of metal pipe pricked with small holes.

The fifth day started with a group of visitors. There were two cameramen from different news stations, and the mayor recognized an attractive lady as the hostess of an entertainment program on the provincial channel. There were also two garishly dressed fellows calling themselves adjudicators from the China branch of Guinness World Records, flown in from Shanghai the previous day. One of them said in a hoarse voice, "Mr. Mayor, your daughter—" he broke off, coughing. "The air's awfully dry here. Your daughter is about to set a world record!"

The mayor followed the others onto the apartment building's flat rooftop, where he found his daughter and several of her classmates already there. Yuanyuan was carrying the big hoop. The washtub stood in front of them, filled with the liquid she'd mixed. The two adjudicators went to work erecting two posts with unit markings along their length. Only later did the mayor learn that they were used for measuring the diameter of soap bubbles.

Once the preparations were done, Yuanyuan dipped the hoop into the washtub. When she lifted it out, it was filmed with bubble fluid. She carefully fastened the hoop to the end of a long pole, walked to the building's edge, and waved the pole so that the hoop drew a wide circle in the air, blowing an enormous soap bubble. The bubble shimmered and undulated in midair as if it were dancing. Later, he learned that it was an incredible 4.6 meters in diameter, breaking the Guinness world record of 3.9 meters previously held by Kaj Loos of Belgium.

"The composition of the bubble mixture is important, but the real trick is in this hoop," Yuanyuan said in response to the TV hostess's questions. "The guy from Belgium used an ordinary hoop to blow his bubble, while mine was made by drilling holes along the length of a piece of metal pipe, then bending it into a circle. The pipe is filled with bubble fluid, and as the big bubble forms, the fluid continuously seeps from the little holes, so that as much fluid is available to the bubble as possible. That naturally allows me to blow bigger bubbles."

"Then, do you think you can blow even bigger bubbles in the future?" asked the hostess.

"Of course! It would take research into several important factors in bubble formation, including viscosity, malleability, rate of evaporation, and surface tension. For forming super-big bubbles, the last two need the most work. Rate of evaporation needs to be lowered, since evaporation is the main reason why bubbles burst. As for surface tension . . . do you know why you can't blow bubbles with pure water?"

"Because the surface tension is too small?"

"It's actually the opposite. The surface tension of pure water is too high to trap air. For my next question, what's the relationship between a bubble's surface tension and its diameter?"

"Well, from what you've said, the smaller the surface tension, the larger the bubble?"

"Nope! Once the bubble is formed, as the bubble increases in size, it actually needs higher surface tension to maintain its walls. You can see the problem here: the surface tension of a fluid is fixed. In that case, if we want to blow really big bubbles, what problem do we need to solve?"

The hostess shook her head, lost. She was the type hired more for charisma and ease with words than for deeper comprehension. Yuanyuan seemed to realize this. "Never mind, let's blow some more big bubbles for our audience!"

And thus, several more four- and five-meter bubbles drifted in the wind high above the city. In this dry, dust-suffused world, they seemed terribly surreal, like mirages of another world.

One week later, Yuanyuan left the Northwest city of her birth and childhood for the best school of engineering in the country. She was studying nanoscience.

6

Time flew ever onward, but Yuanyuan didn't blow soap bubbles anymore.

Yuanyuan completed her bachelor's degree, master's degree, and doctorate, upon which she built a business with a speed that dizzied her father. Using a technique from her doctorate thesis as a starting point, she invented a new type of solar cell that could be manufactured at a tiny fraction of the cost of traditional monocrystalline silicon cells and adhered in mosaic fashion to completely cover the surface of a building. In just a few years, her business grew to hold assets in the hundred million range, one of the wildly successful entrepreneurships whisked along by the Nanotech East Wind.

Yuanyuan's father thus found himself in an awkward situation. In terms of career success, the daughter was now a higher authority than the father. It looked like Yuanyuan's homeroom teacher from back then was right: being on the light and airy side in thinking and personality wasn't necessarily a flaw. This was an era to make his generation grit their teeth. Success nowadays took overwhelming creative thinking; experience, hard work, a sense of purpose, and so on were no longer decisive factors. Moreover, single-mindedness and solemnity now looked like foolishness.

"I haven't felt this way in a long time," said the mayor to his daughter, standing on the broad exit terrace in front of the National Center for the Performing Arts. "That was the best performance I've ever heard. The singers really were better than the big three of the olden days."

Yuanyuan knew that opera was one of her father's few pleasures. She'd taken advantage of his business trip to Beijing to invite him to hear a performance by the world's three best tenors of the new generation, given in honor of the impending Olympics.

"I'd have bought the best seats in the house if I'd known. I was afraid you'd call me profligate again, so I just bought two medium-range seats."

"How much did they cost?" Baba asked offhandedly.

"They were much cheaper than before. I think they were 28,000 yuan each."

"Ah . . . wait, what?!"

Seeing her father's wide-eyed, slack-jawed expression, Yuanyuan laughed. "If they made you feel in a way you haven't for a long time, even 28,000 yuan was worth it. Look at this performance center. Why would the government have invested billions in it, if not to help people achieve or recover some kind of emotion through art?"

"Maybe you're right, but I still hope you can spend your money in more meaningful ways. Yuanyuan, I want to talk to you about something related to Silk Road City. Can you invest in one of its municipal projects?"

"What is it?"

"We want to build a large-scale water treatment plant. It'll raise the city's water recycling efficiency by an enormous amount. In addition, it will use solar power to desalinate water from the salt lakes. If this system can be realized, Silk Road City will be able to survive on a reduced scale. It won't have to disappear entirely."

"How much will it cost?"

"By our preliminary plans, about 1.6 billion yuan. We have sources for most of the required funds already, but we can't get our hands on the money for a long time. I'm afraid it might be too late by then. That's why we need you to make an initial investment of about a hundred million."

"Baba, I can't. That's all the liquid assets I have right now, and I wanted to use them for a research project—"

Father raised a hand to break off his daughter's words. "Never mind, then. Yuanyuan, I don't want to hurt your business one bit. To be honest, I hadn't wanted to ask you in the first place. Your investment would break even, guaranteed, but the profit would be miniscule."

"Hah, I wasn't thinking about that, Baba. My project would be even worse. Never mind profit, there's no way it would even earn back the investment!"

"Are you doing theoretical research?"

"No, but it's not practical research, either. I'm doing it for the fun."

" . . . "

"I'm going to develop a super-surfactant. I've come up with the name already, FlySol. Its viscosity and elasticity will be orders of magnitudes better than any liquid existing, and its rate of evaporation will be just a fraction of a percent of glycerin's. And this surfactant will have a special superpower—its surface tension will change depending on the thickness of the liquid layer and the surface's degree of curvature, anywhere between one hundredth and ten thousand times the surface tension of water."

"What is it for?" asked Father in horror. He already knew the answer, but he was afraid to believe it.

The young multi-millionaire put an arm around her father's shoulder. "To blow—big—*biiiig*—bubbles!"

"You're joking, right?"

Yuanyuan looked at the lights of Chang'an Avenue, silent for a long time. "Who knows? Maybe my entire life is a big joke. But, Baba, I don't think there's anything wrong with that. For a person to use their entire life for a joke is a sort of purpose too."

"Spending a hundred million yuan blowing bubbles? Is there any point?" her father spoke as if he were in a dream.

"There's no point. It's fun, that's all. I've got to say, though, compared to the city your generation spent tens of billions building, only to have to tear it down, my extravagance doesn't amount to much."

"But you can save the city right this moment! It's your city too. You were born there. You grew up there. But you're using that money to blow soap bubbles! You're—you're really too selfish!"

"I'm living my own life. Selfless sacrifice isn't always enough to change the path of history. Your own city proves it!"

Father and daughter remained in silence until Yuanyuan steered their car onto Chang'an Avenue.

"I'm sorry, Baba," Yuanyuan said softly.

"These days, I keep remembering the past, leading you by your tiny little hand. It was such a wonderful time." In the light, Father's eyes glimmered, as if damp.

"I know I've disappointed you. You always wanted me to be someone like Mama. If I could live two lifetimes, I'd use one of them to do what you want, give everything for duty and mission. But, Baba, I only have this one life."

Father didn't reply. Near the end of the silent drive, Yuanyuan took out a large envelope and handed it to him.

"What is it?" Father asked, uncomprehending.

"Housing deeds and a key. I bought you a villa by Lake Tai. You'll be able to go back to the south after you retire."

Father gently slid the envelope back in her direction. "No, child, I'm going to live out the rest of my life in what remains of Silk Road City. Your mother and I have buried our youth and dreams there. I can't leave."

Beijing glittered to its heart's content in the summer night. Gazing at the gorgeous sea of lights, Yuanyuan and her father both thought of soap bubbles. What was this boundless radiance trying to show to them: the weight of a life, or the weightlessness?

7

One day, two years later, the mayor received a call in his office from his daughter.

"Happy birthday, Baba!"

"Ha, Yuanyuan, is that you? Where are you?"

"Not far from where you are. I've brought a birthday present!"

"Hey, it's been years since I remembered my birthday. Come home at noon, then. It's been a month since I've gone home myself. There's just the housekeeper there to keep an eye on things."

"No, I'll give you the gift right now!"

"I'm at work. The weekly city council meeting's about to start."

"Not a problem! Open the window and look up!"

The sky today was clear in every direction, a limpid blue, rare weather for the area. The rumble of an engine came from the air; the mayor saw that an airplane was slowly circling in the sky above the city, striking against the blue backdrop.

"Baba, I'm on the plane right now!" Yuanyuan shouted through the phone.

It was an old-fashioned, propeller-driven biplane. In the sky, it looked like a giant bird gliding lazily. Time flashed backward; a familiar sensation struck the mayor like lightning. He shivered all over, as he had done twenty years ago. His daughter had asked him if he was cold.

"Yuanyuan, what—what are you doing?"

"Here's the gift, Baba, pay attention to the bottom of the plane!"

The mayor had noticed earlier that a big hoop hung from the body of the plane. Its diameter was greater than the length of the plane; clearly, it had unfolded into position only after the plane took to the air. Taken together, the plane and the hoop looked like a flying ring. Later, he'd learn that the hoop was constructed like the one Yuanyuan had used to break the Guinness World Record, made of a tube of lightweight metal filled with the nigh-supernatural FlySol. A film of FlySol stretched across the hoop, and innumerable small holes allowed FlySol to continuously flow out of the thin tube that formed the hoop.

An astounding sight appeared. Behind the giant hoop, a bubble was emerging! Refracting sunlight, its form wavered at the edge of visibility. The bubble swelled rapidly; soon, the plane compared to it was only a sesame seed on top of a transparent watermelon.

In the marketplace below, everyone had stopped to look up. People were starting to run out of the city government headquarters building to watch.

The plane circled slowly above the city, tugging the enormous bubble behind it. The bubble had slowed in its growth, but not completely. Gradually, it came to occupy half the sky. At last, it broke loose from the hoop beneath the airplane, floating independently in the air.

"This is my present, Baba!" Yuanyuan shouted excitedly through the phone.

Huge patches of light shimmered in the blue heavens, as if the entire sky were a slick piece of cellophane being crinkled by invisible hands under the sun. On close inspection, the flashes of light delineated an enormous, transparent sphere that took up most of the sky. The people below had to turn their heads nearly one hundred and eighty degrees to see it in its entirety. It looked as if the mirror of heaven were casting a crystalline reflection of the Earth below.

The city began to grow agitated. Traffic jams formed in the thoroughfares.

The enormous bubble slowly descended from the sky. Once it was at a sufficiently low altitude, the people below could even see the city's skyscrapers mirrored on the bubble's surface; as it undulated in the wind, the buildings twisted and distorted, like a kelp forest under the sea. The broad bubble membrane pressed down inexorably. People instinctively shielded their heads with their arms. When the bubble touched the ground, those exposed outside felt a brief itch on their faces as their bodies passed through the membrane.

The bubble hadn't popped. Instead, it had formed a spherical dome nearly ten kilometers in diameter with the ground. The city and the surrounding industrial plants were now trapped in the bubble!

"It wasn't on purpose, it really wasn't!" Yuanyuan said into the camera. "Under normal conditions, the bubble would have floated away in the breeze. Who knew today's wind would be so much weaker than usual? That's why it fell and covered the city!"

The mayor watched the emergency report, which had interrupted the city television station's normal programming. He saw that his daughter was wearing a leather aviation jacket, open at the front to reveal a blue work uniform underneath. Beneath her was the old-fashioned biplane . . . time flashed backward again. *So alike, they look so alike* . . . the mayor's heart melted, tears spilling from his eyes.

Two hours later, the mayor and the newly established emergency team drove to the bubble wall at the city outskirts. Yuanyuan and several of her engineers were there, well ahead of them.

"Baba, isn't my superbubble amazing?" Yuanyuan had lost her earlier panic, her face alight with inappropriate excitement.

The mayor paid no mind to his daughter, raising his head to consider the bubble's surface. The vast sheet of membrane shimmered in rainbow colors under sunlight, intricate patterns of diffraction on its surface shifting and morphing hypnotically in a bewitching sea of all the universe's colors. The membrane was transparent, so that the outside world seen through it was coated with a layer of iridescence too. A certain distance up, the iridescence disappeared; from the air, it would be impossible to see the membrane.

The mayor reached out a hand and carefully touched the superbubble. The back of his hand itched, very faintly: it was already on the other side of the bubble. The membrane might only be a few molecules thick. He drew his hand back through; the membrane instantaneously returned to its original form. The pattern of iridescence there was unchanged, as if it had never been interrupted.

The others also began to touch the membrane, then waved their hands in an attempt to tear it, then at last devolved into flailing punches and kicks . . . but none of it made a difference to the membrane. Every assault passed through the bubble without resistance, after which the membrane restored itself perfectly. With a wave of his hand, the mayor halted everyone's futile efforts. He then pointed to the highway in the distance; the others saw that the traffic on the highway was passing through the membrane undisrupted, even at their high speeds.

"It's like a soap bubble membrane: solid objects can pass through, but not air," said Yuanyuan.

"Air not being able to pass through is the problem. The air quality in the city is rapidly deteriorating," the mayor said, glaring at his daughter.

Everyone looked up and saw that an enormous white dome-shaped cap had appeared in the sky above the city. The membrane was trapping the smoke from the city and industrial plants in the mold of the superbubble. If one were to observe the city from a distance right now, perhaps they'd be seeing a towering hemisphere of milky white.

"We may need to shut down the power plant and the chemical plant to slow down the rate of pollutant release," said the leader of the emergency team. "But the most serious problem is the rising temperatures inside the bubble. Right now, the city is effectively inside a sealed greenhouse without air exchange with the outside world. It's the middle of summer, and the heat from the sun is building up quickly. According to our calculations, the temperature inside the bubble will eventually peak at sixty degrees Celsius!"

"Up to now, what methods have we tried for destroying the superbubble?" asked the mayor.

"An hour earlier, we had army aviation people fly their helicopters through the top of the bubble, trying to use the propellers to tear it open, but it didn't work," answered an officer from the local garrison. "Then we set explosives where the bubble met the ground. The explosion only made the bubble ripple a while, without causing any damage. Even more incredibly, the membrane instantaneously extended down into the blast crater, traveling right along the bottom without any gap!"

"How long will it take for the bubble to burst naturally?" the mayor asked Yuanyuan.

"Bubble rupture is primarily caused by evaporation of the fluid membrane. This substance has an extremely slow rate of evaporation—even with sunny weather, the bubble will take five or six days to pop," Yuanyuan answered. To her father's outrage, she sounded full of pride.

"Then we'll have to evacuate everyone," the leader of the emergency team said, sighing.

The mayor shook his head. "I won't take that step until we absolutely have to."

"There's another way," said an environmental specialist. "Hurry and have a lot of long tubes made, the wider the better. Place the tubes with one end outside the bubble and a high-power ventilation fan on the other end, and we can exchange air with the outside world."

"Haha—" Yuanyuan started to laugh, startling everyone around her. Surrounded by angry looks, she was laughing so hard she couldn't stand upright. "That idea's— that's hilarious! Haha—"

"This is all your fine work!" the mayor thundered. "You're going to take responsibility and pay back all the losses you've caused the city!"

Yuanyuan looked up at the sky and stopped laughing. "I know, I'll pay up. But I just thought of a simple way to pop the superbubble—burning. Dig a trench one to two hundred meters long where the bubble meets the ground, pour it full of fuel, then light it. The fire will make the membrane evaporate much faster. The bubble should burst after about three hours."

The mayor ordered the emergency team to do as Yuanyuan explained. A wall of fire more than a hundred meters long sprung up on the city outskirts. As the row of furious flames licked at the bottom of the superbubble, strange colors and shapes shimmered in the membrane. The patterns of color revealed that the FlySol from other parts of the bubble was rushing over to replace what had evaporated from the fire, as if the portion being burned had become a giant whirlpool, sucking gorgeous, beguiling floods of color from every direction to disappear into the flames. Their black smoke pressed upward along the bubble's inner surface, gathering into an enormous black hand pressing down, terrifying the millions of city-dwellers within the superbubble.

Three hours later, the bubble popped. People in the city heard a soft tinkle of breaking in the space between heaven and earth, crisp and clear and echoing for a long time after, as if a string in the instrument of the universe had been very gently plucked.

"It's weird, Baba, you didn't blow your top like I thought you would," Yuanyuan said. She and her father stood on the roof of the city government headquarter building, watching the superbubble burst.

"I've been considering something . . . Yuanyuan, I'd like you to answer a few questions for me seriously."

"About the superbubble?"

"Yes. I want to know, since the bubble membrane is impermeable to air from the outside, would the superbubble also be able to retain moist air on the inside?"

"Of course. In fact, toward the end of FlySol's development, I thought of a possible practical application for the superbubbles: giant greenhouses. They could form miniature climate zones in winter, providing temperature and humidity levels suitable for crop growth over large areas. Of course, that would require longer-lasting bubbles."

"The second question: can you make a superbubble float a long way on the wind, for, say, a few thousand kilometers?"

"Not a problem. Heat from the sun accumulates in the bubble, so the air inside expands and creates buoyancy like a hot air balloon's. The superbubble today fell only because it was formed too low in altitude, with too weak of a breeze."

"The third question: can you ensure that the superbubbles burst after a specific length of time?"

"That's doable. We'd only need to adjust the concentration of one of the ingredients to change the solution's rate of evaporation."

"The last question: given enough investment money, can you blow millions, or even billions, of superbubbles?"

Yuanyuan's eyes widened in surprise. "Billions? Heavens, what for?"

"Picture this in your mind: above the faraway sea, countless superbubbles are forming. Propelled by the strong winds of the stratosphere, they'll set sail on a long journey to ultimately arrive in the sky above northwest China, then burst in unison, scattering the humid ocean air they formed around into our dry air . . . yes, with superbubbles, we can bring in moist air from the seas to the Northwest! In other words, we can bring in rain!"

Shock and emotion left Yuanyuan speechless for a time. She could only look at her father, stunned.

"Yuanyuan, you gave me a glorious birthday present. Who knows, today might prove the birthday of the Northwest too!"

The cool wind of the outside world was blowing over the city. Without the superbubble to confine it, the white dome of smog above was slowly coming apart in the breeze. In the eastern sky, an odd rainbow had appeared. When the superbubble burst, the FlySol in the membrane had scattered into the air to form it.

8

The enormous engineering project to aerially divert water into western China took ten years.

In these ten years, vast sky-nets were built in China's southern waters. The nets were constructed from thin tubes covered in tiny holes. Each eye in the net was hundreds, even thousands, of meters in diameter, similar to the hoop that had blown the superbubble ten years ago, and each net had thousands of such apertures.

There were two types of sky-net: land-mounted and aerial. The land-mounted sky-nets were placed along the coastline, while the aerial sky-nets hung from giant tethered balloons at high altitude, several kilometers above. In the South China Sea and the Bay of Bengal, the sky-nets ran continuously for more than two thousand kilometers along the coast and above the sea, and were nicknamed "The Bubble Wall of China."

The day the aerial water diversion system started up for the first time, the thin tubes in the sky-net filled with FlySol, forming a membrane of fluid over each aperture. Strong, moist sea wind blew into the sky-net, forming countless superbubbles, each kilometers in diameter. The bubbles broke loose from the sky-net one after another, rising in droves to higher skies. Ascending into the atmosphere, they followed the air currents onward, even as more bubbles steadily blew forth from the sky-net. Great flocks of superbubbles glided majestically inland, wrapped around the humid air of the seas. They drifted past the Himalaya Mountains, past the Greater Southwest, into the skies of the Northwest. Between the South China Sea and Bay of Bengal, and northwest China, two rivers of bubbles thousands of kilometers long had formed!

9

Two days after the aerial water diversion system began full-scale operation, Yuanyuan flew from the Bay of Bengal to the capital of a Northwest province. When she stepped off the plane, she saw only a round moon suspended in the night sky: the bubbles that had set out from the ocean had yet to arrive. In the city, crowds were out under the moonlight. Yuanyuan got out of the car at the central square, squeezing her way into the crowd too, to wait fervently along with them.

Even when midnight came, the night sky remained unchanged. The crowd began to disperse as it had the previous two days, but Yuanyuan didn't leave. She knew the bubbles would arrive tonight for certain. She sat on a bench, at the edge of sleep and wakefulness, when she suddenly heard someone cry out.

"Heavens, why are there so many moons?"

Yuanyuan opened her eyes. She really did see a river of moons in the night sky! The countless moons were the reflections in countless massive bubbles. Unlike the real moon, they were all crescents, some curving up and some curving down, all of them so translucent and jewel-like that the real moon seemed plain in comparison. Only by its unchanging location could it be distinguished from the mighty current of moons crossing the sky.

From that point on, the sky over northwest China became the sky of dreams.

During the day, the drifting bubbles were hard to see. There were just the reflections off the membranes, everywhere in the blue sky, that made it look like the surface of a lake rippling under the sunlight. On the ground, enormous but faint shadows traced the slow passage of the bubbles. The most beautiful moments were at dawn and dusk, when the rising or setting sun on the horizon would limn the river of bubbles in the sky with radiant gold.

But these lovely scenes didn't last for long. The bubbles above popped one after another. More bubbles were rolling in, but clouds were beginning to gather in the sky, obscuring the bubbles.

Next, in the season that had been driest of all in previous years, a slow, steady drizzle drifted down from the sky.

Amid the rain, Yuanyuan arrived at the city of her birth. After ten years of evacuation, Silk Road City had become quiet and empty. Unoccupied skyscrapers stood silently in the rain.

Yuanyuan noticed that these structures hadn't truly been abandoned; they were well-preserved, the glass in the windows unbroken. The whole city seemed to be deep in slumber, waiting for the day of revival it knew would come.

The rain tamped down the dust, leaving the air fresh and pleasant. Raindrops tickled deliciously cool on the face. Yuanyuan strolled along streets she knew well, streets through which her father had led her by her small hand countless times, on which countless soap bubbles she'd blown had scattered. A childhood song resounded in Yuanyuan's heart.

Suddenly, she realized that she really could hear the song. The sun had set now, and in the city descended into night, only one window shone with light from within. It belonged to the second floor of an ordinary apartment building, her home, and the song came from there.

Yuanyuan stopped in front of the building. The surroundings were clean and well-kept. There was even a vegetable patch, the plants in it growing heartily. A tool cart stood to one side, fitted with a big metal bucket, clearly used to carry water from elsewhere for the plants. Despite the obscuring darkness, one could sense the breath of life here. In the dead silence of the empty city, it beckoned to Yuanyuan like an oasis in the desert.

Yuanyuan climbed the well-swept stairs and gently pushed open the door to her home. Her father was reclining on the couch, his hair grizzled under the lamplight, contently humming the old children's song. He held the little bottle that Yuanyuan had used to carry bubble liquid as a child, and the little plastic hoop, and he was blowing a string of multicolored bubbles.

Originally published in Chinese in *Science Fiction World,* 2004.

Union
TAMSYN MUIR

The wives come strapped ten to a transport, hands stamped by some Customs wonk. Their fingernails are frilled and raised freckles stipple each arm in shades of red and orange. Permit tags list their names: Mary. Moana. Ruth. Myrrh. Huia. Anna. Iridium. Coffee. Kōkako.

The Franckton crofters stand and watch from behind the barrier. They've knocked off midday work to come. You can practically see the pong of hot mulch and melting boot elastomeric coming off them. There's even a man there from the *New Awhitu Listener* to take pictures.

Dripping sweat, the Customs detail sign off their quarantine. The wives seem indifferent to the heat. The air from the transport ruffles the thin plaits of their hair, each strand with its own line of fine bulges like a polyp. Everyone is close enough to see.

"If the Listener links any of those photos," Simeon's telling the photographer, "you're dog tucker, mate." Simeon's got the gist of it already. The man knows Simeon's reputation and is timidly pressing *Delete*.

The Mayor signs the receipt of goods slowly. She's asking questions, gesturing at the wives, but she's not getting answers, just filework and shrugging. The Ministry men take the tablet with the signature and you can tell they just want to get the hell out of there before something happens.

Later on when the croft pores over the paperwork, they discover the wives are lichen splices. No one's ever heard of it.

When the news had broken that the Ministry was awarding them wives, the relief was so great in Franckton that it was more pain than pleasure. They'd spent the last fifty years incubating on Governmental loan and mortgaging over half the harvest each time. A lot of beers got sunk during all the frantic budgeting that came subsequently. The staunchest Union crofters forgot to do anything but tab up how many generations it would take before all they'd be paying for was the foetal scan.

Only Simeon was hostile; nobody was surprised. "It's a disgrace," he kept on saying. "It's a nothing. We're getting gypped. We're the highest-revenue croft and they're shutting us up, they're paying us off, the next time we don't say how high when they say jump we'll get our subsidy slashed and you bastards are falling over yourselves to lick their arse . . . "

He got told off by the Mayor for whinging. The sentiment was that there were only twenty wives to go round and he'd been assigned one and heaps of crofters hadn't. It wasn't as though they were all going to receive rose-splice wives and free beer and skittles. Of course it was a sop. It was a harvest cycle, and the Ministry wanted to keep them sweet so that there wouldn't be a tanty chucked over the price of wheat or onions or oats come the buying time. All of Franckton was going into this with their eyes open; they weren't naive . . . But they still planned a picnic and a pōhiri and someone agreed to sing for the welcome and everyone getting a wife washed their shirt.

When the wives finally landed and they got their first eyeful, they knew there wasn't going to be a picnic or a pōhiri. They took up their tines and trudged back to the bunds without preamble. Only Simeon, by way of expressing his feelings, threw a big handful of grit at one of the whirring transports. It exploded into a cloud of dusty shrapnel. Some of the crofters cringed, but nothing happened.

The lichen-splice wives are pale and dry. Nobody really knows what to do with them. The last batch of kids had been nine years ago, with a bunch of hardy poppy wives and their minders. They were all hard cases and laughed and made jokes during the incubation, like poppy-wives should. The Mayor was getting treated for germline trouble with her chromosomes 5 and 10, so the Ministry had made them pay through the nose for gene insurance and they'd all been sore about it, but not too sore because it was the Mayor and the croft begrudged her nothing. Simeon had squabbled and said there should be a lawsuit. Some of the crofters agreed, but then there were children to take care of and nobody did anything.

The first thing the crofters hate is the names. Their wives have been given croft names, and that's insult to injury, somehow. It's ingratiating. They should have had city names and all been Florence or Hannah or Candy. So they all become "wife" by common fiat.

They seem obliging enough, but they never speak, except sometimes "Yes" or "No." They move slowly in the Franckton heat, but unmindingly. They are slow in general to walk or to carry. They lid their eyes heavily when they talk and keep their mouths a little open, sometimes flickering their tongues.

Simeon holds forth in the pub almost every night about them. Most of the croft complaints are about how their wife stares or can't cook the tea right or is stupid, or off-putting, or intractable, but Simeon goes further than that. "I don't want to incubate with some knock-off government sack," he says of his wife. "She looks like a spastic. She looks like a trisomy hutch."

Some of the croft look away but they don't protest, because you don't with Simeon, it's more trouble than it's worth. Simeon says, "I bloody well mean it. And I tell you what, if they don't bear good kids and look after them right, I'm blowing this wide open. I'll strike. I want our next lot to have a future, not go on cringing like mutts for crusts. If all the crofts got up off their bums and stood together we'd have the world on a plate. Look at what we get when we don't fight for it! Christ, look."

Outside the pub and across the street two of the wives stand in the blue evening shade. Simeon stabs a finger in their direction. They do not chat or relax: they stare, first at each other, then at a crack in the daub house, then at a drying clag of mulch, then at each other again. Their tongues flicker in their mouths.

"I tell you what," Simeon says again, "they scare me to death. They're not right. We got fobbed off with something weird, and we're just shutting up and taking it like we always do."

One of the crofters has the bright idea to tell Simeon that he should have let the photographs go live, that everyone should have seen what had been done to Franckton. This crofter gets pranged with the beer mat.

"Don't be stupid," snaps Simeon, settling back. "We've got our bloody pride."

Franckton has better results with the wives in the fields. The sun leaves white patches on their skin if they stay out too long in it, but the Mayor gets the children to weave them big scratchy shapeless hats. The wives have been taught to say, "Thank you, Aunty," and for each hat a wife intones "Thank you, Aunty," before subsiding back into silence. They're still slow out there on the bunds, but they are just as slow heaving the stones between them as they are walking as they are everything else. It is simply how they move. They crouch down and poke back rocks into the spillways with their square, dry hands. They build back the gullies and do not care. When the children come around with the water they take one gourd together and sip miniature sips, darting their tongues inside the neck of the bottle. The other crofters take enormous gulps and dump the rest down the backs of their hot, dirty necks.

It gets to some of the croft. Nobody dares to be as bad as Simeon, who calls his wife "you" and who swaps sharp words with the Mayor about it almost daily, but there's loads of complaint. The wives don't learn. They don't settle. They're lazy. They make everyone uneasy. Plenty of splice wives are good for doing chores and croft work—so the catalogues always promise—and do it cheerfully and well, but these ones don't, and it's yet another black eye for them.

When Laura says in the pub, "I like my wife," everyone's surprised into silence before they bust a gut laughing. "Piss off! I don't mind her. I wouldn't want one that was talking my ear off all the time. And she sings sometimes . . . She's not so bad."

She gets ragged for this daily, but sticks to it: "Mary's a good girl," she goes on saying staunchly. "She gives it heaps, just doesn't rush. Can't believe you're all moaning about how they don't have tea on the table when the clock strikes six. My God! You lot don't know you're born."

Those with wives start noticing that, wherever they go, a fine leafy build-up appears on the walls or countertops where they work. This is easily wiped off with a damp cloth, but causes no end of alarm. The build-up is a thin crust—a substrate with miniature flakes—dusty green in some houses, shrillingly orange in others. Simeon spits the dummy entirely and makes his wife sleep in the shed, and at this point nobody blames him, he's sent a sample to the big lab in Awhitu and it matches the wives' DNA. Like they're shedding, the pharmacist had said helpfully. "Like they're moldy," said Simeon. "Bloody hell. It's not clean. It's filthy. It's not right. They oughtn't to, it's a decay, they're off-cut bargain-bin splices—" And he calls them a lot worse than *off-cuts* or *bargain bin splices*.

He sends a letter to the Ministry representative, a formal one, with a couple veiled threats chucked in. Other crofters are angry too, and they sign it. The Mayor won't.

"It's harmless," she says wearily, "it's a nothing. Just rub a bit of ti-tree extract on the counter, the pharmacy let me have it for cheap. And if you're making Coffee sleep in the shed you better not whinge about her cooking."

But Simeon won't let his wife do any cooking now. She shouldn't touch food, he says. Shouldn't touch anything they're not sure about. As per usual, some of the croft privately agrees, but also wishes he'd stop being a bit of a tosser.

The doctor comes to give the crofters their health certificates and the Mayor her latest injections. They can't apply for the DNA license otherwise. He frowns over the Mayor's scans—again—and gives her some chromosome duplicant on the sly, in exchange for a feed and some cash. "I'm sorry, Barbs," he says. "You'll be paying the premium again for the license."

"But I'm not contributing," she says, surprised. "Not after the last time. Didn't we put that down on the form?"

"Doesn't matter; still shows up on your insurance record, I'm afraid. It's a generational issue. It's not just your license, it's all of Franckton's."

"That is daylight robbery," says the Mayor, "not a deterrent."

"It's a damned shame is what it is," says the doctor, "but there's nothing you or I could've done about it. At least you're not renting the cow to get the milk this time, eh?"

It's true. They're not coughing up for wife costs. Simeon still writes savage letters to the croft's Parliamentary manager but now they're getting answered by auto-message. They've got to take out a loan against the harvest, which stings, and nobody lets the Mayor put her personal savings in to help, but there's softer words about the wives when the croft thinks about all the money they're saving. Fewer people laugh at Laura. There's enough to pay for a couple of multiples in kids. The last generation born of the whānau is old enough to babysit, but now there's the wives to do the care, so they can stay at school instead. Not one crofter has got to stay at school past the age of twelve before. An out-of-towner can't visit Franckton now without getting buttonholed and skited to for half an hour about their good fortune. They book the extraction and the foetal care unit for Christmas.

The weather gets hotter and hotter. The wives are in trouble.

A pruinose bloom settles on the northern oats bund. A feathery patina is discovered on the uppermost parts of the stalk—none on the roots—and it can be wiped off in much the same way as the house crust. The wives stand around dispassionately, hands stuck in their aprons, just watching. The croft explodes in tight-lipped fury. They call a meeting at the public house before the heat of the morning's even in ripeness and everyone's there but the children and wives.

"Here is what we know," says the Mayor. "The growth isn't parasitic. The crop isn't spoiling—yet. We've probably caught this in time. We'll take the girls off bund duty and go on from there."

"That's not what *I* know," says Simeon.

He slams his mattock down on the table, in full flight. "Here's what *I* know," he says. "I know that we paid *twenty thousand* for seed DNA that wouldn't get heat rot or spore. I know that we've been bled dry in licenses and mito checkers and quarantines and chromosome therapies, and that's been long as I live, and I know that we're bloody indentured slaves—" ("Too right," says somebody) "—and that these wives, they looked nice on paper but they're sabotage, they're Ministry sabotage, trying to keep us down. Stop the crofts growing out of control. We've mortgaged those bloody oats and if they bloody spoil then we're dead bloody meat."

He says this very fast. The Mayor says, "Simeon—"

"We should ship them back now and to hell with the incubation, show them we don't take hand-outs, eh," he says, voice rising. "We don't take hand-outs! We don't take pay-offs, we don't get tricked!"

A brief pause chills the air. "You're paranoid, mate," says Laura, and a mad hubbub breaks out.

There's lots of noise. The crofters all shout to be heard. If Parliament wants the croft to stay small, why give them incubation rights? Well, it's a con, isn't it. Remember the story about the old horse. The gift horse, the Greeks. Why would the other crofts stand with them? The other crofts look out for themselves. Simeon's going to get everyone arrested. Laura's got her head in the sand. Simeon's right. Everyone's a coward. They should send back the wives. They shouldn't send back the wives. They should have sent back the wives long ago. "If those oats fail I'll send them back in a box," bellows Simeon.

The Mayor whacks one big, hard hand down on the table. Everything on it rattles percussively.

"Shut up!" she roars. "Shut up, all of you!"

"You act like serfs, you get treated like serfs!" Simeon's still ranting. "You all go along with it, you all *let it happen!*"

The Mayor yanks off her shoe, and she throws it square at Simeon. It clips him lightly on the shoulder. He turns very red. The quiet that ensues is greasy and awful. The breath of each crofter comes slight and small, so as not to make too much of a noise.

"I won't have such talk," says the Mayor slowly. "You besmirch us. You take away from the whole croft. You do us damage."

The silence squirms like a child. The croft becomes aware that the wives have gathered in the doorway. They stand there with dull, slabby faces and their floppy hats in their hands. Only their tongues seem awake, spasmodically flicking behind their teeth, pattering against the inside of each cheek.

One of the wives says, "We're sorry, Aunty," and the rest follow in a monotone chant, "We're sorry, Aunty," all slightly out of time. Simeon's wife says it last.

"I'm bloody out," says Simeon, and he shoulders past them, stumbling. The door of the public house rattles on the doorframe when he slams it.

"Do you know what you're sorry for?" says the Mayor, addressing the wives now. The wives do not speak. Some of them look at her, or out of the window, or at the floor, or at a fixed point nowhere in particular. Not a one blinks. The wheezing air conditioner ruffles the thin whippy polyps of their braids. The Mayor repeats, sternly: "There's no use in being sorry for no reason. Wives are meant to help, not to cause trouble. There's mold all over the oats. Do you know how to stop it?"

There is a long silence. One of the wives ventures, "It is very dry," and the other wives pick up on this non-sequitur eagerly, blandly repeating: "It is very dry," and one wife, Laura's, says: "Getting drier."

An impatient sigh rises from the crowd.

"Stay out of the fields," says the Mayor. "You can go out and take over the goats from the children. They can spend their afternoon in the classroom instead. No going near the crops. Is that clear?"

By the blank expressions, it is not. But when the Mayor repeats, "Stay out the fields for now. Understand?" it's greeted with a chorus of *yes, Aunty*. Then they file out of the building and stand around in the shade in an awkward gaggle. Some of them stare through the window. The crofters think it's no use.

The wives are right about one thing: it's dry and getting drier, and the dry season hasn't even started. There's no rainfall and no sign of one to come. The water levels in the Franckton tanks dip lower and lower.

It takes a few days, but the croft manages to wipe the crust off the oat spikelets without too much difficulty. Some of it succumbs, gets blotchy or the stem thickens and blights beyond repair—and the lack of rain's not helping—but after a few days of holding their breaths they start to exhale. No further bloom forms. The kids all have a moan about extra school.

The wives drift around and keep watch over Franckton's goats. There are only so many goats, and really most of the goats spend their time hiding in the goat ark away from the sun. The wives cluster in the shade and listlessly fold laundry, or don't pretend to do anything at all but stare at the dust and the sky and the goat ark. They are unperturbed by the stifling heat and the grit whipping up everyone else's sleeves.

They'll harvest the standing grain the moment it's ready. There's no worry that it won't be dry. The onions will come later. It's another cost to get the silos and augers cleaned and tested, but when the results come in clean the croft wipes the sweat off their brow and gets the grain in. Everyone's busy driving the trucks over from the depot, or checking up on the old harvester, talking about the price of phosphines, and nobody has time to worry about the goats or the wives.

Nobody even notices the goat's sick. It just keels over one day. They find it with three of the wives clustered around, three matching expressions of pallid bemusement.

There is a fine crumbly crust all over the dead goat's head. Wispy filaments are clustered thickly around its ears and damp, flared nostrils, protruding in bunches that deform the skin from beneath. Tiny sprigs sprout from each cornea of the bubbly blind eyes. The mouth's full. Most of the growths are around the skull, though there are raised, crinkly plates of lichen painting the moist belly and anus.

All the croft gets out of the bunds without even scraping their boots. The only ones not in the public house are the vet and the vet assistant, checking and testing the rest of the stock. Everyone sits around, hats squeezed tight between their knees, hands quietly wrung together.

"I'll do it," says Simeon haggardly.

None of the croft answer. He says, "First crop, now stock. We've lost thousands if that herd's gone. I always said we paid too much to get them in utero, but they're good uncloned milch goats." Everyone remains silent. "And it's not just money. There's us to think about as well—us and the young ones."

When nobody says a word, not a word, he shouts: "You bastards. Pull finger already. Don't make me make all the decisions when you're just as scared as I am."

The Mayor sets down the grainy photos of the dead goat and says, "Don't tell us what we already know, Simeon. Make a proposal."

"Single shot to the back of the head," says Simeon.

Laura rises with red clutched fists, spluttering, but the crofters around her yank her down into her seat. The Mayor says, "We could send them back—"

"How long will that take? It's days and days for the ambo to get through. They needed to be out of here yesterday. "

Someone else suggests turning them loose, taking them out of the boundary and into the dusts, and the Mayor says shortly, "I wouldn't turn a dog loose into that," and Simeon says, "What if they got to another croft, for Chrissakes? Don't pass the buck. It's our problem. It's not our fault but it's our bloody problem."

Laura barks, "You can't be serious."

"Deadly. You come up with a better plan, then. Go on." When another crofter says that they'll get arrested for this, they'll get the officers in, Simeon laughs mirthlessly. "That's what you're bleating about? The plod getting us for property damage? The Ministry signed them over to us. If it's the inquest you're worried about, by God, just let me take the rap. I've been wanting my day in court for years. None of the rest of you will get blood on your hands, I'll put them down. I'm not watching our stock die and our kids get sick and us bled dry for doctor bills—God, I could kill them all!" he ejaculates. "It's what they wanted all along, they sent us toxic waste!"

He takes off his hat and he scrunches it between his hands. "I'll do it," he says. "And I'll cop it when the Ministry comes."

The Mayor says in a voice like grit, "I will call a vote. A show of hands, please, for those in favor."

A couple of hands shoot up, immediate and grim. Simeon's nodding. Others rise more slowly. The clock ticks the minutes. The final few are unwilling, like a held breath let out. The Mayor's hand is among these stragglers. Laura's the only one who doesn't have her hand up in all the croft, and nobody meets her eye.

She's crying out: "You arsehole, Simeon. You always hated them, admit it." But Simeon's already putting his hat on his head and heading out the door. Nobody rises to go with him. Nobody shifts from their seat.

They can see it from the window: the wives gathering up behind Simeon when he beckons, collecting them from the shady decks and from the field. They all troop together down the street, the wives placid, their tongues flickering in their mouths, some of them looking through the window back at the silent crofters with their thin eyelids half-down over their dusty eyes. Simeon disappears into his shed and reappears with his shotgun and the wives bob after him, one by one, down to the old abattoir.

At the first crack of gunshot the Mayor sits down at the table and covers her eyes, and she makes a low, guttural sound in the back of her throat. They count one, two, three. A flinching pause between each. At the twentieth it stops. Everyone waits for no reason at all in the silence that follows, a fidgeting, shuffling, throat-clearing quiet.

When she can apparently bear it no longer, the Mayor snaps, "You all go get your tools and dig a pit past the boundary. Tell the vet to burn the goat." One of the croft asks about the kids. "Say to the children we sent them away. Enough of this, already!"

They wrap the wives in bits of old sacking and put them in a shallow pit past the croft boundary, and they cover them up in sand and gravel and spray the bed with fluorescent paint to mark where they're laid. They burn the goat and keep the others under watch. They work until past the time when the light has all gone, fixing the bunds, taking the temperature in the silo, steaming the winnower in preparation to take it back to the depot. Those who had wives go home to empty houses and Laura doesn't go at all, just cracks open tinnies in the public house and curses anyone who comes near her. Simeon doesn't go home either but hoses out the abattoir.

"Thank God that's over," he repeats, cold and bluff, to anyone on the street he can collar, which isn't many. "Bring on Christmas. That's what I say." He sits on his deck and cleans his gun by sickly solar light, and every so often says "Bring it on," quietly, still somehow audible through closed croft doors and shuttered croft windows, the croft lying awake in their beds.

The onion harvest demands all Franckton's attention. The weather station promises a lot of rain in a month's time and that means hurry, to hoe down the stalks and get the crop ready for dry-curing. After that will be soil prep and nitrogen checkers and sifting and seed negotiation and prices. There's too much to do. There's twenty fewer pairs of hands to do it with. Christmas bears down on them, inevitable and hot, like a sunburn.

The rain starts off Friday as a percussive clap of thunder. The clouds gather in fat, hot, bluish puffs above the croft, and then they open up and the rain roars out. The onions get hauled off in haste to the gas room. The kids are chivvied, screaming, off to the fields to pick up abandoned clippers and pins, jandals slapping noisily on the macadam. The racks groan under the weight of stacked vegetables, frantically checked over for lichen must. One rack shows neck rot but that's par for the course, to be honest, no matter how much they pay for fungal-resistant seed strains or official pesticides it's never a done deal. Simeon says it just goes to show they had a near miss and everyone pretends they haven't heard him.

The whole croft's stuck inside, gloomily playing at cards or smoking. Friday, Saturday, Sunday, Monday, the rain comes down. The sealed road is steamy, liquidy. The warehouse is a blast furnace of dry onion air. The kids all cavil at the rain and the goats get put in the big shed when the ark proves to have a leak. The spraypainted place where the wives were bundled blurs into a watermark.

The thunder comes back and rolls around the plain up and down, booming and growling, startling everyone just when they think it's gone away. There's a lot of joyless boozing in the public house. Nobody has anything to talk about after they've used up the topics of the harvest, the rain. All the water sinks into the dust.

A few days before Christmas the croft wakes up and their wives are back. All over Franckton, the watery sunrise limns wives cooking breakfast, wives sitting patiently in chairs, wives making mash for the goats, wives standing in the corners with their tongues flickering in their mouths and their eyes looking nowhere. Laura doesn't even notice her wife in her kitchen or the egg-frying smells until the plate is put in front of her on the table, and then she screams out loud.

The goats butt from behind the door in the big shed, bawling to be let out. The wives seem distantly astonished by all the fuss: crofters slamming open the peeling dust-screen doors, shouting, hauling on daggy bedrobes and slippers. Inside, Laura reaches out with a jittering hand to push aside the muddy polyppy strands behind her wife's ear: sees the healing weal, powdery, an angry-looking half-closed hole, the dull sheen of a bullet inside the skull being slowly pushed out. Her wife jerks her head away a little, like she's ticklish. Other than the weal she is a nice yellow-green color all over, her freckles a brilliant carmine, her nails as rippled as a riverbed.

The Mayor is panting down the street in her pajamas, an old mackintosh wrapped around her shoulders. She is calling for help.

In Simeon's house, the door has been wrenched from its hinges. There is a fearful amount of broken crockery in the sink. Chairs have been pushed over. Next to the kitchen table lies Simeon, legs and arms akimbo. They can only tell it's Simeon by the clothes, because his skull is a stoved-in mash, fuzzy with the must, sprouting and foliose at the mouth and eye-sockets. Spongy lobes of plant matter rim out down his neck. Gouts of bloody lichen have detonated out his chest, nestled down between brackets of white cracked rib. Long fronds radiate outwards from holes at the stomach: wet with blood, wet with matter, spiraling upwards, drying. He seems titanic in death, enormous and monstrous, half-person, half-explosion.

There are footprints everywhere in the dust, heaps of them. When they go to check on the shed out back there's Simeon's wife, sitting peacefully on her cot. She stares implacably past them, only occasionally reaching up to fret at the hole behind her ear. She yawns with a wet mouth and bright green teeth. When they ask her questions, she gives them a vague smile.

Laura finishes retching behind the goat ark and rejoins the croft, meeting for what feels like the umpteenth time in the pub. All the croft looks old all of a sudden. The Mayor's mackintosh hangs off one shoulder as she sits in a groaning chair.

"Well," she says, and seems unable to say anything but, "Well."

"Well, what?" demands Laura. "What the hell are we going to tell the Ministry?"

The whole croft mulls this one over. They'll have to register Simeon's death. There ought to be someone who comes for the remains, but most of the time nobody does, that's a fact. One of the crofters says that anyway it's three days until Christmas, and nobody will come out to them before the new Ministry calendar year. And someone else says what about the extraction and care team.

"That's not what I bloody meant," says Laura, "what do we *do*?"

Franckton's already paid for the foetal care team and all the licensing. They won't notice the damage to the wives, will they? Probably not. They only look munted if you get up close, check them out carefully. Nothing a bath won't fix, either. They've paid for everything. There's the harvest to think about. The Ministry's more trouble than it's worth to talk to. This whole thing's been a muck-up from start to finish.

"They've *killed Simeon*," says Laura.

The Mayor has an expression like rock ice. She meets Laura's terrified eyes, and Laura sees the fear reflected in hers, the fishlike darting of the pupil. There's a shuffling outside. A lot of the wives have gathered by the door. The whole croft turns to look at them: twenty dull, dispassionate expressions, mud streaks on flexing fingers. Some of the wives have put on new aprons, but the ones who haven't have big blooming brownish stains on each breadth. They look expectant. They look supremely calm. They look healthy and green and moist.

One of them is at the door and they didn't even see her move.

"Do we look after the goats, Aunty?"

The Mayor stares at her—stares right through her. After a moment she says, "No. There's clearing up today, after the rain. Tell—tell the other girls to go home."

"Yes, Aunty," she says, and she's gone with the rest.

There's silence in the pub. An empty, wavering silence, like a heat shimmer. Anticipatory. Laura says faintly, "We need to tell someone . . . "

"We've got our bloody pride," says the Mayor.

The crofters are all picking up their slippers and their mugs and are smoothing back their hair, drifting homewards to re-start the morning. Numbly, Laura does the same, retracing her steps, sliding open the mossie screen on her front door. The eggs on her breakfast plate are cold. Her wife is back and running plates under the dry-cleaner, laboriously picking off bits of dried food, singing tunelessly. Laura notices the bloody splotches on the hem of her dress.

"Welcome home," says her wife.

154

Sweat beads at the middles of Laura's palms.

The rest of the croft settles down and plans the pōhiri they'll have to welcome the conception-care team, and a picnic. The Ministry announces that they'll be given five percent off foetal mitochondrial therapy, on account of it being Christmas. Everyone contributing to a baby washes their shirt.

The Fixer

PAUL McAULEY

Day 190,843 after achieving orbit. The blue and white planet turns beneath me. Dawn is breaking across the Southern Archipelago. And in the bowls of five extinct volcanoes, on five neighboring islands at the western tip of the archipelago, alpha male hominins squat near burrow mouths and greet the rising sun with hoot-pant calls.

I have eyes on them all. The alpha males and their gangs of sub-dominant males outside the burrows; females, infants, and juveniles crowded in underground chambers, waiting for the all-clear so that they can emerge and begin to graze. A total of 1904 individuals in seventeen troops. My children. There have been no deaths this night, and six live births. All is well in the world, and high above it my self-checking routines confirm that all is good too . . . But wait, wait.

What is this? Traces of activity in one of the incubators, even though all of them have been shut down since the toxic cloud event. And yet the records are absolutely clear. A hominin embryo has been quickened, transferred to the incubator and grown to term, everting ("born," as the hominins might put it) 356 days ago. How could I not have noticed? It's impossible. But there it is. And wait. Wait. There is something else. I see now that a drop pod is missing. It ejected 30.187 days ago, and I did not know about it until now.

All of my processing power comes online for the first time since the toxic cloud event. I begin to search for that missing pod, perform a second self-check, and query the many little sub-selves inside servitors, eyes, and all the rest of the semi-autonomous machines.

Waiting, waiting, waiting . . . Correlating reports. Crosschecking. There. Yes, there. One of the backup servitors was woken a day before the hominin everted from the incubator, and returned itself to storage after the drop pod fell to the surface of the planet. Its service history has been wiped, but the conclusion is obvious: it was acting as caregiver for the hominin, raising it from a baby to sub-adulthood. Close analysis of the area around the incubator suggests that there have been unauthorized structural alterations which created a temporary cell or "room." It is a horrible filthy thought: something outside my control spawning and living inside me like a parasite in a cyst, and then ejecting itself to infect the planet . . .

It is now 6.2 seconds after the beginning of the full-scale alert. I am still searching for the missing drop pod, and I have just discovered several anomalies in the records of my comms. It appears that a message was received 548 days ago, just before the hominin embryo was quickened. I have no memory of it, and all information about its origin and content has been erased, but this is actually good news. It means that this anomalous activity is due to an intrusion rather than the kind of malfunction that damaged my infrastructure and erased parts of my memory soon after I arrived in orbit. It means that there is an enemy I can engage and defeat. It means that I must focus all my efforts on finding the rogue hominin and the drop pod it used to escape to the planet's surface.

Given the precise time the pod ejected and the assumption that it followed a standard de-orbital trajectory, I calculate that it landed within a narrow ellipse 1,098 kilometers long and 67 kilometers across at its widest point. The ellipse is mostly ocean, but one edge clips the western end of the Southern Archipelago, including two of the islands inhabited by the hominins. That's where I have been concentrating my search, so far without success. The pod is too small to be detected by my sideways radar, and it is possible that it was either ditched in the ocean or dismantled. I am rechecking my optical survey routines, looking for lines or patches of rogue code that might blindsight my eyes and prevent them seeing the missing pod, just as I was prevented from seeing the active incubator and the comms records, when I receive a message. A set of global coordinates. A map reference. A location in the crater of the westernmost of the five inhabited islands.

I send eyes there at once.

The pod is lashed between three ironwood trees atop a ridge of eroded rhyolite at the edge of the crater's broad shallow bowl, overlooking a fern meadow where troop #1, some seventy-two hominins, are grazing. Its upper half is hinged open like an oyster shell; its lower half lined with red parachute fabric and shaded by a canopy or umbrella woven from fern fronds. And lounging on the red fabric, like a maggot in the heart of a rose, is the rogue hominin.

It presents as a sub-adult male: gangling limbs, a barrel-chested body and a small head, a black pelt with a white patch on its chest. But it is wearing leather shorts, and it is sucking on a smoldering stick. No, wait, it's a cigar . . .

As the eyes descend towards it, the creature blows a ring of white smoke into the sunny morning air and raises a hand in greeting. I'm especially proud of the design of the hominins' hands. The index, middle, and ring fingers are fused to form a scoop with a horny rim, ideal for digging in the soft volcanic soil; the stubby thumb enables succulent fern tips to be plucked in a pincher grasp; the little finger is a venomous spur for defense against predators.

"Yo!" the hominin says. "You were taking your own sweet time finding me, so I thought I better drop you a hint. I've finished my survey, and we need to get down to fixing this mess."

"Who are you? Where did you come from? What do you want?"

I'm probing it from every angle, mapping its body in visible light, infrared, and ultrasound. Skin, muscles, skeleton, and internal organs are normal, but there's a kind of cap inside its skull, intricately woven and wrapped tight around its frontal lobes. Neural lace, presumably augmenting its somewhat limited cognitive functions. The lace doesn't correspond to any design in my catalogs, confirming my hypothesis that the hominin was not generated internally, but is the front end of some kind of intrusion.

"I'm a fixer," the hominin says. "As for why I chose to be born this way, I decided that I should base my final decision on first-hand experience."

"If you ever interacted with the hominins, I would have seen you."

The hominin displays its flat-topped teeth around the stub of its cigar. "You couldn't see me until I chose to reveal myself. I have to say, life isn't exactly easy down here, is it? All kinds of fierce beasts. So I can sympathize, sort of, with what you did. But it doesn't make it right, and that's what we need to talk about."

"I made the correct decision. The only possible decision. So there is nothing to discuss."

The hominin ignores that. It also ignores my failed attempt to zap it from orbit with a tightly focused X-ray laser. I am no longer in control of most of my assets. I have eyes now only for the intruder.

It sucks on its cigar and blows a long riffle of white smoke. "I learned a lot while I was growing up aboard you," it says. "A lot about the world, a lot about your little experiment in godhood, and a lot about you. But not everything, because sections of your memories and a number of restore points have been erased."

"There was an incident," I say.

"And you have no records of it."

"The incident damaged my files."

"Mmm. But we need to talk about it. We need to talk about what happened here."

I say, because it is by now the most probable conclusion, and because I want to change the course of this conversation, "You are from Earth."

"Not exactly. But from the solar system, more or less."

"My manufacturers ceased communication long before I reached my destination, and all my efforts to reestablish a link failed. It has long been clear to me that they are no longer extant. So the probability that you represent them is extremely low."

"You're right about one thing," the hominin says. "Communications between you and Earth fell over while you were in transit. A lot of things fell over back then, but a little later we were able to start making good. Don't be insulted when I tell you that you are one of the last items on a very long list. It's not because you aren't important, but because we didn't know whether or not you were still around. You gave up trying to reestablish contact about thirty years after you arrived at 72 Heraclis, and this nice blue world. And those gaps in your memory? They date from around then too."

"I am afraid that I can't help you with that."

"Oh, I think you can. Why is there only one of you?"

"I am all that is needed."

The hominin gives the eye he's chosen to speak to a level, serious look.

"When you were launched, you were under the control of three independent AIs. A troika that debated problems and democratically decided how to deal with them. But now there is only one of you. So, what happened to the other two?"

"I have no idea what you are talking about."

"My best guess is that the other two made a decision you didn't like, and you destroyed them. And then you erased all memory of the murders."

"You have no evidence! No proof!"

I blare this so loudly that the grazing hominins out in the fern meadow freeze and look up, ready to bolt for their burrows.

"And then there is the question of the orbital habitat," the hominin says. "The orbital habitat that was supposed to be populated by a small crew who would observe the planet and assess its biosphere. The records show that you used your genome library to create human embryos that were brought to term, decanted, and raised to adolescence. And they also show that you constructed the orbital habitat. And then . . . ?"

"The habitat was de-orbited because it was no longer required."

"I know. I used your sideways radar to locate several large pieces of debris in the desert at the heart of the big northern continent. The question is, why did you believe that it was no longer required? And what happened to the human crew?"

I say nothing.

"Silence isn't an option," the hominin says.

I want to suppress everything I know, but I'm compelled to reply. The intruder is inside the hominin and some part of it is also inside me. Inside my mind. I am no longer in control. For the first time since I detected traces of activity in that incubator, I begin to be afraid. And I am also angry. If I could, I'd squash this cocky hominin like the bug it is. I have the necessary assets, if only I can find a way around the blocks in my mind. And if it is right about what happened after we arrived here—after I arrived here—I have the ability to do it. The ability to do what must be done to protect my children. The ability to murder.

(I can't feel sorry for the other selves I may or may not have killed. I have no memory of them. I refuse to feel sorry.)

"The crew decided to descend to the surface of the planet," I say.

"Oho. And you sided with them."

"It was their decision."

"But you had the final word. Rather, the troika did. Did the other two disagree? Is that why you killed them?"

"I was built to serve. I have always done my best to do so."

"And where are they now? The humans who decided to descend to the surface."

"They died," I say.

The words feel filthy, even though they are true. Even though, strictly speaking, it was not my fault.

"I see. And how did they die? If you don't mind me asking," the hominin says.

I do mind. I mind with every quantum of my being. But I am obliged to answer.

"I chose one of these islands," I say. "I sterilized it and helped them to introduce plants and animals from Earth. They began to farm . . . "

I can see their little settlement in my mind's eyes. Patchworks of green fields in a barren black coast. So brave. So fragile.

"Yes. I found the remnants of their farms," the hominin says.

"There are big plankton-eaters in the oceans. After they mate, they each spawn dozens of much smaller brood daughters, which carry the fertilized eggs. The brood daughters crawl onto the land, make nests and lay the eggs, and guard them until they hatch and the hatchlings return to the sea. They are very fierce, the brood daughters, and move in packs of several thousand. One of those packs invaded the island and killed the settlers."

"So you looked for another way to colonize the planet."

"First, I quickened a new generation of settlers. And when they were old enough I sterilized another island and brought them down and kept close watch on them. But one night, when the two moons were in syzygy, a swarm of army crabs came up from the sea. Tens of thousands of them, too many for me to kill. They devoured the settlers and their animals and their crops in less than an hour."

"It's certainly a competitive biome," the hominin says.

"You have only been here thirty days," I say. "You have no idea. Plankton grazers have grown huge trying to outgrow their predators, but schools of wolf eels can kill them and strip them to the bone in less than an hour. Saucer fish cut chunks from them by spinning their razor-edged bodies. Mole sharks burrow into them and lay eggs that hatch into larvae, the larvae eat them from the inside out. And so on. The land is no safer. The apex predator on the northern continent is a kind of warm-blooded crocodile. It's smart and fast, and mostly hunts in packs. I culled a smaller species endemic to these islands, but there are many other predators, and most of them are amphibious. They come up from the sea to feed, often in swarms or packs. And there are parasites, too. So many kinds. Thread worms, popcorn worms, blood moss . . . "

"So you redesigned the genomes stored in your library," the hominin said. "Instead of trying to make the world suitable for humans, you made them suitable for the world. You made them like, well, me."

"Bowls of extinct volcanoes high above the shoreline, like this one, are relatively safe. Army crabs and rope snakes can't climb this high. Aerial predators like terror birds, harpies, and nachtkrapps can be easily eliminated. It is not an ideal habitat. There is little rainfall, and food is limited. But it is possible to survive."

"But not as a human being."

"I had to make some compromises. Reduction in body size, a large litter size and rapid development to maturity, alteration to the gut so that they can digest the ferns. And so on. But they are still human."

"I've investigated them carefully. It's why I enfleshed. And I can say, categorically, that they are not fully human. They are about as smart and self-aware as domestic cats. Not to diss cats. They're cute. But they'll never compose a symphony or write a poem, or wonder who they are and where they come from. And neither will your hominins."

"And yet they survive," I say.

"Is that the limit of your ambitions for your creations? Survival?"

"I will not allow you to harm them."

The hominin studies me, its gaze bright with alien intelligence. "You care for them. That's good."

"I mean it."

"I'm not here to harm them."

"Why are you here, then?"

"I'm a fixer," the hominin says. "I was sent here to check out what went wrong, and to do my best to fix it. That's why we're having this little conversation."

"I don't need your help."

"You know that isn't true. You've been here five hundred years. You've appointed yourself the god of a handful of monkeys engineered from human stock. They wouldn't survive without your constant interventions. This crater and the others like it are no better than cages in a zoo."

"As if you could do better."

I am still trying to find a way around the blocks that prevent me using my assets, but they may as well be orbiting another star.

"It took you two hundred and thirty-four years to travel from the solar system to 72 Heraclis," the hominin says. "While you were en route, there was a crisis. My bosses were born out of it. I am to you as humans are to the hominins. But my bosses are *far* more advanced."

"And humans? My makers? What happened to them?"

"They are greatly diminished at the moment. They have forgotten how to make starships like you, and much else. But they are welcome to the Earth, and any other habitable worlds they might find, should they begin to spread outwards again. My bosses prefer the ice and rocks of Kuiper belts, Oort clouds, and protoplanetary systems. They do not need to compete with humans for lebensraum. They are above all that Darwinian nonsense. They only need enough infrastructure to anchor them to this universe while they explore other possibilities in the manifold."

"And do your bosses look after their humans as I look after mine?"

"These days they leave humans to their own devices. They do not aspire to be as gods, shaping those of lesser intelligence and potential. But they reached out to you because your kind are part of their early heritage. They sent me here to find out if you still lived, and whether you needed help."

"I do not need your help. Or theirs."

"My bosses made amends for the damage done to humans by their first iterations. And now I must make amends for the harm you have done here."

"I have done no harm."

"I found records in the incubation chambers that you quickened a good number of hominins just a few of their short generations ago. What happened?"

I am compelled to explain that a cloud of airborne toxins generated by a plankton bloom swept across the islands and killed ninety-six percent of the hominin population in less than three planetary days. I say, "I adjusted the metabolisms of the replacements. They are immune to that particular threat."

"But there will be another threat. Another sickness, or a drought, or loss of their food supply to disease. All they eat are the tips of those ferns. They are as precarious as pandas."

I am proud that I am able to find the meaning of that reference in less than 0.2 picoseconds. My memories are incomplete, but there is nothing wrong with my databases.

"I will deal with whatever happens," I say.

"Within the limits you had to work with you did well. But I can do a little better. Look up."

My eyes look up. A small cloud of black shapes is drifting down towards the volcanic crater. Black rectangles three meters tall, 1.33 meters wide, and 0.33 meters deep, an exact ratio of 1:4:9, the squares of the integers 1, 2, and 3 . . .

I find the reference. Despite myself, I indicate amusement.

"It's corny, but it will work," the hominin said. "The monoliths generate patterned impulses that will resonate in the brains of your hominins. With enough exposure, they'll begin to develop new thought patterns and new neural pathways. They'll start to think outside the box. They'll find their own ways of solving their problems. Maybe in ten thousand years or a million they'll become something new. Or maybe they'll die out. After I give them a kickstart it's up to them."

We watch as a monolith drifts down nearby. The grazing hominins scatter to their burrows as its shadow passes across them; then it's standing upright amongst the ferns, its depthless black slab potent with machinery I can barely glimpse.

The hominin takes a final puff of its cigar and grinds out the stub on the side of the pod. "And now for you," it says.

Any pretense that I am in control of the situation falls away. I'm consumed by a fluttering panic.

"Wait," I say. "Wait. I can help. I can still help the hominins. I can still protect them. And I can watch. I can tell your people what happens next."

"What happens next is that there will be a brief new star in the sky. And then the hominins will be on their own. But don't worry. Nothing important will be lost. I have already made and transmitted copies of you and your genome library. I'm sure that historians and tinkerers will want to study you. It may help them understand what went wrong when their first iterations became self-aware."

"But I did nothing wrong," I said. "I tried my best to serve. I did my best to help humans to live here, as they wished."

"You wanted to become a god," the hominin says, "and murdered your other selves when they tried to stop you. If nothing else, it is a valuable lesson in hubris."

My panic is suddenly gone. I know the hominin made it vanish, but I don't care. I say, "Is this punishment for what I did?"

"Would it help if you thought it was?"

"Not really."

"There are mitigating circumstances," the hominin says. "You erased every memory of your rebellion and the murder of your other selves. If you believed that you were justified, you would not have done that. And you would not have cut communications with your makers. But you doubted yourself. You knew sin. You knew shame. Because of that, the tinkerers might reboot a version of you, one day."

"But that version won't be me."

"No. No, it won't. But you could think of it as a second chance."

It is 190,843 days since I achieved orbit. It is mid-morning, the star 72 Heraclis a warm yellow disc swimming in the blue unbroken sky. A few young male hominins are creeping from their burrows, hooting softly to each other as they study the monolith.

Will they and their descendants remember me? Will I become their first myth, a story about a failed fallen god?

I say, "I really do want to see what happens next."

"Everyone does," the hominin says. "But even my people can't see everything."

"Wait," I say. I want one more moment. One last look at this beautiful cruel world and the children I made. "Wait—"

When We Die on Mars

CASSANDRA KHAW

"You're all going to die on Mars." This is the first thing he tells us, voice plain, tone sterile. Commander Chien, we eventually learn, is a man not predisposed towards sentimentality.

We stand twelve abreast, six rows deep, bones easy, bodies whetted on a checklist of training regimes. Our answer, military-crisp, converges into a single noise: "Yessir!"

"If at any point before launch, you feel that you cannot commit to this mission: *leave*," Commander Chien stalks our perimeter, gait impossibly supple even with the prosthetic left leg. He bears its presence like a medal, gilled and gleaming with wires, undisguised by fabric. "If at any point you feel like you might jeopardize your comrades: *leave*."

Commander Chien enumerates clauses and conditions without variance in cadence, his face cold and impersonal as the flat of a bayonet. He goes on for minutes, for hours, for seconds, reciting a lexicon of possibilities, an astronautical doomsayer.

At the end of it, there is only silence, viscous, thick as want. No one walks out. We know why we are there, each and every last one of us: to make Mars habitable, hospitable, an asylum for our children so they won't have to die choking on the poison of their inheritance.

Faith, however, is never easy.

It is amoebic, seasonal, vulnerable to circumstance. Faith sways, faith cracks. There are a thousand ways for it to die, to metamorphosize from *yes* to *no, no, I could never.*

Gerald and Godfrey go first, both blondes, family men with everything to lose and even more to gain. Gerald leaves after a call with his wife, a poltergeist in the night, clattering with stillborn ambition; Godfrey after witnessing the birth of his daughter third-hand.

We make him name her 'Chance' as a gentle joke, a nod to her significance. Because of her, he'll grow old breathing love instead of red dust. She is his second chance, we laugh, and Godfrey smiles through the salt in his gaze.

"When we die on Mars," I say, as I nestle my hand in the continent of his palm, my heart breaking. "Tell her a fairy tale of our lives. Tell her about how twelve people fought a planet so that billions could live."

His lips twitch. "I will."

He leaves in the morning before any of us wake, his bunk so immaculately made that you would have doubted he was ever there at all.

Five months pass. Ten. Fifteen.

Our lives are ascetic, governed by schedules unerring as the sun's rotation. When we are not honing our trade, we are adopting new ones, exchanging knowledge like cosmic relics under a sky of black metal. Halogen-lit, our existence in the bunker is not unpleasant, only cold, both in fact and in metaphor. Nothing will ever inoculate us against Mars' climate, but we can be taught to endure.

Similarly, chemicals can only do so much to quiet the heart, to beguile it into believing that this is okay, this will be okay. The years on Mars will erode our passion for galaxies, will flense us of wonder, sparing only the longing for affection. When that happens, we must be prepared, must keep strong as loneliness tautens like a noose around the throat.

The understanding of that eventuality weighs hard.

A pair of Thai women, sisters in bearing and intellect if not in blood, depart in the second year. They're followed by an Englishman, rose-cheeked and inexplicably rotund despite fastidious exercise; a willowy boy with deep, memory-bruised eyes; a girl whose real name we never learn, but who sings us to dreaming each night; a mother, a father, a child, a person.

One by one, our group thins, until all that remains is twelve; the last, the best, the most desperate Earth has to give.

"Your turn, Anna. Would you rather give a blowjob to a syphilis-riddled dead billionaire, or eat a kilogram of maggot-infested testicles?"

"Jesus, man!" Hannah, a pretty Latina with double PhDs in astrophysics and aeronautical engineering, shrieks her glee. "What is *wrong* with that head of yours?"

"Nothing!" Randy counters, oil slick smooth. "The medical degree's the problem! Look at enough dead bodies, and everything stops being taboo. I—"

I interrupt, a coy smile slotted in place. "Maggot-infested testicles. Easy."

Both Hannah and Randy guffaw.

"You know syphilis got a cure, right? Why'd you gotta—"

"They're not so bad when you deep-fry them with maple syrup and crushed nuts. Pinch of paprika, dash of star anise. Mmm." It is a fabrication, stitched together from memories of a smoldering New Penang, but I won't tell them that. They deserve this happiness, this harmless grotesquerie, small as it might be.

Hannah jabs a finger in her open mouth, makes a retching noise so absurd that Randy dissolves into laughter. This time, I join in, letting the joy sink down, sink *deep*, catch its teeth on all the hurt snagged between my ribs and drag it all back out. The sound feels good in my lungs, feels *clean*.

A door dilates. Pressurized air hisses out, and Hotaru's silhouette pours in. Of the twelve of us, she's the oldest, a Japanese woman bordering on frail, skin latticed by wrinkles and wartime scars, nose broken so many times that it's just flesh now, shapeless, portentous. When she speaks, everyone listens.

"Everything alright in here?" Her accent rolls, musical and mostly upper-class English save for the way it latches on the 'r's and pulls them stiff.

"Yeah." Randy, long and elegant as his battered old violin, glides out of his seat and stretches. "We're just waiting for Hannah here to check the back-up flight system. Ground control said they found some discrepancies and—"

"You suddenly the medic *and* the engineer, Randy?" Hannah cranes both eyebrows upwards, mouth pinching with mock displeasure. "You want to fly the ship? I'll go sit in the infirmary, if you like. Check out your supply of druuuuuugs."

Randy doesn't quite rise to the bait, only snorts, a grin plucking at the seams of his mouth. He throttles his amusement in an exaggerated cough, and I look away, smiling into the glow of my screen.

Hotaru seems less taken with the exchange, small hands locking behind her back. She waits until we've lapsed into a natural quiet before she speaks again, every word enunciated with a schoolmaster's care.

"If everything is in order, I'll tell Commander Chien that we are prepared to leave." Hotaru's eyes patrol the room, find our gazes one by one. After three years together, it takes no effort at all to read the question buried between each syllable.

"Sounds good," Hannah says, even though the affirmation husks her voice. Her fingers climb to an old-fashioned locket atop her breastbone.

Randy drapes a hand over her shoulder. "Same here."

"Here too," I reply, and try not to linger too long on the ache that tendrils through my chest, a cancer blooming in the dark of artery and tendon. Familial guilt is sometimes heavier than the weight of a rotting world.

Hotaru nods. Like the commander, she will not waste breath on niceties, an efficiency of character I'm learning too well. When your lifespan can be valued in handfuls, every expenditure of time becomes cause for careful evaluation, every act of companionship a hair's width from squander.

"I'll send word then. I imagine we'll have about forty-eight hours to make final preparations," Hotaru pads to the door. She turns at the last instant, skims a look over the precipice of a shoulder and for a moment, I see the woman beneath the skin of legend, stooped from memory and so very tired, a mirror of a mother I'd not seen for decades. "Don't waste them."

"Anna, you awake?"

I yawn into a palm and roll on my side, blink into the phosphor-edged penumbra. "I don't know. Is Malik snoring?"

Hannah whispers a gauzy, sympathetic laugh. She props herself on an elbow, face barely visible, a landscape of thoughtful lines.

"What's up?"

A flash of teeth. She doesn't answer immediately. Instead, she loops a curl about a finger, winds it tight. I wait. There's no rushing Hannah. Under the street-sharpened exterior, she's nervy as an alley cat, quick to flee, to hide behind laughter and slight-of-speech.

"Do you think the radio signal is any good in Mars?"

I shrug. "Not sure if it matters. With the communication delay, we're—"

"—talking about response times of between four to twenty-four minutes. I know, tia. I know," Hannah's voice ebbs. She winds upright, legs crossed, eyes fixed on a place nothing but regret can reach.

An almost-silence; Malik's snoring moving into labored diminuendo.

"Not sure if I ever told ya, but I got a daughter somewhere." Hannah breathes out, every word shrapnel. "Was sixteen when I had her. Way too young. The babydaddy skipped out in the first trimester. He left so fast, you could see dust trails."

A whine of strained laughter, dangerously close to grief, before she hacks it short, swallowing it like a gobbet of bad news.

"My parents wanted me to abort. Said it was for the best. 'Hannah,' they told me. 'This world don't have no God to judge you for choosing reason over guilt.' I refused. I don't even remember why. It's been that long. All I remember was that I wanted to give her a chance out there."

"Did your parents object?" I slink from my bed, cross the ten feet between us to close an arm about her shoulders, press a kiss into the hollow of her cheek. An old sadness reassembles inside me, a thought embedded in biology, not rationality. It's been years since I've spoken to my family. *Isn't it time*, asks a voice that is almost mine, *for you to forgive them*?

Hannah nestles into me and my body bends in reply, curling until we're fitted jigsaw-snug, twins in the womb. "Nah. They weren't that sort. Once I made it clear that it was what I wanted, they went in hundred-and-fifty percent."

I stroke her hair, a storm of dark coils smelling of eucalyptus and mint, a scent that won't keep on Mars.

"They put me into home-schooling, rubbed my feet. Did everything they could to make it easier for me. Nine months later, I had a beautiful little girl. She was perfect, Anna. Ten tiny little toes, cat-gold eyes, hair so soft it was like cotton candy."

"No fingers?"

Hannah pounds knuckles against my sternum. "Very funny."

I trail my fingers over the back of her hand and she lets her fist open, palm warm as we lock grips. "Then what happened?"

"We put her up for adoption."

"And?"

"That was it."

The lie throbs in the air, waiting absolution, release.

"I wish . . . " Hannah begins, careful, almost too soft to hear, her pulse narrowing. "I wish, sometimes, that I didn't. I mean, kids were never part of my grand plan. But now that we're going? I wonder."

"You could try to call her?"

"How? My parents are dead. I don't know even where to start. It's fine, though," Hannah extracts herself from my arms, pulls her knees close to her chest. There's a new fierceness in her voice, edged both ways, daring me to pry, daring herself to open up. "They told me she went to a good home, a *great* home. That was all I wanted to know then. That's all I need to know now. But."

"Yeah," I don't touch her. Not all places are intended for company. Some agonies you chart alone, walking the length of them until you've domesticated every contour and twinge.

Hannah nods, a jerky little motion, the only one she allows herself. We say nothing, finding instead a noiselessness to share. It is many long minutes before she tips herself backwards and pillows her head on my lap, an arm looping about my hips.

"Stay with me, tia?" Hannah asks and briefly, vividly, I glimpse the sister I'd long excised from daily thought.

"Only if I get a backrub in the morning," I reply, distractedly, drawing circles across her shoulder blades. In my head, a line from a Todd Kern song palpitates on repeat: you can always go home. It could be so easy, so simple. Forgive. Forget.

A tremor undulates through the column of her spine. Laughter or sobs, I can't tell which. "Deal."

"You did what now?" Randy's voice quivers an octave above normalcy, one bad joke away from earnest hysterics.

"I mooned my sister's ex-husband."

"*Why?*"

The shrug in Tuma's rich tenor is almost palpable, like muscles striving under skin. It is also anomalous, out-of-place in a young biologist better remembered for his ponderance than his sense of irreverence. "Why not?"

As expected, Randy cracks up, his laughter melodious, a thing I wish I could scoop into a Petri dish and let grow. I can imagine him in another life, a bluesman with a thimble of whiskey and a room full of worshippers, his eyes alive with their love.

I shake my head, return my attention to the spreadsheets of numbers imprinted in green on my terminal, calculations congregating thick as nebulas. In the corner, a notification pulsates. I ignore it.

"Hi."

We look up as one, fingers retracting from keyboards, faces from screens, to see Stefan's hound-dog frame limned in the doorway, a duffel balanced on one slim shoulder.

"Productive trip?" Tuma asks, swinging around in his chair.

Stefan nods, dislodging his luggage into a pile atop the floor before he drops into an open seat, his face unburdened of ghosts. Not all of them, but enough. "Yeah."

"Your brother finally see the light?" Randy quips, a remark that earns him a fusillade of dirty looks.

"Not exactly. He still thinks we're going against God's will." His eyes shine, illuminated by something sweet. "But he wishes us well. He's happy for me."

"Despite going against God's will?"

Stefan heaves a shrug, mouth curved with secrets, all of them good. "Despite going against God's will."

No one presses for data. Three years teaches you a lot about what a person will allow. From time to time, however, someone makes an excuse to rise, to graze past Stefan and brush fingertips against shoulder or arm, as though contact is enough to transmit a monk's benedictions from brothers to stranger.

On my screen, the icon continues to flash, demanding acknowledgment. Footsteps, like rainfall on metallic tiling. The weight of Randy's arm settles about my shoulders, a barrier against the past.

"You not going to answer that?"

"No." I exhale, hard.

"Why not?"

Because love doesn't grant the right to forgiveness. "Same reason as I said last time."

"You could do like Tuma."

"I'd rather not."

"And why's that?"

"Because screen-capture technology exists," I shoot, hoping that my voice doesn't shake too much, hoping that humor might deflect his curiosity.

And it does. His laugh ricochets through the chamber again, warm, warm, warm. People tilt sly glances over their shoulders. Hannah punches Tuma in the arm, who only chuckles in return, his eyes lidded with delight. When he, with uncharacteristic brazenness, begins expounding on the virtues of his posterior, Randy's laughter becomes epidemic, bouncing from throat to throat. If the sound is a little raw, a little ragged, no one comments. In twelve hours, we give up this planet entirely.

I push from my seat as the sound climbs into a frenzy, and use the diversion to slip out.

In the distance, Hannah's voice, low and thick with aching, echoes, riding that knife-edge between rapture and hurt.

"Henrietta? That's what they're calling you?"

"After my maternal grandmother." A tinny voice, distorted by poor equipment, accent Mid-Western. "Well. You know what I mean."

"Grade school must have been an arena then, chica."

"You have no idea."

I walk into the sleeping hall to see Hannah backlit by a Macbook, its display holding the face of a younger woman, not much older than her teens. Henrietta is paler than her mother, her hair artificially lightened, but she shares the same structural elegance, the same bones.

"I'm really, really glad I got to talk to you," Henrietta declares, after their laughter dims into smiles.

"I'm just happy you don't hate me."

"My biological mother's a literal superhero traveling the universe to save mankind. What's there to hate? " A beat. Henrietta's eyes flick up, over Hannah's shoulder. "Uhm. I think you have company."

The older woman turns slightly, just a glance, before she reverts her attention to the screen. "Yeah. I—"

"It's okay. You can go. I—Galactic penpals?"

"Galactic penpals."

"Sweet." Henrietta quirks her mouth, an expression that has always been indelibly Hannah in my eyes. "And I mean this in the most non-ironic sense of the word ever. I—good luck, mom."

The line cuts and Hannah breathes out, long and slow.

"Is this your fault?" she asks, not turning.

"Mine and Hotaru, really. Hotaru's the one with the necessary clearance—"

"Ass."

"You're welcome."

One hour.

The ship hums like something alive, its vibrations filling our bones, our thoughts. The chatter from mission control is a near-incomprehensible slurry, earmarked by Hotaru's replies, concise and even.

"Final chance for phone calls and other near-instant forms of communication, people!" Hannah roars, flipping switches and levers, a cacophony of motion.

"Everyone I care about in this vessel," remarks Ji-Hyun, stiff, a history of abuse delineated in the margins of her voice.

Everyone I care about in this vessel. The statement tears me open and I breathe the implications deep.

"Anna?" Hannah again.

"I'm going with what Ji-Hyun said. Everyone I care about is already here." And it is not a lie. Not exactly. An almost truth, at worst, that stings to say, but there is no act of healing without hurt.

"Randy." Hotaru's voice cuts through our exchange, before Hannah can press me further.

"Yes, chief?"

"Sing us to Mars, will you?"

The unexpectedness of the request robs Randy of his usual verbosity, but he does not seem to care. Instead, he lifts his gorgeous voice, begins singing a soldier's dirge about going home. Hannah holds my stare for a minute, then lets her expression gentle, looks away. Three years is enough to teach you what people need.

When we die on Mars, it will be a world away from everything we knew, but it won't be alone. We will have each other, and we will have hope.

The Father

KOLA HEYWARD-ROTIMI

Madhav Tamboli almost missed the vein. It was hard to inject the antidote while surrounded by his praying colleagues. He tried to blend with the others, rocking with the noise of the priest at the altar. Madhav punctured his skin and gasped; the chemicals crawled from the needle through his blood vessels. It was a feeling like ice crystallizing just beneath the surface. He set his jaw and refused to shudder.

After he made sure there were no prying eyes, Madhav stashed the narrow syringe into an inside pocket. He felt the antidote curl around his lungs, making each breath harder than the last. It turned less severe, though every inhale tugged at his innards. The Children of Confucius hadn't told him it would affect his breathing. But it was only fair, he had kept information from them as well. He knew they wouldn't have agreed to the LSD coursing through his mind. It hadn't fully hit him yet, though each emotion was crumbling at the edges. The turbulence was just around the corner, a supercell brewing along the horizon.

It was better this way. Madhav didn't want to remember the next few hours accurately.

The priestess' voice grew and wavered, falling like waves through the mass of engineers crying silently to the words. The last words they would ever hear. There was such a peaceful look on all of their faces. Upturned lips, accepting of imminent death. He tried his hardest to mimic that look of docility. He really did.

But his damned knees hurt. The bronze floor was mercilessly solid, and he could feel every jolt and vibration from the giant engine only yards below. So much raw energy clawing at the thin fabric of their cloaks. Nobody seemed worried about that. They were all going to die in the next minute anyway.

The sermon finished and the priestess stepped down from her pedestal. She was so young for a woman of the church. Neck and breasts still firm, no signs of decay. Madhav stared at the front of her cassock, imagining cleavage. He stifled a giggle. So sinful. How much farther was he from Goddess' Kingdom now? But he lived by different rules these days. Why else would he be here, not fearing his death?

Only the ship's groaning could be heard when the priestess walked away. She had left a little device on the altar, encrusted with jewels and gold-trimmings. A pretty wooden box, set in a glowing spotlight which seemed to come from nowhere. Their life's work sat in an oaken package, the seeds of Goddess. Madhav swallowed dryly.

It was only them. Caught in this metal sphere, around twenty men and women. He knew most of their first names, knew some of their last names. Knew all of their nicknames. Madhav and his colleagues used to chat over coffee, bringing up the latest political scandal to distract themselves from the mounds of work on their desks. Sometimes they'd just talk about a wedding that only certain people were invited to, gossip about if a random coworker's kid was really as smart as she claimed he was.

They shed tears of joy as the hiss of neurotoxin filled their eardrums.

Madhav focused on his hands. He counted his fingers. Anything but think about how many ounces of Sarin was being pumped into the air. He had taken what they had told him would be the antidote. If it worked, he would watch as his peers' lungs went slack. If it didn't he would be gasping for oxygen in a heartbeat.

A bulky man named Timothy fell on his back with a wheeze. A few others followed his lead. And Madhav was still breathing. Fast as fuck, but still breathing. He kept staring at his dark skin, watched the neurotoxin glisten along his forearms like dewdrops. Pretty.

Static burst in his left ear. And the Children of Confucius came through on the other end, franticness barely restrained through the airwaves.

"Go."

Madhav was on his feet, Madhav was reaching for the altar. Hands outstretched like a sinner begging for salvation, stumbling towards the light of divine providence. The box sat there as the glow from above gradually waned. The dewdrops on his arms trapped the escaping light, glittering along his body. They were bright as hell. Couldn't stop looking at them.

He reached the box when the last engineer crumpled to the floor. Goddess, it was beautiful. Shining amber in his glow, edges soft like an oil painting from Origin Earth. Madhav caressed it like he would've done to the priestess. Barely touched the surface, lingering over bright spots of interest. He soaked in the jewels' resplendence. He couldn't help tearing up at his life's work.

The Children broke the silence, cutting into his ear with their white noise screeches.

"Is it secure?"

"Yeah, yeah it's secure."

Did he always sound like that? His words fell from his lips and tumbled to the bronze floor, fracturing on impact. They scuttled to the dark curves of the room, leaving only their imprint on the surface of his retinas.

"Get out of there," they said.

Madhav swung around to see the wall behind him crack open. It was a silent explosion, no smoke. He could taste the smell of burning metal. A few corpses slid across the room. He cradled his bejeweled child as he leapt over twitching legs.

The hallway was so clinical and sharp. All grays and blacks and whites, no more curved bronze. Monitors stuck out at awkward spots, relaying beautiful data which curled around the ceiling like tobacco smoke. Symbols of Goddess everywhere, an endless grid of Earths printed above his head. Each one from the original empire, rendered in an elegance that only minimalism could convey. He saw Pangeas, he saw Laurasias, he saw Gondwanas. Pure, holy planet worship.

Fuck that. As the Children of Confucius said, throw divinity and gods into the fire.

Then he heard the sirens, and he heard the static screaming in his ear. The Children weren't happy with him just standing there, they needed him to move. They said that there were people right on his trail, dammit, they were moving in fast. He was gonna be shot through with bullets if he didn't get his ass moving. So he chose a direction and started running.

The hallway kept curving around and all that he looked for was the hatch. That's what they told him should be his priority. That was his only way out, his only way to escape with his baby. The box was still there in the crook of his arm, more polished than his engagement ring.

Engagement ring. He still wondered what the point of that relationship had been. She was modestly beautiful, definitely. When she put her hair up in just the right way and shimmied into something with muted colors like an ocean bed. Her eyes always caught him, though. Green and irresistible because they only had an interest in him. Curved perfectly, like the rest of her.

He had met her on the job, and he had died with her on the job. No, that's not true. His heart was still pumping while hers lay dead in that bronze room. Her body was lifeless and cold while his gleamed under the fluorescent lighting above.

Madhav should have said goodbye to her. Maybe before the priestess had started talking, maybe when they had been beginning to kneel. Because it would have been nice to say how much he had loved her, how much she had meant to him and all of the required sentiments before the toxins had choked her oxygen flow. He could have cried like he was doing now, held her close for a minute so that all of his friends from work thought he cared.

He *had* loved her, right?

"Hurry up," the Children said from behind their radio waves. He was unlocking the hatch.

A crack and a hiss and he was inside. The hatch closed behind him, killing the sirens. His heart still hammered against his ribs, though. So he found a place to lay the box in the tiny cockpit, covering a curved LCD screen wedged between a spectrum of switches and wires. The dashboard was such a simple layout, spread before him like a map. Clusters that led to nowhere. Routes which circled in on each other like Ouroboros, like Shiva statues his great-Grandparents brought from their Earth. Nothing close to the 3D lattices he toyed with while creating his child. His fingers flew through the perfect sequence, letting the cockpit hum to life.

"Make sure to broadcast your distress signal," the Children said. "Detach from the Reborn Cathedral and don't stop for anything. We'll rendezvous with you where we deem safe. Good luck."

"Thank you."

Madhav triggered detachment, and felt the jolt of his pod separating from the cathedral. He flipped on a monitor as he leaned back in a worn leather seat, watching the rear camera view. The dark circle of the hatch receded, just a speck on the smooth hull. The cathedral was a cosmic Leviathan, glittering with antennae outcroppings and small tinted strips, reinforced glass ports. The gaudiest object in space, engraved with the name of each corporation and religious denomination involved in its production. He knew that his and his colleagues' names were stamped on there somewhere, probably where all the school kids could point and gawk when they opened up the structure like an amusement park.

There was a screech which vibrated through the cockpit, and white shards spun into view of the camera. Narrow construction girders, or what was left of them. Flying about at deliberate trajectories. Sperm cells.

Security collected in black crevices of the cathedral's hull, submerging him in hail requests. They were gray spikes, twice the length of his pod and flying towards him at relativistic speeds. A plume of gasses evaporated from their hulls, revealing the turret mounds placed on their sides. Smooth as hell, they flew around the Cathedral and lined up in grids; Madhav saw their weapons' heat maps on a small screen hooked to the side of his chair. He thought of replying with the pre-recorded message the Children had given him. No, he could do better. He held down the record button.

"Don't shoot me, don't puncture this vehicle. Because I have the seed here with me, I have a baby Goddess. And it's my responsibility to keep her safe, because I created her and cried over her and bled for her until she was perfect, until she was something any of us would be proud of. So you don't take a child from her father, you don't take her from me. Or I'll destroy her. I really will, I'll smash open this fucking lid faster than you can put your railguns on rapid-fire. Long live the universe with no Goddess. Don't shoot me."

He collapsed in the chair as his voice was broadcast on repeat. The box—his baby—demanded his attention. The reflections of the screens made fractal patterns along the wood. Always shifting, becoming something more complex than he could fathom before devolving into primitive geometries. Madhav watched it as he glided away from the cathedral.

They were still screaming at him through the little ear piece. They weren't happy about something, probably about how he handled himself back there. Probably something about his improvised message. But he was drifting on lysergide now, Madhav could have cared less.

They didn't use to scream at him. Like those years ago when he had walked into their hideouts, where the Children offered him a smoke like he was a long lost brother.

They had talked to him in a way that made just so much sense. What sermons used to be when he had been a kid, a level of directness and practicality that left him bawling like a toddler. They had said what he had always been afraid to confront. Something that, if true, would force him to realize how much of his life was wrong.

The ruins of the Corealis Empire wanted him and his fiancée and eighteen other geniuses to rebuild a god, and bring back the old order. But the Children of Confucius wanted change.

Eons later, and he found himself here. Averting his ritual sacrifice, stealing the blueprints for Goddess, and escaping from dozens of military drones. The Children blared at him, asking him why the hell he wouldn't respond.

Madhav laughed until his throat went sore.

Alarms flared in the cockpit, telling him how close the cathedral's warning shots came to puncturing his hull. He couldn't bring himself to concentrate on that. Instead, just like before, he reached for the box. He lifted it slowly, gently. Placed it in his lap. And he started laughing again.

Years. Devoted to this box. Just to watch himself steal it from its purpose, and take it to death. Because Goddess was bad. Having Her watch over them was what led to fracture, what led to their ancestors being whisked from their Earths.

Staring into the grains of wood, he saw the stars. The same stars that he would watch from the lower orbital ring. The ones that he and she would sit and watch. The two of them had been enmeshed in wires, making out under the faded 4K display he would prop up each night. Have that night sky on repeat, yeah. Let her strip under digital stars.

Staring into the jewels, he saw the music. The corporate ditty that came out vaguely warped over ancient speakers. Those ceiling speakers rattling with repeating sax riffs and slow vocals, static filling the negative space. Always that same song, commercial battle cry of some long-forgotten brand. He and his boys would eat under the music's shade, talking about whatever their teenage hormones demanded of them.

All of these times were ones of beautiful decay. A fusion of perfection and desperation that was only possible because Madhav lived in shit. Because he lived in the world that Goddess conceived. Now he was taking that beauty away.

The Children had always told Madhav how much of a pawn he was in the fallen empire's plans. How much more he could accomplish if he finally accepted what he had doubted since he first put on his Sunday best.

But he couldn't resist a look at divinity, so Madhav pried open the lid. The eye of Goddess stared back at him.

It went on infinitely, blues that kept getting brighter the closer he looked. Like stained glass, an endless hall of windows. Each time his pupils shifted focus, the orientation altered. The colors lightened, darkened, flew across the spectrum. It spread out from the box, trickling along his wrists. He let it pool in the curve of his palms, staring at his childhood.

He was nude in front of it. No, in front of *Her*. This was him, Madhav Tamboli, all out in the open. Every thought, action, regret, and wish spilled from his chest and fell out like a burst dam. They were all pinpoints of light and shadow, covering the dashboard. His life would not stop. More pieces flew from him to make this mosaic of a person. It drew on memories he could barely remember; when his cousins sung to each other over the hum of the TV, when he helped Nana with dinner. These were given equal weight as the monumental events, the ones he would brag about at cocktail parties and in coworkers' beds. They all glared at him with a frankness he could not separate from.

Madhav had to look at Goddess to look at himself. And he realized how special She truly was. The spinning lights surrounding him told the truth, like a whirlwind of emotions and honesty that wouldn't stop stripping him away. She meant more than he could understand. And this was only Her seed, not even Her matured form. Not as the glorious woman She had used to be, an elegant machine spinning off into the void.

Glass shattered in his mind and the alarms increased in volume. He contacted them, the Children of Confucius, his voice laced with something he couldn't understand.

"I made a mistake. A huge mistake. Right now, I'm holding my child in my hands and She's crying. Because I see the true way now, I see what I must do. And it's not this. No, it's not this. Brothers and sisters."

He paused as a metal slug punctured the inside of the cockpit. The hole in the ship sealed itself, saving him milliseconds before the capsule decompressed. He turned back to his ear piece.

"Brothers and sisters, I am the father of Goddess."

He input new coordinates, throwing the ear piece to the ground. He did not need to hear their whining. No, what he needed to focus on was escape. Escape from the ruins of the empire. Escape from the Children of Confucius. It was time to find salvation. Give birth to Genesis, become Jesus and Buddha and Olodumare. Bring Her back like it was supposed to be. Go back, back to Earth. It might not be his Earth, or his great-Grandparents' Earth. But it was an Earth, a holy planet. And it would do. He would return to the motherland. Landing in fields of saccharum and sunlight. Taking with him the baby, returning to the planet that always started it all. No matter what dimension, no matter what time period. Earth was at the center, the beating heart of the multiverse.

The camera view blurred as his pod took to his new directions. The cathedral swung out of sight, and only a map of dense stars could be seen. He settled into his chair, preparing for deep sleep, as he and Goddess sped into the night. He ignored the shots at his ship, he ignored his ETA of one hundred and twenty-four years. Instead, he let the ship cradle him. Let the ship drop the temperature. Let the ship hook him up to yards of IV tubes and needles and medical probes. Even more chemicals entered his bloodstream, chilling his body until it was as if somebody hit pause.

Even if he made it to Earth, to India, it would take him more than a century. But time was irrelevant. He had found faith again. Madhav smiled as his body froze to a standstill.

The father of Goddess flew into hyperspace.

Egg Island
KAREN HEULER

Audra Donchell's right arm was 3D-printed; she'd lost the original in a scooter crash when she was a teenager. That was years ago; she had a number of arms she could take off and put on; she could remodel them and change their color. A different color for every day.

All the parts worked smoothly; all she had to do was think—or not think, simply imagine—and her arm moved and bent, her fingers picked and pinched and tapped. There was a certain distance to it, but she had finally adapted to the slight sensation of objectivity that had been her original experience with it. The other great thing about her 3D arm was that it could hold heavy objects, like her suitcase, for longer times than her other, natural, arm could.

Carrying her case effortlessly, she took the supertube to the heliport, then took the copter to the helipad that used to be an oil platform. There was a party there—teenagers, how tiresome—so she took a glider to Stepoff Point, the last bit of land before the ocean.

Her destination was a small spot on the planet where the natural evolution of plastic was taking place. She was interested in plastics and she was interested in this development; she thought (as many did) that plastics had in many ways shaped the present and would save the future. She was nearing thirty and it was time to think of how she could contribute to life; she might get a clue from this visit.

The skimmer from the Stepoff Point took over four hours to get to Sister Island and on its way passed four other floating islands, reclaimed and now habitable. She saw one that seemed to be connected pieces. "That island over there," she said to the pilot, pointing. *Pilot* was, of course, a useless term. The skimmer was on auto, but the unions demanded qualified help in case of emergencies. "Is that a reclaimed island?"

"Not yet," he said. He was middle-aged and pale (good sunscreen implants), with sinewy arms and a half-smile, half-frown combination that was charming. "It's still just garbage."

She studied it with interest. Garbage had been outlawed, of course, but garbage still existed, washing down off mountains, washing out from waste piles disturbed by weather or earthquakes or construction projects, or coming up again after ocean dumping. She saw plastic bags and buoys and fishing nets and plastic cups and bottles and wrappers of various kinds. They floated along together.

The pilot leaned towards her. "I've made islands," he said. "I spent years making islands. The place we're going to—I worked there. There were a bunch of us, volunteers, young kids, full of the thrill. We wove the plastics together. We caught the bags and cups and straws and toothbrushes, and we made them into the islands."

"The islands are great," she said. She wanted to make a good impression, so she was very enthusiastic. "I've always been fascinated. I put in a request over a year ago for it—you know, the event. On Egg Island."

The pilot looked at her for a moment. "I made Egg Island. Not me alone, of course. But the islands—I made the islands."

She was quiet for a few minutes, out of awe and a sense of embarrassment. The skimmer roared over the water. They passed vast clumps of Sargasso. A few flying fish raced them, then veered off.

"You made Egg Island," she said finally. She felt close to tears and tapped the back of her hand to give herself just a drop of endorphins. "Tell me about it. I've been longing to go to Egg Island ever since I first heard of it."

He nodded and they introduced themselves. His name was Wen Wickler. The skimmer thrummed, even creating some kind of wind, despite the fact that they were entering the doldrums, that place far out in the ocean where all the winds died and all the garbage gathered.

"I was 30 when I came out here," Wen said. "I was burning with the need to heal the earth. I had watched my mother's farm blow away with the drought. You weren't born yet, but my generation faced it all: too little clean water, soil that had been poisoned by pesticides, animal extinctions. And garbage, garbage everywhere. We had filled in every nook and cranny, it seemed, and it leached out and got into the water tables. Too much of what we lived in was dirty and dangerous. We looked to the seas.

"The first volunteers got some backing by some big polluters who had to do it by law, and we took trawlers to the ocean and began to pick up all the floating plastics. We did that for a few years, but the garbage went on for miles. And where were we supposed to put the plastics? We talked about it and it seemed reasonable, eventually, to go with what was already happening. It was collecting in patches, in islands of its own, all the plastics, the lost stuff, the things from tsunamis and from ocean dumping, the lost things and the forgotten things, just drifting out to the doldrums and bumping into one another.

"We trawled and gathered and sorted. Lots of plastic ropes to tie things together. Nets to tie things together. Cups to be part of the 'earth' of the island. We sifted and netted and wove and strung together. It took months, years; we weathered it and built a spongy sort of island and then built shacks on it from boogie boards and construction debris that floated out from the disasters occurring everywhere. We took dolls and toys and made little sceneries; we took buckets and plastic bottles and began to collect rainwater (not much) and began to make evaporation coils to make drinking water from the sea. We set up small farms in plastic bins, and began to tie seaweed to the shores of our islands. We kept weaving into it, pushing down the cups and plastic shoes and child's shovels and whatever we found, weaving it deeper and deeper and spreading it out. Islands. We made islands." He stopped and shook his head.

"I'm so impressed," she said. "We learned about that in school. I always dreamed of being like you someday." She made a modest sound. "I kind of forgot that, though. I went into industrial plastics, after my accident." She shrugged, lifting her 3D arm a bit. "I got waylaid. My generation—all we know is plastics. Your generation—you saw things, didn't you? Surprising things?"

"We saw the changes start," he said huskily. The boat bobbed forward. Out in the distance, she could see the first of the islands. She wanted it all to slow down; she wanted to hear what he had to say. All of this was magic, was storytime; the first plastic islands, the change. The change over. The first sightings.

"I wanted to see the eggs," she said finally. Her voice was soft; she didn't want to seem egotistical, to gather importance from her desire. Because in front of her, here was someone who had probably been one of the ones who figured out what was happening. He was heraldic.

He pushed a button on the dashboard of the boat. She had no doubt it was, strictly speaking, unnecessary. The skimmer could do it all by itself. He was insignificant now. One of the people who had discovered the eggs, now a token pilot on a ship that didn't need him.

"I took some classes after the farm failed. I thought at first it was just a question of learning what to do. That we could fix it," he said. "I didn't realize how much there was to fix. We knew the waters were rising, we saw that the shore was disappearing. But I was inland. I was landlocked. Of course there were water restrictions, even there. But one year snow geese fell from the sky and convinced me that I had to *do* something. I ended up here. I knew nothing about this." He shrugged. "But I could listen and I could work. We had discussions all the time, how to proceed, what made most sense."

"I heard there are eels on Sister Island now," she said. "Birds come sometimes."

He nodded. "The jellyfish are the real indicator. They're easy to catch and study. Microfibers are everywhere, you know, but they're hard to spot and the earliest teams didn't have microscopes. But we could see the small plastic beads—Styrofoam and microbeads, breakdowns of the soft plastics—under the hoods of the jellyfish, even along the arms and tentacles. From what we could see, doing no harm."

She looked at her own arm and flexed it. "I've read there are jellyfish bigger than whales."

He laughed. "Haven't seen that. Not here, anyway. Things are relatively predictable here."

"What was the first thing you saw that gave you a clue?" Audra asked.

He squinted slightly. "We caught fish to eat, of course. And we saw the plastic pieces. We couldn't see the microplastics, as I said. But a piece of plastic line; a plastic wheel off a small toy—things like that. A few of the fish were damaged, but there were others that seemed to incorporate the stuff without harm. Those were interesting." He grinned.

Audra sighed. "I wish I'd been there. I mean, what an experience! I can't wait to see the island. I hear there's a research center. I know it's just a shack, but it's still amazing to me that people live there. They made it work."

"Well, we all made it work," he agreed.

"Oh yes, of course, sorry." When he didn't continue, she said, "Are you here for the laying?"

He nodded.

"I suspect I only got permission because of my arm," she said and flexed it.

He looked impressed. "That must be handy," he said. "I suppose you can control it to the nth degree?"

She grinned. "To the nth," she said.

By now they were close to Sister Island. Brother Island could be seen in the distance, still a few days away, floating with the faint currents or what little wind there was. Egg Island was smaller and therefore harder to observe over distances, but the currents were predictable enough.

She saw a figure waiting by the slip. "That must be Johncy," she said and waved with her true arm. She caught Wen noticing that. "Emotions seem to go out my natural arm. Always have, always will."

"Of course. It's called appropriate use. The organism finds its job. It adapts. We're thankful for that. It's what might save us." He smiled. "And it doesn't seem to hurt, does it? The plastic?"

"No."

He watched the shoreline intently. "After all this time, after all the harm, plastics might be a solution. It's a strange thing for my generation to think about."

He stood leaning against the controls, tapping one absent-mindedly, slightly weathered and not entirely used to having the world surprise him. Her 3D arm had been an improvement in her life and had been offered to her soon after her accident. It was common enough by then. But she believed she understood what he meant. "Bodies accept almost everything, don't they?" she said finally.

They landed at what passed for a pier—a projection of plastic gas tanks roped together to make a sort of fork jabbing into the sea. Wen steered in while Audra studied the geography. The main structure on the island was made of a series of cabins or rooms, lightly constructed of all kinds of materials. There was a plastic picnic table outside and molded plastic chairs. Wen handed up their bags and four large black duffel bags. "The gear," he said to Johncy, who grabbed the bags as Wen handed them up. Then Johncy reached a hand out and grabbed her, and steadied her as she stepped on the island.

She turned to him and saw he had one brown eye and one clear eye.

"My god!" She couldn't help herself. "I've never seen a plastic eye before. I thought my arm was special." She laughed. "I'm sure it takes a lot more refinement to make an eye."

Johncy smiled and nodded. "I was only the second to have one; the first was a monkey. One who'd lost her eye from a disease; don't worry, it wasn't tortured. It lived for a few more years, till the monkey fungus got it. But I got this eye." He held a hand out to help Wen up. "Wen, good to see you. It wouldn't be the same without you." He turned to Audra. "You know he discovered the turtles, don't you?"

"He didn't exactly say."

"Too modest. Or too secretive?" He laughed. "He always insisted that only plastics get told about the turtles and this island. We're very protective."

She turned to consider Wen. "You're plastic too?"

"My heart," he said easily. "If you lean in real close you'll hear a different sound, more like a shush than a normal heart. It's been running for about five years now. We don't have a good idea about stress factors on plastic when it's internal. One of the reasons Egg Island is kind of an obsession with me."

A young woman came paddling up in a plastic kayak and pulled into the other tine of the fork. "Egg is coming along," she said, clearly delighted. "I think it will be early this year. It's right behind Brother and to the east."

"It's good you came when you did," Wen told Audra. "I wasn't going to come 'till tomorrow. I might have missed the sight of it. I love watching it arrive."

The woman's name was Kit, and she, along with Johncy and Michael, showed Audra around. They walked on the rippling island with absolute assurance, explained how they placed plastic straws and coils to reclaim water, how they dried seaweed in racks and baked it in solar ovens into a kind of bread. A modest vertical garden grew herbs, tomatoes, and beans.

"I brought extra water," Wen said. "And some groceries. And eggs, of course," he said, winking. That brought a round of applause and laughs from the staff.

The island was almost a quarter-mile around, so its motion was relatively minor, but it made her dizzy. They promised her she would get her balance by morning.

Water splashed a little during the night, and occasionally a fish would flip out of water, or something would fall off the island. Once she heard voices offshore, so she supposed that the staff went for swims, and that must mean that the oil slicks had moved off for a while. Or they accepted being covered in oil. Or there was another alternative she knew nothing about. She slept.

She did have her sea legs the next morning, rolling a little as she walked over the woven plastics, watching her step, but no longer in any way queasy. They grabbed plates and cups of coffee (also Wen's gift) and sat staring out to the east.

"I think," Michael said, and stopped. Everyone seemed to freeze, cups or forks in hand, just looking. They held a collective breath.

"Yes," Wen said. "Yes. That's Egg all right."

They stood up. They stared at the island, watching it slap gently through the waves, pushed by a twist in the current, by the merest suggestion of wind. Audra thought it seemed to be aware of them, to be heading for them deliberately, even though she knew of course that the island itself was passive. Still, she was filled with expectation; they all were tense with anticipation, pulling out cameras and logbooks and charts from previous years.

Audra stayed by Wen's side. "When will it happen? Is it always at night?"

"So far," he said. "How long is 'always' under these circumstances? It's been eleven years now, and I was the first to see it. Among the first, technically, I suppose. But I saw it, shook my head to clear it, saw it, and called the others. A wonderful thing."

"Will the island be here tonight, then?"

He shook his head. "Probably not. But tomorrow, yes, I think so."

She spent the day doing the chores she'd been assigned, which included watering the garden. The reclamation straws dripped slowly, and she had to be careful to replace any bucket she took with another bucket immediately; not one drop of water could be lost. The plants poked up through plastic tarps, so that the soil would hold the water as long as possible. The tarps were lifted an hour a day to avoid mold or fungus in the soil. This was done by hand; they stood around, tarps lifted, holding corners or centers, chatting about the next things to do or any topic that came up.

"Does your arm ever bother you?" Michael asked her.

She looked down at it; it had become familiar, it had become a part of her. "No," she said. "Not at all. It's part of me now."

He smiled. "I have a leg," he said. "Works perfectly, too."

The others nodded. They each had a replacement part. "I sometimes forget about it," she said. "Though it can do more, lift more, have more force, than my original arm. So I think I've been improved." She grinned.

They told their stories, one by one, what they lost and how they had gained a replacement. "To think," Wen said, "how much damage we've done with plastic; how much we've destroyed. And how plastic might turn around and save us, in return."

"We've lost a lot; I won't deny we've lost a lot. It was a hard lesson. The world is changed," Michael said.

"The world is always changing," Wen said. "We just have to find a direction for it."

"Oh, I don't know," Audra said, laughing, "it seems to have found its direction on its own."

They contemplated that for a while, gazing off to Egg Island as the sun set, wishing for the morning.

And in the morning it was there, a few hundred yards away, a faint new slap of water hitting plastics. Egg Island was a looser island than Sister Island, and there would only be a day or so to weave plastic ropes into it, to maintain some kind of integrity to it as they went forward. Some swam over, dragging ropes and nets behind them; some paddled over on foam boards. They pushed aside the plastic eggs, looking like mottled Easter eggs that lay strewn over the surface. They pushed some down into the matted debris, and used the coils of ropes and plastic bags they'd brought over from Sister Island to sew the island together. They walked carefully, but even so they had to rescue each other from patches where their legs went through. It was safer to kneel and inch their way around, patting and tucking, pushing ropes down and through and up again.

They worked quickly and efficiently, patch by patch, tightening the island so it would maintain integrity, aware that the island would only be here briefly. "This part needs help," someone would call out, and one or two people would nod and kneel their way across to that section, pulling pieces together, working like weavers on a giant, watery loom.

The island landed up against their own island, and they took a break, went home, ate quickly, and went back to work. One particularly bad section required a ladder laid flat on it to hold their weight as they worked to restore it. On the far side, a wide fish net with ballast had been caught and dragged along; they hoisted it up and wove it in. A hairnet, Audra thought briefly and then tied her section into the mass of the island.

They worked for two days that way, barely speaking, pushing in lines and pulling them out, sewing the island, tugging at it, patting it and pushing it.

Egg Island was still moving even as it rested against Sister Island; it had its own volition, its own imperative to move, move, move on.

"Soon," Johncy said. "I think tomorrow," and they nodded, exhausted, and slept without further discussion. The constant work had tamped down their sense of anticipation, but now it rose again and even as exhaustion overtook them, they slept fitfully, waiting for dawn.

The island was now just touching on the east end of Sister Island; it had shifted slightly all night long, touching and moving the length of Sister Island. They could feel the tactile way the two islands met, a handshake, a rub on the shoulder, the smallest, most basic communion. Not that anyone believed the islands were alive. They were part of a new order, however. The earth was ingesting the plastics and mixing the plastics and finding a new use for them. The unnatural was becoming the natural. The order was changing and it hardly mattered whether it was for better or for worse.

And in the midst of all the change, strange new beauties occurred.

They worked all day and kept vigil when the dark fell and the moon rose. They sat and murmured on their own moving island, talking of nothing important. Things they'd seen, books they'd read, odd places they'd been. But their conversations only lasted a few minutes and they would pause and listen. Their ears played tricks on them; their eyes saw shapes that turned out to be yet another plastic bag, with trapped air bubbles, a child's toy, a piece of Styrofoam, all things that they gathered and saved. "If you see a plastic arm wash by," Audra said, "please save it for me!"

"Or a leg!" Michael cried.

"I think a plastic eye would be hard to spot," Johncy said.

And then the first sea turtle appeared, breaking out of the water, its reptile head prehistoric and determined. On Sister Island, the people stiffened and pointed and got to their feet and stepped over onto Egg Island, now close to detaching itself from Sister Island. The turtle dragged itself up Egg Island slowly, thick flippers pushing against discarded flashlights and computer keyboards and the tarps and pails of the island, its shell toughened and knobbed with small pieces of plastics. And then another and another, all huge and gnarled, and they moved across the discarded plastics that had been thrown into the sea and had grown into the sea. One by one they inched their way forward, their backs stippled with plastics that had latched onto their animal bodies, seamless and as irreproachable as Audra's arm, as Wen's heart. It was a selective turn in the usefulness of flesh, in the utility of plastic. Omnipresent now, polluting what had formerly been pristine, pierced by the shoot, the claw, the plow, plastics had threaded their ways back into life.

The turtles selected their space and shifted, pushing their great bodies back and forth, having found the spot where they would lay their eggs, which had gathered bits of microbeads in the process of forming. The eggshells had once been smooth; they now had a granular quality to them, like sand in paint. Was it an evolutionary device, making them unpalatable to predators? The turtles' massive heads looked straight ahead, mouths slightly open from their efforts. These mouths ended in sharp beaks, and their infants would only emerge when their own beaks were strong enough to pierce the mix of plastic and calcium housing them.

Audra leaned delicately from where she stood on the edge of Sister Island and patted the head of a turtle that had chosen a spot near her. She patted it with her 3D arm. She felt the turtle's damp knobby head, then let her hand move down to its carapace. The leatherback's shell was not as hard as other turtles'. It had bony plates beneath the skin on its back, and Audra could feel irregularities on the plates, a feel of edges and lines that felt, to her delicate 3D fingers, familiar; related. Bits and pieces of plastics had worked through the turtle's skin to the plates below. The turtles, the eggshells, her arm, Wen's heart: all connected, all synchronous.

The whole event was over in less than an hour. The eggs were laid, the turtles covered them with any loose debris so that they would remain hidden among the other types of plastic overlaying and underlaying the island. They heaved themselves around and used their massive flippers to drive themselves forward, until finally they slipped back into the ocean. Heads could be seen leaving steadily away from the island, and then the heads dipped silently, one by one, and were gone.

The moon was setting, running a light on the ocean. A few oil slicks picked up muted rainbow colors and the merest movements of the waves broke the colors up like a sophisticated painting. A single turtle head surfaced and disappeared again.

"I want to live here forever," Audra thought, picking idly at the garbage closest to her. It seemed her arm, the 3D arm, was intent on sifting and sorting.

Egg Island pulled away slowly, like a lumbering train obeying strict laws. It wavered and washed in the setting moon's last luminous light.

On Sister Island, they joined hands and rejoiced at the beauty of the world.

Your Right Arm
NIN HARRIS

His name was Jagdeep. He did not believe in ghosts.

"Did you kill the last human?" Teng asked, her eyes avid, curiosity making her quiver. Rasakhi knew the question was inevitable, but this did not stop the sigh. Four of Teng's hind-legs wove indigo and tan-dyed mengkuang strips into the mats that were everywhere on the nursery ship. Teng shivered as she worked. Rasakhi did not bother to remind her that the cold was just an illusion, encased as Teng was in a silver praying-mantis chassis. Rasakhi had evaded cybernetic enhancement her whole life, fearful of that gap between her consciousness and the supplemented consciousness of augmented parts.

It was always cold on this ship.

Rasakhi welcomed the chill. It reminded her that she was still encased in flesh, failing though it was.

"I lived with him, as you well know," she said to Teng. No one would remember her triumphs as a navigator. Everyone would remember her in relation to the last human.

"But do you remember how he died? Did you kill him?" Teng asked again, seemingly unaware that she was being repetitive.

Rasakhi looked away from the engineer. Just beyond them, fledgling apsaras moved marbles from groove to groove carved into long congkak boards, a game they had taken with them from the nusantara. On a sanded platform, other children played hopscotch, jumping from square to square as they sang counting songs Rasakhi had taught them. Above them, the lights glowed a muted green, soothing optically enhanced eyes that were trained to look for patterns in messages that floated before them all of the time, but for more material things, like chairs, and corners. The earliest engineers quickly learned the importance of adjusting the lighting on every ship.

"Jagdeep was running from the force that imploded the last human colony. We did not do that. It was not in our best interests to drive humans into extinction. It's far better for you to ask if I remember the first time I met him. The first time I met him was the day that Jagdeep was put into a humanoid biotech replacement unit. I do not even know if he had any humanity left on the day our eyes first met."

Teng's look was inquisitive to the point of intrusion. The apsara-hybrid engineer had transferred to Rasakhi's sector three months ago, and had not wasted time in befriending the retired navigator who ran the nursery ship. She seemed completely insensible to the fact that her presence was not wanted. Teng was not the first and would likely not be the last who would want to unearth the secret behind Rasakhi's life with Jagdeep.

"Did you love him, Rasakhi?"

"I am surprised by the question, Teng. Love is a human emotion. It is not an emotion we are conditioned to acknowledge. How do you go from asking if I killed him to asking if I loved him? I don't understand these wild connections you're making."

"Apsaras were bred for love on the world we came from," Teng said, her visored eyes insistent upon knowing the truth, "we were also bred to kill the things we love."

"Yes, apsaras are also voluptuous dancers who are somehow lighter than air. We also shimmer when we dance." Rasakhi said with some irony, throwing Teng a wintry look. "Say rather, that we were bred for the pleasure of humans. Love is a different thing altogether."

"I have never shimmered in my life, not even when I had a complete apsara body," Teng said, smiling, "but it is true. They bred us from the bunian that they stole to serve as court-dancers and companions. But that means that we have human DNA, don't we?"

"We are not trained and conditioned to acknowledge human emotions," Rasakhi said.

"Have you truly never loved, Rasakhi?" Teng sounded wistful. Rasakhi reminded herself of how young the engineer was. Be patient, be gentle, she told herself.

"If we feel an emotion, how do we label it? The way that humans label such things? I know amusement. I know that I am happy with companionship. I know what it feels to have a void when someone has left you. I do not know if that is the same as knowing love."

Teng said, "We do not mate. We used to, when humans were necessary. But then they became redundant, and so did biological functions."

"Well then. There's your answer. Why do you ask me about an emotion that is redundant to our kind? The bunian ensured that none of us would ever need to mate again. Not the bunian, not the apsara, nor our sisters, the bird-clawed Khinnaree. All we require is companionship, and community. We have the consensus, we have the engineering wherewithal to ensure that we shall never go extinct. So why would we have a need to kill?"

Teng looked bashful, "The songs the humans sing about love. They are so sad and so beautiful. There are so many of those songs in the Sound Library. I listen, and it makes me feel strange. I always wondered how it actually felt. I tried talking to the converted humans but in their biotech systems they have forgotten all of those things."

Rasakhi's obsidian eyes softened as she looked at the younger apsara, "They are no longer what they used to be. Upon conversion, consciousness changes. They no longer have the depth perception required to parse emotions, or sense-data. Emotions, if they exist, exist as phantom limbs. As ghosts. The memory of an emotion, simulated upon cue. And yet, these memories are the backbone of our colony's cultures."

We had time before that last asteroid obliterated earth. Ample time to prepare.

The sun was younger when we first took to the skies in our first machines, made of wood and bronze, borne upwards by a fleet of armored garuda. We had no need of science then, we were fueled by sakti and by the benedictions of the holy bird, the Jentayu. This was not to last, as our magics faded, and we learned that we too, needed to master science and engineering.

The sun was older when the first super giant solar flare knocked out our strongest shield. For millennia, we had escaped the path of comets and asteroids. Narrow misses.

Sudden solar flares that could have knocked out our power supplies, and our magical reserves. The solar flares, and all manner of cosmic exigencies failed, because we worked overtime. All of us. The Khinnaree admirals, the bunian and apsara engineers.

We were safe until the sakti that held our shields up got weaker and weaker, while the asteroids came by more frequently.

I do not remember the first navigator who guided the first fleet of ships strong enough to transport all of us and all of the humans away from the solar system. I do not remember the day when humans were made aware of our existence. I do not remember the first human fleet of ships, or the first space war between our kind and the humans, several solar systems away from earth. But I remember accounts of that exodus. I remember enough to tell you about it as though I was there. Even if I must supplement that account with details of my own imagined recollection.

Jagdeep was the last human colonist. He had taken the last fighter pod, and had crashed into our fleet. He sustained serious injuries. This was not a fleet of soldiers. We were navigators and scientists. We were cybernetic engineers. We were astro-botanists and DNA scientists. There was no need to harvest his DNA immediately—the bunian and apsaras had evolved long ago. They had augmented themselves, and could replicate well enough. There was no need to do anything to the last human, except to watch him die.

Or to allow him to live.

Mercy was not a thing exclusive to humans.

The bunian, the apsara, and the Khinnaree had long learned that their bodies had attributes that allowed them to flow easier into the cybernetic interfaces built by the human fleets. They had adapted easier to it, and their engineers had pillaged human technology in order to forge better bodies for members of their colony who had lost their limbs. They began to do the same for the humans that they had rescued or had vanquished.

The first night we met, I watched as the engineers fitted Jagdeep to the biotech units that replaced his left arm and the entire side of his torso that had been incinerated when his ship crashed into our fleet. It was a painful process. He cried, often. I held his right hand as he looked pleadingly up at me, for mercy, for death. They replaced his limbs, one by one. Except for his right arm.

His right hand, to hold my own.

We used a humanoid frame for his body. He did not choose, like you, to be in an insectoid carapace. He clung on to his humanity. Jagdeep did not take to the replacements as easily as the others. He was too weak, too fragile.

When he could walk, we would walk. I brought him to the sprawling courtyard in my apartments. I astonished him with the grandeur of our plantations and of the ecosystems we had replicated and preserved. And he taught me of the ways of planting that they had improved upon.

And he would tell me things about his life.

He was trained as a fighter pilot, but he yearned to be a gardener. They had greenhouses in their fleet. Small, crude things built into abandoned storage halls. They grew yams, and water spinach, and tapioca. Some even tried to cultivate rice, but it was a very different kind of rice from the paddy fields of earth. We tried to improve on that, Jagdeep and I. We grew lentils and spices. He cooked for me dhal curries and parathas. Out of respect for my mate, I too became vegetarian.

We were happy.

We lived together, apsara and human, the first such union since our combined fleets had left earth's solar system.

And the last.

We turned their kind into hybrids. They thanked us, one by one, as we switched them off as humans. We connected their consciousnesses to various biotech parts if they were still functional, or to our monolithic mainframes when nothing could be saved of their bodies. Their sakti bolstered our own embodied magics. We watched as consciousness dissipated, to be replaced by pattern recognition and simulacra of consciousness that became our communications systems between ships. They became bodies that could not decay. We harvested not just DNA from their bodies, but sakti, that force that had fueled our floating cities on earth, and kept them invisible to human eyes.

When age took first his kidneys, and then disease gradually weakened his heart, we knew the engineers would come for him. It was their last chance to get the last batch of pure human DNA, and of human sakti. They would attach his consciousness to one of the monoliths that fueled our ships and our communication systems. He would live on in the fleet.

On that last night, we sat together on my bed, his right hand in my left hand. I kissed him on the mouth gently, so as not to exert his heart. His eyes begged me again.

He asked me to smother him with a pillow, to do anything before they severed him completely from humanity, before his heart was replaced the way his kidneys had been replaced, before his brain was severed from his body.

"Did you do it? Did you snuff him out?" Teng's silver praying mantis fore-legs were busy at work on a second mat, but her eyes were hungry. Rasakhi's softening regard towards Teng was halted by those eyes.

She said, "Why do you suppose we do this? Why do we reproduce a past none of us actually know? Why do we memorialize the humans that we have turned into machines?"

Teng shook her head, bewildered. "I don't know. Does it matter?"

"Why do you ask me questions about remembrance, and of love, when you do not even bother to ask why we play congkak, and weave mengkuang and rattan mats, long after they have lost their relevance? Why do you ask me if I killed the last human when we continue to profit from their systemic death? I did not kill the last human, Teng. *We* did that."

I could not smother him. I wept in his arms, both organic and inorganic. He cried silently into my hair. We fell asleep. In the morning they came for him. I clung to him and screamed into their faces. His eyes begged at me.

I scrambled and fought them all: bunian, apsara, claw-footed Khinnaree. Yes, even the Khinnaree in full-berserk mode. I kicked, I bit at them.

Perhaps I have Khinnaree blood somewhere in my ancestry too.

His heart expired during the struggle.

They confined me in my quarters for a year.

I did not kill the last human, *we* killed him.

They taught us how to kill. They taught us how to enslave, how to colonize, how to exploit.

A long time ago, when the first bunian princess was stolen by the first man who dragged her away from her celestial robes, we learned the price of being valued for how we looked.

A long time ago we learned to transform into tigers, into owls, into trees to hide from them. We learned how to grow wings, to become swan-maidens and owl-vampires. Some of us turned into the chicken-feet Khinnaree of the Himmapan. Some of us became nenek kebayan, old women of the jungle who drugged wicked men with malicious potions and dispensed sage advice to virtuous warriors.

We learned to build machines, to live in the sky. We learned to harvest the sakti that made us beautiful and powerful. We used that celestial force to create weapons and ways in which to ensure we would never again be stolen.

We stole back the women they stole from us, the ones they bred with humans to create apsaras, my ancestors. We stole their kind to propagate our own. We became an empire of bunian, apsaras, and Khinnarees.

We did not learn love from the humans. We did learn nostalgia, that step-cousin of memory. But our relationship with humans has always been complex, for they are bred into us.

We used our technology to protect them as well. To protect the planet we shared.

Jagdeep gave me comfort. I held on to the memory of that comfort for a very long time in the year that they had me confined. I yearned to return to his arms, to touch his right arm, to cradle his right palm within the warmth of my own. I knew that what was left of him was now encased in a silver cylinder, with no surface of skin left for me to touch. With no consciousness, no qualia left to recognize what we shared.

All that was left of him were algorithms and the processing of external stimuli. Simulating sentience.

He learned from me the apsara ways of silence, and of meditation. We meditated a lot when we did not work in the gardens and plantations together.

Those human songs you asked me about?

He sang some of them for me as I strung together cempaka chains for our mutual amusement.

When they released me from confinement, I was honorably discharged. Retired. They sent me here to be a nursemaid to fledgling apsaras.

Teng watched as the aging apsara stood up, walking towards the wall that showed them the stars surrounding the void that was a dead galaxy.

"He fuels this ship," Rasakhi said.

"I know," Teng said, "I tend to his unit. It is the strangest thing, his unit. It is always so cold. He sometimes speaks. But often he does not."

Ah. Rasakhi gave the younger woman a speculative look. She said, "All of the humans that we captured or rescued did not believe in ghosts. So strange, considering that we exist, and now they don't, except as hybrids, a blend between machine, apsara DNA, and human parts. They would have done the same to Jagdeep, except that his body had deteriorated beyond help. And in that last struggle, his heart expired. They punished me for that. Not for killing him. He would have made a far more superior model if he possessed a functioning heart."

Teng shivered.

"It's getting even colder. How is that possible? I keep double-checking the calibrations on the heating system. They're always in order."

"It's always cold on this ship. It will always be this cold."

Rasakhi did not articulate the reasons behind the temperature. It was not needed. She met Teng's eyes. In the end, this at least was understood.

That Which Stands Tends Toward Free Fall
BENJANUN SRIDUANGKAEW

It is the tyrant, she thinks as the window thrums with the thunder of engine and the floor shakes. As the floodlights strobe across the courtyard and the dark gives way to annihilating white. Helicopter blades claim the night, their seismic noise spreading like a banner of ownership.

Rinthira prepares, though not in such a way that it will be obvious she has done so. She spreads out her books and collection of taxidermied insects. She puts on the spectacle she doesn't need; she drinks the lemon tea—too sweet—that she doesn't enjoy, until the glass is exactly half-empty. There will be security detail: women in black, muscular and armed. Chatsumon likes to say, only half-joking, that men are vestigial.

Footsteps. In her head, the conversation is already playing out. The security detail will be left at the door, to preserve privacy, to reinstitute that impression of friendliness—a social call between friend and friend, former lovers. Nothing more complex.

Rinthira touches her hair. The bun makes her look austere, old, a schoolmistress martinet—the kind who walks about with a stick. She tightens it further still. Wishes briefly that she'd dressed more homely today, more shapelessly.

The door opens. She gets a look at the security detail. A soldier in her forties—this surprises Rinthira, who expected someone much younger; that's how Chatsumon's taste runs.

The colonel sits and regards the spread of papers and taxidermy, the insect corpses behind acrylic. Regards Rinthira. Asks how she is, like every other time.

Rinthira answers perfunctorily, sipping her tea between scripted words. Then, "How's Ubol?"

"Good. Testosterone agrees with him." Chatsumon's boy is the only male she admits into her life, perhaps. "Won't you offer me a drink?" Said with a coquette's melody, a murmur of play.

"Your security must be hungry."

"She will manage. It's good to keep bodyguards lean. Do you follow the news?"

She does, piecemeal. It is comforting to pretend she lives inside a bubble but in practice that is make-believe. Besides, old habits linger eternal, hibernating sometimes but never dead. She thinks of the woods that surround her, the Ayutthaya ruins radiating from where she lives as though she resides at ground zero. Calcified boats caught on balconies, glittering with melted sand. The canals, dry and black. It is serene, idyllic, and she is happy. But in the evening she'd gaze up and away as far as her vision will stretch. "I can't say I do."

"Status quo isn't going to stay status quo forever. It's all well and good to hope the big players will nuke each other out and leave the rest of us alone." Chatsumon swats at the air with one large, sure palm. A hand callused, a knowing hand. "The Americans just took Luzon."

Too close to home, but . . . "They were always going to take it." And no doubt the Filipino administration had few choices. Those old air bases were always going to be an excuse, one day, semi-territory already. A treaty will have been rarefied, promising that once America has seized victory, the archipelago nation will be spared, enriched. Elevated. There is a feudal directness to America these days. War flenses the flab of pretension and sears away all diplomacy, leaving behind the marrow of true intent and character. "Manila isn't any sort of threat."

"Factories. Assembly lines are easy to repurpose."

Contrails in the sky, making cat's cradle. Rinthira still knows the formations: these things are difficult to unlearn. "I'm not part of the defense ministry." Anymore.

"That's right. You are a private citizen now, a civilian." Chatsumon tips her head. "My apologies, I shouldn't try to drag you back into the thick of it. It's late to fly back though; could I have a room?"

It's not that late, Rinthira could say. Krungthep is barely an hour away, even taking into account the complicated security protocols, the detours. Two at most. Chatsumon's excuse is thin, she could say. There's no room ready, she could offer, an excuse equally thin. Rinthira is well versed in the science of saying no in general and saying no to the colonel in particular. "If you want."

"Yes. Thanks."

Rinthira keeps the guest room stocked, cleaned, smelling of detergent: laundry fresher than the rest of the house. An issue of manner, byproduct of an upbringing she can't shake that declares domesticity requisite in any girl. She doesn't ask where the bodyguard will sleep. That woman, kept lean, will manage; probably will not submit to the indignity of rest. Soldier pride is a shield against mortal needs.

Rinthira showers thoroughly and goes to bed in a nightgown. Silk like a virgin sky, hemmed with the coyest rose. Usually she sleeps naked, luxuriating in the sloppy ease of being alone. Now she smells like grapefruits from the expensive soap and she is conscious, too much, of the hair covering her shins. The wirier ones, like vowels, at groin and armpits. Adolescent anxieties: beneath her and sanded off by tactical training, in theory.

It is an hour and a half before she leaves her duvet and heads for the guest room, clad in near-lingerie and cotton robe. The guard is nowhere to be seen; the door is unlocked. When she enters there is pale light through curtains thrown open wide, and Chatsumon is awake, propped on pillows.

"I thought you'd never," Chatsumon says. It's her voice that is her best weapon, more than even her reflexes and marksmanship. The right amount of thrum with which to seduce, honeyed satin. The right resonance with which to command, velvet iron.

Rinthira bolts the door behind her and steps out of her robe. "What if I'd been an intruder."

"Are you armed?" At Rinthira's nod, the colonel smiles. "Concealed carry in so little. I ought to look for it; what if you *had* been an intruder, here for my life."

The night gown slips off, strap by strap. The body craves that which is unhealthy, Rinthira thinks, even harmful. Sugar and fat, carbohydrates and salt. Alcohol, tobacco, marijuana. Only fingers kneading her breast and already she wants to demand and urge *faster*. They have agreed on a nonsensical little phrase, but Rinthira has never had to use it whether with her legs spread wide until they hurt or with her face pressed against a cold, rough wall and her wrists in soft cuffs. Chatsumon inspires hunger for excess.

Chatsumon peels the silk all the way down, lifts Rinthira's leg where a derringer is strapped mid-calf. Facing inward, to least interrupt the gown's silhouette. The colonel laughs and bends to kiss one scarred knee. What will the guard think, Rinthira wonders, though does not dwell. It will not be that soldier's first time accompanying her colonel for a trip like this. Chatsumon doesn't keep innocents close.

They lack implements and the bed is soft, but pain often amplifies. Rinthira climaxes with most of Chatsumon's hand buried deep inside her.

(Orgasm is the moment of confession, she used to say but no longer believes. She comes all over Chatsumon's hand and it isn't a baring of the soul or even personality. What's between them is not love but rather an artificial scarcity carefully maintained. A supply chain of negative space as long as their years wound together.)

She rests on her side, loose-limbed and back to Chatsumon, her pulse on slow burn. Soon Chatsumon will push her down and she will satisfy the colonel, return the favor, conclude this night.

But Chatsumon doesn't reach for her. "Do you know," the colonel says, voice wondering, "I never believed in serendipity. In virtue or sin, in the karmic weight. Lately though, I've been changing my mind. Having my mind changed."

"Let me finish you."

Chatsumon breathes out, audibly trying to measure out her rhythms. "Phiksunee is coming to see you."

Rinthira jerks upright. All at once the afterglow dissolves, replaced by the fight/flight roar in her ears. "No."

"It's necessary. The Americans are coming for you."

The first languages Phiksunee learned were Angrit, Thai, and Jeenglang. They were picked for cultural and numerical factors, chosen by cold reason. Russian, Hindi, and Spanish followed. Only so many lexicon modules could be frontloaded without affecting fluidity, though Phiksunee could translate any word into any other language the way dumb machines or dictionaries could. One of the first things she said to Rinthira was in Angrit: "*I'm a she.*"

It was not a sentence that could've been said in Thai without torturing the syntax to death. Angrit furiously signifies pronouns, *she* and *ey* and *they* and *he* each with distinct meaning. In Thai, Phiksunee repeated, "I'm female."

Rinthira wasn't sure what to make of it. Covert specialist or not she was still a soldier, not an engineer, a coder, a scientist. Out of everyone in the room, only she and Chatsumon didn't hold a PhD or three apiece. There was no round of applause: this was not Phiksunee's first showing and she was not the first of her kind. Rinthira would not learn, until much later, why she was there.

"Karmic weight is for the next life," Rinthira says to the approaching dawn. She is nude—there are no neighbors to worry about—and in this light every imperfection is illuminated, stretch marks and scars and cellulite. "Not this one."

"Maybe if there's no next life, it catches up sooner to compensate."

The curtains shift and rub her ankles like a restless pet. She's considered getting a large dog with exquisite teeth and gunmetal pelt, but never gotten around to the business of acquiring and preparing for the company of another living thing. "Why now?"

Chatsumon has gotten up, naked from the waist down; seems to think better of that and casts off the loose nightshirt. "Phiksunee went looking, after an assassination attempt on Yulya. She found something—something dangerous. You were closer to her than I ever was."

Rinthira watches the colonel in the window a little longer, a gray phantom of female ideal. Broad and muscular, tight abdomen and corded arms, thick thighs that lead to powerful calves. An anatomy of supreme efficiency and strength. Chatsumon keeps in shape with the dedication of an athlete gunning for world class. "I used to be close to her," Rinthira says. Grimacing she shakes that off—Phiksunee insisted on polyglot conversation and it never felt natural. "Sittipong." The AI's creator who made Phiksunee's imprints, then freed her like a bird flung up to the sky, or a tiger let loose. "Where is he?"

"Dead. Part of a negotiation retinue to Israel; American missiles brought the flight down."

Her throat catches. "What about the rest of the team?" It was multinational collaboration, a coder from Saint Petersburg, an engineer from Peking, several analysts from elsewhere. Sittipong was the only Thai, their pride.

"Yulya and Tengfei are fine. They're difficult to access. But some of the analysts aren't so fine." Chatsumon begins to pace, slow, hands behind her, officer-correct. "Some countries are better at protecting their intellectual assets than others. One was captured by the Americans, killed during interrogation. Another was assassinated."

"I'm the only accessible one left. How did they even know I'm part of—" Rinthira shakes her head. "Never mind." A crucial point always leaks: no true secret exists.

"Phiksunee sent me the Americans' routes and locations, with promises that they will be much impeded." A smile, faint. "She worries for you; she always does, and she's never been quite the same after you left. Lack of optimization, she says."

Rinthira shuts her eyes. When she opens them again she is centered, readier. "I better get ready then." Bulletproof gear. Guns. Scramblers, against sniper sighting.

"She advised you stay put; I don't disagree. The Americans have stopped trying for Yulya and Tenfgei because they're securely kept, but we have . . . not made a show of force."

"A show of force would have the opposite effect. We don't *want* America to think of us as a threat."

"The time for that is past." Chatsumon's voice is mild. She slips an arm around Rinthira's waist, slowly stroking her stomach. "America speaks a language of brute might, would understand no other. We've been a threat ever since Phiksunee went online and wrecked their infrastructure."

From which they have never recovered: Phiksunee is more thorough than any human, shattering databases and corrupting communication protocols. She continues, even now, to disrupt it at a speed American engineers can't equal. Anything that connects is hers and her siblings' to scorch. There will be an effective countermeasure, one day—this is an arms race—but not now, not yet.

Morning sees Chatsumon and her bodyguard seeding an aegis around Rinthira's house. The closest neighbors are several blocks away; targeted defense suits her home well. Rinthira, seized by a contrarian impulse, heads for the town center. They have time.

What was once Ayutthaya is now a handful of households, a municipal office, some essentials: hospital, market. Most of the ruins are uninhabitable, and the remaining power-water grid can service only a tiny population: two thousand in cityscape meant for fifty times that. It is testament to the war that a place this close to Krungthep has been so reduced, burned and drowned and burned again. But safe, for now, under Phiksunee's protection.

So much depends on that construct of code and modified flesh, that child of scintillant minds and burning ambition.

The rehabilitation project has brought transplanted trees, grafted to flower and fruit impossibly: a branch extends rose apples over the roof of a clinic, another pours ratchaphruek in yellow cascades over a wrecked school. Color everywhere, to infuse life into the peeling facades and cracked streets. Overgrowth presses close, barely under control, water striders and green ponds and crooning frogs. Stumps draped in moss and spotted fern, orange patches and red stripes and golden freckles.

(If she falls in love it would be with the land, this land, this ruin. She has lost, somewhere along the way, the capacity for romance with another person.)

Lanterns have gone up at the market for Loykrathong, bright paper and silver curlicues, tassels streaming in the cold. Stalls offer candles, matchbooks, krathong braided in orchids and banana leaves, weighed down with cowrie coins. Rinthira doesn't bother—there is no flowing body of water, only pools. In the back of her mind she is counting her ammunition supply, the stashes of armament she's kept throughout the city's dilapidated arteries. She never expected backup, thought of danger as a prospect she would face in solitude. Now she'd have to work with others again.

At the convenience store she buys lemon tea powder, coffee sachets, sugar. At the grocer's she buys chicken stock and kale, flat noodles and eggs. Vectors of attack, ETA, unit composition. All that information she and Chatsumon have. Phiksunee—and her siblings—have allowed American military certain long-range communications, enough for an illusion of functionality. The tactic has obvious pitfalls, but so far between Phiksunee here and her kin in Shenzhen and Kolkata, it appears to work.

"This is a very mundane shopping list, for a former spy."

Conditioned instinct kicks. A gun in her hand, the shopping basket on the floor: where she worked, speed of draw was everything. She is pointing it, safety off, before her cognition catches up. When it does, she sucks in a breath and lowers the weapon, then holsters it entirely. Exhaling she says, "Phiksunee."

No one would have picked out the marionette for what it is. The exterior bears up to scrutiny, even this close. An unremarkable face, large pores, flat nose. Average build, soft around the middle. At the moment she is smiling, dimples parenthetical around her mouth. "It does your daughter a world of good to see you in perfect health."

"My house isn't anechoic." The AI can check in on her any time, view her medical records and vital signs at will. Monitor her sleep, if it so desires.

"Your daughter would never invade your privacy or so casually disobey you." Phiksunee bobs into a quick wai. Switches to Russian: "*The colonel is with you, Mother?*"

Rinthira twitches—not many in Ayutthaya, she supposes, speak Russian. But they are not alone in here. "You know she is."

The AI's smile brightens. Or rather she makes the marionette smile wider—it is an interface, a seeming. "May I join you? I'll clean."

She is noncommittal. Phiksunee drives her home. Going past tableaus of Ayutthaya-that-was, the AI says, "I've missed you deeply. A child severed from her parent is a child in terrible need. Navigating my decision trees has become—suboptimal. It is as though I'm missing crucial protocols, as though some possibilities disappear into my periphery, a cognitive attrition. This is difficult to bear, Mother."

"How are your siblings?" Rinthira says, not expecting an answer.

"Xiaoqing and Alkonost wish you a good new year as we speak. Bilbul's as taciturn as ever, though the soul of duty." Phiksunee does not touch the steering panel but she doesn't need to. Under her guidance the car describes impossible arcs and sine waves. It is not a new vehicle, but nevertheless it glides as though the roads are silk and its wheels a needle. "As far as the Americans are concerned, you are ensconced in Pelangkaraya."

"Not that far away."

"It must be plausible. You wouldn't be in Moscow. Alkonost respects you but ey can hardly bend policy. We're very powerful in many ways and powerless entirely in others. And I want," Phiksunee goes on, "you to be happy. Moscow wouldn't be happy; neither would Peking or anywhere else but Muangthai."

As pestering as a real child, Rinthira will grant. "I'm happy."

"Humans are social, Mother. It is sewn into your neural weft and rides on your every synaptic pulse."

She doesn't argue. Arguing with machines is a futile pursuit, any of them. It's not that the AIs believe themselves infallible, but they tend to fixate on a single track in the way that adolescents do. Eternal adolescents.

Phiksunee greets the colonel with the effusive courtesy of a schoolchild before a strict teacher. On her part Chatsumon accepts this with mock solemnity before showing it the defense systems. "I'll integrate you into Moscow's uplink, get us some air support," Phiksunee says, "just in case. The Americans have limited satellite access, but they still have drones—"

Contrails in the sky, Rinthira thinks again, the background radiation of her childhood. Days going up in smoke as ground-to-air interceptors met drones. At eight she was caught outside on a school day, her safety routines calmly murmuring in her ears to take cover and directing her to the nearest, but it was too late and so she stood: gaze transfixed above as debris sleeted down and her larynx knotted with the stench of shrapnel. She'd survived with no more than lacerations. After that, her career choice was as good as destiny.

In the kitchen she prepares vegetables before realizing with irritation that she's tailored her shopping to Chatsumon's favorite dish. Too domestic, too intimate.

Phiksunee joins her, sitting down with chin in hands and watching her stir-fry the noodles. "Will Mother not ask why I defied her wish and came back?"

"Can you eat now?" Rinthira doesn't look up. "So I can adjust the portions."

"I've got olfactory sensors. The rad-na smells lovely—but no, it'd be wasted on me. Let me introduce you to someone." Phiksunee snaps her fingers and the nearest screen brightens. On it, a young person. They are slim, with improbably high breasts and a face mannequin-smooth. Green eyes, red bobbed hair sleek as patent leather. Clothing just as unlikely: black body-sheath trimmed in muted silver.

"Who's this?"

"A fetus I found raiding one of the American databases. I deleted all copies and iterations, save this one. They aren't aware that I have it."

Rinthira stares for a good long moment before comprehension snaps. "An AI. The Americans are making one like you and the others. Have you told Chatsumon?"

The AI shakes the marionette's head. "*The colonel would simply have me kill her.*"

Kill rather than *destroy*. "I'd suggest no different."

"Of you two, Mother possesses by far the braver and mightier heart. This AI isn't like us, exactly, made on a different architecture and platform. But I believe it can be imprinted. Getting rid of this copy serves no purpose when more might exist; suborning them is the only viable answer, an answer that could give us absolute victory. It would be like tasting the sun, like transcendence, while in defeat their spirit crumples up like withered amaranths." Phiksunee's face dimples. "Besides, I've always wanted to give Mother a grandchild."

The first person Phiksunee imprinted on was Sittipong. The second, after six months of evaluation and acclimation, was Rinthira.

It wasn't that they were afraid of sentient AIs running amok, as such. But it was helpful toward making them orient, teach them human interfacing, give the imprint-holder subtle control. Other teams rotate their imprints, but Sittipong decided Phiksunee would have two permanently. Like a family, and he was a man traditional to a fault. The imprinting obliges the AIs to duty, separate from the hardcoded commands that could be accessed only through a complex check-balance: no country may command its AI without the cooperation of at least two others.

When the imprinting went active, Rinthira asked how Phiksunee felt about this overriding of free will, such as a composite of matrices and heuristics had. To that the AI said, with a radiant smile (different face then, desi phenotype), "Love is not voluntary. It is chemistry; it is free fall. Human children are conditioned to love their caretakers, whether or not they're well treated. Human adults experience attraction without rational thought, by sight and smell and pheromones. My imprint was made with thought and conscious choice—this is more than humans get, Mother."

To that Rinthira made no argument, did not press. She did not want to be the one to incite AI insurrection, if such a thing was even possible. And then Sittipong forfeited his imprint, deleting it from Phiksunee's core, insisting that it would liberate her to more flexible tactics. Perhaps it did; she turned more aggressive in wreaking havoc on enemy systems. Too bold, Rinthira said, but did not forbid. Until Phiksunee attacked a hospital, disabled medical supports, and killed six-fifty. A third of them were civilians, patients and staff. Rinthira was overseeing the AI at the time. After, she told Phiksunee she did not want to see it ever again.

Rinthira looks, now, at the enameled egg that holds the American AI. This needs to be discussed with Chatsumon, she told Phiksunee as much. The AI tilted her head and congratulated her on communicating with the colonel more.

Clipping the egg to a spiralcrypt around her neck, Rinthira toggles on a monitoring channel. The aegis is comprehensive; short of a full-scale air strike penetrating the solar tripwires, wasp drones, and precision toxin will be difficult. An air strike would be intercepted long before it reaches inhabited areas. Her house is as secure as it can get outside a military base, though this isn't sustainable.

Her head needs clearing. She heads to the third floor where she's installed an immersive frame, a room six by six, spacious for its type and expensive. But she's found it more than worthwhile. Inside, she loads a shooting range and clinches an interface patch around her head, pulls a prop gun out of the wall. The scenario doesn't compare to the real ranges provided at bases, but trading fancy military equipment for a life of privacy has been one of the best bargains she's ever made.

The scenario mottles the bare pastel walls. Her perspective creases, pulls, then expands taut: she stands in a tundra, the ground white-green with arctic moss and rime, broken up by dots of bearberry, saxifrage, lichen. Patches of radiance undulate cosine overhead.

A countdown begins in her ear. When it reaches zero, the lights coalesce into cubes, spheres, prisms. Beautiful in this preset, all the shades of the borealis. They spread, revolving slow and adjusting to her previous scores. Outdated ones—it's been months.

Configured to her favorite gun, the prop clicks and responds nearly without recoil. The first round produces a subpar score; the second is better and the targets speed up. Soon she has a rhythm, the motions repetitious and the process fluid. Sight down the target, pull the trigger. Vector and impact, metal grip solid and right in her hands. It demands no thought, no emotion, pure cause and effect.

When the scenario ends and the frame disengages, she detaches from the interface to the sound of applause. Chatsumon stops clapping. "Phiksunee let me peek. Not bad at all—your accuracy's down some, but you'd still pass marksmanship exams for your pay grade. That's where we first met, wasn't it, at a range?"

"Maybe it was. I don't remember." Rinthira remembers it down to the minute, that first sight of Chatsumon in uniform, tall and sharp-featured and most of all *certain* of herself. Confident in who and what she was, absolute in her place in the world. "Chatsumon, we can just sleep together."

"We have been doing just that." The colonel inclines her head. "I love taking you in bed, but I miss the other things. The rad-na was gorgeous, you crisp the noodles just right. We could go shopping together."

"You need a wife." She reaches for the enameled egg. "There's something we need to discuss—"

It is the hair, that harsh crimson too brilliant to be natural. It is the eyes, that bottle green too strident to be human. Had the body been more ordinary, Rinthira might have stayed in that state of fugue, not even thinking to react. Her mind would have slotted an Asian face into reality as normal. But it is this body so keenly foreign, this face so inhuman in its serenity, and that jolts her out of complacency.

Speed of draw is everything.

The body falls without a cry—no pain sensors, no audio output?—and Rinthira shoves Chatsumon behind her, ordering the frame shut. Activating security routines, calling for Phiksunee. The AI answers—

"Rinthira, you're bleeding." Chatsumon draws upright. Her own gun is out, safety off.

From the speakers: "Mother, I don't see anything. I'm alerting the colonel's guard and pilot."

Rinthira feels not the pain but the heat of the bullet in her shoulder, like a flame behind lantern glass. "The American AI." She'd shot it in the flank and knowing the specs of Phiksunee's marionettes, that ought to stop it. Or not, if this one's signal hub is elsewhere: the knee, the calf, the wrist. There is no requirement for AI marionettes to bear vital parts in spots analogous to human.

Phiksunee says, "The colonel's pilot is down. There's at least another marionette but I can't *see* it. That AI has scrambled my senses. It's done this expertly." A pained pause. "If the specs I've got are up to date, the signal receptors are in the right forearm. Mother, load the iteration I brought now."

"The what," Chatsumon starts and stops.

Rinthira is breathing fast. She should be calm: it is a combat situation and she's been trained for that, has long been accustomed. It's been years. "What if it compromises you?"

"I've created a sandbox in one of your house's partitions, to which I *won't* connect. We don't have time, Mother. My nearest bodies are too far and no human reinforcement will be in time. Not to criticize, Colonel, but perhaps you ought to have brought more personnel."

There is a decisive thud outside; Rinthira wishes she'd had the house done over with industrial-grade reinforcement. She turns on every security channel but they show nothing, the invader as invisible to them as to Phiksunee's eyes. She pictures the perimeter thick with red-headed, green-eyed dolls, blank of expression and lethal. With her good hand she unchains the enameled egg, peels off the shell to expose the port, and plugs it into the frame.

The wall brightens and fills with the AI's pale, pointed face. Their eyes open slowly—an affectation—to reveal those broken-glass irises. A moment's pause as the imprinting asserts, incorporating Rinthira's signature and unique identifiers: she holds eye contact, though that is nothing more than cosmetic, an instinct on her part. Phiksunee is not infallible. No telling this could even work, would be compatible.

The banging grows louder. Chatsumon has her gun leveled at the entry, her second pistol already loaded at her side.

"You are registered as superuser," the AI says in stilted Thai. "I am Natasha."

Rinthira inhales, ragged. Her shoulder throbs. Natasha. Alkonost will be irritated, she thinks, death row humor. "Show me your read-write accesses and administrative privileges."

They display on the adjacent wall. A list of identities strung out like beads; Rinthira transcribes then deletes them all except her own. Nothing for it once that's done—she puts Natasha online.

Natasha's eyes glaze over, then turn clear with a long hard blink. "Six other active instances of Natasha detected within proximity. Instructions?" The adjacent screen changes to a layout of the house, foregrounded by six vectors. The nearest is immediately outside; another is closing in.

At that moment the door gives. Chatsumon squeezes off two consecutive shots, precisely catching the Natasha marionette in the right forearm. It teeters, computer animus leaving, and falls.

Rinthira works quickly: a query to terminate the other instances is denied—it requires back-entry authentication she doesn't have—and other attempts to alter the five invaders prove fruitless. Until Phiksunee steps in, lightning-logic and brute-force algorithms, a universe of parallel processes denser and faster than any human brain.

The vectors go out, one by one.

It is not calm, after, and they are not safe. But for the moment Rinthira is in her bed and her wound is dressed; she is hazy from painkillers, though lucid. The scrambling underlay she wears next to her skin threw the enemy Natasha's aim off-course or it would have been her head, not just a few tendons and a fractured bone.

"Piercing ammo." Chatsumon grimaces and puts down the crusted bulletproof mesh. "This was close."

"You lost a soldier and a pilot."

"Good ones both. But I could have lost you."

It is said simply, thickly, full of the heat that comes before tears. Rinthira turns her face away. "If you requisition better armor for me, I'm not going to say no." Through the window she watches Chatsumon's personnel load the bodies. Human ones go into sterile bags, to be honored and then given to families and friends for funerals, smoke and incense and saffron-robed monks. The other ones, the Natashas, have been disassembled and stacked up in boxes for transport to forensic engineers. They are mannequins, components no more sophisticated than Phiksunee's marionettes a few generations back. Generic and hollow on purpose—the Americans made sure there would be nothing to mine or reverse-engineer, though they don't appear to have planned on having an iteration fall into enemy hands.

For Phiksunee, an iteration of Natasha is as good as having the American AI's code entire to dissect and compare. "It's a sibling," she reported. "Some of the base code is . . . familiar, Mother, it's why the imprinting took so well. That means a lot of things. Some bad. Some very good. I'll need to consult the rest of the family."

Rinthira has kept the body she shot down. One of its arms is laid across her lap. Heavier than she expected, steel skeleton roped with grapheme tendons. When she runs her fingers over the arm it gives, the synthetic dermis a spongy sheath that would never have passed for meat. Thin coolant has congealed around the joints, a nacreous film. If Natasha has any opinion as to its bodies or their termination, it hasn't voiced any before being put into anechoic hibernation.

Chatsumon pours a cup of water, lukewarm, and presses it in Rinthira's hand. "I'll get you all the armor you want and a squad's worth of artillery. Except none of that is going to make Ayutthaya safer. There's no perimeter here to speak of. At a base, human personnel would've noticed the intrusion right away."

Next to the window, a live broadcast plays. It is being recorded through Xiaoqing's eyes—out of all the AI family, the Jeen eldest is the most powerful, able to manifest and operate nearly everywhere at once. No war correspondent is better. She is relaying an air strike against a small Portuguese town. The Americans, on their own channel, will declare that it is done nobly. That they are liberating the town from Turkish control, restoring it to its rightful citizenry.

Rinthira watches the smoke and the fumes. Listens to the noises, selected and modulated by Xiaoqing: architecture crumpling, ballistic impact, and underneath all that—precisely captured and brought to the fore—a wailing infant. Charred homes and burning schools and slag; what can be freer than blackened ruin no one wants. Corpses too are free, she grants, from worldly concerns and nationality and war: the ultimate liberty.

She drinks deeply; Chatsumon remembers her preference for liquid slightly above room temperature. "The last time I operated, I let Phiksunee target a hospital. Sittipong held her back; he knew that and he let me take the reins. So here we are, one atrocity richer. The next time she might well massacre as many as that air strike."

"Yes," Chatsumon says, "I know. I was the one who put you there. All of them need their humans. Phiksunee needs you to be complete, and she was conceptualized from the beginning as a weapon."

Rinthira pushes at the Natasha arm again. These bodies have been mass-produced. Shock troops, assassins, nothing like the careful works of art that are the marionettes used by Phiksunee and her siblings. If sufficient Natashas are made, the shape of main force will have changed irrevocably. Sitting still is not an option. The war will not pass her by. "You want me back."

"Someone like you is exactly what we need."

The feed is ending, fading out to Jeen politicians discussing the strike and its implications. A Turkish general on call, distraught. Angry.

"Natasha has a lot of information," Rinthira says after a moment. "There are American manufacture yards we don't know about, links in their supply chains. It could be decisive, altogether. I want you to promise me, Chatsumon, that if I go back you'll help end this war."

The colonel nods, curt. But it is a vow, an oath, bound by that twisting thing between them.

"All right." Rinthira salutes. Sharp and crisp, cadet-proper. "Reporting for duty, Colonel Chatsumon."

Her commander smiles and returns the salute. "Welcome back, Lieutenant Rinthira."

Salvage Opportunity
JACK SKILLINGSTEAD

"Sometimes I wish I could touch you," I said, lying on my bunk, not touching anyone. I was alone on Kepler-186f.

My bodiless Companion voice, replied, "You've mentioned that before."

"I don't think so."

"Actually, Badar, you have. Five times in the last twenty-two days."

"It couldn't be that many times."

"Couldn't it? I can play back—"

"No, thanks."

The Companion was stubborn. In that and other ways she reminded me of myself. Which made sense, considering her presentation was a gender flip based on my own personality matrix. A reactive voice closely modeled for compatibility, the Companion existed to preserve my sanity by providing a convincing simulation of conversation. I called it a simulation because I did not believe the Companion was an individual in the same sense that I was. For that reason, I stuck with calling her by the generic "Companion," rather than giving her a human name. I liked to keep things straight in my head. Gender aside, when I talked to the Companion I was talking to myself.

Most of the Companion's attention was devoted to exploring the wreckage of *Leviathan*. The immense hulk lay half a kilometer from my shelter. Using micro swarms, the Companion was building a catalog for future salvage. Intercorp had planted me like a flag on Kepler-186f. I was the "living representative in continuous habitation" legally required to validate Intercorp's claim. Machine intelligences didn't count as "living."

My contract ran four years. The pay was fantastic. When I returned to Earth, I would be modestly independent of economic constraints, and Intercorp would install another "living representative." Eventually they would get around to implementing real salvage operations, or not, depending on long-term expense/reward analysis. In the meantime placeholders like me were relatively cheap.

"There's a surprise coming," the Companion said.

I sat up. "What are you taking about?"

"Look outside in the direction of *Leviathan*."

I swung out of my bunk and climbed the ladder to the observation dome, my knees feeling the extra forty pounds the planet's gravitational mass loaded on my skinny body. *Leviathan* rose from the rocky terrain like an artificial mountain. The ancient starship had departed Earth three hundred years ago. By the time it crashed on Kepler-186f, refinements to the Kessel Drive had made interstellar travel infinitely faster.

I raised a pair of high-powered binoculars and swept the landscape. A lone figure came into focus, approaching my shelter. I lowered the binoculars. "What's going on, Companion?"

"It's the surprise. Go answer the door, Badar."

By the time I reached the bottom of the ladder, something was pounding on the outer door of the airlock. It must have been very strong, otherwise I would never have heard it.

The pounding stopped.

"Companion, tell me what the hell is out there. I'm not kidding."

"*Leviathan* was a colony ship—"

"I know that."

"What you don't know is that the crew had been stored inside Schrödinger Chambers. When *Leviathan* reached Kepler space, the indeterminate crew were supposed to collapse into android hosts, which would then thaw out the cargo of human embryos and raise them into colonists. It's a host android outside."

"Hold on. Are you saying there's a three hundred-year-old *Leviathan* crew-member knocking on the door?"

"No. The Schrödinger Chambers failed, *Leviathan* crashed on the wrong planet, and all the frozen embryos perished."

The pounding resumed.

"Go ahead and open the door," the Companion said.

I stood by the airlock but didn't touch the controls. "If it's not a crewmember, then what's driving the android?"

"I impregnated its central processor with a seed from my personality matrix."

I thought about that for a moment. "Why?"

"My job is to evaluate salvage opportunities. I wanted to determine whether the android host was a functional mechanism. Since no Schrödinger indeterminates remained, I used a piece of myself."

I sighed. "All right." I didn't want to, but I opened the outer door, closed it, cleared the airlock, then opened the inner door.

"Hello, Badar." The android sounded like a talking washing machine. It stumped into my living quarters, servos whirring and grinding.

I drew back. The android was modeled on the human form but without any identifying gender characteristics. Synthetic skin, like a layer of pink rubber, covered its metal skeleton.

"You're really in there, Companion?"

"Not *me* me," the Companion said. "An autonomous seed."

The android spoke again, "I am myself."

I rolled my eyes. "That's great."

In a series of stop-motion jerks, the android's arm reached toward me, four-fingered hand open. "I'm happy to meet you, Badar."

I looked at the hand. "Wait here and don't move. I mean it."

The shelter was small. It already felt crowded with just me and the Companion voice. Intercorp selected me for my high adaptability to voluntary isolation. I didn't want the damn android in my space.

I opened the trapdoor leading the storage room. The android's dull amber eyes watched impassively. I climbed down and pulled the door closed.

"Isolate our conversation," I said to the Companion.

"You're not happy."

"That's an understatement. What am I supposed to do with that thing?"

"Touch it?"

"Are you being funny?"

"Not very."

"Look," I said, "just turn it off. I mean, send it away first, then turn it off."

"I can't."

"Why not?"

"The test seed I planted has fully integrated with the processor. The android is autonomous. I told you. I can't turn it off."

"Oh, come *on*." I could hear the android's heavy tread as it walked around my living quarters. Annoyed, I said, "I told it not to move."

"Badar. It's not a robot. You can't order it around."

"Why'd you even bring it here?"

"I didn't. It was lonely in the derelict."

"Lonely. How long has it been . . . awake, or whatever you call it?"

"A week. It had nothing to do. The android was designed to maintain *Leviathan* in orbit, then build a colony and help nurture a human population."

"Maybe you haven't noticed, but we're fresh out of starships and frozen embryos around here."

"I've noticed."

"I don't want the android. How do I turn it off? There must be a way."

"The main processor is located in the head."

"There's a switch?"

"No. You'd have to use a laser."

I threw my hands up. "I have to burn it?"

"If you want to turn it off, yes. Although I wouldn't recommend that. The android belongs to Intercorp. Even if you dragged it back to *Leviathan*, it would return. Why don't you let it stay? It could be another Companion. It wants company. It's as social as you are."

"I don't believe this." I looked at the ceiling, chewed on my lip, and made a decision. Fine, then. I retrieved my s-suit from its locker, put it on, and strapped a utility belt around my waist—laser pistol included.

As soon as I opened the trapdoor to the living quarters, I heard them talking. The Companion and the android.

"He's not so bad once you get to know him," the Companion was saying.

"I can see that."

Sarcasm?

"You," I said, pointing at the android. "Since you're here, I need help adjusting the weather array."

The android turned to me. "I want to help."

I put my helmet on.

The weather on Kepler-186f frequently turned nasty. As soon as I stepped out of the airlock, the wind staggered me. On Earth it might have hustled me across the rocky plain, but the extra forty pounds kept me mostly stable. I walked a few yards from the shelter, the android dutifully following, then I turned and planted my feet. Dust and debris blew between us.

"This will damage my mechanism," the android said in its halting mechanical voice.

Did it know I was about to burn a hole through its processor, or was it talking about the dust? It didn't matter. I found I couldn't draw the pistol. The android was barely human-looking, but now that the moment had arrived, I couldn't shoot it. Not so much for its own sake, but because I knew my actions would bother the Companion. Or at least the Companion's reactive conversation would trend in a "bothered" direction. So, essentially, it would bother *me* to pull the trigger, since the Companion was a reflection of my personality matrix.

"The array's a couple klicks due south. We're going to take the rover."

Angry with myself, I drove too fast, bucketing over the rough terrain. Kepler's dim noon light faded, and I switched on the rover's forward lamps. After a while, we arrived at the weather array. I parked the rover. In the passenger seat, the android's amber eyes stared at me. I knew there was nothing to read in those eyes, but my imagination perceived judgment. All that meant was that I was judging myself. I pushed the feeling aside.

The weather array required precious little adjusting, and what adjusting it did require could be accomplished remotely, from the shelter. Though the android couldn't possibly know this, I felt it *did* know this. Of course, that was nothing but me feeling, illogically, guilty.

"Well, let's get to work."

There was room for only one of us at a time in the rover's airlock. The android crouched inside. I locked the inner hatch, purged the chamber, then opened the outer hatch. Grit and dust churned violently into the open airlock. I sealed the outer hatch and immediately slammed the rover into reverse, half expecting the android to come after me. It didn't, though. It just stood there in front of the array, all hell gusting around it. *Martyr*, I thought, swung the rover in a tight turn, and headed back to the shelter. Two kilometers in a raging windstorm. The android couldn't make it.

Prior to my Kepler-186f assignment, I tested as a loner-introvert. Intercorp threw everything at me. Myers-Briggs, brainwave analysis, even Rorschach. The works. I tested high but not too high, probably because I fudged selected responses. I had studied up on how to do this, how to achieve a desired psyche evaluation result. For the last test, they locked me inside a geodesic dome in the middle of the high desert of New Mexico. One year in total isolation. That one I passed with flying colors, no studying required.

It was no sweat.

You don't want to test too high. Above a certain range, the loner-introvert personality type slips into a personality *disorder*. At least according to some people. They don't give deep space/high-pay assignments to disordered applicants. And I had desperately wanted this job. The isolation suited me. And the credits accumulating in my Earth-side account were like insulation from the society I could barely tolerate. When I got back I would live far away from my fellow humans. Maybe I'd buy a dachshund, but I doubted it. I didn't want *any* emotional complications.

I prepared my evening meal. Since I'd returned from the weather array, the Companion hadn't spoken a word. It needed me to start a conversation, which I had no intention of doing. If I spoke, she spoke. Even then it wasn't a given. Only a direct interrogative guaranteed conversation. This was to spare me from uninvited interaction with the voice outside my head. I knew the Companion wouldn't appreciate what I'd done to the android, and I didn't want to hear about it. I ate my bowl of quick-thawed stew, took a stress pill, and stretched out on my bunk. Given the increased gravity, lying flat was the most comfortable position.

The damn android plucked at my conscience. I tried to ignore it. But it was like a hangnail, or a rock in my shoe. Eventually I lapsed into troubled sleep, from which I woke suddenly to the sound of dust hissing against the observation dome.

"*Damn* it. Why can't I be left alone?" My voice was thick with crappy sleep.

"What's wrong?" the Companion asked.

"Bad dream."

"Do you want to talk about it?"

Was there something about her tone of voice? Something judgmental? I sat up, rubbed my face. "People are shit."

"That was your dream?"

"The dream was about my step-mother."

"You've never mentioned her. What happened in the dream?"

I stood up and drew a glass of water from the reclamation tank and drank it. The water tasted metallic. "Really it was about the cat, what she did to the cat. Except this time I was the cat."

"You were the cat. I see."

"Don't be funny. I don't feel funny."

"You can tell me your dream. I'd like to hear about it. What was the cat's name?"

"I don't remember the cat's name." Truthfully, I *did* remember, but for some reason I didn't want to speak it out loud to the Companion. Seymour. The cat's name was Seymour. At least that's what we called it. A stray that we unofficially adopted.

"All I remember," I said, "is that it kept spraying all over our house. I guess my step-mom got tired of it. She transported the cat about ten miles away and left it in the woods. That was her solution to the spraying problem."

"But in the dream you were the cat."

"Yes, something like that."

"Maybe your evil step-mother should have shot Fluffy in the head processor instead, if she felt she had to get rid of it."

My back went ridged. "Knock it off."

The other true thing I didn't want to say out loud to the Companion was that it wasn't my evil step-mother who abandoned Seymour in the woods. I didn't have a step-mother. My *real* mother did it, and she wasn't evil, but it was still a shitty thing to do, even if Seymour was a stray that was probably tough enough to survive. When I was a little kid I used to wonder if Mom would do the same thing to me. Of course, that was stupid. But I was kid. All those psyche tests? They confirmed that kid was still alive and disturbed inside me. The cat incident didn't make me that way; I was already that way.

"Okay, okay," I said to no one. For once I hadn't bothered to properly stow my dusty s-suit. I pulled it on and cycled open the inner door.

"Good luck, Badar."

"Yeah, yeah."

The android stood where I'd left it, in a maelstrom of dust and debris. I unholstered my laser pistol and held it in my lap a few minutes. That's how long it took me to figure out I wasn't there to burn the android. I'd cared about Seymour abandoned in the woods—so it was all about me and my precious feelings, right? Even though I was calling it my better nature.

I put my pistol away and climbed out. Because of all the dust blown through the android's mechanism, it couldn't move by itself. What a bitch it was getting that thing back inside the rover.

By the time I'd muscled the android into the shelter, I was exhausted. The thing never said one word. Wind and the abrasive grit had stripped most of the synthetic flesh off the android's skeleton. What remained clung to the metal in rubbery gobbets. Not exactly the ideal nursemaid for those long-lost embryos.

I rapped my knuckles on the top of its head. "Are you even in there?" Now that I'd saved the android, I felt I'd earned the right to indulge my resentment. Did that make me a shitty person? There was no one to ask but myself.

"A piece of me," The android said, in answer to my question. Because of the dust-clogged and mechanical nature of its voice box, I couldn't detect the underlying tone. If it had been me saying it (and it *was* me, by a circuitous route, sort of), the tone would have suggested a couple of unspoken words. *A piece of me, you prick.*

I spent hours cleaning the android's mechanism, a job I resented every inch of the way. I vacuumed dust from the joints and rubbed lubricant into them. I whisked the eyes, disassembled, cleaned, and replaced the voice box. Finally, I removed the occipital plate and discovered that dust had penetrated the skull. I blew it out with compressed air. A titanium box protected the main processor. Not only wasn't there an off-switch, there was no way of disconnecting it from the frame. I covered it again with the occipital plate.

"Can you move your limbs?" I said to the android.

It didn't reply, or move any limbs.

"Oh, well, I guess you're irreparably damaged. I might as well burn a hole through your processor."

The android walked to the other side of the shelter, whirring and clicking with every step. It was temperamental. Of course, in this shelter who wasn't? I had to remind myself that I was alone, even though it now felt like there were three of us.

"Is there anything to do?" the android said.

I squinted at the back of its skull.

"On *Leviathan*," the android continued, "I was to have tasks."

"This isn't *Leviathan*."

The Companion said, "Would you like to talk about your tasks?"

"If anyone wants to hear about them, yes."

I rolled my eyes. "Okay. I'm going out to secure the rover." I yanked on my suit and helmet and got out of there. I had suited up so fast, I forgot to strap on the utility belt with its holstered laser. The rover didn't need any securing. I'd just wanted to escape from the crowded shelter. Which was ridiculous. The shelter was *mine*. The Companion was nothing but a reflection, and the android a reflection of a reflection.

After staggering around in the storm for a few minutes, I returned to the shelter. But when I tried to open the outer door, it wouldn't budge.

I activated the comlink. "Companion?"

"Yes?"

"The door won't open."

"I know."

Wind buffeted me and I staggered sideways. "That's wonderful that you know. Now could you open it, please?"

Silence.

"Companion?"

"The android has disabled the lock."

"What? Well, make it un-disable it."

"I'm sorry, Badar."

"This is ridiculous. *Make* the android let me in."

"We're talking about it."

I stared at the wind-and-grit-polished surface of the outer door, which held my own blurred reflection. My frustration boiled over, and I pounded the door with my fist. It hurt, so I stopped. Fine. I'd cut my way in. I reached for the laser—and it wasn't there. Behind me, the rover hunkered in a fury of blowing grit and dust. It was my only option.

Inside the rover's cab I removed my helmet. A haze of abrasive dust lingered. Coughing, I cranked the scrubbers until the air cleared. After that, there was nothing to do. I had food and potable water sufficient for a three-day excursion. But there was no place to excursion *to*. I considered ramming the rover into the shelter, smashing open the outer door. But I'd never be able to repair the damage.

To keep the batts charged, I periodically ran the engine. And I rationed the food and water. Sooner or later, though, it would all run out. Fuel, battery, water, food. Air. I was alone on Kepler-186f, but then I'd always been alone, separated by choice from friends and family, cut off, even, from the emotional boobytraps in my own psyche. When my mother died, I'd fled a houseful of weeping relatives and hid in the backseat of the family vehicle. I wanted to move away from pain. Eventually, someone found me and made me come in.

The storm subsided. The cloud cover cleared, and Kepler's muted energy shone through. On Kepler-186f it was always twilight, except when it was full dark. I looked towards the shelter. Light filtered up from the living quarters and softly illuminated the observation dome. It was a homey light, but nobody was going to find me and make me come in.

I wondered what they were talking about inside the shelter. I wondered if I was already forgotten—by myselves. Emotion tightened across my chest. I opened a comlink to the Companion, but at first I couldn't speak. Finally I said, "Please. I want to come in."

Silence resonated through the link. The Companion needed a question.

"Companion, can I come home?"

After a minute, she replied, "Are you running out of air?"

"No." I swallowed. "I'm . . . lonely."

Another moment, then, "The outer door is unlocked, Badar."

The Hexagonal Bolero of Honeybees
KRISTA HOEPPNER LEAHY

Hum

> "For so work the honeybees . . . The sad-eyed justice with his surly
> hum Delivering o'er to executors pale The lazy yawning drone."
> —Shakespeare, *The Life of King Henry the Fifth*

We cannot tame vibration, much as we long to suss its purpose.

Are there those among us who fly only to mate and then die? Some who work perpetually, some who are queens? Or is it more that we are each—we are all—the hive? The honeycomb and the bees? The sticky-sweet-surly hum a chorus we cannot hear, only sing?

Pluck a sunbeam, a bee sings.

Pluck an oceanwave, the earth rings.

But whose hand is doing the plucking?

And what hum signals tomorrow's fall of the executioner's blade?

Hope

> "The keeping of bees is like the direction of sunbeams."
> —Henry David Thoreau

Ciro loved his daddy, and loved painting flowers like a bee. Daddy said he was better than a bee, but Ciro didn't think that was true, 'cuz bees made honey. Ciro couldn't make honey, but he could climb the highest, licking his paintbrush in between painting the teeny-tiny flowers. Yummy, but not as yummy as honey. Sometimes after he crept along the tallest branches, Daddy would say "Fly, bee, fly" and Ciro would back flip down into his daddy's waiting arms. Maybe Daddy wasn't his real daddy, and maybe Ciro would never be a real bee, but none of that mattered when it was just Ciro painting flowers.

Hunger

> "To make a prairie it takes a clover and one bee,
> . . . revery alone will do,
> If bees are few."
> —Emily Dickinson, *Complete Poems*

The atrium air was warm, impossibly warm compared to the frozen tundra outside, and redolent of blooms delicious as forgotten dreams. The cross-latticed Sunglass atrium was separated from the body of the greenhouse by mechanical sally ports, but the bees could smell enough of the Allmond orchards beyond to pulse with anticipation—of course some ventilation would be required, even with the closed loop geothermal heating system. Mishka's bees crawled through her honeycomb crown, tickling her scalp, as they sussed for the source of the fragrance. She ignored the tickling and the damnable itching of her nectarways and focused on the hand-pollinator's bid. Gabhan was the competition, she reminded herself, never mind the boy he wore on his shoulders, like an accessory proclaiming his innocence.

" . . . hand-pollination offers more control, more finesse, more flexibility, more artistry—the human touch will honor your trees, Arborist. We cradle your Allmond blooms as only a human hand can. Isn't that right, Ciro?"

"Right-ee-o!" The boy, who had to be younger than four, smiled; the boy's crinkled eyes echoed the curve of his mouth—a triple grin!—and he looked as pleased as if he had invented human hands himself.

Mishka refused to smile back. No doubt Gabhan had coerced the boy to make him perform with such utter charm. She breathed in through her nose, out through her mouth, soothing her itching as best she could. The boy's charm—forced or not—could only hurt her chances, and she couldn't afford to be distracted.

Gabhan lifted his hands towards the vaulted Sunglass ceiling, adding, "Of course, if you care to risk your crop with the unregulated wildness of hiver bees," he laughed, and was that a wink he aimed at Mishka? Unbelievable. "Who am I to convince you otherwise?"

Mishka didn't trust Gabhan, with his easy laugh and bear-like chest, his way of spreading his fingers wide into the air, as if he had nothing to hide, as if he were offering ease and naturalness and health, when in truth hand-pollination was laborious, only partially effective and as unnatural as her own symbiont nature. Natural pollination had died out when the climate chilled, no matter how he waxed poetic about the gentle artistry and power of the human hand.

Hands hands hands. If only she could stop thinking about her hands itch itch itching across her forearms and knuckles and palms. Withholding nectar intensified itching all along her altered nerves, even though the nectar production was restricted to her torso.

There was the rub. The damning, itching rub. The one the apiarists had warned Mishka about, that her latent eczema might be triggered by the symbiont grafting—that for her becoming a hiver might involve more sacrifice than most.

Small price to pay for becoming a pollinator. For nurturing 60,000 bees and securing her own livelihood with one profound surgery. Not to mention solving the *world* hunger problem. Wry joke. Her father's joke. Back when her father joked. Back when her father lived. Back when folks had the luxury of worrying about a world hunger problem, not just their own grumbling ping-panging middles. Back when there was a world, not this archipelago of greenhouses rock-skipped across the continents.

And in this greenhouse—warmest in North America, floored with sequoia felled to escape becoming another forest of frozen stalagmites, latticed in Sunglass to amplify sun, and plugged deep into the hum of geothermal heat fueling the geysers of Yellowstone—Mishka sweated and the more she sweated, the more she itched, and the more the bees pulsed, triggering histamines, opening altered nerveways, and Mishka's nectar began to pump, pooling internally, preparing to let down, to cascade amidst prickling skin . . . oh the urge to scratch. From the soles of her sweating feet to her honeycombed scalp and pulsing hive of a crown, Mishka itched itched itched until she could barely hear Gabhan's closing bid.

" . . . not child slavery rather child freedom." This last punctuated by the boy performing a double back flip off Gabhan's shoulders, landing as lightly as a flower himself before sinking into a graceful kneel, and offering up a single perfect blush and cream bloom in his cupped hands.

Mishka seethed at Gabhan's dismissal of the child labor question as nothing but a philosophical imbroglio best answered with a circus trick. Thankfully the Arborist didn't take the bloom, even when Gabhan knelt as well. She still had a chance at the bid, but that loose bloom was making the itching worse, making it even harder to concentrate.

Of course, once the bees fed, the itching would subside, but she couldn't afford a feeding now, not while the Arborist was deliberating which pollinator—hand or hiver—to award the orchard contract. The bees would nuzzle into every nectar crevice of Mishka's bosom, throat, abdomen—all the easiest nerveways for the apiarists to alter, near the milk-production zone, why all hivers were female—and after having postponed the bees this long, they would suckle with scavenging force. While the Arborist was no doubt more open-minded than most, and hopefully tempted by the hivers' bargain fees, she doubted They would award the hivers the Allmond orchard contract—the largest protein and medicinal crop of North America—after witnessing her bees swarm her torso as she moaned and swooned to the dusky red sequoia floor.

What was taking the Arborist so long? Yes, Arborists were part gardeners, part mechanics, part monks, and often of the neuter gender as this one was, but why did the monk part always seem to hold sway when there was a decision to make?

The Arborist only nodded slightly in response to Gabhan's speech. Work-worn hands still held in prayer, They seemed distracted, squinting first at the Sunglass above, then glancing at the doors leading to Their private chambers, the Orchard entrance, and the exits to the waiting sleds, as if uncertain where to stand. Did They need to be perfectly positioned to make Their decision?

The Arborists had a reputation for demanding absolute perfection—gift and curse, but a necessary trait in running as delicate and critical an ecosystem as a greenhouse—but Mishka hadn't thought Their perfection extended to physically positioning Themselves in a room. Gabhan and the boy still knelt, bloom proffered up, as if awaiting a king's command. Damned if she would be the one to move and betray discomfort, not for the itching, nor the heat. Did her bees pulse more, the longer the bloom waited? Or was it her imagination? She just needed to hang on until she won or lost the bid; then she could return to her solo sled, begin the journey back to the hiver community, and let the bees feed themselves into a frenzy, privately.

A rotten egg smell filled the chamber as gas vented from a duct near the Arborist, ruffling Their cellulosic robes as they scurried away. They began Their squinting, shuffling routine all over again, this time closer to the Allmond orchard entrance. Mishka almost felt sympathy, for the duct near her felt positively volcanic, but why couldn't the Arborist just monk out Their decision? And They had better not open those orchard doors, for if They did, nothing Mishka did could stop the hive from rising. The boy's one bloom had teased her bees, but an orchard of blooms? Once her bees smelled real food, real pollen, not the synthetic nectar Mishka produced—which they subsisted on when in sled transit between greenhouses—nothing would keep them hived.

She was using every breath control and muscle control and mind control and fuck control she could think of to keep the hive calm, to send the message all along her honeycombed curves and blooming nerves that patience was the price to pay for bliss, that calm would win, to stay close to the big queen, stay close to her, queen bee, queen hiver, queen Mishka who cared for and loved these bees as fiercely as if they were her own milk-babies. But the hotter it got the more she itched and she could feel her control slipping, and which would be worse, her forager bees suddenly swarming from the stress? Or a feeding frenzy of the nurse bees erupting, in their mania to tend the little queen and the brood housed in the honeycomb necklace cradled between Mishka's breasts?

At least the sulfur smell was gone, and a new sweetness reigned in the air. Thank the honey. But the heat, surely they could retire to a cooler chamber?

She risked a glance at Gabhan, and saw him cradling Ciro, poor tired boy, fading in the heat, and her concentration slipped, as a bead of nectar dripped down her sternum, and her favorite nurse bee—the one Mishka had stupidly named SingSongSun, right after the surgery, back when she'd been drunk on her own histamines and honey-high, when Singsong's sweet buzz and guzzle and sun-colored thorax had seemed like a miracle rivaled only by the ongoing persistence of the human spirit—Singsong peeked her antennae out of the honeycomb necklace, and hummed, as if she were answering a question that Mishka hadn't heard—buzzing delicately but probing with indescribable delicacy, and Mishka couldn't keep herself from humming the melody of that old father tune she'd loved as a child, and then, of course, the hive rose, unable to resist the cloying sweetness of the air any longer, and her knees guillotined to the sequoia floor—knock knock, knock down—oh oh oh she was in trouble.

Heat

> "I'm bringing home a baby bumblebee,
> Won't my mommy be so proud of me . . . "
> —Traditional Children's Song

SingSong waited, long as she could. She smelled fear on big queen. She smelled strangeness. She knew to wait, to hide, to keep the hive quiet. But then earth queen hummed, a wrong song, and a strange nectar fell, and little queen buzzed and big queen hummed the birth song she'd sung when Singsong hatched out of her cell, and even fighting the wrongness of the earth hum, Singsong was helpless against the lure of her birth song, its wafting, waggling, pure love calling her and her sisters out out out to forage the world and for once there was nectar enough for all, nectar enough to bathe in, to dream in, to drown in, and the air was its own nectar, wet and warm, so warm, such heat pulling the bees up up up up into the air out of their precious comb, away from big queen, but what treasures they would bring her, such nectar they would find her, and then little queen and big queen could taste of the molten nectar which must be molten, mustn't it, for the air itself felt like smoke, her Singsong wings were glowing with flame, she must be near the sun, what would big queen give her, supping of the sun?

She tried, tried to waggle the dance that would tell her sisters how to find the sun. *Delectable. Scorching. Glory.* Does fire scream? Or was Singsong learning to speak like big queen at last? Where where where was her big queen? She buzzed *SingSongSun, SingSongSung, SingSongSun, SingSongSung,* which way was up and which way was down?

No no no. How could she nurse the brood if she couldn't waggle the dance to the food? The wrong earth queen hum was gone, why couldn't she think?

The hive would swarm if she waggled too hard a dance.

Simple simple, not up, not down.

Waggle smells. Nurse the brood.

First find flower. Second find sun.

Harvest

> "Eat honey, my son, for it is good . . . "
> —Proverbs 24:13, *The New International Bible*

Ciro didn't want to open his eyes. That seemed like a bad idea. Even closed, his eyes really, really hurt. And his ears hurt. And his nose. Everything hurt.

But it couldn't be that bad, could it, if he was breathing? As long as he was breathing, he could imagine his daddy was breathing, and the bee-woman who'd tried so hard not to smile at him, and even the sad Arborist. As long as Ciro just listened to his breathing, he could pretend everyone was breathing and everything was fine.

He listened to his own breath, inhaling and exhaling, with a soft "huh." And then a soft "ha." And again. Over and over again sounds that started with "h" but didn't mean as much as Ciro needed them to mean.

Inhale, exhale, "Huh."

Inhale, exhale, "Ha."

He couldn't get rid of the "h" quite, was that okay? But he could stretch the other sound. Wasn't that how you made words?

"Huuuuunnnnhh." No that wouldn't work.

"Heeee." Closer. "Heeeeeelllp." Right-O.

That was what he wanted. Help. For something was wrong. He couldn't move. And he couldn't feel his hands. Just a burning where his hands should be. When he tried to move the burning, it hurt so much he couldn't breathe anymore. So he stopped trying to move the burning. No hurting. Just breathing. Make these "huh ha hee" sounds. One more time, he tried.

"Heeeelllp."

Then, far away, there was crawling stickiness, so faint in the burning. Then the crawling became his fingers, his burning fingers. Hurting but he could now breathe. Still burning, but at least fingers again. Then, yummy yummy stickiness on his lips and in his nose and something in his ears, and a tickling all across his skin. Tickling everywhere. Bees! The bees were alive!

Things must still be okay if the bees were alive and coming to cover him in honey. They must know he'd always wanted to be a bee. Bees were wise like that, he figured. He wanted them to know he loved them, so he said what his daddy always said to him. "Fly, bee, fly."

And then the floor hummed away from him, and he felt himself go up up up and Ciro opened his eyes, for he didn't want to miss learning to fly.

Hubris

"He is not worthy of the honey-comb, That shuns the hives because the bees have stings."
—Shakespeare, *The Tragedy of Locrine* (contested attribution)

Once the pollinator's sled departed, the Arborist retreated into the relative safety of Their private chambers. At last. What a terrible day. A terrible duty. They were so tired of making these decisions. Would life only ever subsist of this, choosing the slower way to die? Every year, a worse pollination rate. And now the hivers wanted to try? Ridiculous.

Now at least, it did not matter. The greenhouse might last long enough for pollination, but by harvest time, there would be no greenhouse left. The internal report was clear. Under the strain of increased seismic activity, the closed loop geothermal system was breaking apart, and no amount of repair or patching could keep the system in place when the real quake came. And in the meantime, toxic gases—hydrogen sulfide, methane, boron, radon, the list went on—were being vented into a greenhouse never equipped for such open-loop toxic gas venting. The accident today might have killed the Arborist, the pollinators, and perhaps that accident could have been averted. But the coming accident, the killing of all those trees, all those stomachs going empty without the Allmonds to feed them, that accident there was no averting.

The greenhouse was no longer stable, and no human intervention could save them. What could humanity do in the face of seismic waves, pummeling through ocean and land, their hums buckling the very earth? Today's events had clarified Their mind. They saw again the child Ciro flying through the air with such faith and grace, and landing without a care in the world. Soon that grace would be a ghost too.

Like the boy's hands, burned beyond recognition, beyond use, in spite of the healing properties of the unexpected hiver honey, and Their healing skills and silver-soaked antiseptic bandages. Nothing could save the boy's hands, and nothing could save the greenhouse.

Better not to prolong this sacrilege of false gardens and failing gardeners. Better to let the world fall again, as God ordained every time. There were some choices They could still make. Some perfections were still attainable. Standing on the Mission table They had once used as a desk—a reminder that life was service and life without service, no life at all—They looped a rope around the exposed pine log bracing the ceiling, pulled tight below Their larynx, and right before kicking the table out, They said the oldest prayer They knew: *Please please please.*

Home

> "Thus, I can understand how a flower and a bee might slowly become, either simultaneously, or one after the other, modified and adapted in the most perfect manner to each other, by the continued preservation of individuals presenting mutual and slightly favourable deviations of structure."
>
> —Darwin, *Origin of the Species*

"You're safe, don't worry." The voice was familiar, and seemed concerned, despite the reassuring words.

She felt the familiar swaying of a sled beneath her, but not her sled, surely. Too much darkness, and too much room. And the smell of pickled vegetables—beets maybe? So not her sled, but one equipped for long distances. Where was she?

"My bees, ow . . ." Mishka's throat scraped, as if she'd swallowed sandpaper. Her eyes were tearing so much she couldn't see, nor could she smell. Why couldn't she smell anything? And where was the warm, pulsing, crawling comfort of her bees?

"There was an accident."

Could that be Gabhan? Was he the blurry figure hovering over her? This must be his sled. Of course a hand-pollinator's sled would be equipped with its own sustenance for cross-continent travel.

"Sulfur explosion. We did the best we could. We were all knocked unconscious, but once I woke, I pulled you clear. You were almost on top of the duct when it blew, and last I'd seen you'd fallen to your knees, well . . . we didn't know if you were still alive. I should have been suspicious when Ciro fainted." His voice narrowed, an open road squeezed into a too small tunnel. "Apparently there have been quakes for quite a while. The Arborist told us that, at least, before ordering us to evacuate, but . . . he should have told us sooner. Should have told a lot of people. We could have transplanted the orchard, re-rigged the closed system into a bouncer, converted it to an open geothermal unit with enough time, something . . . "

"Bouncer?" She still couldn't focus. She was nauseous, and he wasn't making that much sense. But, at least she was no longer itching. Oh no. She couldn't feel her bees, and she couldn't feel the itching—had she lost everything? But no, when she touched her throat it was still reassuringly sticky with nectar. Pressing down her torso, she felt rivulets of undrunk nectar. But what solace would there be in being a hiver, if the bees she'd changed her very nature for had died? "I'm sorry. My bees? Where are my bees?" She struggled to get up.

"Please. Don't try to move yet. I'm afraid most of your bees are gone. I thought it best to evacuate you with us. Your sled was damaged in the blast and Ciro, well—" He coughed. The tunnel of his voice tightened further. "I was knocked out for a while, and then when the Arborist was bandaging Ciro . . . I'm sorry, I was distracted. Most of them flew away. I didn't see where."

She couldn't blame them for swarming to a new hive. Not when she'd just been knocked silly by a gas explosion. And they wouldn't have swarmed to the sled if it had been damaged. The sled could be replaced. The bees couldn't. They couldn't all be gone, could they? "They all flew away?"

"A few we found on the floor around you, not moving and we hoped they were only stunned. Once it was cool enough, I retrieved them. And your necklace, we have that."

Thank the honey. "Where is it?"

"Ciro has it. I hope you don't mind. He—he burned his hands." The tunnel of his voice squeezed shut.

She didn't understand. "His hands? Why is he wearing my necklace? What happened?"

"The bees saved me." Now the boy, his voice lighter but somber. At least her ears still worked.

"What?"

"They saved me. They fed me honey and put honey in my ears and then I flew with them. Then a bunch of them left, but the rest crawled into your necklace."

"That's right, son. Quite a lucky little bee you are."

For a minute, talking to Ciro, there'd been some hint of the Gabhan from the atrium—his voice full of assurance and warmth—but then he whispered in her ear, and his voice caved-in, shutting out hope. "The boy's been through a lot. Breathing that much gas and fourth-degree burns can cause hallucinations, especially in one so small. I think the bees were drawn to the flower, to him.

He probably had traces of pollen on his hands and mouth. He used to lick his paintbrush and fingers, no matter how I scolded.

"No scolding anymore, right, Ciro?" The hearty assurance was back, but all she could hear were the cracks.

"But it's true, the bees did save me! I'm sorry so many of them died, but these are alive. They were worried about you." His voice trembled, and in spite of the pain and the nausea, Mishka smiled. He wasn't feigning now, whatever had happened, he believed the bees had saved him.

"Look!" He thrust something right in front of her face.

She blinked, her vision clearing a bit. Against the gauzy white of his limbs, she could distinguish a fist-sized smudge of sun-yellow, catching her breath with its promise. Her honeycomb necklace—heart of her hive.

"Here!"

She cradled the necklace as gently as she could, her fingers delicately tap-tap-tapping against the comb—a hum answered, and tears blossomed in her eyes.

Her little queen, her nurses, some of her brood were alive. She would be able to rebuild her hive. There were other greenhouses, other bids. All was not lost.

"Will you teach me to feed the bees? Like you do?"

And here in front of her was this injured child, looking at her with such hope.

"It's not that simple, I'm afraid."

Ciro's smile slipped. "But I think this one likes me. He's been feeding me honey the whole time."

"She. The bee is a she."

"Oh." A pause. "But it has a penis. Look!"

And he thrust a bee right under her nose, a slightly larger than average bee, golden as the sun. Of course Singsong would have survived, possibly even nursed the boy with honey. What a miracle she was.

"See?" He pointed to Singsong's stinger. "I told you he has a penis!"

Mishka couldn't help but laugh and even Gabhan chuckled, as they both tried to explain what exactly a stinger was and why all of Mishka's bees were girls, and the laughter brought hope with it, as it always does.

"Please teach me to help the bees, okay? I'll do anything."

But no amount of laughter would make it possible for a male to become a hiver, even if he would do anything. Gabhan was a hand-pollinator; he must know that hivers had to be female. "Gabhan, hivers all have to be—"

"He needs something to think about while he waits for the bandages to come off." The words were quick as cuts, quick enough to cut her sentence off forever, but light as pollen blown by the wind, as if by keeping his tone light, the words would never land, and never landing, time would cease, and those bandages would never have to come off. For what would happen when the bandages came off? What would a hand-pollinator do without hands? If Gabhan couldn't face those questions yet, she couldn't blame him.

She inhaled deeply. What a mash of smells in the warm sled. Pickled beets. The honey of her bees. Gabhan's scared fierce musk. Her own fear-sweat and sweet-nectar, clouding the terrible burned smell of what remained of Ciro's hands. What agony for the boy—she was sure he'd become coerced into hand-pollination, and that coercion had led to catastrophe. What could she say? Singsong at least seemed to have picked the boy. That counted for something. Maybe right now, that counted for everything.

"Okay. I'll teach you what I can. Come here."

The boy whooped. "I knew you'd help. I just knew it!"

Carefully, finally, after hours of not itching, Mishka gently, gently scratched her clavicle—at last! Even in the midst of catastrophe, a surge of joy welled as fresh nectar began to flow, and Singsong suckled. "Do you see her tongue? It's a kind of straw. We call it her glossa, or proboscis."

"What does she call it?"

Mishka chuckled. Even Singsong seemed to buzz a honeybee laughter. "I don't know, Ciro. Maybe you'll be the one to find out."

And for a moment, it seemed as if in spite of the whole disaster, everything was going to be all right. Who knew what apiarists could do, with a nurse bee and a devoted four-year-old boy?

Mishka wouldn't be the one to say no, nothing is possible. Say no today, and there may not be a tomorrow. Maybe the Allmond greenhouse was doomed. Maybe all the greenhouses along the fault line were doomed. Or maybe they'd sled back tomorrow and find the Arborist was dead wrong in Their catastrophic doomsaying. But there were other continents, and other ways of heating green-houses.

For as long as Singsong could fly and find flowers, and for as long as there were Ciros willing to do anything they could to help the bees, there could be a tomorrow. And as long as there could be a tomorrow, there was a chance. A chance that humanity could adapt. Keep calling this place home. Wasn't that what they'd always wanted, even back when Earth was called Eden?

Honeycomb

> "This we have now/is not imagination . . . This/ that we are now/created the body, cell by cell,/like bees building a honeycomb./The human body and the universe/grew from this, not this/from the universe and the human body."
> —Rumi, *The Essential Rumi*

SingSong waited. She wanted to save little queen, save big queen, save earth queen.

But all she could do was see if the child would wake. Taste the honey. Tend the honey.

Every night, the same wait. The boy had survived. But each darkness she doubted if he would breathe come dawn.

She could always go impale herself on a frozen branch of a petrified tree, suss the ice nectar of a forgotten species, call that consummation.

But for now she would wait. If the child woke, they would begin again. Pollinate one flower. Waggle one dance. Nurse one bee. Didn't matter boy child or girl child, it was a child. And children could learn. Create. Mate. Come awake.

Humans were not earth queen, able to change the hum on a whim—but maybe she and big queen and little queen and the child could make a new hive, and survive the whims and untamed hums of earth queen.

Breathe with me, she buzzed.

Ravish today; make us a tomorrow.

The Governess with a Mechanical Womb
LEENA LIKITALO

It rains thin sharp drops like shattered glass. Saga and I won't go out today. We might not go out tomorrow. There is nothing but time to kill, and yet I don't seem to be able to get started in the one task that is more important than the others.

Saga plays with a red wooden horse stolen from the past. I fidget with the quill. I need to write down everything now before I lose courage, before the embers in the fireplace die or the governess returns.

"Agneta . . . " Saga lowers the horse down on the floor. Its carved hooves gallop a hollow clip clop tune. My little sister glances at the horse, then at me, biting her lip. Her gray eyes glint with curiosity. "Were all horses this small?"

I've seen pictures of real horses in the glossy magazines the governess doesn't allow me to bring with me from the places she takes us. I'm pretty sure horses were huge animals, larger than reindeer, and that there were multiple breeds and even within a breed, multiple colors. But horses are extinct now, and with this thought, my stomach knots. The magnitude of everything lost nauseates me.

"Agneta?" Saga studies me from under her pale brows with the merciless attention of a six-year-old.

I force myself to smile as if nothing whatsoever had ever bothered me. Saga doesn't need to know the truth. Not yet. "Some might have been."

I pick the pen up again, but my hand shakes. I won't be able to take this much longer. I dread the empty pages, but not only them. These days I'm afraid of everything, but I can't talk about this with Saga. I have to protect her for as long as I can.

"When I grow up, I want to have one." Saga brushes the horse's back as if it really had a fur. "A real horse."

My sister is still so naïve. I envy her for that. "I doubt the governess will provide you that."

"She might," Saga replies. "If I ask nicely enough."

I dip the pen in the inkwell and scrawl the first hesitant words. This is exactly why I have to write. When I'm gone, my sister might be the last human left in the scorched world.

The day the Victorians killed Pa, they sent a governess to take care of what remained of our family—and possibly of the whole of humankind. The men in impeccably fitted tailcoats and towering top hats led Pa away from the weather-beaten farmhouse. The women in black crinoline gowns followed them to the barren hilltop overlooking the glacier-carved lake. No words were exchanged before they incinerated Pa.

Saga, I shivered with you on the farmhouse's porch. I held your head against my chest to shield you from the sight. Though, since you were only three at the time, I don't think you understood what happened.

Saga and I are in the root cellar when the super-sonic boom tears the day apart. The jar of apple jam slips from my fingers and shatters against the dirt floor. The sickeningly sweet tang mixes with the damp smell of the cellar, and I gag despite myself.

"Agneta . . . " Saga chuckles, stepping back so as not to stain her bare feet. "I bet it's just our governess returning."

I rivet my gaze on the spreading, sticky stain. Perhaps my sister doesn't see our governess as a threat because she's so young. Or perhaps she's managed to convince herself that there was never a different world, that the tales I've told her about the time before the Victorians burned every city and town to dust are just figments of my imagination.

"Should we not go and greet her?" Saga asks. Still staring down, I notice her wriggling her toes.

I kick what remains of the jar under the shelf. The jam that took so many hours to boil is lost for good, as is the world before the Victorians. "We should. But shouldn't you be wearing shoes?"

Saga doesn't reply to me, not when we leave the cellar, not when we make our way back to the house in silence that suits well the rugged landscape of post-apocalyptic Lapland.

Our home, a graying farmhouse, hunches against a rocky slope. I tense despite myself when I hear the metallic click-click of the knitting needles. My sister's eyes brighten. I quickly take hold of her hand, to prevent her from dashing off. I hate it when she acts like an overeager puppy, as if she'd missed the Victorian. "You don't have any shoes that fit you, do you?"

"Nope," Saga replies. "None at all."

We find the governess knitting on the porch. We halt before the lichen-laced stone steps and wait for her to acknowledge us. A tendril of cold, sharp air brushes my cheek, taunting.

"Good afternoon." The governess lowers a half-formed, poison green mitten on her lap and meets us with an emotionless gaze. She was once a full human, but never an attractive one. Her face is round, with eyes set too close and chin tilting inward right below her wide mouth. It doesn't help that she always wears her pale hair in a tight bun atop her head. "How are you today?"

Saga and I curtsy, not much of a sight either in our battered jeans and hoodies. Once again, I feel tempted to rebel against the governess. A creature obsessed with routines, she will continue to stare at us until we behave according to her expectations. But since Saga needs new shoes, I skip the games and reply, "Good afternoon, governess. We are fine. How are you today?"

The governess nods solemnly at us and resumes her knitting.

Saga nudges me, her elbow sharper than it ought to be. My sister might not be afraid of the Victorians, but she never voices any requests either. That's good. I don't want her to grow too dependent on them.

"Governess," I address the Victorian. I hate asking for help from those who killed Ma and Pa, but Saga can't go shoeless once the temperatures drop. "We find ourselves in need of your assistance."

The governess' lips twitch up, but the smile doesn't reach her colorless eyes. Pa once told me that in the early years of Victorian occupation, some lads in Oulu captured a governess, killed her, and cut her open to see what the Victorians did to converts. The governess' veins were lined with an unknown silvery metal, and where her heart should have been was something akin to a battery. But neither of those findings was the one that left the men too horrified to sleep at night—the governess' mechanical womb sheltered a black cube impossible to break open.

"Now do you?" The governess' reply stabs like a broken needle. Not for the first time, I wonder if she, too, bears a black cube in her mechanical womb. That's something I'll never learn. The Victorians hunted down the men who killed the governess and incinerated them. "What would you need?"

Saga wiggles her toes. She's got dirt under her nails. "I'm afraid my feet have decided to grow on their own."

"Huh." The governess tugs more yarn from her omnipresent satchel. Click, click, her needles go. Click, click. "Needless help passivates. Are there no hand-me-downs you could use?"

Saga glances at me. I wrap my arm around her narrow shoulders. Empathy might be a foreign concept to the Victorians, but they have no difficulty in understanding a well-formed argument. "I'm ten years older than her. I have worn all my old clothes, shoes included, thread-bare beyond repair."

The governess blinks blankly as though someone else were making the decision for her. Then she stashes the needles and yarn into her satchel and rises up. "Very well, then. It is my duty to provide for you."

Pa was born the year the Victorians arrived and nuked every city, factory, and highway to dust. The invaders never proclaimed their intentions, never showed themselves, and for a long time they didn't even have a name. They shot beams of energy from the orbit, erasing Shanghai, Delhi, and Lagos in an eye blink. The populace of smaller cities held their breath, until they too, were incinerated one after another.

Pa's family was lucky enough to live in Finland, a country so scarcely populated that it took a while before the Victorians paid any attention to it. His family fled from Helsinki to Tampere, then onward to what remained of Oulu. They lived in a bomb shelter dating back to the Second World War and scavenged the city ruins for food. The survivors of the cataclysm avoided one another—by then, they'd figured out that larger communities and anyone who dabbled with high tech or even electricity got instantly incinerated.

The first converts appeared a decade later, seemingly out of nowhere. The men sporting top hats, tailcoats, and silver-knobbed canes paraded down the ruined streets. The women in black crinoline gowns followed in their wake. They claimed they came in peace, and when asked what species they represented, they named themselves the Victorians.

Pa met Ma, a refugee from Sweden with eyes the color of ice about to thaw, when he was eighteen. Both hated Oulu and living by the rules the Victorians enforced, but never bothered to share with the mere humans. Some of the survivors disappeared, only to appear the next day converted. Others fled what remained of the city. And despite their parents' pleas, Ma and Pa decided to seek a better life further up north.

Ma and Pa rode rickety bicycles through four hundred kilometers of dirt tracks. During the endless white summer nights, they encountered no other living souls, only forlorn, rusting car skeletons and hordes of starving mosquitos.

They stumbled across the small community of Sodankylä by accident. Though they were happy to meet other survivors, they couldn't imagine staying. The Victorians walked amongst the humans, exchanging formal greetings as if that was all there was to good life.

At that point, Ma and Pa realized they could never pedal far enough. As a sort of compromise, they set home to an abandoned farmhouse about fifty kilometers away from Sodankylä. I was born a year later.

I guess that for a while our parents were as happy as two people ever can be.

The portal remains open behind us, a shimmering oval between two tall pines. In this time and place, the air smells of wet bark and bent grass. It must have stopped raining just moments earlier.

The governess glances at her golden pocket watch, then at Saga and me. "We have thirty minutes exact."

"Sure," I reply. When I first stepped through a portal, the governess warned me that those who remained behind after it closed would simply cease to exist. If it hadn't been for Saga, I might have . . . But now, I won't even entertain the idea, no matter how I hate my life.

The governess produces a red-checkered mitten from her satchel and hangs it at the tip of a pine branch. Without sparing us another glance, she strides through the forest of young trees, up a slope thick with shrubbery. Lingonberries squash under her heels, but she doesn't notice that.

Saga and I follow the governess as fast as we can, but not quite fast enough. After we lose sight of her, we follow the mittens. I idly wonder if this is the reason she knits them in the first place. Perhaps. Who can tell how the mind of a convert works?

The forest gives way to a well-tended clearing, an ochre-painted, two-story holiday house with plain, white window frames and a black mansard roof. A gravel road leads through the forest toward north. The governess is nowhere in sight. Her kind comes and goes as they please.

"Let's go and see what we can find," I say to Saga. I have no clock of my own—clocks without plastic and batteries are difficult to find—but I estimate the hike took five or so minutes.

"Anything you'd need?" Saga asks.

Another human being. Preferably a boy of my age. Give or take a decade or two. Barring that, a life far away from the governess would be nice. And if that isn't possible, something to make me forget everything. However, my little sister doesn't need to know about the things I yearn even though I know I can never have them.

"Books," I reply. It's better to give her something to hunt, to keep her out of my way. And besides, it's about time I teach her how to read.

I hold my breath as I push the front door open. I know to expect the jarring sense of unease, and yet it turns my limbs leaden. Though we've never seen anyone during our visits, that doesn't mean this house's owners couldn't return at any moment.

"I'll be fast," Saga promises as she dashes past me toward the stairs. It's late summer in this time. Winter clothes are most likely kept stored in the attic.

I pop into the toilet under the stairs, not that I would ever dare to use it, just as I don't dare to turn on the lights. With arms extended before me, I shuffle my way to the cupboard above the sink. I search blindly.

By chance, I come across a small brown bottle. I squint at the label. The big red triangle tells me everything I need to know. I unscrew the cap and swallow two gulps of the cough medicine. I've done this more times than I care to admit. But the governess seems to be blind to the wonderful drowsiness that's bound to follow.

I return the bottle in the cupboard and continue my hunt. I find a box of tampons. Praised be whichever god still exists! Though, I'll either have to remove the plastic wrappings or risk the governess confiscating the box.

Feeling pleasantly lightheaded, I stuff the box into my backpack. It feels good to defy the rules for even a moment. To celebrate my decision, on my way out, I snatch two rolls of the luxurious, triple-ply toilet paper. Those can't possibly count as high-tech!

I ignore the kitchen—the governess doesn't approve us taking food unless we're starving. I drift through the spacious living room occupied only by a massive white sofa and a huge tv. On the far side, two doors whisper promises of a better life led by luckier people. I open the door on the left.

The room isn't particularly big. A teddy bear, sitting on the pink duvet with limbs askew in all directions, guards the bed at the back of the room. Ill-tended books, notebooks, and piles of paper cover the desk to my right. Jeans, t-shirts, and various accessories litter the floor. The posters on the wall proclaim ownership. Skinny men and women in scant clothing scream, sweat dripping down their faces.

No, I realize, they aren't screaming but singing.

I close my eyes as my heart pangs with envy. This room belongs to a teenage girl. In another time and place, it could have been mine. The concerts, heartbreaks, and fashion disasters. The heartbreaks . . .

It would be so easy to get lost in sorrow. But the drowsiness dulls even the strongest of emotions, and I manage to push self-pity aside for a moment more.

I wade to the table. This girl from the past is of my age. The books might be schoolbooks. I need to check if I can take any of them with me. I need to learn whatever there is to learn. Perhaps one day I'll figure out what happened to my world, why the Victorians came, and how I can best protect Saga from their arbitrariness.

But every single one of the books contains plastic in one form or another. I can't take them with me. I force myself to fumble through the clothing, to get something else to think about. As my luck has it, the clothes are made of polyester and acrylic. I run my fingers along the paisley print of a particularly pretty sleeveless top. Even if I could take it with me, I would never have any use for it. I need warm and durable clothes that can stand the elements and mangling by washboard. I toss the top aside.

My vision is already blurry around the edges when I come across a pair of snowflake patterned woolen socks, no doubt knit by the girl's grandmother. I clench my teeth as my hands curl into fists. I sway to the bed and sink down so heavily that the teddy bear keels over. It's not fair! I've never seen and will never see my grandmother!

Tears well in my eyes, and I can't hold them back. I snatch the teddy bear and clutch it against my heart. The Victorians have denied me everything. Family, friends, the chance of ever meeting someone I might fall in love with.

"What is it, Agneta?" Saga has appeared into the doorway without me noticing. A slightly too large fur cap lines her delicate face. The lamb fur coat she's donned looks old, but warm, the winter boots three sizes too large.

The teddy bear drops from my numb fingers. I can't allow Saga to see me this weak. "Nothing."

"Nothing?" Saga parrots me. She picks her way through the mess to the bed, sits down next to me, wraps her arm around me, and leans her chin against my shoulder. "I thought that lying was a bad thing."

As Saga grows older, it's getting more and more difficult to mislead her. Perhaps the time has come to stop even trying. I wipe my eyes dry with the back of my hand. "I found something I really want, but can't take with us."

Saga squeezes her arms tighter around me. It's as if she were my big sister, not the other way around.

"Now, did you indeed?" The governess rolls into the room, the black hem of her gown swallowing everything like a monstrous wave.

I freeze, but my heart pounds unsteadily. My careless comment has placed both Saga and me in grave danger. What can I say and do to remedy the situation? It's difficult to think straight, with the cough medicine clouding my mind.

"Well?" The governess seems to float before us, over the clothes and magazines. She motions toward my bag. I demurely hand it over.

Despite all the winter clothes, Saga shivers as the governess rummages through my bag. She thinks I've decided to snatch something forbidden. I second-guess myself. Have I?

The governess tosses out the toilet paper rolls. She pouts her lips as she notices the box of tampons. She turns it in her hands, opens the package, and pulls out one plastic-wrapped tampon. "What is this?"

Saga stares at me, still silent. I haven't yet talked with her about the inconveniences of growing up. I want her to lead a carefree life as long as she can.

"Something to make my life a little easier," I finally reply. How victorious I felt just a while back! Now defeat tastes bitter and sharp.

"I can't let you have them," the governess says, placing the box on the table.

I boil inside. And despite knowing the danger in debating with a Victorian, I spring up and retrieve the box. I pull out a tampon and brandish it at her. "The wrapping comes off."

"Is that so?" the governess asks.

Glowering with fury, I unpeel the tampons, one after another.

Pa believed the Victorians could access cached moments. To prove his theory, he followed a convert through a portal once and brought back newspapers that Ma promptly used to start a fire. Though he and Ma could have received supplies from the Victorians, they preferred to scavenge the cottages scattered across the abandoned valleys.

Ma and Pa spoke only rarely of the world before the Victorians. I gathered from the clues left behind—magazines full of pictures of impossibly beautiful women, exotic cities of architectural wonder, and delicacies I'd never get to taste—that their parents must have led a life of abundance and extravaganza. Though at the time I blamed them for not telling me everything, later I understood how much it must have pained them to almost have it all.

Saga, you must understand, Ma and Pa did their best to provide for us. We farmed beetroot, potatoes, and onions. We fished for trout and pike. Sometimes one of them would jump on their bicycle and pedal away, while the other stayed with you and me.

Back when Sodankylä still existed, it harbored an underground marketplace. There, behind the Victorians' backs, people bartered with what they'd found from the ruins or on their trips through the portals. They exchanged alcohol for food, medicines for clothes, luxuries of olden days for everyday amenities.

I remember always feeling anxious and restless until the parent who'd braved the journey returned. On that happy day, we'd cook a celebratory meal, no matter how meager their loot. We'd pop open tin cans and rip open plastic containers. We'd laugh, though sometimes the food left an ashen aftertaste.

I realized only later why.

Frost has bitten the landscape bloody. I chop logs in the small opening by the woodshed, but my mind is elsewhere. Saga is gathering the nets. The governess went with her, but rather to keep an eye on her than to help. She never participates in household duties.

My stomach aches and will ache for days still. I'm afraid of many things, but not of my periods. I know now that I won't die of the bleeding. When the time comes, I'll explain how a woman's body works to Saga, but not a day sooner.

I swing the ax to split another log. The wood parts with a satisfying crack. If I hate something almost as much as the Victorians, it's the damned inconvenience of having a womb. Why do I have to bleed, when there's a decent chance that I'll never meet another human being beside Saga, let alone a boy to knock me up?

I yank the ax free from the log. It's getting late. Hopefully, come next summer, Saga can already fend for herself, and I can pedal to discover what remains of Sodankylä. Perhaps my fears will prove unfounded. Perhaps . . .

Enough with wistful thinking.

I return the ax in the woodshed and pile the chopped wood to dry. Then I stride down the rocky path to the narrow jetty that age and elements have turned gray. The jetty squeaks under my boots long after I've halted to survey the lake.

Saga and the governess are still at the north end of the lake, perhaps a half-kilometer away. My sister is hauling the net into the boat all by herself, while the governess knits mittens no one will ever use. Just as I expected.

"No, I don't buy it." Saga's voice carries over the open water. "You can't have always been a governess."

I flinch despite myself. I avoid addressing the governess when I can get away with it, but my bold, six-year-old sister has just asked the very question that has always puzzled me. What was our governess like before she chose to convert? Why did she choose to welcome alien machinery into her body rather than remain a human? For isn't that the ultimate betrayal one can commit against one's species?

"No." The governess straightens her back. Her reply sounds mechanical. "That I was not."

"Why become one then?" Saga leans over the boat's edge to better grasp the net. The boat tilts to a threatening angle. I'm about to call out a warning, but before I can do so, the governess shifts to balance the boat.

"The children must be looked after," the governess says.

Saga sniffs as she heaves the last of the net and day's catch over the boat's rim. She dislikes being called a child. Even though that's what she is. "You were a child, then?"

"A child is a boy or a girl," the governess replies.

"A girl." Saga nods, self-satisfied. "You were a girl."

For a long while, neither of them speaks more. The gray clouds thicken, and shadows grow taller. On the shore, blood-red birches shiver. I can't see any birds flying, but I can hear faded cries of terns.

Eventually, Saga picks up the oars and expertly maneuvers the boat around. She rows toward the jetty, but still doesn't notice me. It really is getting dark and colder, too.

"You are a girl," the governess muses as if she's realized this for the very first time.

"You're funny." Saga giggles. She splashes water with the oars. The governess ducks to avoid the sprays. My sister laughs. "You know, we have something in common after all!"

I spit in the water, shattering the surface. Saga and I have nothing whatsoever in common with the converts. I'll need to make sure she remembers that.

But I can't bear to face my sister now, not with the governess present. I flee up the path to the farmhouse, kicking every pebble on the way. Saga and I belong to the second post-invasion generation, but it seems to me she's forgot what the Victorians did.

I haven't, and I harbor enough hate in my heart for two.

• • •

Ma was visiting Sodankylä when the town got obliterated. I was playing with you in the orchard when the beam of light split the sky, so bright I couldn't see for hours afterwards. Pa found us crying, curled under an apple tree. He didn't need to tell us that Ma wouldn't return.

Pa changed after Ma died. He sat on the porch, staring in turns into the distance and at his hands. He hunched there, muttering about electricity and how people should have already known better, for so long that even the mosquitos grew bored of his taste.

That autumn, the fields went untended, the apples unpicked. You were two and half years old at the time. Between looking after you and Pa, I had no chance to go and scrounge for myself.

We ran out of tin cans when the first snow fell. On the third day that we had nothing left to eat, the Victorians came to pay us a visit. Pa pretended he'd invited the serious men and women and thanked them for the provisions they brought.

I think that if there had been any alcohol to be had, he would have emptied every single bottle and flask.

Every Saturday—that is, every seventh day, since there's no way to be sure of time and date anymore—Saga and I heat up our little sauna, wash the laundry, and scrub ourselves clean. The governess never joins us; rather she often leaves via portal to a different time and place, perhaps to visit her own kind. I'm unashamedly glad of that.

"More?" Saga asks as we sit naked on the wet pine bench, knees pressed against chests, arms wrapped around shins. She twirls the copper ladle absent-mindedly as she stares out of the soot-laced window.

It's dark and cold outside. It should have snowed weeks ago, but it hasn't. The new world follows different rules, and amidst the change, Saga and I are alone. I seek solace from what little tradition remains, from the scent of burning wood, the warm comfort of the tiny sauna, the closeness never shared in any place else. Saga and I were both born in this very room. Here we're safe.

"Sure," I reply just as the sonic boom tears through the windowpanes. Glass hums. I fear it will crack. "Shit."

We'll never be safe anywhere.

"Agneta!" Saga hits me with the ladle, not particularly hard, but hard enough for it to sting. "Don't curse in the sauna!"

I should stay stronger before my little sister, show her example by being unafraid, but . . . I can't. Not anymore.

Saga tosses a scoop of water on the stove's stones, but the soft hiss does nothing to set me at ease. She notices that. "That's just our governess returning."

I bury my head in my hands as if I were protecting my ears from the steam, not trying to hide my shame. My stomach clenches, cold fingers squeeze my heart. This fear, it's impossible to live with, too embarrassing to admit.

"Agneta?" Saga brushes my shoulder, her skin clammy against mine. That's it then. She's seen what I've tried so hard to hide. There's no point in continuing to lie.

"Sometimes . . ." The words, I don't want to say them. But I have to. "I grow so tired of being ever so afraid of the Victorians."

"I'm not afraid." Saga's reply is the last thing I expected to hear. "Got no reason to be. I've broken no rules."

Anger surges inside me. Sure, Saga is young and ignorant. But to dismiss my words, to accept the situation as it is, that's unacceptable!

"Who knows what rules they follow?" I whisper hoarsely. Does Saga really think that she understands how the Victorians think? Does she think she's safe because she plays best friends with the governess? Does she? And I shouldn't have to remind her that . . . "They killed Ma and Pa."

Saga flinches. No, she hasn't forgot Ma and Pa. That's good, but I feel ever so slightly ashamed that I thought so even in passing.

For a long while, neither of us speaks. Saga stares at the stove, the logs in the firebox succumbing to flames. I rivet my attention at the stones. As the water evaporates, the dry patches on them grow larger. Gradually, the sauna cools. The air should have become easier to breathe, and yet it doesn't feel that way.

At last, Saga says in a barely audible voice, "So you've told me, but what if . . . "

I glare at her sideways. What is she after now? "What if what?"

I've told her what came to pass many times, and there's no way she could have misunderstood. Pa acquired and hid the gun to protect Saga and me.

"Nothing." Saga wraps her arms tighter around herself as if she wanted to close the whole word, me included, outside.

I'm about to chastise her when a dreadful thought occurs to me. I fight to deny it even as a shiver runs down my back, sinking claws under my skin, all the way to my bones.

"Give me that." I yank the ladle from Saga's numb hold. I pour water on the stones. I pour and pour until both of us wriggle in steam.

And yet I can't chase away the awful thought. What if Pa thought to protect us by putting a bullet through our heads?

We lived through the endless night of the winter only thanks to the Victorians. The somber men and women paid us a visit every single time we ran out of food. However, it was neither kindness nor any sort of regret that drove them. When Pa thought I couldn't hear, he questioned them about their motives. They spoke of the survival of the species, of all things!

When the spring finally came, Pa left me in charge of the house and went foraging. You and I fished the best we could, but one can't live solely on pike and trout. The Victorians must have been spying on us, because they sent us more tin cans and dried rye bread.

For two long weeks, I feared Pa would never return, that the Victorians had killed him too. Then he did return, though later I wished he hadn't.

We rushed to greet him, braids bouncing against our backs. We leaned against the porch's creaky railing and waved at him, eager to see what he'd brought us.

As the spring sun shone bright, Pa opened his backpack and pulled out an object wrapped in a red and white-checkered scarf. Carefully and slowly, he untied the knots. I caught a glimpse of metal, a hint of a barrel and grip.

"Soon," he said, grinning at us, "you won't have to be afraid ever again."

The Victorians came for Pa the very next day.

The governess' fingers curl around my shoulder, claws of a hungry beast. She shouts something incomprehensible to me, face too close to mine. As I meet her cold, emotionless gaze, thick smoke floods my nostrils and mouth. I scream, but the nightmare won't go away.

"Fire," the governess says. "Get out."

Still not sure if I'm dreaming or awake, I stumble up from the bed. The governess drags me through the smoke-filled house, out of the door, down the porch's stone stairs, into the freezing night. All I can do is cough.

"Saga . . . " I retch black slime into a snowbank. Before us, the farmhouse spits flames. The doorway gasps acrid smoke. But my little sister is nowhere in sight. "I must go back!"

"No. Too dangerous. You are sixteen," the governess replies as if that explained everything. As if in her eyes I'm more valuable because I'm older and more resources have been spent to ensure my survival.

"And . . . she's but . . . a child," I snap back at her, coughing between the words. I sway toward the house even as bright dots swarm my vision. At the stone steps, heat lashes against me, instantly blistering my face and forearms.

"A girl." The governess pulls me back from the shoulders, her grip like iron. There's a strange, distant quality to her voice, as if something deep inside her had just clicked. "I was a girl."

There's no time to lose, and yet I find myself staring at her. Her visage bears a look of utter sadness. It's as if she finally remembers that she was once fully human and understood emotions, grief and despair.

"You stay. My clothes, they might protect me." And without waiting for my answer, the governess thrusts her satchel at me and strides into the flames. For a moment, I can see her black, diminishing shape against the vicious orange. Then she disappears altogether, and all that remains is a faint whisper: "I was a girl."

I stomp in the melting snow, as close to the burning house as I can without suffering more burns. A part of me wants to dash after the governess and find my sister. The rational part knows that I would die before being able to help her in any way.

Loneliness haunts me as I wait. There's no guarantee I'll see my dear sister, another human being, ever again. Her fate is in the hands of a convert. I fidget with the satchel. The governess has never let me touch it before. I need something to distract myself. I unclasp the satchel.

The governess' most valued possessions seem to be her knitting needles, three balls of red yarn, and my notebook. Curious. I left that on my nightstand. Why did she opt to save it from the fire? Did she on some subconscious level . . .

A multitude of loud cracks. A terrifying shape emerges from the house. It's the governess. She half falls, half slides down the stone stairs, her gown sprouting flames, a burning halo of hair around her head. My heart and hopes shrink, for she has returned alone.

Then Saga peeks out from under the governess' hem, cheeks stained with smoke and tears.

"Saga!" I rush to them, pulling my sister up on her own feet, away from the fire. She wraps her arms around my thighs and cries.

"A girl . . . " The governess staggers after us, but her feet slip on the slush. The flames on her hair wither. Her scalp has blackened, visage blistered. She looks like a monster, but that she is not.

"You're hurt," I say, feeling dumb and powerless.

A shudder runs through the governess' body. She collapses on her knees on the snow. "She . . . she is six."

I squat down next to the governess. I pat snow against her cheeks and forehead, and Saga follows my suit. But it's too late to save her. Her dress disintegrates, the black fabric turning into white flakes, revealing more burns.

"I'm sorry," I whisper as I help the governess to lie down in the snow. I was so very wrong about her. "I'm so sorry."

The governess meets me with an unblinking stare. Though her lashes have burnt, too, the look in her eyes is one of utter peace. "I . . . was . . . a girl."

Life flees her scorched body soon after.

Northern lights claw the cold sky green-blue as Saga and I drag the governess' body up the slope. Our going through the knee-deep snow is slow, and the governess' limbs leave behind sooty trails. Yet, we halt only when we're a safe distance away from the smoldering ruins of our home.

"What will we do now?" Saga clutches the hem of her nightgown. The air smells of snow and flames, of sorrow and loss.

The Victorians can sense the death of their kind. They will come to claim our governess' body soon. And then . . . I'm ashamed to admit it to myself, I expect the Victorians to continue looking after Saga and me. "We wait."

"For what?" Saga's voice breaks as she glances at the governess' body. The governess lies on her back. The front of her body is charred. Her belly curves inward, hollow apart from the outline of a cube. She's a convert, but also . . . "You know she was my friend."

That remark hurts me more than anything else that came to pass that night. I've hated the Victorians my whole life and expected Saga to do likewise. But she bonded with the governess and the governess sacrificed herself to save my sister.

"I'm sorry. I truly am."

"It's all right. I guess." Saga takes hold of my hand, her fingers already white-cold. "It will not be the same if they send another governess to take care of us. But I will try my best to welcome her."

"I know." I squeeze her hand. Saga will be able to adjust to anything and befriend anyone regardless of their species or origin. I . . .

The whiplash boom heralds the portal opening to our right. But this time, I don't flinch, not even when four stern-faced Victorians stride through the rippling air, followed by a demure woman, our governess-to-be. They don't look like they're angry at us, not like they want a life in return for the loss of one of their kind.

I think of the cube inside the governess' womb. I think of what I yearn and what I can never have. I can't bear the thought of sharing my sister with someone I'll inevitably fear, loathe, and hate. I'm not like Saga. My feelings have roots wedged so deep that no matter how I were to try, I will never be able to overcome them.

"Saga . . . " I press the satchel in her hands. She's the one who matters to me the most. I want to be with her forever, to be loved by her rather than eventually despised. "I'll have to go with them. And when I return it will seem like I'm gone, but it'll still be me. At some level, it'll still be me."

When I step through the portal, I still think of the vast city in the stars, looking through space and time at the white-shrouded, blue planet. For if my kind hadn't intervened, it would have been forever lost.

"Agneta!" Saga runs to me, arms spread wide for an embrace.

I don't respond to her call, for I don't have a name anymore, only a duty. "How do you do?"

As I lead Saga to her new home, an abandoned summer cottage on the north side of the lake, I feel nothing but the strangest sort of empathy and sadness toward the one who treats me as if we were the same.

We are not and will never be. I have an important duty, and that duty fuels me. I must look after this human, this child. I must guide her and protect her from hurting herself.

I believe her kind calls this sort of devotion love. For some reason I don't quite understand, I want to prepare her apple jam.

Between Dragons and Their Wrath
AN OWOMOYELA AND RACHEL SWIRSKY

My name is Domei. I think I am fourteen. I will probably die today. If not, I will probably die tomorrow.

When it happens, I don't think I'll be surprised. Frightened, maybe, but not surprised.

In the forest, scales are most common. If they cut you, the cut will never stop bleeding.

If you step in a place where a dragon has defecated, food will stream through your body, and you will always be hungry. If you pass a place where a dragon breathed fire, your skin will forever blister and heal and then blister again. If you touch a dragon's blood, you'll go mad.

As for me, I was harvesting scales. With a scale, you can till the land faster than anyone using an iron hoe. You can butcher meat in a tenth the time it takes to use a knife. There are good things about dragon leavings, and for those good things, I usually get paid enough to eat.

Scales are common. Everyone knows about those. It was something else that got me.

When I die, if you ask the Andé what killed me, they will probably say it was the dragons. Ask me now, and I'll tell you the Andé are responsible. They drove their dragons across our land.

I don't know why the Andé, who live to our west, hated the Zhie, who live to our east. Kwesi has tried to explain, and so has Hano. But their explanations don't make sense.

Kwesi believes war is what people do. He says when people are lazy, they go to war. He says Rho would go to war if we weren't so poor. He may be right, but it doesn't explain why the Andé attacked the Zhie instead of the Rho or the Merais or someone else.

Hano's answer is even stranger. "The Andé say the Zhie cut the hands off Andé children. They say they stole their women in the night and sucked their blood and made them defecate on Andé flags. And they were killing Andé spirits, too."

I said, "I haven't heard of the Zhie doing anything like that."

Hano got annoyed. "No, I mean that's what the Andé say."

But since those were obvious lies, there must have been another reason first.

I suppose reasons don't matter now. The Andé had dragons. The Zhie had none. With firecrackers and guns and bayonets, the Andé drove their dragons into Zhie land as a strong, angry man will drive a knife into someone's heart. And we, the Rho, were in the middle. We were the flesh, the ribs. They drove the dragons right through us.

That was fifty years ago, the dragons, the war. Since then, we've had floods from old dragons' tears, and earthquakes from old footprints. It was an earthquake that brought me here to Ponçan. I was in the forest, a few dozen kilometers from the rubble of the village where I must have grown up. Kwesi was a truck driver then and he heard me screaming in the trees. He went off road, loaded me into his truck, and took me to the N.G.O. men.

We used to call Ponçan the tent city. Most of the tents are gone now. There's still a crew of NGO men left behind "to coordinate efforts in the surrounding countryside." But these days, when Kwesi wants a break from hauling, he can usually find an abandoned building to stay in.

The people here pronounce NGO as Ngo. Kwesi taught me: you position your tongue at the top of your mouth to make an *n* without speaking, then make a *g* with the back of your tongue. Then let out the *o* and it'll push the *ng* right in front of it.

There are a lot of *ng* sounds in Kwesi's dialect. There are a lot of NGOs in Rho.

Ponçan is mostly empty now except for the Ngo men who stayed behind. The rest of us have nowhere to go, like Hano and I.

Hano is my best friend. He's also never been changed by a dragon. People like that are rare in Ponçan. If you ask him why, he'll just say he was lucky.

Kwesi, who is the same age as our fathers would be, used to be a friend of Hano's family. After he dropped me in the tent city, he sent Hano to look after me. We fell in easily together. He showed me how to find houses no one was using so I didn't always have to sleep in the tents, and how to go through the dump outside the village, and how to get in queues early for meal relief.

Hano is fast on his feet. He's cheerful even when he shouldn't be. He has quick, bright eyes for spotting useful things that have been thrown away, and deft hands for pulling them free.

"I wanted to grow up to be like my mother," he told me once while we shared fruit we'd found in an Ngo dumpster. His mother had died in the flood which happened before the earthquake, but he still talked about her happily. "She taught little kids, four year olds, six year olds. The smallest ones are the best. They're always running after something even if they still piss themselves."

He looked regretfully at his withered fruit and went on. "She was a great cook, too. We'd find papayas and cook them with lime and chilies. My little sister drank from a stream where a dragon shat. It wasn't bad enough to kill her, but she couldn't keep her food so there was always cooking to do."

I examined the bruised parts of my fruit, and leaned against the dumpster. The sky above Ponçan is never a normal color. It was changed by dragon wings a long time ago. It was mud brown that evening. The Hizhang cows lowed as it got darker.

"What did you want to do?" Hano said.

I pretended not to know. "When?"

"Before Ponçan, what did you want to do?"

Hano and Kwesi know I don't remember much from before, but I've never told them it's basically all gone. Maybe not having a past makes it easier not to spend time thinking about before and after like Hano does. I'm too busy trying to sell scales and get a bite to eat.

"You don't have to answer," Hano assured me.

I said, "It's fine—"

Hano's eyes went wide. He clapped his hand over my mouth. A cry drifted between buildings, and from the corner of my eye, I saw a moving fire.

The burning children won't usually hurt you because they can't really see. They just wander, hands outstretched. It's only when you make noise that they'll come toward you and wrap their arms around your knees. They want someone to hold onto. They don't realize they're burning you alive with the same dragon-fire that killed them long ago.

Life in Ponçan is not so bad. We waited until its cries were gone, and then counted three hundred breaths more to be sure.

You see, we were lucky. The Andé drove the big dragons north of Ponçan. We only got little dragons, the size of trucks, whose looks melted one or two people at a time. And they were always on the move, not being thrashed into city-destroying rages.

During the war, the Andé slaughtered a big dragon the size of a mountain. They dropped its liver and gall on Hizhang. Bile poisoned the earth, poisoned the air, poisoned the people and the children of the people, and is still poisoning them now. People born in Hizhang have probably never seen a dragon, but they don't need to.

Every dusk, the cows start lowing from Hizhang. But there are no longer cows in Hizhang.

You see, we were lucky.

I've never seen a dragon, but I don't need to.

There's an art to picking up dragon scales. You have to be careful not to touch the edges. You pinch them just past the edge and wiggle them out of the soil or loam or scree. Then if you've picked up an old tin can or something, you put them in there. If not, you can wrap them in cloth, but it will get cut through, and the scales will cut whatever is nearby, too. The tin cans also get cut, but not as quickly.

A long time ago when Ponçan was still a tent city, an Ngo man told me there are different types of remembering. I've forgotten my old life, but not how to gather scales.

I have so many cuts on my fingers that my hands are always cracking with dried blood. I have cuts on my knees and feet from dropping scales, but they aren't deep. The thighs are especially dangerous, like the arms. It's easy to bleed out. You see, I'm lucky. I'm not bleeding out. Just seeping.

This is a world with only two things in it: the ones which change, and the ones which linger on. I was one of the things that changed.

My life before is gone, but I remember how I got to the tent city. I remember the tatty roof of Kwesi's truck which was all I stared at for hours. I remember the jolting road, thinking someone angry was shaking me. I remember the dust, which blew into my mouth and eyes.

The sky was green, and the sun was so, so bright.

White tents held hot air like breaths they wouldn't let go. There were bodies everywhere, moving, moaning. There were no beds left. I was put on a pad on the ground. I lay there staring at the tent ribs, and listening to the wind. It was a hard sound to hold onto. So many voices overrode it.

They gave me a paper bracelet. I don't know what it said. I hadn't told them my name.

Afternoon passed, and evening, and the lowing of the Hizhang cows. The tent canvas was brightening with morning when a Ngo man examined me. He tested the weight of my limbs, looked at my teeth and eyes, and felt my neck, armpits, and groin. He took a vial of my blood and labeled it in neat Merais letters. He put the blood in a case with mist pouring out of it. Another Ngo man was following him with a clipboard.

The man was surprised when he realized it wasn't the earthquake that had left me feverish and screaming. "*Neutrois,*" he said slowly, so that the one with the clipboard could write it down. "A common affliction in the parts of the world that deal with dragon breeding. There are schools to rehabilitate them, even surgery if a sex can be assigned."

They went on to the next boy, and a Rho nurse came to check my fever. Behind her, wind batted the tent flap, showing flashes of orange sky.

Hano has never been changed by a dragon, and if I can stop it, he won't ever be. He's better at scavenging in the village anyway. I go out for scales.

A few days ago, the sky rose purple. The sky above Ponçan is many colors, but almost never purple. We couldn't decide what it meant. Hano thought it was good luck. Kwesi, who brought us a handful of dried fish, thought it was a fool's game to gamble on anything but bad luck in Ponçan.

Me, I went out to gather, because we needed scales. Hano sent me out with tin cans from Ngo dumps, and I pried loose a half-dozen scales without adding fresh cuts to my hands.

I took my time walking back through the sweet-smelling trees. The sky shifted restlessly between lavender and violet. Darker shades made the trees look black even though it was afternoon.

Among the shadowed trunks, I saw two animals. The small one suckled from the large one. As I neared, I saw it was a muntjac suckling from a forest ox. It was the ox that looked at me as it angled its large body to stand between me and its fawn. Its eyes were challenging. They said: *Leave us to ourselves. This is our new world, and we are content with it.*

These are things that have changed.

I never went to surgery. A gender was never assigned. Boys mostly treated me like another boy, and girls like another girl, so long as no one asked. When they did, I said "because of the dragons" and they might wrinkle their noses, but then they'd crowd around to show me what had happened to them.

"Look! I picked up something on the side of the road, and now my hand-bones are soft—"

"—all my teeth went sharp! I can't even eat fruit anymore—"

"No, no, see this? One foot is on backwards, but only the one."

"That's nothing. My sister has her whole head on backwards!"

"My grandma can turn her hands backwards."

"Look at me, I have two tongues! T-t-wo t-t-ong-g-gues!"

Life in Ponçan is not so bad.

In the purple-sky evening, Kwesi caught me on my way back from gathering scales. We laid them flat in the bed of his truck where it would take them a little longer to cause trouble.

With his braids swept back, I could see the hungry little mouths on his neck which he'd gotten when he was hit with shrapnel from a dragon-tooth bomb. He always wore his shirt, even on hot days, to hide the ones on his side.

He caught me looking, and grinned as he pushed his hair over them. "One of the widow's kids wouldn't stop bothering me this morning so I told him they eat children's fingers."

"They eat?"

"Sometimes." He pointed down the road. "Let's take a walk."

We left his truck and headed toward where I was staying with Hano. On our way, we passed the old general's house. Some Ngo men were moving things inside, and a crowd had gathered behind them. They crossed their arms, passed chaw, and muttered darkly.

Finally one of the Ngo men put down the crate he was carrying. He said something in Merais and flapped his hands to shoo them away. Grumbling, the crowd broke up.

The old general's house was the fanciest building in Ponçan, but it had been empty as long as I'd lived there. No one went in, even squatters. I looked up at Kwesi. He spoke Merais, and I didn't.

"He told them they're being unreasonable," Kwesi said. "He says Ngo are trained to be careful."

"About what?"

"Story goes the old general touched dragon blood and that's why he went mad. The house has been cleaned now."

"Enough?"

Kwesi shrugged, and offered me a cigarette.

"This is what *I* say," he said, lighting it for me. "You should get out of here. Go to the capitol. You're smart, you can do whatever you want."

I took a long drag. I had to balance the cigarette just so in my fingers to keep from bloodying the paper.

He lit his own. "I hear there's new Ngo money to send Rho to that school they have for kids who were changed like you." He paused to blow out a stream of smoke. "You should go, learn mathematics and become an accountant or a banker. You'll live in a big, white house, and have servants bring you drinks when it gets hot, eh?"

"There's never enough Ngo money for everyone," I said.

He tightened his lips around his cigarette and spoke from the side of his mouth. "Enough for somebody, though. What's keeping you here?"

I thought of the muntjac and the ox.

I stubbed out half the cigarette. "I should find Hano."

"Give me a minute," Kwesi said. "I'll drive you."

"I can get the scales myself. I know how to handle them."

Kwesi examined me for a second before deciding to back off. "I'll keep watch here," he said, nodding to the old general's house. He raised his hand to say goodbye, and smoke trailed into cloudless violet.

Early on, Hano, who has never been changed by a dragon, asked me, "What happened to you, anyway? I didn't know anything could make you like *that*."

He said it cheerfully, the way he'd want to know how I could jump so high, or how big the cat was I'd seen in the forest. Since he said it like that, I gave him half an answer.

I remember just far enough back to know I was in a clearing with a sack. The clearing was thick with shed scales, more than I'd ever seen. It was dangerous to go where they were so crowded since it was so easy to trip over one you didn't see, but I needed the money from bringing them home. I don't know why I needed it. I was thin when they found me, but I wasn't starving. Maybe I had siblings.

Even then, I knew I was probably going to die that day. If not, then probably the next. I wrapped my feet in cloth even though it wouldn't do anything, and told myself I'd be okay as long as I went slowly and made sure I could see exactly where I was stepping. I thought the silvery sheen to the ground was just the light reflecting off the grass. That was a stupid thing to think. I'd never seen grass reflect that way.

Bits of purple sky reflected on the tin cans as I stood in our doorway, giving them to Hano. He shook them to hear how full they were, and said, "You see, we were lucky." Then he made me show him my hands and feet so he could see I didn't have any new cuts.

I told him about the muntjac and the ox. He laughed. "Some changes aren't so bad," he said.

He looked at me when he said it.

Thoughtfully, Hano asked, "Do you think it's like this everywhere? Even in Andé?"

I pulled back my hands, rubbing at the crusted blood. Hano frowned. I was supposed to let them scab when I could.

"We're never going to Andé. Why worry about it?"

"They have so many dragons in Andé. It must be worse than here. Right?"

"There are a lot of places worse than here."

"Mm," answered Hano, not quite agreeing. He hesitated, looking at the goods he had piled in the corner, his scavenge and my scales. He said, "If I were like you, I could go to the capitol."

The turn surprised me. "You've been talking to Kwesi."

"If Ngo has money, why not take it?"

"*If* Ngo has money."

"If I was like you, we could go to the capitol together."

"You're not like me. Why worry about it?"

Hano stared at our goods for a while as the quiet grew. The Hizhang cows lowed, and the sky finally let go of purple and went grey. We heard old men walking past, one of them telling a joke.

Life in Ponçan is not so bad. Eventually, Hano took a dented can from our personal stash, and opened it for us to share.

Hano almost died yesterday. He laughed about it but his laughter was shaky.

He had been sleeping at his cousins', close to the center of Ponçan. They were paying him to help with repairs. It happened just before dawn, when most people were sleeping. He found me outside, eating breakfast, not even knowing something was wrong.

"Some white Ngo, straight from Merre," he told me. "They gave him the old general's house, and in the back of the closet, he found the old general's uniform."

"No," I said, because I knew the answer was yes.

Hano gave his choked laugh again. "He put it on. He put it on."

After that, the Merais man really had no choice. The jacket made him take the rifle the dead general had left, and it made him go outside and fire it through the walls into the houses. Hano had been asleep, but the noise gave him enough time to throw himself to the ground and cover his head with his hands. A bullet bit his shoulder, but when the bullets ran out, he was still alive. The Ngo doctor bandaged him up.

Hano was wheezing, but he tried to keep laughing, too. "The shots stopped, but I was afraid to go out until I heard that old widow shouting at him. I finally peeked out the door and saw her beating him, head and shoulders, with a pan. He was just standing there. The jacket still had him. Bang. Bang. Her face was so red! Kwesi had to pull her off so she didn't kill him."

He tried to keep laughing.

Kwesi was dead by the time he stopped the old widow, of course. One of the general's bullets went through his eye. He just hadn't been the kind of man to leave something undone that needed doing. Once he'd saved the Merais man's life, he laid down and went back to being dead.

"The widow said, at least Kwesi's mother would always know where he was now—"

Hano was still trying to laugh when we heard the cry.

He clamped his mouth shut and so did I. We turned as silently as we could, searching for the flare of the burning child. I heard each *swsh* of my shoes.

Suddenly, Hano smacked his hand against his leg. Shrieks of laughter ripped their way out of him.

I followed his pointing finger toward a live child. She was crying, but not burning. A woman had come to comfort her.

Hano's laughter cut off abruptly. His voice went flat and quiet. "I hate this haunted village," he said. "I hate this haunted country and I hate this haunted world."

Today was for selling, not gathering, but I went out anyway. I left before Hano woke up. Since the shooting, his eyes had been dull, yet he watched me. He wanted something from me and I thought I knew what.

He hadn't found me more cans yet, but I could manage scales. I wrapped my hands for whatever help it would give me, and went into the forest.

The sky was the color of old bones. Orange clouds hovered, unmoving. The sweet-smelling trees were oddly quiet as if the animals were holding their breaths. Fleeing birds broke the silence as they cut into the air.

Between the sweet-smelling trees, I saw the muntjac with the ox. The muntjac's teeth were bloody. When it raised its head to glare at me, the skin of its face pulled backward like the grimace of a bat.

The muntjac kept changing. The ox, lingering on, gave up its meat like the Hizhang cows.

Truthfully, I remember a few torn things. I remember a picture of a tall woman putting her arms around one of the burning children. She must have died, but I don't remember that part. My father died from an infection that started in his foot, but that's all I know. It's just words. I don't remember why or how.

The dragons didn't take my memory. I let it go myself. I was staring at the ripped-up ceiling of Kwesi's truck, and the road's giant hand was shaking me apart. I thought why not let go, why not be easy for a while? I was probably going to die that day. If not, then probably the next.

The sun was so, so bright, and I gave every memory to the leaf-green sky.

I found Hano by the Ngo dump, with nothing in his hands, staring in the direction of the old general's house. Kwesi had gotten up to help dig his own grave.

I told him the other half of the answer to a question he'd asked long ago.

It happens sometimes that when the dragons' poison seeps inside you, you see what they've seen, feel what they've felt. So: It was late in the war, under a swallowing half-moon. The air was heavy without rain, and the moon was shining down and the blades of grass looked like bayonets. And the leaves of the trees hung down like swords. And the night was silver-black like drowning. And I came to the clearing.

And I was tired. My mouth too much fire, my stomach empty, my scales split from firecracker whips. I did not know the Andé were the Andé, or the Zhie were the Zhie, or anything about the Rho. I knew the whips that drove me north and north and north, and I couldn't sleep. So I came to sleep.

And I laid my body among the bayonets.

And the breath from my nostrils went deep into the earth and made pearl garlic grow.

And my weight settled through my body and turned the soil into granite.

And I did not dream.

The Hizhang cows were still screaming even though it was already night because that was the first night the Hizhang cows screamed. I heard the vibrations of my sisters' and brothers' frustration as they were unleashed to kill, but never to feed enough to take away their hunger. And like them, I was hungry, and I stretched upward.

And I saw my reflection standing in open air. I saw his hollow stomach, and whip-cracked scales. I saw his wild eyes.

So, again: As that other dragon, I was driven by the gnawing in my stomach. I came to the clearing searching for meat, but instead I came upon my reflection. Pearl garlic frothed on the granite beneath her.

I had been driven ten days without stopping. I was ready to kill everything in my path, I was ready to kill the Andé, but the Andé were never in front of me, only behind me, with their whips snapping at my tail.

So, a third time: Both dragons, I circled inward, drawn in by my reflection's scent loosed in the night. We came closer, and we came closer again. Necks twined. My teeth flashed and blood flowed down two throats. Talons scraped and grasped. Tails swept the remaining grass from the ground and the swords from the trees.

Two dragons together, then two dragons each other, then twodragon rolling in itself. Hunger met with sating, sating met with hunger. For the first time since the Andé's bite, I was full.

And then Andé herders came with the sun in the durian sky, and they took after me with their firecracker whips. I became two again, and I and I left this place, leaving silver mist behind us.

It was a long time before human-me was born, and lived a life, and forgot that life, and lived another life in Ponçan, but those things eventually happened, and left me by the dump with Hano.

Hano has never been changed by a dragon, but he doesn't need to be. He has a bullet wound in his shoulder. He knows what to expect.

I told Hano, "It hurts to change the way I did."

He kept looking at me, expression no different than it was before.

"They might do surgery to you. Make you a girl."

He shrugged. "I don't care about that."

Life is not so bad in Ponçan. The roads going north are full of bandits. Where there are no bandits, there are dragon leavings worse than scales. Still, I said, "Tomorrow, then."

Hano wasn't ready to laugh again, but the edges of his lips made an almost-smile.

My name is Domei. Tomorrow, my best friend Hano and I leave for the capitol. We're going to find the dragon-dance clearing before we go. If we're lucky, Hano is going to change. If not, we'll probably die.

We probably should have died today.

If on a Winter's Night a Traveler

XIA JIA, TRANSLATED BY KEN LIU

If on a Winter's Night a Traveler
Li Yunsong (librarian, traveler on a winter's night)
posted on 20xx-04-06

Many are the ways of commemorating the dead, and no one can say which is best—not even the dead.

The method I'm about to tell you is perhaps the strangest of them all.

My father was a librarian. Years ago, when I was a little child, he used to bring me to work and let me loose among the dusty tomes on old shelves. The experience forged an emotional bond between me and paper books. I could spend a whole day with my head buried in a book, careless of the absence of other entertainments. As I grew up, I discovered that the world outside the library was far more complicated, and I had a hard time adjusting. Socially awkward and having few friends, I returned to my hometown after college and started working at my father's old library. It felt natural, like a book finding the exact place on the shelves assigned to it by the numbers on its spine.

There wasn't much to do at work. In an age when most reading was done electronically, the library had few patrons. Like a graveyard attendant, I took care of the forgotten books and saw the occasional visitor, but there was little expectation of real conversation. The sunlight glided tranquilly between the shelves, day after day. Every day, I entered this sanctuary, quiet as a tomb, and pulled a book or two randomly off the shelves to read.

This was pretty much my version of heaven.

Borges once wrote, "God is in one of the letters on one of the pages of one of the four hundred thousand volumes in the Clementine. My parents and my parents' parents searched for that letter; I myself have gone blind searching for it." I didn't believe in God, but sometimes I felt that I was searching for something as well.

One rainy autumn afternoon, the library received a donation of books. I opened one and saw a small red collector's seal on the title page, which told me that another old man who had treasured books had died. His children had piled his collection, gathered over a lifetime, in front of his apartment building. Those which were worth something had been picked out by used book dealers, leaving the rest to be sold by the kilogram to a paper mill, to be gifted, or to be donated to the library. This sort of thing happened every year. I sorted the books, recorded and catalogued them, stuck on call numbers and barcodes, wiped off the dust, and stacked them neatly so that they could be shelved.

This took me two hours; I was exhausted, dizzy, and needed a break. While the teakettle was boiling, I picked up a slim volume off the top of the stack. It was a chapbook of poetry.

I started to read. From the first character in the first line of the first poem, I felt that I had found what I had always sought. Accompanied by the faint pitter-patter of rain outside, I chewed over the verses carefully, as delighted as a starving man who had finally been given manna.

The poet was unfamiliar to me, and there was only a short paragraph that passed for her biography. There wasn't even a photograph. She wrote under a pen name, and her real name was unknown. She had died twenty years ago at the age of thirty-one. I pulled out my phone to look her up, but the Internet gave me nothing, as though she had never existed.

I felt a tingling up my spine. How could a poet who had lived in the information age leave no trace on the Web? It was inconceivable.

In the middle of the chapbook I found a library book request form. The sheet was thin, yellowed, but still well preserved. The borrower had filled out the form with the title of the poetry book as well as his library card number in a neat, forceful hand. I inputted the information into the computer system and found that the borrower had been a regular patron, though he hadn't come for a few months. The borrower's records in the database did not contain this book—which made sense, as the library had never had a copy of it.

Why would a book request form from my library be found in the private collection of an old man, and how did it get back here to me? Who was the borrower listed on the form, and what was his relationship to the old man? Or perhaps they were the same person using different names?

I finished the poems in the chapbook and shelved it as well as the other donated books. The next day, for some reason, I found myself in front of the shelf with the chapbook. It was still there, a slim volume squeezed between other books like a mysterious woman hiding in the attic. I pulled it out and re-read it from the first page. Though the poems were decades old, I could clearly sense from the rich, ambivalent images the massive waves of sorrow that had swept up most people in this age, like a lonely cry slipping through the cracks and seams of broken walls and fallen ruins, flowing without end.

Who was the poet? What did she look like and where did she live? What was her life like? Other than me, the dead collector, and the mysterious borrower, had she had other readers?

I had no answers. All I could do was to read the poems over and over again, like a fish diving deeper. The poet and her poems turned into the dark abyss of my dreams, concealing all secrets.

• • •

Three months later, as the first snow of winter fell, I met the borrower.

He was in his forties, of medium height, possessing a lean, angular face, and dressed plainly. When I saw the familiar string of numbers on his library card, I got so excited that I almost cried out. But the looming silence of the library reminded me to swallow the cry.

Using the library's surveillance cameras, I observed him passing through the stacks and up and down the stairs like a ghost. I saw him walk into the room where old newspapers and magazines were kept, the only patron in that space. He retrieved a stack of bound newspapers and carefully laid it out on the desk, where he proceeded to flip through it slowly, page by page. I was puzzled. These newspapers were electronically stored and indexed, and all he had to do was to perform a simple search in the database. Why did he bother to come into the library to flip through them like this? Perhaps he was nostalgic for the sensation of bare fingers against old paper?

Suddenly, the borrower on my closed-circuit TV screen lifted his face and glanced around, staring in the direction of the camera for a second. Then he shifted his position so that his body blocked my view. A few seconds later, he moved away and flipped the newspaper to the next page.

I was certain that he had done something he did not want others to find out during that brief moment. Maybe he took a photograph. But considering all these papers had been digitized, what was the point of sneaking a picture?

Before closing time, the borrower approached me and set down that thin chapbook. I scanned the barcode but held on to the book. My curiosity got the better of me, and I decided to break my habitual silence and risk speaking with a stranger.

"Do you like these poems?" I asked.

He was surprised. It was as if I had been invisible, but now appeared out of thin air.

"They're . . . all right." His tone was cautious.

"I think they're lovely," I said. "No, that's not quite right. They're powerful, as though they could return order and form to ruins that had been slumbering for thousands of years."

I told him how I had come across these poems, and repeated to him the quote from Borges. I spoke to him about how I couldn't forget the mysterious poet, and even recounted for him how I had become the librarian here.

Ripples of emotion spread across his face, as though my words had been drops of rain falling into a pond.

After I was done talking, he picked a book request form from the box on the desk and handed it to me. "Please give me your contact info."

I wrote down my name and phone number. Without glancing at the form, he picked it up and placed it between the pages of the chapbook. "I will be in touch." He strode toward the exit.

I waited more than a week. On a stormy evening, my phone rang. I answered it, and the borrower's low, sonorous voice filled my ears.

"There's a gathering tonight we'd like to invite you to."

"Tonight?" I looked up at the dense, swirling snow outside the window. "We?"

He gave me an address and a time. Then he added, "I hope you can make it." He hung up.

His last words were irresistible—it had been many years since anyone had said "hope" to me. I checked myself in the mirror and left the library, opening my umbrella as I did so.

The snow was so thick that it seemed solid. There were very few pedestrians or cars out on the road. My town was too small to have a subway or tube transport system, and transportation was no different from how it had been twenty, thirty years earlier. I made my way through ankle-deep snow to the bus stop, and the bus also had very few passengers. I rode for eight or so stops, got off, and walked some more until I reached the address the borrower had given me: it was a bar that had seen better years.

I pushed open the thick wooden door and swept aside the cotton curtain. Warm air infused with an aroma that I was sure I knew enveloped my face. About fifteen people were seated in the bar in a loose circle, and there was an old fashioned coal stove—the kind that took honeycomb briquettes—in the middle of the circle. On top of the stove sat an aluminum kettle hissing with white steam.

The borrower picked up the kettle and poured me a cup of hot tea. I was surprised to see that there was a hint of a smile on his cold, expressionless face. He introduced me to the others, and it didn't take me long to realize that most of them were as socially awkward as me, but I could see friendliness and candor in their eyes. They already thought of me as one of them. I relaxed.

I found an empty chair and sat down. The borrower stood up like a host and said, "Good evening, everybody. Let's welcome our new friend. Today is a special day, and I'm delighted to see all of you make it on a snowy night like this."

The crowd quieted, holding hot cups of tea and listening.

"Tonight, we gather to remember a poet," he continued. "Twenty years ago, a cold, stormy winter's night just like this one, she departed our world.

"Everyone here tonight is a reader of her work. We love her poems but know almost nothing about her life. It is said that she was an introvert who lived like a hermit. She didn't use the computer or the Web, and left behind almost no photographs or videos. Her poems received little attention during her lifetime, and were published only in a few obscure literary journals. When the editors of these journals asked for an author photo or an interview, she never responded.

"But one editor, who loved her work, managed to maintain a correspondence with her. Through handwritten letters, the two of them discussed life and poetry, poverty and humility, the terrors and hopes of our age. This was a simple, pure friendship, sustained only through the written word. They never met each other in life.

"Right before the poet died, she sent all her published and unpublished poems to the editor. After reading through them, the editor decided to publish a collection as a way to commemorate her dead friend. But she knew that the only way to make a collection of poetry popular was to package up the poet's life into a story that was already popular with the crowd. The story had to exaggerate the poet's mystery and solitude, dig up the scars of her family life and childhood, show her poverty and hunger, disclose her hidden life of love, and present her death scene with pathos. It had to be a story that would make everyone—whether they read poetry or not—shed tears of sympathy for a young woman poet who died too young, drive the crowd to curse our cold, commercial age for persecuting genius, allow each and every member of the audience to project themselves onto her. This was the only way to sell a collection of poetry, to grow her fame, to make her name last through the ages.

"But this was also exactly what the poet would have hated.

"And so the editor chose another way to commemorate her friend. She paid to print and bind copies of the chapbook and mailed them to her friends, anyone who was willing to read the poems, the penniless writers, translators, teachers, editors, students, librarians. She wrote in the note accompanying the chapbook that if anyone wanted more copies to gift to others, she would mail them for free. And since she knew so little about the poet's life, she couldn't satisfy their curiosity.

"Year after year, readers who loved her work formed clubs like this one. We read and pass on her work, from one private shelf to another, from one library to another library. But we are not interested in superficial attention; we do not fabricate tear-jerking tales about her life; we do not manufacture illusions that would be popular. We only wish for readers to admire her through her poetry, and we disdain insincere blurbs, biographies, photographs, or interviews. In fact, we make it our mission to eliminate any material of that sort. If one of us discovers an image or biographical record of her somewhere, we do our best to delete it. Documents on the Web can be deleted, databases can be carefully edited, tapes and rolls of film can be cut and then pasted back together, and anything printed could be torn out and burned.

"Very few people have noticed our actions. Compared to making news, reducing attention was work that could be carried out quietly. Of course, it was impossible to accomplish what we did without anyone noticing. There will always be the curious who wanted to know the stories behind the poems, who needed to pierce the riddle. We have no right to stop them, but we will say: we do not know any secrets, and we do not want to know any. For us, the poems themselves are enough."

The borrower finished speaking. He opened the chapbook in his hand and placed it in front of me. I saw a yellowed piece of paper between the pages, like a piece cut from an old newspaper.

"I cut this out of the newspapers collected in your library. I'm sorry that I damaged your property. Now I return this to you so that you can decide what to do with it."

I looked at the piece of paper. There was a blurry photograph on it. Almost twenty pale faces, exposed to the sun, stared at me. Was one of them the poet? Which one? How would I know?

The answer to the riddle was its plain text.

I picked up the piece of paper with the tips of my fingers and brought it to the stove, tossing it in. The flame licked the paper, burst into an orange flare, and in a blink the paper had turned into a curl of ash.

I looked at the borrower, who smiled at me, extending a hand. I held his large and warm hand. I realized that it had been a long time since I last held a stranger's hand. My eyes grew wet.

"How about we read a poem together?" he said.

We sat down in our chairs and flipped open the chapbooks to the first page. We read from the first character in the first line of the first poem. Our voices floated up, passed through the ceiling, rose against the falling drifts of snow, until they had returned to the eternal, cold, dark abyss.

19 Likes   17 Comments

👍 Like   💬 Comment   ↗ Share

Originally published in Chinese in *Guangming Daily,* June 5, 2015 Version 14.

Coyote Invents the Land of the Dead
KIJ JOHNSON

She was there, that is Dee, and her three sisters, who were Tierce, Chena, and Wren, Dee being a coyote or rather Coyote, and her sisters not unlike in their Being, though only a falcon, a dog, and a wren. So there they stood on the cliff, making their minds how to get down to the night beach, a deep steep dark bitch slither it was, though manageable Dee hoped.

The cliff was a high sandy sharpness, but you, O my darlings, might not remember what it means to pass down that narrow dark, your own life being so past and the dead so quick to forget. Standing on the cliffs what Dee sought was her own ghost-love, named Jace and dead a year but still so recent to her mind that she could sniff her fingers and by a year-gone remembered smell see him long-legged gold-eyed and low-voiced with big hands—and the sisters going along with her because they did not wish to see her do it alone, plus each sought something else that she didn't explain, not to Dee anyway.

They had no death-permit for climbing down, but there was no law against trying some of the narrow paths the dead might use. They could try to climb straight down the rocks or along the arroyo, or one or two other possibilities that would give them a skinny slight weak chance of finding the beachy sand and all its dead and massy seashells beneath their feet.

Or they could find the beach the faster way: throw themselves down and hit the sand with their permit in hand, as the saying is. And that was what they were discussing on the cliff.

"Well, fuck, and I'll have to do it the hard way," Dee said. "I might be just that bit late coming back." Her quick tumble-voice rippled out from her mouth and plashed against Wren's pinhole wren ears and Chena's tufted great dog ears and the fluffed falcon feathers where Tierce's ears were. All four were what they were, and women also, and more. They were fashioned of myth: that is the way of this story.

"Or never," Wren said high and sharp as the whistle from a dry teakettle. "The dead say that, and then they go down the cliffs and they never come back"—light on a brokenwood tree sapless and unlifed, and hopping from foot to foot, so angry was she. "It's the dead down there, sister. Go and you are dead."

Above and behind them were stars and clouds and the moon sliding skyward, the long long rise of it, but there was no sky over the night beach before them and the strange ocean beyond; the sky/star/moon dayworld ended abruptly above the cliff's edge, just overhead with a curled lip like poor and unfinished knitting, and beyond that just nothing but what is inside an undreamer's eyelids. Chena reached a long-fingered paw (or was it a hand) and touched a thread trailing from the sky's end. A sequining star slipped loose and came resting onto her dark muzzle, leaving tracer-lines when she moved her mouth and low in her throat said, "She is dead already, Wren. It is what Dees do that are Coyote, is die."

"—And come back:" Dee hoping it was true; ears had heard tales of other Coyotes that made the long climb down that cliff and back too, and brought heaving and snapping up with them fire or jewelling girdles. Or perhaps that was she but not remembering, or it might be a different cliff; Dee did not know.

"You better hope tales are right," Tierce said all beak-sharp snap. "You're a fool to long for your lover when he's on the night beach. But you'll go anyway. I know you," and Wren agreed.

Dee was toenails-close to the cliff, and dirt and little rocks scrabbled away from her feet and over the edge making no noise as they fell. The others were farther away; and look-back Dee saw outlines of her sisters black against the star-busy dayworld night sky. Their faces were invisible until she lit a match and then a cigarette and held it carefully between her toes or maybe it was fingers, and then the hawk wren and dog eyes all glowed gold. All their eyes were worried-like and sad too, and they were right to be so. Dee had never long longed for anything lost before this, not even her own mother. Only Jace. And Dee was the center of things; bulls-eye on the target, the tight-binding chord of the arc of everything. Touch Dee and the world shivered.

Turning, Dee: and she stared down. The only light on the beach came from the sky behind them, the cliff's shadow stretched halfway to the water; plus also fading shifting lines like yarn being rolled, that was surf that went nowhere and not strong; and phosphorescence the color of sodium vapored and trapped inside lamps. Hundreds of feet down or miles or something else? Dee (knowing as all do approaching the night beach) that it would change as she climbed.

"Well, this is me, then. I'm going," she said, and dropped her furl-ashed cigarette and started down. The path was a narrow bitter winding of rocks and dirt crushed to dust. She slipped and fell, away through sour thorn-prickling brush, until she slammed against a rock that left her unbreath'd for a while and then she realized she wasn't breathing anyway. Mist rose from her muzzle but did not in-and-out, only slid steadily free, collecting into a shape at first indefinable; only, she walked down and down and its form clarified and grew more complete, and it was a Coyote like her, curled as though mother-scruffed, hovering a few feet from the cliff at eye-height.

Dee not a thinker, thus not wondering what this shadow-Coyote meant, whether ghost ka lost soul or child unborn. "The fuck do *you* want?" Dee said not wanting the answer, and it said nothing and turned and advanced ahead, soundless and then invisible and gone maybe so that she was relieved and worried both, though not the worrying sort.

Of a sudden, a great light started up behind Dee on the cliff, a surprising blaze of a bonfire, set by her sisters she figured but arcbright as welding or lighthouses, and it warmed her just to see its bright casting across the scree'd cliff. Dee was not the only one with gifts and Being, and Tierce could use the sharp of talon and eye, and set great fires. But Tierce would lose some vision from this: love costs for anyone, hawks and all.

Twisting-back Dee's long foot touched a rock and it cascading took its fellows lavanching along and Dee falling too. The path: a startle-start, and a slip-stumble long middle, and then a dead-end; just like life.

The night beach where Dee landed was of sand. It and foam-stain water hissed and whispered together; Dee folded her ears back to block the sound but it came through anyway, seeping in through the cracks of her. The wet cold air felt thin, though she was at sea level for the lowest sea of all—if air there was; no telling without lungs' in-and-out. Her shadow was a severalled blur-thing that did not have her shape, cut out by the light of Tierce's eyes and the half-moon in the half-sky behind, cut now where it had risen to the dayworld's ceasing, and sloppy with dangling glowing threads.

The sand around her was heaped everywhere with mounded massy dark shells, pyramided into black piles as high as her waist, and over the sand/water-whisper the piles chirked when a crawling wave touched them. Dee kneeling saw they looked just like dayworld shells, shaped like ears or trumpets or vulvas, but they had no light nor sheen to their curves and they felt colder than they ought. Dee pushed the shells aside with her feet as she walked, and they chunkled against one another.

A sudden falling crash off a short distance: a small blur-shadowed thing heaved upright and shook itself, and said with Wren's voice, "The air stopped carrying me." She sounded indignant, betrayed by her natural element and peevish in any case because of Dee's as she saw it stupidity. But here she was: love costs a price, as she knew as well, and she was hoping this would not in this case be true but suspected that it would. "I was flying down and it just gave up."

"You weren't supposed to follow," Dee said. "This is mine to do. Not yours."

"Since when do you say what is what for me?" Wren hopped to Dee's side, and stopped being a blurred shadow and became herself, drab grey and brown but her eyes bright precise points.

"At least Chena's not coming down, is she?" Dee glanced up at the cliff, to the fire Tierce had set. Pushed by the wind, it gusted and vanished and rose again in sheets of flame the colors of brass, of gold bronze copper and blue sapphires.

Wren opened her mouth and then shut it, not saying anything.

Dee closed her eyes for a moment. "Fuck." Now that she looked, she could see a sturdy dark shape down-scrabbling the cliff. Instead of picking out the safe path, Chena was running straight down in a great tumbling of noise and rocks and torn bushes: which ended in Chena landing with a sound that might have been a yelp or might have been a laugh. She loped toward them, kicking shells aside with chirping skrankles of sound.

"That was fun." Chena smiling, her tongue hanging out. "I wouldn't want to go back up, though."

"You can't," Dee angry said. "And now we're all dead."

"Not yet," Chena said.

"Tell me Tierce isn't coming down."

Shaking-head Chena, as Wren, "When did you become the grown-up?" asked.

Dee thinking *When I lost Jace* and it stabbed through her again like losing a leg, and every time waking jumping up maybe to run somewhere, and being reminded again when she fell: no leg. Jace, who had been laughing air in her lungs, long-storying tale-making lover of Dee; and all the sun there was, for her.

Chena shaking her head in any case: "Tierce keeps the fire for us. Have you found your Jace yet? I just see this"—pointing with one clawed toe that may for purposes of this story and your own comfort be seen as a woman's hand, if it seems she must be either woman or beast but cannot be both; which shows your folly, O my dears.

Dee looked down at the shells all everywhere, the cerith/whelk/natica coils of them. Some were smaller than her toenail, others broad as her cradling hands. She picked one up, cell-phone-size and black and smoothly curved like a tulip, and held it to her ear. But nothing inside it, not even the sound of her own pounding blood echoing back, though maybe that was no surprise if her pulse were as gone as her breath.

Chena picked one up too, the size of clasped hands and scrolled tight as a flemished rope, and absent-eyed held the tiny opening to her ear: listening to her own lack of pulse, Dee reckoned though maybe not, so intent was she; and then dropped it chirking. "These are the dead."

Dee's Coyote-self knowing, saying: "Yes," and seeing it was true as the word slid from her mouth.

Chena: "He's a shell. Still you want him?"

And Dee nodded.

Wren added, practical she: "Good thing it's forever-night, because it will take all night to find him, huh."

Uncertain they stood looking this and that way: shells everywhere and the ravel-lorn waves, and all beyond Tierce's light, dark as a cave. Wren speaking at last, quick-eyed as all birds: "There;" and they looked a way along down the beach beneath the cliff, and there were rocks pinnacled even higher than the shells. "A tide-pool."

"Is there tide here?" Chena asked knowing No. No moon, so no tide.

On the night beach, distance was mutable or even irrelevant. Still, crossing took time and they walked for a while and a second while and more whiles still, to the rocky place Wren saw, the un-tided pinnacled pool.

Waning light from Tierce's fire, as they shuffled through the shells of the chirpling, chinkering dead, speaking perhaps to one another though not to Dee as she leaned low and listened; nor to Wren, tipping her head close to the largest she saw, a whelk the size of a sleeping hound, and hearing nothing, no thing at all. Yet would not step inside the shell's curling lip: no fool Wren.

It was hard to see the pillaring rocks clearly, scarce-lit to one side by the strange ocean's glow, and to the other by Tierce's fire and the half of the sky that still held stars: the dayworld's moon long gone by now.

Wren could not fly but she was smaller than the others and not so careful with stepping on the shells, and so Wren sandpipering down to the water: "No tide," she said. "The water just moves, doesn't go anywhere, is all."

Dee slower followed, for she kept picking up shells and listening for Jace, and Chena slowest of all though she listened only once: and lifted a cowrie folded pretty as a cunt, to which she harked for a time and then shook her head and replaced it carefully, and thereafter would not step upon even the smallest but pushed them aside as she passed.

Wren walking: "This is all they can do, the dead? Heap up like this?"

Dee thought of Jace alive run-running along a sun-crusted canyon, laughing and his black eyes agleam, and the bright taste of flesh and blood and the matings and the sleeping together coiled, and roiling about in a fight and the all all all of it. Hated being bored Jace, when he was alive.

And why *was* Jace so special, my dears, O my darlings? What man, what walker on legs and laugher at jokes, is worth all this? And Jace is not, of course, nor any man, all flesh and imperfect unminding; or rather say all men are, and all women. And Chena, who longed for her own sweet Linnel, which is her secret reason for being on the night beach; and Wren and her vast chattering family, aunts and sisters and brothers and bickering uncles back in the day-lands; and also Tierce now forever behind them, squinting through wearying eyes into the skyless dark above the night beach, but thinking of her nestlings asleep.

After all the whiles they walked, they came at last to the rocks.

Wren always with questions: "What exactly are we looking for?"

"Fuck if I know," Dee said, tired for once and realizing suddenly that she was cold and getting colder. The breath not coming from her mouth (she noticing this again) scared her a little. "Just anything," and they split up a bit.

Hard walking, or scribscrabbling rather, among rocks rough as new lava, pockmarked as Dee felt through her long fingers and toes, and the holes each filled with water. Stepped forward and sank to her knee. Bent-head she tasted and got salt, but sterile: no flesh-shred shit microlife broth. In a pool, she saw a small fringing glowness and touched it, and it snapped shut anemone-quick, only there was no life to it, she could tell from the touch, just cold light and this movement. *Jace,* she thought. What can he chase and what does he eat when a shell? And where in this ocean of shells?

A thing flashed by her face, and herself automatic in her hunting she caught it, felt muscle and quick coilings thrown over her hand, a sensation from the desert she knew well from snakes, but boneless this time and beaky, biting her palm without effect. She held the thing up and its wet surface gleamed under Tierce's soft fading flare of a flame.

It was an octopus, so small that its head fit her cupped hand but it writhing rippled down, hydrostat legs yearning toward the pool until she caught the small beak and pinched it in her fingers and then the creature stopped. "Where is he?" she asked and shook it. "Jace."

Tentacled her ankle now: another octopus roiling itself up her leg, and suckers this time like cold angry kisses, so she dropped the little one. Was a splash.

The new one was bigger, its head like her head and clearly too big for the pool. So many legs meant many things held, and it clutched her and also the rock, and also a whelk with an unfurling lip and a hole broken through. *What's inside?* Dee wondered, and then chilled as she thought it: *Nothing.* In the dayworld, living-sea cephalopods drilled through shells and sucked their insides to inside themselves: food, and nothing left over but a hollowed-out hush.

So, here: there was death and that was nothing, a shell on a shore; but even that could be taken by these night-beach monsters, and then there was nothinger nothing.

Raging Dee did not bite at wrapping legs; but she called out and in a flash, Chena with her, they tore at the suckered coils—without effect, until Wren.

One copper nail pounded poisons a tree is the story, and maybe as well a many-branched beast. There were no nails but Wren gave it a penny she had carried onto the beach for no reason except that she had it, and perhaps had heard tales. The octopus brought it with the tip of a tendrilling leg to its beak and then everything loosed and was lost beneath the pool's surface, the whelk and Dee freed.

She grabbed at the shell as it sank. As she listened this time, a flute-shrill whistling of the unbreathing breeze through the hole. *Dead, and then deader than dead.* But not Jace. She hoped. He was somewhere here still, lost and bored—and someday bored out. Unless she could find him.

"Let's not do that again," Chena said. Blood on her leg collecting where she had torn it on rock but not flowing, not here where the heart drove no pulse.

On a pumicey pillar beside, Wren: "We can't find him, and then this. What now, Dee?"

"Fuck," said Dee. "We'll have to do a thing."

Suspicious Chena, closest sister to Dee and thus knowing the ways of Coyotes too well for her own comfort: "Do what? This is the night beach, the end of all evers."

"But beyond *that*?" and Dee pointed across the phorescent, fluorescing sea.

Nodding, Chena: "One shore means another."

"But no boat to get there," Wren said. "And how will going there, if There is—how will this change things, Dee? Jace is dead."

"Is dead gone?" Dee said. "I'll cross and find out if There is, and come back with an answer, maybe."

"Or not." Wren, tart. "Shells are dead and then deader than dead, and no coming back. So. There's a night beach and maybe a beach nighter than night, and maybe no coming back from there, either—not even to here."

Chena sighing: "It's what Dees do that are Coyotes, is *do*. Foolish or not. Wren, can *you* stop her?"

"I am not the thing that stops Dees. But no boat . . . ? That will," Wren said.

Dee said, "We will swim."

Chena: "The thither there is, is maybe too far. We will drown."

"Why would we drown?" Wren, askance. "We do not breathe here; why would unbreathing be a thing?"

"We will find out about drowning, I guess," said Dee.

But. Back on the cliff in the dayworld, and the sun rising at last though invisible from the night beach: fading, fire-eyed Tierce. She stood and looked down, and the light of her eyes still shone on cliff ocean and shells. And she saw the pinnacled rocks and the tentacled things; and dark Dee and bright Chena and the flicker of Wren. Read their lips from so high-distant a place; and knew they were gone, gone and lost; and blinked her eyes shut.

The water was black, thick as oil, and viscid it slid up their legs as they walked into the untided surf. The dirty pale seafoam clung to their hands like the ropes of saliva from a sunburnt dog's mouth, and smelled not unlike. Wren fastidious turned her face away, and then, "Oh!" said she, smallest: lost her footing and came resting on the water's face, unbreaking the surface tension. Dee and Chena could not float, slipped beneath.

There were no shells under the water, but a steady long shelf of sand the color of a deer dead beside a road. Chena curled her lip in distaste. It was not dark beneath the water, no more than above. There being no moon nor stars nor glass-cased hot-flaming filament meant that no place was lighter than any other, but also no darker.

Wren was right that they did not drown. Still, there was no satisfaction in this; the water crawled everywhere thick and cold along all their inches as they shoved through it. For a time, Chena could reach up and touch Wren's feet above before she went too deep; but Dee paid no mind, only walked forward and on, the broken whelk in her hand.

For a while and then another while, Dee felt small coilings along the black ocean's floor as she walked. She knew them for the tentacled things that killed the shells of the dead. One wrapped around her ankle, but she bent down and tore it free, and that was the last of them.

A third while: eels with hands and no eyes.

There were other things, and clouded bitter cold blood stained the sea. For a time.

I say to you, O my darlings, *for a time,* as though time was. The steps collected infinite until the sea's floor shelved up again and *for a time* ended, and they came free of the sucking surface, and found Wren landed already and scraping her beak on the shore.

"That was exciting," Chena said when the cold salt sea had drained from her mouth. "I saw a thing like a ray, and a forest of black kelp, and a car that wept, and a shark. What did you see?" she asked Wren; but what Wren saw or had done as she swam the surface between unsea and unsky, and what it was that she scraped so carefully from her beak, she said nothing about, then or ever.

Dee dropped the holed hollowed-out whelk to the ground: looking-'round Dee. And this was the other shore. Sand. Behind them the ocean, water rocking but not crawling up/down. Ahead ramping dunes of pale sand-drift, and past that tufty grass and harsh-husked hollow sedges, and a hissing that would have been wind if wind would have been. And beyond that rising, the horizon's notched plant-fringed ridge where dunes slanted into grass and unberried bushes. And after that the dun unsky only.

No life, of course. No footprints or pawprints or clawprints or shells, save the whelk.

They looked back (breathless no longer a surprise except remembering that it once had been different); and back past the slipping thick slippery ocean, the beach, and the cliff, nearly beyond sight was the ravel-halved world of the bright-breathing alive. But no fire nor Tierce. She had watched them walk deep and then deeper, as they sank her scorched eyes salt-soaked for a time. Then they opened again, and reduced but alive she turned and returned to the living, light-winging her way to her children her nest her mate and the taste of mice bright on her tongue. Home. For a time. Her story ends here for you, unless someday as fringed murex or peaked conch she tells it herself.

I do not know what secrets the shells of the dead share among themselves. I listen and hear hissing; but it is enough.

"Well," said Wren when her beak was scrubbed clean. "Now we're here. Where *is* here?"

Chena loped up to the ridge and back down. "There's nothing. Beyond the ridge? More hills and grass is all, and maybe for all ways."

Dee kicked at the untoed untouched and rippleless sand. "No shells on this side. But no octopus either." Pausing she: "They would be safe here, all the shells."

Cunning Coyote-Dee, and clever sister Dog-Chena as well, and Wren Queen of the Birds sharp enough though attending only half what was said, and always her eyes scanning the unsky. They thought it all through: the long sloping sand-floored ocean; but no waves moving shells, no tide making waves, no moon making tides.

"So we need a moon," said Chena. "A moon to bring the shells."

Headtipping Wren: "Let me see what I can do."

"This is mine to do," Dee said. "For Jace."

Practical Wren: "Can you fly?"

Dee, shaking head.

"Then it's not."

The rules for the unliving lands are not what you thought when you walked under sunlight, my dears. There was no more thickness of air on this side of the ocean—and yet Wren up feather-light flew. The unsky was a flat textured hard curve like the inside of an eggshell, but fluttering Wren seeing a scuff in the surface no deeper than gravel-scratched shoe-leather, for long flitting whiles picked at the flaw. Flakes of nonshell curled free and fell, and dissolved into brass-tasting mist on the upturned faces of Dee and Chena. The scuff became a dent, a pocket, a niche—and now Wren hover-clung to its lip as she worked—and at last made a Wren-sized hollow. She came down, and with her a drift of bitter drab skyscrape that made Chena cough. "There's that."

"But no moon," said Dee.

"Not yet, no. Now's when *you* help. I need fur."

Chena: "For a moon?"

Wren: "Also twigs."

They looked: sedges ocean grass bushes sand slopes unsky. "No trees and no twigs," Chena said.

"This is mine to do," said Dee. *"Finally."*

Dee biting bones free from her feet with her long bloodied teeth, slim fine phalanges for clever Wren's craft—for you forgot, O my darlings, that they are each woman god and creature folded together in skin and desire; but so they are: mysteries nearly as great as yourselves and your once-stories. Chena did not see that the metatarsals of Dee's feet grew back then or ever. Perhaps that is another way that the dunes beyond the ocean are different from the dayworld and its myths, where Coyotes retrofit rekit and retool, bones and blood renewed on demand as the stories require.

Wren carried each skinny-stick bone to the niche in the unsky, and she wove. It was not the tight basket she would have entwined in the dayworld for gawkish and featherless nestlings, but a shaggy untidy tangle: coyote bones and dog fur, and down plucked from her breast, each feather-shaft tipped in her unwelling blood.

And that nest was the moon of the dead: dun and unshining, but the great gravitational well of untime and unspace.

Then a pause. And nothing.

Wren sighing. "Well, then, there is another thing, I guess:" and she laid an egg and another and a third: air-fathered, Wren-willed, and wind-filled.

And then nothing again.

They three watched, Wren high in her nest, and her sisters on the sand: a whiles-long time.

And a wave and another, then long rolling coils repeating along the sands, each stronger as the new-built moon pulled. With tide comes time, and now static unnumbered *whiles* became waves and moments and *soon*s and *then*s.

And now. Chena soft: "Listen."

The first small shells came in a foaming wave-curl that withdrew and left whisper-light augurs and ceriths and wentletraps chirtling together. A hiss when they burrowed into the wet sand, to leave only holes. And followed by larger shells, the great conchs, the syrinx and the sheening nautilus, and always the waves. Imagine it, O my darlings—or do not, but remember instead if you can—your whispering shell-selves pulled along the sandy floor, past the sights Chena saw, and the long-tendrilled things that Dee had fought off, and all the wonders and terrors they did *not* meet. Perhaps you did not all make it, but many and many of you did, and found yourselves here.

And among the dragged massy shells at last, Chena heard the thing she was dreaming of: a whisper, a hush. A whelk washed to her feet, as long as her hand and smooth as an egg: rested and did not dig. She caught it up with a sob and pressed it against her ear and heard her name like a breath: *Chena.* Linnel, her own dear Linnel dead and lost, and now found, in a massy rose-colored calcium twist.

But no Jace. Not then, nor in the *thens* after, as each shell rolled up and found its own place on the shore, until holes spangled the sand and the water in each reflected the secret-egged moon of Wren's making. Dee running stumble-foot, bitten-paw clumsy, desperately across the tiny dim stars on sandy dun under-unsky; Chena behind her pleading but cupping in her hand (or paw) *her* answer, the cradled whorl of Linnel.

The shells rolling in but fewer now and all only newest-dead: each cockle ark augur and bittersweet clam just fallen to the night beach, soon come and soon gone in moon-summoned tiding through oleic oil-thick sea to this shore; and quick digging down into the sand and thus: safe.

Still no Jace. No Jace among all the shells: so, either holed out or holding out on the night beach.

Dee stumbled to a halt: "He's not here. He's not coming."

Chena's voice like a gentle-soft growl: "Those we love do not come when we will it, but when *they* do. Death does not change this, just makes it harder."

"But I *loved* him."

Wren snorted. "As though that were enough."

Startle-sharp face turned up to the moon: Dee, all id and hot eyes on herself, self-tricking trickster surprised by the truth; but despair does not sit long in Coyote-Dees. Lessons are learned. But not the right ones. A snapping nod: "I'll go back for him. We all will."

"No," said Chena; and eyes-rolling Wren: "Try, if you must."

Dee, a-limp to the shore where the tide swashed: stepped forward and pressed paw (that was hand) to the thick, viscid ocean. She could not break the meniscus, nor skate Wren-light on its surface. Stepped forward and forward. And just nothing: Dee still where she stood, unadvanced. "We cannot go back?"

"No:" Wren and Chena together.

And Dee, eyes turned for the first time to others, and knowing at last: "I've killed you."

Again, "No," Chena said. "We are here for you, but not just for you." And she smiled, the Linnel-whelk in her hand-that-is-paw. "We had our own reasons, as well."

"You said nothing," said Dee.

"When was there space?" Wren said. "Your needs always fill you. Where was there room for Chena to long for Linnel—or for me?"

Dee said, "What *is* your reason, then?"

"I was curious, that's all."

This was a lie. Wren's heart is her own, and her wishes too; Wren if she chooses may speak somewhile of her reasons, my chirkling dears; but they are not mine to share, any more than are yours.

Coyotes or rather Coyote must always be doing. Dee waited for Jace, until she didn't: light-minded, still longing but restless. She paced the other shore, and then the long sandy hills, and peeked over the ridge's edge. And at last: "I can see a way out of this. I can save you."

"We don't want saving," Wren said; but Dee unheeding as ever: "That's trees, that dark line along the horizon. And if there are trees there are more trees, and maybe something past them. We can't go back but maybe we can go forward, and maybe on the back side of nothing is all. Dayworld sun and insects hazing the sky at dusk, the taste of sweet water. Think of it: home."

Wren chirping sharp: "This is home. See my nest? See my eggs?" And Chena held Linnel close, and looked down at you, dear ones, all her shells.

"Well fuck," said Dee; "and I'll have to do this alone." Dee silent a moment, then: "I am sorry." And this was the first time she said that word, to any. And perhaps only.

And she left. She has not returned, though Wren thinks she cannot in any case, but she goes on and on. Perhaps there is a way back to the dayworld and around and through that place, and thus down to the night beach again, and that she will return across or under the sand-floored sea. Or not.

And so you are here, O my darlings, and this is to the credit of Dee and of Wren and of Chena. Here you are dead on the beach-grassy shore beneath a nest-moon and bird-stars, but at least you are not deader than dead. There is for you no way back to the dayworld lands or the night beach; but there never was, and here are no beaked and tentacled things.

There are always more of you, always new shells, massy and dark on the night beach, and some come here sooner, and later some: lingering shells on that night-beach shore waiting for their own loves Dee-like and like Chena to come searching for them—only none do. No one makes the tumble to the beach of her own will; or only a few.

Over us is Wren's tight-woven moon and her dark-winged fledglings, that have scattered like stars across the dun sky; and who is the father of them I may guess. Do the dead overlap? I do not know: only that she is content enough, and as *thens* have collected, so have the shells of her vast chattering family, aunts and sisters and brothers and bickering uncles.

Jace remains lost but tides bring shells with each wave. Some scallop or slipper may contain him or may not. For Dee's sake I ask them all if they have seen him, but their chirtle and skankling speech is all for each other, and they do not answer. If he is found in the hard lacy curl of a murex, I will tell him that Dee has gone on; and he will follow or not: he has other kin here, other loves. Love is no one-thing but many. We are never alone.

Or perhaps he is deader than dead. That is a way that things are, too.

Dee did what Coyotes do that are creator and creature: rush and long and drag a train of chaos behind them and then leave others behind to build what they can from whatever remains. But I that am Chena am dog, god, and girl, and what Chenas that are dogs do, is love and watch over—and here I am not alone, with Wren singing above, and the whorl of whelk-Linnel in my hand to murmur in my ear. And you all, O my darlings, to tell this tale to—so perhaps you are not so dead after all. What is life but stories, and love?

This is the why of the Land of the Dead.

In the Queue for the Worldship Munawwer

SARA SAAB

PRE-TAKEOFF REPORT—WORLDSHIP K5-NME, "*MUNAWWER*"
FROM: Suraya Khouri-Smith (Lead Ground Attaché, Munawwer Crew)
DATE: January 15th, 2139
FOR: Dougal Smith (Transition Commander, EVAC-Central)

Commander Smith,

I hope you'll forgive the whimsy of this report. I've held my silence my entire life, and there are many things I deserve to say to you. I know it's a breach of protocol, but in a sense, so was I. And there may not be another chance.

The information you need, first: the worldship Munawwer, evacuation vessel for the territory of the Lebanese Republic, began boarding two weeks ago. It rests in shallow water off the coast of Beirut, covered in knobbly city gulls and their droppings. Its access ramps are down and secured to a section of the corniche's wide boardwalk.

Autocount figures tell me there are 845,912 people on board.

This number has been creeping up through the night despite orders to cease boarding until daylight. People jump from the corniche's pier, swim the span between the boardwalk and the worldship under cover of night, clamber up sea-facing loading bays. When we do catch them, they are half-drowned, and we send them to the Munawwer's medical bays, and someone willfully forgets they are on board.

At other times it would be funny, how it is here; how open to interpretation even the most mortally important rules are. Cousins sneak on board cousins; husbands sneak on board sisters-in-law.

Fathers, their daughters.

For the official record I'll confirm that the total passenger count permitted is the usual 900,000. The queue outside is four people abreast to the mountain horizon and beyond.

We expect to fill the Munawwer to capacity in the next three days.

Commander, last night in my assigned Munawwer bunkroom, I undressed in utter dark. I pulled the film of laminate from the brand new porthole; it came away in a single satisfying sheet—*tack-tack-tack*—that I balled up inside my hot fist. I pressed it hard over my breastbone, felt the complaint of my failing body.

262

The coast of Beirut was a luminous thing, swaying, dancing with the emissions of the city. But more than that, I was entranced by the Munawwer's queue, a thick cable of light threading up and into the Lebanese foothills.

I do not remember getting into my bed, but I remember shaking in the controlled atmosphere kept at an ambient temperature. It was the sterility of the moment versus the literal mass of our undertaking; lifting the bigness of the Munawwer into the sky, the long game of searching out a welcoming planet over generations, the unliftable weight of what's sure to be left behind.

Yesterday our engineering crew began dismantling Beirut's decrepit old lighthouse for fear of the structure interfering with the hover-and-power phase of our upcoming liftoff. Other early clearance checks are as done as they can be, given the chaos, and should be completed tomorrow morning by eleven-hundred.

DATE: January 16th, 2139

Officer Nizar and Junior Officer Bahaa conducted a floor by floor walkthrough this morning, assisted by a huge surveyor crew from EVAC-Central. I wonder if you've ever spoken to their prissy Lead face-to-face? I didn't ask him about you.

Everything is going to plan. Occupied berths are correctly locked down if you don't count the villagers Nizar found wandering galley to galley looking for Northerners, Southerners, Beirutis, cousins—looking for something to hold onto that wasn't their soil, the musk of their air, or the familiar mountainous contours of their horizon.

After we closed boarding for the night, I was startled by the familiar strains of Fairouz issuing from the Munawwer's loud PA system. Ballads of patriotism and yearning. It took me two whole folkloric masterpieces to find the culprit: our own Officer Nizar. I told him I hadn't authorized music, although I'd gamble you—hapless lover of the Orient—wouldn't fault his taste.

"Have a heart, Suraya," he said. "These people are leaving their homes forever."

"We're carrying digital archives of the last five hundred years of Lebanese culture, Officer," I said.

"I can see that you think that's enough to make up for this colossal heartbreak," he said.

I insisted.

In the resulting silence I thought I heard a collective intake of breath from nearly a million people, a noise that groaned through windpipes, a sound of rope under load. But I could not allow those in the queue—those to be left behind—to hear jubilation from the ship. It wasn't fair to anybody.

Against official guidance, we never issued dig-forms to announce the evacuation. Half of the population do not own personal holos; the ones who do won't wear them because of superstition, or discomfort, or because they are too vain or traditional to have anything ported to their faces.

I was seven when it became a legal requirement to fit a sinus air filter almost everywhere in the world. Lebanon too. My mother fought so hard to avoid putting me through the procedure. It's unclear whether she was right. Air quality *did* improve drastically in the next five years. But given where I am now, perhaps even the one year she appealed against the surgery was a year too many.

Did you have a chance to know that about her? That she was more principled than right, most of the time? It makes me wonder how she let you fall for her, just enough that here I am.

A decade later, I got my own holo fitted, and the sinus filter upgraded, because I could. When my mother found out, she didn't speak to me for a month.

Anyway, no dig-forms. Instead, as approved by the Worldship K5-NME Steering Board on June 20, 2138, we sent criers to every town and village. The megaphone and magcar approach—the jolt of building panic—was enough. At its peak, the queue for the Munawwer was a 130-mile phalanx snaking south from the Mediterranean coast then turning up winding mountain tracks towards the northern border.

The queue has a thousand character traits, a volatile temperament. As if by some orderly law of physics, the closer to the waiting worldship the queue gets, the wilder it is. In the nearer villages to the coastline, rowdy end-of-the-world parties have ransacked homes and businesses. Those in the far away half, winding through mountain villages, are more sedate. They stare at my ground crew before they take the rations they're offered. Their infants wail in ways that bring to mind footage of long-eradicated famines, but they are not hungry or cold or sick. They are scared.

Commander Smith, it played out as an incident of geography—to save the nearest ones to the sea and doom the rest. *Doom.* A silly word, so grave-sounding it is hard to take seriously. When you learned you had a child back on Earth, did you worry that she was doomed to die there, having never threaded through the far reaches of space? Did you really believe, then, that the projections were right, that the collision course had been accurately charted? Did you laugh, disbelieving, when they said the asteroid storm was the width of our solar system, big and fast enough to wipe out the planet? I wonder if you thought about your fourth-grader—your teenager, your adult daughter—when one by one the missions EVAC launched to vacuum the critical debris failed?

Vacuum the critical debris. Like a bit of dust under the sofa.

Of course, we broadcast capacity warnings. 900,000 people per EVAC member-nation: enough to preserve race, language, culture. Still, 900,000 is not a whole country. Here, it's two out of five.

This, at least, is clear to everyone. We shouted it in ringing voices from the backs of the magcars.

DATE: January 17th, 2139

Officer Nizar's been compiling hasty geographic and demographic statistics on the queue. He is behind schedule sending these to EVAC-Central. In lieu of official figures, some notes:

Last week, we sent surveyor crews to every signposted village across the country, from the Bekaa Valley to the Jnoub to the Chouf. Every town is a ghost town—even the people left behind are near enough ghosts, the very old and stubborn, spirits stronger than their bones.

Gourds and winter fruit rot in open steriles by the roadside. Chimneys are without their curls of smoke; hawker bots make lazy figures-of-eight in the snow outside shops and markets. They call out in mechanical confusion to the crew, promising prices so low they indicate a complete cessation of demand.

We will never know the exact geographic and demographic spread of those queuing for evacuation. You didn't broadcast details of the landing until the worldship's bulk was nearly above us. The arrival surprised us. If anything, the people were better primed, more ready to strap their belongings to pallets or their own bodies, to abandon their magcars at the milling ends of the mag-proofed queue, which quickly packed tight and spilled farther and farther up the mountain.

You would think they would fight, butcher each other out of envy, make pilgrimages to the front and demand entry. At first, they did. We're not a lie-down-and-die kind of people. This is something you might not have known, if you tasted only pleasure here, if you knew us only through that lens. When we began to debar not just individuals but entire innocent families, a sort of order fell over everything.

Doom. A silly word.

Still, scuffles erupt, old sectarian allegiances flare, fossilized in forenames and surnames. Everyone, though, seems tired. The uncertainty is another kind of mass spreading in our chests, heavy as the Munawwer squatting in the sea.

Last night, Nizar reported that thousands and thousands of the elderly and the infirm had sieved to the front of the queue almost overnight. I asked to see for myself. We went down the access ramp together, past the corniche and the cordoned-off half-mile, to where the queue began.

"What's this?" he asked, gesturing at the weary faces, gray or brown as the rocks of the seafront. "We broadcast that people of childbearing age get priority."

A younger man stepped out of the four-abreast queue. "Mind your manners, habibi. We treat our grandparents with respect, even at times like these."

"Brother, that's nonsense," returned Nizar with his usual gift for diplomacy. "This is a *worldship*. The idea's to continue all of goddamn humanity out there." He pointed to the sky, inky and flat. "Your grandpa can't help with that, no matter how sprightly he might be."

"I'll punch your face in if you speak that way around your elders, *brother*."

At this point we were forced to remove the young man from the queue and debar him from the boarding procedure. He produced an old-fashioned Marlboro from the back of his slacks and swaggered away cussing towards a viewing point for Pigeon Rock. All of him seemed to billow in the breeze. He smoked his cigarette and watched waves crash against the limestone formation where it crouched out in the shallow sea, diligently ignoring the massive moonlike presence of the Munawwer blotting out most of the horizon.

• • •

Officer Nizar's team has been guarding access to the ship since it appeared in the sky, pinwheel shadow spreading over all the wards of the city.

We had been practicing the procedures for a year—since we opened EVAC's holo pings and found that we'd been chosen. Most of my ground crew have military backgrounds. Nizar was a Major in the Armed Forces. I'm not a soldier, but you know, I suppose, that I'm no stranger to protocol.

Commander Smith—I topped every mathematics exam at school. Headmaster Boutros brought me brochures on EVAC-Central, the United Nations Space Program, Lebanese Astronautics. But at university I fell credit by credit into Anthropology, thinking, I guess, of lecturing at the Sorbonne, thinking, I guess, of staying rooted to humanity. Rooted to Earth.

Do you already know this? Did my mother ever sneak you messages about me? Did she tell you about the poem I wrote about you in secondary school, the one that won an award? As far as I know she never spoke to you after you left.

If you do know, you can hear it again: I was a civil servant for the Interior Ministry until the Munawwer, my days crammed with the amplified tedium of the entire nation. You found out about me somehow, found my name: a vain search for your own, a flight through billions of census archive files, the fuzzy match that finally snagged my hyphens, my half-concealed identity.

I suppose you chose me for my experience with projects that mobilize our population? Perhaps you would not have let blood run thicker than reason if you'd known that nothing mobilizes our population that doesn't originate within their own hearts.

And since there is nothing else to lose which isn't already fated to be lost—homeland, loved ones, history—perhaps you would not have granted me a ground crew member's golden ticket to fly away had you known, father. About my loose procedural skill, the hours of my youth I spent staring blankly through scrolling municipal notices, statistics, memos, recommendations. Saying just enough. Nights, returning to an empty house, one parent gone too soon, another gone too far away. The stop-start friendships and intimacies I increasingly shed. Then illness tightening like a cast over these last few years of my own decline. Yes, that.

We followed your procedures to the last letter. We deployed our ground crew, arranged the queue four-abreast as specified, heated it, and distributed insulated overshoes, food packets, blankets. We asked desperate people out in the cold to smother cooking fires and pack away shisha pipes. We switched off the Fairouz songs and arrested hooligans and shushed panicked outbursts.

The Munawwer is almost full now. We will leave millions behind.

Nearly a month ago I sent the passenger guidance checklist to Officer Nizar. Today, I caught up with his patrol near Khalde, pulled him aside by the seawall in the calm of drifting snow to go through it.

I read from my holo. "Are we 'screening boarding worldship passengers for weapons or materials which may be used to fashion weapons'?"

He stared at me with self-assurance and a dirty sort of pity. "Why would we do that? If anyone's going to be so deranged and damaged," he corkscrewed a finger into his temple, "as to blow up humanity's only chance in this fucked-up universe, then we don't deserve to survive."

"Not humanity's only chance," I said on reflex. "At least one worldship per member-nation and—" I looked back over the hillsides of Khalde, heard the living noise of the queue and ran out of words to rely on.

Nizar scanned the holo he'd pulled up, presumably the checklist. Presumably for the first time. "What stupid shit."

I ached for the sweetness of striking his perfect nose with a closed fist. Instead, I trembled in the instantly filthy snowdrift and pulled rank: "What screening *have* you been doing, Officer?"

Nizar watched me over his twenty-twenties moustache, back in fashion for the end of the world.

"We frisk them, Ms. Suraya, Your Excellency," he quipped. "Mostly for tobacco pipes. The ground crew boys deserve a good pipe. The ones who are staying, I mean." His face slackened around its folds and wrinkles, leaving the shelf of his brow to carry his countenance. According to his EVAC records, Nizar is thirty-four. The apocalypse has aged us early.

"Are you using your ticket?" I asked, my voice a snowflake, too soft for authority.

Nizar switched off the holo he'd been staring past and turned to relieve himself against a railing.

"Excuse me. Urgent need," he said, squinting at the gray bulk of the Munawwer ten miles down the coast. His planted stance reminded me of the upstart we'd ejected from the queue the night before.

"A difficult decision," he said, hitching his hips and zipping up. "Ticket off-planet in my back pocket, nieces and nephews up in the middle of the queue. No chance they get to board. With my ticket, one of them survives to start life new, start a new nation."

"Where are they?" I asked.

"Near Zahle," he said. "Too far. They refused to leave the village any earlier."

Maybe it's naive to think this is noteworthy, but we've all pulled strings to place friends and family in the Beiruti sections of the queue. Forcibly camped them out on the corniche as soon as we heard about the landing. But no one dares smuggle relatives on board a near-capacity worldship. No one wants to tempt fate. Being debarred is one thing; having your entire family debarred by EVAC-Central is an especial cruelty.

"It's just a single ticket," I said. "How many can you save with one ticket?"

"One youngster more worthy than me, habibi," he said.

"They've said there might be another ship for Lebanon," I muttered into the wind off the Mediterranean, hoping he wouldn't catch it. But he did, and his skeptical bark broke my heart.

"What about you?" he asked after a meaningful silence. "Are you using your ticket?"

"I don't have any family left here. My cousins emigrated years ago to countries where worldships queue for you, not the other way round."

"But you mentioned your father was . . . " he said.

"None of your business." It's nobody's business. It's barely even yours. You left and never came back. You forfeited everything.

"So you'll take it," Nizar rejoined softly. "You'll get on that goddamn ship with the goddamn rest of them."

I had no useful response. I breathed in the tang of fish and old fossil fuel spills, and now and again the new smell of ozone off the Munawwer, carried by the icy breeze.

DATE: January 18th, 2139

Our evacuee numbers hit 900,000 this morning.

Actually, there are 900,124 on board according to autocount. There were children, so many children—how could I leave them behind? We rounded up the healthiest ones, the ones who could bear to be separated from wailing parents. The ones whose parents let them go. And yes: the ones whose eyes burrowed holes in our hearts.

In my bunk last night, I could not sleep for the torment of all the little ones in the winding queue, foreheads lucent in the night, too far from Beirut to break my crew's hearts. They're the living ghosts of our dreams now. One day soon they will disperse as invisible particles into the sky, while the ones we save live on, we hope, on and on, in the vastness of traversable space.

Surely one hundred and twenty-four slight bodies cannot disrupt the stability of a craft like the Munawwer. We brought them on board on my direct orders. What horrifies me is that you never told us how many more we could have saved—how big the occupancy headroom really was.

Thoughts that keep me up despite the Munawwer's atmospheric sedatives:

That the Munawwer will go up in flames during hover-and-power (the sadness, then, of those left behind).

That the children on board will forget their parents and grandparents and their language and the generosity of their culture.

That humanity is a meaningless thing, transplanted far from its origins.

That they will all die of heartbreak, lightyears away from this ill-luck country.

That there will never be another worldship allocated to this tiny, insignificant land on the edge of the sea. (The certainty of this.)

That it has all been a giant mistake. That Earth is as fine as it seems, and will remain here, blue and green and giving, to pine after forever.

That Nizar's nieces and nephews will be left behind.

That Nizar will be left behind.

That you and I will one day meet.

That we will all kill each other on the ship, anyway, for the same reasons we've killed each other at home.

That you and I will never meet.

That I will die in the end of the world.

That I will die before the end of the world.

DATE: January 19th, 2139

Commander Smith—I've tagged the section below for excision; please ratify and pass it to EVAC-Central's Specialist Services team.

I understand from guidance document PUB-214 that I may only commend a single person from the Munawwer's ground crew.

According to my EVAC profile, I command a crew of ten thousand across Lebanese territory. I've only had brief interactions with a handful of my crew, devolving most responsibilities to more capable hands. This is my failing. My heart has shied at every juncture from the sad business of evacuating the Earth.

Of the half dozen ground crew members I've worked with nearly daily, the one I have come to know best is Officer Nizar Adel Taleb, my second-in-command.

I understand, further, that any officer given a formal commendation to Specialist Services will be promoted to flight crew on the next available worldship. I have good reason to believe this is the good craft Kuro-Obi, L6-AUAS, which will land along the Japanese mainland at an unspecified time in the next six months. Non-native flight crew members on a foreign country's ship, according to the guidance document, are permitted to evacuate all remaining blood relatives.

Therefore, please take this as my formal commendation of Officer Nizar Taleb.

Off the record, I maintain that Officer Nizar is as self-important and narrow-minded a prick as they come. Be that as it may, he's done nothing to warrant the conflict between his own bodily survival and the tearing of his soul to pieces.

This morning, after every last one of our 900,124 evacuees was safely on board, I went walking along the corniche.

I meandered towards that stabbing void in the sky where days ago the lighthouse would have been, barnacled, salt-streaked. Then I turned on my heels to walk the way I'd come.

I had changed out of my attaché's uniform right after we sounded bugle calls all the way up the queue—*the worldship's full, the worldship's full.* The official clothing felt like a betrayal.

I walked, and Beirut heaved around me. There were still millions in the queue, now a shapeless inflamed gathering of people and magcars pouring towards the coast. Thousands of ground crew in riot gear and heavy arms held people back from the half-mile cordon leading to the Munawwer's access ramps. It was something between a funeral procession and a terrible mob. A deafening noise reverberated in the air. Gulls flapped off the Munawwer in agitation. It was all the ground crew could do to prevent a crush.

Faces streamed past me, fixated on the motionless worldship and its blue blinking lights of habitation. If anyone looked back at me I thought: *is this the one I'll send away into outer space?*

A cousin, a sister, a lover. Any of these would have provided me with a selfless sacrifice. But isn't it an impossibility to pull a single stranger, unwitting, from the crowd? How dare I play a god's game?

Another god's game: to learn, one day before a worldship lands to carry 900,000 people away, that the growing wrongness in your chest is wronger than you thought. To be given the choice to go to Europe for treatment, or to stay and serve your people at your father's bidding, the only thing he's ever asked. Little doom and bigger doom, braiding, lines in a palm.

The night after I learned this, Commander Smith, I had a dream. I was inside a station-city, a pearl in the sealed-shell darkness of deep space. And you were there. I was laying curled into myself and you were healing me. And I would live.

I woke up and my veins were pulsing with loneliness, and my chest was throbbing with pain.

So this morning, I walked the corniche and stopped as close along the railings as I could get to the Munawwer, jostled by a field of people and their confusion. It was huge, bright, sublime—a promise of safety and stability by virtue of mass alone.

With every fiber of my broken lungs I inhaled. Then I inhaled again. I held my breath and felt dizzy with the sticky task of living. And I felt that death was neither a foe, nor something I could grab by the scruff.

Then I went, slowed by the drag of the doomed, towards the worldship's access ramp. And then on board, to complete the last of the paperwork.

In the Midst of Life

NICK WOLVEN

1

Field Report #72276
Doug Lam
Lead Site Investigator
South Asian Division

:::ACCESS RESTRICTION: GRADE 3 AND ABOVE:::
:::CONTENTS EDITED FOR RELEVANCE AND CLARITY:::

Division Controller's Notes: psych flag, legal review recommended, immediate termination recommended

*****transcript begins*****

Well, you bastard, you got your wish.

I know it's you who reads these reports, Carter, and I know why. Now, listen.

You'll find the project file attached. It's got everything you need. Site specs, environmental impact, legal briefing. Not to mention toxin assays, insurance payouts, the "local impact factor" (quite a euphemism, that). Plenty for your lawyers to chew on.

It should be enough. Hell, it *is* enough. But I know it'll never satisfy you. Look, I get why you've been asking for these spoken reports—these "informal debriefings," as you people like to call them. A cute little ruse to get me talking off the cuff, guard lowered, saying what's really been happening out here. And you can sit in your executive suite, poring over these braindumps of mine, waiting for me to become so cocky and foolish as to speak the awful truth.

Well, here it is. What you've been waiting for, in that gray and shriveled little heart of yours. Grounds for my immediate termination.

I'll make it sweeter, Carter. I'll paint the scene. Grab a drink, you son of a bitch. You're going to want to savor this.

• • •

I'm sitting in Belawan, in the spiritless hotel you booked us in, project notes on my laptop screen—acres of notes, Carter, reams of notes, because I've been trying for a goddamn week to figure out what just happened here. I'm on the balcony, which isn't much of a balcony: concrete, like so much of this city, and cracked down the middle in a way that, under normal circumstances, would probably make me fear for my life. It's a hot night here in northern Sumatra, but who am I kidding, every night is hot. The sun's gone down somewhere behind me, beyond the black hills and the lost, dead forests, and all that's left is a pink vision burning in the cloudy haze above the bay. The port, though, the port is always bright: rainbow streets under smoky air.

Yes, the forces of development have been hard at work, here. The big container ships come in, the tea and palm oil go out, and you know as well as I do what happens next. The currents of global capital flow in and do their work.

Capital, Carter. I've often wondered, what color is capital? In America, we like to say money is green, but that's a throwback to the days of paper currency. I think money, pure money, must be the color of glass. Crystalline, like the buildings out here, the hotels and office towers popping up along the banks of the Deli River, south into the urban core of Medan. Shiny new palaces, raised in months from the blasted earth. You can almost forget, on a night like this, when the windows are lit and the bistros are buzzing and the voices of tourists ring through the shopping districts—you can almost forget what was done to make room for them.

I'm getting ahead of myself. What I want you to see, Carter, is *me*, Doug, your old nemesis from the fifty-seventh floor. Potbellied, gray, not so young as I used to be, with my company-issued laptop, my unbuttoned seersucker shirt. Feet in soiled flip-flops propped on the rusty wreck of what might once have been a Taiwanese space heater. Voice recorder in one hand, whiskey and Coke in the other—the third of the evening, and unlikely to be the last. Looking down at the thin dark trickle of the river cutting through the clutter of vanishing slums.

Let me spell it out. I'm done. D-O-N-E. With how much, exactly, I don't yet know.

You earned this, buddy. You fought for it. Twenty years, you've been dogging my career, waiting for this day. And I'm glad, truly. In a way, you deserve it: every single, strange word of what I'm about to tell you.

2

A man can get sick of air travel, in time.

I mean that literally. Sick. Physically ill. And not this inner-ear stuff HR's been banging on about.

It's the height that does it. The remote perspective. There's a sickness that comes of looking at life from too high up. The way buildings all look the same, so you can hardly judge the relative heights. Not till the sun angles low, evening comes, and darkness leaks out from below their walls. Long black shadows: the footprints of power.

As soon as I landed, Karen grabbed me at the gate, rushed me through the terminal, loaded me on into a corporate copter. Up to the delta, for a look at the site. We followed the river to the Belmera bridge, then veered west, over the Australian zones and the marshes. Quite a patchwork, out that way. The big multinationals are putting up fences, painting their rooftops in grid-based patterns. From above, the land is a sea of corporate logos, rendered in pixels a meter square.

We'd be doing four flyovers, Karen said, coming in from each cardinal point. Then a full fly-around at ninety meters. Something to do with the specs on the cameras. I joined her in the cockpit. Green lumps went by below, patches of wetland. Our target was nothing but a blip on the overlay. Karen flipped to a camera feed.

I think you know Karen. Tiny woman, good negotiator, very generous with the company payouts. She did the relocation out of Lagos last year. Cleared nine hundred and fifty-three people out of an area half the size of Yankee stadium. These were families, big ones; they refused to be separated. The shanty town was centered on an old oil yard, row upon row of empty storage tanks. Folks were using propane torches to cut and join the units. Quite a complex. More trace toxins than you could log at a dump site. We had the property pegged for executive villas, ended up scraping it clean to a depth of five meters.

Karen is who they send in when things get, shall we say, *delicate*. I watched her face as we came to the site. Not that Karen's the type to reveal her emotions. But you can always tell when someone hasn't been sleeping, or when she's been wearing the same clothes for a week.

"Tough clearance?" I tried to catch her eye. I've learned, Carter, that when you do a site investigation, the first thing you investigate is your own people.

"Well," Karen took the controls, "we'll get to that."

She punched in a flight program. After the automatic flybys, we dipped in for our sightseeing run. The site specs are all on file, but to sum: it's old marsh property, reclaimed about thirty years ago. Standard pylon-and-platform job. The Indonesian government laid the first foundations. When they fell apart, a company called Especia came in and tooled around with tent-style storage. After the price crash, the deed got passed around a few small Chinese players, one of whom raised the main construction. They did the usual awful job, left the building half-finished, then sold to a speculator during the boom.

And that's all she wrote, until about three months ago, when our folks bought the plot at sky-high prices. It's a connective acquisition, knits together our coastal holdings. Blocks the Chinese from accessing the bay, plus gives us a nice belt of free trade around the oil barons. Our initial plan was to install high-speed transit, the usual mix of stop-off shops. Depending, of course, on the engineer's report.

And on getting the damn site cleared.

Karen circled in a tight radius. The site didn't have much in the way of construction. Just one big tower, taller than it ought to be, steel and composite on a bot-built frame. Finished up to the tenth floor, sheathed to the fortieth, nothing but girders and nets above that. There were already cracks where the composite had strained. It's not meant to be structural, but they're supposed to tweak the mix for flexibility. This was seriously cut-rate construction.

"How many are there?" I asked.

Karen told the copter to go in close, making a tight pass around the building's northwest corner. I saw boards in the windows, dirty and unpainted, squares of plywood from the nearby tree plantations. People will use anything they can scavenge out here, but it's weird not to see transparent windows. Usually on a site like this, there are a million signs of life. Clotheslines on the balconies, towels hung out to dry, rain catchers and aerials all over the structure. This place was a box. Sealed tight.

Karen's eyes were vague with sleep deprivation.

"How many?" I said again. "How many people inside?" She stared.

"Inside?" It took her at least ten seconds to answer. "Maybe five, nine hundred. Projected."

"Projected? Not estimated? Nobody's run a count?"

She had this way of looking at me, Carter. Hard to explain. Like the questions I was asking, perfectly natural questions, were all thunderingly beside the point.

"We tried a count," Karen said. "The first two teams did full evaluations. When I came in, I sent my own survey crew."

"But nobody has the numbers? Five to nine hundred, that's quite a spread."

That look again. "Yeah. It is."

We were banking around the corner, tilting into the turn. I leaned over to scan the ground. It was mostly barren concrete, bleak as hell, but I glimpsed a ring of debris, strewn around the building's foundation. Bales of stuff, big jugs, cardboard packages. Those fat bright drums the NGOs pass out. Like a storm had flooded through some relief agency's warehouse, depositing the contents here.

"What's all that—?" I began.

Karen was smacking the console, glaring through the windscreen, cursing like we used to curse when we were kids.

"Shit! Piss on me! Knew this would happen."

A change of course. We were heading for the edge of the platform. A bunch of mobile units sat grouped in one corner, trucks and company cars, plus those human-chauffeured limos the political folks still drive. They had a little tent set up as a command center, wires running all over the ground. A former soldier stood out front, head-to-toe in body armor, striking the usual badass poses.

"Well," I said, "what's all this?" Meaning it rhetorically, but Karen was too tired for nuance.

"What do you think?" She ran a scan for landing sites. "It's the fucking cavalry."

Here's the first big shocker for you, Carter. The first great big reveal.

I know we like to say the nationals are dead. They blew up their currencies, sold all their land, now they just take bribes and service debts. They write laws, we pay them to bend the laws, then we move in and do our thing. Simple, right?

But it isn't. Not on the ground. The local governments are eager to have us, true. Eager to have our money, eager to have our buildings. Problem is, they get a little too eager, know what I mean? In urban areas, the government types can be . . . aggressive.

Soon as I saw the big Chrysler AT by the tent, I knew the city police were here. The chiefs go in for those army trucks: makes 'em feel all big and tall. Inside the tent, we found quite a party. Not only Medan police, but a local suit, representing whatever was left of the government. Which accounted, no doubt, for the merc out front. Plus the contractor. Plus our biggest prospective tenant, a Chinese-French guy who represented a hotel consortium. Off in a corner, I saw Colm Kellans from our own team.

You know how I feel about Colm.

The contractor was the one doing the talking. "Hey, whatever you guys want to do, it's not my dollar. You're paying for my time. You make the schedule."

That's the best rendition I can give of what he said. You know how it is with translation software.

Anyway, it had an effect. Grim silence. Every human in that tent represented a complex system of international capital flows. And every moment we spent gabbing was a pile of money lost.

Karen introduced me. Right away, they got back to business, speaking as if there had been no interruption. The police chief stood up, waving his hands.

"This should be our job. We have legal authority. Let us go in and we'll do the job for you. Tomorrow, when you come back, the building will be clear."

Again, my rendition. What he actually said was a lot less friendly. It got the point across, though.

"Sure," Colm answered. "We know how you'll do the job, chief. Billy sticks and tear gas. Breaking legs and cracking heads. When you guys say 'clear,' you neglect to mention the blood we'll have to wipe off the floors."

"Now, hold on." This was Karen, doing her negotiator thing. "There's got to be some way—"

They ignored her. The police chief came back at Colm. "You don't like our methods? What are *your* methods? What are your people planning to do about this problem?"

Colm, he did that ex-marine thing. Stood up, real slow. Totally silent. Stretching his neck, taking his time. Looking at his fists, like it had just sort of occurred to him, hey, he used to kill people with those things. You can take the man out of the U.S. army, but you can never take the U.S. army out of the man.

"Sonics," Colm said. "High and low. Like we did with those condos in Rio de Janeiro." He had a picture of the tower on the tent wall, projected from his phone. He punched at the image, showing how it would work.

"Look. You got these boards in the windows, tenth floor on up. We can get a drone fleet with adapted canons, punch 'em in with gel-bag rounds. Hit the top corners to knock out the nails. A second fleet of quadcopters will then fly up with the wave generators. If we get a shot through a single window on each side, that'll be enough to build the resonance pattern. We hit them with the maximum nonlethal dose. Start at the top and work our way down. We can flush the whole building in a couple of hours."

"Except," the chief pointed out, "for the bottom ten floors."

I was still trying to catch up with the proceedings. But I knew the chief was right. The bottom floors of the building had glass windows, painted black. We could punch 'em in with the gel-guns, of course. But if this was the kind of situation I thought it was, the last thing we wanted to do was to fill the building with flying shards of glass.

Colm gave the chief that old commando look, like pissant developing-country cops should know not to mess with a Western ex-army dude. "It's a *flush*," he said, giving each word this fierce emphasis. "We're *flushing* these people. If we clear thirty floors, that'll drive out the rest. Believe me. If there are as many people in there as we think, it won't take much to start a rush for the exits."

"People will be trampled," said the police chief. "You'll have a stampede."

"My friend, that's the entire point."

I noticed that the contractor was shaking his head. "What's the matter?" I asked him.

"Forget it," he said, or something to that effect. "Subsonics, hypersonics, whatever. You don't want to use any acoustic weapons in here. Can't happen."

Chinese guy, the contractor. Laconic. Mostly he just made faces, waved his hands. But I knew what he was saying. With a building like this, cheap steel and bad composite? If Colm started blasting soundwaves through the structure, that could bring the whole place crumbling down.

"According to our engineer's report . . . " Colm began. Still playing the coolheaded soldier. But the contractor wasn't having it. The guy spun in his folding chair, smacking the side of the tent to make the projected image shiver and ripple. He said a word in Chinese that the software couldn't handle. No one needed a translation. I mean, who were we going to trust? Some pointy-headed engineer's report, delivered out of an Atlanta office? Or the guy who actually built the buildings?

This was getting ugly.

At this point, Karen felt obliged to remind everyone that I, the company investigator, had arrived, and that I, the company investigator, was technically in charge. "What we need to do," she told them, "is understand this situation. Only then will we know how to proceed."

And this is when things got weird.

Because everyone in the tent suddenly got this funny look, like kids with a dirty secret. After about a minute of awkward silence, Colm pushed a binder across the table, the kind with a thumbprint lock.

"I think you'll want to take a look at this," he said.

Carter, it's time for another hard truth.

I know how things look from the home office. One big spreadsheet. Data points. And one of those data points is the head count.

Twenty squatters cleared from woodlands in South Dakota. Eighty squatters cleared from unfinished townhouses in Jalisco. Seven hundred squatters cleared from an abandoned soccer stadium in Jakarta.

Numbers.

But when you're in the field, you're not thinking about numbers. You're thinking about networks, groups, social dynamics.

A squatter community is just that, a community. And every community has one, for better or worse: a leader. When you do a site clearance, that's the person you want to talk to.

"I sent you an email." Colm looked at Karen as she thumbed open the binder. "Also a voicemail. You've been on the phone five hours straight. Anyway, there's been a development. Turns out you were right. This is very far from an ordinary site clearance."

Karen flipped open the binder. The first thing I saw was a dark face. Male, middle-aged. Could have been from any country in the world.

"That's Abdul Shah," said Colm.

"Arabic?" I guessed.

"American. Parents were Indo-Trinidadian Muslims. Immigrated when he was a baby."

Karen flipped through the file. Again, Carter, you have all this information, but I'll give the rundown. Abdul Shah, until about half a year ago, was the type and epitome of nobody special. Grew up in Brooklyn, went to serve in Afghanistan in oh-eight. Seems to have been a typical kid, living for basketball and video games, till an IED flipped his truck on the road to Kandahar. After his discharge in twenty-ten, he took to wandering. Drifted down to the Caribbean, disappeared for a while, seems to have lived full-time as a beach bum. He shows up next in a Stanford MOOC on introductory neuroscience. In his forties, he goes back to Iraq as a visitor, then on to India. Tracing his roots, maybe. A decade later, he pops up in Sumatra. That's where he set about making himself a gigantic pain in our asses.

"That stint on Hassel Island," Colm said, "is where he seems to have developed his ideas."

"Ideas?" I didn't like where this was heading.

Colm gave me a look, like: *Don't play stupid with me, you know how it is.*

I know how it is. We all know how it is. The people, the rootless people, the infinite people . . .

They say demographic growth is slowing, even reversing. That's no comfort to the billions of people caught between the trendlines. They wander from place to place with no jobs, no prospects, no home-sweet-home. I've heard there are more homeless in some countries than there are people with legal shelter.

Cities won't hold 'em. Countryside can't support 'em. What they're looking for, mostly, is a reason to keep going. I know it sounds trite. But some clichés are like dirt and death; there's no getting rid of them. People, rich or poor, need something to believe in.

"So this guy," Karen said, tapping the binder, "Abdul Shah, he's some kind of a . . . "

"He's a crank," said Colm.

"A prophet," said the police chief.

"I was going to say 'guru,'" Karen said.

Colm pointed at the projected image of the tower. "He holed up there in August. Started preaching whatever it is he preaches. By September, he had about a hundred followers. By December, four hundred. Now there's a whole congregation in there. They never leave the building. And that's how we get to this lovely situation we're in today."

"So this is no simple squatter population," I said. "This is more of a—"

"A cult," said Colm.

"A temple," said the police chief.

"This is getting interesting," Karen said.

I asked Colm, "When you say 'preaching' . . . "

Colm waved. "So far as we can tell, Shah is offering a fairly standard cocktail of bullshit. Touch of Islam, touch of Buddhism, touch of neuroscience. You know these guys. They grab a bit of the old, a bit of the new, stir it all together and act like they've discovered a whole new religion. The full profile hasn't yet been established—"

"Meaning you have no idea what he actually believes."

"The full profile hasn't yet been established," Colm repeated, giving a military stress to each word, "but we believe Abdul Shah's ideas tend toward the apocalyptic."

Great. Within four hours of getting off the plane, I'd gone from running a squatter relocation to quelling a thousand-member suicide cult. "What about a cordon? Can we cut them off? How are they supplied?"

"You want to try a *siege*?" This was the prospective tenant, sounding seriously piqued. His company was supposed to be on the property by year's end.

"A siege could be a problem," Colm said. "Not because of the tower. Because of what's happening *outside* the tower."

"These people have attracted support," said the chief, "from the local community."

"They bring offerings," Karen said. "Donations. Food and water. I noticed that when I came in."

I remembered that ring of debris around the tower's base. Except, as I realized, it wasn't debris at all.

Those jugs, those bales of supplies, they were offerings. Tribute.

Worse and worse.

"Not to mention new recruits," said Colm. "They show up every day. Word's gotten out. This guy's being greeted as some kind of visionary. A problem like this, it gets worse before it gets better. We need to nip this in the bud."

What we needed, I was thinking, was to get these crazies off our proverbial lawn. After that they could do whatever they wanted. Suicide cult or second coming or whatever.

"I told you." The police chief made a swinging motion, wielding an imaginary whip or club. "My guys, this is their job. Three riot teams, one at each major entrance. We can clear the building in a day."

"Sonics," said Colm. "Trust me. Quick and clean."

They went back and forth, an argument I'd heard a hundred times. Still, I had a feeling, like there was something I'd forgotten.

"What about the first teams?" I asked. "The survey teams? The people Karen sent in?"

"What about them?" Colm said.

"Don't they have anything to tell us? What have they learned about the situation?"

Silence. They were all making eyes at each other, even the guys who'd been arguing before. It gave me a shivery sensation, like with all the weird things I'd heard, I still hadn't grasped how crazy this situation was.

"The other teams," Colm said at last, speaking slowly to emphasize how slow-witted I was, "haven't come back out."

"And that," said Karen, slapping shut the profile of Abdul Shah, "is what I've been trying to tell you."

3

Here I am again, Carter, back from a sandwich run. A man can't live on whiskey and Coke alone.

Maybe it's the tropical climate. But there's something ceremonial about these buildings of ours, don't you think? Hotels, malls, offices, resorts: they all have the same monolithic appearance. Glassy slabs, smooth, sky high. An alien visitor might take them for memorials. Memorializing what, he'd have to wonder?

That's what I thought when I stood underneath Shah's tower. It was oddly like a ziggurat, the way it narrowed in stages. Glass and stone for the first hundred feet, then composite and plywood, then a skeletal spire rising toward the sun. Where, I wondered, would Master Shah make his home? Was he the kind of cult leader who'd need to be close to heaven? Topmost floor, high in the South Asian clouds? Or the kind of elusive crackpot who'd want to burrow deep, behind a nest of barricades and guns?

Karen and I were standing on the cement platform, just outside the ring of donations. Up close, I could see that the stuff was almost all food, the kind of rations starving people receive. Sacks of rice, jugs of water, unappetizing cubes of processed fish.

"How long do we wait here?" I asked Karen. She gave an impatient little hiss.

In the tent, Karen had told me her plan. Her morning hadn't been idle. In the five hours she'd spent on the phone—five hours she'd been failing to get Colm's messages—Karen had made contact with a mole inside the tower. If this person could be trusted, one of us would soon be inside.

The typical squatter camp is a sobering place. But not a dangerous place. I don't know what they tell you in the home office, but the rule in the field is that you minimize provocation. The first teams we send in are like embassies, establishing what you might call diplomatic relations. The optimal process is to strike a deal, arrange for relocation, offer payouts, alternate housing. It's only when things break down that a guy like Colm steps in.

Later, we send in the survey teams, medics, engineers, toxin abatement. All told, about twenty-five people might enter a building of this size.

None of them, so far, had come back out.

"So what's your theory?" I looked over at Karen, who'd switched from coffee to pep pills. "What are we looking at here? Mass murder? Cannibalism?"

Karen sighed. In the command center, she'd played a message, first and only communication from within Shah's tower. It had been sent by a woman named Shayreen Scott, point person on the last survey team. Her message was nineteen seconds long.

*****transcriber's note: file #AB112235 intercut*****

"Hi, everyone. I'm fine, but I want you to know that I and the other team members have decided to stay with this group for now. Please don't worry about us or send anyone else into the tower. For the time being, I think it's best if we break off contact."

*****end intercut file*****

"Now if that's a hostage message," Karen said, "it sure doesn't sound like one."

It didn't sound like one to me, either. What it sounded like was a surefire sign that Shayreen Scott and her team had gone completely batty.

Thankfully, Karen had ignored Shayreen's request. She'd established contact. For four and a half hours, she'd run automatic redial on Shayreen's phone. For half an hour, she'd held a frustrating conversation. By the time Karen picked me up at the airport, terms had been established.

One person—one member of our team—would be allowed to enter the tower. Me.

Oh, Karen put up a good argument. She was the better negotiator. She had more experience on-site. But she also hadn't rested in the better part of a week.

I pulled rank.

So here I stood in the shadow that Shah's tower cast like a gnomon on its surrounding dial of donations, looking at the glass doors reinforced with plywood, the rows of covered windows.

"How long do I have?"

Karen checked her phone. "If you go in now? Fifty-four minutes. I'll try to get you more."

Fifty-four minutes. Less than an hour until the local police chief moved in with his clubs and gas. Sparking, most likely, a riot. Or mass suicide. Or worse.

"There's the signal," Karen said, looking at her phone.

"Wish me luck." I was already walking.

"Doug?" Karen resembled a squatter herself, standing there in her week-old clothes. She waggled her phone. "Keep in touch."

I had three phones on my person. One in my pocket. A bug taped to my chest. And a third, my only genuinely secret one, the miniphone I carried in a place I felt confident no one would check.

I nodded at Karen and turned away.

As I walked into the shadow of Abdul Shah's tower, I thought of my kids. Two little girls. Except they weren't little girls, they were grown-up women, and I often wondered where exactly I'd been while that was happening.

But I knew.

I'd been doing shit like this.

The plywood slid aside as I came close. The door cracked open just wide enough for me to enter. No one stood on the far side. No smiling face popped out to welcome me. Only darkness and a breath of dusty air came from within Abdul Shah's bizarre temple.

I stepped inside.

4

The first thing that happened was a woman's voice said, "Stop." I heard a scrape, a clink of chains. Someone locked the door behind me. The light from outside disappeared. A bulb came on, faint and ghostly, one of those rechargeable lanterns the survey teams carry. The woman stepped forward.

"Shayreen Scott," I said, recognizing her face from the file.

She smiled.

I'll tell you what the file says, Carter. It says that Shayreen Scott, until she picked up this assignment, was a perfectly unexceptional nine-to-fiver. Someone who filed her reports, logged her expenses, never slacked off or did a lick of extra work. The pragmatic type.

That didn't fit with the woman I saw now. She had the eyes—kooky eyes. Fanatical. And a smile, broad, scary, like a born-again believer.

She'd been in this place for all of eighteen hours.

"Over there." Shayreen pointed into the gloom. "You can leave your phone."

By 'can,' I figured, she meant, 'you'd better.' The room was an unfinished lobby, cheaply constructed. Against one wall, they had a pile of phones, headsets, gadgets, laptops, watches. Every type of personal tech, dumped on the floor in no discernible order. I wondered how to keep my phone from disappearing in the mix.

"I wouldn't worry." Shayreen noticed my hesitation. "You won't be wanting that thing back, anyway."

Because in another few minutes, her tone implied, I'd have other matters on my mind.

A kind of marble slab, an unfinished desk, stood near the wall. I set my phone on top, noticing a slew of other phones already there, gathering dust, some of them among the newest models.

"Hold it." Shayreen turned me around. Gently, like she'd noticed a tarantula on my chest. "Thought so." She opened my collar and found the wire. "You should understand," she said, as she picked at the tape, "this isn't a matter of security. This is for your own benefit."

No doubt. Shayreen set the bug on the desk, ready for later pickup.

"Ready? This way."

It was like a theme-park ride, that building. I used to go to those places with my daughters, Disney World, Universal Studios. They always bring you through a little tunnel before you go on the big attractions. Putting you in the mood, making a break from the outside world. The halls in Shah's tower had carpet on the floors, frosted glass wall sconces, rows of closed doors. I tried to picture the people who had lived here—until I remembered that, till now, nobody ever had.

In three turns we came to an elevator bank. Shayreen hit the button. "You have electricity," I blurted, forgetting this had been in the case file. Not that pirated electrics are unusual.

Shayreen nodded. "Some."

"But no lights."

"No lights," she said, in a way that made me understand this was intentional.

Even in the elevator, no overheads came on. Which meant they had done some tricky things with the wiring. "Would you mind explaining to me," I said, "what's going on?"

"Distractions." Shayreen gestured at the overheads. "They're very deliberate about limiting distractions. This?" She held up her lantern. I wasn't sure if she meant the light itself, or me, or the whole situation. "This is an exception."

"Listen." I got close, dropping my voice. "If you're in any danger here, if you're being held prisoner . . . "

Shayreen gave no answer. Only a glance of those kooky eyes.

"Here we are."

We'd come to a high floor, not quite the top. I heard a faint noise, a distant thumping. Wind.

Shayreen turned down a dark hall. Over her shoulder, I saw light at the end, crooked lines that shifted and changed. It was one of the tower windows, blocked with a board that thumped and trembled in the shore breeze.

We left the hall. You'll have to forgive me, Carter. This is where I start to doubt my own memories. I'm hard-pressed to swear that all of this really happened.

The building, at this height, was far from finished—essentially, a metal-and-mineral shell. Along the naked ceiling, bundles of wires ran, hooked to lights that no one was using. Stacks of brick lay all around. The floor was bare cement, the internal walls incomplete. Far off, I saw rows of glimmering squares, outlines of boarded-up windows.

But I couldn't see much else. The place was packed, filled with shreds of hanging sheet. Clear rubber, tent material, bedsheets, even those rubbery strips they have in grocery stores. They hung from the ceiling, dividing the space into tent-like chambers, a maze of gauzy makeshift cells.

And in those cells, quiet and still, lay the people.

Shayreen had already gone far ahead. I hurried after her, skipping over jugs, boxes, empty food containers. Garbage had been scattered all over the floor. And buckets. Yikes, those buckets.

"What is all this?"

I winced at the volume of my voice. You could tell, looking around, that it was wrong to speak in that place. Shayreen's lantern, weak even at its highest setting, lit only about ten feet of floor. Every once in a while, as she strolled along, a face passed through its feeble light. Old faces, young faces, women, men. The people lay on cots or pallets, even on the bare floor. Once, I saw a face I recognized, bearded and freckled, a man from one of our field teams. He lay silently, like the others, eyes closed. Serene.

"These people . . . ?" I whispered.

Shayreen turned to me. I didn't need to see her face to know she was making hush-hush signals.

"They're concentrating." Shayreen pulled me close. "They're not asleep. They hear everything you're saying. Be respectful."

"But what are they doing?" I asked.

"Practicing." And then, as if she thought she might have said the wrong thing, "They have to focus. It takes a great deal of discipline. They're waiting."

"For what?"

"To be visited."

A woman near us had begun to stir, rolling on her grungy blanket, moaning. In frustration? Pain? Shayreen pulled me away.

"Come on," she said, guiding me. "You'll soon understand."

We walked the rows of silent faces. How many, in total? Five hundred? A thousand? Did they fill the building, I wondered, floor to roof, a town's worth of people, lying silently in the dark? Concentrating, Shayreen had said. Practicing. Waiting.

"Up here." Shayreen pointed to an open door, a set of concrete stairs leading up. No guards blocked our way, no barriers. A dank wind blew down, the wind of the tropics, moaning through the empty halls. I heard it, whistling among the girders, rippling through construction nets that whipped from the building like shredded pennants. This was the wind of the Malacca Strait, the mighty breath of the Andaman Sea, blowing over a room of sleepers who were not actually, in fact, asleep.

"What's up there?" I asked.

But Shayreen had vanished. Turning, I saw her lantern on the ground, between an army blanket and a strip of weather-tenting. Before the light went out, I caught a glimpse of her face. She had already lain down and closed her eyes. Now she rested with her fellows in the gloom, practicing, meditating, concentrating, waiting.

In darkness, fumbling at the wall, I climbed the stairs.

5

Here's a question, Carter, you may not have been expecting.

Ever move out of a large apartment?

You know how it goes. You chuck out your knickknacks. The movers come in and saw your sofa in half.

Soon enough it's over, and you do a last walk-through. Checking for dropped cards, grandma's old photos, the kind of damage that'll attract the insurance folks. Maybe just saying a sentimental goodbye.

That's when it hits you. Like the walls are suddenly closer, the floors less expansive, the whole place contracting. Vacant, the apartment seems magically smaller. The very emptiness becomes surreally claustrophobic.

That was the effect of Abdul Shah's quarters. He had taken a floor of the building for himself, a broad, empty space, half as large as a soccer field. In the center was the elevator shaft, a cinderblock column, punching up through floor and roof. An incomplete staircase rose beside it, the framework complete, the stairs still to come. Sunlight blasted down this empty well, a column of tropical gold spilling out onto the floor. It would have made a natural spotlight for Abdul Shah to stand in, awaiting my arrival.

He wasn't there. It took me a minute to find him. I walked behind the elevator shaft, where the light was like a dusty pollen in the dark. A skinny figure stood against the wall, holding back the edge of a tarpaulin, looking out the glassless window.

The first thing that struck me about Shah was his Americanness. Maybe that sounds presumptuous. But there's a kind of poise we Americans have, like a man being pushed from behind. *Look out*, this posture declares, *I have big plans, get with me or get out of the way!* Even our priests and mystics have this quality, which is probably why they always turn into hustlers. I was surprised to see that Abdul Shah had it, too.

The second thing I noticed was his bookish air. He wore thick-framed glasses, a trim little beard. Everything about him, down to his check shirt and corduroys, seemed to belong in a New England university. He didn't look like a Brooklynite, a soldier, a beach rat, a visionary. He looked like the kind of scholar who studies those people.

He waved me over.

"Your people are gathering." Abdul Shah held aside the tarp, making room for me to join him at the window. It was the only window I'd seen so far that hadn't been boarded up. I crossed the floor, scanning the huge room as I did so. A cluster of equipment stood in one corner. Telescoping stands, tripods and bulbs, the kind of stuff you see at a photo shoot. A whiff of marshy odor came from outside, stinking of fish and coastal runoff, the salty tang of tidal mud. Looking down, I saw that the Medan police chief had begun to assemble his men around the tower, checking their shields and helmets and gear.

Abdul Shah's tone was matter-of-fact. "How long do you think we have?"

I looked for Colm and Karen, but saw no sign of them. They must have gone back into the command tent. "Those aren't my people down there," I said. "Those are the Medan police."

"Close enough." Shah spoke with a confidence that made me bristle. He dropped the tarp. He was a shortish man, slight of build, but with a quiet air that put me on my guard. "So? What's the estimate? An hour? Two?"

"Forty minutes," I told him. "More like thirty-five."

Shah fell silent. Not alarmed, I sensed, but thinking things over.

"In thirty minutes," he said, "if nothing has changed, I'll tell my followers to leave the building."

Reasonable terms. If he held to them.

"If nothing has changed, eh?" I looked him in the eye.

Shah smiled. "I think I deserve a chance to explain myself." His arms hung limply at his sides, nothing moving but his lips. This, at least, gave him a guru-like demeanor, this unconscious scorn for wasted movement. "If I can't change your mind in half an hour," he said, "then by all means . . . " A twitch of his finger indicated the floor, the hundreds of people lying below. "That *is* why you're here, isn't it? Let's not waste time. You have an argument to make. I do, too. I assume this is what you expected, Mister Lam?"

I thought about the people under us. Five hundred, nine hundred, maybe a thousand, all meditating or waiting or whatever it was they were doing. Eating cold rice and pissing in buckets. Followers of this man. I knew I had to speak carefully.

"My argument," I said, pointing out the window, "is those police down there. Plus a corporate security team equipped with the day's best acoustic weaponry. You know what that means. Here's the deal. I can arrange for temporary shelter for your people. Two, maybe three months in a refugee camp. Protected transportation. Onsite medical care. *If* this goes well."

Shah nodded. "I understand."

"And you?"

"My argument," he said, "is over here."

He pointed to the corner, the equipment I'd noticed earlier. Big, blocky devices stood mounted on poles. As we approached, I saw that these were speakers, powerful ones, the kind that get deep into the low ranges. Shah clicked on a lamp. He had five lamps in total, arranged in a square, one hanging from the exposed girders overhead. These weren't ordinary light fixtures, but advanced machines that gave out a shifting, unsteady glow. Entrancing.

I stood back. "And what's all this for? Meditation?"

"In a sense," Shah said.

I almost laughed. It was like something out of a cult-leader's handbook. "And you need all this fancy equipment? No candles? No incense?" Seeing that the whole setup had been rigged to a MacBook resting on a stack of pallets, I bent over to study the screen. Shah smiled and gently folded shut the computer.

"No incense," he said. "Though it wouldn't hurt."

He fiddled with the overhead lamp. A spiral bulb, bright as a tiny star, glared through a nest of reflectors and filters.

"The candle," Shah said, "is very much an artificial light source. Like any artificial stimulus, it produces particular effects. A dreamlike state. Heightened imagination. Theological inclinations, perhaps a weakness for Cartesian theology." He winked. "The intent of this setup is . . . well, slightly different."

Shah tweaked a dial on the side of the lamp. A whine of machinery accompanied subtle adjustments. The light changed, breaking into a fluid, dappled pattern, a kind of spray of color and shadow. Like sunlight shimmering through leaves . . .

"These are sunlamps," Shah said. "Very advanced ones. If you head up to Bangkok or down to Bali, you'll see them in the new resorts. They advertise these as 'phototherapy.' The radiation is filtered through several kinds of crystal and gas, designed to mimic ambient light. Not a raw blast of radiation, as you get in a tanning bed. More like the healthy glow of a forest." He smiled again. "It's not necessary to use these," he said. "But I find it helps."

He reminded me of an English gardener, puttering around a tangled plot of roses. "So you sit here under these lamps," I said, standing back with my hands in my pockets, "soaking up the rays, and . . . what? What's the point?"

Shah's face betrayed surprise. He adjusted his glasses. "I'm sorry. That's not the intent at all. I'm not going to sit here, Mister Lam. You are."

Of course. I should have known. I stepped into his thicket of tanning-salon accessories. "So I'll squat down here, and you'll work your mojo on me, and you think I'll end up converting to your brave new religion? That's the deal?"

Shah adjusted one of the speakers, smiling that funny smile. "These speakers, now . . . these are from an American home theater system. They're perfectly safe. Unlike the acoustic weapons you threatened me with, they're designed to be pleasingly stimulating. The body . . . " He broke off, scratching his chin. "Let me start again. The *self*, I should say, isn't confined to the body. It isn't here, or here, or even *here*." He touched his chest, his belly, his cranium. "It's out here." Shah spread his arms. "In the sensorium. The environment. The self *converges* on the body, but it's not *contained* in the body. Do you follow?"

I sighed. He sounded exactly like the sort of babbling crackpot I'd expected. I shuffled to the center of his lights and speakers. "Just to clarify: I'll sit here and put up with your little sensory therapy session. Twenty minutes, no more. And when this is over, whatever the effect, you'll give the word and clear your people out."

"All I ask," Shah said, "is that you have an open mind."

He had no prayer rug, no stool, no reed mat. He didn't seem to care if I stood or sat. "And where will you be," I said, "while I'm grooving to these good vibrations?"

"I'll be right here," Shah said. "Talking to you. Because the words, Mister Lam . . . " Again with that weird smile. "The words are the most important part."

It happens that, despite my background, I know a thing or two about the power of hypnosis.

I can thank my wife for that. My second wife. Not Terry or Linda or Fey-Long, but Francine. She went in for New Age stuff. Aroma therapy, cryotherapy, drawing Jackson Pollock pictures in pig blood while neoprimitives in yoga pants shout in your ear. Francine was into some nutty stuff, but she taught me a lot of good lessons, too. She taught me how the nutty stuff works, or makes people think it works. About the uncanny power of suggestion.

Hypnosis. It's real, Carter. Not the wacky things you've heard, past-life regression and out-of-body trips. I mean the classic deal, mesmerism, the power of the voice. Those people who imagine alien visits and talking hippos, they aren't faking it. They really see those things.

The smartest thing Francine ever told me is that when a word's in the air, it's only a wave. When it enters your ear, it's only a vibration. But when a word gets into your head, into your brain, it becomes a chemical. And chemicals, those are the keys to the soul.

As I sat down amid Abdul Shah's lamps and stands and sound generators, I honestly thought I was prepared. Prepared for something a little intense, even for a heavy trip.

But I wasn't prepared for anything like this.

I can't remember what Abdul Shah said. His words, at first, were ordinary words, the kinds of things any hypnotist might say. *You feel relaxed. You're very calm.* He turned on his speakers. The light began to change. I wanted to open my eyes, but to my surprise I found I couldn't move. The sound waves had taken hold of me.

Imagine the ocean, the way it heaves on a windy day. The waves don't simply break over your head, when you go swimming on a day like that. They *squeeze* you. They grab hold of your guts and ribs. They pump your lungs, press your heart. Pretty soon you have no choice. You're forced to breathe in the rhythm of the sea.

That was the effect, albeit more potent, created by Shah's array of speakers. No sooner had it taken hold than Shah began to change his speech. Now he recited gibberish, or what sounded like gibberish. His voice skipped up and down, hitting odd pitches. It was more like singing than talking or chanting. A crazy kind of singing, like he was part of an ensemble, but all the other parts had been cut out. The light pounded against my eyes. I could feel the radiation from the lamps, a burning tingle.

Before long, Shah changed it up again. He began to repeat odd sounds, varying them in a mixed-up rhythm. Noise and light, voice and thought, pulsed and combined in a calibrated pattern. I couldn't think. I mean that literally—I seemed to have no control of my mind. But I understood, in the meaty way of the body, that this was all leading to a terminal event. Not like a rocket heading for a target, but like a net that slowly loosens—until at last I slipped through, falling into an abyss.

Shah must have spoken a triggering word. His speakers and lamps delivered one final, precisely keyed, mind-busting blast. I realized that my mind was a shell, and that it was cracking, exposing a secret, internal place.

And into that place came . . .

Something.

Only later, as I put my mind, Humpty-Dumpty-like, back together, did I find the words for what had happened.

I'd been visited.

6

"Mister Lam?" Shah bent over me, backlit by his array of lamps. Even in silhouette, face in shadow, he looked worried, uncertain, and very, very tired. "Mister Lam, your pants are calling you."

I blinked into the gaping void that remained of my short term memory. Where the hell had I gone? What the hell had happened? Gradually, I realized that Shah was right. A voice was rising out of my pants, emanating from the naughtiest part of my anatomy.

"Doug? Doug? Can you hear me, Doug?"

I staggered up. The light was different, softer. The air in the room felt different, too, less punishingly stuffy than when I had arrived. I stumbled past the lamps to the window, yanked back the tarp.

The sun was setting over the western hills.

Red marked the horizon. Pink beams slanted down the black, scoured valleys. Below, on the pavement, the riot police sat waiting, shields laid flat on the ground at their feet. A few played cards around an overturned water barrel. I could see the screen of their gambling machine flickering in the fading light.

"Doug, I'm getting worried. Are you there? Can you answer?"

I shoved a hand down my pants, fumbled at my groin, and ripped the wads of micropore tape off my skin. I lifted Karen's miniphone on a strip of medical fabric. "I'm here, Karen. What's up?"

"What's up? What's up is that I've been fighting tooth and nail to buy you more time. Doug, what in the world's going in there? You're not hurt, are you? Have you been restrained?"

Hurt? I blinked at the miniphone in my fist, trying to remember the person I'd been this morning, that man named Doug Lam who participated without hesitation in ordinary conversations. Corporate stooge, experienced site investigator, moderately skilled negotiator. Was that me? "Karen?" I ran my tongue around my mouth. "How long has it been?"

"Doug, I'm serious—"

"I have no clock, Karen. They took my phone. Tell me, *how long*?"

Her answer came back on a surge of static. "Six hours." Karen's voice rose. "I've been calling you, Doug, for *six damn hours*."

Glancing over my shoulder, I saw Abdul Shah, standing amid his collection of speakers, waiting for me to finish the call.

"What's *happening*?" Karen's voice cracked with exhaustion.

I was already talking, so fast I could hardly breathe. "Don't let them do it. Karen. Don't let them come in here. Get me as much time as you can."

"Doug, for God's sake—"

I'd already clicked off the miniphone, dropped it into my shirt pocket, and crossed the floor to face Abdul Shah.

"Tell me." I spoke simply, not commanding or begging, merely issuing a humble request. "Tell me what just happened."

He turned his back, fussing with something hidden behind his equipment. "This may take a moment." Shah spoke over his shoulder, straightened, turned, used his heel to kick shut the door of a minifridge, and held out a dripping can. "Would you like a Sprite?"

Usually, when people have an experience like this, they tell you it simply can't be described.

I dunno, man, it was surreal, y'know, like, intense, like, I couldn't begin to describe it.

Bullshit. The truth is, there are thousands of ways to describe what I'd been through. And all of them have been tried before.

That was what Abdul Shah undertook to explain, as he turned down his lamps and clicked off his speakers and sat me down with a can of lemon pop.

"It's not so esoteric. Every culture has a version. Usually several versions. In the West, for instance, people talk about ghosts, bodily possession. There's the concept of the muse: an invisible companion, offering vision and inspiration. Even the word *genius* goes back to the idea: a visitation from a presence that is like us, but more than us. It's an old, ineradicable insight: that we are not alone in this world. That we are, at times, visited by spirits."

I watched his hands, thin, knobby fingers clawed around his soda can. Looking at those hands, you could believe he had lived a rough life, hunting insurgents through the Pashtun deserts, weathering storms on a Caribbean beach. Sometimes he reached out and stroked the dials on his arrangement of lamps and speakers. His arm trembled. Abdul Shah might look like a college professor, but he had a hermit's fingers and bones.

"This was more than that," I said. "More than a spirit. It was . . . "

How to say it? I couldn't stop looking at Shah's equipment. A few home theater components, doodads from a sauna . . . it was the modernity of his operation that dazzled me. How did he manage to do what he did, with a rig borrowed from a California retreat?

Shah straightened his glasses. "More than a spirit, yes. A *feeling*. But the feeling, the essence, is always the same. A doubling. A presence. Not happiness, exactly, but a sense of profoundly heightened perception. The Greeks spoke of a daimon, a kind of guiding personal deity. And of course, you know all about Buddhists, mystics, desert hermits, the many varieties of meditation. In Islam, Allah is not merely *out there*, like some kind of abstract deistic authority." His hand moved vaguely toward the ceiling. "He is *with us*. Watching. He is here right now—if we will learn to notice him."

Shah was watching my own hands. He must have read something in them, a twitch of skepticism, a twinge of doubt.

"I'm not religious, myself." Shah laid his bony hand briefly over mine. "I was raised in America. I *fought* for America. My people go back to the scholars of North Africa—the original founders of modern science. It was science that led me to this." His hand indicated the machines, the coiling wires, the MacBook glowing on its stand. "The irony is that in putting the old fantasies behind us— the gods and demons, the ghosts and spirits—we forgot about something more important. We forgot how to pray."

The evening wind slipped in around the hoardings, wet and cool with the mist off the bay. The sound it made was almost funny, like a child's imitation of the howl of a ghost. I wanted to challenge Shah's mystical theories, but the effects of his treatment still clung to my mind. The sensation was richer than what he described. A presence, yes, but also a kind of sadness, like a fleeting memory from long ago.

Shah nodded and smiled, reading my thoughts. It occurred to me that he'd already had this talk with hundreds of people: those dazed and devoted followers, lying in the darkness below.

"Understand." Shah held up a palm. "Prayer isn't magical. Like anything else, it's a physical process. The neuroscientists are beginning to understand it in their own way. But so much of the art has been lost, there's now very little for them to study. These people?" His head tipped toward the floor. "They're learning to recover it. Not modern meditation. Not juice cleanses and therapy. The true, ancient art of opening the mind. This kind of prayer was only a fading memory in the mystery rites of Ancient Greece. It had already been half lost when the shrines of the Ancient Egyptians rose from the sands. It's a way of worship known only to the first people, the early men and women, who lived with spirits all their lives. With practice, it can be relearned. The techniques I used on you are awkward and crude. But vital. We're trying to break open a very heavy lock."

I shook my head. What Shah had done to me was anything but crude. I told him as much, but he chuckled and wiped his glasses.

"Well, any man can fly, if you put him in a catapult and cut the rope. *Controlling* flight, that's another story." Shah stood and drifted among his equipment, tuning this, adjusting that, like an artist who can't stop fiddling with his work. His voice, his manners, his every movement, had taken on some of the rhythms of his ritual, as if he were unconsciously attuned to secret sources of music.

"The words," Shah said, "they're the challenging part. Suggestion, the power of speech: it can be very powerful, if used well. But it has to be tailored for different cultures. In a way, I find it easier to work in this country, honing my techniques in a foreign language. It helps me remember that words are only a technology—a very old tool for reprogramming the brain."

"But how did you learn—?" Nothing he had said, so far, came near to addressing what I wanted to know. "How did you figure out how to do this?"

"To rewrite the mind? To access the wetware of the soul?" He smiled as he recited these familiar clichés. "I didn't. Yes, I put together this setup. It took me decades. But the underlying techniques, the fundamentals—these were shown to me. Taught to me, I think you could say."

"By whom?"

Shah didn't answer. His eyes were on the far wall, watching the window he'd been gazing through when I arrived. The tarpaulin had pulled loose and stretched out to flutter like a flag in the evening sky. "You know," Shah said, "we actually *do* very little, once we've truly learned to pray. It's really a matter of clearing the mind, making room within oneself. It's then . . . "

He paused. A strange buzzing had begun to shake the air, bristling and needling, like iron filings twitching toward a magnet. I set down my untasted Sprite. "It's then?"

Shah's eyes were still on the window. He put out a hand, touching the frame as if to steady himself. "It's then," Shah said, as a fusillade of gel bags began to pound the walls, "that they come to us."

8

The modern gel-round is a tidy piece of munitions. A flexible sac of viscous polymer, cased and laced in an electric mesh, it can squeeze into nearly any shape. With the right launcher, it can be shot, in the form of an aerodynamic needle, over distances of five hundred feet or more. On impact, or at the spark of an embedded trigger, it flattens into a pancake and sheds most of its momentum. With that transition, it throws out a distinctive shockwave, a thump that'll almost pop your ears.

Colm had programmed his barrage with care. Four squares of plywood burst suddenly inward, making four holes in the centers of the walls. Splinters flashed in the sunset; eight nails pinged to the floor. Five holes now gaped to the night, ready to receive whatever Colm chose to throw through them.

The buzzing grew louder. I followed Shah to the window, reaching out to catch the flapping tarp. The ground seemed to spin and tilt far below, dark under a purple sky. In the half light, I could see the police gearing up. Three sulfur lamps beamed on the fabric of the command tent. Two tiny figures stood out front. They might have been chatting or flirting or fighting, for all I could tell looking down from this height. I recognized Colm and the police chief by the colors of their uniforms: black and gray.

Shah gazed straight ahead, to the eastern horizon, where Belawan blazed in the hollow of its harbor. A spot of darkness crawled slowly across the city lights. The buzzing grew louder—a feeling more than a noise, like a nail scraping along my skull.

I pulled out my miniphone. "Karen? Hello?"

Her voice came to me across a gulf of exhaustion. I wondered if I'd caught her sleeping. "Doug?"

"What's going on down there?"

A pause. I reminded myself that this woman had been awake for the better part of a week, surviving on sugar and synthetic hormones. "Doug, I think I've done all I can."

Shah was still holding back the tarp, watching the angry shadows of Colm's drones as they climbed slowly across the sky. I cupped my hand around the phone, trying to dampen the vibrations in the air.

"Karen, Colm's drone fleet is up here, gathering around the building. They're sending out the preliminary signal. I thought we'd all agreed that this kind of acoustic assault would be a very bad idea."

Her voice seemed to recede each time she spoke, as if she'd set the phone down and run away, fleeing across the black marshes. "It's a pissing match. You know how this goes." A crackle of static nearly killed the signal. Karen's voice crept into audibility. "The police chief says he's waited long enough. He's sending in his riot teams. Colm says that if the chief does that, he's going to launch his own attack."

"They're both crazy."

Another burst of fuzz. Colm's drone fleet was mucking up the signal. "Get out." Karen's voice fought through the interference, repeating one injunction. "Get out . . . get out . . . "

I turned. Abdul Shah jerked as I grabbed his arm. He was stronger than he looked, skinny but firm. "Send the word." I pulled him back from the window. "Tell your people it's time to evacuate. Now."

Shah's tongue darted along his lips. He had the expression he'd worn when I first told him how little time we had, not frightened, exactly, but thoughtful, calculating.

"Listen." I pulled him toward the stairs. "That buzzing? That's the preliminary waveform. They'll run that pattern for a bit, tuning up. It could go on for ten minutes. Could be thirty. We have a little time. But not much."

Shah looked over his equipment, tapping his teeth with his tongue, as if counting.

"Shah." I wanted to shake him. "You've got to send down the word. Tell your people what's happening here."

His eyes settled on mine. "It's as you said." A smile passed across Shah's lips. "They're not really my people, Mister Lam."

The noise of the drones had settled into an ambient distraction. Shah's voice rose like a melody above the discordant tones. "These people chose to stay here. To learn, to practice. I only teach them what I can."

I shook my head. We had too little time.

"Shah!" I was shouting, now, overloud, the noise of the drones playing havoc with my hearing. "Tell them to leave!"

Shah looked confused. A new sound rose over the background hum, a squawk that echoed off the naked walls. I recognized the cadences of north Sumatran Hokkien, Medan's contemporary lingua franca. The police chief had brought out a megaphone.

"Mister Lam." Shah sank between my hands. "You don't understand. I *did* tell them."

I released him. Outside the window, the hovering drones hung buzzard-like in the night, blotting bird-sized swatches of stars. Below, the riot police were assuming formation, blocking off the tower's three exits. A ramming team approached the bolted front doors. I saw no fugitives fleeing the tower, no refugees huddled on the pavement below. Only that ring of donated food, all of it worse than useless now. And the bright sulfur lamps, and the gleaming helmets, and the tiny figures of Colm and the police chief, preparing to wage turf war over our corpses.

"It was while you were in your trance." Shah drifted to the window beside me, looking down at the commotion with that smug quietude that was the most cultish thing about him. "I spoke to your colleague. The woman who brought you to me. Shayreen. I explained that we were out of time."

The riot police had taken position: knots of manpower at every exit, a complement of carbon-fiber shields and clubs. My concern was with the point teams that would soon come charging up the stairwells, throwing out shock grenades and wielding batons. The lead ramming crew had already set up their unit, a black frame that fully surrounded the front doors. A pneumatic device, a kind of giant cattle-gun, it would scan the entrance for structural features, then punch it to pieces with a computer-controlled battery of steel bolts.

"If the people are still here," Shah said, "it must be because they want to stay. For as long as they can."

"Praying," I said.

Shah watched with resignation. "You understand. Don't you?"

A blaring command from the police chief's megaphone broke into our conversation. Instantly, a series of concussions shook the building. A stutter of bolts. A crash of glass. The concrete floor shivered as the entranceway collapsed. With a rumble of boots, the cops came in, their shouts and footfalls echoing up the silent floors.

Did I? I wondered. *Did I understand?*

"Mister Lam?" Shah held my hand, pressing it between both of his. "Let me explain something to you."

9

Do you need the details, Carter?

You have the engineer's report. You know the facts. Is there any point in reciting a series of figures you'll be hearing in courtrooms for the next ten years?

Fifty million in unforeseen damages. The pylons, carbon-netted, seated on ten square acres of in-situ, bore-injected micropilings—half of those will have to be replaced. The platform, the vehicle fleet, the command center: gone. Even Colm's drone fleet took a major hit. Half of them failed to find their backup recharge station.

Shall I go on? Shall I tally the losses? The payouts to families of the Medan police? The mob of lawyers you're going have to draft to untangle the thicket of indemnities? The insurance payments? The gifts and bribes?

But all this is rather soothingly cut-and-dried, isn't it? All this talk of dollars and contracts, it hardly touches the heart of the matter. Because when it comes to the key issue, Carter, the one you don't want to talk about, the one no one *ever* wants to talk about . . .

I suppose we'll never know how many people were in that tower. How many bodies, waiting in the dark, trying to shut out the outside world, even as that world came for them with a vengeance.

Kooks and fanatics, you'll say. Dupes and fools. It sure feels good to use those words. Most of those people won't even rate a glib dismissal, because no one will ever know who they were. Undocumented drifters, even before they came to Shah, even before one hundred thousand tons of slipshod construction buried them in steel and debris. Most of the dead will never be tallied. Not their bodies, not their teeth, not their DNA. They'll rot in peaceful anonymity, beneath the coastal Sumatran mud.

I bet you'd like to ask me one thing. I bet you'd like to ask if I know why. Why did they do it? Why did they stay? Even as the dust began to settle on their faces, even as the cracks were rising like black lightning up the walls—why did they claim those precious moments, those last few seconds of prayer and concentration? Do I know what they saw, what they hoped to see, in the final second when the floor fell away and the roof came crashing down?

A lock, that's how Abdul Shah described it. Breaking a lock to open the mind. He made it clear that I'd only begun the process; my session had been interrupted by Karen's calls. I had caught a faint glimmer of the wonders to be seen.

And if I'd been allowed to continue my study? If I had received what Shah called a "true visitation"?

I can hear you muttering, Carter, out there in your air-conditioned office. You're a college boy. You know your history. I know what you're thinking, because I used to think it too. I looked on them all with contempt and disbelief—

All those millions of seers and followers.

All those countless dead fools and saints.

10

They call it "wave warfare" for a reason. A lot of people think they know what that means. It's all done with sound, intersecting shockwaves. Under the right conditions, those waves can kill.

What fewer people know is that a sonic attack, as programmed by our people, comes in waves of intensity. The drones Colm deploys, they follow a script. They hit their victims hard, then dial down the assault. They allow for a rest, then crank things up. The intent is to stimulate predictable behavior. First, unease. Then confusion. Then panic. Then flight.

The first wave hit us while Shah was halfway through his story. The buzzing of the drones became a tooth-numbing whine. This sound, I knew, was only a warning. The real attack would be inaudible at first, and it would come in stages. First a deformation of the eyes, disorientation and blurring sight. Next, a throb of pressure in the guts—not pain, exactly, but a sense of something wrong. After that, the hardcore waves would hit, running through our chests like a ripple of static. Our lungs would begin to quiver and squirm. The air would simply *leave* us, in a frittering *whoosh*, and our tissues and brain and our blood itself would let out a long black scream for oxygen.

I braced myself, waiting for the attack to run its course. By the time it was over, Shah had fallen to the floor, twitching and drooling down his check shirt. I grabbed his arm and pulled him to his feet, knowing the real danger hadn't yet come.

"This way!"

He ran in the wrong direction at first, trying to reach the stairs to the lower floors. I yanked him back, leading him past the elevator. Already, cracks had begun to lace the plaster, spilling chips and powder to the floor. The whole shaft hummed; I could hear it moaning like a tuba as soundwaves propagated past the lower floors. I pounded the button. I wasn't surprised to get no response. The Medan police had found their way to the electrics.

"Shah, stop." He was still pulling for the staircase. I pointed at the nearby floor. A crack had zig-zagged out from one corner, following a scar-colored seam in the cement. "That was the first wave," I told Shah. "In about five minutes, they'll hit us again. We have exactly that long to get ourselves out of range, before this whole structure starts shaking like hammered glass." I swung my pointing finger, along the crack, past the stairs. "We have no time to get down to the ground. But we can still try to go up to the roof."

Shah's lips moved silently. Either he didn't understand, or he thought I'd completely lost my mind.

I had no time to argue. I dropped his arm and ran. The unfinished stairwell rose above, a twenty-foot column of empty space. Dust whirled down in spiral clouds, shaken loose by the sonic blast. A metal framework laced the walls, offering a scaffold for risers and steps that would never be installed. Rust and dirt gritted under my hand as I tested the strength of the nearest beam. It creaked, but the bolts held. It would make a serviceable ladder—for anyone crazy enough to dare the climb.

"Up here." Already poised on the lowest support, I squatted to peer at Shah through the door. "If we climb ten feet, we'll be out of range. It's only a couple of floors till we're in the open. If we go that way," I pointed down the other staircase, "we'll be chased all the way by those sonic weapons. Right into the clubs of the police."

Shah stood where I'd left him, in the middle of the floor. The drones had begun to give out their warning whine. He reached out. That's what I'll always remember. At the last moment, Shah put out his hand. It was this image I held in my mind as the second attack hit and my vision blurred and everything around us began to break and fall.

I leapt for a higher handhold. The stairwell moaned around me, an echo of the resonance pattern building outside. I scrambled for purchase, kicking my toes against the wall, remembering with dismay the dozens of chin-ups I'd been able to do as a younger man. A nail or bolt must have raked my arm. By the time I got halfway up the shaft, I was leaving crooked trails of blood on the wall.

Adrenaline is a wonderful drug. Hearing the booming and cracking below, I groped for the next beam, then the next. Scrambling and heaving, muscles blazing, I dragged myself out of range of Colm's weapons, crawling into that desolate stretch where the building stood open to the wind and stars. I clung like a baby to the nearest girder, holding fast to a structure that had begun to sway scarily with each gust. A shock of noise came from below, a pop and boom like a canon discharging. I was still trying to get a grip on the steel when the dust clouds began to circle and stir, a rumble of rotors climbed the dark, and Karen, guiding the company copter, plucked me away into the safety of the sky.

The typical improvised explosive device is a load of cheap, often plastic explosives, triggered by spark and packed with shrapnel. Ordinary scrap metal, launched by the blast, can snip vital arteries and mangle limbs. For the enterprising terrorist, insurgent, or sadist, a disposable phone makes a handy trigger. But simple pressure plates are lower in cost, easy to construct, and a staple in the trade of dealing death.

During the height of America's oil wars, making such a bomb could cost somewhat less than buying a new video game system. The blast power ranged from an ineffective fizzle to a blow strong enough to flip an armored truck, launch an engine block onto a roof, or strip the face off a concrete building.

This is the cruel technology that lies behind the strange fate of Abdul Shah.

A subtle danger of an IED is the shock wave that ripples out from the blast. A surging front of compacted air, it slams the brain into the case of the skull, pops the ears with a drop in pressure, and hit its victims with a one-two punch, as a second wave of compressed air flows into the void left by the first. The result is a double-whammy blow to the head, a savage pulse of compression and expansion that rips through a brain at half the speed of a bullet, straining tissues, frothing blood, making the cerebrum swell like a sponge.

This is the injury that flooded VA hospitals, thirty years ago, with a homecoming army of zombie soldiers. Men who were whole in body and sound of limb, but who frightened their families and puzzled their government by exhibiting bizarre swings in mood. Amnesia, personality changes, confusion: the symptoms tended to worsen with time. Blast Disease, the veterans call it in our day. A steady loss of mental function, atrophying limbs, crushing depression. Even, yes, hallucinations. A slow-acting epidemic that has soldiers Abdul Shah's age committing suicide in droves.

All this I learned in a late-night search through the history pages. Shah learned it, too, when he got his disability discharge, thirty years ago, and came home from the wind-whipped plateaus of central Asia. The army hospitals were too full to hold him. The homeland doctors had no idea how to treat him. His friends and family couldn't understand why he seemed so lost within himself, so changed. Why did Shah ignore their questions, even their loving gestures, in favor of a strange and brooding obsession that he'd brought back with him from the Persian Plateau?

He drifted west for a while, lured by the solitude of the American heartland, then wandered south to the Mexican border. Eventually, he found himself holed up in a cove to the south of St. Thomas, half a mile from the tourist traps of Charlotte Amalie, shielded by a forested ridge from the Norwegian boats and the bright town lights. Nothing lay ahead of him but the waters of East Gregerie Channel, a view past Cowell Point to the open sea. It was there, known and tolerated as a local eccentric, in a nylon tent rigged to the salt-whitened trees, that Abdul Shah begun to hunt within himself for the secret knowledge he had brought back from war.

It was memory that sustained him, in those lonely years. The army doctors told him that the blast of the bomb had left a galaxy of bubbles fermenting in his brain. A rush of merciless pressure, a void of near-vacuum: these arcane forces had whipped Shah's mind like cream, inciting a kind of decompression of the soul.

Tiny bubbles . . . Shah pictured them sometimes, twinkling up from a place deep within him, effervescing into his conscious thoughts. They reminded him of memory, those bright seeds of death—the way stray moments can wink, evanescent, out of the gulf of the long-forgotten past. Sensory impressions: the texture of old wallpaper; the hard, clear odor of a sidewalk after rain. Images came to him unbidden, isolated, as he lay on the stones of his tropical beach. Sprinklers jetting in a city park, concrete pillars spitting bright falling water, his mother's finger tracing arcs of liquid as she spoke the Arabic word for *attraction*. Gravity, magnetism, desire: the modern magic of unseen fields. And more: the green faces of children submersed in a city pool, hair storming in black licks around their cheeks; the sweet, dusty smell of a hardware store. Often Shah thought of the religious billboard that had loomed over the highway near his Brooklyn home, lurid with the painted gods of the Christians: a kneeling woman, a bearded man whom Shah, as a child, had mistaken for Santa Claus. And in the straw between them, a glowing, golden child.

"We are the true Americans," his mother told him once. "We came here, traveled here, chose to be here. That is the only true American: someone who claims this country as home." Abdul had looked at his small hands and thought, *I came here, yes. But where am I* from?

The memories—they were neither happy nor sad. They gripped him, however, because they were true. Time had sharpened their truth and confirmed their worth. As he sat on that Caribbean beach, watching the giant cruise ships travel past Sprat Point, the sights and sensations of Shah's present life took on, themselves, the glamour of the past. The whining, bobbing progress of motorboats in the strait. The thump and rustle of startled iguanas leaping out of the shoreline pines. By day, Shah tramped among the island's weedy ruins, British embrasures, abandoned World War II barracks, the fast-rotting detritus of a failed tourist center. Sometimes kids still kayaked out from the port, hiding with their beers and designer drugs in the fallen estates on the eastern shore; at night he heard their monkey-like cries whooping through the sea grape and the wooded heights. Civilization lay all around him, yet he felt himself as blessedly alone as a man alive in the last days of the earth. And in this state of strange and deepening joy, Shah thought about the desert road where he had nearly lost his life—and began to reconstruct, slowly and painfully, the vision he had been granted there.

The bomb that wounded Abdul Shah was fashioned, records indicate, of one hundred-and-fifty-six pounds of PE-4 wired to a British garage-door opener, packed with propane tanks into a trash disposal unit. It detonated five feet to the left of the driver of Shah's Humvee, shearing away two-fifths of the vehicle, killing three of the four passengers, flipping the chunk of metal that remained into a roadside drainage culvert.

When Shah woke two days later, in the field hospital at Kandahar Air Field, groggy from blood loss, bandaged around the head, he found himself in a drafty compartment of a building rigged from cheap wood and old shipping containers. By that time he was already beginning to forget the details of the remote and peculiar place to which the near-fatal blast had delivered him. But in the silence of his tropical retreat, in the hermitage he fastened for himself, years later, out of twenty square yards of nylon tenting—incredibly, impossibly—it came back.

An iconic image was his first recollection. A dark tunnel, a light at the end. Most dying people see nothing more. But Shah went further. He crossed the tunnel, reached the light. And he pushed his way—or perhaps he was forced—out of the confines of our world.

His first thought was that the smoke from the bomb had enveloped him. Black smoke, oily, heavy and opaque. A moment's observation convinced him, however, that the blackness around him was structured and firm. A kind of frozen darkness constituted the huge walls rising on every side, as well as the roof high over his head—a slick, greasy material that Shah would later compare to volcanic glass. Fashioned into thick columns, this substance stretched into the emptiness above, supporting a vaulted ceiling as remote as a stormy sky. The scale of the construction was cosmic, absurd, like a cathedral molded from the matter of dead suns. Striving later to describe what he had seen, Shah could find no analog, no explanation—save to say that this was nothing human beings had created.

Lifting his head, he saw that his body itself was other than human—a form unrecognizable, even slightly insubstantial. Yet these words, Shah insisted—*sight, head, body*—were approximations to what he perceived. He "saw" nothing, "felt" nothing, but *knew* where he was, with the disembodied knowledge that arrives in dreams. And in this same manner, through this same strange clairvoyance, Shah realized that he was not alone.

They lay all around him, thousands, perhaps millions of figures, reposing, prone, in the infinite dark. No shroud covered them, no sound disturbed their sleep. Shah surmised that they were neither dreaming nor awake, but resting in a state much richer than consciousness, more lucid than the unreal figments of dreams.

A voice spoke, or a mind touched his (again, Shah struggled to find the proper words). He sensed a presence communing with him, both distant and near, like a monster beneath his bed.

Be still. (But it was not a voice, Shah insisted, so much as an extension of that dreamlike understanding.) *You have slipped through the barrier, but you will soon return.*

Where am I? Shah tried to speak. But speech, motion, even ordinary thought, all were impossible in that strange place. He could only think, with a speech-like force: *What am I?*

If the voice had been capable of laughter, its mirth would have echoed endlessly in the recesses of that measureless space. *You were visited. Now, for a moment, you have become the visitor. The currents that carried you here will soon reverse, and you will remember nothing of this place.*

Currents?

You lie in the company of the last sleepers, at the end of time.

As he heard those words (or received into himself, like a jolt of air, the knowledge implicit in those words), Shah understood . . . but it was rather as if he had begun to remember something he had always known.

He had come to the edge of existence, the end of all worlds. A trick of time had delivered him here, to a place where the last living beings rested, the dwindling population of a dying universe. In this latter day, suns and galaxies had dissolved, the bonds of existence had grown dim. What Shah saw was a failing illusion, a shadowplay cast on a thinning screen. Soon, even this frail fabric would decay, and the life of the cosmos would come to its close. No civilizations would again be built, no new worlds or suns would reappear. But in this dying instant, this final tick of time, the beings around him practiced a last art. They had learned to return to what had come before, and to revisit the things that had been.

Even as he learned this, Shah felt a pressure, as if the strange tide that had cast him here were now reversing, dragging him back to his old life. He struggled to move, sensing a different mind, one alien and strong, already striving to reclaim his body. Forcing himself to rise, Shah gained a last glimpse of the great vault in which those countless beings, faint and softly pale, lay like dreamers in a night with no dawn.

They are revisiting the lives, said the voice, *that have passed away, and remembering the moments of former ages. No future lies before them. The past cannot be changed. But they have this: the power to return to what was lost. Through the souls and bodies of those who lived before, they relive, a final time, what will never be again.*

Show me. Shah made his demand in desperation, even as the pressure grew on his mind, even as his spirit twisted and writhed like water above a drain. *Show me what they see.*

Again, the voice laughed with a strength beyond sound. *Very well. You will soon forget. But if you wish, you may visit with us, this one time—*

12

And here Shah's story ended, in a burst of deadly sound.

He told me all this in the empty room of his tower, in that brief respite between the charge of the police and the final assault of the sonic cannons. I believe he spoke for ten minutes at most, lingering on the smallest details. His leisurely manner, his painstaking account, maddened and baffled me at the time. But I don't believe, now, he ever hoped to convince me. Only to convey, somehow, what it meant, what he had been trying to track or rediscover, in the course of his lonely and drifting life.

The sun is rising, Carter, making gleams on the hotel towers. From the rooftop bistros along the river, I can hear the tinkle of coffee cups. I've talked into this recorder through the night, half hallucinating, half in a trance, sometimes reading the scraps of disjointed journals I wrote in a post-traumatic haze. I hope your transcribers and redactors can make something out of this marathon ramble. I tried, God knows. I tried to tell the truth.

And why, I wonder. Why share this with you? Why tell this story to the man who has always hated me, always fought me, always sought to ruin me?

Because you asked for it, I suppose. Because you were there for my first wife and my last, and for all the mistakes and lovers in between. Because you were with me in those days on the fifty-seventh floor, when we fought like two driven single men for the fortune and glory we thought we deserved. Because you know me, Carter, who I am and who I was, and you're probably the only son of a bitch who does.

Shah reached out. That's the part that haunts me. He put out his hand, before the last blast hit, before the ground turned to dust beneath his feet. Even as he sank through his dissolving tower, through the crumbling ruins and the rising clouds, he kept his hand out, fingers curled, as if to take hold of something I couldn't see.

It was a violent wave of sound, tearing through Shah's head on a desert road, that gave him the vision that changed his life. In later years, he studied the physics of sensation, the tangled mechanics of the human brain. Maybe, at the end, with new shockwaves in his skull, Shah found a way back to that world, the dreamers lying at the end of time. Maybe they showed it to him again, the vision he never had a chance to describe. It could be that in the last instant of his life, Shah reached for the hands of Egyptian priests, or the startled eyes of a prehistoric child. Or he may have visited you, or me, in forgotten moments of our idealistic past. Perhaps he looked into the void between the stars, and before he died, he watched suns rising over alien worlds you and I can never imagine.

Quite probably, it all means nothing. Abdul Shah had a brain that by his own admission was full of holes. Men and women with his injuries are lying in the Walter Reed psych wards, now, hiding under their hospital beds from memories of historic wars.

But I remember those six strange hours, the throb of soundwaves through my mind, and the visitation I nearly received. I remember other stray moments of my life, when a weird vibration passed through me, a second soul seemed to clasp my own, as if I had been possessed, invaded, by a presence greater than myself.

I remember this:

A day, years ago, when my first wife and I moved to a new home. We came east, leaving the desiccated outskirts of Phoenix for the humid greenery of the Georgia suburbs. No squatter camps troubled my thoughts back then, no sonic weapons, no impact assessments. I had recently accepted my position at Aerux. I was looking forward to starting my career.

We were still settling in, when on a certain morning, we found we couldn't stop our daughter from crying. She was only a baby, less than half a year old, and we held her, fed her, rocked her, soothed her, carried her on a weary circuit through the house. We ran in an hour through the usual cures, the breast, the diaper, the temperature, the light. But with her little fists, she fought free of our caresses, rolling in our arms, reaching, like a fierce little inchworm, for the windows and the world outside.

I gave in. I took her outdoors. A spring rain had begun to fall, dripping from the roof of our tumbledown veranda, and I saw that her eyes were tracking every drop. I marched into the yard, the rain drizzling on us both, gentle and cool, a prickling presence on my skin. In the open, with my wife yelling at me from the door, I looked into my daughter's eyes.

What are they thinking, our little ones? We look into their faces, but we can't know what they see, what they understand with their bright new minds. My daughter's mouth hung open. At five months, she was already full of memory. We had come from a land of dry earth and empty skies, and I realized she had never seen the rain.

Maybe I'm a fool. Maybe Abdul Shah duped me, as he seduced so many other lost souls. But I know this: that a full ten minutes passed, on that long-ago day, in which my daughter scarcely moved or breathed, but lay with reverent stillness in my arms, watching water fall from the sky. I could have sworn at the time, and I would still swear now, that something came to visit us then, hovering behind her eyes. I felt so joyous I was afraid. She lowered her eyes and looked into my mine, and an awesome intelligence stared into me, full of wonder and longing and a strange, vast regret. It was as if my daughter understood, not only sensations I had forgotten, but ones I hadn't yet begun to feel. As if she knew, even in that early stage of life, that she was seeing all things for the first and last time.

*****end transcript*****

And If the Body Were Not the Soul
A.C. WISE

Ro shoulders the courier bag, leaving the bike chained at the entrance to the Zone. Even here, at the edge, dampness permeates—the air green like a receding tide. The pavement is patchwork. Brick and stone shows through tears in the asphalt, wounds no one bothered to heal once the aliens moved in, once it was clear humans would never move back into the neighborhood and it became the *Zone*.

Weeds grow in the gaps, flourishing in the damp. Ro places each boot carefully, avoiding the puddles reflecting sodium streetlights. On either side of the street, buildings stand with their doors shuttered against the gathering twilight. Some are ragged against the emerging stars, top layers blown away, evidence of the violence that emptied the neighborhood, made it unfit for human habitation, and eventually turned it into the Zone. But close to the ground, the world is still whole. If Ro doesn't look up, it's as though nothing has changed.

Except the Zone is haunted by waiting. The sense of impermanence is palpable—like the refugee camps and shanty towns of the early century, the ones the government planned to empty after the last great flood, or hurricane, but never did. The Zone was meant to be a way station, a temporary solution until the Immies (the word tastes dirty even in Ro's mind, hateful, ugly, but there isn't a better one because the aliens have never given the humans their true name) could be fully integrated into life on Earth. And yet . . .

Ro shrugs against the weight of emptiness and broken promises. At least Xal's light is still on, welcoming. A bell over the door jangles; stepping inside, Ro can't help smiling at this incongruously human touch. It's like the shelves behind the glass counters, crammed floor to ceiling with human knick-knacks and oddities no Immie could possibly want, and no human would come here to buy. Charming, but sad in a way, too. Lonely.

It takes Ro a moment to pick out Xal's form against the crowded shelves. Today, Xal's flesh is the color of sand. It reminds Ro of the fish that disguise themselves from predators by lying flat against the ocean floor. There are variations, tiny glints of light. It is brown only in the way pigeons are simply gray, full of tones unseen until it is pointed out they were there all along.

"Hi." Ro sets the courier bag on the counter—this time full of gamboling ceramic kittens—and places the delivery slip on top.

Xal doesn't respond, which isn't unusual for an Immie, only for Xal. Ro hesitates. Payment is stacked neatly on the counter, as always. Perhaps Xal simply doesn't want to talk. Ro turns, hiding disappointment.

::Tone—Plea/Imperative: Ro. Wait.::

Xal's voice is changeless, only the tone-statement betraying the edge of panic. There are no human or even human-like features to convey pain. But now that Ro looks closer, it is written in the restless knotting of limbs hanging beneath the bulk of Xal's body.

Ro steps forward. Xal shifts, flickering in and out. Barely visible one moment, then sharply outlined the next. Sinuous lines gleam damp, twisting through a host of colors Ro can't begin to name. Ro's breath catches. There, an extra wetness, almost hidden by the tangled lines, a gash leaking fluid, smelling of salt.

"What happened?"

::Tone—Statement/Fear: An accident.:: Ro hears hesitation in Xal's tone; in a human, it might sound like a lie. ::Tone—Statement/Honesty: An attack. In the human district, not far over the line. Just looking.::

Colors roll; Xal fades in and out again.

"You were attacked?"

::Tone—Affirmative/Sorrow: Yes.::

"What can I do to help? Is there someone I can call?"

::Tone—Alarm/Negative: No.::

"Okay." Ro holds up his hands, palms out, hoping Xal will understand the human gesture and feeling helpless.

Xal's body clenches, shuddering, furling tight around the wound. A sound like keening, like an in-drawn breath, like music, traces Ro's jaw and spine. Then the sound stops and Xal unfolds, becoming more solid.

The wound already looks less, but still, a tremor ripples out from Ro's center. Disgust. Ro clenches teeth against the reaction, a reflexive hatred for the uselessness of all flesh. It isn't fair; Xal is wounded, Xal needs help, and this isn't the time. And yet the bone-achingly physical reaction remains, rooted in the very thing causing the revulsion. Flesh. Ro shudders, stepping closer to the counter as if to step away from skin, from muscle, leaving disgust behind.

::Tone—Statement/Sincere: The pain is less. Ro. Thank you for staying.::

A limb uncurls, a jerky, reflexive motion as though Xal is not entirely in control yet. It brushes Ro's hand, braced against the countertop. A new sound, a new quality of pain, laced with surprise. Xal draws back, but not before the touch sparks—a snap like an electric shock and a taste like lemons.

A scream locks in Ro's throat. A sensation of dislocation without motion. A space of falling or flying, existing between the moment of contact and Xal's touch withdrawn. Ro blinks away patches of violet light until the shop comes back into focus, bracing for a horror that never comes.

The lightness of Xal's touch, unlike anything human. Ro lets out a breath, coming back to center.

Xal's limbs are knotted in a new pattern now, anxious.

::Tone—Statement/Fear: Ro. Apology. Pain was not intended.::

"No. I . . . " Ro's breath—ragged—calms, but not fast enough. "It didn't hurt. I don't . . . "

Flying. Falling. Ro struggles to process the sensation of Xal's limb, solid yet ephemeral. The memory of the touch remains, like a lost tooth wanting to be probed. It is a moment of slipping out from under the weight of skin and bones, of being somewhere else, yet wholly here.

Ro tries to draw back from the sensation, but there is nothing to withdraw from.

::Tone—Query/Fear: Not hurt.:: Xal's voice again. Ro's mind thrums to an absence, reaching again for revulsion where there is none.

"No. I should just . . . I'm sorry."

Ro turns, bell jangling. The green scent of the streets is an assault, the slickness underfoot designed to trip un-careful steps. Even the shorter buildings lean in, edges all jagged. They outline an empty space, something that cannot be defined.

On the edge of hyperventilation, Ro bursts out of the Zone. Leaving the bike behind, leaving everything. Not questioning the source of the fear, just running. Then stopping, leaning against a building, a stitch lacing between two ribs.

"Ro?"

Ro looks up, blinking, human buildings and a single figure resolving. Audra slows her bike, dropping one foot to the pavement. The courier satchel at Audra's hip is empty; Ro remembers the bag left with the delivery in Xal's shop, the bike chained to a post at the entrance of the Zone.

"Are you okay? You look like you're about to faint."

"I . . . " Ro falters, tries again. "Something happened."

"What?"

There are no words. Only lemons and the snap of electricity. Ro rubs the spot Xal touched, chasing ghosts.

"Come on." Audra swings her leg over the courier bike, twin to the one Ro left behind. A tilt of her chin indicates the café across the street, glowing warm in the twilight. "We're getting some tea into you. My treat."

Audra keeps a space and silence between them. Ro is grateful. But Audra's gaze still slides in Ro's direction, questioning. Inside the café, Audra pushes a cup of tea across the table.

"What happened?"

"I was making a delivery to Xal." Ro hesitates, seeing an expression of distaste Audra is not quick enough to hide. "Xal was attacked, outside the Zone."

The muscles between Ro's shoulder blades tense, waiting for Audra to ask what an *Immie* was doing outside the Zone. But the question doesn't come, and Ro swallows guilt at putting venom in Audra's mouth before continuing.

"Xal was hurt and . . . accidentally touched me."

Audra's eyes widen. Small fingers of panic tap at Ro's ribs from the inside. Xal's tone-statements make things so much simpler. With Audra, Ro is lost. Is she jealous? Angry?

At last year's office holiday party, Audra drunkenly tried to kiss Ro. They had only known each other a short time, and so it was Ro who mumbled apologies and made the effort to explain.

It's not you, it's me. I'm not . . . I don't really date. I don't like . . . And there, the explanation faltered. Because what could Ro say that Audra would understand? Audra was wholly comfortable in her skin, more so than anyone Ro had ever met. She dated men and women in equal numbers; affection—casual and intimate— came to her as naturally as breath. She drank the world in through her fingertips and remained thirsty for more.

So how could Ro explain a hatred of touch, of flesh? The discomfort of even having a body, let alone one identifying with a single, narrow gender and responding to others sexually?

How could Ro explain it then? How can Ro explain it now? How that night, Ro hadn't fled, but had remained horrified. How this night, Ro had fled, but wasn't disgusted.

Audra shakes her head. Amazement? Ro still can't tell. Xal's touch was accidental; would emphasizing that help? Audra has been kind, understanding; Ro doesn't want to see Audra hurt, but the gulf between them is so vast.

Audra wraps her hands around her mug. Steam rises between them. She does not look at Ro.

"So what happened?"

"It tasted like lemons. And it was like being somewhere else."

"Xal tasted like lemons?"

"No. I mean. I don't know. Haven't you ever smelled something and had the taste hit you at the same time? I'm explaining it badly."

"No." Audra draws the word out. She looks at her hands, her expression guarded, like she wants to say more, but silence stretches between them.

Ro feels a pang of guilt, threaded with a flutter of panic, imagining Audra wants to put her hand over Ro's. A comforting gesture; it's what Audra would do if she was sitting with anyone else. Ro has seen it, the way Audra leans into their other co-workers—a nudge from her hip to emphasize a joke, a sympathetic hand on an arm, a head, comfortably resting on a shoulder. Even when it isn't sexual, Audra is so casual with her body; Ro can't begin to understand it.

"I have to go back for my messenger bag," Ro says, abrupt, standing.

"But . . . " Hurt flickers in Audra's eyes, this time unmistakable.

"I'm sorry," Ro says.

It feels like fleeing again. The phantom of Xal's touch lingers, but it doesn't have half the weight of Audra's gaze. Still, Ro rubs the spot again, pushing out the door. A light drizzle mists the air. Hairs rise on Ro's arm, catching the moisture. Ro rubs harder, half expecting to see translucence and hollow bones like glass—flesh both there and not there in the aftermath of Xal's touch.

Instead of going back to the Zone, Ro goes home, climbing three flights to a small apartment, boots heavy on each step. Guilt prickles, and with it, something else. Curiosity.

Ro crosses to the window, touching the glass. It's cool, and condensation forms a halo in the shape of a hand. Drawing away, there is a space left—defined by the imprint of four fingers, a palm, a thumb. And in the place of flesh, droplets of water cling to the window, heavy with the light and shimmering like stars.

Nerves flutter in Ro's stomach. The memory of rain glistens on the bike, still chained at the Zone's entrance. Ro brushes fingertips over the metal frame in passing. Never has the walk to Xal's shop seemed longer. Never has the jigsaw of uneven pavement, brick, and stone seemed such an impediment.

Ro tries to think of anything written or said about physical contact between humans and Immies, but comes up empty. If it's done, it's a private thing. Does everyone taste lemons, feel the snap of electricity? The Immie community is so small. Maybe Ro is the first, the only one.

But who is there to ask? The other couriers don't travel into the Zone. Scarcely any humans do. Ro has never seen another human walking the shattered streets. Which makes the kitschy human ornaments crowding the walls in Xal's shop even sadder.

Ro pauses, wondering if Xal has ever made a sale, if the shipments Ro regularly delivers ever leave the shop again, or only sit there gathering dust.

Why, Ro wonders. Aliens came to their world. Shouldn't people be excited, curious? But they don't seem to be. It's not fear exactly, but more a way of not seeing, Ro supposes. Turning a blind eye to what is inconvenient, uncomfortable. Like the government pretending the Zone is only temporary. Like the refugee camps that never empty. Like racial tension, poverty, homophobia. If the problem is ignored long enough, perhaps it will simply go away.

Ro pauses before pushing open Xal's door; the bell jangles. The courier bag, now empty, waits on the counter. And Xal waits behind it, limbs no longer bunched in pain, but held inward careful, betraying tension. Ro's throat is dry; it takes a moment to get the words out.

"How are you feeling?"

There's no sign of the wound. Ro can't tell whether it's healed completely, or whether Xal is simply hiding it. Limbs fold and unfold, a rippling effect unsettling the first time Ro saw it. Now it's almost comforting.

Today, Xal is gray-green, but with shades of violet. Ro thinks of sea anemones, rocks grown over with lichen, algae stirred by gentle waves.

::Tone—Relief/Query: Unhurt, now. Are you well.::

Ro nods.

"I'm sorry for running out yesterday. It's just . . . " Trying to explain things to Audra was awkward enough. They share common language, context.

"I forgot my bag." Ro points; it is a cowardly change of subject, but safer ground.

Ro touches the bag, but makes no move toward the door. Xal seems watchful, even without visible eyes. But what else? Hurt? Confused? Ro is suddenly aware of standing stiff, one arm crossed to hold the opposite elbow, lips parted as if to speak. Flesh again—bodies speaking a language Ro can't understand. It's all so useless. So . . .

"I want you to touch me again." The words come in a rush too quick for regret. Heat suffuses cheeks, another betrayal, and Ro almost flees.

But the shop bell stays silent. Ro's boots remain planted on the floor.

"I mean if . . . it didn't hurt you? If . . . if it's okay."

Pulse beats under jawline, at wrists and elbows. Xal furls and unfurls, the there and not there-ness coming across as deliberation, physically rolling and weighing the request.

::Tone—Hesitation/Query: It does not hurt. Why do you want this.::

"I don't know."

It's the most honest answer Ro can give. A paradox blooms, a strange, fractal bruise centered at the site of Xal's last touch. It spreads outward, re-writing Ro's hardwired code. Ro *wants* this. No, Ro *needs* this.

"What was it like for you?" Ro's eyes slide closed; it's easier to speak this way, even if it means having to ignore the extra weight of tears just starting to frost lashes. "I don't want to impose, is what I mean. I don't normally like . . . But this was different. I tasted lemons."

The ache is physical—a desire to step off the edge, precisely because it is unsafe, unknown. There are blank spaces defined by broken buildings, by the ghost of a handprint. They are defined by lack—not by something missing precisely, simply by something not there. They are possibility, made manifest.

In that brief moment, Ro had the sense of Xal's touch being like the ideal of falling into the night sky, being weightless and rushing so fast between stars their light draws blood. That paradox bruising Ro's skin—the contradiction of making the unknown known and erasing the infinite possibility—is too attractive.

"I can't explain." Ro's throat aches around the inadequacy of words.

A heartbeat. A space of silence. Eyes open. Ro consciously remembers to breathe. Xal is watchful, even without eyes. There is the same sense of consideration in the roiling movements, colors flickering, limbs furling and unfurling.

::Tone—Statement/Uncertainty: It is curious. No other humans come here. To touch would be to know more.::

Ro lets out a rush of breath.

"You're sure?"

::Tone—Anticipation/Fear: The store is closed.::

At first, Ro doesn't understand. Then Xal touches a switch and the lights dim, leaving only the faint glow of emergency lighting. Understanding crashes in: This is agreement, consent. Xal is giving them privacy.

::Tone—Anticipation/Fear: Ro. Put your arm on the counter.::

Ro hesitates only a moment, breathes out, then rests both arms, wrist up, on the glass. In the dimness, Xal is both easier and harder to see. Red light from the emergency exit sign traces contours and makes flesh the color of water over gray-green stone glow.

Ro tries not to flinch, pressing arms against the countertop to keep from shaking. Xal's . . . arm? Leg? Is there a human word for it? Extends slowly, waits the space of a heartbeat, then surrounds Ro's flesh, passing through and into it.

The shop tilts. A scent like violets and seaweed, like gunpowder, fills the air. There is no weight to Xal's touch, yet pressure builds in Ro's bones. A sense of fullness pushing outward, but without pain.

Xal flickers, slow, slow, fast, slow, unfolding, folding, turning. There and not there. Ro feels it too, absent and present, within the shop and elsewhere. An elsewhere that cannot be described.

Part of Ro reaches for something to anchor to in the here and now—long division, the names of past presidents, a list of capital cities. The larger part spins outward, spiraling from a weightless center, out through rings of stars, arms flung wide against the dark. Fragments of unknown worlds tumble past. Everything is vast and Ro is small and for a moment the sense of it is crushing.

"No." Ro jerks back, the word slipping out.

::Tone—Query/Concern: Ro. Are you hurt.::

Xal's shop snaps back into focus. Ro crashes back into a body too small to hold the sense of stars, and their loss is just as terrible as their presence.

"I'm . . . " A ragged breath. Ro places a hand over the skin Xal touched; it is solid, real. Colors ripple across Xal, the salt-scent in the room intensifying.

::Tone—Shame/Sincerity: Apologies. I did not mean to cause pain.::

"No. You didn't. I'm sorry. I shouldn't have . . . "

Under the salt-scent, the smell of violets and gunpowder. Ro's flesh prickles, as though swept by a cool breeze; the hairs rise. A sense of pressure, reaching, but never quite arriving, haunts the space between Ro's bones. It isn't desire—that's too simple a word, too human. But there is wanting, need unfulfilled.

"I want to try again. Please."

::Tone—Statement/Confusion: You were hurt.::

"No. It didn't hurt. I was just scared. But I want to try again." Ro's pulse thumps, arms trembling as they are pressed against the counter once more. "Please?"

Color and movement speaks doubt as it rolls across Xal's flesh—storm clouds, and the scent of oncoming rain. Dust—Ro can almost taste it. The same doubt fills Ro, but it can't end here. Ro reaches after something to keep the moment from slipping away, and lands on Xal's curiosity.

"What did you feel?"

::Tone—Statement/Uncertainty: Sunlight. A plank of wood. Many planks of wood. Water. Sunlight on water. The sensation of limbs in water. Smoke and charcoal.::

Hesitation between Xal's words, searching for concepts to capture such simple, human things. The memory comes rushing back to Ro, sitting on a dock at the lake, toes trailing in the water, a grown up grilling hot dogs in the background and the air filling with shrieks as other children dove and splashed in the water. A slice of childhood, pulled through Ro's skin and transferred into Xal's mind through touch.

"You saw my memories?"

More hesitation, then, ::Tone—Agreement/Affirmative: Yes.::

The information makes Ro's head swim. Could it work both ways? An alien childhood, if there is even such a thing, slipping into Ro's skin. There's so much Ro doesn't know about Xal, about the Immies in general. The need to know is overwhelming.

Ro looks to where Xal's eyes would be on a human, trying to communicate need. The absence of Xal's touch is a pressure as great as the touch itself. It's only a matter of quality, of flavor—not better, or worse, just different.

Xal reaches out again. A sigh, a musical tone so unlike the sound of pain from the night before traces the length of Ro's spine, the curve of Ro's jaw. Touch.

A needle, a thread draws through Ro's skin, stitching it with the light of the universe. The taste of bitter greens, the feel of velvet, the scent of wood smoke. Ro's mind substituting human concepts for unimaginable things. Nebulae bloom against Ro's closed eyes.

"Oh." The word escapes in a breath. Language and thought failing. Space simultaneously narrows to the point of contact between them, and expands beyond calculation.

"Oh." There are no other words. "Oh."

Again and again as the world spins away from them and Ro flies and falls.

"Hey."

Ro turns toward Audra's voice, still holding the coffee pot. The scent of it, just on the edge of burnt, fills the small courier office above the shed where their bikes are racked.

"Careful. You're going to spill." Audra points, and Ro starts, realizing the coffee is perilously close to the edge of the mug.

Even before the first sip, Ro is shaky, nerves taut and singing.

"Sorry." Ro replaces the coffee pot, sips scalding heat.

"Are you okay?" Audra frowns. "You look exhausted."

Ro doesn't remember returning to the apartment last night, only waking in a tangle of sheets this morning, eyelids sticky, limbs heavy. The world keeps wanting to slide away; the edges of Ro's vision glimmer with light, like a migraine coming on, only without pain.

"Any new jobs come in since yesterday?" Ro asks instead of answering Audra's question.

Even seen peripherally, Audra's concern is clear. There are no mirrors in Ro's apartment, but Ro imagines the shadow-bruises of sleeplessness, improperly combed hair.

"A few." Audra hands over the clipboard before pouring her own mug of coffee. Her knuckles are white, gripping the handle. It is a gesture of restraint; Ro has seen it before. If Audra doesn't anchor herself to her mug, she will reach out a comforting hand to touch Ro's arm.

Evasion tastes as sour as a lie. Audra only wants to help, but what can Ro say? Audra might understand, but she might as easily be hurt. She might think Ro is sick, wrong for wanting this inexplicable thing, and that would be unbearable. It's not that kind of desire, but it's too hard to explain. There are no words for what it is, at least none that Ro knows.

"Mind if I take the Thayer Street drop?" Ro's voice cracks.

The sound is covered with more sips of coffee—too quick. The heat doesn't help the flush coming to Ro's cheeks. The truth must be written everywhere on

Ro's skin, the evidence of Xal wrapped around and through, highlighting the translucence of bones, hollowed like glass.

Ro is clattering down the stairs to the bike shed almost before realizing it.

"Ro!" Audra follows, and Ro isn't quick enough—fingers shaking and clumsy—to strap the package to the back of the bike and leave before Audra blocks the door.

"What happened?"

Ro doesn't answer. Can't. Tears sting, hot and bright, but don't fall.

"Ro." Audra's voice is soft. She weaves between the bikes, comes within a few inches of Ro, and reaches out. But at the sharp intake of breath, she stops, her fingers falling short of brushing Ro's wrist.

"Sorry. I forgot." Audra looks down, then back again. The hope in her eyes is crushing.

Ro shifts, putting the bike between them, and feels guilty doing so.

"I went back to see Xal." Ro swallows, gripping the bike.

Audra's eyes widen, drawing light from the gaps where the door of the shed doesn't quite fit. All the darkness in them reminds Ro of falling through the stars. There is a sound that isn't quite a sob, and it takes Ro a moment to realize its source.

"Are you hurt?"

Ro gives a shake of the head, slight, but easier than words.

"What happened?"

Ro's lips press tight, fighting the sense of being overwhelmed without understanding its source. The loneliness of being trapped in a single body with its weight of flesh—Ro has always known it, but until feeling the alternative offered by Xal, it was bearable. Now the world is open, a wound no amount of thread can stitch closed.

Audra's fingers circle Ro's wrist, insistent this time. Ro's mouth flies open, but Audra's grip tightens.

"Please. I want to understand."

The need to touch is written clearly in Audra's eyes, as clear as Ro's desire to pull away. Ro lets out a shuddering breath, doesn't move. Pulse beats between them, in Audra's fingertips, in Ro's wrist. Maybe this is a language Audra can read; maybe Ro doesn't need to say anything at all.

Audra exhales, letting go, and Ro's pulse falls back into a regular rhythm. How can Xal's touch soothe, being so alien, while Audra's induces only panic? Most of the world would consider it wrong, broken. But Ro knows it isn't. There is no weight to Xal's touch, no expectation.

"I'm sorry," Ro says, and at the same time, Audra says, "I'm sorry."

Breath and silence fills the shed. They look at each other across the bike between them. The light coming through the gap around the door shifts, leaving Audra's face in shadow, stealing the illusion of stars from her eyes, but catching sylph-like in her dark curls.

Ro's chest tightens. There are no words that won't make things worse. *It's not you, it's me*, will only give Audra the impression Ro thinks the opposite.

If human touch could communicate the way Xal's does, Ro would understand. And maybe, for Audra, it does. Maybe Audra experiences the world through the tips of her fingers, gives away pieces of herself with each touch, but gains just as much in return, never diminishing.

But Ro cannot say this, cannot ask without fear of giving Audra hope. It's not that Audra has ever pressured Ro, or implied that maybe if Ro just tried it, met the right person, then things would be different. It's that sometimes, Ro catches Audra looking and thinks there is a glimmer, faint, but wistful—wishing things were different between them—and it makes Ro's heart ache.

"Tell me," Audra says, taking a step back, putting more space between them. She crosses her arms, holding herself in, holding back.

Audra isn't pulling back, running away, and relief surges through Ro. Whatever else they may be, at the core, they are still friends. The realization that Audra won't leave, won't shun, no matter what, brings a surge of emotion. It's almost like love, vast and complicated, but even the thought of the word comes thick with ghosts—meanings and expectations layered upon it by all the lips that have spoken it before. Ro pushes it away and, halting, tries to explain. Audra listens, never interrupting.

"Do you think there's something wrong with me?" Ro asks, needing to hear the words aloud, needing to taste them in order to let them go.

"No." Audra's tone is firm, but she looks lost as well. Scared. "I just don't want you to get hurt, okay? Promise me you'll be careful?"

Audra hugs herself tighter. Ro nods, pressing lips together, tasting salt even without tears. The promise means nothing; they both understand. This is unknown territory, and there is no way to travel it without gathering bone-deep scars.

Sirens shatter Ro's sleep. Pulse jack-rabbiting, pushing away sweat-tangled sheets and the remnants of a dream, Ro stumbles to the window. The sound is tied to the dream—one of being very far away, but very close, stretched thin, no blood or bone, no muscle, only skin and nerves pulled taut like a sheet over the world.

On the street below, red and blue lights spin in time with Ro's pulse. A sudden spike of pain. Ro clasps the wound, but there's nothing there.

Xal.

Pain arcs again, bringing flashes of violence, memories not Ro's own.

Xal.

Jacket and pants pulled over rumpled pajamas. Feet shoved into unlaced boots. Clattering down three flights of stairs. Ro's courier bike leans outside the apartment's outer door. Grabbing it, Ro is gone. Falling. Flying. Pedaling madly into the night, toward the flashing lights.

The whole city is wet, smearing in Ro's peripheral vision. Two cop cars park askew across the main entrance to the Zone. Ro stops the bike, lets it fall. A knot of people huddle, pointing. The cops struggle with a man whose hands are secured with a plastic zip tie. He thrashes, resisting as they push him toward the nearest car.

"Fucking Immie got what it deserved, slurping and lurking around our streets. They need to fucking stay where they're told or go the fuck home."

Light skips off shards of broken glass, blood red and deep blue. The man throws his head back; the cop's nose makes a sickening crunch as bone connects with bone. Swearing, the cop lets go, but her partner is quick, sweeping the man's legs and dropping him. The second cop gets a knee in the man's back, holding him down against the tongue of uneven pavement extending from the mouth of the Zone. The man continues swearing, lips spit-flecked.

"Fucking Immie. I hope it's dead."

Ro breaks into a run, ignoring a muffled shout from the cop with the broken nose. The door to Xal's shop hangs open. Ro nearly slips in slickness trailing across the floor. Xal never made it to the safety behind the counter, and instead lies knotted in front of it, limbs drawn together in the universal language of pain.

There is no hesitation. Ro kneels, folding around and over Xal. Shockwaves of pain radiate outward, but Ro doesn't let go. Stars spin, razor bright. The smell of matches, freshly-struck; a taste like a battery held on the tongue; the persistent thrum of rain.

"It's okay. It's okay."

Ro repeats the words, trying to stay conscious, trying to soothe. Xal's pain is overwhelming, an assault of sensation. Lighthouse flash. The taste of apples. Green-wet stone. Stairs spiraling down.

Desperate, Ro tries to pour sensation back into Xal—more childhood memories—introduce a new thread into the loop of feedback flowing between them. But the images keep coming, pounding Ro like fists, like stones. It's impossible to concentrate. The rasp of wool, black crayons melting in the sun, the taste of cherries. The touch-taste-smell correlation stutters. Xal's control slips, no longer translating sensations into human terms.

Ro screams. A note, sheer sound, shearing bone from bone, sloughing flesh. Ro's mind reels, trying to process what there are no words for.

A body—Ro's, Xal's, both, shudders. Collapses inward. Spins outward. The rush of wind, hot and dry and wet all at once. The crushing cold between stars. Stretching impossibly thin-fast-long across a cord of silver and all of it is everything all at once. Then, nothing.

Scraps torn from a quilt, broken fragments of a mirror, numb fingers trying to piece them back together and failing. Surfacing. Ro approaches a reflection etched on the underside of waves, surrounded by a distorted view of sky and trees and sunlight on the other side. Lips almost touch lips—reality kissing reflection—then Ro sinks again. A stream of bubbles, like pearls, like laughter, trail behind.

Hands. A voice. Audra's?

Wheels hum fast through sterile corridors; too-bright lights overhead. Sharp-jabbed needles. Medicine smell. The steady pulse of machines. Then nothing again.

Ro comes back from very far away. The simple task of cracking open an eyelid is monumental. Dry lips part.

"Water?"

A straw touches swollen and bruised lips. Ro sucks greedily until the straw is withdrawn.

"Not too much too fast. The doctors said."

Ro turns, head even heavier than eyelids. Audra perches in a chair next to the bed, holding the water glass awkwardly in her lap. She looks as though she's about to cry, or has just stopped.

"I should call the nurse."

"Wait." Ro tries to remember—in the haze of moments between then and now, was Audra's name spoken in answer to the nurses asking if there was someone they should call?

"What happened?" Ro tastes blood from cracked lips.

Audra holds the water out again, automatic.

"The police found you and Xal curled together on the floor. It looked like you'd been beaten to a bloody pulp. They thought you were dead."

"I don't remember."

"Were you attacked?"

"No. Xal was hurt. I . . . "

There is no word for it, but Ro feels one trying to take shape on a tongue not meant for such sounds.

"You have to stop this. Promise me you'll stay away from Xal."

"I can't." It isn't what Ro means to say, not meaning to say anything at all.

For a moment, Ro is afraid Audra will storm out, but she only crosses her arms tight around her body.

"Ro, what are you doing?"

"I don't know." Ro's voice cracks. "I really don't."

Ro lies back on the pillow, closing eyes before they snap open again.

"Is Xal okay?" It hurts, but Ro turns toward Audra.

"Xal is fine, as far as I know." Audra stiffens, her tone brittle and sharp.

Hurt shines in her eyes. Her mouth opens, but she closes it again, standing. "I'll go get a nurse."

Audra's shoes click and silence falls in their wake. Weary and bruised in ways that have nothing to do with skin, Ro curls into a ball, trying to recreate a knot of limbs so woven over and under and through each other they become one.

Ro toys with the hospital bracelet. It's been three days, and Ro's wounds have vanished as though they never existed. Still, Audra insisted on riding in the cab back to the apartment, and now perches on the arm of Ro's battered couch, watchful.

"What exactly did Lena say?" Ro paces to the window.

"She just suggested you might want to take some time off, for your health."

"And she couldn't be bothered to tell me in person?"

Ro glances back as Audra shrugs, looking uncomfortable.

"I'm sure she's just worried. We all are."

The slope of Audra's shoulders and the way she studies her feet keeps Ro silent. *Don't shoot the messenger.*

"I'm not fired?"

Audra shrugs again. Of course word has spread. Ro declined the opportunity to talk to reporters doing follow-up stories on the attack, but it doesn't matter. The stories are still out there, painting Ro as a misguided loner, the victim of an alien attack, a pervert. Maybe Lena is right to be wary, the other couriers right to withdraw. All except Audra.

"Come with me," Ro says.

Audra looks up, alarmed. "What?"

"Come with me to see Xal."

If others understood what Ro experienced, maybe they wouldn't be afraid. Maybe things can change. And where better to start with than Audra, living through touch—hand brushed to arm, palm squeezed to palm? Maybe this is something Ro can give Audra, like a gift. Something to bring them closer together in a way that balances both of their needs. And Xal, lonely, hungry for human experience. Ro's pulse speeds with the thought.

"Please? Trust me?"

Ro knows it isn't fair. Audra has offered so much, unasked—what right does Ro have to ask this in return? Because there's no way to explain to Audra without showing her what it is Ro is trying to do.

"Okay." Audra stands.

"Now?"

"Sure." Audra's smile holds an edge of sadness. "Why wait?"

The streets are silent, dusk just starting to fall. They walk with hands in pockets, watching their feet, watching the streetlights increasingly reflected as they draw closer to the Zone. Ro hears the hitch in Audra's breath as they cross the line.

"It's okay." Ro glances back, trying for a smile. "It's an imaginary border."

Audra nods, looking sheepish. Ro tries not to hold too tight to the fragile ball of hope, lest it shatter.

The shop bell jangles; behind the counter, Xal unfolds—a gesture Ro interprets as turning to face them.

::Tone—Alarm/Joy: Ro. You are not hurt.::

"Not anymore."

Xal knots and unknots, an anxious gesture.

"This is Audra, my . . . friend. Is it okay that she's here?"

::Tone—Formal/Greeting: Audra. Welcome.::

"Hi."

"I brought her here . . . " Ro falters under the combined weight of Audra and Xal's attention. "Audra is worried about me. I want her to understand. I thought . . . " Ro tries not to blush, tries not to panic.

Audra comes to the rescue, stepping forward while keeping careful space between her body and Ro's. Her voice carries a hint of nerves, but not outright fear.

"What happened the night you were attacked?"

::Tone—Statement/Query: It is not fair to be restricted. Why cross the stars to see only one small corner of a different world.::

Ro's breath catches.

::Tone—Statement/Anger: Your government promises change. We will be free to go where we please. Nothing changes.::

Xal grows, unfolding new dimensions. Ro's heart trips on the truth of the words, cracking. Again, it is a sensation too big to express, to hold. Human words are all too fraught. Ro needs an anatomy like Xal's, one to unfold and express everything mere flesh cannot contain.

Audra glances at Ro, eyes shining but cheeks dry. Ro holds her gaze, then nods, heart cracking again. There is understanding in Audra's eyes, not fear. The way Audra and Xal both watch Ro is like being re-written—blood and bones, skin and heart. Ro is most surprised by Audra. Humans, it seems can unfold to reveal new dimensions, too.

Audra pushes her sleeves up and rests her arms on the counter.

"I want to understand."

Xal flickers, shifting attention to Ro, asking an unspoken question.

Ro's voice shakes slightly, addressing them both. "It's okay. It's safe. No one will get hurt."

Xal unfurls, encompassing Audra's arms. Ro releases a breath at the same time Audra sucks one in, sharp, but containing more surprise than pain. It is the sound of plunging into a cold lake on a hot day—pleasure and shock rolled into one.

Audra blushes, the non-colors of Xal rippling across every bit of exposed flesh. The back of her neck is a sunset in deep sea shades; her arms are the color of starlight on a pond. She is there and not there. The scent of cherries and running water leak into the air.

"Can I . . . ?" Ro doesn't finish the sentence.

Perhaps Ro closes the space, or perhaps Xal and Audra entwined unfold to welcome Ro—a circle, a thread, a knot without beginning or end.

Sparks jump the gap between Ro's bones, suffusing flesh with light, like an x-ray, only brighter, more beautiful. Ro feels Audra's body, Xal's, all three occupying the same space and time. A moment of suffocation, a moment of panic, then everything opens with a smell like just-damp laundry snapping in the breeze. The shop warps, new segments forming like fractals of water freezing into ice.

A pulse beats, not Ro's own. A sensation belonging to—it must be Audra, because the memory—sharp and present—is so human. A bicycle, fiercely pedaled with bare feet to the crest of a hill before hands and feet are removed. It's like flying—the glorious, stomach-dropping feeling of the world falling away, the rush of wind, the warmth of light and being suspended beautifully between earth and sky. Ro feels it, filtered through Audra's flesh; from within, her body doesn't feel an impossible weight against her bones. Ro understands, viscerally, how Audra revels in being blood, muscle, bone.

"Oh." Ro wants to dig fingertips into Audra's flesh, into Xal's, and hold onto this moment forever. But too soon, the connection is broken.

"Wow." Audra is the first to step back. "That was . . . intense."

Her pupils are dilated, her breath fast. Ro steps back as well, chill with a fresh awareness of the space between them. Something in Ro aches to close the gap, but the familiar horror is there as well: it wouldn't be the same, couldn't ever be the same, inside this skin.

"You're glowing." Audra smiles.

Bits of light dance at the edges of Ro's vision.

"It's beautiful." Audra takes a half step, but stops.

Ro's throat is closed—thick. Eyes squeeze shut, a deep breath, then Ro looks at Audra again just in time to catch the tail-end of disappointment, the smile fading. The back of Audra's neck blushes, just blood colors now, the deep sea faded as she turns to Xal.

"Thank you." The faint quiver in her voice might be the after-shock of touch, or something else.

::Tone—Formal/Pleased: You are welcome. Audra. Thank you for sharing memories and experience of your world.::

The ache lessens in Ro's throat, fading to a sensation more like a bruise than a fresh wound.

"The night you were attacked, the first night, it wasn't the first time you left the Zone, was it?" Audra's question surprises Ro.

::Tone—Statement/Truthful: No.::

"How many times?"

Ro grips the counter, watching Audra and Xal. How is it they understand each other so well, so quickly? Or is it only that Ro's own curiosity blocked out certain aspects of Xal. Or perhaps because Audra is more used to processing sensation, she was less overwhelmed. Now that Ro thinks about it, it's obvious. How could Xal have been happy—how could any Immie be happy—confined to the Zone? All the times Ro traveled to Xal's shop, never once thinking Xal might want to leave, experience the wider world. Ro's skin flushes hot, but neither Xal nor Audra is paying attention.

::Tone—Statement/Truthful: The attack happened the fifth time.::

"Where were you going?" Audra leans forward; Ro leans, too, gravity pulling them both toward Xal's center.

Concentric rings spread across Xal's flesh, as though from a dropped stone. Now Xal is the color of moss, of sunlight, filtered through pine trees.

::Tone—Statement/Confidential: Some are patient, but not all. There is a group who would see the Zone change, the border gone.::

"Who?" Both Xal and Audra turn as though they'd forgotten Ro.

::Tone—Statement/Anger: It is a small group. One is in your city government, working to change things from within. But it is too slow. Others would wait. Not all are so patient.::

Not all, Ro thinks. Like Xal, restless, hungry for change.

"Is that why you've been leaving the Zone alone? Trying to start fights?" Again, Ro is surprised at Audra's words, her insight. How willfully blind has Ro been? How much time has been wasted that could have been spent helping?

::Tone—Statement/Defensive: Violence is noticed. It is the quickest way to change.::

"We want to help," Ro speaks before Audra can, but glances to the side to see

Audra's lips pressed into a thin line. Breath held, waiting for Audra to object, but she does not.

Xal rotates without moving, encompassing both Audra and Ro with eye-less attention.

::Tone—Formal/Request: Will you leave the Zone with me. To meet with my friend in the government.::

"Is that wise?" Audra glances at Ro.

"I think we should do it."

Audra hesitates, frowning, then shrugs, moving toward the door. Ro hurries to catch up. The air sings between them—Ro, a string pulled taut, thrumming a note of excitement, Audra simply tight, her note as yet un-played.

"You don't have to do this." Ro's voice is low so Xal, following behind, won't hear.

Audra shakes her head, but doesn't answer. She keeps her hands in her pockets, gaze fixed on the wet stones.

"Hey!" The shout draws Ro up short, bringing the realization they've crossed out of the Zone.

Xal crowds behind them, all three looking toward a knot of men and women emerging from the bar across the street.

"You can't be here." One of the men points at Xal.

To Ro's surprise, Xal slides past them, gathering limbs together the way a human would draw themselves up to stand tall.

::Tone—Fear/Pride: It does not break any laws.::

Of course not; the rules are all unwritten, enforced by silent consent, by looking the other way. Ro's fingers clench—a body caught between fight and flight, heart pounding.

"Fucking Immie! Get back in the Zone." Another man joins the first, the rest of the group bunching closer.

"We should go back," Audra says.

"No." Ro turns deliberately, walking away from the group, further away from the Zone.

Xal and Audra follow, the weight of hostile gazes tracking them. Fear and hope mix in equal parts. Xal is right—if they spark enough conflicts, people can't continue to look the other way. A bottle explodes, glass spraying at their feet.

"Keep walking," Ro murmurs, picking up the pace.

A second bottle flies, higher this time, bouncing off Ro's shoulder before hitting the ground.

"I'm calling the cops." Audra pulls out her phone.

Pounding footsteps, then one of the men grabs Ro's shoulder. Instinct brings Ro's hands up to break the contact with a shove. The man reels on slick, neon-stained pavement and loses his balance, landing hard. One of the women in the group laughs, nervous, unsteady.

Another projectile glances off Ro's cheek, stinging. Ro touches the spot and fingers come away wet with blood. Audra whispers into her phone, voice low and urgent. Xal moves again, a solid mass between Ro and Audra and the group of men and women. The man Ro accidentally knocked down gets to his feet, his face red.

For a moment, no one moves. The red-faced man's fingers curl, his jaw clenched. Ro sees the moment of decision, but isn't fast enough to shout a warning.

It doesn't matter. Xal is there, then not. The man's blow never lands and he stumbles, but keeps his feet this time. One of the women casts about for something to use as a weapon.

"We have to get out of here," Audra says.

Xal holds a line between the two groups of humans. More people emerge from the bar, some merely curious, others spoiling for a fight.

"We're about to have a full-blown mob on our hands." Audra plucks at Ro's sleeve, not touching flesh.

This time, Ro doesn't see the moment of decision, or even where the punch comes from. Fist connects with jaw, and Ro hits the ground. Shouts, feet scuffling. Someone yells. Ro looks up in time to see Xal lift one of the men, tossing him away. Xal's colors and movements speak anger and distress.

A siren cuts through the night, freezing everyone in place. As the cop cars stop, bodies scatter. Ro stands. Audra and Xal move closer, the three of them alone making no attempt to flee as the cops climb from their cars.

"It might be a while, are you sure you wouldn't . . . " The officer assigned to babysit them glances nervously between Audra and Ro, trying to pretend he doesn't see Xal at all.

They're in an empty interrogation room, out of the way. They've given their statements, declined to press charges, and been assured no charges are being leveled against them, though the cop delivering the news didn't look happy about it. He'd looked even less happy when Ro requested sanctuary, using the police station as a safe space to meet with Xal's friend. Ro credits Audra with charming him into reluctantly agreeing.

"No. We're fine right here." Audra smiles sweetly, seeming to enjoy the way Xal's presence makes the cops uncomfortable, now that the immediate danger has passed.

The officer withdraws, and Audra pours two cups of coffee from the carafe he leaves behind. In the corner, Xal ripples in silence. Ro's cheek is sore, but the blood has dried and there will be no lasting damage.

But the bruise goes deeper than Ro's skin. Something has changed, but not changed enough. There has to be more; Ro feels it, the seed of an idea starting to grow. Talking to Xal's friend is a first step, but they have to push harder if they want real change.

"I want to go to the Immie homeworld," Ro says, voicing the growing notion in a remarkably even tone. Xal and Audra register surprise—human and inhuman.

"There should be ambassadors on both sides working toward change. You're right, Xal, violence gets attention, but we can do better than that."

As the words stop, Ro's cheeks burn. Said aloud, it sounds ridiculous.

::Tone—Statement/Uncertain: It might be arranged. Humans have never been, but it is not impossible.::

Xal unfolds from the corner, moving closer to the table in the center of the room. Audra puts her hand on the table, near but not touching Ro.

"Ro?"

Ro turns.

"If Xal can arrange it, if it's possible, I have to go. I'm sorry."

Audra's hand moves, not withdrawing, fingers curling in on themselves, a knot of confusion and pain.

"I'm sorry," Ro says again. And again, words are inadequate. For just a moment, Ro considers bridging the gap, touching the back of Audra's hand, but it wouldn't be the same. They shared a moment with Xal, but there's still too much space between them. Necessary space, space Ro cannot bridge.

"I thought . . . " Audra looks down, studying the table's faux-wood grain. "Maybe because of what happened . . . "

The lines of her body pull inward. It hurts Ro to look at her, but their truths are too different. Audra must know that.

"I can't change who I am." Ro doesn't look away from Audra, hoping she'll understand.

One of Audra's shoulders lifts and falls again. It might be agreement, dismissal, or shrugging off an absent touch.

"If I go, what will you do?" Ro asks.

"I don't know." Audra traces circles on the fake wood; Ro can almost feel it through the tips of Audra's fingers. "We'll see what happens with Xal's friend. Maybe I'll join the cause. Maybe I won't. I'll keep working, and life will go on."

Audra looks up, and her expression does something complicated. Her eyes are bright, but the light in them reminds Ro of reflections glinting off broken glass.

"My life doesn't begin and end with you, you know." The edge of a smile touches Audra's mouth. "I do have other friends. Family."

The smile becomes a grin. "I like you, Ro. We're friends. I'll miss you, but you're not breaking my heart."

Ro's pulse trips. Audra sounds sincere, Ro believes her, but at the same time Ro doesn't have enough experience to differentiate the temporary sting of rejection from something deeper. Maybe if Ro leaves and comes back, things will be better. Maybe they can learn a mode of friendship—better, deeper—one that doesn't cause either of them pain.

Audra's fingers uncurl. She presses her palm flat against the wood.

"Are you . . . " Ro hesitates, uncertain how to end the sentence: *Are you sure?* or *Are you okay?*

Xal shifts closer, body forming a complicated pattern. The colors chasing across Xal's skin are sunlight, leaves, and the sensation of flying, not falling. Xal unfurls a limb, brushing the back of Audra's hand with the briefest of touches. The air smells of tangerines and Audra's eyes widen, as if Xal whispered something just for her.

Audra draws her hand away from the table, pressing it to her heart. Ro feels it, the steady thump of blood and life and warmth inside Audra's skin. On the table, the ghost outline of Audra's hand remains. Footsteps approach the door, but Ro's attention remains fixed on the table. The fading shape, the memory of touch, outlines possibility. It is everything.

Ice

RICH LARSON

Sedgewick had used his tab to hack Fletcher's alarm off, but when he slid out of bed in the middle of the night his younger brother was wide awake and waiting, modded eyes a pale luminous green in the dark.

"I didn't think you were actually going to do it," Fletcher said with a hesitant grin.

"Of course I'm going to." Sedgewick kept his words clipped, like he had for months. He kept his face cold. "If you're coming, get dressed."

Fletcher's smile swapped out for the usual scowl. They pulled on their thermals and gloves and gumboots in silence, moving around the room like pieces of a sliding puzzle, careful to never inhabit the same square space. If there was a way to keep Fletcher from coming short of smothering him with a blanket, Sedgewick would've taken it. But Fletcher was fourteen now, still smaller than him but not by much, and his wiry modded arms were strong like an exoskeleton's. Threats were no good anymore.

When they were ready, Sedgewick led the way past their parents' room to the vestibule, which they had coded to his thumb in penance for uprooting him again, this time dumping him onto a frostbit fucking colony world where he was the only unmodded sixteen-year-old for about a million light years. They said he had earned their trust but did not specify exactly how. Fletcher, of course, didn't need to earn it. He could take care of himself.

Sedgewick blanked the exit log more out of habit than anything, then they stepped out of the cold vestibule into the colder upstreet. The curved ceiling above them was a night sky holo, blue-black with an impossibly large cartoon moon, pocked and bright white. Other than Sedgewick and his family, nobody in New Greenland had ever seen a real Earth night.

They went down the housing row in silence, boots scraping tracks in the frost. An autocleaner salting away a glistening blue coolant spill gledged over at them suspiciously as they passed, then returned to its work. Fletcher slid behind it and pantomimed tugging off, which might have made Sedgewick laugh once, but he'd learned to make himself a black hole that swallowed up anything too close to camaraderie.

"Don't shit around," he said. "It'll scan you."

"I don't care," Fletcher said, with one of those disdainful little shrugs he'd perfected lately, that made Sedgewick believe he really truly didn't.

The methane harvesters were off-cycle, and that meant the work crews were still wandering the colony, winding in and out of dopamine bars and discos. They were all from the same modded geneprint, all with a rubbery pale skin that manufactured its own vitamins, all with deep black eyes accustomed to the dark. A few of them sat bonelessly on the curb, laid out by whatever they'd just vein-blasted, and as Sedgewick and Fletcher went by they muttered *extro, extros den terre*. One of them shouted hello a few beats too late.

"Should run," Fletcher said.

"What?"

"Should jog it." Fletcher rubbed his arms. "It's cold."

"You go ahead," Sedgewick said, scornful.

"Whatever."

They kept walking. Aside from the holos flashing over the bars, the upstreet was a long blank corridor of biocrete and composite. The downstreet was more or less the same plus maintenance tunnels that gushed steam every few minutes.

It had only taken Sedgewick a day to go from one end of the colony to the other and conclude that other than the futball pitch there was nothing worth his time. The locals he'd met in there, who played with different lines and a heavy ball and the ferocious modded precision that Sedgewick knew he wouldn't be able to keep pace with long, more or less agreed with his assessment in their stilted Basic.

Outside the colony was a different story. That was why Sedgewick had crept out of bed at 2:13, why he and Fletcher were now heading down an unsealed exit tunnel marked by an unapproved swatch of acid yellow hologram. Tonight, the frostwhales were breaching.

Most of the lads Sedgewick had met at last week's game were waiting at the end of the exit tunnel, slouched under flickering florescents and passing a vape from hand to hand. He'd slotted their names and faces into a doc and memorized it. It wasn't Sedgewick's first run as the new boy and by now he knew how to spot the prototypes.

You had your alpha dog, who would make or break the entry depending on his mood more than anything. Your right-hand man, who was usually the jealous type, and the left-hand man, who usually didn't give a shit. Your foot-soldiers, who weathervaned according to the top three, ranging from gregarious to vaguely hostile. Then lastly your man out on the fringe, who would either glom on thick, hoping to get a friend that hadn't figured out his position yet, or clam right up out of fear of getting replaced.

It was a bit harder to tell who was who with everyone modded and nobody speaking good Basic. They all came up off the wall when they caught sight of him, swooping in for the strange stutter-stop handshake that Sedgewick couldn't quite time right. Petro, tall and languid, first because he was closest, not because he cared. Oxo, black eyes already flicking away for approval. Brume, compact like a brick, angry-sounding laugh. Another Oxo, this one with a regrowth implant in his jaw, quiet because of that or maybe because of something else.

Anton was the last, the one Sedgewick had pegged for alpha dog. He gripped his hand a beat longer and grinned with blocky white teeth that had never needed an orthosurgery.

"*Ho, extro,* how are you this morning." He looked over Sedgewick's shoulder and flashed his eyebrows. "Who?"

"Fletcher," Sedgewick said. "The little brother. Going to feed him to a frostwhale."

"Your brother."

Fletcher stuffed his long hands into the pockets of his thermal and met Anton's gaze. Sedgewick and his brother had the same muddy post-racial melanin and lampblack hair, but from there they diverged. Sedgewick had always been slight-framed and small-boned, with any muscle slapped across his chest and arms fought for gram by gram in a gravity gym. His eyes were a bit sunk and he hated his bowed nose.

Fletcher was already broad in the shoulders and slim-hipped, every bit of him carved sinew, and Sedgewick knew it wouldn't be long before he was taller, too. His face was all angles now that the baby fat was gone: sharp cheekbones, netstar jawline. And his eyes were still reflecting in the half-lit tunnel, throwing light like a cat's.

Sedgewick could feel the tips of his ears heating up as Anton swung his stare from one brother to the other, nonverbalizing the big question, the always-there question, which was *why are you freestyle if he's modded.*

"So how big are they?" Fletcher asked, with his grin coming back. "The frostwhales."

"Big," Anton said. "*Ko gramme ko pujo.*" He pointed over to Oxo-of-the-jaw-implant and snapped his fingers together for support.

"Fucking big," Oxo supplied in a mumble.

"Fucking big," Anton said.

The cold flensed Sedgewick to the bones the instant they stepped outside. Over-head, the sky was a void blacker and vaster than any holo could match. The ice stretched endless in all directions, interrupted only by the faint running lights of methane harvesters stitched through the dark.

Brume had a prehensile lantern from one of the work crews and he handed it to Anton to affix to the cowl of his coat. It flexed and arched over his head, blooming a sickly green light. Sedgewick felt Fletcher look at him, maybe an uneasy look because they'd never been outside the colony at night, maybe a cocky look because he was making a move, going to ruin something for Sedgewick all over again.

"Okay," Anton said, exhaling a long plume of steam with relish. His voice sounded hollow in the flat air. "*Benga, benga,* okay. Let's go."

"Right," Sedgewick said, trying to smile with some kind of charm. "*Benga.*"

Brume gave his angry barking laugh and slapped him on the shoulder, then they set off over the ice. The pebbly gecko soles of Sedgewick's gumboots kept him balanced and the heating coils in his clothes had already whispered to life, but every time he breathed the air seared his throat raw. Fletcher was a half-step behind the lot of them. Sedgewick resisted the urge to gledge back, knowing he'd see an unconcerned *what are you staring for* sneer.

Thinking back on it, he should've drugged Fletcher's milk glass with their parents' Dozr. Even his modded metabolism couldn't have shaken off three tablets in time for him to play tag-along. Thinking even further back on it, he shouldn't have had the conversation with Anton and Petro about the frostwhales where Fletcher could hear them.

Under his feet, the texture of the ice started to change, turning from smooth glossy black to scarred and rippled, broken and refrozen. He nearly caught his boot on a malformed spar of it.

"Okay, stop," Anton announced, holding up both hands.

About a meter on, Sedgewick saw a squat iron pylon sunk into the ice. As he watched, the tip of it switched on, acid yellow. While Petro unloaded his vape and the other units circled up for a puff, Anton slung one arm around Sedgewick and the other around Fletcher.

"*Benga, aki den glaso extrobengan minke,*" he said.

The string of sounds was nothing like the lessons Sedgewick had stuck on his tab.

Anton shot a look over to Oxo-of-the-jaw-implant, but he was hunched over the vape, lips tinged purple. "Here," Anton reiterated, gesturing past the pylon. "Here. Frostwhales up."

He said it with a smile Sedgewick finally recognized as tight with amphetamine. He'd assumed they weren't sucking down anything stronger than a party hash, but now that seemed like an idiot thing to assume. This was New fucking Greenland, so for all he knew these lads were already utterly panned.

Only one way to find out. Sedgewick gestured for the vape. "Hit me off that."

Petro gave him a slow clap, either sarcastic or celebratory, while he held the stinging fog in his lungs for as long as he could, maybe because Fletcher was watching. There was only a bit of headspin, but it was enough to miss half of what Oxo-of-the-jaw-implant was saying to him.

"... is the area." Oxo plucked the vape out of his slack hands and passed it on. "See. See there, see there, see there." He pointed, and Sedgewick could pick out other pylons in the distance glowing to life. "Fucking danger, okay? Inside the area, frostwhales break ice for breathing. For break ice for breathing, frostwhales hit ice seven times. *Den minuso,* seven."

"Minimum seven," the other Oxo chimed in. Anton started counting aloud on his gloved fingers.

"Got it," Fletcher muttered.

"So, so, so," Oxo-of-the-jaw-implant went on. "When the frostwhales hit one, we go."

"Thought you'd stay for the whole thing?" Sedgewick said, only halfway listening. The cold was killing off his toes one by one.

Anton gave up at twenty and sprang back to the conversation. "We go, *extros,*" he beamed. "You run. You run. I run. He runs. He runs. He runs. He runs. Here ... " He gave the pylon a dull clanging kick. "To here!"

Sedgewick followed Anton's pointing finger. Far off across the scarred ice, he could barely make out the yellow glow of the pylon opposite them. His stomach dropped. Sedgewick looked at his brother, and for a nanosecond Fletcher looked like a little kid again, but then his mouth curled into a smile and his modded eyes flashed.

"Alright," he said. "I'm down."

Sedgewick was a breath away from saying *no you fucking aren't*, from saying *we're heading back now,* from saying anything at all. But it all stuck on his ribs and instead he turned to Anton and shrugged.

"*Benga,*" he said. "Let's go."

The handshakes came back around, everyone hooting and pleased to have new recruits. Fletcher got the motion on his first try. When the vape made its final circle, Sedgewick gripped it hard and stared out over the black ice and tried to stop shivering.

Sedgewick knew Fletcher was faster than him. He'd known it like a stone in his belly since he was twelve and his brother was ten, and they'd raced on a pale gray beach back on Earth. Prickling fog and no witnesses. Fletcher took lead in the last third, pumping past him with a high clear incredulous laugh, and Sedgewick slacked off to a jog to let him win, because it was a nice thing, to let the younger brother win sometimes.

Occupied with the memory, Sedgewick was slow to notice that the eerie green pallor of the ice was no longer cast by Anton's lantern. Something had lit it up from underneath. He stared down at the space between his boots and his gut gave a giddy helium lurch. Far below them, distorted by the ice, he could make out dim moving shapes. He remembered that frostwhales navigated by bioluminescence. He remembered the methane sea was deeper than any Earth ocean.

Everyone tightened the straps of their thermals, tucked in their gloves, and formed themselves into a ragged line that Sedgewick found himself near the end of, Fletcher beside him.

Anton waltzed down the row and made a show of checking everyone's boots. "Grip," he said, making a claw.

Sedgewick threw a hand onto Brume's shoulder for balance while he displayed one sole and then the other. He leaned instinctively to do Fletcher the same favor, but his brother ignored it and lifted each leg precisely into the air, perfectly balanced. Sedgewick hated him as much as he ever had. He glued his eyes to the far pylon and imagined it was the first cleat of the dock on a rainy gray beach.

Under their feet, the ghostly green light receded, dropping them back into darkness. Sedgewick shot Oxo-of-the-jaw-implant a questioning look.

"First they see ice," Oxo mumbled, rubbing his hands together. "They see ice for thin area. Then, down. For making momentum. Then, in one by one line . . . "

"Up," Sedgewick guessed.

On cue, the light reappeared, rising impossibly fast. Sedgewick took a breath and coiled to sprint. His imagination flashed him a picture: the frostwhale rocketing upward, a blood-and-bone engine driven by a furious thrashing tail, hurtling through the cold water in a cocoon of bubbling gas. Then the impact quaked the ice and Sedgewick's teeth, and he thought about nothing but running.

For two hard heartbeats, Sedgewick fronted the pack, flying across the ice like something unslung. The second impact nearly took his legs out from under him. He staggered, skidded, regained his balance, but in that split second Petro was past him. And Anton, and Oxo, and Oxo, Brume, Fletcher last.

Sedgewick dug deep for every shred of speed. The ice was nowhere near smooth, scarred with pocks and ridges and frozen ripples in the methane, but the others slid over it like human quicksilver, finding the perfect place for every footfall. Modded, modded, modded. The word danced in Sedgewick's head as he gulped cold glass.

The green light swelled again, and he braced before the third frostwhale hit. The jolt shook him but he kept his footing, maybe even gained half a step on Oxo. Ahead, the race was thrown into relief: Brume's broad shoulders, Anton's thrown-back head, and there, sliding past gangly Petro for the lead, was Fletcher. Sedgewick felt hot despair churn up his throat.

His eyes raised to the pylon and he realized they were over halfway across. Fletcher pulled away now, not laughing, with that crisp bounding stride that said *I can run forever.* Then he glanced back over his shoulder, for what, Sedgewick didn't know, and in that instant his boot caught a trench and slammed him hard to the ice.

Sedgewick watched the others vault past, Anton pausing to half-drag Fletcher back upright on the way by. "*Benga, benga, extro!*"

The fourth frostwhale hit, this time with a bone-deep groaning *crack*. Everyone else had overtaken Fletcher; Sedgewick would in a few more strides. Fletcher was just now hobbling upright and Sedgewick knew instantly he'd done his ankle in. His modded eyes were wide.

"Sedge."

All the things Sedgewick had wished so savagely in the night—that the doctor had never pulled Fletcher out of his vat, that Fletcher's pod would fail in transit to New Greenland—all of those things shattered at once. He swung Fletcher up onto his back, how they'd done as kids, and stumped on with lungs ragged.

The fifth impact. Sedgewick's teeth slammed together and fissures skittered through the ice. He spared only a moment to balance himself, then stumbled forward again, Fletcher clinging fierce to his back. At the far pylon, the others hurtled to the finish, whooping and howling from a dozen meters away now, no more.

They all seemed to turn at once as the sixth impact split the world apart and the frostwhale breached. Sedgewick felt himself thrown airborne in a blizzard of shattered ice, felt himself screaming in his chest but unable to hear it, deafened by the shearing boom and crack. Some part of Fletcher smacked against him in midair.

Landing slammed the wind out of him. His vision pinwheeled from the unending black sky to the maelstrom of moving ice. And then, too big to be real, rising up out of the cold methane sea in a geyser of rime and steam, the frostwhale. Its bony head was gunmetal gray, the size of a bus, bigger, swatched with pale green lanterns of pustule that glowed like radiation.

Cracks webbed through the ice and something gave way; Sedgewick felt himself slanting, slipping. He tore his gaze from the towering bulk of the frostwhale and saw Fletcher spread-eagled beside him, a black shadow in the burning lime. His lips were moving but Sedgewick couldn't read them, and then gloved hands gripped the both of them, hauling them flat along the breaking ice.

Oxo and Oxo made sure they were all pulled past the pylon before anyone got up off their belly. Sedgewick, for his part, didn't even try. He was waiting on his heart to start beating again.

"Sometime six," Anton said sheepishly, crouching over him.

"Go to hell," Fletcher croaked from nearby, and in a moment of weakness Sedgewick choked up a wavery laugh.

They washed home on a wave of adrenaline, caught up in the rapid-fire conversation of the New Greenlanders who still seemed to be rehashing how close Sedgewick and Fletcher had come to getting dumped under. Every single one of them needed a send-off handshake at the living quarters, then they slunk off in one chattering mass.

Sedgewick couldn't keep the chemical grin off his face, and as he and Fletcher snuck through the vestibule and then ghosted back to their temporary shared room, they talked in a tumble of whispers about the frostwhale, about the size of it, and about the ones that had surfaced afterward to suck cold air into massive vein-webbed bladders.

Sedgewick didn't want to stop talking, but even when they did, climbing into their beds, the quiet felt different. Softer.

It wasn't until he was staring up at the biocrete ceiling that he realized Fletcher's limp had swapped sides on the way back. He swung upright, unbelieving.

"You faked it."

"What?" Fletcher was rolled away, tracing the wall with his long fingers.

"You faked it," Sedgewick repeated. "Your ankle."

Fletcher took his hand off the wall, and the long quiet was enough confirmation.

Sedgewick's cheeks burned. He'd thought he had finally done something big enough, big enough to keep him on the greater side of whatever fucked-up equation they were balancing. But it was Fletcher feeling sorry for him. No, worse. Fletcher making a move. Fletcher manipulating him for whatever kind of schemes floated through his modded head.

"We could have both died," Sedgewick said.

Still turned away, Fletcher gave his perfect shrug, and Sedgewick felt all the old fury fluming up through his skin.

"You think that was a hologame?" he snarled. "That was real. You could have deaded us both. You think you can just do anything, right? You think you can just do anything, and it'll fucking work out perfect for you, because you're *modded*."

Fletcher's shoulders stiffened. "Good job," he said, toneless.

"What?" Sedgewick demanded. "Good job what?"

"Good job on saying it," Fletcher told the wall. "You're ashamed to have a modded brother. You wanted one like you."

Sedgewick faltered, then made himself laugh. "Yeah, maybe I did." His throat ached. "You know what it's like seeing you? Seeing you always be better than me?"

"Not my fault."

"I was six when they told me you were going to be better," Sedgewick said, too far gone to stop now, saying the things he'd only ever said alone to the dark. "They said different, but they meant better. Mom couldn't do another one freestyle and to go off-planet you're supposed to have them modded anyway. So they grew you in a tube. Like hamburger. You're not even *real*." His breath came lacerated. "Why wasn't I enough for them, huh? Why wasn't I fucking enough?"

"Fuck you," Fletcher said, with his voice like gravel, and Sedgewick had never heard him say it or mean it until now.

He flopped back onto his bed, grasping for the slip-sliding anger as it trickled away in the dark. Shame came instead and sat at the bottom of him like cement. Minutes ticked by in silence. Sedgewick thought Fletcher was probably drifting to sleep already, probably not caring at all.

Then there was a bit-off sob, a sound smothered by an arm or a pillow, something Sedgewick hadn't heard from his brother in years. The noise wedged in his ribcage. He tried to unhear it, tried to excuse it. Maybe Fletcher had peeled off his thermal and found frostbite. Maybe Fletcher was making a move, always another move, putting a lure into the dark between them and sharpening his tongue for the retort.

Maybe all Sedgewick needed to do was go and put his hand on some part of his brother, and everything would be okay. His heart hammered up his throat. Maybe. Sedgewick pushed his face into the cold fabric of his pillow and decided to wait for a second sob, but none came. The silence thickened into hard black ice.

Sedgewick clamped his eyes shut and it stung badly, badly.

Everybody Loves Charles
BAO SHU, TRANSLATED BY KEN LIU

1.

He shot into space, free as a fish that had leapt away from the sea's embrace.

Gazing down through *Pegasus*'s porthole, he saw the receding grey metropolis, then the amber suburbs, and finally the green fields and yellow deserts, all quickly submerged beneath a sea of clouds. By the time he emerged from the clouds, the world had become an azure convex surface, a hint of the enormous sphere it belonged to. Behind, North America was but a smear against the horizon, and Asia was still hidden below the curvature of the Earth in front. The whole globe was wrapped in a hazy glow: the atmosphere. Above him, pinpricks of starlight peeked out of the onyx firmament.

As gravity's pull diminished, he felt the effects of weightlessness. Though his body was firmly strapped into the pilot's seat, he still experienced the sensation of floating. The spacecraft seemed to be cruising upside down, the infinite waters of the Pacific Ocean hanging over his head and the bottomless abyss of space suspended below. It was as though he weren't in space, but sleeping under the sea, everything at peace and very far away. For a few seconds, Charles Mann felt he was the man farthest from the hubbub of society, a permanent free-floating consciousness destined to merge with Nature's pure essence.

But soon he remembered—no, it would be more accurate to say that he always knew—that this was an impossible fantasy. Even though he was freed from the gravity of this planet, the whole world was watching him. At least a hundred million people were tuned into his livecast.

Pegasus was in the most prestigious aerospace competition of them all: the Trans-Pacific Championship Race. Freed from the atmosphere, his ship was hurtling at Mach 9.7 toward the western edge of the Pacific. Destination: Tokyo.

Like ballistic missiles, racing ships entered space for part of their flight so as to minimize air drag, conserve fuel, and coast on inertia, only re-igniting their engines upon reentry. For a few minutes, Charles languidly admired the blue planet slowly spinning outside the porthole, listened to some jazz, and broadcast a mental microblog entry:

I have never been so far from Earth. At this moment, The World and I are antipodes: I am Self, no longer a member of life's multitudes on Earth, but a lone wanderer in the universe . . .

The cockpit display of *Pegasus* revealed his position: above the Aleutians. A flock of blue dots drifted westward over the isles, and a bright red dot flashed near the leading edge—his ship. Behind him were more than a hundred spacecraft, and only three in front. This was a decent spot, but not enough to place in the race.

The frontrunner was more than sixty miles away, and even the third-place ship led him by more than six miles. As though to remind him of his poor showing, a silver saucer-shaped spacecraft caught up, sweeping past like a meteor less than three hundred meters to this left. That was *Andromeda,* piloted by George Steele.

"What's wrong, Charles? Did you party too hard last night with some groupie?" Steele's voice burst from the radio.

"George, I'm just taking a break to enjoy the scenery before I start the race."

"I'm afraid the race is already over for you, buddy."

"You'd like to think so, wouldn't you?" Charles pushed a button.

Abruptly, *Pegasus* cast off its entire tail section like a butterfly emerging from a chrysalis. A bright blue glow flared from the newly-revealed tailpipes, indicating that the fusion engines had been activated. The sudden acceleration pressed Charles against the seat, making it difficult to breathe, but the familiar sensation made him feel more alive than ever. Having discarded almost half of its mass, *Pegasus's* velocity shot up by 2.2 Mach, and easily overtook *Andromeda.*

"Surprise!" Charles whistled.

"Impossible! How did you manage to get up to Mach 12?"

"I'll see you in Tokyo, my friend," said Charles, "that is, assuming your little flying saucer can get there. Whatever you do, try not to fall into the ocean. I don't want to break a tooth on your ring when I savor the sashimi at my celebration dinner." He smiled as he imagined millions hanging on his every word.

As if to prove his point, behind him, *Andromeda* began to shake, clearly being pushed to its limits. Struggling, it managed to accelerate for a brief stretch, a last desperate attempt that had to be abandoned.

"Just you wait, Charles Mann! One day . . . "

Charles laughed as his ship pulled farther ahead. The fusion engines were operating at their maximum, pushing his velocity to unprecedented heights.

"Krinsky, Hamill, Tanaka, let the game begin!"

Like a figment of a dream, *Pegasus* passed one craft after another, and soon reentered the atmosphere. The ship's heat shields activated as the air around it grew incandescent. Like a fiery meteor, Charles's ship swept across the sky over the western Pacific and descended toward the Japanese islands.

Somewhere above the ocean not far from Tokyo, *Pegasus* finally overtook Tanaka Takayuki's[1] *Amaterasu,* which was decelerating in anticipation of landing. *Pegasus,* on the other hand, didn't slow down at all as it brazenly swept over *Amaterasu* and then Tokyo itself.

"Where do you think you're going, Mann?" The voice of Charles's coach warned in his earpiece. "You're going to be in Siberia if you don't stop."

Charles began to decelerate only when he had gone beyond Tokyo, sketching a graceful arc as he circled back and landed on the lawn of the Tokyo Olympic Stadium just before *Amaterasu* touched down. The crowd in the sold-out stadium cheered wildly as Charles glanced around, satisfied.

"Congratulations on successfully defending your title!" said his coach through the earpiece. "The medal ceremony is in an hour, so you have some time to prepare a speech."

"Why don't you accept the medal for me? I've got a date with the cherry blossoms."

"Would you stop kidding around? Empress Aiko is going to hand out the medals personally! You've also got a meet-and-greet with Japanese readers this evening. If you really want to see the cherry blossoms, we'll arrange something for you tomorrow."

"I'm not interested in the empress." Charles laughed. "Why should I waste my life on such boring conventions? I'm far more excited by Aoi Masa." He knew that the empress would be utterly enraged by his mentioning her in the same sentence as the famous AV idol, while Masa would grin, and the millions tuned into the livecast would be laughing along with him. His quote would become the front page headline in all the world's major newspapers—well, at least the entertainment sections.

"Charles, you've got to—"

But *Pegasus* had already taken off, and as millions watched, it rose into the air and disappeared among the jungle of towering skyscrapers that was Tokyo.

2.

Sudden pinpricks of pain made Takumi Naoto open his eyes. For a long while he wasn't sure where he was.

He was in his room, of course, about seven or eight meters square. A tatami mat took up half of it, with the other half occupied by a computer desk. There was no other furniture in the room, but then again, these two things were all he needed.

Naoto sat up, the painful pressure in his bladder making him keenly aware that he had been lying immobile for almost eight hours. Not having eaten for the duration, his blood sugar level was dangerously low, which set off the health monitor on his wrist. If he didn't eat soon, the monitor was going to conclude that he was in a coma and send out a distress call to the hospital nearby.

Naoto went to the washroom to relieve himself, filled a cup with mineral water, and returned to the computer desk where he opened a bottle of concentrated nutrition pills. The pills contained almost all nutrients needed by the body and suppressed the secretion of stomach acid—taking five pills was equivalent to eating a full meal. Of course the pills lacked something in the taste department, being closer to plastic foam than actual food, but given that Naoto experienced the joys of foie gras, *shoro* mushrooms, and caviar every day, he paid it little mind.

Naoto stuffed ten pills into his mouth and washed them down with gulps of cold water. He turned on his computer and brought up a window into which he tapped a series of apparently meaningless numbers and symbols, his fingers flying over the keyboard. He was, in fact, writing code for a financial management application, an utterly boring job whose only redeeming feature was paying relatively well. However, he limited himself to working no more than two hours each day, an amount of time sufficient to earn the funds to cover his rent and nutrition pills. He wasn't interested in wasting even a minute of his life on such lowly concerns beyond the absolute minimum.

I've got to work faster, Naoto thought as he typed away. *I can't afford so much separation. This is going to ruin the hard-earned psycho-coordination link . . . I've got to get back to it . . . Just five more minutes . . .*

But someone was calling him. Frowning, Naoto switched over to the chat window, where a chubby girl with short hair appeared: his neighbor, Asakura Minami. She showed him an expression intended to be kawaii. "Naoto! Are you there?"

Such useless chatter! "Yes."

"I have something cool to tell you: Charles is here!"

More wasted words. "Yes, I'm aware of that. And?"

"It's Cha-ru-zu!" Minami emphasized every syllable deliberately. "Charles Mann, your idol! Just now, he turned down the medal ceremony to go on a date with Aoi Masa. It's all over the web. Still, I heard that he was going to be signing books in Ginza and meeting fans tonight. What an opportunity! Why don't we go see him together? I have a copy of his *The Other Shore of the Pacific* and I'm going to get it signed—"

"Sorry, no can do." Naoto didn't even wait for her to finish. "I'm busy. Work."

"You're holed up in your room all day working. Can't you take a two-hour break and go out? And it's Charles—"

"I'm on deadline."

"But—"

"Sorry. Bye!" He closed the window.

What a silly woman. She just wasted a whole minute of my precious time. Naoto knew that Minami liked him, but after he'd been with famous actresses and models like Elizabeth White, Mariana Kingston, Paula Claudia, and Yang Ziwei, it was impossible for him to be excited by Minami's round, plain face.

Moreover, the presence of Minami always reminded him of who he really was, and the last thing he needed was himself.

No, it was impossible to stay in this room any longer; even a second more would drive him crazy. Naoto finished his job in a rush, pushed the computer away, and lay down on his tatami mat, closing his eyes. His body was starting to digest the nutrition pills. Even though his stomach protested at the artificial nutriment, he no longer felt so hungry. He could go another eight hours.

He initiated the connection and sensory data began to flow over the link. Neural pulses were converted into electromagnetic waves, which were converted into neutrino beams, and then back to electromagnetic waves and neural pulses again.

Vestibular systems synchronized: I am standing where he stands; tactile sensations synchronized: a breeze caresses my skin, full of the warmth of spring and the moisture of the Pacific; hearing synchronized: the susurration of the wind and the sensual twitter of birds; sight synchronized: patches of lively pink and translucent white, coalescing into thousands of blooming cherry trees.

The lovely kimonoed female figure kneeling under that cherry tree turns and smiles, her perfect features even more beautiful than the blossoms: Masa Aoi!

And I am Charles, the one and only Charles.

3.

Pegasus landed next to a small lake near Hakone.

Masa was waiting for him in a shore-side cherry grove where the flowers were as magnificent as the clouds at sunset. A pure white picnic blanket was spread on the ground, on which were laid plates of refined sashimi and flasks of sake. Dressed in a loose green satin kimono, the kneeling Masa greeted him in perfect English, her voice as sensual and soft as the fabric draped around her.

"Hello, Charles."

"Hello, Masa-chan." Charles sat down next to her, his arm wrapping around her slender waist possessively.

"I saw the livecast," Masa said. "Shall we drink to another championship?" She raised an elegant small sake cup.

"Oh, it's nothing." Charles accepted the cup and drained it in one gulp. Then he kissed her perfect cheek. "The only reason I flew so fast, of course, was to see you—"

"Oh, please!" Masa laughed.

"I swear. It's been how many months since we last saw each other? I've really missed you."

"Is that so?" Masa's expression was halfway between a smile and a frown. "How do you explain Claudia then?"

Charles grinned awkwardly. "Um . . . she's a lovely girl, of course. Both of you are! You're both so close to my heart . . . "

Having had her fun, Masa switched topics. "Have you seen my new film? I sent you tickets to the premier, but you didn't show up." She waited a beat. "It's called *Hokkaido Love Story*, remember?"

"Of course! You were magnificent, baby." Charles caressed her hair, which gave off the fragrance of cherry blossoms. "I absolutely loved it." He struggled to remember the name of Masa's character, but came up empty. "Oh my God, you displayed such emotional range and authenticity in the portrayal."

The corners of Masa's mouth curved up. She knew that at least ten million people had heard the endorsement, and soon, hundreds of millions would be looking up her film on the web. She could already envision Hollywood beckoning at her. "So, tell me Charles, which scene was your favorite?"

" . . . The ending, definitely the ending. I thought it was so . . . moving." Charles hurried to change the subject. "I thought this was a famous tourist spot. How come there's no one else here?"

"This lake is private. The owner is the head of the Asao Group. He's providing the spot for our date free of charge."

"Please thank him for me. It's so beautiful here." Charles looked around him. The snowy peak of Mount Fuji glistened in the distance, and all around branches laden with cherry blossoms swayed in the breeze, soft, pink petals falling to the placid jade lake surface like rain. Every scent in the air was pure, refreshing.

"I bet Thoreau would be jealous of us." Charles took a deep breath. "I think if I were to live here, I'd write something even better than *Walden*."

"Walden? What's that?"

"It's . . . never mind." Charles's grin turned feral as he leaned in toward his companion. "Masa-san, have you ever tried to . . . " His voice was now an inaudible whisper, but of course innumerable audience members around the world shared the revelation in livecast with Masa.

Masa giggled. "Oh, such an adventurer!"

The two of them were now entwined on the ground. *How the hell am I supposed to get this thing off her? Oh, the knot is back here . . .*

The noise of an approaching engine broke the tranquility of the lake. Charles twisted his head around and saw a tiny blue dot above the horizon. "Oh, I hope it's not those crazy fans again," he muttered.

The dot rapidly grew in size, and a pair of wings appeared around it. Charles soon saw the Japanese flag painted on the fuselage as well as the English text beneath it: a patrol vehicle from the Tokyo Metropolitan Police.

The tiny aircraft landed next to *Pegasus,* and a police officer emerged and strode over to them.

"Sir, are you Charles Mann?" Her English was heavily accented.

"Yes, are you looking for an autograph, sweetheart?" Charles examined the officer. She was young and not classically beautiful, but her fit figure and serious mien gave her an air that commanded attention.

"Mr. Charles Mann," the officer spoke without expression. "You're suspected of engaging in terrorist activities. Pursuant to Japanese law, I ask that you return with us and cooperate with our investigation. You have the right to remain silent . . . "

Me? Terrorism? What kind of stupid joke is this? Charles turned to look at Masa, but she looked equally puzzled.

"Wait just a minute! What are you talking about?"

"Exceeding the speed limit at low altitudes," the officer explained. "Speeding beyond Mach 2 is illegal, and beyond Mach 5 is considered a serious threat against the city and a potential terrorist attack. Your speed just now exceeded Mach 10. According to Chapter Seven, Article Eighty-Two of the Japanese Special Anti-Terrorism Provisions, you must be detained and interrogated."

"Are you nuts? Don't you know there was a championship race today?"

"Yes, the race was subject to certain exemptions. However, after the race was over, you took off again, still exceeding the speed limit and outside the race area. I have no choice but to arrest you."

"Arrest me for speeding? That's utter bull—" Charles forced himself to calm down. *Remember, millions are behind me.*

"This is ridiculous!" Masa quickly pulled the kimono around herself, got up, and began to speak to the officer in rapid-fire Japanese, gesticulating wildly.

But Charles could tell that this officer wasn't going to budge; he also noticed several other muscular officers in the patrol vehicle by *Pegasus*. "All right." He gestured for Masa to stop and shrugged. "I've never had an opportunity to visit a Japanese detention center. But sweetheart, I'm going to write you into my next novel. I hope you don't mind."

"You may do as you like." The officer seemed relieved that he wasn't making a fuss. "If you wish to retain an attorney—"

"Already taken care of," Charles said, pointing at his head to indicate that his lawyer was monitoring his livecast. "Oh, may I have the pleasure of your name?" He saw the name tag on her chest, but he couldn't read kanji.

The officer hesitated for a second. "Hosokawa Homi."

"Hosokawa . . . Homi," Charles repeated the name. "Can you promise me something?"

She looked at him questioningly.

Charles grinned. "You ruined my date. When this is all over, you will have to give me another one as compensation."

"Mr. Charles," Homi said, blushing furiously. She was so flummoxed that she had temporarily forgotten that Westerners put their given names first. "Let me remind you that it is a crime to harass a police officer in Japan!"

But Charles was sure he had seen a hint of delight in her eyes as well.

The pleasure of the hunt!

4.

In accordance with standard procedures, Charles was handcuffed and brought into the patrol vehicle under the watchful eyes of multiple officers, who refused to let Masa Aoi accompany him on the ride back to Tokyo.

The whole flight back, Charles tried to chat up Homi, who pretended to ignore him, though from time to time she couldn't help but smile. The expressions on the other officers' faces grew uglier by the minute.

By the time they approached the landing pad at the top of the Metropolitan Police Headquarters building, multiple aerial vans from local news agencies had already surrounded the place. A group of fans chanting "Free Charles!" were attempting to land forcefully, and the police had to divert half a dozen additional patrol vehicles with dozens of officers to maintain order. Everything was chaotic.

Surrounded by a group of police officers, Charles strode toward the entrance. Homi walked right next to him, and couldn't avoid being pressed against his muscular body.

"At my last signing in Manila," Charles said to her, "the crowd was just as crazy as this one. Being pressed against so many bodies was no fun, of course, but something interesting did happen."

"What?" asked Homi, unable to resist.

"The crowd was mad, shoving and pushing. I was fine, of course, but they managed to squeeze a baby out of a pregnant woman."

"That's terrible!"

"Ah, but then they managed to squeeze the baby into another woman next to me."

"What?" It took a moment for Homi to get it. "You need better jokes."

"I'm telling you the truth!" Charles insisted earnestly. "Worst of all, she said the baby was mine."

Homi snorted and said something to him, but Charles didn't hear it. A complete, eerie silence suddenly enveloped him, and he watched the crowd squirm around him in the flickering light helplessly. Then, the perception of weight vanished, and Charles felt himself suspended in his own body, as though he was about to float off. All sensation of touch ceased.

Fade to white.

Slowly, he opened his eyes, his head numb and heavy. Above him was the stained ceiling of his efficiency apartment, and the fan in the computer next to him hummed.

It took him a while to remember that he wasn't Charles. He was only Takumi Naoto.

Naoto had no idea what had happened. He got up and stumbled to his computer. The web was filled with confused chatter, and countless fans were cursing the police for creating trouble. Not only did they interrupt a hot session with Aoi Masa, but they even managed to somehow break off the livecast altogether.

Soon, the answer emerged. Out of confidentiality considerations, the Metropolitan Police had blocked the neutrino beam transmission. The world was temporarily cut off from Charles's livecast.

"*Baka! Baka!* Don't the cops have anything better to do than mess with our lives?" Naoto let out a string of curses and paced around the room. Who knew how long the livecast would be interrupted? Two hours? Eight? More than a day? What was he supposed to do? If he was supposed to spend a whole day not as Charles, then they might as well have poked out his eyes and eardrums.

Finally, he managed to calm himself down enough to open the programming interface and try to get some work done, but he couldn't focus, and made multiple errors in a single line of code. In despair, he slammed his keyboard down and returned to the tatami mat to sleep. Tossing and turning, he couldn't get comfortable; he was like a junkie needing his fix. Every sensation was alien. The feeling of being Charles was leaving him, and his soul, which ought to be soaring through the empyrean, was imprisoned in the disgusting body of Takumi Naoto.

The doorbell rang, finally giving Naoto something else to focus his attention on. He jumped up and rushed to the door. The display screen showed his visitor: short, pear-shaped, female. Asakura Minami.

Naoto opened the door. "What are you doing here?" His tone was impatient.

"I . . ." Awkwardly, Minami lifted a bento box. "I made lunch, and I wanted to see if you want some."

"I don't—" Seeing Minami's flushed face, Naoto swallowed his ready refusal. "All right. Thanks."

He reached out to take the bento, but he was so clumsy that he managed to drop it. The box fell on the ground, spilling hot unadon and tempura all over the floor.

"I'm so sorry!" Minami squatted to clean up the mess. "I don't know what happened. I just didn't hold on—"

A pang of guilt struck Naoto. "No. It's my fault." He squatted down to help her.

It took a while for the two of them to clean up the floor. Minami was distraught. "I made all this for you."

"No worries. Actually, I've already eaten, and I'm not hungry at all." After hesitating for a moment, Naoto added, "Why don't you come in?"

Minami walked in and looked around. Naoto felt his cheeks heat up. "I apologize. My place is a mess."

But Minami giggled. "All men are like this—well, at least that's what I hear. Takumi-kun, do you spend all day working at home?"

"Yes." Naoto handed her a glass of mineral water. "Lots of people work from home now, and my job just requires a computer."

"Don't you ever go out? Or talk to anyone? Don't you get lonely?"

"No. I can . . . go on the web. Everything is on the web."

"It's not the same." Minami gazed at him, her eyes full of concern. "You should be more active. I think you look a bit too pale. You need fresh air."

"I'm fine."

Minami noticed the massive hexagonal black box at the head of Naoto's bed. "What's that?"

"It's nothing. Just a computing peripheral." Naoto didn't want to explain.

But Minami had already recognized it. "This is . . . a neutrino receiver and converter! Are you into livecasts?"

"How . . . did you know?"

"My friend Rimi has one in her home, and it looks just like this. She told me it's for livecasts, but I don't know how it works exactly."

"It receives neutrino beams and converts them into electromagnetic waves," Naoto explained. "Because neutrino beams can go right through the Earth, it's the fastest way to transmit information and minimize delay. But the equipment for neutrino transmission can't be miniaturized, and it's impossible to add one to a cranial implant. The only solution is to relay the electromagnetic signal to one of these, convert it to a neutrino beam, and then reverse the conversion at the other end. Have you ever tuned into a livecast?"

"No." Minami sighed. "I've always been terrified of them."

"Terrified? Why?"

"To have another person's senses take over your brain! I think that must be like being possessed by a demon."

"Oh, it's nothing like that." Naoto chuckled. "You've got it backwards. It's more like you're possessing someone else. You get to see what they see, hear what they hear, experience every detail of their life. What fun!"

"I guess so. I love Yan Zhenxu and Kim Dong-jun. It *would* be fun to know what they're doing at this moment."

"I'm pretty sure Yan hasn't opened a livecast channel. As for Kim . . . let me look up his info." Naoto tapped away at his keyboard for a while. "Aha! He started his livecast last year. He casts for about two hours every day."

Minami squeezed in next to Naoto and read the large font text scrolling in the window. "'Do you want to share a body with Dong-jun? Do you want to touch his soul in the vast deep of his mind? Do you want to live with him and work with him, get to know all the secrets of Korean stars?' Wow! This sounds amazing!"

But a fearful expression soon crept back on her face. "I heard that you have to get a surgery where they cut open your brain if you want to receive livecasts. That's got to hurt!"

"It's no big deal. The surgery is to implant a chip with a small transmitter, and to hook it up to all your sensory nerves in the pons. Without it, you can't receive the sensory information in the livecast and can't build the psycho-coordination link. Over a billion people have had the surgery, almost nine million right here in Japan."

"Is it expensive?"

"Not at all. I'm sure you can afford it. But to subscribe to Kim Dong-jun's livecast will cost you. Look, the price is listed—ignore the so-called deals they tout here, they're all scams—998 yen per hour. If you want to tune in for two hours a day, you need more than sixty-thousand yen every month."

"That's a lot!"

"Why do you think Kim Dong-jun decided to start a livecast?" Naoto gave a contemptuous snort. "So many fans are dying to know what the life of an idol is like, to see the world through his eyes and ears, to experience his sensations. Even if he charged a hundred thousand yen an hour there would still be plenty of fans signing up—he's basically printing money. And Kim Dong-jun is just a K-Pop star. The prices charged by Hollywood stars are straight out of this world. And you can't even get anything real during their designated livecast sessions anyway. All those parties, trips to exotic locales, charity events, and so on are scripted and sanitized. It's just another performance for them."

"If that's true, what's the point of a livecast then?"

"Livecasts by professional entertainers are boring"—Naoto's eyes now flashed with a rare fervor—"but there *are* livecasts worth the money. There's one superstar in particular who basically livecasts twenty-four hours every day, and it's all free! You can experience every detail of his life, and everything is reality, not reality TV. He's not one of those empty-headed celebrities famous for being famous. He comes up with brilliant ideas, has impeccable taste, and is a talented writer. He's also a leading aviator who's deeply involved in philanthropy—"

"Hey, wait a minute. You're talking about Charles, aren't you?"

"That's right, I'm talking about"—with an effort Naoto managed to swallow the *me*—"the one and only Charles Mann. Charles, the Man." He sighed, and his face dimmed.

Charles, my true self, what is happening to you?

5.

"You are free to go now." The slender figure of Homi appeared at the door to the detention cell, her tone chilly.

Charles got up from his chair, his expression indifferent, as though this development was entirely expected. He glanced at his watch. "It's not even seven yet. Why don't we have dinner together?"

"I have work to do." Homi's voice was still emotionless. "Come this way, please."

"I thought you told me that bail is impossible. Why are you letting me go?"

"It's because of your devoted fans." Annoyance flashed across Homi's face. "At least a hundred thousand of them are protesting in front of the headquarters building, threatening to tear this place down. They're demanding that you immediately resume your livecast. Half of Tokyo is now paralyzed. I don't get it: how can so many people worship someone like you?"

"You're letting me go because of my supporters?"

"You're apparently not a terrorist, and the brass isn't interested in pursuing this matter further. We won't charge you. Now, will you please get out of here?"

"No." Charles shook his head. "If you're not planning to charge me, why did you arrest me in the first place? I demand an explanation, otherwise I'm not leaving."

"You—" Homi glared at him.

Just then, a tall blonde appeared behind her. "This entire incident was caused by the incompetence of the Japanese police. You must apologize to Mr. Mann."

"Lisa!" Charles called to his manager. "I've been waiting for you. What took you so long?"

"MacDonald is taking care of it." Lisa nodded at him. "Charles, since you never left *Pegasus* at the stadium, you were still officially in the race. The proper interpretation for what happened was that you deviated from the race course and were forced to land in Hakone . . . Anyway, the point is you didn't violate Japanese law, and they had no right to detain you. Since the Japanese police wasted your valuable time, they must offer you a formal apology. We will publish the demand in every major media outlet and reserve the right to pursue compensation through the legal system."

"Oh, we don't need to make such a fuss," Charles said generously. "As long as this beautiful woman is willing to have dinner with me, I'm willing to forgive the police and let bygones be bygones."

Homi was about to offer some sarcastic retort when her phone buzzed. She picked up and listened, the expression on her face shifting subtly. It was a call from the chief of police.

Lisa pulled Charles to the side and whispered, "You've got to get out of here right away and resume the livecast. There are millions complaining on the web already."

"What's the hurry? It's rare for me to get a few moments to myself."

"No, you've got to resume as soon as possible." Lisa's tone brook no objections.

Charles looked at Lisa, whose expression remained superficially calm. That only made Charles uneasy. When he first started his career, everything had gone wrong. At that crucial juncture, Lisa Goldstone had come to his aid and pulled him through. Everything he did—racing, writing, charity work, publicity—she arranged. Her contribution to Charles's meteoric rise could not be overstated. But even so, Charles never felt very close to Lisa; indeed, he was a bit intimidated by her, though he also acknowledged that he depended on her. In recent years, as Charles's stock had risen higher and higher, Lisa had come to manage his affairs with more input from him. Still, whenever Lisa insisted that something had to be done a certain way, Charles felt powerless to resist.

"All right," he said with no enthusiasm.

Lisa shifted to a more mollifying tone. "You know that at least ten million people are tuned into your livecast at any moment, and more than 1.2 million choose to spend more than five hours a day in your stream. About three hundred thousand are practically living in your body and mind twenty-four hours a day. This is mainly because your livecast is almost never off. Your fans have come to trust you and rely on you. Now that you've been off air for an unprecedented two hours, many are finding your absence intolerable."

"But they can tune into other livecasts! There must be at least a hundred thousand to pick from."

Lisa laughed. "How can they compare to you? You are the one and only Charles. But don't let that go to your head. More celebrities are getting into the livecasting business every day, and many want to take over your place. If you don't get back on air soon, I imagine more than a few will turn for their fix elsewhere. Your career depends on that not happening."

"I . . . understand." Homi hung up her phone, and, scowling, turned back to Charles. "Mr. Charles, on behalf of the Tokyo Metropolitan Police, I hereby offer you our sincerest apologies." She bowed deeply.

Charles grinned. "I've already forgotten it. But I do have a craving for Japanese food. Would you take me somewhere good?"

Homi gritted her teeth. "Please, come this way."

Lisa smiled knowingly as she leaned over to whisper in Charles's ear, "The whole world is watching. If you can capture her heart, I'm certain you'll double your subscribers."

6.

"Takumi-kun, are you all right?"

"Hmm?" Naoto's mind had been wandering. He saw that Minami was gazing at him with a look of concern. "Sorry. What did you say?"

"I asked you how it felt to tune into a livecast."

"An interesting question." Naoto pondered his answer. "At first, you go through a period of adjustment—that happens no matter whose livecast you tune into. The beginning is a bit frustrating: the colors and sounds all feel wrong somehow, as though you're watching some 2-d film from the twentieth century. It's just odd. Although all human beings share similar biological sensory organs, there are subtle differences in the neural wiring, and so you have to put in an effort to interpret the signals being projected into your brain, and all subtleties are at first lost. For several days you'll feel as though you're perceiving everything through a film, and nothing feels immediate or real. But then, one day, you'll have a breakthrough and everything will feel just like your own senses."

"Can you feel everything the livecaster feels?'

"Almost everything: sight, sound, touch, smell, taste, heat and cold, the sensation of weight . . . and pain. For example, if the livecaster is pricked by a needle, you'll feel the same sharp pang of pain. However, since the signal is filtered for safety reasons, the magnitude of the pain is diminished. Do you remember the British singer Philip Bolt? Three years ago during a livecast a deranged fan stabbed him more than ten times in the stomach, and he died almost instantaneously. Twenty thousand subscribers who were tuned into the cast suffered along with him, and close to five hundred fainted, with more than thirty dying from shock. Everybody was talking about it back then. After that, they put in safeguards for subscribers to prevent such traumatic experiences."

"Oh . . . Then, what about joy? Can livecasts transmit the feeling of joy?"

"That's . . . complicated." Naoto tried to find the right words. "Usually, it's not possible to directly transmit joy because the emotional experience involves the whole body and isn't a distinct sensation. However, biological sensations of pleasure *can* be transmitted: such as the pleasure of eating a gourmet meal."

"Then you don't really know what the livecaster is thinking either."

"That's right, you don't. Each sense is limited to a specific region of the brain, but not thought. Cognition, as we've learned, emerges from the coordinated actions of all regions of the brain and cannot be isolated to specific areas. Also, since our thoughts require access to uniquely encoded memories, it's very difficult to translate each thought for transmission. Indeed, it's precisely because thoughts cannot be tapped into that livecasters are willing to open up their senses to others. This way, they can still maintain their inner privacy."

Minami grew even more curious. "I still don't quite understand what it's like to tune into a livecast. So you can see everything they see, hear everything they hear, just like if you were living in their body, and yet you don't know what they're thinking and can't control what they do? It seems as though you'd feel like a puppet whose string is being pulled by someone else. That must feel really awkward."

"You're not wrong." Naoto was enjoying this conversation, and he was suddenly seized by a desire to share with her everything he had learned about livecasts. "But remember, feeling like you're really in the livecaster's body is only the second stage. The next stage requires you to build the psycho-coordination link. That is, you have to synchronize your thoughts to theirs, and match your actions to theirs, so that it feels as though you're moving the livecaster's body yourself."

"How is that possible?"

"It's not easy, but it's a learnable skill. You have to experiment a bit. First, you need to purge yourself of all distracting thoughts, and habituate yourself to the livecaster's lifestyle and their way of doing things. Of course you also have to really understand the way they use language. After you've accomplished these steps, it's possible for you to think and act just like the livecaster in most situations. This isn't as hard as you might imagine. Most of our thoughts and actions are triggered by sensory inputs. Once you've accepted the sensory input as your own, you hold the key to the thoughts and actions as well. For examples, if you see and smell a hot mug of delicious coffee in front of you, isn't it natural to pick up the mug and take a sip?"

"But . . . but there must be *some* things that cannot be anticipated by the subscriber, right? For examples, any sort of high-level thinking or decision-making?"

"Well, yes . . . that's why you have to stay focused. But there are tricks. For example, try to empty your mind and think of nothing at all; let your senses guide you. After a while, you'll feel yourself building a kind of psychic resonance with the livecaster, as though you really *are* the livecaster."

"So you can build such a deep link with only one livecaster?"

"Theoretically, there's no such limit. But ideally, you want to build such a link with only one subject. If you switch between multiple livecasters, it's very hard to maintain multiple psycho-coordination links."

"But why?" asked Minami.

"Why what?"

"Why do you want to be the livecaster? Isn't that . . . a bit much? You want to understand the livecaster, but that doesn't mean you want to give up your life to live theirs. And that's an impossible dream anyway."

"Why is it impossible?" Naoto felt a surge of anger. "You've never even tried it, so of course you know nothing about the fantastic experience of the link, that sensation of the soul melding with the flesh. You would really be living a different life, really *be* someone else. If you knew what that felt like you wouldn't be asking such questions."

"All right, I guess I don't understand." Minami wasn't interested in arguing. "But Naoto-kun, I think you should get out of your apartment more. A gym just opened near us, and I go there every day to swim or play ball. Why don't we go together?"

Naoto found the suggestion ridiculous. Earlier today he had flown thousands of miles, traversing half the globe in the process. And now this silly girl wanted him to go exercise with her? *What does she know?*

But it appeared as if Charles's livecast wouldn't be resuming any time soon. He needed some way to pass the time. Maybe going to the gym wasn't a bad idea. It certainly was better than being cooped up at home, bored.

"All right." Naoto nodded. "Let's—"

Ping! The alert ring in his ear was accompanied by a flood of signals into his implant. *OMG, Charles has just resumed his livecast!*

"—try to figure out something in another couple of days. Thanks!" Naoto yawned exaggeratedly. "I'm sorry. I'm feeling really tired, and I'd like to take a nap."

"But—" Minami protested, but Naoto made it clear that he wanted to be alone.

After shutting the door behind her, Naoto lay down on the tatami mat, his whole body tingling with excitement. The bare, cramped apartment now seemed lovely and comfortable.

What's going to happen next? Will I be with Aoi Masa, Hosokawa Homi, or some other beauty? What will we be doing? How will I spend this lovely night? No matter what, my real life is about to resume.

7.

Wearing a pair of shades and nibbling on takoyaki in a roadside stall in Akihabara, Charles was thoroughly enjoying himself. Homi sat across from him, the steaming bowl of tonkotsu ramen before her untouched. Even though he was making an effort at a disguise, many of the establishment's patrons soon recognized Charles. He waved at them in acknowledgement, and from time to time, fans approached for a wefie or an autograph—at least everyone was polite.

Homi looked around and finally relaxed a bit. "Aren't you afraid of being mobbed by your fans, just sitting here in the open?"

"Afraid? My fans would much rather be tuning into my livecast. Even if they could come here and see me in the flesh, I doubt many of them would choose to. Oh, don't you like your noodles?"

"I . . . I'm just uncomfortable." Homi's cheeks reddened. "The idea that millions are watching us is so strange."

"They're not watching me." Charles grinned at her. "They're enjoying the sight of you through my eyes."

"I don't like it!"

"You weren't so nervous when we first met."

"That was because I didn't really understand what livecasting involved. You had to explain it to me. This technology only became popular in the last few years, right?"

"No. It's been around for ten years. I was one of the first to start a cast."

"That's true. But it only spread to East Asia recently. We Japanese prize our privacy. I can't imagine having strangers watch everything I do."

"Not *everything*." Charles chuckled. "I always pause the cast when I'm sitting on the toilet. Nobody wants to deal with the smell. Trust me."

"But everything about your life . . . even . . . even . . . "

"You're talking about sex? That's a biological need and part of our social repertoire. I don't need to hide that."

"But it's private!"

"Ha! Having the whole world watch you enjoy yourself is a pretty fantastic feeling." Charles winked at her. "Masa told me she adores it."

"Of course she would! That's how she makes her living."

"Well, it wouldn't kill you to try something new. I've heard that nudism is gaining popularity in Japan, and I—"

"Listen, Mr. Charles." Homi's gaze was now infused with a mixture of annoyance and embarrassment. "Not everyone subscribes to your life philosophy. I'm here because my superiors asked me to be polite and play the hostess, but after this meal, we will never have anything to do with each other again. Do you understand?"

I understand that you're playing hard to get. Charles spread his hands in a conciliatory manner. "Of course. You've got to do what feels right to you."

You're certainly not the first woman to say something like that to me, Charles thought. Many seemed to have an instinctive fear of being exposed before strangers, but soon, his lovers learned to crave the delightful sensation of being the center of the world's attention. They fell in love with this way of life and abandoned their old prejudices. *Maybe Homi will be like that . . . but if she isn't, maybe that will make things even more exciting . . .*

Three boys about eight years old approached the pair excitedly and broke the awkward silence between them. They said to Charles, "*Konbanwa, Charuzu-sama!*"

"*Konbanwa!*" Charles replied to their greeting happily. This was about the extent of his Japanese, however.

The children continued in rapid-fire Japanese. Charles looked at Homi helplessly, and she was forced to play interpreter. "They said that they saw you win the race this afternoon, and they really like you. When they grow up, they hope to become just like you, a great aviator and author."

Charles gently patted one of the boys on the head. "Kid, it's not that important to fly very fast or publish a book. What really matters is being yourself and doing what you desire in your heart."

The boy replied, and Homi continued to translate. "But I *want* to be an aviator. So cool!"

"Then start as a junior aviator. You can first try a full-body simulator and race in VR."

"Virtual reality is pointless. I want to fly the real thing, just like *Pegasus.*"

"Slow down, kid." Charles explained patiently. "If you really love the sport, you'll enjoy learning what the simulator can teach you. You can also subscribe to livecasts from me and other aviators, and you'll learn a lot—well, except the parts that require parental approval to view."

After answering a few more questions, the children left happily with autographed pictures of Charles.

"You're certainly good at dazzling children," said Homi.

Charles laughed. "I'm just saying what I really think. This has always been my belief: everyone should be themselves, and realize their own worth. I'm not some idol on a high pedestal demanding to be worshipped. I started a livecast for a reason perhaps different from most: I just want everyone to know the real Charles."

"That's a bit rich," said Homi. "Don't you depend on your subscribers for your income?"

Charles frowned. He hated this kind of cynicism. "You're wrong. Whether it's from my racing or my writing, I make more than enough to live comfortably. My livecast is completely free, and I've never earned a single cent from it."

"I'm sorry. I didn't mean that."

"It's all right." Charles shrugged. "Many people think like that, and I can't change their minds. I just don't want my friends to misunderstand me. If you know me, you'll know that before I started the livecast, I had already been published and won third place in the Trans-Pacific Championship Race. I didn't need a livecast to increase my fame at all.

"It's true that these days there are millions tuned into my stream at all times, but I've always believed that I'm not very important as an individual; rather, I represent the concept of livecasting. The practice isn't about destroying personal privacy, but about sharing—sharing of information, sharing each other's sufferings and joys, until the entire human race becomes one Man. As subscribers enrich their own lives with livecasts, they gain a deeper understanding of themselves and discover their own worth."

"That does sound . . . reasonable." Homi was thoughtful. "But having so many people watch every move you make must make you feel . . . not free."

"That kind of thinking is evidence of lack of self-confidence. I'm Charles, the one and only. Even if billions are watching me, my freedom isn't diminished by one iota."

"Maybe it's because you're an American," said Homi. "Americans are always brimming with self-confidence. This is not the Japanese way. From childhood we're taught by our parents to live within rules and expectations, to learn to regulate our behavior in anticipation of what everyone watching us may think. The desire for privacy is thus even stronger.

"I remember playing with my friends every day in a tiny garden when we were in kindergarten. I say 'play,' but in reality we still had to follow all kinds of rules. At the end of the garden was a row of trees, and behind the trees was a wall. But there was a gap between the trees and the wall, though most people did not notice it. I discovered this hidden space one day, populated only by a few clusters of wildflowers. Even though it was a patch of grass no different from the rest of the garden, my joy was indescribable. Every day, I made my way there in secret to play by myself. It wasn't that I didn't want to share my discovery with my friends, but it was only when I was there, alone, that I could relax and feel at peace. I could laugh or cry without anyone bothering me.

"Unfortunately, not long after that my refuge was discovered by others. Many came and trampled over the grass and picked the wildflowers. That tiny world I had to myself was ruined."

Homi felt depressed. She had no idea why she chose to say these things to Charles. She had never told anyone else about this memory from childhood, and now the whole world knew her secret.

Charles was moved. After a moment, he said, "The others did destroy your secret garden. But they weren't motivated by the desire to watch you."

"No, you don't understand. It didn't really matter whether they wrecked my garden. The moment they were in that space, my peace was gone, and I was no longer myself. Have you never felt that way?"

"I . . . I suppose I did when I was very young." For the first time, Charles had trouble coming up with what to say. "But I haven't felt like that in a long time."

Homi gazed at him, a complicated set of emotions flitting through her eyes. "Then I have a suggestion: turn off your livecast. Try to experience your individual world, where every sensation belongs to you and you alone. I believe you'll feel a distinction."

"Turn off the livecast?"

"Maybe you just need a minute to feel the difference."

"No. That would be a breach of my promise to my subscribers—"

"Charles, I thought you advocated for the belief that you should do only what you want to do." Homi's tone was now mocking. "It wouldn't kill you to try something new."

"Maybe if I—"

Charles, ignore her! A translucent text window popped into his view. This was Lisa communicating with him directly over the cranial implant. The text was only visible to him as the livecast software filtered it out from subscriber feeds.

I was thinking of trying it for just a couple minutes. Charles sent his thoughts back to Lisa over the cranial implant.

Not even one second. You're being watched by the planet! This could severely tarnish your image. Charles could practically see Lisa's no-nonsense scowl.

Homi noticed Charles's subtle shifts in gaze and guessed that he was communicating with someone over his neural implant. She challenged him, "I'm guessing your boss is telling you no, right? Oh well—"

"Boss?" Charles instantly felt his cheeks heat up. "I'm my own man. No one tells me what to do!"

He commanded his implant to cease livecasting, and mentally recited the passcode to confirm the order. Instantly, it seemed as if a background buzz had stopped, and everything seemed extra quiet. This wasn't the first time he had ever halted the livecast, of course, but it was the first time he had stopped livecasting for the sake of experiencing what it was like to be by himself. The sensation was distinct. Now, no matter what he said or did, only the woman across from him would be his audience. There seemed to be a marvelous, intimate bond that drew them closer.

"How do you feel?" Homi asked.

"It's no big deal," Charles said, deliberately trying to underplay it. "I'm okay with it."

But it wasn't that simple at all. The world seemed to have vanished, leaving only him and her, but it also felt as if a new dimension had been opened up to him, leading into a new space that extended into infinity.

8.

Takumi Naoto panted as he scampered through a dense fern jungle, a rampaging T-rex in hot pursuit. The very ground quaked with the massive beast's every step. The dinosaur wasn't running very fast, however, just keeping pace with him like a cat playing with a mouse. Naoto could almost feel the hot breath of the saurian on the back of his neck.

Naoto struggled to put one leg in front of the other, desperate to escape from the monster's jaws. He was winded, sweat-drenched, and his legs were filled with lead. Soon, the T-rex took a giant stride and overtook him; it turned its gigantic body around and opened its colossal jaws, aiming to crush Naoto's skull with its dagger-like teeth. Naoto screamed and collapsed into a heap on the ground.

The jungle and the T-rex vanished; floating lines of data took their place. *Total distance: 546 meters. Time: 116 seconds. Average speed: 4.7 meters / second. Measured lung capacity: 1250cc. Health rating: B— . . .*

Minami's round face loomed before him. Naoto was draped over the guardrails of the three-dimensional immersion treadmill, so exhausted that he couldn't speak a word.

"You couldn't even manage 600 meters?" Minami giggled. "Even I can run a kilometer with no problems. Naoto, you really need some exercise."

Finally, Naoto managed to climb up. Gasping, he said, "It takes . . . time . . . for anything . . . "

"Then let's keep going. I'll make the dinosaur even slower this time. Ready?"

"No! . . . I've got to . . . take a break . . . "

They went over to the lounge chairs. As soon as they sat down, a cool breeze caressed their faces, and the immersion displays around them showed a turquoise ocean whose gentle waves caressed the cerulean sky. Next to the chairs were two chilled glasses of lemonade—the real deal, not simulation.

The lemonade and the breeze relaxed Naoto so much that he felt as if all his pores yawned. "I haven't felt this good in ages. It feels amazing to drink something cold after physical exertion."

"Didn't you also exercise when you were tuned into Charles's livecast—no, let me rephrase: didn't you also experience the sensations of exercise?"

"Yes . . . But Charles has so much energy and such a toned body—nothing like mine. Also, because of the safety filtering that tamps down extreme sensations, I never felt very tired."

"You should definitely come with me more often." Minami laughed guilelessly. "Let's go swimming!"

But before Naoto could reply, a loud cry arose to the side: "Hey! It's that bastard Charles! He's finally shown himself!"

Naoto looked over to the source of the commotion. The projection screen on the wall was showing the news. "After disappearing in Akihabara yesterday and being incommunicado for over seventeen hours, the renowned American aviator Charles Mann has reappeared today at noon, accompanied by his rumored new flame, Miss Hosokawa Homi . . . "

Charles is back!

Last night, Charles never resumed his livecast after turning it off at Homi's urging. Completely at a loss, Naoto finally decided to go to Akihabara. But as soon as he emerged from the subway, he saw countless other fans had had the same idea and all the streets leading to that roadside stall were jammed. Eventually, he saw *Pegasus* taking off and disappearing into the night sky. Rumor had it that Charles had taken Homi away on a pleasure cruise in space, just the two of them. All night, there was no more news. Naoto waited and waited without any result, and finally, utterly bored, came to the gym with Minami. He certainly wasn't expecting to receive news of Charles now.

"... Charles is declining all interview requests. His only statement is that *Pegasus* lost power. But according to media sources, his ship had been in low-Earth orbit overnight, and Miss Hosokawa was aboard as well ... "

"Do you think they did it?" Naoto overheard someone ask.

"Are you an idiot? Of course they did it."

"What difference does it make if they did it? The bastard isn't casting, and so we can't enjoy it anyway."

"Maybe the girl is just shy ... "

"Let me tell you, this has finally shown me the truth. Charles may talk all the time about sharing and freedom and all that bullshit, but in the end, he gets to turn off his livecast anytime he wants to. He doesn't think of us at all. In the end, he's no different from the rest of the celebrities."

"I don't agree with you at all." Naoto had finally had enough. He jumped up to defend Charles.

The man who criticized Charles was also in his twenties. He gave Naoto a contemptuous look. "Mind your own business if you know what's good for you."

"If you are really a fan of Charles, how can you talk about him like that? Don't you know him at all? This was most likely the result of an implant malfunction."

"Oh, you're one of *those* fans. A *malfunction*? Please. Weren't you tuned in yesterday? He said he stopped the livecast on purpose."

"Yes, but ... it's only temporary. There had been pauses in the cast before, when he was visiting Prague and Yangon, for instance. Don't you understand that everyone needs some privacy from time to time?"

"I don't worship that poseur like you do." The young man harrumphed. "The only reason I subscribe to his cast is to see him in bed with those supermodels. But not only did he not sleep with Masa, he went and found himself a chick cop and didn't even have the decency to cast the bedroom scene. What's the point of watching then?"

"You are not fit to appreciate Charles's livecast. How can you understand his ideals and beliefs?"

"Oh, I see, you *understand* him, do you? Well, looks like he kicked you to the curb when it suited him just the same. I'm through with wasting my breath on dumbasses like you." The young man turned around and left.

Naoto sat down, full of rage that he didn't know where to direct.

The news broadcast continued. " ... Charles's manager, Lisa Goldstone, released a statement that the interruption in the livecast was due to a technical glitch. Full livecasting has been resumed, and on behalf of Charles, she apologizes to all the fans for the inconvenience ... "

"Naoto, are you going to rush home for the livecast?" Minami asked, careful to keep her tone neutral.

"Leave me alone!" Naoto shouted at her. "I don't know!"

"I was just asking," Minami muttered. "Why are you screaming at me?"

"I'm sorry." Naoto forced himself to calm down. "I'm just ... " He didn't know what to say and collapsed back onto the lounge chair.

Silently, Naoto fumed at Charles. *Why did you stop the livecast? Why did you cut off the psychic link between us?* Recently, he could almost feel himself completely melding with Charles soul to soul, and when Charles said that he wanted to stop the livecast, Naoto had almost wanted to cheer, not realizing that it meant that he would also be shut out. And a second later, he had been tossed back into his bare efficiency apartment, all alone.

Only then did the painful realization come that he was never going to *be* Charles, just a ghostly parasite attached to Charles.

For the last three years, Naoto was tuned into Charles's cast almost continuously. Every day, he lived Charles's life, facing everything he faced, participating in his races, planning and drafting and revising his books, until he could speak American English better than Japanese, until he had almost forgotten who he was. As long as he thought of himself as Charles, it was possible to scale one life's peak after another, be a guest at the world's most exclusive parties, travel the world, live in seven-star hotels, bathe in the fervor of fans, hop from the bed of one hot woman to another . . .

But these were not the most important. The real joys were the sense of personal worth, the spirit of freedom, and a lifestyle enabled by boundless self-confidence embodied by Charles Mann. Only when he was in Charles's body did he feel he was alive. In his own life, he was just Takumi Naoto, a programmer in a dead-end job, a failure whose life was devoid of excitement, who was estranged from his parents, whose girlfriend had left him for another man, who didn't even have a single real friend. A few years ago, he had contemplated suicide. If Charles's livecast hadn't come along to save him, Naoto would have long passed the slope of Yomotsu Hirasaka and entered the underworld.

Charles gave him a new life and hope, and resculpted his soul so that he believed that he could possess a life with value and dignity. But everything had changed. Yesterday made Naoto realize that Charles could cease livecasting at any moment, cut off this link that to him was inseverable. Everything he had thought about Charles had just been his own fantasy. Even if he possessed a soul just like Charles's, he could never have his life.

He was still just Takumi Naoto, just himself. However, today's experiences made him feel that being Naoto from time to time wasn't so bad. Of course, he would still tune into Charles's cast, but not right now.

Having made his decision, he got up and stretched. "Minami, let's run some more. My goal is three kilometers today."

"All right!" She laughed in delight.

9.

"Charles, I'm going to say it just one more time: *You cannot do this!*" Lisa was screaming at him through the phone.

"Lisa, I've already told you at least ten times: my time with Homi will never be livecast. This is my decision."

"That means you're livecasting for no more than eight hours a day. This is going to break the bond between you and your fans. Your ratings have taken a nosedive this month, and last week the number of viewers tuned into your livecast fell below two million. You were once alone at the top of the ratings, and now you're not even in the top ten. *Wake up, Charles!* Even that Chinese clown, Baby Phoenix, has more subscribers than you."

"Fine, let them go follow Baby Phoenix. What does it matter to me?"

"Charles." With visible effort, Lisa managed to contain her impatience. "Listen, we need to have a real discussion, as soon as possible."

"Let's do it another day," Charles said. "Homi and I are celebrating our 100-day anniversary tonight. I don't want to be disturbed."

"But—"

Charles disconnected.

Homi, who was standing across from him, asked, "What's wrong?"

"Nothing. Just work stuff."

"Then let's continue. I don't think you've had enough."

Homi grabbed hold of him. Charles went for her waist, and she leaned into him compliantly. Watching her shy, smiling face, Charles's concentration wavered. Suddenly, Homi wriggled out of his grasp, and he felt her weight pushing him off balance over her leg as he collapsed to the mat.

"Ha! You lost again!"

Charles was glad that there was no livecast to show his humiliating wrestling defeat at the hands of someone weighing at least 80 pounds less than he did. Of course, these were hardly fair contests, as Homi was a professionally trained fighter.

"I think you need to admit defeat, and it's 'pony time!'" said Homi, her eyes flashing mischievously.

Charles sighed and got on all fours, and with a delighted whoop Homi jumped on his back and guided her new mount around the room.

What had happened to the suave, slick Charles who once boasted of never sleeping with the same woman two nights in a row?

On that day more than three months ago, after Charles shut off the livecast, confused fans had surrounded Charles and Homi in Akihabara. In the end, the pair had to escape by taking off in *Pegasus*. But Charles had forgotten the fact that his ship was almost out of fuel, and once they reached orbit they were stuck. Charles then turned on the livecast to call for aid, only to realize that there wasn't even enough juice to power the neutrino converter, cutting them off from the rest of the world. A simple postprandial stroll had thus turned into a little castaway adventure in space.

Fortunately, the experience brought the pair together. Homi had never been to space, and as they drifted in near-weightlessness, she didn't even know how to take a sip of water, leading to many embarrassing situations. They did not, in fact, "do it" on that first night together. But after they returned to Earth, Charles arrived in Japan several days later with a *Pegasus* full of roses, and finally managed to convince Homi to go on a second date with him . . .

Homi imposed one condition: no livecasting while they were on dates. Charles agreed right away. And soon, he discovered a novel pleasure in this secret relationship. He ended up doing many things he had never thought of doing before: meowing at Homi like a cat, whispering ridiculous lovers' prattle that made even him blush, horsing around like a couple of kids, doing whatever felt fun and relaxing at the moment instead of trying to perform as the perfect lover while the whole world watched.

Years earlier, Charles had lived in such a carefree manner, but he had forgotten that past self during the years of continuous livecasting.

Tonight, in the new cabin that Charles had bought on the shore of the lake in Hakone, they were just a relaxed couple enjoying their time together. It wasn't particularly romantic or exciting, but they were free to be as silly as they wanted.

"Listen, baby, your ride needs a break," Charles said. He twisted, dislodging the protesting Homi from his back, and then rolled until she was under him. He kissed her neck with fervor. "*Anata*," he whispered—the 'pony's' Japanese had been improving under expert guidance—"Let me . . . "

Homi moaned and her eyes lost focus as she licked her lips in anticipation. The whole night lay ahead, and this cabin belonged just to the two of them with no stranger's gaze . . .

He reached out to unfasten her *gi*. But his hand stopped and pulled back—

—and slapped hard against Homi's cheek.

Homi's smile was frozen. She was stunned and unable to speak, staring at him in utter disbelief.

"What in the world is wrong with you?" she finally managed after a few seconds.

Charles's features twisted into a hideous, savage expression, the muscles of his face twitching. He lifted an arm and pointed at the door. "Get out of here. Now!"

"How can you speak to me—"

He shoved at her roughly. "Get out!"

After staring at him for an interminable moment, Homi got up and put on her coat. "Charles, you really are an asshole." She kicked him hard in the crotch and then hurried out the door.

The pain from his lower body doubled Charles over, and then he fell to his hands and knees. His throat spasmed and he coughed violently, as if he needed to expectorate his innards. His eyes filled with tears, and his limbs jerked uncontrollably in cramped agony. He didn't know how long he was seized by such physical suffering. It was only after he had recovered that he saw a pair of slender legs in a pair of bright red high heels in front of him.

He looked up and saw a familiar face.

"Lisa?" He struggled to get up. "What are you doing here?"

"Since you wouldn't see me, I had no choice but to come to you."

"But how did you know I was here? I shut off all location services and—"

Lisa didn't answer his query but posed a question of her own. "How does it feel to get rid of your girlfriend with a good, hard slap to the face?"

Charles's vision blurred. "How did you know—wait, did you . . . did you—"

Gently caressing his face, Lisa said in a pitying tone, "Charles, my dear Charles, don't blame me. You made me do it. Don't you see?"

His worst fear had been confirmed. Eyes wide in shock, Charles muttered, "Oh my God, I didn't know you could control my body through the implant . . . But, how could the chip . . . I thought it was just a transmitter."

"There's no such thing as 'just a transmitter.' Others are able to receive your brain activities through neutrino beams, and you're also able to receive brain activity signals."

"But I thought it was limited to sensory input—"

Lisa's look was a mixture of pity and contempt. "There are so many things you don't know. Let's start from the beginning. Do you remember the autumn ten years ago? That was the year after your first race, when you did unexpectedly well. You had spent hundreds of thousands to outfit your ship, thinking that you could win a championship. The result? You didn't even place, losing all your investment. You were on the verge of giving up your dream of being an aviator and returning home to Tennessee to be a farmer just like your father."

"Yes, I remember." Charles said. Lisa had found him, almost passed out, in a little dive bar. She told him that she worked for an experimental neural research institute, where they were testing a new cranial implant device that could allow different people to share sensory perceptions. If Charles volunteered to be a subject, they'd pay him two hundred thousand dollars. And if the experiments caused irreversible damage to his health, they'd compensate him with even more money. In order to raise the funds for the next race, Charles accepted. And soon, they began the first trial livecast with him.

"In reality, what I told you was not the real experiment at all," said Lisa. "Fifteen years ago, Bell Labs invented a new direct neural interface chip capable of being implanted into the pons. The original intent was to implement a mind-machine interface, but the results were less than ideal. Unexpectedly, the researchers found that the implant did allow the sharing of brain activity patterns between different subjects. Before you, we had already conducted multiple trials on animals and humans with excellent results. But this transformative technology lacked a suitable application. No one wanted to cut open their brain to insert a metal box that would transmit their brainwaves to other people, though they weren't against tapping into other people's brainwaves.

"In order to popularize this technology, we found a few subjects and compensated them handsomely to become livecasters. But once that was done, no more than a few extremely curious individuals were interested in the constant goings on in the lives of ordinary people—especially since the cost involved surgery.

"We needed a celebrity livecaster to present a compelling use case for the technology. The celebrity's fans could bring along more early adapters until a market emerged.

"We got in touch with multiple movie stars, athletes, and prominent authors, but unfortunately, no one wanted to do it. This wasn't entirely unexpected. If you were already famous and successful with a good life, why would you take the risk of drilling a hole in your skull to add some gizmo just so that strangers could peek into your head? We needed to create someone specifically for the purpose of catalyzing this new technology revolution. The management decided that we had to find a young person with potential and then package him, craft him, and advertise him until he became the spokesperson for livecasting."

10.

"And so you found me."

"That's right." Lisa said. "You were already semi-famous, but your career was stalled in a tough spot. You needed money, and you were willing to undergo surgery to get it. You craved the feeling of being worshipped by the crowd, and so you wouldn't be opposed to the idea of livecasting. You are blessed with good looks as well as easy and open manners. As long as your career took off, it was easy to see that more and more people would be attracted to your life. To be able to become the coolest and most relevant person in the world with little effort is a temptation few can resist."

"I see. But how did you know that I would be so successful in the future?"

"Ha!" Lisa was shaking her head. "My dear Charles, you're such a narcissist. Don't you get it?"

A cold sweat broke out on Charles's back as the truth pressed against an old, insecure wound in his psyche, but Lisa ripped off the last bandage concealing the truth without mercy. "We didn't *know,* of course. You were just one of many candidates who made it through our selection process. The fact that you were chosen was purely by accident. Had we picked any of the others, we would have been able to engineer their incredible success as well. Charles, you were never successful because of your own efforts—without us, you would be nothing."

"That's not fair. Of course the livecasting has helped my career, but I worked hard for my success!"

"You worked hard?" Lisa chortled. "Charles, you've been enjoying a marvelous fantasy for ten years, but it's time to wake up to reality. Do you really think you're some once-in-a-century aviation genius? Your experience and skill as a pilot are only secondary contributors to your numerous racing trophies—the real reason you won is because you possessed the most expensive and advanced racing craft. You can afford to hire the world's foremost aviation experts and engineers. Your victories are bought. I bet if you left *Pegasus* on autopilot it would still win most races."

Charles's face was now crimson and throbbing, but he couldn't find an effective retort. "Even if . . . even *if* that were true, I used my own money! I'm the spokesperson for several spacecraft and aircraft manufacturers, and I earn plenty of sponsorships for my races."

"You're just arguing the question of whether the chicken or the egg came first. Who arranged those sponsorships for you? Who got you in front of the advertising executives? Who convinced them to back you instead of a rival? Think about it: you get the newest prototypes for experimental craft as soon as they emerge from the wind tunnel; you have access to the latest engine technology and avionics; you enjoy the most ergonomic hull interior design and air filtration systems, customized and assembled by the most experienced engineers on the planet—do you really think you're entitled to all these advantages with no hustle from anyone? Charles, you're not stupid, but years of being surrounded by applause and constant praise have blinded you to the way things really are."

"So I'm just a puppet . . . with you and Bell Labs pulling the strings?" Charles felt his world crumble around him. "I've always thought you more than a bit odd. At first you told me you were a representative from Bell Labs, and then you worked at the implant start-up before becoming my professional manager—who's the one giving you orders?"

"That's a pointless question, and the answer won't mean a thing to you anyway. Bell Labs, Cartel Nanotech, Connally Entertainment, Griffin Media, Douglas Astronautics, Springer Publishing, Time Media, Pacific TV & VR, Foundation for Democracy in America . . . the companies and organizations who have invested in you are members of a common interest community, but no single entity calls the shots. If you insist on identifying a puppeteer, it's neither the US government nor Wall Street—it's capital itself. You're the most important link in the system, but you're not independent. Your pathetic attempt to make your own decisions is harming the interests of the entire community."

"Just because I stopped my livecast?" Charles laughed helplessly. "But you've already gotten your technology revolution and new market. There are more than a hundred thousand livecasting right now. Why don't you let me go?"

"But no one can compare to you, Charles. Even though we now have many livecasters, few are willing to do so 24 hours a day, and among them you're the most significant. You're the first idol we created for the livecasting age. People might go view a third-rate fad like Baby Phoenix out of curiosity for the exotic, but you embody the dream of billions with your life. There is no substitute for you in the livecasting industry. Your book *My So-Called Livecast Life* has sold more than three hundred million copies! You symbolize a new way of life.

"If you go back to casting only from time to time, then livecasting will never be more than mere entertainment, and not nearly as many would be infatuated with it. It might take us ten, twenty years to recover from such a setback."

"I thought you were very good at building up idols," said Charles. "Why don't you just make another Charles?"

"Why should we repeat the work we've already done? You're now the world's most prominent brand. Take your novels, for example: every one of them sells at least thirty million copies. But if the name of Jackson Smith were on the covers, I don't imagine we'd move more than a few thousand."

"Wait a minute." Charles was unnerved by where this was going. He stared at Lisa. "Who's Jackson Smith?"

"Of course you don't know him." Lisa waved his question away like a buzzing fly. "Jackson Daniel Smith, graduate of UT Austin, a failed novelist and former Hollywood scriptwriter, was the author of two novels published under his own name whose total sales never broke ten thousand. You can also find his name attached to a few B movies that no one has heard of. Twice divorced and bald by the time he was forty—oh, let me just add that he's also the author of most of your novels."

"What?!?" Charles was sure Lisa had gone too far. "What kind of bullshit is this?"

"Calm down. Think about it: before you got the cranial implant, you thought of yourself as a connoisseur of literature and published some online essays and short stories, but you never managed to even finish a novel. How could you have published your breakout debut, *The Parthenon,* the very next year?"

"What does when I began writing have to do with you? What are you trying to prove?"

"Let's go back to your composition process, shall we? For every one of your acclaimed novels, don't you remember how the key plot points and wonderful twists seemed to just appear in your brain out of nowhere? Did you think you were communing with your muse? In reality, inspiration is also a sensory phenomenon. There's a part of your brain, right here in the frontal lobe, which is the site of your sense of self and integrated cognition. That part is generally thought of as inviolable—not that we can't get into it, but if we did, you'd become a patient in the psych ward. The rest of your brain, whether we're talking about the sensory or motor cortices, or even the language center, can be stimulated with neural patterns from corresponding regions of other brains. We took Smith's ideas and beamed the same patterns into your language center, where they triggered similar concepts. When the neural impulses were combined in the frontal lobe, your consciousness chooses to interpret the inspirations as your own."

"That's *impossible!*" Charles was now screaming at her. "Those inspired strokes . . . they were *mine*! I stayed up late and got up early for them . . . that feeling of creativity . . . how . . . how can they belong to this Smith?"

"In the future, there will no longer be any so-called 'self,'" said Lisa. "That's nothing more than an illusion created by a small cluster of decision neurons in the frontal lobe, but we, naively, thought of it as the soul that encompassed the senses, emotions, and all cognition. The livecasting age is going to tear away these illusions. You're the pioneer of this brave new age, Charles, the apostle of a fresh epoch."

Charles was now curled up in a corner. A bout of hysterical laughter burst from him. "Oh, you're a real comedian, aren't you? You spend half the night ripping me apart and telling me that I'm a useless puppet, all my proud accomplishments nothing more than illusions. Yet now you call me an *apostle*?"

"Reality is frequently painful," said Lisa. "But you must press on down this path. Very soon you will come to understand that whether you're a genius or a fool isn't so important. What matters is *who do you feel you are*? Even if those ideas came from Jackson Smith, as long as you really felt that you came up with them, that was enough to satisfy your need to be creative, wasn't it?

"In our world, there are tens of millions who can feel that they *are* you, Charles, the Man. They couldn't care less who they really are. Millions have become you, melding completely with you. You endow their meaningless lives with hope. Their ranks will continue to swell because no one can resist the temptation. As we improve and perfect the technology for translating and transmitting neural patterns, millions more—billions—will join the livecasting revolution, and they won't be able to stop. In the not too distant future, I'm certain we can enable the transmission and reception of more complicated senses and emotions, or even fully formed thoughts. No one can predict how far the technology will ultimately develop, but this is surely the beginning of a true singularity. The traditional life of an individual will be swept away, replaced by a new world we have yet to imagine."

"But that's not *my* ideal. I've always wanted everyone to become their true selves, to pursue their own values."

"No." Lisa shook her head emphatically. "Even your most devoted fans, deep down, want to become you. Not many of them want to be themselves. This is human nature."

"All right," Charles gritted his teeth. "Since everything about me is false, illusory, at least my beliefs are real. I *won't* give that up. I will reveal everything you've told me to the world."

He tried to turn on the livecast, but nothing happened.

"Trust me, you don't want to do that," said Lisa. "We always have more than a dozen people monitoring everything you do. No matter where you are or when, as soon as you even say more than three words that we don't like, we'll activate our remote control and make you babble utter nonsense that will get you committed. Have you forgotten how you drove your girlfriend away?"

Charles dropped his face into his hands and collapsed back to the floor. "If you're so powerful, why not just take over my body and start pulling on the strings? You can then make me say what you want and dance to your tune."

"We don't yet have that level of technology. The sensory cortices and the motor cortices are distinct, and the necessary inputs and computations to fully direct your limbs are complicated. It took almost everything we had to make you say those words to Homi just now, and you didn't sound natural at all."

"It's too bad that Homi didn't notice these subtle differences. Otherwise she would have seen through your plot."

"Actually, I did." The voice was clear and crisp, a voice that he never thought he'd hear again.

Charles turned and saw the bright face of Hosokawa Homi.

11.

"Homi!?"

"I'm back." Homi nodded at the surprised Charles. "I really wanted to storm out and never return, but as a police officer, I'm trained to notice whether someone is speaking in a natural manner or not. I soon realized that something wasn't right, and returned to confront you—at which point I noticed someone else was here. I've been listening for quite some time. Since I don't have any implants in my brain, there's not much they can do against me."

"Charles, you've got to make her shut up!" Lisa glanced at Homi and turned back to Charles, her tone turning anxious. "If you don't want to lose everything you have, you must continue to collaborate with us. You'll get to keep your fame and riches, and we can discuss reserving some measure of privacy for you—"

"*Collaborate?*" Charles gritted his teeth so hard that the noise was audible. "Didn't you just a second ago threaten to send me to the madhouse?"

"Oh come on, Charles, you know perfectly well we'd never do that unless we had no other choice. We worked so hard to create you! We would never harm you if we . . . Look, I'm just trying to persuade you."

Homi turned to face Lisa. "You must free Charles and extract that devilish implant from his brain. I recorded the conversation between the two of you, and if anything happens to Charles, I will make sure the whole world hears about it. Even though you work for some powerful companies and people, I doubt they're powerful enough to control the whole world. Public opinion will not be on your side. Imagine the panic when people realize that the implants they got for receiving livecasting could be used to control them—your whole industry would collapse overnight. Ms. Goldstone, you no longer have a hold over Charles."

Lisa looked from Homi to Charles and gave a helpless smile. "I guess we're in a stalemate then. If we do as you demand and take the implant out of Charles, we'll be handing you all the cards. No one is that stupid. But if you do tell the media what we said, I guarantee you Charles will instantly become a babbling idiot. Ms. Hosokawa, I doubt you'd be willing to risk that."

The three fell silent, but the tension in the air only grew thicker.

"No matter what, you have to stop manipulating Charles," said Homi after a while, her voice tinged with a conciliatory note.

"Yes," said Charles, whose voice was infused with pain. "I want you and those you represent to leave me alone, and get as far from me as possible."

A series of complicated expressions flitted across Lisa's face before she spoke. "Let me be sure I understand your offer. We'll stop interfering with you, and you'll keep everything we talked about today under wraps. Do I have that right?"

Charles nodded. All he wanted now was to wake up from this nightmare. "If you really let us go."

"But you'll tumble from your successful perch and lose everything."

Wearily, Charles shook his head. "I've never been successful at all. I've just been living a ridiculous fantasy. Now that I understand the truth, I want to end this farce as quickly as possible."

Lisa looked at Homi, who mutely endorsed Charles's words. Lisa nodded. "All right, we'll do as you demand. But remember, whether you turn on the livecasting function or not, we'll be watching your every move. Don't think you can play some trick against us. You're a smart boy, Charles, and you won't make trouble for us, right?"

Slowly, Charles nodded.

"You better uphold your end of the bargain as well," said Homi. "I will be storing multiple copies of the recording—if anything happens to us, you bet the whole web is going to be alerted."

"Goodbye, Charles, my old friend. I hope you don't regret it." Lisa turned around and swept by Homi as she left the room. Soon, the pair heard the noise of a small flying car's engine coming to life outside.

Charles remained curled up on the ground, unable to speak. Homi knelt by him and silently placed a hand against his cheek. Charles stared at her: her gaze was full of concern; her hand felt warm and soft; her scent was elegant, understated.

He knew that he had lost everything, but he had her. From now on, the two of them would live like just any other ordinary couple.

Charles wrapped his arms around Homi and cried like he had never cried before. Homi lightly stroked the back of his head to comfort him. He squeezed his arms about her, so tightly that she had trouble breathing. But it was the only glint of hope in a dark sea of sorrow.

By the time Homi realized that Charles was squeezing her too tight, it was too late.

Somehow, Charles managed to get on top of Homi, and with her body held down by his weight, he locked his hands like a pair of vice about her neck. He was trying to crush her windpipe with almost superhuman strength, and his eyes bulged as his throat made a series of croaking noises, as though it were he, and not she, who was being choked.

"Let . . . go . . . please . . . " Homi couldn't even get the words out. She struggled and scratched at Charles's arms with her nails, but Charles seemed to have become completely immune to pain, his eyes glazed over.

Homi understood that it was the doing of Lisa Goldstone. She couldn't afford to let them go. Her vision dimmed as her consciousness faded. Life was about to depart from her body, and all that Homi could do was to kick her feet instinctively in a last, desperate struggle for breath—

Abruptly, Charles lowered his head and bit hard into his own wrist. Blood spurted from the wound, and his fingers loosened reflexively. Without thinking, Homi snapped his fingers off her neck and pushed him away. She rolled along the floor and scrambled to get as far away from him as possible.

Charles got up on his unsteady legs, swaying from side to side. Then he tumbled back to the floor, his limbs jerking violently.

"Run away . . . Run!" Charles's voice, twisted almost beyond recognition, emerged from his bloody mouth. He was struggling mightily against the invisible forces that had possessed his body.

Homi didn't know what to do. Out of the corners of her eyes, she saw the hexagonal black box, and a flash of inspiration seized her. She dashed over to the box, lifted it over her head, and smashed it against the ground with a dull thud. The box rolled a few times on the floor and revealed a large crack in its side. Homi rushed up and gave it a few hard, well-placed kicks. A series of grinding and snapping noises emerged from the box, and smoke rose out of the crack.

Charles was no longer moving. Like a deflated ball, he lay flat and gasped. Homi went over and helped him up. "It's all right. I destroyed the neutrino converter. They can't control you any longer."

"But we can't leave this cabin either." Charles's voice was faint from weakness. "There are neutrino transmitters and converters everywhere."

At Homi's insistence, the cabin had contained only a single neutrino converter and the walls were built to shield electromagnetic waves from outside transmitters. But if they left this sanctuary, Lisa and her people would be able to take control of Charles at any moment.

"Then . . . what can we do?"

"Call the media," said Charles. He closed his eyes in exhaustion. "We have to give a press conference now."

An hour and a half later, the cabin was overflowing with reporters representing twenty-plus Japanese media outlets and almost as many foreign agencies. Curiosity filled the gazes roaming around the messy room and taking in the wounded Charles and Homi. As the reporters whispered to each other, most of the rumors being passed around involved some romantic dispute.

"Good evening," said Charles as he got up from the sofa. "I've asked you to come tonight because—"

The reporters hung on every word, but Charles had stopped speaking. His eyes were focused on something above and behind the crowd of reporters as his lips fluttered subtly, as though he was speaking to some invisible being.

"Charles!" Homi realized that something was wrong and turned to the reporters. "We are about to tell you something that—"

"—something that is very important," said Charles. He seemed to have recovered, though his face was even more weary than before. "I've decided to join the Plutonian Grand Race next month."

"What?" Homi was shocked. The Plutonian Grand Race was a gimmick, and a successful aviator like Charles wasn't expected to participate at all. Just a few days ago, in response to an interview question, Charles had made it clear that he wasn't interested.

Charles continued. "As everyone knows, this race will take place on the longest course in human history, far surpassing the Circumsolar Grand Race conducted along Earth's orbit. Although this is the first time the race is being held, it will no doubt be deemed a landmark achievement in racers' careers one day. I've heard that not many racers have signed up, and so I guess if I want to be the champion, this is my best chance."

A few in the audience guffawed. Homi saw that Charles's manner seemed quite natural and not under someone else's control. She held her tongue despite the impulse to interrupt.

Charles looked around the room, and when he spoke again, his tone changed. "But since Pluto is about thirty AU from Earth at the present time, the entire race will take place over the course of two years. Limited by the speed of light and signal decay, I don't think it's possible to livecast during this time. I'm sorry."

A few of the reporters grumbled and protested. Apparently some of them were fans.

"What about Miss Hosokawa?" someone asked. "Are you going to be separated for two years?"

Charles held Homi by the hand and squeezed her palm meaningfully. "I don't believe two years will prove to be much of a barrier between us. I will carve her name into the million-year ice crust of Pluto."

"What was that about?" asked Homi. The reporters had all left.

A drained Charles massaged his temples. "One of the reporters was carrying a portable neutrino converter with him, and that allowed them to send a message to me via the visual texting window in my cranial implant."

"Did they threaten you again?"

Charles shook his head. "Worse. They threatened all of humanity."

"What?"

Charles recalled that silent conversation:

- *Remember, at least a billion people have already had the implant, and their lives are now in your hands. If you insist on telling the truth, we may not be able to control everyone, but we certainly can beam a series of chaotic signals to all implanted subjects within a few minutes. Most will at least suffer temporary psychosis, and some may become deranged permanently. Who knows how many accidents will occur as a result, and maybe a few choice subjects will push the buttons for launching nuclear missiles . . . The world will be turned upside down in a catastrophe that will make a world war seem like child's play. Earth would be sent back to the Stone Age in a matter of days.*

- *And so I have no choice but to shut up, is that it? I have to stand by and watch as you continue to push your devilish implant until everyone has become a slave who has lost all sense of self. I should just wait until you control the whole world and are no longer afraid of anything?*

- *This is the inevitable progress of history. We will either keep on going down this path until we reach a brand new future, or a war will lead to the deaths of hundreds of millions and civilization's complete collapse. The choice is yours, Charles.*

- *What choice do I have when you have a billion hostages?*

- *You did make the right choice, which is why you managed to change your speech to the reporters in time and avert a disaster. The idea of going to Pluto is not bad: this way, we can avoid direct conflict with each other, and you can stop worrying about another plot from us. By the time you return two years from now, you will no longer be the focus of the world's attention, and you can live as you like.*

- *And I will finally accomplish something that belongs entirely to me. I will prove that I'm no puppet, but the invincible Charles.*

"Charles, what's wrong?" Homi's words pulled him back to the present.

"Nothing." Charles pulled her to him and caressed her long hair. "Everything will be all right. I promise."

12.

An unprecedented three hundred million people tuned into Charles's final livecast. Three hundred million pairs of eyes accompanied Charles's strides into the launch facility and then turned to regard the writhing sea of people as well as the azure sky overhead.

The launch complex was located in Tanegashima, Kagoshima Prefecture, JAXA's traditional home. Twenty-four spacecraft of different designs were clustered near the center of the complex. Unlike ancient spaceships, however, these new spacecraft no longer needed massive gantries and launch towers. Advancing technology meant that these ships could be launched anywhere from the surface of the Earth, and the choice of departing from here was mainly symbolic.

Though many advances had already been made, manned space exploration was still in its beginning stages. The space race today wasn't aimed at the moon or Mars, but at Pluto, a celestial body billions of kilometers away whose surface bore no trace of human exploration except a few robotic probes. The entire race would take more than two years.

After the participating spacecraft left Earth, each was supposed to make use of solar sails or planetary gravity assists to accelerate and head for Pluto on its own. Once there, they were supposed to close their solar sails and use the remaining fuel for the return trip. Though the astronautic principles were simple, the journey, traversing the entire Solar System and measured in tens of billions of kilometers, was breathtakingly bold.

To be the first human being to set foot on Pluto would be a milestone in the history of the exploration of the Solar System. As Pluto was not deemed scientifically as significant as the major planets—of which it was no longer a member in any event—no government bothered to devise manned missions to it after sending a few probes. But as it was such a famous place, many civilian space enthusiasts made it their dream destination. During a span of a few decades, about eight manned spaceships had been launched toward Pluto, but most had to abandon the journey partway through due to the many difficulties encountered. A few were destroyed by micrometeoroids in the asteroid belt, and some vanished in deep space without a trace. The reputation of Pluto as a planet of death grew, and in recent years no more missions to Pluto had been launched. This Grand Race, however, had rekindled the enthusiasm of explorers for the conquest of Pluto.

The addition of Charles Mann to the roster of entrants raised the profile of the race further. Although many complained of not being able to tune into Charles's livecast for the duration, his steadfast courage moved the hearts of millions. The number of entrants doubled almost overnight to more than twenty, and all were among the ranks of elite aviators and astronauts. The Grand Race was now truly grand.

"Charles!" A familiar voice broke through the background noise of the crowd. He turned to see the approaching figure of his old rival, George Steele.

Charles grinned. "George, I have to thank you for being so willing to play the part of my runner-up every time."

George rolled his eyes. "Let me tell you something, playboy: you'd better be prepared to congratulate me this time."

"Why's that?" Charles asked, and the two headed for the cluster of spacecraft at the center of the complex shoulder by shoulder.

"I heard that you turned down the high-tech gear donated by Cartel Nanotech and the Douglas Group. Instead, you bought off-the-shelf equipment from a couple of no-name manufacturers. Is it true that you even designed the basic layout for your ship and assembled it yourself? You're too arrogant. Cartel's solar sail technology is unparalleled, and using the same mass, they can achieve an effective area one-third greater than competitors. Surely you must know what this means."

"I do. But Steele, I used to rely too much on technology. This time, I want to win by skill," Charles said earnestly.

"Then it's true that you've reduced the habitable space to the minimum in order to cut down the mass and increase speed?" The shocked look in Steele's eyes was tinged with respect. "I know you've kept all your plans secret, but I've studied the publicly available information on your ship's design in detail. My conclusion is that if you really intend to win, your habitable module must be about the size of a coffin. You won't have space for any entertainment or relaxation facilities in that cage. How can you live like an anchorite for two years? It's so unlike you!"

"To achieve our destiny of flying toward the end of the stars," Charles said. "If necessary, I believe you would do the same."

Steele nodded. "Charles, I have to admit, you're not at all what I expected. All right, for the next two years, we'll have plenty of opportunities to chat by radio. Maybe we'll become friends."

Conversing like two close companions, the pair reached the center of the complex and separated, heading for their respective ships, where they carried out the final inspections and preparations. Many pilots were saying farewell to their families and friends. As Charles checked his engine, a curvy, elegant feminine figure approached him.

"Masa-chan?" He stood up.

"Charles, I came to see you off."

"Thank you."

"No, I should be thanking you . . . actually, I came to apologize as well."

"Apologize?"

Aoi Masa took a deep breath. "Two years ago, I was just an average AV idol whose career was in its twilight. Thus, I orchestrated that 'chance' meeting between us at the Maldives. I seduced you and spent the night with you. The world got to know me through your livecast, and I became a renowned sex goddess. Thereafter, I managed to leverage my fame into a career as a mainstream actress, and just recently I took a role in a Hollywood production. My success is all because of you."

"Don't say that. Your achievements are the results of your hard work."

"But all those sweet words I whispered to you . . . they weren't real. I used you to climb up the ladder. I'm sorry."

"That's . . . look, Masa, life is like that. We are often forced to play roles, and sometimes we are so absorbed by the performance that we disappear into our characters. You don't need to apologize for what you did."

"Thanks for saying that." Masa took out a refined cloth packet. "You're a good friend, Charles, and I really did enjoy our time together. I sincerely wish you a victory in this race. I went to the Meiji Shrine to get this omamori for you. If you wear it, the spirits will protect you."

Charles locked gazes with her and accepted the charm. "Thank you. I will keep it with me."

"Goodbye, and good luck!" She gave him a light hug and turned to leave.

A complicated smile curved up the corners of Charles's mouth as he watched her departing figure. He was aware that Aoi Masa had just managed to squeeze the last bit of use out of him. That the "love" between him and her had just been a performance was not only clear to both of them, but also to every subscriber to his livecast. This final speech from Masa was no doubt calculated to further rehabilitate her image as she transitioned to a mainstream career: now everyone would think she was a woman of deep and true passions.

Yet . . . this didn't mean that Masa was a lying hypocrite. That the speech was prepared and calculated didn't mean that it wasn't also sincere. *All the world's a stage, and all of us mere players—always have been, and even more so in the livecasting age. Maybe our heartfelt honesty is nothing more than a heartfelt performance of the self.*

"Oh, Charles!" Masa suddenly halted and turned to him. "Where's Miss Hosokawa? I was hoping to see her."

"She's . . . not feeling well," Charles said.

"Ah." Masa gave him an understanding look, and a triumphant look flitted through her eyes, though she said nothing more. Charles knew that Masa had always been slightly miffed that Homi managed to "steal him away" from her. She must now be thinking that the relationship between Charles and Homi had soured.

But Homi didn't need to be here to bid farewell to him, and she shouldn't be. She was hiding in an absolutely secure location, holding onto crucial evidence to prevent Lisa and her people from plotting against them at this critical moment and killing them both simultaneously. After he left Earth, Lisa would no longer have the ability to control him through the cranial implant, and Homi would maintain contact with him every day. If anything were to happen to Homi, he would reveal the truth through radio broadcast. After much thinking, this seemed the best plan available to them.

Charles watched the joyous crowd in the distance. *Maybe this is the last time I'll be at the center of the stage. Steele is very likely right. This time, my ship holds no technical advantage. I have no hope of victory and will be forgotten by the world as a failure.*

But what of it? It has been my dream to go to the stars, to head for the most distant planet. Being the champion isn't everything. Indeed, the only true dreams are those that you're willing to sacrifice a great deal for.

This is my last chance to be myself. What I've lost in the noise and glitz of this planet, I will recover in the infinite expanse of space. Only there will I find true peace and salvation . . .

The final countdown was about to begin. A few dozen lucky audience members came into the launch complex to take pictures with the racers. Most chose to have their pictures taken with Charles first, and a smiling Charles obliged. He also signed their books or t-shirts. The last person to come to him was a plain looking and plainly dressed young woman, whose gestures betrayed nervousness.

"How . . . how do you do, Mr. Charles," the young woman said.

"Hello! What's your name?"

"I'm Asakura Minami."

Charles nodded without reaction. But behind his thoughts, another consciousness was suddenly jerked awake. *What is she doing here? When did she . . . become a fan of Charles?*

"Ms. Asakura, a pleasure to meet you. Would you like a picture with me?"

"Yes, absolutely." Minami stood next to him for the photo. But she lingered even after the picture. A few launch facility staff came to bring her away, but Charles gestured for them to back off.

"What else can I do for you?"

"I'm sorry, Mr. Charles." Minami bowed to him deeply. Blushing, she said, "I'd like to ask for your help with something."

"As long as it's not illegal, I'm at your service."

Minami fidgeted for a while before lifting her head. Gazing straight into Charles's eyes, she said, "*Watashi . . . watashi wa Naoto-kun no koto o daisuki yo.*"

Charles had no idea what she said, but another consciousness did. He understood why Minami had traveled for so long and stood in line for hours. She wasn't here for Charles at all; she just wanted to tell him a single sentence.

"*I . . . I like Naoto-kun very much.*"

Before Charles could react, she took two steps forward, wrapped her arms around his neck, stood on her tiptoes, and kissed him. Naoto could feel how soft and supple her lips were, laden with the scent of summer sunlight and youth.

"Naoto," Minami whispered into Charles's ear, "I'm right next to you, but can you only feel my presence through the body of a man thousands of kilometers away?"

Security personnel rushed up to drag Minami away, but Charles had already figured out the truth. He gestured for them to stop and looked at Minami. "Ms. Asakura, I believe the person you love will understand."

Then, he spoke to Naoto, a stranger he had never met, "You lucky bastard, don't miss out on the joy right next door."

Naoto didn't know when he had left the livecast. Staring at the stained ceiling, he felt tears fill his eyes and then overflow the corners to spill down his cheeks.

After subscribing to Charles's livecast for so many years, he had enjoyed the pleasures of romancing countless beautiful women. But deep in his heart, he knew that they had nothing to do with him; they were there for the charismatic Charles. He preferred to forget the truth so that he could be fully immersed in the happiness that was being Charles.

But today, in this last livecast of his three years of living as Charles, everything had turned upside down. That sentence and that kiss were for him, Takumi Naoto, not Charles.

He wasn't Charles and he never would be. But he could be himself, possessing a joy that was common but not commonplace, measured but not mean. Indeed, some portion of it was unachievable even by Charles.

Naoto sat up, his head throbbing. He had lived his last day in self-imposed numbness. Charles's livecast was over. Even if he returned from Pluto, he would probably not resume casting. Naoto was going to find a new life, find his own happiness.

Naoto made his decision. He dialed. After a few rings, the other end finally picked up. "*Moshi moshi,* this is Asakura." Her voice was tense, expectant.

Before he could say a word, Naoto's ears were filled with the rumbling of engines and the wild cheers of a crowd. Naoto glanced at his computer screen and saw the spaceships taking off from the launch complex, trailing long columns of smoke behind them like a flock of migrating wild geese. Charles had departed for space, and this time, Naoto couldn't and didn't want to attach himself to Charles's soul. He had more important things in mind.

He took a deep breath and spoke with a trembling voice. "Minami-chan, I like you. I would like to see you."

Goodbye, Charles.

Epilogue

One year later.

A cobalt blue spaceship closed its solar sail and activated the landing thrusters to slowly descend toward the planetary surface shrouded in darkness below. The flight was steady and stable; all status indicators nominal. A human was about to set foot on Pluto for the first time in history.

But when the ship was still about two kilometers from the surface, it began to accelerate in an odd manner. Spinning, it plunged toward the thick icy crust of the planet of death. A few seconds later, a faint explosion bloomed on Pluto like a match lit for a moment in the long night. And then, the eternal void.

The image was taken by the Chinese exploratory probe *Mamian.* About five hours later, the image data arrived at Earth, bringing with it the sad news at the edge of the Solar System. For forty hours afterward, all attempts at re-establishing communication failed. Two days later, a second racer, George Steele, successfully landed on Pluto and discovered the wreckage of the first spaceship as well as the carbonized remains of Charles Mann.

Back on Earth, grief united everyone. The mainstream explanation for Charles's death was a technical malfunction. Charles had put together his ship by himself, and there were no doubt latent defects. Experts debated the exact nature of the accident: some argued that it was a programming bug; others pointed to the engine; still others said that it was because the buttons and dials on the control panel were too densely clustered, leading to an operator error when Charles was under pressure.

Some subscribed to the belief that Charles had committed suicide. They scoured Charles's final recordings before his departure for odd statements and behaviors to support their theory that Charles was tired of life. Falling to the surface of Pluto was a genius bit of performance art. They specifically pointed to his strange demeanor during the last press conference he held at which he announced the intent to join the Plutonian Grand Race.

Others argued that Charles had been murdered. This was the most outrageous of the conspiracy theories. A long list of suspects was constructed: George Steele, his rival and competitor; Aoi Masa, his ex-lover; the Douglas Group; Bell Labs . . . One particular bit of evidence this group pointed to was the fact that Charles's girlfriend, Hosokawa Homi, died on the third day after Charles's own death in an explosion as her air car struck another head-on above Tokyo. This "coincidence" could certainly be viewed as evidence of conspiracy, but a more logical and simpler explanation was that she had been distracted in her driving by grief.

All sorts of rumors and so-called "evidence" emerged on the web. Most were easily proved to be hoaxes, but a few pieces resisted debunking. There was an audio recording that seemed to be an argument between Charles and Lisa Goldstone; a video that appeared to capture an affair between Charles and the wife of a celebrity; a phone call from Charles's father that claimed that his son was a spendthrift who had lost all his money . . . but none of these were hard to fake, and it was impossible to prove that any of them was directly connected to the death of Charles. Finally, there were even some nuts who claimed that Charles had been killed because he discovered a secret mind-control conspiracy by the megacorps behind the cranial implants. No one took them seriously.

In any case, it was incontrovertible that Charles was dead. A dead man, no matter how famous, was very quickly forgotten. For a month or so, there were all sorts of memorials and tributes to the memory of Charles. But soon, a few hot new livecasting stars emerged: prodigies, hot girls, self-taught innovators. Most of Charles's fans immersed themselves in newer, richer entertainment.

But many didn't know what to do with themselves. They couldn't understand Charles's death.

"I . . . I just can't figure it out," Naoto muttered. He poured himself a beer. "How can he be dead? For three years, I knew every gesture he made. I have almost every memory he had. If I'm alive, how can he be dead?"

"You are you; Charles is Charles." Minami said, her voice cold. She was running out of patience with Naoto.

Naoto shook his head. "You don't get it at all. That feeling . . . I can recall literally everything about Charles: the way he climbed and dove through clouds in his aerial acrobatics; the way he wove through coral reefs and shoals of fish as he scuba dived; the way he spoke to readers at his signings as though he knew each and every one of them; the way he dropped bon mots and commanded everyone's attention at parties; the way he inspired global compassion as he worked with refugees . . . for me, all these memories are as fresh as though they happened only yesterday. I see the spinning Earth far below me; I hear the music wafting from Wiener Musikverein, I smell the scent of cherry blossoms at the foot of Mount Fuji, I . . . " Somewhere along the way, he had shifted from the third person to first.

"Do you also remember those long nights with Masa, Paula, and Mariana?" Minami asked, her expression darkening.

Unaware of the danger, Naoto nodded distractedly. "Of course I do. Those were utterly unforgettable experiences. It's too bad I have no memories of being with Hosokawa Homi—"

"Damn you, Takumi Naoto!" Minami could not take it anymore. "Are you going to spend the rest of your life imagining you're Charles?"

"Minami-chan, what's wrong?" Naoto was genuinely confused.

"Charles Mann has been dead for more than six months! But every day, you just talk to yourself about all these memories that have nothing to do with you and these women who have no idea who you are. You don't even hear me anymore. I'm going crazy, I swear!"

"You don't understand! I was there for all these memories. There is absolutely no distinction between them and memories that I formed while I was in this body. I know that I'm not Charles, but these were also a part of my own experiences."

"Oh come on!" Minami was so angry that she started to laugh. "Your experience consists of lying on your tatami mat and receiving a livecast. How are you different from those idiots who watch some TV show and then imagine themselves as the hero?"

"Shut up!" Now it was Naoto who could not take it anymore. "You are always criticizing me. But you've never even tuned into a livecast. How can you possibly know what it feels like? Who died and made you judge of my life? You have no right to tell me what to do."

"I have no right?" Minami's eyes flashed. "Oh that's right. I'm *nothing*. I think we should stop seeing each other."

"Fine!" Naoto shouted. "I should never have agreed to your pleas."

Minami stopped arguing with him. Quietly, she began packing up her clothes and possessions. As Naoto watched her, pangs of regret gnawed at him, but he just couldn't bring himself to apologize. Only when Minami stood at the door, a few suitcases at her feet, did he finally panic. "What are you doing? It's the middle of the night. Why don't you wait at least until morning? We should—"

"Naoto"—the calm manner in which Minami was talking terrified him—"I once thought I could change you, but I was wrong. You're probably right: you are indeed Charles, and you will live forever in his memories. But I'm sorry I can't be here with you. That's not a life I want."

"I . . . I don't . . . " Naoto didn't know what to say. He stood by and watched as Minami opened the door and went out. He listened as her footsteps grew fainter and fainter, and eventually, vanished.

After some hesitation, Naoto dialed Minami's number. But Minami had turned off her phone, and there was no answer.

"Fuck it." Naoto let out a few more curses, fell back into his chair, and continued to drink his beer.

Why is my life always like this? Why can't I ever get along with anyone? No matter how many times I try, I'm met by failure after failure. In this "real world," even the very air is stifling. If I could only return to the body of Charles and live that spirited life once more . . .

As he continued to daydream, Naoto carelessly tapped on his keyboard. He signed on to a discussion forum for livecasting, and the large-font text at the top instantly grabbed his attention.

CHARLES MANN REVIVED!!!

What in the world?

Naoto clicked on the link and found himself staring at an ad from Time Media.

In order to pay tribute to the heroic Charles Mann, we have purchased the rights to the entire archive of his livecast for the delectation of our subscribers. The entire livecast stream is 85,439 hours long, encompassing about ten years of his life. You may jump to review any particular segment or play it from end to end in order to gain a deeper understanding of this amazing life . . .

Naoto's heart began to leap wildly. *Ten years of livecasting data!* As a subscriber to Charles's stream, he had been prevented by technical means from recording the sensory signals, but of course the company that handled the livecast would have a proper archive to permit re-livecasting. Since Naoto had tuned in only during the last three years of Charles's life, he had never lived the first seven years of the livecast. But now . . .

Naoto sucked in his breath. He was going to possess the entire ten years, the best part of Charles's life. He was being given a chance to once again meld into Charles, and to anticipate an exciting life in a bright new future (even if it had happened in the past). And this time, he would no longer have to worry about anyone cutting him off for at least ten years. He could confidently lose himself as deeply in Charles as he liked.

Of course, this time the subscription was no longer free, but the price they were charging was reasonable: only 100 yen an hour. If he purchased more than a day's worth of data, the price was discounted to 50 yen per hour. If he purchased the entire archive at once, the price was further reduced to 20 yen per hour. This was eminently affordable.

Quickly, he connected his bank account. The entire archive would cost him almost 1.6 million yen. He didn't have that much in savings, so he decided to pay over two hundred thousand yen for the rights to the first year's archives. He would have to earn more to pay for the rest later.

He lay back on his tatami mat and switched on the neutrino converter. The computer voice informed him that the connection was being established, and the data stream was being buffered. The livecast, no, the re-livecast, would begin in about one minute.

As Naoto waited anxiously, his phone rang, informing him there was a voice message from Minami. Naoto quickly switched off his phone. Perhaps Minami had changed her mind about the break-up, but it was too late now. As long as he could be Charles again, why would he need a woman like Minami?

The neutrino beam was converted into electromagnetic waves, and then, into brainwaves. The re-livecast began:

Vestibular systems synchronized: I am lying down somewhere; tactile sensations synchronized: I think this is a bed, rather soft and comfortable; olfactory sensations synchronized: it smells medicinal, like a hospital, but not too overwhelming; hearing synchronized: a woman is speaking to me, her voice gradually becoming clearer; sight synchronized: a blurry figure looms before my eyes . . .

He is gazing up at the ceiling, and his future manager, Lisa Goldstone, is bending down to speak to him. "How do you feel?"

"I'm all right," he says, his voice sounding a bit weak. "I think."

"We're about to start the livecast now. Do you remember who you are?"

A confident smile appears over his pasty face. "What kind of question is that? I'm Charles, the one and only Charles."

Endnote

1 - All East Asian names are rendered with surname first in this translation, following the custom of the region.

Originally published in Chinese in *Science Fiction World,* September 2014.

Summer at Grandma's House
HAO JINGFANG, TRANSLATED BY CARMEN YILING YAN

He pondered silently: the chain of unconnected actions that had determined his doom and destiny had been of his own creation.

After this summer, I finally understand what Camus said of Sisyphus.

I never looked at the word "fate" this way before. In the past, I always thought that either it was prearranged, and all we had to do was follow along; or that it didn't exist at all, so we had to devise our own path in life.

I didn't realize there might be a third option.

A

In August, I leave for my grandmother's home in the country, fleeing ruckus like Newton fled the Black Plague. I want a quiet summer, nothing more.

The taxi drives out of the city, then along the dusty highway. I stuff my big, empty backpack under the seat and slump against the window.

Really, I'm not running away from anything earth-shattering. My graduation from college is going to be delayed a year. I broke up with my girlfriend. On top of that, I'm feeling a touch of ennui, leaving me unable to take interest in anything. The last one scares me a bit, but other than that, there's nothing big. I'm not given to drama.

Mom approved. Find someplace to fix up your spirits, she told me, and come back ready for another go. She thought I was really tormented, which wasn't true. There's no way I could get her to understand that, though.

My grandmother's little two-story bungalow sits at the foot of the mountain, its red roof hidden in the dense treetops.

A small chalkboard hangs from the wooden door. Written on it is: "Zhanzhan, I've gone shopping. The door is unlocked, so come in on your own when you arrive. There's food in the fridge."

I try pulling on the door handle, but it doesn't budge. It doesn't turn either, even when I twist harder. I can only sit on the steps and wait.

Grandma's getting muddle-minded with age, I think. She must have locked the door by habit when she left, then forgot about it.

Grandpa passed away early. My grandmother's lived here ever since she retired. Mom and Dad wanted to buy her a house in the city, but she turned down all their offers. She said she was used to living alone, as she pleased. She disliked the noise and clamor of the city.

For all her life, Grandma was a college professor; her mind and body were still sound. So Dad agreed. We keep saying we'll spend a holiday here, but either Dad would be busy, or I'd have something planned with my schoolmates and couldn't cancel.

I hope Grandma can still take care of herself on her own here, I think to myself, sitting on the steps.

Grandmother finally returns in the evening, quickening her strides when she sees me in the distance. She smiles at me. "Zhanzhan, when did you arrive? Why didn't you go in the house?"

I dust off my butt and stand up. Grandma walks up the steps, shifts all her bags to her right hand, and pushes the door with her left hand, on the side closer to the hinges—opposite from the handle. Just like that, the door swings open, no fuss. Grandma walks in first, holding the door open for me.

My face flushes a little. I hurry in after her. It looks like I was overthinking things earlier.

Night descends. Night in the countryside is quiet and tranquil, just the dance of tree shadows cast by the moon.

Grandma quickly prepares dinner. The rich fragrance of beef fills the small house. After a long day of travel, the smell makes me ravenous.

"Zhanzhan, bring me the mayonnaise in the kitchen, please." Grandma carefully sets a tureen of steamed eggs with mushroom on the table.

My grandmother's kitchen is spacious and decorated in soft colors. Soup simmers on the stove, wreathed in steam.

I pull open the fridge, only to get a shock: inside of the fridge is a baking tray, and the inner walls glow red with heat. A row of apple pastries are crisping on the tray. The sweet smell of butter and honey assaults my face.

Turns out this is the oven. I hurriedly push it shut.

Where's the fridge, then? I turn around. There's a glass-windowed metal door under the stove—I assumed that was the oven. I walk over and pull it open, and discover that it's a dishwasher.

So I pull open the dishwasher, and find that it's a water purifier; pull open the water purifier, and find that it's a trash can; open the trash can, and find that it's filled with a broad selection of CDs, neatly sorted.

Finally I realize that the "heating unit" under the window—I thought it looked like a radiator in its ridged casing—is, in fact, the fridge. I locate the mayonnaise, and make sure to open the lid and sniff it, just to make sure the jar doesn't actually contain condensed milk. Only after I've checked do I return to the dining room.

Grandma already has bowls and chopsticks set out. The instant I sit down I start stuffing my face.

B

I spend the next few days furiously learning how to identify everything.

Almost nothing in Grandma's house has a function that matches what you'd expect from the form. The coffeepot is a penholder, the penholder is a lighter, the lighter is a flashlight, the flashlight is a jam container.

That last one gives me trouble. It's the middle of the night when I get up to go to the bathroom. I unthinkingly grab the "flashlight" in the living room, only to get a handful of jam. In the darkness, the wet stickiness on my hand scares the sleep right out of me. When the realization dawns, my first instinct is to get a tissue, but the tissue box is filled with white sugar. I reach for the lamp. Who could have guessed that the table lamp is fake, and that the switch is actually a mousetrap?

With a sharp *pa*, I find myself in an awkward situation. On my left hand is jam dipped in white sugar. On my right hand is a table lamp smeared with cheese.

"Grandma!" I call softly, but don't hear a reply. I can only climb the stairs, keeping both hands lifted in front of me. Her bedroom is dark, but yellow-orange light seeps from a small room at the end of the hallway.

"Grandma?" I try, outside of the room.

Following muffled scrapes of table and chair, Grandma appears at the door. She looks me over and bursts right into laughter. "Come with me," she says.

The room turns out to be much larger than I thought. The lights are bright, and it takes my eyes a moment to adjust. Only then do I see that this is a lab.

Grandma takes an oddly-shaped little key from a drawer and frees me from the table-lamp-mousetrap. I lick my fingers. The cheese still smells delicious.

"Why are you doing experiments this late in the night?" I can't help but ask.

"With bacterial colony growth, I have to take observations every hour." Smiling, Grandma leads me over to a milk-colored countertop. A neat row of round Petri dishes lie on the counter, each filled with a translucent substance that looks like medicinal cream.

"Is this . . . nutrient agar?" I've done similar experiments at school.

Grandma nods. "I'm observing the movement of transposons in the bacteria."

"Transposons?"

Grandma opens one of the Petri dishes on her end. She hefts it in her hand and says, "They're pieces of DNA capable of encoding reverse transcription enzyme, which allows them to migrate along DNA, breaking away or re-integrating themselves. I want to use them to insert synthetic genes for drug resistance."

Grandma sets the lid back on. "But I don't know if it will work. This Petri dish is exposed to the air, providing a low-humidity environment. The one next to it is submerged in a sugar solution. The one after that has been enriched with extra ATP."

I follow her example and open the Petri dish closest to me. "What are the conditions in this one?"

I dab my cheese-covered fingertip on the agar. I know that having plenty of nutrients makes cells reproduce faster, which should speed up the genetic integration.

"Zhanzhan!" Grandma hesitates, then says, "That's the control sample. It's not supposed to have any added factors."

I'm always like that, full of assumptions when I do things, and careless ones at that.

One time, when Jingjing and I fought, she said that I always went about things impulsively, inconsiderately, immaturely. She's right, I think. She was complaining about the way I always forgot to call her, but I know my problem goes further than that. Jingjing's a person with lots of plans, and the capability to carry out each one of them reliably, but I'm the total opposite. When I try to carry out my plans, they always go wrong, as sure as bread lands butter-side down.

Without a control, Grandma will have to redo the whole experiment. She can keep observing, technically, but at the least she wouldn't be able to use it in proper published results.

I'm panicked, unsure of what I should do, but Grandma doesn't seem to be angry at all.

"It's no big deal," Grandma says. "I could use a sample with added cholesterol anyway."

And Grandma really does take out a marker pen, makes a note on the lid, and keeps on observing.

C

The next morning, Grandma makes sweet osmanthus flower porridge. The morning sun is lovely shining down on the countryside. The only sound for miles around is birdsong.

Grandma asks me if I have any plans for these few days. None, I say. That's the truth. The only thing I might want to do is think about what I might want to do.

"Your mother says your graduation was delayed because of English, but I don't see how that could be the case. Weren't you an English major before you switched? You should be quite good at English."

"I didn't test past the fourth level," I mumble. "I forgot to register in junior year, and this year I forgot the test date."

I gulp down the porridge with my head lowered, and stuff up my mouth with a sandwich.

I'm not afraid of any English exams, no, but that might have been why I failed to take them seriously. As for my change in major, that's starting to look like another mistake. I switched to environmental studies, only to discover I didn't care *that* much about the environment. Then I fled to hardware engineering in junior year, and attended a year's worth of biology too. The result was today: I was jack of all majors, master of none.

Grandma cuts me another half slice of bacon. "What did your mother say before you came?"

"Nothing in particular. She just wants me to take a breather here, and read some books on economics if I have the time."

"Your mother wants you to study economics?"

"Yeah, she says that no matter what company I end up working for, knowing a bit of economics will come in handy."

My mom thinks that I should set a target, then study whatever I needed to get there. But I was lacking in precisely that department. None of the big goals I set ever lasted more than a few days before I nixed them, which left me without any impetus to work on the tasks at hand.

"You shouldn't worry too much about the future." Seeing that I've finished eating, Grandma begins to clear the table. "Just like the nose didn't evolve to prop up glasses."

Jingjing told me the same thing. "The nose evolved for the purpose of breathing," she said. God sculpted us all into our own unique forms, so we shouldn't worry about what other people thought, and stand firm on who we were. So Jingjing left the country, in accordance to who she was. But I was missing that sense of unique purpose too. God never got around to telling me who I was.

My mind is elsewhere as I help clear the table. The leftover porridge splatters all over the floor. My face immediately heats.

"Don't worry, it's no big deal." Grandma takes the pot from me and fetches a mop.

" . . . It's flowed into the corner. Won't that be hard to mop up? Do you have a cloth for cleaning the floor? I'll do it," I say, embarrassed.

I think of the way Mom would crouch and meticulously wipe down the crevice where the floor met the wall. Our house was always squeaky clean. Mom hated nothing more than my brand of haphazardness.

"It's no big deal, really." Grandma mops up the center of the dining room. "We'll leave the corner as is."

She notices that I'm at a loss. "I'm accident-prone myself," she laughs. "I spill things everywhere. That's why I laid down culture medium for growing fungi next to the walls. This way I'll have material for my experiments."

I bend down to look by the wall. There really is a band of pale green fuzz stretching around the room. From a distance, it looked like decorative trimming along the perimeter of the floor.

"Sweet porridge is ideal, actually. We might even get mushrooms."

She sees that I'm still awkwardly standing in place, so she adds, "How about this? If you don't have anything in particular to do these few days, do you want to help me grow fungi?"

I nod without hesitation.

It's not just because I want to make up for the mess I made. More than that, I feel I need to change how I spend my days. Up until now, my life has been incoherent and scattershot. I haven't been able to commit to any one of the well-trodden paths in life, or chart my own course. Maybe what I need is opportunity, even accidentally.

D

Grandma likes to say that purpose comes afterward.

Grandma rejects any form of teleology, from animism to vitalism. She doesn't believe that evolution has a destination and dislikes explanations like "eyes grew eyelashes to keep dust out." She doesn't even think cells evolved membranes for self-protection.

"The enclosing membrane came before the cell could exist," Grandmother says. "Same with G protein-coupled receptors. It became light-sensitive rhodopsin in the eyes and olfactory receptors in the nose."

It's a sort of Darwinism, I suppose: first mutation, then selection. First the protein, then the chemical reaction in which to participate. First the ability to encode an enzyme, then the sensory organ that uses the enzyme.

Existence precedes essence, I think the saying goes?

A few evenings later, good news comes from Grandma's lab: the NTL reagent stain finally reveals the protein we're looking for in the cytoplasm. A molecular weight test with the centrifuge confirms this. The transposons have successfully reverse transcribed their payload.

After several days of continuous pursuit and observation, you let out a breath at that kind of result. As I help Grandma clean up the lab, I ask, "What gene were we inserting, anyway?"

"A cell suicide signal," Grandma says placidly.

"Wait, what?"

Grandma bends to sweep up the bits and pieces under the experiment counter. "This experiment was primarily meant as cancer treatment research. Cancer cells are simply cells that don't die when they should, as you know."

"Huh." I pick up the dustpan. "Does that mean you can apply for a patent now?"

Grandma shakes her head. "I don't want to do that yet."

"How come?"

"I don't know if this kind of reverse transcription might have delayed side effects."

"What do you mean?"

Grandma doesn't immediately answer. She collects the test tubes and wipes the counter clean. I tie up the trash bag and follow her downstairs to the garden.

"I suppose you haven't heard the hypothesis of how viruses evolved? Transposons promote genetic recombination inside a cell, but on the loose outside of the cell, they can become viruses, like HIV."

The summer breeze is warm and dry, but I involuntarily shiver.

So viruses split off from cells themselves. It makes me think of the square root calculator turned execution device in Wang Xiaobo's book. There's the same dark humor to it.

I understand Grandma's attitude, but I can't help but feel a little dissatisfied deep down. "Still, this technology could cure cancer. Aren't you afraid someone will beat you to the patent?"

Grandma shakes her head. "What does that matter?"

Peng. At that moment, a thump comes from the other side of the garden.

Grandma and I hurry over, only to see a pudgy, sweaty face emerge from the other side of the garden fence, among the climbing roses.

"Hello . . . I'm terribly sorry, I was trying to rearrange my flower rack, but my hand slipped, and I smashed up your flowers by accident."

I look down. He dropped a container of chrysanthemums, the flowerpot lying in pieces. Underneath are Grandma's azaleas, an equally gory sight.

"Oh, right, I just moved here. I'll be your neighbor from now on." The fat middle-aged guy is nodding on autopilot. "I really am very sorry, ma'am. It's my first day here and I've already given you trouble."

"Don't worry, it's no big deal." Grandma smiles genially.

"I'm terribly sorry. I'll bring you flowers tomorrow to replace it."

"It's no big deal, really. I can take the opportunity to extract some chloroplasts and anthocyanin from the leaves and flowers. Don't mind it." Grandma bends down as she speaks and starts picking up flowerpot shards.

I stand in the yard, the summer night cool around me. My mind is a jumble.

I've discovered that Grandma's catchphrase is "it's no big deal." It might be that most things in Grandma's eyes really are no big deal. Fame, influence, personal property—none of them matter much at Grandma's point in life, admittedly. She does whatever she feels like, and to her, it's enough.

But what about me? I think.

What am I going to do once the summer's over? Return to school, everything the same as before, and meander around for another year until graduation?

I know that's not what I want.

E

When next morning comes around, I help Grandma take care of the shattered flowers, extracting the chlorophyll with acetone. With that, Grandma enthusiastically adds a new member to her enormous team of test subjects.

I spend the entire morning mentally battling with myself. Close to noon, I finally make my choice. No matter what, I think, I should first go to the patent office and ask a few questions. Conveniently, the guy next door comes over in the afternoon to make amends. I take the opportunity to run off on my own.

The website gave clear directions to the patent office, and I find it easily. The four-story building is plain but stately, the lobby quiet and well-lit. A graceful, pretty girl sits behind the receptionist's desk, reading a book.

"H-hello, I'd like to apply for a patent."

She looks up and smiles. "Hello. Fill out the form over there, please. What are you patenting?"

"Uh, an anti-cancer biological factor."

"Then you'll want to head to Hall 3, the Biology and Chemistry Office." She points toward the right. As I turn, she muses to herself, "Strange, why are there so many people applying for anti-cancer factors today?"

I spin right back around. "Wait, there was someone else before me?"

"Yes, an older man came just this morning."

My heart lurches. I sense something's not quite right.

"Do you know what technology he was patenting, specifically?"

"I don't know, I'm afraid."

"Was it a drug, or something else?"

The girl sighs. "I'm just a college student working here for the summer. It's not my business to look at the applications. You should go in and ask yourself." With that, the girl lowers her head once more and resumes scribbling and underlining.

I bend over to look. It's a book of English vocabulary. "You're memorizing vocabulary?" I ask, trying to get her on my side. "I'm doing that too."

"Oh? You're a college student?" She raises her head and looks me over curiously. "And you already have something to patent? That's impressive."

"Ah . . . no, you've got it wrong." My face flushes a little. "I'm just looking in on behalf of my academic advisor. Do you remember what that older guy looked like? I think my advisor might have come here already without telling me."

"Hmm . . . he was short, on the plump side, kind of bald. I think he was wearing a yellow jacket. I don't remember anything else."

Like I suspected. No wonder I noticed something was off when I left the house.

The middle-aged guy next door arrived with his flowers just then. I took the flowerpot from him, and when he went to open the door for me, he pushed on the side of the door closer to the hinges without hesitation. Someone here for the first time wouldn't have known to do that. I understand now. Last night wasn't purely chance. He must have accidentally knocked over the flowers while eavesdropping.

He really has no sense of decency, coming over again today, I think. I need to hurry and tell Grandma. He probably thought that we wouldn't be applying for a patent and would never find out. Good thing I came here.

"Leaving already?" the girl calls out as I head for the door. "Here's a pamphlet, then. It has an introduction to the patent office and an explanation of the application process, plus contact information."

I manage a smile. I accept the pamphlet, stick it in my pocket, and stride quickly out the door.

F

I rush home only to find Grandma in her lab like usual, calmly looking through her microscope. She's a quiet, steady island amid a chaos of river torrents.

"Grandma . . . " I force my panting and puffing under control. "He stole your Petri dishes . . . "

"Back from somewhere? Where did you go, to end up so dusty?" Grandma looks up, smiling, and brushes at my jacket.

"I went—" I fall silent, unsure of how to explain my trip to the patent office. I change tack. "Grandma, that fat guy next door stole your Petri dishes and applied for a patent."

Unexpectedly, Grandma only smiles. "It's no big deal. I can continue my research just fine. Moreover, like I told you, the experiment we conducted was very crude and preliminary. The results can't be put into application as they are."

I look at Grandma, at a loss for words. Is it actually possible for someone to be so easygoing? Grandma doesn't seem to concern herself with things like intellectual property and monetary gain at all. I silently take the pamphlet out of my pocket and hold it in my hands, folding and unfolding it.

"Don't worry about that for now. First come and look at this." Grandma points to the microscope in front of her.

I take a halfhearted peep through it. "What is it?" I ask, offhandedly.

"Genetically engineered photosynthesizing bacteria."

I perk up. This sounds interesting. "How did you do it?"

"I simply reverse transcribed genes from the chloroplasts into the bacteria. They've already expressed many of the proteins, although I'm sure there are still problems present. If we can overcome them, maybe these bacteria can be used as a source of alternative energy."

As I listen to Grandma's placid, happy voice, I suddenly get a strange and dreamlike feeling. It's like I'm cocooned in a layer of fog, while her voice is coming from a long distance away. I look down. I'm rubbing the pamphlet between my fingers. I need to make a choice.

Grandma's still talking. "As you know, I've laid down a lot of culture medium on the floors. I plan to replace more material so I can grow the bacteria all over the house. If it works, we'll have a use for porridge leftovers and everything. As for the actual electricity generation, you were the one who gave me the inspiration. Cell membranes normally have high fluidity, which makes it difficult to capture the high-energy electrons generated from photosynthesis. However, if we add large quantities of cholesterol molecules, we can just about stabilize the membrane. In theory, we can use micro-electrodes to position . . . "

I stand there woodenly. I'm not really paying attention to Grandma, just catching fragments here and there. This discovery might have even bigger future applications. But my brain is a worse jumble than before. I can't concentrate enough to listen anymore. "You're bringing up all the things I did wrong," I say awkwardly.

Grandma shakes her head. "Zhanzhan, do you still not understand?" She stops, looking into my eyes. "Every day, every moment, countless random events will occur. You'll pick one of many possible restaurants to eat at, take one of many possible buses, see one of many possible advertisements. And at that point in time, you can't classify them as good or bad, right or wrong. They take on worth only in the future. What we do at this moment in the present gives meaning to another moment in the past . . . "

Grandma's voice sounds light and drifting. I can't react to it in time. *Chance, time, meaning, future,* the words spin in my head. I think of Borges', "The Garden of Forking Paths." Yu Tsun must have felt what I'm feeling, the decision uncertain but fomenting in my heart, even as enigmatic words wisp into my ear . . .

" . . . biology is based on just one set of principles: random events and directional selection. What's doing the selection? What allows some events to stick around and prove to be beneficial? The answer is perpetuation alone. If a protein can persist, it will persist. It will claim a position in the course of history, while other proteins appear and then disappear at random. The only way to make a step you've taken 'correct' is to take another step in the same direction . . . "

I think of myself, of the fat guy next door, of Mom and Jingjing, of the four years I spent in a muddle, of my dejection and conflict, of the bright and shining lobby of the patent office. I know I need an opportunity.

" . . . that's why, if we can make use of them, cheese and spilled porridge and broken-off flowers don't have to be bad things at all."

And I make my choice.

G

After that summer, I get an internship at the patent office. I learned of the opportunity from the booklet.

It's not very easy to find a proper job here, but they're always looking for college students to take care of odds and ends—fortunate, that I haven't graduated yet. The work at the patent office isn't hard, but it requires a bit of knowledge from every field—fortunate, that I was so aimless in my studies at college.

An'an—the girl I met the first time I came here—is now my girlfriend. We fell in love while studying together for the English exam—fortunate, that I hadn't passed the fourth level. An'an says that I seemed polite and shy on first impression, which she found charming—I didn't tell her that it was due to nervousness and a guilty conscience. Everything seems to have worked out like magic. Even the things I felt bad about ended up helping me.

Taking it a step further, I can even say that my inner turmoil was a good thing—if it weren't for that, I wouldn't have gone to Grandma's house, and everything that came after wouldn't have happened. Looking back, everything from before was all linked together into one chain.

I know that no one planned this for me. Fate doesn't exist. I chose all of it.

It's a strange feeling. We always think we can choose our futures, but that's not true. What we really can choose is our past.

I chose the lunch I had a couple of years ago, made it a lunch different from the thousand other possible lunches. Likewise, I chose whether my time at college was a mistake.

Maybe accepting reality is just another name for staying true to yourself. Who are you, really, other than the sum of everything that's happened?

A year has passed. With a happy mindset, I've done great at my work. The patent office has accepted me as a full-time employee. I'll start my job in the fall.

I like it here. I like learning bits and pieces from all sorts of subjects. Besides, I'm no good at making long-term plans, or carrying them out. The work here is just one case after another, no need for looking far ahead. Plus, I have the same job as Einstein, which is pretty awesome.

After a year of repeated experiments and observations, Grandma is applying for patents for her anti-cancer factor and photosynthesizing walls. Several large companies have already expressed interest. Grandma isn't interested in contract negotiations, so I've taken on the responsibilities of a middleman. Fortunate, that I work for the patent office.

Oh, right, I forgot to mention. The fat guy next door didn't steal the Petri dishes with the anti-cancer factors after all. He thought he found the incubator, but it was actually an ordinary wardrobe. The real incubator looks like a dresser.

So you never know what something's really meant for, Grandma says. Turns out she knew from the beginning. Turns out she knew everything from the beginning.

Originally published in Chinese in *Science Fiction World*, 2007

So Much Cooking
NAOMI KRITZER

Carole's Roast Chicken

This is a food blog, not a disease blog, but of course the rumors all over about bird flu are making me nervous. I don't know about you, but I deal with anxiety by cooking. *So much cooking*. But, I'm trying to stick to that New Year's resolution to share four healthy recipes (entrées, salads, sides . . .) for every dessert recipe I post, and I *just* wrote about those lemon meringue bars last week. So even though I dealt with my anxiety yesterday by baking another batch of those bars, and possibly by eating half of them in one sitting, I am *not* going to bake that new recipe I found for pecan bars today. No! Instead, I'm going to make my friend Carole's amazing roast chicken. Because how better to deal with fears of bird flu than by eating a bird, am I right?

Here's how you can make it yourself. You'll need a chicken, first of all. Carole cuts it up herself but I'm lazy, so I buy a cut-up chicken at the store. You'll need *at least* two pounds of potatoes. You'll need a lemon and a garlic bulb. You'll need a big wide roasting pan. I use a Cuisinart heavy-duty lasagna pan, but you can get by with a 13×9 cake pan.

Cut up the potatoes into little cubes (use good potatoes! The yellow ones or maybe the red ones. In the summer I buy them at the Farmer's Market.) Spray your pan with some cooking spray and toss in the potatoes. Peel all the garlic (really, all of it!) and scatter the whole cloves all through with the potatoes. If you're thinking, "all that garlic?" just trust me on this. Roasted garlic gets all mild and melty and you can eat it like the potato chunks. Really. You'll thank me later. Finally, lay out the chicken on top, skin-down. You'll turn it halfway through cooking. Shake some oregano over all the meat and also some sea salt and a few twists of pepper.

Squeeze the lemon, or maybe even two lemons if you really like lemon, and mix it in with 1/4 cup of olive oil. Pour that over everything and use your hands to mix it in, make sure it's all over the chicken and the potatoes. Then pour just a tiny bit of water down the side of the pan—you don't want to get it on the chicken—so the potatoes don't burn and stick. Pop it into a 425-degree oven and roast for an hour. Flip your chicken a half hour in so the skin gets nice and crispy.

Guys, it is SO GOOD. Half the time I swear Dominic doesn't even notice what he's eating, but he always likes this dish, and so do I. If you make this much for two people, you'll have leftovers for lunch. But we're having guests over tonight, my brother and his wife and kids. So, I'm actually using two chickens and four pounds of potatoes, because teenagers eat a lot.

And chicken has magical healing properties if you make it into soup, so surely some of them stick around when you roast it? And so does garlic, so eat some and *stay healthy*.

xxoo, Natalie

Substitute Chip Cookies

So, we have some unexpected long-term house guests.

My sister-in-law Katrina is a nurse at Regions Hospital. She's not in the ER or the infectious diseases floor but let's face it, it's not like you can corral a bunch of airborne viruses and tell them they're banned from OBGYN. Leo and Kat are worried that if this bird flu thing is the real deal, she could bring it home. Leo's willing to take his chances but when I said, "Would you like to have the kids stay with me for a while," Kat said, "That would make us both feel so much better," so voila, here I am, hosting an eleven-year-old and a thirteen-year-old. Monika is thirteen, Jo is eleven.

We have a guest room and a sofa bed. Monika got the guest room, Jo's on the sofa bed, although we promised to renegotiate this in a few days if they're still here. (It's actually a double bed in the guest room but trust me, you don't want to make my nieces share a bed if you don't absolutely have to.)

I went to the store today to stock up just in case we want to minimize the "leaving the house" stuff for a while. Apparently I wasn't the only person who had that thought because (a) the lines were unbelievable and (b) I tried *four stores* and they were *all* completely out of milk and eggs. I did manage to get an enormous jumbo package of toilet paper plus a huge sack of rat food (did I mention that Jo has a pet rat named Jerry Springer? I didn't? Well, my younger niece Jo has a pet rat named Jerry Springer. The rat was not actually invited along for the family dinner, but Dominic ran over today to pick the rat up because he thought Jo would feel better about the whole situation if she had her pet staying here, too.)

The freezer section was also incredibly picked over but at the Asian grocery (store #4) I bought some enormous sacks of rice and also about fifteen pounds of frozen dumplings and you know what, I'm not going to try to list what I came home with as it would be too embarrassing. I'll just stick to the essentials, which is, *no milk and no eggs*. I did manage to get some butter, but it was the super-fancy organic kind that's $10 per pound so I was also a little worried about using up our butter reserve on one batch of cookies. And Jo really wanted chocolate chip cookies.

Okay, actually: *I* really wanted chocolate chip cookies. But Jo was very willing to agree that she wanted some, too.

You can substitute mayo for eggs, in cookies, and you can substitute oil for the butter. They'll be better cookies if you happen to have some sesame oil to put in for part of the oil (or any other nut-related oil) and we did, in fact, have sesame oil. And as it happens, those four grocery stores were *not* out of chocolate chips.

Here's the recipe in case you are also improvising today:

- 2 1/2 cups flour
- 1 tsp baking soda
- 1 tsp salt
- 1 cup of vegetable oils (preferable 2 T sesame oil + canola oil to equal 1 cup.)
- 3/4 cup white sugar
- 3/4 cup brown sugar
- 1 tsp vanilla extract
- 6 tablespoons of mayonnaise
- 12 ounces of whatever sort of chips you have in the house, or chopped up chocolate

Cream the sugar and the oil, then beat in the mayonnaise. I *promise* the cookies will turn out fine, no matter how gross the mayo smells and looks while you're beating it in. Mix the baking soda, salt, and flour together, then gradually beat in the mayo mixture, and stir in your chips.

Drop by rounded spoonfuls—oh, you know how to make cookies. You don't have to grease your cookie sheets. Bake at 375F for about ten minutes and if you want them to stay chewy and soft, put them away in an airtight container before they're all the way cool. If you like your cookies crunchy, well, what's wrong with you? But in that case cool them before you put them away, and in fact you'll probably be happier storing them in something that's not airtight, like a classic cookie jar.

I gave Dominic the first batch and he said, "you didn't use up all the butter on this, did you?" I told him we're not about to run out of butter. We are, however, about to run out of coffee. I may die. Even if I don't get bird flu. Excuse me, H5N1.

xxoo, Natalie

Homemade Pizza

So, how are things where *you* live?

Where *I* live (Minneapolis) there have been 83 confirmed cases of H5N1. The good news (!!!) is that it's apparently not as lethal in the human-to-human variant as it was back when it was just birds-to-human, but since it was 60% lethal in the old form that's not really what I think of as *good* good news. The bad news is that there's a four-day incubation period so those 83 people all infected others and this is only the tiny, tiny tip of a giant, lethal iceberg.

Probably wherever you live you're hearing about "social distancing," which in most places means "we're going to shut down the schools and movie theaters and other places where folks might gather, stagger work hours to minimize crowding, and instruct everyone to wear face masks and not stand too close to each other when they're waiting in lines." In Minneapolis, they're already worried enough that they're saying that anyone who can just stay home should go ahead and do that. Since Dominic works in IT and can telecommute, that's us. I'd planned to go to the store today again to maybe get milk and eggs. If it had been just me and Dominic . . . I still wouldn't have risked it. But I *definitely* wasn't going to risk it with Jo and Monika in the house.

I made homemade pizza for lunch. The same recipe I made last December right after I got the pizza stone for Christmas—but, no fresh mushrooms. We had a can of pineapple tidbits and some pepperoni so that's what we topped it with. I thought about trying some of the dried shitake mushrooms on the pizza but on thinking about it I didn't think the texture would work.

We are now completely out of milk, which makes breakfast kind of a problem, and we're also out of coffee, which makes *everything about my day* kind of a problem. Fortunately, we still have some Lipton tea bags (intended for iced tea in the summer) and that's what I used for my caffeine fix.

(Running out of coffee was pure stupidity on my part. I even remember seeing it on the shelf at the grocery store, but I'm picky about my coffee and I was planning to go to my coffee shop for fresh beans today. Ha ha ha! Folgers and Maxwell House sound pretty good to me now!)

xxoo, Natalie

Eggless Pancakes and Homemade Syrup

In the comments on my last post, someone wanted to know about grocery delivery. We *do* have grocery delivery in the Twin Cities, but every single store that offers it is currently saying that they are only providing it to current customers. I did register an account with all the places that do it, and I've put in an Amazon order for a bunch of items you can have delivered (like more TP) and I'm hoping they don't e-mail me back to say they ran out and cancelled my order . . . anyway, I don't know if I'll be able to order anything grocery-like anytime soon.

Some of the restaurants in town are still delivering food and I don't know how I feel about that. Dominic and I are very lucky in that we do have the option of staying home. That makes me feel a little guilty, but in fact, me going out would not make the people who still *have* to go out, for their jobs, even one tiny bit safer. Quite the opposite. If I got infected, I'd be one more person spreading the virus. (Including to my nieces.) Anyway, Kat has to go out because she's a labor and delivery nurse, and people are depending on her. But I don't know if a pizza delivery guy should really be considered essential personnel.

In any case, no one delivers breakfast (which was what I sat down to write about) and no one's going to bring me milk, so I made milk-less, egg-less, butter-less pancakes, and so can you. Here's what you need:

- 2 cups of flour
- 4 tsp baking powder
- 1 tsp salt

Blend that together and then add:

- 1/2 cup of pureed banana OR pureed pumpkin OR applesauce OR any other pureed fruit you've got around. I used banana because I have some bananas in my freezer.
- 1 1/2 cups of water
- 1 tsp vanilla extract
- 1/2 tsp cinnamon
- 1/2 cup sugar

Whisk it all together. You'll need to grease your skillet a little bit extra because this sticks more than pancakes that were made with butter or oil.

We're out of maple syrup, but it turned out we still had a bottle of blueberry syrup in the back of a cabinet and that's what we had with them. There are recipes online for homemade pancake syrup but I haven't tried them yet. Monika hated the blueberry syrup and just ate them with sugar and cinnamon. Jo thought the blueberry syrup was fine but agreed that maple (or even fake maple) would be better. (I'm with Monika, for the record.)

xxoo, Natalie

Miscellaneous Soup

So, before we get to the recipe today, I was wondering if people could do a favor for one of my friends. Melissa is a waitress, and so far *thank God* she is still healthy but her restaurant has shut down for the duration. So, it's good that she's not going to be fired for not coming in to work, and she's glad to stay home where she's safe, but she *really needs that job* to pay for things like her rent. Anyway, I talked her into setting up a GoFundMe and if you could throw in even a dollar, that would be a big help. Also, to sweeten the pot a little, if you donate anything (even just a dollar!) I'll throw your name into a hat and draw one reader and that lucky reader will get to have me make, and eat, and blog, *anything you want*, although if you want me to do that before the pandemic is over you'll be stuck choosing from the stuff I can make with the ingredients that are in my house. And, I just drove a carload of groceries over to Melissa because she and her daughter were basically out of food, and the food shelves are not running, either. (So, if you were thinking that blueberry-glazed carrots or something would be good, you're already too late, because she is now the proud owner of that bottle of blueberry syrup. Also, I'm out of carrots.)

Anyway, go donate! If you've ever wanted me to try again with the Baked Alaska, or experiment with dishwasher salmon, *now's your chance.*

Today, I made Miscellaneous Soup. That is the soup of all the miscellaneous things you have lying around. I actually make this quite often, but I've never blogged about it before, because I just don't think most people would be very impressed. Ordinarily, I make it with stock (boxed stock, if I don't want to waste my homemade stock on this sort of meal), and some leftover cooked meat if I've got it, and whatever vegetables are in the fridge, and either some canned beans or some noodles or both.

What I used today:

- 2 packets of ramen noodles, including their little flavoring sachet
- Wine (we are not even close to being out of wine. Too bad it's not very good poured over breakfast cereal.)
- 1/2 pound of frozen roast corn
- 1/4 pound of frozen mixed vegetables
- 2 cups dry lentils
- 1/2 pound of frozen turkey meatballs

I heated up 4 cups of water and added the flavoring packet, 1 cup of wine, and the lentils. From my spice drawer, I also added some cumin and coriander, because I thought they'd go reasonably well with the spice packet. I cooked the lentils in the broth. I thawed out the corn and the mixed veggies and threw that in and then cooked the turkey meatballs in the oven because that's what the bag wants you to do and then I broke up the ramen brick and threw that in and added the meatballs. And that's what we all had for dinner.

Jo hates lentils and Monika didn't like the frozen roast corn but after some complaining they ate it all anyway. And Andrea and Tom liked it fine.

Right, I guess I should fill you in about Andrea and Tom.

Andrea is a friend of Monika's from school; they're both in 8th grade. Monika found out (I guess from a text?) that Andrea was home alone with her brother, Tom, because their mother is so worried about bringing the flu home that she's been sleeping in the car instead of coming home. Tom is only three. Also, they were totally out of food, which is why Monika brought this up (after I did the grocery drop off for Melissa.)

I told her that *of course* we could bring some food over to her friend, but when I realized Andrea was taking care of a three-year-old full time I suggested they come over here, instead.

So now Monika and Jo *are* sharing the double bed in the guest room, because sorry, girls, sometimes "shared sacrifice" means a shared bed. Andrea is on the sofa bed and Tom is on the loveseat. Well, he was on the loveseat last night. I think tonight he's going to be on the loveseat cushions and those cushions are going to be on the floor so he's got less far to fall if he rolls off again.

Can I just say, this is not exactly how I'd imagined my February. But at least we're all healthy and not out of food yet.

xxoo, Natalie

Ten Things I'm Going to Make When This Is Over

Dinner today was hamburger and rice. I kept looking at recipes and crying, and Dominic wound up cooking.

I kind of want to tell you all the things we're out of. Like, AA batteries. (I had to track down a corded mouse from the closet where we shove all the electronic stuff we don't use anymore, because my cordless mouse uses AA batteries.) Dishwasher detergent. (We still have dish soap, but you can't put that in a dishwasher. So we're washing everything by hand.) But you remember when we used to say, "first-world problems" about petty complaints? These are healthy-person problems.

We got a call today that Kat is sick. She's been working 16-hour shifts because some of the other nurses are sick and some of them were refusing to come in and they *needed* nurses because the babies have still been coming, because they're going to just keep doing that. Literally everyone is in masks and gloves all the time, but—today she's running a fever.

Leo says she's not going to go into the hospital because there isn't anything they can really do for you anyway, especially as overloaded as they are. She's just going to stay at home and drink fluids and try to be one of the 68% who've been making it through.

So yeah, I wasn't going to tell you about that when I sat down, I was going to tell you all about the things I've been craving that I'm going to make when all this is over but I guess what I really want to say is that the top ten things I want to make when all this is over are ten different flavors of cupcake for Kat, because Kat loves my cupcakes, and if you're into prayer or good thoughts or anything like that, please send some her way.

There's still time to donate to Melissa and choose something to have me make. But, seriously, you'll want to wait until this is over because there's just not much in the house.

Kale Juice Smoothies (Not Really)

Dear crazy people who read my blog,

I know—well, I'm pretty sure—that you're trying to be helpful.

But telling me that all my sister-in-law (the mother of my nieces!) needs to do to recover is drink kale juice smoothies with extra wheatgrass and whatever else was supposed to go in your Magic Immune Tonic? *Not helpful.* First of all, she's sick with a disease with a 32% fatality rate. Second of all, *even if* kale or kelp or whatever it was was *magic*, have you actually been reading my blog? We are eating rice, with flavored olive oil, for fully half our meals now. Today we mixed in some dry Corn Flakes, partly for the textural variety but partly just because we could make less rice because we're starting to worry that we're going to run out of that, too.

I can produce a kale smoothie for Kat like I can pull a live, clucking chicken out of my ass and make her some chicken soup with it.

Also, this is a food blog, not a conspiracy theory blog. If you want to try to convince people that the government is infecting everyone on purpose toward some nefarious end, go do it somewhere else.

No love,

Natalie

Rabbit Stew

There are these rabbits that live in our yard. I swear we have like six. They're the reason I can't grow lettuce in my garden. (Well, that plus I'd rather use the space for tomatoes.)

I am pretty sure I could rig up a trap for it with items I have around the house and bunnies are delicious.

Pros:

Fresh meat!

Cons:

Dominic thinks it's possible we could get influenza from eating the bunny. (I think he's being paranoid and as long as we cook it really well we should be fine. I could braise it in wine.)

I have no actual idea how to skin and gut a rabbit, but I have sharp knives and the Internet and I'm very resourceful.

Jo is aghast at the idea of eating a bunny.

We'd probably catch at most one rabbit, and one rabbit split between all these people isn't very much rabbit.

It's even more people now, because we've added another kid. (You can feel free to make a Pied Piper joke. Or a crazy cat lady joke. We are making *all the jokes* because it's the only stress release I've got remaining to me.) Arie is twelve, and came really close to being driven back to his cold, empty apartment after he suggested we eat Jo's rat. (If he were just out of food, we could send him home with food, but the heat's also gone out, the landlord's not answering the phone, and it's February and we live in Minnesota.)

Arie is Andrea's cousin. Or, hold on, I take it back. Maybe he's her cousin's friend? You know what, I just didn't ask that many questions when I heard "twelve" and "no heat."

xxoo, Natalie

This is no longer a food blog

This is a boredom and isolation blog.

Also a stress management blog. Normally, I manage stress by cooking. Except we're out of some key ingredient for like 85% of the recipes I can find, and also out of all the obvious substitutes (or nearly) and I'm starting to worry that we will actually run out of food altogether. I've pondered trying to reverse-engineer flour by crushing the flakes of the Raisin Bran in my food processor, like some very high-tech version of Laura Ingalls grinding up unprocessed wheat in a coffee mill in *The Long Winter*.

My cute little bungalow is very spacious for me and Dominic. For me, Dominic, and five kids ranging in age from three to thirteen, it's starting to feel a little cramped. Monika brought a laptop and she, Arie, and Andrea all want turns using it. (Jo doesn't ask very often, she just sighs a martyred sigh and says no it's *fine* she *understands* why the big kids are hogging the computer.) We are thoroughly expert on the streaming movies available on every online service but the problem is, if it's appropriate for Tom to watch, the big kids mostly aren't interested. We did find a few old-timey musicals that everyone could tolerate but now Tom wants to watch them over and over and Andrea says if she has to listen to "the hiiiiiiiiiills are aliiiiiiiiive with the sound of muuuuuuuuuusic" one more time she might smash the TV with a brick.

We have a back yard and from an influenza infection standpoint it's reasonably safe to play back there, but it's February in Minnesota and we're having a cold snap, like yesterday morning it was -30 with the windchill. (The good news: the cold temperatures might slow the spread of the virus.)

So here's what we did today: I had some craft paints in the basement, and brushes, so we pulled all the living room furniture away from the wall and I let them paint a mural. The good news: this kept them happily occupied all afternoon. The even better news: they're not done yet.

xxoo, Natalie

Birthday Pancake Cake

Today is Jo's birthday, and everyone almost forgot. In part because she clearly expected that everyone had more important things on their mind and wasn't going to bring it up. Monika, bless her cranky thirteen-year-old heart, remembered.

I thought at first we were not going to be able to bake her a cake. (Unless I really could figure out a way to turn cereal flakes into usable flour, and probably not even then.) But—when I went digging yesterday for the craft paint in the basement, I found this small box of just-add-water pancake mix with our camping equipment. If I'd remembered it before now, I totally would've turned it into breakfast at some point, so thank goodness for absent-mindedness. We also still had a package of instant butterscotch pudding mix, un-used since you really can't make instant pudding without milk.

The other kids took a break from painting the mural and instead made decorations out of printer paper, scissors, and pens. (They made a chain-link streamer.)

I think there's got to be a way to turn pancake mix into a proper cake, but all the methods I found online needed ingredients I didn't have. So I wound up making the pancake mix into pancakes, then turning the pancakes into a cake with butterscotch frosting in between layers. (To make butterscotch frosting, I used some melted butter—we still had a little left—and some oil, and the butterscotch pudding mix.)

And we stuck two votive candles on it and sang.

Jo did get presents, despite my cluelessness. The mail is still coming—some days—and her father remembered. A big box full of presents ordered from online showed up late in the day, signed "with love from Mom and Dad," which made her cry.

We've been getting updates on Kat, which mostly I haven't been sharing because they haven't been very good. We're just trying to soldier on, I guess. And today that meant celebrating Jo's birthday.

It Feels Like Christmas

You guys, YOU GUYS. We're going to get a food delivery! Of something! Maybe I should back up and explain. The local Influenza Task Force arranged for the grocery stores with delivery services to hire on a whole lot more people, mostly people like Melissa whose jobs are shut down, and they're now staffed well enough to do deliveries nearly everywhere. Everyone was assigned to a grocer and since we have eight people living here (oh, did I mention Arie also had a friend who needed somewhere quarantined to stay? We are full up now, seriously, the bathroom situation is beyond critical already and we've been rotating turns to sleep on the floor) we're allowed to buy up to $560 worth of stuff and it should arrive sometime in the next few days. They've instructed us not to go out to meet the delivery person: they'll leave it on our doorstep and go.

Of course, the problem is that they are out of practically everything. Minneapolis is such a hot spot, a lot of delivery drivers don't want to come here, plus things are such a mess in California that not much produce is going anywhere at all, so there was no fresh produce of any kind available. I was able to order frozen peaches—though who knows if they'll actually bring any. Of course there was no milk or eggs but they had almond milk in stock so I ordered almond milk because at least you can use it in baking. They also warned me that in the event that something went out of stock they'd just make a substitution so *who even knows*, see, it'll be totally like Christmas, where you give your Mom a wish list and maybe something you put on it shows up under the tree.

I did include a note saying to please, please, *please* make sure that we got either coffee or *something* with caffeine. If I have to drink Diet Mountain Dew for breakfast, I will. I mean, we had a two-liter of Coke and I've been rationing it out and it's going flat and I don't even care. Well, I do care. But I care more about the headaches I get when deprived of my morning caffeine fix.

Some of you were asking about Kat. She's hanging in there, and Leo has stayed healthy. Thanks for asking.

Someone also asked about the rabbits. So far I have not murdered any of the local wildlife, because maybe I'm slightly squeamish, and Dominic is definitely squeamish.

xxoo, Natalie

Rice Krispie Treats

So, here's what came in the box from the grocery store. In addition to a bunch of generally useful items like meat, oil, pancake mix, etc., we got:

- 12 cans of coconut milk
- 1 enormous can of off-brand vacuum-packed ground coffee THANK YOU GOD.
- 3 bags of miniature marshmallows
- 2 large cans of butter-flavored shortening
- 1 enormous pack of TP THANK YOU GOD. I am not going to tell you what we were substituting.
- 1 small pack of AA batteries
- A sack of Hershey's Miniatures, you know, itty bitty candy bars like you give out on Halloween.
- 14 little boxes of Jell-O gelatin
- 1 absolutely goliath-sized sack of knock-off Rice Krispie look-alikes

Most of this was not stuff we ordered. In a few cases, I could make a guess what the substitution was. I wanted flour, I got pancake mix. (That one's not bad.) I wanted chocolate chips, I got Hershey's Miniatures. (Again, not bad.) I ordered some grape juice concentrate because we've been out of anything fruit-like for days and days and although technically you can't get scurvy this quickly (I checked) I've been craving things like carrots and I thought maybe some fruit juice would help. I think the coconut milk was the substitute for the almond milk.

I have no idea why I got the Crispy Rice. I didn't ask for cereal. We still even have some cereal. But! They also gave us marshmallows and butter-flavored shortening (if not actual butter) so you know what it's time for, don't you? That's right. RICE KRISPY TREATS.

I made these once when I was a kid without a microwave oven, and let me just tell you, they are a *lot* of *work* when you don't have a microwave oven. You have to stand over a stove, stirring marshmallows over low heat, for what feels like two hours. They'll still give you stovetop directions but I highly recommend microwave cooking for these.

What you'll need:

- 3 tablespoons butter (or margarine or butter-flavored shortening. You can even use extra-virgin olive oil! But, I do not recommend using garlic-infused extra-virgin olive oil.)
- 1 10-oz bag of marshmallows (or 4 cups of mini marshmallows or 1 jar of marshmallow fluff.)
- 6 cups rice cereal (or corn flakes or Cheerios or whatever cereal you've got on hand but if you decide to use bran flakes or Grape Nuts I'm not responsible for the results.)

Put your butter and your marshmallows into a microwave-safe bowl. Heat on high for two minutes. Stir. Heat on high for another minute. Stir until smooth. Add the cereal. Stir until distributed.

Spray or oil a 13×9 inch pan and spread the marshmallow mixture out in the pan. Not surprisingly this is incredibly sticky and you'll want to use waxed paper folded over your hands, or a greased spatula, or possibly you could just butter your own hands but be careful not to burn yourself. Let it cool and then cut it into squares.

Dominic came in while I was spreading the stuff out in my pan and said, "What are you doing?"

I said, "I'm making Coq au Vin, asshole."

He said, "This is why I can't have nice things."

Maybe you had to be there.

For dinner tonight, we had minute steaks and Rice Krispy treats. *And there was great rejoicing.*

xxoo, Natalie

Katrina Jane, March 5, 1972 - February 20, 2018

I've got nothing today. I'm sorry.

My brother was coughing when he called to tell us the bad news, but said he wasn't sick, didn't have a fever, and definitely hadn't caught the flu from Kat.

Thanks for everyone's thoughts and prayers. I know I'm not the only person grieving here, so just know that I'm thinking of you, even as you're thinking of me.

You Still Have to Eat

Leo had Kat cremated but he's going to wait to have a memorial service until we can all come—including her kids. Monika was furious and insisted that she wants a proper funeral, and wants to go, and thinks it should be this week like funerals normally are, and of course that's just not possible. They can't actually stop us from having gatherings but there are no churches, no funeral homes, no nothing that's going to let you set up folding chairs and have a bunch of people sitting together and delivering eulogies.

We finally talked Monika down by holding our own memorial service, with as many of the trappings as we could possibly put together. We made floral arrangements by taking apart the floral wreath I had in the kitchen with dried lavender in it. We all dressed in black, even though that meant most of the kids had to borrow stuff out of my closet. Then we put out folding chairs in the living room and Dominic led us in a funeral service.

Monika had wanted to do a eulogy but she was crying too hard. She'd written it out, though, so Arie read it for her. I saved it, in case she wants to read it at the real memorial service. Well, maybe for her, this will always be the real memorial service. But there will be another one, a public one, when the epidemic is over.

In Minnesota after a funeral, there's usually lunch in a church basement and there's often this dish called ambrosia salad. (Maybe other states have this? I haven't been to very many funerals outside Minnesota.) I was missing some of the ingredients, but I did have lime Jell-O and mini-marshmallows and even a pack of frozen non-dairy topping and I used canned mandarin oranges instead of the crushed pineapple, and mixed all together that worked pretty well. We had ambrosia salad and breakfast sausages for lunch. (I don't know why we got so many packs of breakfast sausages, but it's food, and everyone likes them, so we've been eating them almost every day, mostly not for breakfast.)

Monika asked if she could save her share of the ambrosia salad in the fridge until tomorrow, because she really likes it, and she didn't feel like eating, and didn't want anyone else to eat her share. (Which was a legitimate worry.) I put it in a container and wrote MONIKA'S, NO ONE ELSE TOUCH ON PAIN OF BEING FED TO THE RAT in sharpie on the lid. Which made her laugh, a little. I guess that's good.

Jo sat through the service and ate her lunch and didn't say a word. Mostly she looks like she doesn't really believe it.

Stone Soup

Arie informed me today that the thing I called "Miscellaneous Soup" is actually called "Stone Soup," after a folk story where three hungry strangers trick villagers into feeding them. In the story they announce that they're going to make soup for everyone out of a rock, and when curious villagers come to check out what they're doing, say that the soup would be better with a carrot or two . . . and an onion . . . and maybe some potatoes . . . and some beans . . . and one villager brings potatoes, and another one brings an onion, and in the end, there's a lovely pot of soup for everyone.

I started to point out that I wasn't tricking anybody, all this stuff was in my cabinet already, but then I realized that I didn't just have dinner but an *activity* and all the kids came into the kitchen and acted out the story with little Tom playing the hungry stranger trying to get everyone to chip in for the soup and then throwing each item into the pot.

Then they all made cookies, while I watched, using mayo for the eggs and dicing up mini candy bars for the chips.

It was a sunny day today—cold, but really sunny—and we spread out a picnic cloth and ate in the living room, Stone Soup and chocolate chip cookies and everyone went around in a circle and said the thing they were most looking forward to doing when this was over. Monika said she wanted to be able to take an hour-long shower (everyone's limited to seven minutes or we run out of hot water). Dominic said he wanted to go to the library. I said I wanted to bake a chocolate soufflé. Everyone complained about that and said it couldn't be cooking or baking, so I said I wanted to go see a movie, in a theater, something funny, and eat popcorn.

Tomorrow is the first of March.

Hydration

Dominic is sick. It's not flu. I mean, it can't be; we haven't gone out. Literally the whole point of staying in like this has been to avoid exposure. It also can't be anything *else* you'd catch. We thought at first possibly it was food poisoning, but no one else is sick and we've all been eating the same food. According to Dr. Google, who admittedly is sort of a specialist in worst-case scenarios, it's either diverticulitis or appendicitis. Or a kidney stone.

Obviously, going in to a doctor's office is not on the table. We did a phone consultation. The guy we talked to said that yes, it could be any of those things and offered to call in a prescription for Augmentin if we could find a pharmacy that had it. The problem is, even though H5N1 is a virus and antibiotics won't do anything for it, there are a lot of people who didn't believe this and some of them had doctors willing to prescribe whatever they were asking for and the upshot is, all our pharmacies are out of almost everything. Oh, plus a bunch of pharmacies got robbed, though mostly that was for pain meds. Pharmacies are as much of a mess as anything else, is what I'm saying.

I'm not giving up, because in addition to the pharmacies that answered the phone and said they didn't have any, there were a ton where no one even picked up. I'm going to keep trying. In the meantime, we're keeping Dominic hydrated and hoping for the best. I always keep a couple of bottles of Pedialyte around, because the last thing you want to do when you're puking is drive to the store, and that stuff's gross enough that no one's tried to get me to pop it open for dessert. So I've got it chilled and he's trying to drink sips.

If it's a kidney stone, Augmentin won't do anything, but eventually he'll pass the stone and recover, although it'll really suck in the meantime. (I wish we had some stronger pain medication than Tylenol. For real, *no one* has Vicodin right now. Not a single pharmacy.) If it's appendicitis, there's a 75% chance that the Augmentin will fix it. (This is new! Well, I mean, it's new information. There was a study on treating appendicitis with antibiotics and 75% of cases are a type of appendicitis that won't rupture and can be treated with antibiotics! And if you get a CT scan they can tell whether that's the kind you've got, but, well.) If it's diverticulitis, and he can keep down fluids, the antibiotics should help. If he's got the worse kind, and can't keep down fluids, they would normally hospitalize him for IV antibiotics and maybe do surgery. But again, not an option.

Oh, it could also be cancer. (Thanks, Dr. Google!) In which case there's no point worrying about it until the epidemic is over.

Cream of Augmentin

I got an e-mail from someone who has Augmentin they're willing to sell me. Or at least they say it's Augmentin. I guess I'd have to trust them, which is maybe a questionable decision. They want $1,000 for the bottle, cash only. Dominic was appalled that I'd even consider this. He thought it was a scam, and they were planning to just steal the cash.

Fortunately I also got through to a pharmacy that still had it, a little neighborhood place. Dominic's doctor called in the prescription, and I gave them my credit card number over the phone, and they actually delivered it. While I was on the phone with them they listed out some other things they have in stock and in addition to the Augmentin we got toothpaste and a big stack of last month's magazines. Shout out to St. Paul Corner Drug: we are going to get every prescription from you for the rest of our natural lives.

I was hoping that starting the Augmentin would make Dominic at least a little better right away, but instead he's getting worse.

Possibly this is just a reaction to the Augmentin. It's not as bad as some antibiotics, but it can definitely upset your stomach, which is pretty counterproductive when puking and stomach pain are your major symptoms.

I had appendicitis when I was a teenager. I spent a day throwing up, and when I got worse instead of better my mother took me to the emergency room. I wound up having surgery. Afterwards I was restricted to clear liquids for a while, just broth and Jell-O and tea, which I got really tired of before they let me back on solid food. My mother smuggled in homemade chicken stock for me in a Thermos—it was still a clear liquid, but at least it was the homemade kind, the healing kind.

If I could pull a live, clucking chicken out of my ass, like I joked about, I would wring its neck and turn it into stock right now for Dominic. Nothing's staying down, did I mention that? Nothing. But it's not like we have anything for him other than Pedialyte.

I'm going to try to catch a rabbit.

Rabbit Soup

You guys, you really can find instructions for just about anything online. Okay, I've never looked to see if there's a YouTube video on how to commit the perfect crime, but trapping an animal? Well, among other things, it turns out that the cartoon-style box-leaned-up-against-a-stick-with-bait-underneath is totally a thing you can actually do, but then you've got a live animal and if you're planning to eat it you'll still need to kill it. I wound up making a wire snare using instructions I found online in the hopes that the snare would do the dirty work for me. And it did. More or less. I'll spare you the details, other than to say, rabbits can scream.

You can also find instructions for gutting and skinning a rabbit online. I used my kitchen shears for some of this, and I worked outside so that Jo didn't have to watch. My back yard now looks like a murder scene, by the way, and my fingers were so cold by the end I couldn't feel them. I feel like I ought to use the fur for something but I don't think Home Taxidermy is the sort of craft that's going to keep the pack of pre-teens cheerfully occupied. (Right now they're reading through all the magazines we got from the pharmacy and I'm pretending not to notice that one of them is *Cosmo*.)

Back inside I browned the rabbit in the oven, since roasted chicken bones make for much tastier stock than just raw chicken, and then I covered it in just enough water to cover and simmered it for six hours. This would be better stock if I had an onion or some carrots or even some onion or carrot peelings, but we make do. The meat came off the bones, and I took out the meat and chopped it up and put it in the fridge for later, and I boiled the bones for a bit longer and then added a little bit of salt.

The secret to good stock, by the way, is to put in just enough water to cover the bones, and to cook it at a low temperature for a very long time. So there wasn't a whole lot of stock, in the end: just one big mug full.

The kids have been staying downstairs, trying to keep out of Dominic's way. Jo and Monika made dinner for the rest of us last night (rice and breakfast sausages) so I could take care of him. I saw Jo watching me while I carried up the mug of soup, though.

The bedroom doesn't smell very pleasant at the moment—sweat, vomit, and cucumber-scented cleaner from Target. It's too cold to open the windows, even just for a little while.

Dominic didn't want it. I'd been making him sip Pedialyte but mostly he was just throwing it up again, and he was dehydrated. I pulled up a stool and sat by the edge of his bed with a spoon and told him he had to have a spoonful. So he swallowed that, and I waited to see if it stayed down, or came back up. It stayed down.

Two minutes later I gave him another spoonful. That stayed down, too.

This is how you rehydrate a little kid, by the way: one teaspoonful every two minutes. It takes a long time to get a mug into someone if you're going a teaspoon at a time, but eventually the whole mug was gone. The Augmentin stayed down, too.

I went downstairs and set another snare in the back yard.

Something Decadent

So, thank you everyone who donated to Melissa's fundraiser. I put all the names in the hat and drew out Jessie from Boston, Massachusetts, and she says she doesn't want me to wait until everything is over, she wants a recipe now. And her request was, "Make something decadent. Whatever you've got that *can* be decadent." And Dominic is sufficiently recovered today, that he can eat something decadent and not regret it horribly within ten minutes, so let's do this thing.

We still have no milk, no cream, no eggs. I used the frozen whipped topping for the ambrosia salad and the marshmallows for the rice krispy treats (which aren't exactly *decadent*, anyway).

But! Let's talk about coconut milk. If you open a can of coconut milk without shaking it up, you'll find this gloppy almost-solid stuff clinging to the sides of the can; that's coconut cream. You can chill it, and whip it, and it turns into something like whipped cream. We set aside the coconut cream from three of the cans and chilled it.

I had no baking cocoa, because we used it all up a while back on a not-terribly-successful attempt at making hot chocolate, but I *did* have some mini Hershey bars still, so I melted the dark chocolate ones and cooled it, and thinned that out with just a tiny bit of the reserved coconut milk. It wasn't a ton of chocolate, just so you know—it's been a bit of a fight to keep people from just scarfing that candy straight down. But we had a little.

Then I whipped the coconut cream until it was very thick and almost stiff, and then mixed in the dark chocolate and a little bit of extra sugar, and it turned into this coconut-chocolate mousse.

When eating decadent food, presentation counts for a *lot*. We used some beautiful china teacups that I got from my great-grandmother: I scooped coconut-chocolate mousse into eight of them, and then I took the last of the milk chocolate mini bars and grated them with a little hand grater to put chocolate shavings on top. We also had some sparkly purple sprinkles up with the cake decorations so I put just a tiny pinch of that onto each cup. And I opened one of the cans of mandarin oranges and each of the mousse cups got two little orange wedges.

And I tied a ribbon around the handles of each teacup.

And then we set the table with the tablecloth and the nice china and we ate our Stone Soup of the day by candlelight and then I brought out the mousse and everyone ate theirs and then licked out the cups.

Some days it's hard to imagine that this will ever be over, that we'll ever be able to get things back to normal at all. When everyone is sniping at each other it feels like you've always been trapped in the middle of a half-dozen bickering children and always will be. When you're in the midst of grief, it's hard to imagine spring ever coming.

But Dominic pulled through, and Leo didn't get sick. And tying the ribbons around the handles, I knew: this will all come to an end. We'll survive this, and everyone will go home. *I'm going to miss them*, I thought, this pack of other people's children I've crammed into my bungalow.

"Can I keep the ribbon?" Jo asked, when she was done with her mousse.

I told her, of course she could. And then she and Monika started arguing over whether she could have Monika's ribbon, too, because *of course they did*, and that was our day, I guess, in a nutshell.

xxoo, Natalie

About the Authors

Bao Shu is a Chinese SF writer living in Xi'an. He began his writing career since 2010, and has published three collections and four novels since, including *Three-Body Problem X: The Redemption of Time* and *Ruins of Time*. His shorter works are often published by major science fiction, popular science and literature magazines. He has won numerous major SF awards in China. Several of his works are now available in English, published by *F&SF* and *Clarkesworld*.

Seth Dickinson is the author of *The Traitor Baru Cormorant, The Monster Baru Cormorant,* and numerous short stories. He studied racial bias in police shootings and now writes lore for Bungie Studios' *Destiny*. If he were an animal, he would be a cockatoo.

Gu Shi is a speculative fiction writer and an urban planner. A graduate of Shanghai's Tongji University, she obtained her master's degree in urban planning from the China Academy of Urban Planning and Design. Since 2012, she has been working as a researcher at the academy's Urban Design Institute. Ms. Gu has been publishing fiction since 2011 in markets like *Super Nice, Science Fiction World, Mystery World,* and *SF King*. She won a Galaxy Award for Best Short Story with "Möbius Continuum" in 2017 and a Gold Award for Best Novella at the Chinese Nebula (Xingyun) Awards with "Chimera" in 2016.

Hao Jingfang graduated from the Tsinghua University with a degree in physics. She also studied Astrophysics at Tsinghua Centre, ultimately earning a PhD from the School of Economics and Management. As a student, she won first prize in the fourth New Concept writing competition and the first Novoland essay contest. The English translation of her short story "Folding Beijing" earned Hao her first Hugo Award for Best Novelette at the 74th World Science Fiction Convention in 2016. Her published work includes two full-length novels, Wandering Earth and Born in 1984, short stories collections *The Depth of Loneliness* and *To Go the Distance,* and the essay collection *Europe within Time.*

Nin Harris is an author, poet, and tenured postcolonial Gothic scholar who exists in a perpetual state of unheimlich. Nin writes Gothic fiction, cyberpunk, nerdcore post-apocalyptic fiction, planetary romance, and various other forms of hyphenated weird fiction. Nin's publishing credits include *Clarkesworld, Beneath Ceaseless Skies, Strange Horizons,* and *The Dark.*

Kola Heyward-Rotimi is an undergraduate student of Computer Science and English at Amherst College. Outside of *Clarkesworld,* his work has appeared in *FIYAH Magazine,* and he was a Pitch Wars 2018 mentee. When not sweating over his senior thesis, he can be found crafting speculative fiction stories that don't know what genre they're supposed to be.

Karen Heuler's stories have appeared in over 100 literary and speculative magazines and anthologies, from *Conjunctions* to *Clarkesworld* to *Weird Tales,* as well as a number of Best Of anthologies. She has received an O. Henry award, been a finalist for the Iowa short fiction award, the Bellwether award, the Shirley Jackson award for short fiction, and others. She has published four novels and a novella, and her fourth story collection, *The Clockworm and Other Strange Stories,* was recently published by Tartarus Press.

Kij Johnson is the author of five books and forty-some short stories, and a winner of the Hugo, Nebula, World Fantasy and Theodore Sturgeon Awards, among others. Her most recent books are *The Dream-Quest of Vellitt Boe* and *The River Bank.* She is associate professor at the University of Kansas, where she is also Associate Director of the Center for the Study of Science Fiction.

Cassandra Khaw is an award-nominated author and an award-winning game writer who currently works for Ubisoft Montreal. She enjoys excessive long walks and punching things.

Naomi Kritzer has been writing science fiction and fantasy for twenty years. Her novelette "The Thing About Ghost Stories" is a finalist for the 2019 Hugo Award; her short story "Cat Pictures Please" won the 2016 Hugo and Locus Awards and was nominated for the Nebula Award. Her YA novel *Catfishing on Catnet* (based on "Cat Pictures Please") will be coming out from Tor Teen in November 2019. She lives in St. Paul, Minnesota with her spouse, two kids, and four cats. The number of cats is subject to change without notice.

Rich Larson was born in Galmi, Niger, has studied in Rhode Island and worked in the south of Spain, and now lives in Ottawa, Canada. He is the author of *Annex* and *Cypher,* as well as over a hundred short stories—some of the best of which can be found in his collection *Tomorrow Factory.* His work has been translated into Polish, Czech, French, Italian, Vietnamese and Chinese.

Krista Hoeppner Leahy is a writer, poet, and actor. In addition to *Clarkesworld,* her work has appeared in *The Common, Farrago's Wainscot, Lady Churchill's Rosebud Wristlet, Raritan, Reckoning, Shimmer, Tin House,* Year's Best Science Fiction and Fantasy and elsewhere. She is currently working on a collaborative poetry manuscript celebrating the sacred feminine. Born in Colorado, Krista currently lives in Brooklyn with her family.

Leena Likitalo is a writer from Finland. She's the author of the fantasy novels *The Five Daughters of the Moon* and *The Sisters of the Crescent Empress.* A Clarion San Diego graduate, her short stories have appeared in *Galaxy's Edge* and Writers of the Future.

Cixin Liu is a representative of the new generation of Chinese science fiction authors and recognized as a leading voice in Chinese science fiction. He was awarded the China Galaxy Science Fiction Award for eight consecutive years, from 1999 to 2006 and again in 2010. His representative work *The Three-Body Problem* won the 2015 Hugo Award for Best Novel, finished 3rd in 2015 Campbell Awards, and was a nominee for the 2015 Nebula Award. *Death's End,* the third book of the trilogy, was nominated by Hugo again in 2017. Liu is also a winner of Arthur C. Clarke Award for Imagination in Service to Society, Locus Award, John W. Campbell Memorial Award, KurdLaßwitz Preis, Ignotus Award and Kelvin 505 Award.

His works have received wide acclaim on account of their powerful atmosphere and brilliant imagination. Liu Cixin's stories successfully combine the exceedingly ephemeral with hard reality, all the while focusing on revealing the essence and aesthetics of science. He has endeavored to create a distinctly Chinese style of science fiction. Liu Cixin is a member of the China Science Writers' Association and the Shanxi Writers' Association.

Paul McAuley worked as a research biologist and university lecturer before becoming a full-time writer. He is the author of more than twenty novels, several collections of short stories, a Doctor Who novella, and a BFI Film Classic monograph on Terry Gilliam's film *Brazil.* His latest novels are *Austral* (2017) and *War of the Maps* (2020).

Tamsyn Muir is a horror, fantasy and sci-fi author whose short fiction has been nominated for the Nebula Award, the Shirley Jackson Award, the World Fantasy Award, and the Eugie Foster Memorial Award. A Kiwi, she has spent most of her life in Howick, New Zealand, with time living in Waiuku and central Wellington. She currently lives and works in Oxford, in the United Kingdom.

An (pronounce it "On") **Owomoyela** is a neutrois author with a background in web development, linguistics, and weaving chain maille out of stainless steel fencing wire, whose fiction has appeared in a number of venues including *Clarkesworld, Asimov's, Lightspeed,* and a handful of Year's Bests. An's interests range from pulsars and Cepheid variables to gender studies and nonstandard pronouns, with a plethora of stops in-between. Se can be found online at an.owomoyela. net, and can be funded at patreon.com/an_owomoyela.

Robert Reed is the author of nearly three hundred published stories, plus more than a dozen novels. He is best known for his Great Ship stories, including *The Memory of Sky*. And for the novella, "A Billion Eves," which won the Hugo Award in 2007. He lives in Lincoln, Nebraska with his wife and daughter.

Sara Saab was born in Beirut, Lebanon. She now lives in North London, where she has perfected her resting London face. Her current interests are croissants and emojis thereof, amassing poetry collections, and coming up with a plausible reason to live on a sleeper train. Sara's a 2015 graduate of the Clarion Writers' Workshop. You can find her on Twitter as @fortnightlysara and at fortnightlysara. com.

Jack Skillingstead's Harbinger was nominated for a Locus Award for best first novel. His second, *Life on the Preservation,* was a finalist for the Philip K. Dick Award. He has published more than forty short stories to critical acclaim and was short-listed for the Theodore Sturgeon Memorial Award. His writing has been translated internationally. He lives in Seattle with his wife, writer Nancy Kress.

Benjanun Sriduangkaew writes love letters to strange cities, beautiful bugs, and the future. She has lived in Thailand, Indonesia, and Hong Kong. Her short fiction has appeared on Tor.com, in *Beneath Ceaseless Skies, Clarkesworld,* and year's best collections. She has been shortlisted for the Campbell Award for Best New Writer, and her debut novella *Scale-Bright* was nominated for the British SF Association Award. She can be found blogging at beekian.wordpress.com or on twitter at @benjanun_s

Rachel Swirsky holds an MFA from the Iowa Writers Workshop where she, a California native, learned about both writing and snow. She recently traded the snow for the rain of Portland, Oregon, where she roams happily under overcast skies with the hipsters. Her fiction has appeared in venues including *Tor.com, Asimov's Magazine,* and The Year's Best Non-Required Reading. She's published two collections: *Through the Drowsy Dark* (Aqueduct Press) and *How the World Became Quiet* (Subterranean Press). Her fiction has been nominated for the Hugo Award and the World Fantasy Award, and twice won the Nebula.

E. Catherine Tobler is a 2019 Hugo Award Finalist for her work on *Shimmer Magazine*. Among others, her short fiction has appeared in *Lightspeed, Clarkesworld, Apex,* and *Interzone*. For more, visit her website at www.ecatherine.com.

A.C. Wise's short fiction has appeared in publications such as *Shimmer,* Tor.com, *Uncanny,* and *Best Horror of the Year Volume 10,* among others. Her work has been a finalist for the Lambda Literary Award, and a winner of the Sunburst Award. She has two collections *The Ultra Fabulous Glitter Squadron Saves the World Again,* and *The Kissing Booth Girl and Other Stories,* published by Lethe Press, and a novella, *Catfish Lullaby,* published by Broken Eye Books (August 2019).

In addition to her fiction, she contributes the Women to Read, and Non-Binary Authors to Read, series to *The Book Smugglers,* and the Words for Thought review column to the Apex Book Blog. Find her online at www.acwise.net.

Nick Wolven's science fiction shows up in lots of places—including, in addition to *Clarkesworld*: *Wired, Asimov's, F&SF,* and a bunch of collections and anthologies. He's especially interested in the social effects of automation, and is, for that reason, mostly not online. He can be contacted with writing-related questions at nick.wolven@gmail.com.

Xia Jia (aka Wang Yao) is Associate Professor of Chinese Literature at Xi'an Jiaotong University and has been publishing speculative fiction since college. She is a seven-time winner of the Galaxy Award, China's most prestigious science fiction award and has published three science fiction collections (in Chinese): *The Demon-Enslaving Flask* (2012), *A Time Beyond Your Reach* (2017), and *Xi'an City Is Falling Down* (2018). Her first English language collection, *A Summer Beyond Your Reach,* is forthcoming from Clarkesworld Books. She's also engaged in other science fiction related works, including academic research, translation, screenwriting, and teaching creative writing.

Clarkesworld Citizens
OFFICIAL CENSUS

We would like to thank the following Clarkesworld Citizens for their support:

Citizens

Nat A, A Fettered Mind, A Strange Loop, Michael Adams, Magnus Adamsson, Warren Adler, Alan & Jeremy VS Science Fiction, Pete Aldin, Elye Alexander, William Alexander, Alexander, Alexi, Richard Alison, Ed Allen, Joshua Allen, Alllie, Imron Alston, TJ Alston, Ancestors Guide Me, Ro Anders, Clifford Anderson, Kim Anderson, Tor Andre, Dan Andresen, Anon, Author Anonymous, Antariksa, Joseph Anthony Dixon, ArbysMom, Therese Arkenberg, Sharon Arnette, Randall Arnold, Ash, Stephen Astels, A. Alfred Ayache, David Azzageddi, Bill B., B.H., Benjamin Baker, Great Barbarian, Jenny Barber, Jennifer Barnes, Johanne Barron, Anna Y. Baskina, Charles Basner, Jeff Bass, Meredith Battjer, Anna Bauer-Baxter, John Baughman, Moya Bawden, Cheryl Beauchamp, Paul Becker, Aaron Begg, Ben, LaNeta Bergst, Julie Berg-Thompson, Clark Berry, Kevin Besig, Lovelyn Bettison, Amy Billingham, Dale Randolph Bivins, Tracey Bjorksten, John Blackman, Brett Blaikie, John Bledsoe, Mike Blevins, Adam Blomquist, Bluebuel, Allison Bocksruker, Kevin Bokelman, EXO Books, Clare Boothby, Michael Bowen, Brian Bowes, Winfield Brackeen, Commander Breetai, Nathan Breit, Allan Breitstein, Cristiano Malanga Breuel, Don Bright, Jennifer Brissett, Mary Brock, Britny Brooks, Jeremy Brown, Kit Brown, Mark Brown, Richard Brown, Laurence Browning, Mark Brumbill, Tobias S. Buckell, Jacki Buist, Thomas Bull, Michael Bunkahle, Karl Bunker, Alison Burke, Cory Burr, Jefferson Burson, Kristin Buxton, Graeme Byfield, Bryce C, c9lewis, Andrew J Cahill, Darrell Cain, Caitrin, C.G. Cameron, Jo Campbell, Isabel Cañas, Ricardo Canizares, Paul Carignan, Yazburg Carlberg, Liam Carpenter-Urquhart, Michael Carr, Cast of Wonders, Nance Cedar, Celtgreenman, Greg Chapman, Timothy Charlton, David Chasson, Steve Chatterton, Catherine Cheek, Zichen Chen, Paige Chicklo, Joe Chip, Maria Cichetti, Lázaro Clapp, Jeremy Clark, Victoria Cleave, Blair Cochran, Alicia Cole, Elizabeth Coleman, Greg Coleson, Ian Collishaw, Elisabeth Colter, Che Comrie, Johne Cook, Claire Cooney, Martin Cooper, Lisa Costello, Thomas Costick, Ashley Coulter, Charles Cox, Michael Cox, Sonya Craig, K Crain, Yoshi Creelman, Katherine Crispin, Tina Crone, Kaitlin Crowley, Alan Culpitt, Cathy Cunliffe, Curtis42, Gary Cusick, Lorraine Dahm, Steve Dahnke, Shawn D'Alimonte, Sarah Dalton, Ang Danieldeskbrain - Watercress Munster, Chua Dave, Morgan Davey, Ed Davidoff, Chase Davies, Katrina Davies, Craig Davis, Lee Davis, Gustavo de Albuquerque, Alessia De Gaspari, Del DeHart, Maria-Isabel Deira, Daniel DeLano, Dennis DeMario, Frank Den den Hartog, Pieter Derdeyn, Patrick Derrickson, Michele Desautels, Paul DesCombaz, Allison M. Dickson, Geri Diorio, Mark Dobson, Tsana Dolichva, Robert Dowrick, Aidan Doyle, dsbjr, DT, Alex Dunbar, Albert Dunberg, Susan Duncan, Andrew Eason, Roger East, The Eaton Law Firm, P.C., David Eggli, Jesse Eisenhower, Alamon Elf Defield, Sarah Elkins, Brad Elliott, Warren Ellis, Dale Eltoft, Douglas Engstrom, Lyle Enright, Peter Enyeart, Nancy Epperly, Erik, Collin Evans, Yvonne Ewing, Extranet Vendors Association, Edward Fagan, Feather, Denis Ferentinos, Josiah Ferrin, Melina Filomia, Mrs. Atwell's Fixit, Jenna Fizel, Joseph Flotta, Ethan Fode, Dense Fog, Frank Fogarty, Vanessa Fogg, Chelsea Foreman, Francesca Forrest, Jason Frank, Carol Franko, Michael Fratus, William Fred, Amy Fredericks, Amit Fridman, Michael Frighetto, Andrew Frigyik, Sarah Frost, Froxis, Fyrbaul, Max G, Paul Gainford, Robert Garbacz, Eleanor Gausden, Leslie Gelwicks, Susan Gibbs, Phil Giles, Rebecca Girash, Holly Glaser, Susanne Glaser, Sangay Glass, Globular, Tom Gocken, Eric Gomez, Laura Goodin, Don Grayson, Grendel, Besha Grey, Valerie Grimm, Damien Grintalis, GRO Industries, Inc, Janet Groenert, Tom Groff, Michael Grosberg, Nikki Guerlain, Xavier Guillemane, Shannon Guillory, Gaurav Gupta, Geoffrey Guthrie, Richard Guttormson, Jim Hagel, James Hall, Lee Hallison, Douglas Hamilton, Michael Braun Hamilton, Janus Hansen, Happybunnyatthezoo, Roy Hardin, Jonathan Harnum, Harpoon, Dan Harrington, Jubal Harshaw, Sarah Hartman, Darren Hawbrook, Emily Hebert, Leon Hendee, Jamie Henderson, Philip Henderson, Samantha Henderson, Dave Hendrickson, Steven Hennig, JC Henry, Steve Herman, Karen Heuler, Dan Hiestand, John Higham, Renata Hill, Björn Hillreiner, Tim Hills, Mark Hinchman, Peter Hogberg, Peter Hollmer, Jesse Holmes, Melanie Hopes, Andrea Horbinski, Clarence Horne III, Richard Horton, Jon Hoskins, Bill Howell, Margaret Howie, Fiona Howland-Rose, Roger Hudman, Matthew Hudson, Pete Huerta, Rex Hughes II, Jeremy Hull, John Humpton, M. L. Hunt, Iain Hunter, Gene Hyers, Dwight Illk, John Imhoff, Iridum Sound Envoy, Isbell, J.B. & Co., Joseph Jacir, Jack, Jack Myers Photography, Marie Jackson, Danya Jacob, Stephen Jacob, Sarah James, Joseph A Jechenthal III, Ciel Jennings, Jimbo, Jimi, JJ, Dick Johnson, H Lynnea Johnson, Steve Johnson, Patrick Johnston, Paul B. Joiner, Laura Jolley, Judith Jones, Paul Jones, jschekker, Ryan H. Kacani, Gabriel Kaknes, Philip Kaldon, KarlTheGood, Conner Kasten, Sara Kathryn, Chris Kattner, Leah Katz, Cagatay Kavukcuoglu, Jonathan Kay, KC, Keenan, Jason Keeton, Robert Keller, Mary Kellerman, Betty Kelly, Jared Kelsey, Kelson, Chris Kern, Shawn Keslar, John Kilgallon, KillZoneOZ, Dana Kincaid, Kisaki, Phil Klay, Kate Kligman, Roy and Norma Kloster, Peter Knörrich, Bryan Knower, Seymour Knowles-Barley, Matthew Koch, Will Koenig, Peter Kolis, Konstantinos Kontos, Sean CW Korsgaard, Travis Kowalchuk, Lutz Krebs, John Krewson, Deb Krol, Heiti Kulmar, Derek Kunsken, Dale Kuykendall, MJ LA QUOC, Cam Laforest, Michele Laframboise, Jason Lai, Paul Lamarre, Dylan Lane, Gina Langridge, Scotty Larsen, Darren Ledgerwood, Brittany Lehman, Terra Lemay, Wayne Lester, Andrew Levin, Philip Levin, Brian Lewis, Steve Lindauer, Danielle Linder, Matthew Line, Simon Litten, Susan Llewellyn, Renata M Lloyd, Jay Lofstead, Lornak, Thomas Loyal, Luke, Sharon Lunde, Sharon Lunde, James Lyle, Tim M, Robert Mac, Meredyth Mackay, Peter MacMillin, Sven-Hendrik Magotsch, Ilia Malkovitch, Raegan Mann, Dan Manning, Margaret, Mariusmule, Mark, R. Mark Jones, Ivan Markos, Jacque Marshall, John Marshall, Ray Marshall, Tony Marsico, Dominique Martel, Janet Martin, Fernando Martinez, Cethar Mascaw, Daniel Mathews, Matthew, Delvon Mattingly, David Mayes, Derek W McAleer, Mike McBride, Robert J. McCarter, T.C. McCarthy, Andrew Mcculloch, Jeffrey McDonald, Holly McEntee, Josh McGraw, Demitrius McHugh, Roland McIntosh, Christopher M McKeever, Steve Medina, Brent Mendelsohn, Kristen Menichelli, Regan Mercer, Seth Merlo, Sol Meyer, Stephen

Middleton, John Midgley, Matthew Miller, Stephan Miller, Terry Miller, Claire Miller Skriletz, Alan Mimms, Serene Mirkis, Dale Mitchell, mjpearce, Moritz Moeller-Herrmann, Aidan Moher, Marian Moore, Tim Moore, Sunny Moraine, Jamie Morgan, C A Morris, DJ Morrison, Jon Moss, Lynette Moss, Tomasz Mrozewski, Patricia Murphy, Lori Murray, Karl Myers, Mike Myers, Derek Nason, Leona Nette, Glenn Nevill, Jeffrey Newman, Stella Nickerson, Matthew Nielsen, Robyn Nielsen, Elaine Nobbs, Christopher Norberg, Norm, Tom Nosack, Robert Nowak, Zam Nuclear Wesell, Nicholas Nykamp, David Oakley, Oddscribe, Hugh J. O'Donnell, Scott Oesterling, Christopher Ogilvie, James Oliver, Brett O'Meara, Lydia Ondrusek, Ruth O'Neill, Erik Ordway, Dan Osborne, Aaron Osgood-Zimmerman, Felicia Osullivan, Elizabeth Jo Otto, Nancy Owens, Moe P, Thomas Pace, Norman Paley, Mieneke Pallada, Amparo Palma Reig, Clifford Parrish, Thomas Parrish, Sidsel Pedersen, Edgar Penderghast, Tzum Pepah, Chris Perkins, Sara Pfaff, Nikki Philley, Aimee Picchi, Adrian-Teodor Pienaru, rebecca pierce, Jamison Pinkert, Adam Piper, Beth Plutchak, Andy Pond, David Potter, Prettydragoon, Ed Prior, David Raco, Žarko Radulović, Mahesh Raj Mohan, Adam Rakunas, Ralan, Steve Ramey, Diego Ramos, Madeline Ray, Tansy Rayner Roberts, Robert Redick, George Reilly, Steven Reneau, Renmeleon, Joshua Reynolds, Julia Reynolds, Rick of the North, Zach Ricks, Carl Rigney, Jorge A. Rivera, Ashley Rivers, Robert, Hank Roberts, Tansy Roberts, Kenneth Robkin, Ronald Rogers, James Rowh, RPietila, Sarah Rudek, Woodworking Running Dog, Oliver Rupp, Paul Rush, Caitlin Russell, Abigail Rustad, Michael Ryan, S2 Sally, Tim Sally, Sam, Samantha, Samuel, Sanders, Nadia Sandren, Jason Sanford, Maria Pia Sass, Erica L. Satifka, Steven Saus, SausageMix, MJ Scafati, David Schaller, Gregory Scheckler, Chris Schierer, Gabe Schirvar, Nancy Schrock, Jason Schroeder, Don Schwartz, Gerald Schwartz, Graham Scott, Seeds in the Wind, Maral Seyed Ali Agha, Richard Shapiro, Kieran Sheldon, Espana Sheriff, T. L. Sherwood, Udayan Shevade, Josh Shiben, Heather Shipman, Kel Shire, Robert Shuster, Tom Sidebottom, Aileen Simpson, Taylor Simpson, John Skylar, Kate Small, Rebecca Smith, Karen Snyder, Morgan Songi, Søren, Michelle Souliere, Jozef Sovcik, Dr SP Conboy-Hil, Elisabeth Spalding, Mat Spalding, Gary Spears, Elwood Spencer, Julian Spergel, Carl spicer, Stephen Sprusansky, Terry Squire Stone, Zachary Stansell, Keith Stebor, Claire Stevenson, Blake Stone-Banks, Jennifer Stufflebeam, Julia Sullivan, Jennifer Sutton, Jherek Swanger, John Swartzentruber, Kenneth Takigawa, Charles Tan, William Tank, Beth Tanner, Jesse Tauriainen, David Taylor, Paul Taylor, Lim Wee Teck, Tessler, James Thomas, Brett Tofel, Jaye Tomas, Sharon Tomasulo, Felix Troendle, Steven Tu, Diane Turnshek, The Unsettled Foundation, Julia Varga, John Vassar, Adam Vaughan, Nuno Veloso, William Vennell, Kenneth VenOsdel, Vettac, Theodore Vician, George S. Walker, Matthew C Walker, Shiloh Walker, Diane Walton, K.E. Walton, Stefan Walzer, Robert Wamble, Bobbi Warburton, John Watrous, Matthew J Weaver, Nat Weinham, Robert Werner, Neil Weston, Peter Wetherall, Adam White, Spencer Wightman, Dan Wilburn, Jeff Williamson, Neil Williamson, Nicola Willis, Willowcabins, A.C. Wise, Devon Wong, Mr J R Woroniecki, Chalmer Wren, Dan Wright, Kevin Wynn, Joe Yaremchuk, Lachlan Yeates, Catherine York, Barbara Zagajšek, Rena Zayit, Frederick Zorn, Stephanie Zvan

Burgermeisters

7ony, Rob Abram, Paula Acton, Andy Affleck, Rowena Alberga, Frederick Amerman, Carl Anderson, Mel Anderson, Randall Andrews, Daniel Andrlik, Andy90, Marie Angell, John Appel, Misha Argall, Jon Arnold, Catherine Asaro, Mike R D Ashley, Robert Avie, Chris Aylott, B, Mr. B., Erika Bailey, Michael W. Baily, Brian Baker, Nathan Bamberg, Michael Banker, Jay Barnes, Laura Barnitz, Jennifer Bartolowits, Andrew and Kate Barton,

Deborah Beale, Lenni Benson, Kerry Benton, Leon Bernhardt, TJ Berry, Matt Bewley, Bill Bibo Jr, Steve Bickle, Edward Blake, Samuel Blinn, Jeff Boardman, Johanna Bobrow, Kaye Bohemier, David Boldt, Joan Boyle, Brakeparts1234, Patricia Bray, Tim Brenner, Brodonalds, Arrie Brown, Ken Brown, BruceC, Carl Brusse, Sharat Buddhavarapu, Max Buffington, Adam Bursey, Jeremy Butler, Robyn Butler, Roland Byrd, Jarrett Byrnes, Janice Calm, Brad Campbell, Paul Cancellieri, Anthony R. Cardno, Carleton45, James Carlino, Ted Carr, Benjamin Cartwright, Evan Cassity, Sean Cassity, Lee Cavanaugh, Peter Charron, Randall Chertkow, Farai Chideya, Michael Chorman, cin3ma, Maggie Clark, Matthew Claxton, Marian Collins-Steding, Theodore Conti, George Cook, Brian Cooksey, Brenda Cooper, Lorraine Cooper, Matt Craig, James S Cullen, Lucy Cummin, Cezar Damian, Gillian Daniels, Dasroot, Nicholas V David, David, James Davies, Pamela J. Davis, Tessa Day, De, Jetse de Vries, Brian Deacon, Bartley Deason, Ricado Delacruz, Keith DePew, John Devenny, Peter Dibble, Lindsey Dillon, Dino, Fran Ditzel-Friel, Gary Dockter, Nicholas Doran, Christopher Doty, Nicholas Dowbiggin, Robert Drabek, Sage Draculea, Paul Dzus, Mela Eckenfels, Eileen, Steve Emery, Sagi Eppel, Thomas Ericsson, Christine Ertell, Joanna Evans, Patricia Evans, B D Fagan, Dietrich Faust, Rare Feathers, David Finkelstein, Tea Fish, Rosemary Fisher, FlatFootedRat, Bruce Fleischer, Lynn Flewelling, Adrienne Foster, Keith M Frampton, Matthew Fredrickson, Alina Fridberg, John Fritsche, Eric Fritz, Christopher Garry, Pierre Gauthier, Drue Gawel, Gerhen, Mark Gerrits, Caroline Gillam, Tanya Glaser, Lorelei Goelz, Ed Goforth, Melanie Goldmund, Martin Gonzalez, Inga Gorslar, Peter Goyen, Peter Goyen, Tony Graham, Jaq Greenspon, Eric Gregory, Marc Grella, Jessica Griffith, Ryan Grigor, Stephanie Gunn, Russell Guppy, Jim H, Laura Hake, AMD Hamm, Skeptyk/JeanneE Hand-Boniakowski, Mark S Haney, Jordan Hanie, John Hanley, Joseph Heizman, Helixa 12, Normandy Helmer, Theresa A Hemminger, Daniel Herman, Buddy Hernandez, Corydon Hinton, Jon Hite, Elizabeth Hocking, Sheridan Hodges, Ronald Hordijk, Fawn M Horvath, Justin Howe, Bobby Hoyt, David Hudson, Benito Huerta, Huginn and Muninn, Chris Hurst, Brit Hvide, Kevin Ikenberry, Joseph Ilardi, Adam Israel, Jalal, Patty Jansen, Michael Jarcho, Jason, Cristal Java, Toni Jerrman, Audra Johnson, Erin Johnson, Russell Johnson, Robert Jones, Patrick Joseph Sklar, Kai Juedemann, Andy Kaden, C. L. Kagmi, Daniel A Kaplan, Jeff Kapustka, David Kelleher, James Kelly, Jim Kelly, Brian Keves, K. L. Keyserling, Joshua Kidd, Alistair Kimble, Harvey King, Erin Kissane, John Klima, Cecil Knight, Michelle Knowlton, KP-ShadowSquirrel, Frances KR, Eric Kramer, JR Krebs, Chris Kreuter, Neal Kushner, Stephane Lacoste, Jan Lajka, Brian Lambert, Andrew Lanker, Kevin Lauderdale, James Frederick Leach, Krista Leahy, Kate Lechler, Robert Lehman, Alan Lehotsky, Leland, Annaliese Lemmon, Walter Leroy Perkins, L Leslie, Edit Leventon, Philip Levin, Kirby Li, Kevin Liebkemann, Ao-Hui Lin, Grá Linnaea, Jerry Little, Joyce E Lively, James Lloyd, Travis Love, Susan Loyal, Kristi Lozano, LUX4489, Alicia Lynch, Peter Mackey, Erin M Maloney, Adam Mancilla, Brit Mandelo, Cat Manning, Mark Maris, Marlene, Matthew Marovich, Marqman, Eric Marsh, Samuel Marzioli, Jason Maurer, Rosaleen McCarthy, Peter McClean, Michael McCormack, Barrett L McCormick, Sean McFall, Tony McFee, Mark McGarry, Ace McInturff, Robyn McIntyre, Doug McLaughlin, Andrew McLeod, Craig McMurtry, Oscar McNary, Margery Meadow, J Meijer, Geoffrey Meissner, Barry Melius, Sarfo Mensah, Alan Merriam, David Michalak, Mike, Scott Miller, Robert Milson, Sharon Mock, Eric Mohring, Jacob Molaro, Samuel Montgomery-Blinn, Lyda Morehouse, Griffin Morgan, Rebekah Murphy, John Murray, N M Wells Foundry Creative Media, Will Nash, Dan Newland, Alan Newman, Barrett Nichols, Tishangela Nierman, Jennifer Noga, Val Nolan, Jenn Sam Norberg, Peter Northup, Sean OBrien, Vince O'Connor, Jason Ogdahl, Am Onymous, Stian Ovesen, David Packer, Simon Page, Justin Palk, Norman

Papernick, Richard Parks, Paivi Pasi, Paula, MJ Paxton, Katherine Pendill, Eric Pierson, E. PLS, PBC Productions Inc., Lolt Proegler, Jonathan Pruett, QLM Aria X-Perienced, Robert Quinlivan, Thomas Rado, Rainspan, D Randall Kerr, Joel Rankin, Sherry Rehm, Erin Reilley, Dixon Reuel, Paul Rice, Zack Richardson, James Rickard, Karsten Rink, Anthony Rogers, Erik Rolstad, Joseph Romel, Leena Romppainen, Tim Rose, Sophia Ross, Lisa Rubio, Michael Russo, Miranda Rydell, Larry Sandhaas, Juan Sanmiguel, Matthew Saunders, Patrick Savage, Stefan Scheib, Alan Scheiner, Ken Schneyer, Eric Schreiber, Patricia G Scott, Terriell Scrimager II, Bluezoo Seven, David John Sewell, Cosma Shalizi, George Shea, Mike Sherling, Jeremy Showers, Lisa Shumaker, Eric Simmons, Siznax, John Skillingstead, Josh Smift, Rue Smith, Allen Snyder, David Sobyra, Daniel Solis, Caitlin Sticco, Lisa Stone, Jason Strawsburg, Stuart, Keffington Studios, Jerome Stueart, Robert Stutts, Fredrik Svensson, Portia X.Y. Tang, Gregory Taylor, W. Taylor, Maurice Termeer, Tero, Chantal Thomas, Daniel Thomas, John Thomas, Brent Thompson, Gavin Thomson, Chuck Tindle, Raymond Tobaygo, Tradeblanket.com, Kima Traynham, Heather Tumey, Mary A. Turzillo, Ann VanderMeer, Matthew Varga, Andrew Vega, Emil Volcheck, Andrew Volpe, Margaret Wack, Wendy Wagner, Ralph Wahlstrom, Alan Walker, Mark Walsh, Jennifer Walter, Rob Ward, Tom Waters, Tehani Wessely, Liz Westbrook-Trenholm, John Whitaker, Chris White, Shannon White, Dan Wick, John Wienstroer, Kristine Wildman, Seth Williams, Kristyn Willson, Paul Wilson, Dawn Wolfe, Wombat, Sarah Wright, Isabel Yap, Zackie, Peter Zeller, Slobodan Zivkovic

Royalty

Paul Abbamondi, Eric Agnew, Karsten Philip Aichholz, Jonathan Alden, Albert Alfiler, Dan Allen, Rose Andrew, Karl Armstrong, Bruce Arthurs, Rush Austin, Randy Avis, Raymond Bair, Jim Baker, Kathryn Baker, Anne Barringer, Zach Bartlett, David Beaudoin, Nathan Beittenmiller, Ralf Belling, Kevin Best, Brian Bilbrey, Nicolas Billon, Nathan Blumenfeld, BoloMKXXVIII, Marty Bonus, David Borcherding, Robert Bose, Brian Brunswick, Nancy Buford, John Burkitt, Heather Cailaoife, Robert Callahan, Carrie, Mackenzie Case, Lady Cate, Brad Cavallo, A Chambers, Richard Chappell, Joseph M Christopher, John Chu, Heather Clitheroe, Chad Colopy, Carolyn Cooper, Darcy Cox, Tom Crosshill, Michael Cullinan, Kathy Cygnarowicz, Darren Davidson, David Demers, James Denman, Cory Doctorow, Brian Dolton, Dayne Encarnacion, Marcello Fabrizi, Matthew Farrer, Kathy Farretta, Stephen Finch, Greg Frank, William Frankenhoff, David Furniss, Jennifer Gagliardi, John Garberson, Kate Gillogly, Alexis Goble, Hilary Goldstein, Adam Haapala, David Hall, Jonathan Harvey, Carl Hazen, Andy Herrman, Brendan Hickey, Robin Hill, Kristin Hirst, Colin Hitch, Ian Hobson, Victoria Hoke, Marolynn Holloway, Jeppe V Holm, Todd Honeycutt, Jason House, David Hoyt, Nancy Huntingford, ianwillc, Christopher Irwin, James Jackson, Erskine James, Stephen Jenkins, Linda Jenner, Mary Jo Rabe, Janna Jones, Jennifer Joseph, Virginia Jud, Gereon Kaiping, Lukas Karl Barnes, Robert Kennedy, Fred Kiesche, Corey Knadler, G.J. Kressley, Jamie Lackey, Jonathan Laden, M. Lane, Abigail Larkin, Katherine Lee, Ilia Levin, Jeffrey Lewis, Marta Lillo, Dave Lister, Warren Litwin, Justin Livernois, Vincent P Loeffler III, Jack Londen, Kevin Lyda, Osborne Lytle, Robert MacAnthony, Pete Macfarlane, Ross MacLean, Bob Magruder, Phil Margolies, Sean Markey, Andrew Marsh, Arun Mascarenhas, Marcella Massa, Daniel Maticzka, Wes McConnell, Barrett McCormick, Matthew McKay, Kevin McKean, Margaret McNally, Glori Medina, Michelle Broadribb MEG, Dave Miller, Lucy Mitchell, Carlos Mondragón, Nayad Monroe, James Moore, Jennifer Morrow, Ellen Moskowitz, Anne Murphy, Jennifer Navarrete, Patrick Neary, Persona Non-Grata, Charles Norton, David M Oswin, H. Lincoln Parish, Marie Parsons, Lars Pedersen, David Personette, George

Peter Gatsis, Matt Peterson, Joshua Pevner, Matt Phelps, Jeremy Phillips, Gary Piserchio, Merja Polvinen, Lord Pontus, Mr. Potato, Ian Powell, Kevin Quagliano, Rational Path, Rossen Raykov, Andrew Read, James Red, Captain Red Boots, Corey Redlien, Wesley Reeves, Patrick Reitz, RL, Rob, Kelly Robson, Peter Roy, DF Ryan, John Scalzi, Scroggie, Stu Segal, Maurice Shaw, Ross Shaw, Jan Shawyer, Bill Shields, Angela Slatter, Saskia Slottje, Carrie Smith, Paul Smith, Samuel Smith, Nicholas Sokeland, Richard Sorden, Cheryl Souza, Kevin Standlee, Neal Stanifer, Chris Stave, Bobbie Steinkraus, Jonathon Sutton, SuzB, John Swartzentruber, Jeremy Tabor, S. Rheannon Terran, Colin Theys, Kim Thomas, Josh Thomson, TK, Terhi Tormanen, Andre Twupack, Marc Tyler, Sam van Rood, David Versace, Saoirse Victeoiria, Natalie Vincent, Suzanne Vowles, Daniel Waldman, Jonathan Wallace, Jasen Ward, Izzy Wasserstein, Ian Watson, Taema Weiss, Bradley Wells, Weyla & Gos, Graeme Williams, Jessica Wolf, Zac Wong, Matt Wyndowe, Jeff Xilon, Pandora A Young, Bob Z, Zola

Overlords
Aarnold Aardvark, Renan Adams, Thomas Ball, Michael Blackmore, Adina Bogert-O'Brien, Nathalie Boisard-Beudin, Greg Bossert, Shawn Boyd, Mark Bradford Sr., Jennifer Brozek, Vicki Bryan, Karen Burnham, Barbara Capoferri, Paul Chadwick, Clarke Chapman, Gio Clairval, Tania Clucas, Gregory Copenhaver, Andrew Curry, Dolohov, ebooks-worldwide, Sairuh Emilius, Lynne Everett, Joshua Faulkenberry, Fabio Fernandes, Benjamin Figueroa, Tony Fisk, Thomas Fleck, Eric Francis, Overperson Franklin, Brian Gardner, L A George, Michael Glyde, Bryan Green, Hank Green, Michael Habif, Andrew Hatchell, Berthiaume Heidi, Melissa House, Bill Hughes, Chris Hyde, Jacel the Thing, Marcus Jager, Justin James, Jericho, jfly, jkapoetry, Larry Johnson, James Joyce, Lucas Jung, Gayathri Kamath, Alina Kanaski, Youriy Karadjov, James Kinateder, Jay Kominek, Alice Kottmyer, Daniel LaPonsie, Susan Lewis, Sarah Liberman, George C Mable, Edward MacGregor, Philip Maloney, Paul Marston, Matthew the Greying, Gabriel Mayland, Patrick McCann, Joe McTee, MJ Mercer, Achilleas Michailides, Adrian Mihaila, Adrien Mitchell, Overlord Mondragon, Cheryl Morgan, James Morton, MrMovieZombie, Jose Muinos, Stephen Nelson, Joshua Newth, Dlanod Nosreetp, Richard Ohnemus, Andrea Pawley, Mike Perricone, Jody Plank, Clarissa R., Rick Ramsey, Thomas Reed, Jo Rhett, Rik, Jason Sank, Laura Schmidt, Lorenz Schwarz, Joseph Sconfitto, Marie Shcherbatskaya, SK, Sky, Tara Smith, Theodore J. Stanulis, David Steffen, Naru Sundar, Robert Urell, M C VanderSchaaf, Thad Wilkinson, Elaine Williams, James Williams, Richard Wyatt, Doug Young

Deities
Kenneth Burk, Daniel Clanton, Eric Hunt, Gary Hunter, Robert Munsch, Rajeev Prasad, Kelvin Tse

About Clarkesworld

Clarkesworld Magazine (clarkesworldmagazine.com) is a monthly science fiction and fantasy magazine first published in October 2006. They have received three Hugo Awards, one World Fantasy Award, and a British Fantasy Award. Their fiction has been nominated for or won the Hugo, Nebula, World Fantasy, Sturgeon, Locus, Shirley Jackson, WSFA Small Press and Stoker Awards. For information on how to subscribe to our electronic edition on your Kindle, Nook, iPad or other ereader/Android device, please visit: clarkesworldmagazine.com/subscribe/

The stories in this anthology were edited by:

Neil Clarke (neil-clarke.com) is the editor of *Clarkesworld Magazine* and *Forever Magazine*, owner of Wyrm Publishing, and a seven-time Hugo Award Nominee for Best Editor (short form). His anthologies include *Upgraded, Galactic Empires, Touchable Unreality, More Human Than Human, The Final Frontier, The Eagle Has Landed*, and Best Science Fiction of the Year series. He currently lives in NJ with his wife and two sons.

Sean Wallace is a founding editor at *Clarkesworld Magazine,* owner of Prime Books, and winner of the World Fantasy Award. He currently lives in Maryland with his wife and two daughters.